A Mirror of Stones
Book One

The matrix settles.

A crystal grows
In centered stillness.

And from out of
The dreamtime chaos,
A token appears.

Now, tell me this,
If you can:
Who am I?

A Mirror of Stones
Book One

Herein Lies
A Looking-glass
With Which to Reflect Upon
The Lore Hidden in Stones and Metals

By:
Dvalinn

Foreword by:
J.M. Mickelson

Illustrations by:
Anonymous

EVERGREEN
Silver Spruce Lane
MMXX

First published in 2020
by
J.M. Mickelson

Printed in the United States of America

ISBN: 9781082399862

Design by Jeannette Stutzman

This is Book One in a series.

https://jmmickelson.com/
https://www.instagram.com/joanmmickelson/

FORWARD

One evening, when I was about to close the antique shop for the night, a woman walked in carrying two paper shopping bags. Dressed in peculiar, outdated fashion, she wore a long skirt and, though it was too light for the weather, a jacket made of thin, faded green fabric. Complaining about the bags' weight, she set them on the floor in front of the counter and, after rubbing her hands together, held her palms out for my inspection. She pointed to the red lines, which the string handles had dug into her white, tissue paper-like skin, and were left, like painful scars, on her hands.

She was a collector of oddities, she told me and, as she walked around the shop, in an accent, which I could not place, commented distractedly on several of the antiques on display. She began to describe the sort of items she was seeking, with which she hoped to fill a particular hole in her collection, when in the midst of our discussion, for no apparent reason, she turned and hurriedly headed for the door. Though I yelled after her, "Do not forget your bags," she was already on her way out.

She paused on the threshold, glanced over her shoulder, and asked, "Could I leave them with you for safe-keeping while I go about my errands?

"But, I am closing up for the night," I replied.

"Before I return," she answered, "if you care to browse through the bags, feel free to take a look."

I agreed, somewhat hesitantly, to look after her bags but, by then, the door had shut behind her. I made room for the bags behind the counter and locked up for the night.

Several days later, it became apparent that she was never going to return. I dug through the bags and discovered they were filled with what appeared to be worthless scraps of paper. Some of the sheets were either bundled with twine or loosely held together with rubber bands. Most were covered with a text written in a scratchy, cursive script. There were, also, a few drawings among the loose sheets.

The shopkeeper who owned the store told me to get rid of the bags. But, because the papers had been important to whoever had gone to the trouble of writing and collating the pages of what appeared to be a manuscript of some kind, I did not have the heart to dump them in the trash.

I carried the bags home and, that very night, began to sort through the papers. To make sense of the manuscript, I began to pile the pages on chairs and tables. Eventually, they spilled onto the floor and, over time, filled an entire room. Occasionally, I swore there were more stacks of paper in the morning than there had been the night before. At other times, I awoke in the middle of the night with additional text dictated in a dream.

I have now taken the liberty of editing the manuscript and publishing these books in a limited edition. For historians who study the seventh century, the author offers a unique, first-hand perspective on life in Northern Europe. At that time, the depleted population was still recovering from the devastating effects of an abrupt change in the weather, and the famine, constant warfare, and rapidly spreading plague that had resulted from the volcanic eruptions in 536, 540, and 547 AD.

—J.M. Mickelson

In memory of:

Captain Milo S. Mickelson
Navigator B-24 Liberator
US Army Air Force
World War II
Commissioned April 1, 1943
&
Melva Teubner Mickelson
Married May 9, 1943

Private Joseph Teubner
Infantry Wisconsin Company C
American Civil War
Entered service May 13, 1861
Received Land Grant for Homestead
August 1, 1872
&
Elizabeth Sherman Teubner
Married June 9, 1861

Private Elihu Sherman
Captain Joseph Parker's Company
Ebenezer Sproat's Regiment
Continental Troops
Entered service January 9, 1778
&
Susannah Haight Sherman
Married, date unknown

A Mirror of Stones
Book One

Oh,
Mountain Mother
Who spins the clouds,
And Lord of the Whirlwind,
Whose furious passage alters
The lives of all those who lay in his path,
Let us now begin our song.

Part One

INTRODUCTION

Steel

If you will make a wounding knife
So sharp that, were a hair to fall across it, the strand shall be cut.

Take nuggets which are called bog iron. It is a crumbly stone the color of rust.
If this stone be heated in a charcoal fire and the ore be beaten with a hammer
to weld the metal, then annealed to soften, and quenched to harden, the knife
shall resist fracture and hold a sharp edge. For as long as a man does bear the
blade, it is good against fear and he shall have victory. And this has been proven
of certain men in our time.

The Truth of Rocks, by Aluiss the Wise

I.

Strange purposes were at play that night as I was making my usual
rounds. When, for no apparent reason, instead of taking my typical
route, I chanced to go another way and knocked on an unfamiliar merchant's door.

He opened it directly, said, "I have something to show you," and welcomed me
inside.

In the back room, he handed me the candle he carried and asked me to hold it
above his workbench to give him better light. He pulled a long, narrow packet from
a battered wooden crate and carefully unwound the greasy rags wrapped around a
well-crafted long-knife. Though he apologized for the lack of a hilt on the old blade, I,
nonetheless, assured him that the loss mattered not the least to me. My final appraisal
of the knife's value would rest primarily upon the quality of the steel.

"Then you will like this one," he said with a wide grin.

To hold it out for my inspection, the blade's weight forced the man to lift it by
the tang with one hand and, with the other, to prop the point against a handful of
dirty rags. Up until then, I had seen no reason to distrust the merchant's judgment.
But when he told me the knife had been a gift to the bogman who resided in the waters from which it was dug, I suspected him of playing me for a fool.

"Hold on," I said. "If the blade has lain buried in a swamp for countless years, the
bogman should have gnawed on the steel and turned it to rust. But, as you can plainly
see, the cutting edges are still intact, and the blade remains untarnished. There can be
no other explanation than to say the blade is newly forged."

To counter my skepticism of both its provenance and its undisputable age, he
drew my attention to the strangely branching letters embedded in the steel. Tapping
them, lightly, with his finger, he said, "The reason for its uncorrupted state can be

found here, in these letters."

Though it was reasonable to ask whether he could read them, instead of answering the question directly, he offered additional proof of the knife's great age. "The last man to forge blades, such as this one, failed to pass on the manufacturing secrets before he died. The knowledge went with him to the grave, you see. His craftsmanship has gone unduplicated for several hundred years. You can rest assured, this is an old one."

As it turned out, the merchant's first statement was false. Earlier in the day I had seen a man who could forge a blade such as this one. But any attempt to convince him otherwise would have taken me half the night. Besides, he never would have believed me even had I tried. As for the last statement: it was true. The blade was an old one. And, by implication, for the time being anyhow, the explanation for the long-knife's pristine condition would remain a mystery.

To inspect it in greater detail, I held the flame to the flat side of the blade and leaned in closely to get a better view of the rippling designs imbedded in the blade's skin. It was then that my immediate identification of Berling's signature, herringbone patterns caused the hairs on my arms to stand on end and the scalp behind my ears to prickle.

Convinced this blade could only have been made by either my colleague or one of the lucky few who had worked beside him at his forge, I wished to learn the name of the one who had crafted it. I rubbed my finger across the secret signs embedded in the steel and was left weak-kneed by the shocking recognition. Not only had I known the smith who had forged this blade, I had known her intimately, in fact. And now, after all this time that we had thought her long-knife was lost forever, here it was.

To see this blade, which once hung from a renowned chieftain's belt, in its currently humiliated state, wrapped in rags and stored in an old crate, as if it were cast into a dungeon, nearly drove me to tears. Hurrying to complete our transaction, I harbored no qualms about paying the merchant whatever he asked. After my coins were counted out and had changed hands, I wrapped the knife in the same dirty rags and, feeling as though I was disguising a king in a beggar's clothing, left the merchant's shop.

II.

Back in my rooms, I was polishing the blade with powdered iron rouge when a fit of unbearable yearning overwhelmed me. To share this poignant moment with the long-knife's maker—to see her just once again—was all I asked. I began to frantically rub and caress the steel. My vision blurred with tears. I became short of breath, was overcome with dizziness, carelessly cut myself, and was forced to stop and bandage my hand.

When satisfied that the long-knife had been restored to its former glory, I laid the blade where it belonged in a place of honor at the far edge of my table. Because this knife was made here in these chambers, this is its rightful home. No one shall ever claim it. Not Berling. Not Grerr. No emperor, king, nor chieftain. If others threaten to take this blade, before I allow it to leave this room, I swear to use Allfrigg's explosive powders to bury the entrance beneath a pile of boulders. It will not happen; it cannot happen—not until the Endtime.

I stood back to admire the long-knife and to relish the accomplishment of a job well done but was unable to leave it alone. Drawn to study its interwoven patterns more closely, I picked up the crystal ball. It was then, when I was looking at the long-knife through the lens-like ball that a peculiar thing happened—the blade spoke. Although the voice I heard seemed to have come from somewhere deep inside me, I knew it was not my own. This blade, which once had stood for a famed chieftain's source of power, had just spoken to me in its own voice.

Granted, there are those who will attribute this strange occurrence to a momentary loss of my senses. Yet, I have never disputed what happened—I heard the blade's deep, metallic vibrato demand I tell the story of its birth.

Taken aback by this startling new development, I pondered its meaning. Because the few drops of blood I had spilled had awakened the blade, I could no longer view this long-knife as just another collectible. Rather, it was a proud and unfettered creature with a mind and a will of its own. Even now, whenever I look at the blade, I hear its thrumming tones demand I complete the task assigned me.

At first I was hesitant to set out upon this quest and pleaded for leniency. Because I had no way to collect information from men and women who inhabit realms, to which I have no access, failure was a certainty. Besides, there were both shameful memories, which I preferred to keep hidden, and secretive encounters I had held onto like treasured artifacts and heirlooms. Furthermore, living apart in tunnels, as we do, we are cut off in the daytime from whatever goes on above our heads.

Yet, this unwelcome event soon gave way to an unleashed curiosity. And so, by means of these so-called stone mirrors, the tale of the long-knife's origins follows three generations, or four if you count the child's.

III.

Though there are those who have forgotten me, and others who have rashly disproven that I was ever here at all, I urge you to refuse belief in such spurious allegations. I am still here. Thus, let these writings serve as proof of my enduring presence in this world.

I, Dvalinn the Learned, have written this in my own hand.

Rock Crystal

If you will learn of secret themes and overcome adversaries.

Take this stone which is called Rock Crystal. It is very clear and shining throughout and plain. It does offer comfort and when borne makes a man expound upon and understand dark questions hard to otherwise resolve

The Truth of Rocks, by Alviss the Wise

I.

Time and again, I strove to catch sight of the shadowy forms being cast so fleetingly inside my room. But, unable to account for their strange appearances, I dismissed the manifestation as a mere shadow-play caused by the dim, flickering lights. It was not until I saw similar spots floating inside the crystal ball that I questioned whether the two sightings might be related, somehow.

Drawn to inspect the previously clear ball more closely, I stared at the tiny intrusions. The confounding spots then grew in size, began to move about and looked, quite shockingly, like a flock of birds in flight. The peculiar occurrence led me to surmise that, by some strange, synchronized leakage between the worlds, the dark shapes inside the ball had simultaneously cast those same blurred shadows inside my room. Admittedly, one may dispute my interpretation of both manifestations being one and the same but, for whatever it is worth, that was how I had thought of it at the time.

About the size of a child's closed fist, the ball makes a good lens for magnifying small objects. But for peering into the past or future, as some folks do, or for becoming privy to other's thoughts and motivations, I had never before had an occasion to use it—not until that night, that is. However, this opportunity to peek furtively at something secretive, even forbidden, increased my curiosity until the possibility became irresistibly seductive.

For those who are unfamiliar with the act of scrying—as I was at the time—I can only describe the experience as one that is similar to looking into a mirror. But instead of seeing things transposed right to left, this invaluable tool allows me to learn about things that, otherwise, lie hidden behind everyday appearances. The only note of caution to keep in mind is this: when putting one's trust in the overlapping layers between both the visible and the invisible worlds, one wants to cultivate a modicum of comfort with the uncertainty, which the crystal ball reveals.

II.

To get a better view of the intrusions, I held the ball close to my face. When one of the black birds came straight at me, growing in size until it seemed to filled the ball, I inadvertently jerked back and nearly dropped it. Yet, despite the apparent threat, I remained undeterred. I looked right into the bird's small, onyx-like, black eyes and stared it down until it squawked and veered off to the side.

The crystal began to take on a color mildly reminiscent of the rinse water in which I dip my quill when I cleanse it of iron-salts and oak gall. Inside the sphere, the crow-shaped silhouettes circled lazily against the inky-looking sky. Above them were eddying, low-hung clouds. Beneath them were the rows of turned, black dirt clods making up a recently harrowed field. One by one, each bird dropped down and, after landing on the soil, tucked in its wings, walked about, and pecked at the farmer's recently sown grain seeds.

Then, without warning, the display of busyness, so common to their kind, was interrupted. The crows gave full voice to their disapproval, flapped their wings, and took off all at once. After the birds had dispersed in all directions, my view widened to include the far-reaching fields and meadows. It was then that I saw what had alarmed them so. In the distance, a dust cloud broke through the space between two hedge-rows. And, at the center of the swirling field debris, rushing headlong across the field, I identified a woman at the reins of a leopard-driven, two-wheeled cart.

I knew of only one woman who could tame and harness such ferociously spirited beasts. With her snow-white hair clouding around her head and dressed in a dark green gown and a brown woolen wrapper, the driver of the cart had to be none other than the wide-hipped, big-bosomed, double-chinned Mountain Mother herself, Lady Blessed.

Scanning the thickets at the far edge of the field, whilst urging her cats to run faster, she shook the reins and shouted desperately. When she spotted whatever or whomever she was after, she pulled back on the reins to slow the cats' movement, directed them to turn and circle back the way they had come, and brought her cats to a halt near a stand of thin-trunked, scrubby trees. She pulled up her skirts and jumped down from the cart's open back-end. Irritably brushing dust from her sleeves and shelf-like upper chest, she walked several steps before crouching down amidst a clump of tall, sun-bleached weeds, and bent over a man who was wrapped up in a bedroll and sleeping, apparently.

"You good-for-nothing derelict, wake up," she screamed, shaking him by the shoulders. "Why do I put up with you? Wake up."

The man, who lay on his side with his back turned toward her and the hood on his cape pulled over his head, began to slowly come around. Lady Blessed grabbed the hood, pulled it down, struck the back of his head with the broad side of her palm, and began to pick out bits of straw from his matted hair. "Look at you. You are a shameful mess."

It was then, when he groggily rolled over that I caught sight of his face and knew my hunch had been correct. A jagged, white scar streaked from one side of his forehead to his cheek, and another angled across the bridge of his flattened nose—both the results of the injury that had partially blinded him. Indeed, who else would Lady Blessed be seeking-out in a crow-scavenged field but her spouse, Lord Fury?

He opened his one good eye but a sliver's width, saw her, and struggled to release his arms from the tightly wrapped blanket folds. Once he was freed, he grabbed his wife in a clumsy attempt to pull her down and to kiss her hard on the mouth.

But she was having none of it and impatiently pushed him aside. "Look at you. You were to feast with us tonight. Instead, I find you wandering about like a common beggar and sleeping in a field." She stood up, set her feet apart, stuck her fists to her hips, and said, "Get up."

"Just give me a moment, Blessed." Arms and legs all akimbo, he struggled to free himself from the cloak and blanket. "Are you sure? I do not recall plans for a feast. I cannot leave now. There are things I need to do here. I am not done surveying the region for Lord Glory."

"Something has come up that demands your attention."

"Is that so?"

Though his voice sounded testy, one sidelong glance at his wife's face quickly suggested he might want to change his tone. Convinced of her determination, he sighed, stood upright and, with straightened knees, bent awkwardly from the waist. Though he struggled to fold his blanket and to do as his wife directed, he was, nonetheless, determined to make one final attempt to change her mind before he gave in to her whims so easily. He glanced back over his shoulder, peered up at her from his bent-over posture, and said, "The sun has barely risen, and dew is on the grass. I know what you want. Come lay with me. Then we can go our separate ways again."

"You do not know what I want," she said. "That is what you want." She pushed him aside, knelt down, rolled up the woolen blanket, and tied it with a rope. She picked up the worn leather satchel he had used for a pillow and held it out to him.

He grabbed it from her hand and said churlishly, "I would like to know what you do that is more important than what I do."

"That discussion comes later. Right now, you are coming with me."

Easily more than a head taller than she was and able to put up a good fight using arms and legs taut as thickly braided rope, he nonetheless gave in and let her take him by the elbow. She pulled him, stumbling, toward her cart and brusquely pushed him into the open back end. He crawled in on hands and knees, sprawled into the corner between the side and front rails, and stretched out his long legs.

Lady Blessed grasped the top rail with one hand and with the other pulled up her skirts. Lifting a leg, she hoisted herself up. On the way to the front, she stepped over Lord Fury's legs at the exact same moment that he noticed his feet were dangling over the back edge. To right that condition, he tucked up his knees and, in so doing, tripped Lady Blessed. To catch her balance, she reached for the front rail with one hand and, with the other, grabbed at his shoulder. Squeezing harder than was needed, she elicited a sharp "Ouch" from him.

She grabbed hold of the reins, took a wide-spread stance, glared at her troublesome husband, and asked, "Why do I put up with you? Just give me one good reason."

Lord Fury shrugged off the question, settled himself into the corner, and wrapped his arms around his tucked-up legs. A horseman himself, he travelled light. He had no talent for driving wagons. That was a woman's way of getting around, (after all, they had so much household gear to haul). Confident that he was in good hands—his wife had strong, square hands with thick, short fingers—he closed his eye to take a nap.

Tonight, he would lay in a woman's bed. For one night, in a plentiful world run by women, he would live and feast her way. Lord Glory could wait another day for his report on men who get continually caught-up in a world of their own making and doom themselves to perpetually waging war.

A series of sudden gusts caught the edges of the Lady's cloak to make it flap and billow. She paused briefly to study the skyline. A squall was blowing in from the southwest. She hastily flicked the reins and called out to her cats, "Let's go."

The two spotted creatures began to pull the heavily laden cart. Once they had picked up speed, they zigzagged across the fields and cut swathes through the dried meadow grasses, swaying like swells of the sea. Unable to outrun the wind gathering around them, the cats and the cart were soon enveloped in a stormy vortex. And, curtained off by a sudden downpour, the crystal ball's interior went dark.

III.

By now the crystal ball lay cradled in the palm of the hand that was resting placidly in my lap. Bewildered momentarily, uncertain of where I was or even who I was, I seemed to be both asleep and awake at the same time.

I guessed that I had seen an encounter between Lord Fury and his wife at the same time that it was happening but, other than that, was uncertain of which of the realms I had observed. Because the visible and invisible realms overlap, most folks' ordinary vision obscures the ruling powers and the hidden folk. But if a man, a woman, or even a child, is blessed with second sight or, apparently, has the use of a crystal ball, he or she may see the hiddens anywhere and everywhere.

Though some folks prefer to divide the otherworlds into nine distinct regions, I am reluctant to do so. The worlds are not isolated but continuously overlap, often in hierarchical order: the hiddens fill the bottommost ranks, and the ruling powers fill the ranks nearest the top. To disguise themselves, the otherworlds can bring about confusion and ambiguity in the minds of those who seek them. Then too, there are the unlimited worlds of simultaneously occurring future possibilities, all of which are ripe for exploration. Anyway one wants to looks at it, words are insufficient descriptors of the many interlocking worlds. Because the borders between these realms are murky, to know them first hand, somehow, is the best way to fully grasp their meaning. If the way-farer is adept at navigating the shifting boundaries between them, it may be possible to move from one world to the other at will.

To do so, however, does not preclude the possibility of running into dangerous encounters. Wherever one finds the ruling powers and the hidden folk, violent competition for dominance and survival is rampant. They rule at every level. To keep from getting caught up in their conflicts, to prevent oneself from becoming either lost or injured, or from incurring their wrath, whenever one chooses to walk between the worlds, caution, protection, and guidance are required, or, at least, recommended. It is, also, a good idea to offer a few gifts to the hiddens, now and then, just to keep them friendly.

Generally speaking, the location of each of the otherworlds may be found in reference to the earth's surface, to the ocean surrounding it, and to the sky above it. For example, without ever leaving this world, one might travel far to the north to see the

Land of Mist where the Frost Devourers and the Wind-bringers dwell. But, even so, those creatures will remain invisible to anyone who is not gifted with the sight.

There is another world located far beneath the earth's surface. That is where the Sons of the Fiery Realm are found. It is so terribly hot there, rock melts. Berling and other metal-smiths of our own kind have invented a means by which to put those everlasting fires to use. Their network of pipes and valves channels the small flames that light and heat our underground rooms. Berling tells me that the everlasting fires are tricky to manage though, especially, when he must control the high heat required for ironmongery. Too much heat, he says, will melt the walls that line our living chambers. If that were to happen, those of us who were inside would turn to a form of molten lava similar to basalt. Though it is not an end I care to dwell on, it would be a curious transformation of sorts.

Then there are the places where the dead go. Among them are the two mead-halls, which are located at the far end of the skybridge. The one where the Lord of Rich-Waters dwells is on the coastline; the Sky Lord's Victory Hall is on a nearby hill. Lady Blessed's hall seems to be neither here nor there but, at any given moment, may be disguised as a mountainous island or, at other times, as fields and pastures surrounded by impenetrable forest. Lastly, there is the lowest land of the dead, ruled by Mother Torment, the daughter of Spider the Entangler. That is where the oath breakers dwell. No one wants to go there, believe me.

Otherwise, death does not, necessarily, end a man or woman's sojourn with this hard and fast world. There are lost and restless seekers who can find nowhere to settle. Cursed to wander between the worlds, they are lost forever. If they feel abandoned, they will wander the world of the living while seeking to get back at those against whom they hold grudges. Or they may look for something they miss, have lost and still long for, have forgotten, or have never known, but still desire.

And now that I have at hand the means with which to learn more about those realms, without revealing my own presence there—or even without leaving my own private reading room—after I shake off the confusion and get my bearings, I will take another look.

IV.

Staring into the murky depths inside the crystal ball, I saw numerous glittering lights the size of tiny pinpricks. Within this light-punctured darkness were three blazing hearths throwing sparks in the open space between two parallel rows of tall timbers that supported the lower, crosswise beams inside a huge meadhall. A number of flaming torches were set into iron brackets nailed to the walls and, even more rush lamps, all of which were set on wheels, hung from chains hooked into the high, central roof beam.

Lining the two longest walls, narrow platforms raised two rows of tables and benches from the earthen floor. The wooden tables were well-oiled and polished with bee's wax until their surfaces shone. To add to the glimmer, the tables were covered with patterned woven runners that had been embroidered with sparkling threads of gold. The bronze platters, silver cups and pitchers were polished to such a high sheen that the sparkling glints they threw seemed bright enough to rival the nighttime stars.

Lord Fury, easily the tallest man in the hall, could be spotted standing in the center of the long row of tables on the left side, along with the men and women who were members of his warband. Across from the central hearth fires, on the right side of the hall, were those men and women who made up his wife's warband.

From the looks of Lord Fury's appearance, I gathered that Lady Blessed had hustled her husband off to their private chambers and overseen his freshening-up. After he had thrown off his earlier disguise as a common outcast, he had now become a remarkably stately looking man. His dark hair, streaked with grey, fell to mid-back in waves. The full beard hung to mid-chest, and his mustache's long, turned-up ends had been properly combed and waxed. He had exchanged his beggar's clothing for a suitably fine, dark red woolen tunic. Its mid-thigh length was hemmed with decoratively woven trim, as were the neck and wrists. His lower trouser legs were wrapped tightly with narrow cloth bands. A cloak was thrown dashingly over his shoulders and pinned on the left with a jeweled, gold brooch. His long-knife was sheathed in a scabbard decorated with a silver chape shaped like a crow's head whose beak ended in a spiral. It hung from a wide leather belt that was riveted with gold plaques and drawn closed, in the center, with a massive gold buckle.

Everyone turned to face the far end of the hall where the doors stood open to the clear blue, early evening twilight. Lady Blessed appeared. Framed by the wide, double doorway, she paused a moment before she made her entrance. The floor-length green gown she wore was hemmed with a series of wide bands. An additional, narrow, pale green, linen apron had been decorated on the bottom half with a wide, elaborately embroidered knot-design stitched in many colors. It was pinned at each shoulder with a large, domed, shield-like gold ornament from which multiple strands of beads hung. Her shoulders were draped with a dark green cloak that had been trimmed with woven bands at the hem. Disdaining the married woman's headscarf, her white hair went uncovered. Braided with red and green ribbons the plait hung well past her hips like a long, thick rope.

She cradled in her hands a golden bowl. Filled with mead, the cup was ripe and round as a new mother's breast when her milk first comes in. Its rim was inscribed with swirls ending in small flowers. Suggestive of the Mountain Mother's promise of plentiful game in the forests, the cup was decorated with five engraved medallions, each of which depicted a leaping stag. And to remind her followers of the bountiful fields she gave them, the spaces between the roundels were filled with tied grain sheaves.

Lady Blessed walked down the center of the hall, came to a stop directly across from her husband, and turned to face him.

"Tell me again," he grumbled beneath his breath, "why am I here?"

"To be honored for your wisdom," she hissed back. "So, do your best to act like an intelligent, respectable chieftain. I know that you can do it once you put your mind to it."

He blew out through his lips, disgustedly. "No matter what you say, I know this feast was hastily put together this morning. Whatever you are up to, I promise to have it out of you before the night is over."

A gentle smile graced Lady Blessed's lips. She looked him straight in the eye, and the ceremony began with these words: "Tonight, all the men and women who gather around the tables in this Hall of Many Seats are here to celebrate their bold and valorous leader, Lord Fury the Whirlwind."

She handed the cup to Lord Fury, after which he supped and begrudgingly handed it back.

She then sidestepped and handed the cup to the man who stood beside Lord Fury, on his right. The man raised the cup and praised Lord Fury: "It is a great honor to serve in your warband, all-knowing, all-powerful Lord Fury. You offer men comfort, blessings and hope." After he finished speaking, he supped and handed it back to Lady Blessed. She then handed the cup to the next man, and he, too, did the same.

One after another, they kept up the game. As Lady Blessed carried the cup around the tables, they called Lord Fury a fighter of rectitude. They were honored to serve in his warband, they said. After each man had done his best to outdo the others with his florid praise, Lord Fury nodded approvingly. Even the men in Lady Blessed's warband praised Lord Fury's forthright leadership and swore to be the mightiest of warriors whenever they were called upon to fight.

Admiration of his success went on and on until Lord Fury became quite giddy with all the praise. After the last man had handed the cup to Lady Blessed, she again offered it to her husband. Lord Fury accepted the cup with a bemused expression, lifted it, gazed out upon his guests, and said, "Indeed, all of you have spoken so well tonight and, I might add, so truthfully, that I shall often think of every word you said."

He then raised the cup to honor his wife. "My Lady Blessed the Mountain Mother, I honor and serve you: mistress of the animals, you who soften the wild places' ferocity, just as you tamed your cats; protector of the places where men and women dwell; lady of both life and death and of those places between; you who mediate the boundaries between the known and the unknown; you who manage the borders between the cultivated and the wild; you who arrange the alliance between summertime's life-giving fertility and wintertime's death-dealing destruction; we praise your merciful and boundless goodness."

After Lord Fury handed her the cup, she supped and, to offer her bounty to all the men and women who stood around the tables, extended the golden cup to the full reach of her arms. Raising it high overhead, she turned in a complete circle, shouting, "There is plenty to go around. Eat up."

Food immediately appeared. Carried in by a seemingly endless parade of serving girls and boys, there were trenchers of pork stew, platters covered with round breads and cheeses, bowls of pickles and fruits, and pitchers filled with either sweet mead or bitter ale.

Lady Blessed walked from table to table overseeing the bountiful serving of all those who were seated. Not until she was satisfied that her guests had all been well fed did she take her place at the center of the long tables directly opposite of where Lord Fury was seated. She demurely spread her skirts and sat amongst those men and women who served in her warband, a place from which she could keep a wary eye on her husband throughout the rest of the meal.

Once everyone's hunger was sated, Lord Fury stood. Walking around the far side of the tables, he passed the high, raised platform at the far end of the hall. On his approach to Lady Blessed, he courteously held out his hand. She gently touched him with her fingertips and stood. Together, they walked around the perimeter of the tables, informally greeting the men and women in their service until they had come to the far end of the hall. When they were standing before the closed doors, the men and women quieted. The Lord and Lady then walked up the center, arm in arm, and took their places upon the two elaborately carved, wooden high seats.

Meant to represent Lady Blessed and Lord Fury's combined leadership, the two boxy chairs were both the same height. Neither was higher than the other, for their duties were equally important. It was Lady Blessed's role to pass the praise-and-promise cup that was so important to their holy alliance and, in this way, to bring together both the men and women who were loyal to her, and those who were loyal to Lord Fury. And, whereas, it was Lady Blessed who, as their wisewoman, counseled her husband's leadership, foretold the outcome of the fight, and through her ability to walk between the worlds, granted victory whenever their forces were combined, it was Lord Fury who, in the role of their chieftain, led them into battle.

Lady Blessed looked out over all those who were seated on the benches and clapped her hands. "I have a wish, Lord Fury."

"Whatever you ask, it shall be done. What is your wish?"

"I want to hear a story."

In response to her request, all the men and women cheered enthusiastically. Lord Fury crooked a finger to call two of his attendants forward. He asked them to bring him the box housing the Rememberer, and they left the hall for his private chambers.

V.

Lord Fury's request reminds me of a time when the Remember was a well-known traveling, meadhall storyteller. In itself, his story makes a curious tale:

Back in the day, it was said that the Rememberer's talent for cleverly concealing hidden truths within his stories went unmatched. Because of his ability to bring together things that had never before been seen nor heard, his listeners pictured worlds with their mind's eye that were, otherwise, unknowable to their ordinary senses. With his telling, they comprehended places they had never been, and the stories he told changed people's lives irrevocably and forevermore.

Although his talents for storytelling still remain true to form, unfortunately, he is no longer capable of travel. For, even those who live in the vast forever are not completely free of Mother Necessity's injunctions and Father Time's corruption; even the immortals may be blinded, injured irreversibly, or doomed to exile in the nether regions.

And so it was, one night, when the Rememberer told a tale of treachery, his account of the hero's feats were so skillfully described that his listeners believed that they, themselves, were the ones who were acting out the story. As great as were his talents, there was, also, a dark and dangerous side of the Rememberer's gift. For on that unfortunate night, one man in the crowd was so caught up in the action that he believed that he, himself, was the wrong-doer. We cannot know for certain, but, whatever were his reasons, he thought that the storyteller's words had singled him out as the culprit. Perhaps, in some long-ago time, he had done something treacherous and feared being sent to Mother Torment's hall if he were blamed for the betrayal.

No one saw death coming. But before anyone could stop the man, he had drawn his long-knife from its sheath, run up to the Rememberer and, with a single blow, lopped off the storyteller's head. It was a tragic mistake. But once a man has unsheathed his blade and swung it, there is no way to take it back. Such are the laws of Time and Necessity. Done is done, forever.

Lord Fury had loved that storyteller with all his heart. But even so, he was unable to stop the horror he saw happening before him. He leapt to his feet and ran screaming, "No-o-o-o-o-o-o," to the center of the hall. But once he got there, there was nothing he could do but stand beside the blazing hearth and stare at the Rememberer's head. There it lay, alone and separated from its body, in the puddle of blood draining from both ends of the dead man's severed neck. Fury fell to his knees, picked up the head, and cradled it in his arms.

It was the weeping, the keening back and forth, and the animal-like wails echoing so frightfully from the high roof-beams that sent chills down the spines of all those who heard them. Yet, when Lord Fury quieted, all those who were gathered around him agreed that his silence was even more terrifying. No one moved, so fearful were they of what Lord Fury might do. What crazed punishment might he mete out?

All the men and women stared with hollow eyes as Lord Fury solemnly walked out the doors. No one spoke a word. Carrying the head, he crossed the yard, went directly into his private chambers and closed and barred the door. Not even Lady Blessed was allowed entrance. And there Lord Fury stayed, for many nights and days. He did not open the doors again until he had completed the task that he had originally set out to do—to make the Rememberer open his eyes and to tell him a story.

No one knows how he accomplished the feat (although I do have my suspicions). It was said that he wrote secret signs and spoke spells over the head and, along with the use of his collection of both rare and common herbs and minerals, he was able to preserve the head from rot and decay. Since then, Lord Fury has kept the Rememberer in a lidded box.

VI.

Lifting the hinged lid, Lord Fury quietly greeted the Rememberer with the affectionate and familiar terms one generally reserves for close friends and relations. He set the box on a small tripod and gently tipped it on end. The storyteller opened his eyes, switched them back and forth, and looked out over the hall. He smiled at the gathered crowd and asked what story they wished to hear.

Lady Blessed screamed in a high-pitched voice, "I want to hear a story about the day when Lord Fury first rode into our village. A-n-n-n-n-d," she added, dragging out the last word as her eyes darted playfully, first in Lord Fury's direction, and then toward all those who were seated on the benches awaiting what she would say next, "how I pulled him into my bed and made him my everlasting captive." Her mouth opened wide and her arms wrapped around her belly. Crying and laughing so hard at her own joke, she was forced to wipe away the tears streaming down her cheeks.

When all the men and women saw their Lady having so much fun, they joined in her laughter. Lord Fury tossed his head back and roared with equal pleasure. He slipped his arm behind Lady Blessed's back and draped it across her shoulders. With only the arms of their side-by-side chairs between them, he pulled his wife in toward himself and kissed her just above the ear. She, in turn, snuggled into his embrace, took hold of his hand and raised it affectionately to her lips.

And with that final gesture, the men and women, who were seated on the benches, quieted. And no other sounds could be heard in the hall but for an occasional burst of sparks or settling ashes in the hearths.

The Rememberer blinked his lazy, half-closed eyelids. His brows pulled together to form a deep crease down the center of his forehead. He breathed in hard, let his head tip back and, with an audible out-breath, his soft cheeks trembled. His gaze became unfocused. His eyes closed. And he began:

There was a time when things were different for Lord Fury. It was said that, in his earlier days, he covered himself with so much gold that he blazed as brightly as the sun. He lived in the lands called Scythia and was a wealthy grain trader. The wagons, with which his wives hauled the grain, numbered more than forty. His horses, goats, and sheep grazed the grasslands unhindered. His wives fermented the sheep's milk and felted their fleece. And the children they gave him crowded all around him. In his earlier days, he lived both night and day on the back of his horse and never set foot upon the earth. Wherever he went he was the center of his family, his herds, and the grasslands so vast they extended from one skyline to the other.

And that was how things were for Lord Fury until the day when he and his followers looked out and saw a long line of horsemen riding toward them. His men armed themselves for fighting but, in the end, they took a beating.

When the fighting was over, Lord Fury's enemies stripped him of his gold and weaponry, stole his wives and herds, hung him by his ankles from a tree branch, and left him there for dead.

In time, the rope gave way and he fell head first. There he lay, beneath the tree, like a dead man, reeling from blood-loss, and missing one eye. A puddle of clear water welled up from beneath the tree roots and, at the bottom of that pool, he spotted his eye. He crawled over to the water, knelt at the pool's edge, and reached in, but his eye rolled away. No matter how desperate he was to have it back, his eye remained beyond his grasp.

He asked himself, how he could live with only half his sight? Up until then, he had been a champion. He had won every fight that he had ever engaged in, all but for the last one, that is. How would he fare now? His grief was so great that he could have cried that puddle himself.

A small man then appeared beside him. Indeed, the man appeared to be a bit soft. The skin on his cheeks hung loosely and, because of his lazy eyelids, he looked like he was half-asleep.

The Rememberer then made all his listeners laugh by mimicking the little man's high, squeaky voice. "I see that you are dabbling your hands in my well," he said. "Are you thirsty? Do you wish to drink from my well?"

But when the storyteller spoke for Lord Fury, everyone trembled at the way he bellowed, "No, I want my eye back."

So the little man and Lord Fury sat there, gazing into the well, and thinking over what they might do to get his eye back. But when they saw a big, thick-bodied fish come out of the shadows and open its mouth, they gazed in horror at its rows of sharp, pointy teeth.

The fish snatched his eye and ate it.

Lord Fury sprang to his feet and howled.

But the little man responded, "Ho, you will never get it back now. That lies in the past. It is gone." He patted the tree root and said, "But if you sit beside me, I will dress your wounds."

So there the two men sat beneath the tree. Whenever the little man dipped the blood-stained cloths in the water, the redness scattered, and the pool remained clear. Lord Fury stirred the water with his hand, and asked, "How can that be?"

"Wise judgment comes from loss. This is what you seek," the little man said.

Up until then, the youthful Lord Fury had directed all his efforts toward tests of courage and skill with weaponry. He had lived to accumulate wealth and personal esteem and to retaliate against his enemies. He had lived for strife. What did he care about wisdom or the capacity to judge rightly? The enemy clan had taken his wives and herds and left him for dead. Lord Fury planned to redress the wrongs.

"What is this soundness of judgment you speak of?" he asked the man. "How do you know that I seek it?"

"This water is like the tears that are shed from the tree above," the little man said. "Grief settles like dew upon the leaves, falls to the ground, soaks in and wells to the surface, just as do your tears. Yet it carries with it all that has befallen."

Lord Fury hastily pulled his hand from the water. He shook off the drops and wiped his fingers on his trouser legs. He wanted nothing more to do with tears. There was only one cure for grief, and its name was revenge.

The little man continued, "This is no ordinary wellspring. Healing and thirst for wisdom may be had from its waters." He took a drinking horn from beneath his cloak, dipped it in the water, and gave Lord Fury a drink.

After Lord Fury had supped, he felt the old power surge inside himself again. And, along with the ascendancy of a new thirst for wisdom, his old need for vengeance receded into the past. The little man told Lord Fury to get up and to try his strength. When he did so, except for the partial blindness, he felt as though he had never been hurt.

"You only acquire wisdom through the search itself," the little man told Lord Fury. "Like a never-ending spiral, wisdom is both sought and found at the same time. There is no end-point to the search, and there will be no end-point to the wisdom you may obtain."

"You speak in riddles," Lord Fury said.

"Like an endlessly twisting spiral, this riddle has no answer," the little man replied.

Lord Fury and the little man then parted company the best of friends. Lord Fury set out to discover the unanswerable answer to the riddle that endless acquisition of wisdom posed, and the little man continued to tend his well beneath the tree.

Over time, Lord Fury came to understand that the first clue to the riddle's answer lay with the fish, inside of whose belly his eye would remain lodged forever. As it swims through all the waters that flow continuously between the worlds, his eye becomes aware of all things that the fish can see and informs him of all things that matter most to him. In this way, the eye, he lost, has the power to look into the hidden things that remain concealed from the view of others, to reveal secret knowledge, and to direct his actions.

Soon after Lord Fury set out, he spotted a glimmer in the tall grass. Upon investigating, he discovered a spear. When Lord Fury threw it, he found it was well balanced, was fast as a gale wind, would strike any target he aimed at and, of its own accord, would come back to his hand. Because of its unusual powers, he named his cunning spear Attacker. So, although his luck had nearly left him, now that he had the means to catch game, he was confident that he would not die of hunger. He wandered until the sky turned dark and, that night, slept with only Attacker at his side to comfort and befriend him.

The following morning, he espied his horse Slippery, still bridled and saddled, and grazing on a low hill nearby. Slippery was fast and shifty as the wind to ride and, no doubt, because no man but Lord Fury could mount him, had escaped capture. When Lord Fury whistled, Slippery perked up his ears. When Lord Fury whistled again, Slippery raised his head and looked about. When he whistled a third time, Slippery spotted him and trotted over. Lord Fury wrapped his arms around his horse's neck and kissed him. After he checked the bridle and saddle, he jumped onto his horse's back.

Lord Fury was so glad to have found Slippery, he began to sing. And when other voices began to harmonize with his own, he knew he was no longer alone.

From behind a low hill several of his former companions came out of hiding, riding horseback. Though Lord Fury suspected they had escaped capture because they had turned their backs to the enemy and had run, because he was lonely and had no other men from whom to choose, he agreed to be their leader.

The ragged bunch then headed northwest to stay beyond the reach of their foes. After they had traveled for several days, they came to a dark line of trees. Standing against the horsemen like a stockade without an entrance, it extended from one skyline to the other to mark the place where the grassland met the forest.

Because the men's skittish horses were accustomed to the open steppes, they were wary of the woodland's closed-in spaces. They tossed their heads, reared up, and tried to throw their riders.

But with the enemy clans at their backs, the men had no choice but to go into the woods. Lord Fury raised Attacker and threw it into the forest. A terrible gale began to blow. And as his spear passed through the woods, the trees bowed to both sides to open a wide road before the men. Attacker then circled and returned to Lord Fury's upraised hand.

Lord Thunder then appeared in the western sky and struck his shield with his hammer to make a great din. A lightning bolt spat from a cloud to set fire to a single, massive oak where it grew like a watchman at the edge of the forest. A second lightning strike touched a low-hanging cloud and released a heavy downpour.

Lord Fury said, "Lord Thunder is with us today. Let's go."

And at his command, they entered the forest. As each man bid a silent farewell to the grasslands, the rain struck the leafy canopy above his head, the thunder rolled across the sky, and his horse's hooves crushed the sticks and branches covering the forest floor.

Within a short time, a line of fighters emerged to defend the forest. Lord Fury and his men had never seen such men before. "What kind of men are these?" the horsemen asked.

One man wore a helmet made from a boar's skull and tusks; the others wore helmets made from coarse boar hides. They were clothed in thick leather vests, and cords strung with boar teeth hung around their necks. The forest-dwellers easily outnumbered the horsemen. Goaded to fight by their yelling, Lord Fury and his men took their shields and weaponry in hand, jumped from their mounts, and engaged the forest-dwellers in their foe's preferred style of combat.

The air thrummed and clattered with the clang of metal striking metal. Though the horsemen were unaccustomed to fighting within the closed-in spaces between the trees, their steel knives and spears went unmatched by the forest dwellers' bronze weaponry. Yet, they all put up a good fight and men on both sides were killed.

In the end, the few forest-dwellers who were still alive called the retreat, ducked in amongst the trees, and disappeared. As for the horsemen, after they had picked up their dead and wounded and thrown them over the backs of their horses, they mounted and continued on their way. Soon they came to a village made of small, round houses. Half-buried beneath thatched roofs, each one looked like a large mushroom poking up from the forest floor.

The women who had been left to defend themselves responded to the threat the horsemen posed. They came out of their houses in a great flurry, screaming, and waving their ladles, brooms, and cooking knives.

When Lord Fury spotted full-figured Lady Blessed, he knew immediately she was the one he would take to be his wife. Where he came from, on the grasslands, it was proper to kidnap a woman after the bride-price had been settled and to carry her off, on horseback, to his mother's round, felt-covered tent. But since he had neither asked for her hand in marriage, nor had he presented her father with the goats, sheep, and horses equal to her value, and neither did he have a tent to bring her to, he figured that he would work out those troublesome details later. First, he had to capture her before she got away.

Lord Fury charged forward, jumped from his horse, and landed atop her. During the ensuing scuffle, she was forced to drop her knife. They set about each other and, between them, there was a fierce struggle. They rolled around in the mud. She beat him with her fists and spat in his blind eye.

"You will need to aim better than that," Lord Fury laughed.

She gathered more spittle in her mouth and pursed her lips, but he covered her mouth with his. He took that spit into his mouth, kissed her hard, and said, "Just as the wild horse is broken to the saddle, a woman needs to be tamed and ridden."

Lady Blessed then showed Lord Fury how faulty was his reasoning. There was a tussle between them. She struck and kicked him hard until he could hold onto her no longer. Sometimes he was atop her and, at other times, she knocked him flat on his back.

When he lay beneath Lady Blessed, two other women took hold of Lord Fury's arms, and pushed them down hard into the mud. A fourth woman grabbed both their knives and held them to Lord Fury's throat.

Lady Blessed then pulled down his trousers. Aroused as he was by their grappling, she sat upon his pillar and rode him as if he were a stallion. "Where I come from, this is how women wed their men," she said. "Now tell me this: who will protect our children? For who is to say that you are not siring one of your own right now?"

As for Lord Fury, who had one woman holding two knives at his throat, two women holding his arms, and a fourth woman sitting atop him, what else could he do but answer, "By my cunning spear, I promise to protect your children and mine."

"And who will work my field?"

"Not I," he said, drawing a line, which she dared not cross. "I do not work the soil, I am a herdsman."

"Then will you herd the cows?"

"Not I," he said, continuing to dispute her. "Where I come from, cows are no good." Instead, he proclaimed proudly, "I am a horseman," and like a wild mustang, he bucked his rider hard.

But Lady Blessed was having none of it. Refusing to be tossed off so easily, she said, "Oh husband, now answer me this: who has been broken to the saddle and who is riding her mount?"

Though he pulled hard against the women who were holding his arms, he was unable to loosen their grip. Yet he refused to give in. "You have me wrong. I am a wanderer," he said, "and will keep to my old ways. I roam from land to land gathering wisdom." And, holding fast to his position, he added, "Either take me as I am, or cut my throat and be done with me for good. Take your pick."

By then, the melee between the horsemen and the forest-dwelling women had ended. Lord Fury's men swept the yard, disarmed the women, and chased them back into their houses. Some of the men began to walk the perimeter. Those, who were uncertain of Lord Fury's intentions regarding the woman who was sitting astride him, stood off to the side, watching the strange encounter. None dared to second guess Lord Fury's reasoning, nor to interrupt the stand-off. And so, they awaited their orders.

Lord Fury looked from man to man. To indicate that he had the situation covered and, might even be enjoying himself, he winked his good eye. Upon seeing this confident gesture, the men stood back and left the outcome to their enigmatic leader.

So, there they lay, in the mud, soaked by the rain, and thinking over their choices. Finally, Lady Blessed gave in to Lord Fury's demands, and said, "All right then, have it your own way."

The Lady rolled off and took back her cooking knife. Once she was up and standing, she waved the blade in the direction of her house. "Now, come along husband," she said, "and dry yourself off by my hearth."

Lord Fury did as he was ordered. He stood, pulled up his trousers, and picked up his spear. And, ever since that day, Lord Fury has never understood whether it was he who took her, or whether it was she who took him. But common wisdom says that Lady Blessed is the only one who can hold Lord Fury on the short lead and draw him in.

Inside her hut, Lord Fury sat undressed by her fire. Vulnerable as a new-born babe, wrapped in a blanket while his clothes were drying, his eye never left her knife. Nor did her eyes ever leave his spear.

"What metal is this made from?" she asked, and pointed lustily to its tip.

"My spear is made from iron," he told her. "But your knife is made from bronze. Bronze shatters when it comes up against iron."

"The likes of iron are not to be found around here."

"You are wrong," Lord Fury said. "There is plenty of iron in the bogs around here. When I was passing through your forest, I saw the red-colored waters in the marshy terrain where bog-iron grows. Iron is valuable and worthy of protection. But to make things from this metal requires special know-how and the high heat of a charcoal fire. Give me and my men a place to live and we will harvest the bog-iron for you and will teach your men how to make steel weaponry."

The spear's silvery, blue-black sheen appealed very strongly to Lady Blessed and, being a woman with a practical nature, she knew that this was what she had to have.

That night, when Lady Blessed invited Lord Fury to share her bed, he willingly accepted her offer.

Meanwhile, the other horsemen lit fires, tended to their wounded, and kept the watch against attack by those forest-dwellers who were still hiding in amongst the trees.

Lord Fury and Lady Blessed were lying beneath her fur bed covers when someone came inside. She picked up her knife and asked, "Who is there?"

It was Grerr, the man who made her bronze weaponry and jewelry, and with whom she had gone to bed at times. "I snuck in past the invaders," he said.

"Grerr, you are no longer wanted in my bed."

Hearing that, he went away.

The next to enter was her brother, Lord Benevolent. He was the one whose helmet was made from a boar's skull.

"Brother put down your knife and spear when you are in my house," Lady Blessed said.

"You shelter an enemy."

"He is no enemy. He is now my husband."

Her brother spat at her feet and called her a traitor.

She told him to hold his spittle until the next day.

He answered, "Have it your own way," and went out again.

Early the following morning, Lady Blessed picked up her bronze kettle and rattle. First, she set the kettle at the foot of the pillar that was erected at the center of their village. Then she walked from house to house with her rattle, calling everyone to join her. Women, children, and those men who had snuck into their homes under the cover of darkness sat in the circle. Others, who were still in the trees, came out of hiding. Lord Fury ordered his men to join them.

All the men removed their axes, throwing hammers, and long and short knives from their belts, and placed their weaponry behind their backs. Lady Blessed's brother, Lord Benevolent, sat cross-legged, removed his helmet and placed it between his knees.

When all the forest-dwellers and the horsemen were gathered, Lady Blessed addressed them. She began by saying that despair was in all their hearts. The antagonism between the forest dwellers and the horsemen had gone on for a long time. Lord Fury and his men were not the first to threaten their borders. Over time, the casualties on both sides had mounted. There had been no winners. Everyone had lost. Now was the time to leave those age-old grievances behind. Regardless of their differences, the forest-dwellers should settle their quarrel with the horsemen.

"This is how things are with us," she said. "Lest the fighting begin anew, I challenge those of you who resent the unfair treatment they have suffered to collect your righteous spit. Just as spittle comes from your mouth, so do words that express hatred, fear, anger, and scorn. Today I instruct you to spit into the common pot. In this way we will bring about friendly relations between all men and women who are seated here today. We all have something to contribute to the well-being of our village. When we all spit into the cauldron, we make peace. Our spittle will spawn understanding between us.

"We may either continue the fight or we may end the fight. I, for one, do not seek to get back at those who hurt us. I have taken stock of the situation and chosen to end the killing. We know that an empire is amassing strength in the south. I worry that our lands will be overrun and our people will be taken captive and forced into servitude. If we do not adapt to the horsemen's ways, we will fall prey to others who, also, make iron knives. The time of bronze weaponry is over."

Lady Blessed was the first to rise. She walked to the center of the circle and knelt beside the kettle. She spoke of their losses and of her grief for those who had died. After she was finished speaking, she spat a great wad of saliva. She stood and faced them all. She admonished them, saying, "To bring about the success of this trust between us, we must all agree. I remind you, there can be no breach, or the circle will not hold."

She began to hum in a low guttural tone. It was so steady and so deep, it sounded as though it rose from the earth upon which they were sitting. Men and women picked from her earth-song echoes of both joy and sorrow. And, one by one, each man, woman, and child rose and walked to the kettle. Before they spat, their tears and blood flowed into that kettle. The villagers begrudged the victors for beating them so badly. The fighters were ashamed of running and hiding in the trees. The horsemen missed the grasslands, their herds, their families, and their dead war companions.

In the end, the last two men to spit into the kettle were Lord Fury and Lord Benevolent. The Lady's brother stared at Lord Fury. But Lord Fury was determined to go last, and he met his opponent's gaze. As each man thought it over, he asked himself who would be the first to reach behind his back and to grab a weapon.

To break the standoff, Lady Blessed said, "Brother, will you agree to behave accordingly and to stay with us? Or will you run into the woods and, like a wild boar, grovel for your supper among the tree roots?"

Lord Fury's hands tingled with anticipation. And though they rested on his knees, he was ready to grab his weaponry if her brother tried to take him on.

Finally, Lord Benevolent stood and, without so much as a glance behind his back, walked to the kettle, knelt, and spat.

Lord Fury, grinning broadly, stood, walked to the kettle, and spat last.

Now that they had come full circle, Lady Blessed ended her song. She wrapped her arms around the kettle and hugged it close to her chest. She covered it with a towel and bound it in place with a rope. Holding the two long ends of rope in her hands, she lifted her skirts and tied the ends together at the back. When she was finished, she looked like she was heavy with child. Stroking the kettle, she seemed to be patting an unborn babe. And, whilst she walked around the circle, she smiled and laughed and extended her arms out to her sides.

Over time, the men who had previously lived on the grasslands, married forest-dwelling women. The horsemen learned how to plow and harvest; and the forest-dwellers learned how to ride horses and to forge iron weaponry.

As for Lord Fury, he waited to take up wandering until the spittle in the kettle had fermented. In nine months, a son was born, and his mother named him Wise. When he was one week old he drank from a cup. When he was one month old he walked and ran and jumped. When he was one year old he spoke. Wise knows the answer to all questions and travels far and wide. He tells stories about friendship born from belligerence and acceptance born from heartache.

And though it is said that Lady Blessed had never been beholden to any man but was beholden only to herself, after Lord Fury's arrival the two pledged to be fully true to one another. She named her husband her Furious Lord and he named his wife his Blessed Lady. And over time, they had many more children.

Lord Fury and Lady Blessed are the ancestors of all their followers. They give them rich harvests from their grain fields, and assure them of glorious victory on the battlefield. They gather the souls of those men and women who await their wild hunt. And afterward, they lead their followers to the place where the dead go, here, in this Hall of Many Seats where they join in our endless celebration.

And thus, my story ends. Now go in peace.

VII.

Lord Fury thanked the Rememberer and closed the box lid. This celebration of their union had so changed his earlier misgivings to an affirmation of their deep, abiding love, that he no longer questioned the reasons for which his wife had sought him out that morning. Instead, he was grateful to Lady Blessed for the surprise feast and expected even more delights awaited him. He leaned in close to his wife and whispered in her ear, "My dear, what additional, private amusements have you in store for me tonight?" He licked his lips and squeezed her hand suggestively. "Perhaps you wish to lead me to the soft featherbed in your bower?"

She smiled beguilingly, gazed appealingly into his eye, and gently placed her hand upon his wrist. "I do have something in mind for you."

The fingers of her other hand felt their way beneath her pale green apron. Sight unseen, her hand slipped slowly into the bag that hung from her belt, and she pulled out a bronze disk. To cleanse it, Lady Blessed held the edges with her fingertips and exaggerated the way she rubbed it across the linen.

Lifting the mirror to her mouth, she pursed her lips and blew. Her warm, moist breath fogged the cold metal. She glanced briefly at the images that were slowly coming to its surface, lowered her chin to peek coyly at her husband, and with a tilt of her head, she subtly invited him to move in closer so that he, too, could look.

In hopes of seeing something enticingly arousing, Lord Fury raised an eyebrow. Might the mirror reveal a picture of his Lady combing out her long, lustrous hair? That tempting thought then led him to imagine the way that he would like to unplait the tresses himself. He would bury his face in handfuls of her sweetly scented hair, before he first unpinned the apron, and then undid the belt, and then lifted the dress over her head. Moved by his arousal, he placed one hand upon her arm. He leaned in closely until their cheeks were nearly touching. His breath wended its way beneath the fabric of her bodice to become a gentle, summertime breeze, a small whirling zephyr skipping merrily across a field with child-like abandon. Tossing up dried leaves and grasses before he snuck in, playfully, between his wife's hillock-shaped breasts to assert his rights to warm her bare skin with his breath—.

Lady Blessed interrupted his reverie with a sharp tap on the mirror's edge to draw his wandering attention back to her mirror, and said, "Look here."

Forced to attend to the images coming into focus on the disk's surface, Lord Fury saw nothing at all resembling his earlier expectations. "A family of farmers?" he asked. "What is the meaning of this?"

"Look more closely. Tell me what you see."

"A man and a woman, who I assume is his wife, are resting beneath a tree on the edge of a field. Since I also see a team of oxen grazing nearby, I assume they are taking a break from their fieldwork. The man is sprawled out on his side with his back to me. He leans on an elbow and lazily extends his legs. An older girl kneels beside her mother to help unpack their basketful of food. A small boy comes running at them and pushes his father in the chest. The man laughs, grabs the boy, and rolls onto his back. He pulls his son down atop himself. Then he and the boy roll around, wrestling. Who are these people?"

"Do you remember, Lord Fury, a night when our hunting party came upon an entire warband after it had been wiped out in an ambush? A lone survivor was left to take care of his dead war companions' bodies. It was quite some time ago, and perhaps you have forgotten. But this is the same man who, after he recovered from his wounds, burned their bones on the funeral pyre. That night, all the freed souls joined our hunt."

"So, it was. I do recall that night. Afterward, we celebrated in this hall. Is this the unfortunate man we left behind? I have given him little thought since then. Why bring it up now? I take it he found a home?"

"He did and, yes, even though he was destitute, abandoned by his kinsmen, and declared an outlaw, I found him a wife. But before I could arrange his marriage, I was forced to prod him several times and to push him in the right direction. Finally, he wandered into the farming hamlet where this woman lived. After that, my plans fell into place."

"What plans?"

"I am getting to that. The woman was the youngest daughter in her family and, because she cared for her elderly father, had been deemed unmarriageable. The poor dear was terribly lonely and fearful for her future. She pleaded with me to send her a man of good heart whom she might wed. Day and night that desperate woman prayed. She never quit. Just the sound of that woman's persistent pleas was so annoying, I was nearly driven to distraction. Until that night, that is. When I spotted the man, I realized that he was the perfect solution to my problem.

"Out of all those who were standing around the pyres that night, reminiscing about the good times they had had fighting together, he was the only one still alive. I figured he was ripe for the taking. The outlaw was so available, and the woman was so pitiable. I had no choice but to solve the poor dear's problem. I had grown so dreadfully weary of her insistent begging, you see."

"If you ask me, the man sounds pitifully unattractive, too," Lord Fury said. "You say he was destitute, abandoned by his kinsmen, and declared an outlaw? When you add it all up, it leaves him with less than nothing to offer a woman's father in the way of bride price."

"Oh, quite right and besides, he had been badly hurt and did not look very pretty anymore."

"Did you pity me, too, because I was hurt? I do not look very pretty either."

"Their marriage was convenient to them both."

"Oh, so you saw something in me you wanted."

"Perhaps, if that is the way you want to look at it. But that is not the way I see it. I had been awaiting your arrival for quite some time."

"You saw me in your mirror?"

"Yes, and you were more attractive than I expected."

"Oh, so you like your men tall."

"Not necessarily."

"Oh, right, I forgot, there was Grerr."

"Yes, he was my wild bull." Her eyes became unfocused and a distant look of longing crossed her face. "He was my green lion. And," she added, pointedly, "he always did whatever I asked him to do."

"He was short, though, wasn't he?"

"Stop mocking me. Listen. Both the man and the woman were lonely people in need of help. Can you not see? It was my duty to care for them. He had lost all his friends and family. No one would help him. Not even his own mother. Besides, because he had outlived them all, only one of his dead war companions had shamed him that night. He felt so hopeless he was about to give up and die."

"I saw no sadness in the pleasant family scene you showed me."

"Apparently, marriage suits him. Though he was not what the poor woman had in mind, in the end, it came down to only one thing: she wanted a husband who would sit at her hearth and warm her bed, and the outlaw needed a place to live and a wife who would feed him. Since each one needed something from the other, they agreed to tie the knot."

"Somehow you pulled it off. You took pity on them both and it was settled." He pecked his wife affectionately on the cheek and, acting as though she were a child who had just completed a simple task, he patted her hand, and said, "You did well, my dear."

He tipped his head to the side, lifted his brows, rubbed his clasped hands between his thighs, and wiggled in his seat. "Now, what do you say we leave the feast and return to our private chambers?"

"I have not finished telling you my story yet."

Lord Fury sat up straight. After he had been so tersely put in his place, he staved off anticipation of lusty delights and listened properly.

"To celebrate their marriage vows, the woman promised me the first girl, who was born from their union, would become one of my devoted followers. Now that she is coming of age, I intend to make their daughter one of the wisewomen who perform divination ceremonies in the chieftain's meadhalls."

"The mother might not have had that possibility in mind, you know."

"So?"

"Is she clever enough to be a wisewoman?"

"As it turns out, the outlaw's mother came from a long line of women who had, over the generations, produced several, notably clever wisewomen. So yes, lineage favors her. Likewise, the girl has the sight and has shown a gift for both reading the signs and for taking flight in the dreamtime. But last night something dreadful happened over which I have no control. You know how I hate to lose. And," Lady Blessed added, peevishly tapping the mirror with her forefinger, "I will lose this girl unless you fix it." She then poked Lord Fury in the chest several times with that same impertinent finger, and said, "I want you to bring her to me—alive that is."

Aggrieved by her suggestion, Lord Fury drew back into his chair. "So, now I see it. This is why I am here. This is the reason for the flattery. I knew something was up. The feast was all a ruse meant to make me more agreeable to your entreaties." He snorted loudly and shook his head.

Leaning back into the far corner of his chair, he straightened out his long legs and crossed them at the ankles. Pretending boredom with the festivities, he looked around the hall. When he spotted one of the serving girls nearby, he considered pulling her down onto his lap just to provoke his wife. But after he had thought better of that bad idea, he crooked his finger, winked his eye, and asked her to bring him a cup of ale.

As for Lady Blessed, she did not look the least bit concerned about her husband's insolent refusal. She lifted her chin and smiled benevolently at all the celebrants who were noisily laughing, gaming, and tossing the dice. When one of her favorites challenged another man to an arm-wrestling match, she clapped her hands and cheered him on.

Whereas Lord Fury, unlike Lady Blessed's favorites, the dogged farmers who could plow and rake and dig and hoe and swing a scythe from morning to night without giving in to the insufferable boredom of it all, was a herdsman from the grasslands. Born with the heart of a nomad, he was always on the watch, was easily distracted from one moment to the next, and unable to remain ignored and on the sidelines for long.

He shrugged indifferently and sat up straight. Resting an elbow on the chair arm, he leaned in toward his wife. "Blessed, if you could fully grasp the challenges that I am up against right now, you would know that I do not have time for this trifling matter. I have a lot on my mind." Pressing his fingertips together and lifting his hands to his chin, he thoughtfully tallied the reasons that would prevent the fulfillment of her request. "Disputes about leadership will be argued at the upcoming Assembly in the Victory Hall. Because the Lords of Battle are in league with Lord Thunder to unseat Lord Glory, I am working out a way to make peace between those who remain loyal to Lord Glory and those who plan to wrest away his leadership. His detractors even go so far as to mock him because the wolf Treachery mangled his right hand."

"That sounds like something Spider the Entangler would do. I will never forgive him for taking our son, White Fire, captive and holding him for ransom. I would like to tie Spider to a rock and drip venom onto his face."

Lord Fury gently patted her on the wrist to calm her. "I promise to get back at him but I can only tackle one enemy at a time. Anyway, Lord Thunder and his allies are up to no good. The stories they tell make Lord Glory look foolish. But he was a hero. He put an end to the Terrible Winter. So, now, I ask you, where were those cowards when he was chasing Treachery? Somehow, your brother, Lord Benevolent, is in on it too. How he ever came to be seated at the high table in the Victory Hall, I will never understand."

"It is no wonder to me. Since your arrival, he has not felt welcome here."

"A man does not like to think that his wife's brother is in bed with her."

"For shame, to say such a thing. That is not true. It is a baseless rumor and you know it."

"It was probably Thunder's doing. He called me a cuckold once—what gall."

"You know Thunder is all bluster and no substance."

"Perhaps. But he is clever enough to bait the chieftains with promises of victory if they agree to offer him blood-gifts and swear to fight in his name. Their ring-leader is a man named Leofar. But now that you have reminded me of that young woman's father, I recall that he and his war companions were among the first victims of Leofar's treachery. I would like to take on that rogue myself, but will need men on the ground who can help me. Besides, Leofar has Lord Thunder's protection. Things will need to change before we can get rid of him for good."

"Maybe the man, of whom we are speaking, will become your man on the ground."

"What an inviting notion. You said that he was hurt. Can he still fight?"

"I believe so."

"Perhaps you are right. But, as I was saying, the alliance as it now stands must remain intact or I fear that everything, as we know it, will come to a crushing end. Thunder's followers forget the goodness that Lord Glory stands for. They abandon the respect and honor freemen deserve and deride fair and just treatment before the law. They supplant those beliefs with strife to benefit their own self-regard and standing.

"Thunder looks for ways to enhance his prestige among men, even if he must appeal to their basest, most animal-like natures. He fuels Leofar's and the other men's greed and hatred. Thunder's followers blame those in the western lands for their troubles, makes them the target of their anger, and the reason for all their failures. The solutions Leofar offers are unsound. He promotes the idea that the chieftains should cease paying the tribute, which their fathers and grandfathers have paid to maintain the peace and to guarantee their freedom. If they stop paying the annual tribute, it will lead to an unwinnable war."

Lady Blessed, in contrast to Lord Fury's building outrage, adopted a feigned disinterest in his grievances. As he continued to describe the underhanded treachery and double-dealing among the Lords and the ensuing risks of war, she turned away. First, she busied herself with the bronze disk. Then she tucked it into her bag and smoothed her apron and skirts. She began to fuss about with her cloak, called over one of her attendants, and requested she pin it again at the shoulders.

It was not until Lord Fury had settled down and the woman had left the dais that Lady Blessed casually mentioned her own counter argument. "I know quite well what you are talking about. But let me remind you that men use talk of troubles between warring factions to diminish women's abilities and concerns. The matters that I oversee, birth and regeneration, are of elemental importance. When the wisewomen in my service carry messages between the realms, they bring about peace and plenty. In an abundant world, where all men and women share alike in the bounty, there is fair treatment for everyone and peaceful resolution of conflicts.

"It is when there is scarcity that men fight. The destruction of lives and farmland that war brings about becomes the cause of more scarcity. Wars breed more wars, and war brings about more scarcity. It becomes an endless cycle of killing, waste, and destruction. To counter scarcity and to bring about peaceful resolution of conflict is the reason that I want this young woman to become one of my followers."

Lord Fury scowled. "To keep scarcity in check, and to maintain peace between warring factions is a heavy burden to place upon a young woman's shoulders." Nor did he agree that war was the only contributor to scarcity. But conflict? Yes. Conflict and competition between all the worlds was the reason. When you had the likes of Spider, Thunder, the Sons of the Fiery Realm, and the wolf named Treachery, just to name a few, there was bound to be trouble. Then, too, there were the Frost Devourers and the Wind-bringers who live in the north; the shadow-walking men who live in the tunnels; and the bogmen who live in the Ironwood. Additionally, there were the men and women who walk the surface of the earth. All of whom on the lookout for ways to benefit their own interests. To keep peace among them all was well-nigh impossible. Nor had he included those who dance creation and destruction into being: Mother Necessity, Father Time and their three daughters, the Matrones of the Becoming.

Since the very beginning, violence has saturated the cosmos. The cosmos was born of chaos. It was hard to accept Lady Blessed's unrealistic notion that endless abundance would bring about peaceful resolution of conflict. But tonight was not a good time to point out the errors in Lady Blessed's thinking. There were other things that he would rather do than argue.

In response to Lord Fury's silent reflections upon doom, Lady Blessed hinted at her own inscrutable foresight by suggesting that she may have heard his thoughts as clearly as if he had spoken them aloud. "Someday, during the troubled times ahead, even you, Lord Fury, may come to this young woman for consultation."

This seeming proof of the young woman's value implied that she might achieve a renown equal to the most cunning of the wisewomen. "But, unless you do something about it now, both of us will be deprived of her invaluable service. You said that you need men on the ground. So, too, do you need a woman for more than housekeeping duties and child-rearing. But, unfortunately, the cord with which I had bound her to me has frayed. I would like you to repair it," she said, and added with a casual lift of one shoulder, "The cause should not concern you."

"Oh, is that right?" he asked, and acting as though he were reeling in a more de-tailed explanation for the problem he was being asked to resolve, he waved his hand, suggestively, in a circular, wheel-like, motion. "What else? Hmm?"

But when she refused to take the hint, he gave up on subtlety and asked point blank, "So you expect me to re-tie the cord? Is that it?"

Still getting no response, he turned his one good eye toward her and, looking down at her from the steep, twisted side of his nose, he asked, "What exactly is this difficulty you say should not concern me? Describe the obstacle that has come between you and the young woman, and tell me why you are unable to take care of it yourself."

"It should be an easy fix. I have the utmost confidence in your knot-tying tricks."

"Now it is you who are mocking me. I am being reasonable, and you are shrug-ging off my questions. If the cord, with which you had tied this young woman to you, has come undone, I want to know if someone is preventing her from taking her vows to be fully true to you. Until you tell me who sliced the cord in two and what tool was used, I refuse to help." Lord Fury frowned, sprawled into the chair corner, folded his arms across his chest, stared at her, and said stubbornly, "Fix it yourself."

Lord Fury knew what would happen next. A shadow would cross Lady Blessed's face. Her eyes would stray and well with tears. Then she would give him a plaintive look, one which she knew from past experience would evoke in him a sense of deep sympathy.

And just as he expected, her shoulders slumped. She spread all ten fingers over her soft, round belly. Wordlessly expressing the sadness that struck at the very center of her empty heart and womb, her eyes pleaded with him to fill the void a childless mother suffers for a missing daughter, and said, "She has refused me."

He shook his head and sighed in consternation. Though he questioned why the girl had refused her, he knew that to fight the inevitable was impossible. He stood up from his high seat and got down on his knees. Kneeling there before her, he looked up into her face. He lifted one hand from her belly and held it to his lips. He kissed each of her fingertips, one by one, as he silently counted the ways that she was playing him for a fool. She was hiding crucial information. She knew quite well who had cut that cord. She knew whether the knife had otherworldly powers. And yet, she had refused to tell him. That fact alone was a sign of trouble. Of course, she knew who had cut the cord and why. She knew the relevant details, and yet, for some reason, had refused to fill him in.

Under those conditions, he would be a fool to accept the task. He knew he was a fool and she knew it, too. She knew he was a fool—an eager fool. He was an eager fool, who wanted to please his Lady. And, here he was, on his knees, begging like a fool to receive her favors.

The Lady reached out with her other hand to caress his cheek, and whispered, "My Lord, if you feel even half the affection I feel for you, please me with this simple request. It was I who created this man and woman's home-life. Now it is my right to claim their daughter for myself."

Quite right. On one hand, Lord Fury had limited understanding of the Lady's request and that did not bode well. But, on the other hand, a vigorous pursuit of his game offered a huntsman, like himself, a promising entertainment. To bring a young, unsuspecting woman to Lady Blessed should be easy.

Lady Blessed's adroit charm and the lure of the hunt had turned him. She had feasted him and flattered him, shamelessly. But the praise had worked its charm and, admittedly, neither was it all that far from the mark. Just as men had said tonight, he never lost a fight. He had the power to lay bonds upon his enemies and to make them helpless in battle. And, to accomplish the opposite for his followers, he loosened the bonds of fear and inspired courage. He skillfully tightened and loosened the bonds that connected men and women to their families, to their chieftains, and to their higher, ruling powers.

How did he it? He was fooling no one more than himself when he said it should be easy. There was a lot more to bringing about these marvelous outcomes than simple knot-tying tricks. It was never easy. Men and women were notorious for having minds of their own and for fouling up the ruling power's intentions.

But the evening was getting on and he was eager to bring this trifling matter to a close. If he agreed to Lady Blessed's request, she would take him by the hand and lead him to her bower. And, once they were there, he would participate in whatever private amusements she had in mind. Gleefully looking forward to crawling naked into his wife's soft featherbed, he licked his lips in anticipation of the lascivious games they would play. He threw back his head and roared.

Lord Fury grasped the arms of Lady Blessed's chair and pulled himself up to standing. He tossed all concerns aside, took his wife by the hand and helped her rise. "I will do the task. I will bring you the young woman. But before I take off in the morning, you had better offer me a bit more incentive this evening."

He stepped behind her back and, while placing one hand upon her shoulder, was extra careful not to touch the gold ring around her neck, his avoidance seemingly similar to the hesitancy with which one approaches an object hot enough to scorch. He wrapped his other hand's fingers around her ample upper arm, and pressed his hard thighs against her soft, pillowy buttocks. The Lady responded in kind by provocatively shaping herself to his lanky frame. He lowered his head and eased in closer. His top hand smoothed her full bosom. He caressed her downhill slope and, knowing fully that he would need to wait until they had entered her bower to complete his hand's journey and its exploration of her innermost, cave-like recesses, he stopped at her cinched-in waist.

Though he may have had his woman well in hand, clearly, it was she who had the strangest hold on her man. She turned to face him, pressed her hips aggressively against his thighs and wriggled side to side. Confident this last, suggestive gesture would ensure his complicity in the matter, she gently caressed his cheek and whispered, "Bring me the girl unsullied and you will be happy with your reward. This is all you need to know: the young woman is named Sunniva the Gifts of the Sun and the father is named Aiken the Strength of Oak. You will find them at Gevehard's village, on the shores of the Merchant Sea. Now turn this thing around before it gets completely out of hand."

"Never fear, my Lady. Slippery runs faster than the wind itself. We will be there before your red cock crows at dawn. But before we leave, you and me have more pressing matters to take care of here."

VIII.

Back when Fury spent some time with us perusing my book collection, I had always meant to ask him whether he had died on that tree or if, like us, he had managed to outwit death. But, somehow, the time never seemed right.

We did learn, however, that he was undeserving of our trust. Before we had wised-up to his trickery and had caught on to his talent for disguises, we had inadvertently empowered the imposter with all the information he needed for succeeding at the task that Lady Blessed had assigned him.

If he were he to succeed, I knew that nothing good would come of the pact that we had made with Aiken. Though there were convincing arguments favoring our rights, I, also, knew that Lady Blessed would remain indifferent toward anyone else who had laid a claim against the girl. She would never budge from her opinion that the pitiful woman's promise undermined our demand for due payment from Aiken, the very man whom the woman had wed.

Deeply invested, as we were at the time, in making good on Aiken's promise, I was deeply disturbed by what I had seen in the crystal ball. I grabbed a scrap of parchment, picked up my quill, unstoppered my ink bottle, and took note of everything I had witnessed. Then, after I was done, I marched through the tunnels and notified the men, with whom I share these living quarters, of the upcoming dispute.

Among the four us, Berling understood, better than the rest of us, what Lady Blessed was referring to when she told Fury that the cord had been cut. But instead of filling us in on the details, he told us not to worry. Foolishly and regrettably, I trusted his assurances that everything had been taken care of.

Disappointed that my report had generated so little interest, I set aside the scrap. But a comparison with the story of Rumbleshanks alarmed me with the number of similarities between them. A summary of the cautionary tale goes something like this:

> It all began when a man named Rumbleshanks heard a woman weeping. Curious and kindly by nature, he slipped through a crack in the wall, appeared before her, and asked why she was crying. She told him that her father had seen her talking to the boy whom she was sweet on. And, because her father disapproved of marriage to her young suitor, he had vowed to keep her away from the boy by locking her up this shed filled with raw flax. Because of her talent for spinning flax threads so fine that they were said to be worth their weight in gold, her greedy father had made her spin till her fingers turned bloody.
>
> The poor girl pleaded for help from the kindly man who had appeared so mysteriously before her. After he heard her dreadful tale, Rumbleshanks offered

to do whatever he could to alleviate her suffering. When he asked what she would give him in exchange for helping her spin the flax, the desperate woman promised to give him her first-born child in lieu of payment. The man agreed, took charge of the spinning and, overnight, filled the shed with threads so fine they were said to be worth their weight in gold.

The girl's father sold the thread and became a rich man. In gratitude, he gave in to his daughter's persistent pleas and allowed her to wed the youth. But before she agreed to marry him, she forced her betrothed to promise that he would never make her spin flax.

In time, she gave birth to a fine baby. When the strange man came to collect his due, the young mother clutched the child to her breast and pleaded with him not to take her baby. He agreed to give up his claim on one condition: she must guess his true name.

She asked one of Lady Blessed's wisewomen to spy on the strange man and to learn the answer to this puzzle. The wisewoman was successful and, thus, empowered the young woman with the means to gain control over her creditor. The following night, when the strange man appeared before the young woman, she uttered a vengeful curse and spoke Rumbleshanks's true name. The sound of his name passing her lips made Rumbleshanks so angry he drove his foot into the floor. He caused a small earthquake, fell into a crack in the earth, and disappeared.

It is a cautionary tale, indeed. But unfortunately, Berling, Grerr, and Allfrigg were unwilling to listen to my fearful prognostications. Even to this day, no one has acknowledged the accuracy of my prescience on the matter.

As for the slip of parchment, it lay hidden and forgotten until the fortuitous discovery of the long-knife jarred me from complacency. I set out to find my scribbled notations, and, true to form, after I had dug around in my reading room, discovered the text beneath a heap of books.

ONE

Jasper
If you will eschew all perils
and all terrible things and have a strong heart.

Take this stone which is called Jasper. If this stone has a blue color, it makes a
man mighty and helps him against adversaries and to understand dark questions
when visiting the afterworlds.

The Truth of Rocks, by Aluiss the Wise

I.

If someone were to ask me when I first began collecting things, truly, I could not say. Not in confidence, anyhow. I only know that I have always been here, surrounded by the things I collected for as long as I remember.

In the beginning, there was just the detritus I scrounged from the streambeds and the forest floor: the shells, horns and antlers, bones and teeth, bits of bark, leaves, feathers, and stones—the curiosities a child brings home; the things I valued enough to keep and wanted badly enough to assure their safety.

Now that I include in my collection the things a man of learning wants to keep, its entirety has grown so large that I must sort my collectibles into several different categories. Among them are both the items men and women made, including their artwork, books, and scrolls, and the curiosities Nature made.

Among those things that Nature made are the stones in my collection. Some I sort by kind, some I sort by color, and some I sort according to the likenesses and the landscapes I can see in their designs. Among them there are pictures of birds in flight, ocean waves, and moonlit skies. On some, there are pictures of trees, animals, or fishes. Others even have eyes.

Figured stones like these have been favored by collectors for quite some time. I have heard that the renowned painter, Leonardo Da Vinci, was known to gaze at figured stones and to study walls that had been marred by spots and stains. Seeing in them resemblances to landscapes, figures wearing fancy costumes, or men and women's faces, they frequently inspired the pictures he painted, including the one in which a sitting woman is smiling at the viewer in an especially intriguing manner.

Likewise, there is a picture of a man on one of my stones. He and the sky are colored dark gray-brown. The earth is pale ochre. An artist could have painted this small, round illumination by drawing broad, blocky brush strokes on the diagonal. In the background, flat, angular shapes represent mountain peaks. In the foreground, at the far-right edge, a few lines roughly indicate tree branches. The man in the picture is seen from the side, wearing a pointed cap and a heavy, full-skirted tunic. Because one knee is bent, he looks as though he has been caught forever in mid-step.

According to Pliny the Elder, there was a king named Pyrrhus who owned an agate upon which the nine muses were pictured dancing to a song that the Lord of Music was playing on his lyre. In my own collection I have a stone picturing a naked woman dancing ecstatically near a fire. A red-yellow flame in the foreground highlights the dancing figure. Her spine is arched and her head thrown back. The way her legs are spread apart and her knees are bent in a crouch, she appears to be seductively exposing her private parts to the fire. When I turn the stone over, she disappears in a white, crystalline cloud of smoke.

There are several stones on which I can identify writing in strange letters, glyphs and signs. According to Isidore of Seville's Etymologies, Nature records the things that happen in this world by painting pictures and writing texts on stone. The way in which Nature connects the individual letters in loops makes her cursive penmanship look like curvilinear, Arabic script. It is enticing to imagine that one could read these looping lines, but unfortunately, the text has been written in a language of stones no one but Nature understands.

Nonetheless, there are certain resemblances between both the script and the patterns, which Nature has drawn and written upon these stones, and the snake, which I have seen in the herringbone patterns that the smith made when she forged the long-knife. This observation leads me to wonder whether the glyphs and pictures, which I can see on my stones, may also communicate with me in the same way that the blade spoke and, additionally, will seem to come alive in the same way that the snake rears its head when I study the patterns on the blade's skin. And, furthermore, if such a thing were truly possible, I believe I may have found the solution to my quandary.

My thinking goes like this: if I could, indeed, read the writing on stones, and if my figured stones become the means with which I can decode a message, I might discover the story of the long-knife's birth. It is certainly worth a try. And, guided, either by chance or by design, I pick a round, stone bead out of my collection. Studying it in greater detail, I conclude that Nature has drawn a curled cypher using dark, blue-green ink upon a pale ochre-colored surface and outlined it with thin, yellow brush strokes.

When I hold my crystal lens above the bead to magnify the cypher, I notice its similarity to a fragment of a pictorial sign that either an Egyptian or a Sumerian scribe may have written. If Nature, like the scribe, had intended to abstract a symbol of a stag's most defining feature, she would have drawn an antler. But because it is only part of the glyph, which an Egyptian scribe would have drawn to represent a stag, I set out to help Nature along. By drawing imaginary lines between a series of dots with blue ink, I pretend to sketch an invisible outline of a deer with an invisible brush. A picture of an antler, head, neck, and body appears. This imaginary stag seems to have been caught forever at the height of its leap over a low hanging vine. It is outrunning a cat. The cat's tail is curled up over its body. And at the tip of its tail there is a snake-head.

Now, what should I make of that uncanny detail? To believe that I could read a glyph, which Nature had painted on a round, jasper bead, and furthermore, that I could translate its meaning, may seem far-fetched, indeed. But the strange appearance of a deer outrunning a cat with a snake head on the tip of its tail is convincing proof enough. This image carries a message from another, otherworldly source. I could not have made it up. Not at all. It was simply meant to be.

As my reverie deepens, I realize, with a start, that the blue vine, which the deer is leaping across, is in fact a blue tattoo wrapped around a man's suntanned forearm.

In my struggle to make sense of this strange apparition and to decipher its meaning, I conclude that, just as Isidore wrote, this way of gaining knowledge is simply another form of understanding. It just differs from the awareness that comes from either ordinary sensation, or from book-learning.

Encouraged by this strange revelation, along with a deepening faith in the unfolding narrative, I widen my line of sight. And now, I see that the man with the tattooed forearm is holding a goad in his left hand. What originally had been shaped like a small, round pebble has grown beyond its material borders and, through this correspondence, has taken on the form and bearing of a tattooed man who is riding in an oxcart. And seated beside him, on his right, there is a young woman.

II.

The man's cart rounded the corner of a cliff wall and entered a quarry yard. Cleared of all other vegetation, only a single oak provided shade. Several large, rough-cut, red stone slabs were either laid on the ground or stood on end in the yard. There were heaps of red gravel piled at the far end. Off to the right, beneath a thatched lean-to, two men were hammering red, stone chunks into rectangular blocks. This was a red world. The bare earth was red and even the tree leaves were coated with red dust.

To bring the cart to a halt, the man flicked the goad and spoke a word to the oxen. With the lithe, graceful precision of a dancer he leapt over the side and landed lightly on the balls of his feet. Since the day was getting hot, he pulled the tunic he wore over his head and threw it onto the bench. If I had known no better, now that I had been given a full view of the elaborate designs that were drawn upon his arms and back with blue ink, I could easily have concluded that he had taken off a plain, homespun shirt to show off an embroidered one.

He was a well-built man, broad across his shoulders and narrow through the hips. His light brown, shoulder length hair was neatly trimmed. It was when he turned to face me that I recognized the broad cheekbones, heavy brow, and the strong jawline that gave his head a square shape. His well-proportioned features and thick, straight eyebrows would have given him a pleasing look had it not been for the fact that the right-side of his face was badly disfigured by heavy scarring and the loss of an eye.

I know who these people are. Or rather, I knew who they were, back when they were alive. The man was named Aiken the Strength of Oak, and the girl was his daughter, Sunniva the Gifts of the Sun. This much I know for certain: these were the forebears of the woman who forged the long-knife that, even now, lays resting here on my table.

Aiken led the oxen to the single tree in the yard and tied them in the shade. He picked up a ball of cheese and the round bread his wife, Mildred, had packed for him. Holding them out to show his daughter, he said, "This is for the little men who live here beneath the earth."

"How little are they?"

"Oh, about knee high," he said, bending to the side to pat his knee.

"That is the size of a doll. I would like to see one."

"Then you will be sadly disappointed. One time, I heard a man say that he had caught sight of a little fellow from the corner of his eye. But when he turned to get a better look at him, the little man slipped through a crack in the rock and disappeared. I doubt that you will see one."

"If you cannot see them, why are you giving them bread and cheese?"

Gesturing broadly enough to encompass the entire quarry yard, he said, "Since all the stone around here belongs to them, the men who work the quarry say the little fellows demand payback in return for the stone they take. If you do not honor them with gifts, they will accuse you of thievery and play nasty tricks on you."

"Are you stealing their stone?"

"No. You see, if a man like me makes a fair exchange, the little fellows will show him where to find the best stone. But do not concern yourself with the little men. I will be here for a while, looking for the stone that Shipmaster Gevehard asked me to carve for him. While I am busy, you stay near the cart and do as your mother told you. Do not go wandering off, Sunniva," he added, with a shake of his finger, "the quarry is a dangerous place. You hear me?"

After he turned away, he walked several steps before glancing back to tease her, "You better watch out Sunniva. Do not let the little men play nasty tricks on you." And, after that final warning, he strode off, carrying his gifts and laughing at his little joke.

Though Sunniva nodded obediently, she was in no hurry to pick up the womanly work that her mother demanded she carry wherever she went. She gave the basket holding her fleece, spindle, and distaff a distasteful look. And since there was no reason to obey her mother, now that she was well beyond the range of Mildred's watchful eye, Sunniva gave the basket a good firm kick to shove it beneath the bench. She was ready for an adventure. And when as she saw her father talking with the men who worked beneath the lean-to, she jumped down from the cart.

A footpath that wound between the piles of gravel appeared to be a good a place to start her search. Determined to catch sight of the little men, she walked slowly, switching her eyes side to side. But, just as her father had told her, they were nowhere to be found. Disappointed when she came to the end of the path, her toes pointed to the edge of the deep pit. Looking down, she spotted, not a tiny earth-dwelling man, but Wybert at the bottom of the quarry.

Wybert was a distant cousin who, until recently, had lived in the same hamlet that Sunniva did. His skin glistened with the sweat that he had worked up as he pried at a crack with a pickaxe. Because of his slow, stammering speech, and his inability to learn anything but the simplest tasks, Wybert's father had sold him to a man who worked in the quarry.

Wybert caught sight of Sunniva, put down his tool, and grabbed a handful of pebbles lying nearby.

A spiraling terrace edged the large hole. Each descending level was lower than the one above by over half the height of a man and was wider than a man was tall. Sunniva jumped down as Wybert clambered up the makeshift steps contrived from boulders, and they met on a terrace mid-way between the top and the bottom.

Wybert held out his hand to show her his little chunks of gravel. "The colors d-d-darken and shine when I-I-I spits on them," he said, and showed Sunniva how he rubbed the spit into one of the little, red pebbles.

"I agree, Wybert, the patterns do become more apparent."

When he offered to give her the pretty stones, Sunniva cupped her hands together. He held his closed fist above her hands, and when he opened his fingers the pebbles fell into her palms. They felt refreshingly cool.

Heads together, they looked at each of the stones. Wybert's thick, paddle shaped finger pointed at one of the red pebbles. "The-the-the thin, white streak l-l-l-looks like a cloud."

Sunniva nodded enthusiastically. Though she had never seen a red land until that day, when she looked at the pebble she saw a tiny picture of the quarry yard. It was right there, on the pebble she held in her hand. "Yes, Wybert, I can see it. The streak looks like a white cloud floating above the quarry yard. It is just as you say." She glanced up at the sky to see if it, too, had a few thready-looking clouds floating past and was delighted to see there were.

Wybert pointed to another stone. "W-w-what do you see in this one?"

She touched it with her fingertip, and said, "There, I see a hovering bird."

"It comes s-s-so easy for you. D-d-do you think that you could spread your arms and fly like a bird?"

Prompted by this thought, Sunniva told Wybert that she had always wanted to fly like a goshawk. That was what her father had called her when she was small—his little goshawk. When he had been a man-at-arms, who served in a chieftain's warband, and had lived in a fort town—that was before he had come to live in their hamlet and married her mother—he had taught a hawk to perch on his gloved fist and to hunt for pigeons, doves, and hares.

When she was a baby crawling around on the floor, her father would grab her, hold her little feet in his hand, and carry her around the same way that he had carried the hawk on his fist. He would toss her up—frightening her mother—and catch her. Then he would raise her above his head, tell her to spread her arms, and race around while she was pretending to fly. It was the very first thing she remembered. It had been great fun until she grew too big. When the day came that her father told her that she was too heavy to lift anymore, she cried.

Remembering how it felt to fly, Sunniva closed her eyes, and, before she even knew what was happening, she was disguised as a bird-like girl. Her wings caught an updraft, and she lifted effortlessly on the spiraling sun-drenched air. She was flying in the red sky, past white, thread-like clouds, when, without a warning, a hand, big as a club, slapped her palms hard. Shaken from her reverie, the stinging blow jarred her arms all the way to her shoulders. The stones fell through the spaces between her fingers and made little tinkling sounds when they hit the terrace floor. She opened her eyes and saw, towering above her, the man to whom Wybert's labor had been sold.

Looking back and forth between the two men, one darting glance at Wybert's face convinced her of his outright fear. And, from the sight of the quarryman's hateful glare and bared teeth, she concluded that he wanted to hurt her.

Plainly, she and Wybert were in trouble.

But, she asked herself, what had they done wrong? Certainly, to look at a pebble deserved no greater punishment than a sharp reprimand and a reminder to get back to work.

She stepped backward, but her heels struck and scraped the terrace wall. When she tried to get past the man, he stepped to the side to block her passage.

"You are going nowhere, girly. Not till I say so."

Directing his anger at Wybert, he asked, "What are you doing with this whore?"

Unable to comprehend the question, Wybert stared back and slowly shook his head side to side.

"Men do with whores what boars do with sows, you pig-nose."

Wybert answered, "Oh," without seeming to grasp either the accusation or the explanation.

The quarryman turned next on Sunniva. Standing so close that his spit-spray hit her in the face, he said, "Any whore who is daft enough to give her body to a fool, even a pig-nosed one, in trade for little chunks of gravel, deserves a beating."

He was lifting his hand, ready to strike, and Sunniva was cringing from the on-coming blow when her father shouted from the top of the pit, "Stop."

Aiken came bounding down in a series of running leaps from one terrace to the next, yelling, "Do not lay hands upon my girl." He jumped from the terrace, just above where Wybert and Sunniva stood, to land in the space between them.

She scooted up close to her father, and said, "He hit me when I was looking at the stones that Wybert gave me."

Aiken looked directly at the quarryman, pushed his jaw forward, and said, "Then, you had better pick up those stones and hand them back. Do it now. Do as I say."

"This whore lured my man away from his work," the quarryman said. "Now, get out of my way, outlaw. It is my right to beat her."

"I, too, am protecting my own," Aiken rasped, and stepped in closer. He may have been a slight man and blind on one side, facing off against a larger, two-eyed quarryman, but Aiken had no fear of big, loutish men. Stiff and clumsy, such men were slow to move, but Aiken was quicker by more than half. He was used to fighting in tight spaces and knew how to use them to his advantage. If given no choice but to enforce his command, he was ready to grab the man by the back of the neck, to push him down, and to force him to do exactly as he was told. Within easy reach of the man, Aiken raised his fist, and said, "Pick up the stones."

To egg Aiken on, the quarryman swayed side-to-side, saying, "You want to brawl, do you? I know who you are, Crackpot. No one wants you here, you good-for-nothing outlaw. You lawless, oath-breaking, skulking monster, everyone loathes and detests you." The quarryman's lips curled in a sneer and, pointing with a sideways jerk of his head toward the top of the pit, he said, "You are so little, I could pick you up, sling you over my shoulder, and hang you by the neck from the tree in the yard."

As if the insult to Aiken's size, manliness, and honor were not enough to rattle him, the quarryman additionally accused Aiken of hiding behind the skirts of a woman to whom he was not lawfully wed. "And now, you come here to pander your half-breed bastard. Take her and get out of here. You disgust me." He finished his tirade by spitting in Aiken's face.

Aiken's mouth and nostrils filled with the sour stench of the bog. He felt a sharp stitch in his side as though he had been kicked. And in that single moment, the man who was staring at him with bulging eyes and bared teeth became a man he had killed before. No longer the quarryman's face, it was now Gerard's taut and twisted features glowering at him.

The past invaded the present. Left with no way out, Aiken was cornered. Then and there, the night, which he had lived through, years before, replaced the day in which he was currently living. Aiken asked himself: how many times does it take to kill a man? A man who refuses to stay dead but comes back to haunt the living, time and again? At times like this, Aiken no longer knew what was real to touch and sight, sound and smell. Even in the daytime, the dreamtime did not stop. Whether he was awake or asleep, it made no difference. His missing eye played tricks on him by sneaking things into his line of sight that should not have been there.

Hobbled by shock and indecision, Aiken was unable to move. There was nothing he could do but stare at the man who had risen from the land of the dead to take the quarryman's place.

Spewing insults, trying to get a rise out of him, the taunting voice was saying, "No one takes me down without paying-up with his life."

Gerard and his war companions were coming at him, front and center. If Aiken turned and ran, like the fleeing stag chased by a wild cat, he would be cut down from behind. Instead, he had been taught to never show fear or weakness. When he was a boy, he had been taught to build his rage. He had learned to take on the beast's hardened strength. To embody the cat's fearlessness, he had become a marauder, a predator, a slayer. There was no way to go but forward. To work his way into the enemy line, accompanied by rage, anger became his protector.

His blood brother, Alger, was there beside him. "Take him down, I have you covered."

The only way to protect himself was to strike out first. Aiken's hand hovered over the short-bladed combat knife that hung at his hip. His fingers wrapped around the hilt. He did what years of daily training had taught him—to respond to danger without thinking.

Ready to lash out, Aiken's eye shifted side-to-side. After a quick assessment, he knew where he would strike. He wished he had four arms and a blade in each hand.

And then, just as quickly as the memory had come over him—gone—it was gone. He was no longer in Torwald's meadhall facing off against a pack of trained killers who were coming at him from all sides, he was in the quarry pit. Aiken grunted in horror. He might have mistakenly lunged at either Wybert or Sunniva, thinking they were the enemy. A quick glance to either side assured him that they were both alive and unharmed.

And so, too, was the quarryman. Aiken was not facing off against a battle-hardened warrior, but a pit-worker. The hulking man, who had foolishly spat at him, demeaned his manhood, and called his girl a whore, gripped, not a weapon, but the handle of the sledgehammer resting at the side of his leg.

To test his blade's readiness and to prepare it to enforce its master's command, Aiken slid his knife back and forth in the scabbard. "I warn you," he growled, "You have only one chance. Do not try my patience—not if you know what is good for you. Bend down and pick up those stones. Do it now."

Unperturbed by Aiken's threat, the quarryman leered and tilted his head side to side. Taunting Aiken about his one-eyed blindness, he said in a singsong voice, "So, out-law, do you need your little girly to lead you around? To help you find your way?" And to further goad his rival, he tipped his head back and imitated the red gamecock, who was said to reside in the land of the dead, by crowing with loud, gloating laughter.

At times like this, even Aiken feared what the wild cat inside of him might do—a man who has a wild cat's power lying dormant in his weaponry, when un-leashed, is the most dangerous animal on earth. And now that the quarryman had gotten the rise out of him that he had been going for from the beginning, that last, demeaning mockery had done the trick. It was more than Aiken could take.

The beast's wrath blazed up with claws extended. Once fueled, that wrath be-came unstoppable. A controlled and explosive rage, brought on by hate of the enemy, was difficult to master but vital to staying alive. To stay one slash ahead of an oppo-nent's blade was all he needed. That and the wrath-given stamina to stay standing until the end of a fight.

Aiken and his knife did what they had been trained to do when an armed man was in his face. Man and weapon worked together in perfect harmony. The blade named Rushing Harm leapt at blurred speed from its sheath and homed in on its target. The sinewy patterns that Berling had forged in the blade caught the light and threw glints from what appeared to be the eddying waters in a fast-moving stream. The snake hiding beneath the blade's fluid surface eyed its victim. It lifted its head, poised to strike. And, when it was within a hair's breadth of the throbbing artery beneath the man's jawbone, Aiken stopped the blade from biting its prey in the neck.

The quarryman stood at the edge of the terrace. If he took a step backward, he would fall. He shifted to the side, but the blade moved with him. In an aggressive show of his hammer's heft, he lifted it from its place beside his foot.

But Aiken's knife had no fear of a quarryman who was armed with an unwieldy hammer. The comparison was laughable. A sledgehammer was not intended for use as a weapon. No one but Lord Thunder could wield such a hammer with the control that was necessary to take on Aiken. He was armed with Rushing Harm, an invinci-ble blade named for its speedy attack. There was no contest between them. It was not even close.

So, there they were, in a stand-off. Who would be the first to move? Aiken had waited a long time to get back at every insult that he had been forced to endure. After all these years, this was an opportunity to make up for all the demeaning names that he had been called. If he killed this quarryman now, it would be a good lesson to all those who had called him an ugly crackpot and laughed at him behind his back. They would know that it was better not to pick a fight with Aiken the Strength of Oak.

Not if they wanted to stay alive, that is. They would know that he was a man to be feared.

But on the other hand, Aiken knew what they did with outlaws. They hung them. And now was not a good time to get strung up from a tree branch. He had promised Gevehard that he would carve that standing stone. Besides, there was one last thing that he had to do before he was finished with this world. Then they could hang him.

But, right now, Aiken needed to find a way out of this unforeseen predicament. To make it right, to turn it around somehow, he had to dampfer the rage. But before that could happen, it was imperative to come out the victor. He could not walk away. Not after he had suffered such a demeaning verbal assault in front of his daughter. Never before had he lost a challenge over an insult. Nor could he turn away from this one now.

"Do you want proof of this blind man's aim?" Aiken warned the man in cold, measured tones, "Or will you pick up those stones and put them back in my daughter's hand? I will tell you one last time. Drop down on your knees. Do it now. You will not have another chance."

The quarryman's eyes pivoted to stare at the blade. The sinews in his jawline twitched. One breath away from death, even a tiny movement could justify a slash of the blade. His blood would gush and drain into a pool. Within a short time, his strength would leave him. His knees would buckle. His red blood would seep into the cracks and gravel here, where they ripped the red stone from the earth. His life would be spent and over. All because he had challenged an outlawed warrior, who was reputed to have been an unbeaten champion, over a handful of gravel. It was hardly worth the trouble, let alone his death. But he did have his pride, and he refused to back down. Not just yet, anyhow.

The quarryman lifted the hammer, slightly. "I can smash your knife with a single blow."

"Such feeble prods mean nothing. I was told by the smith who made this blade that no man's weapon could shatter it. Even the Sons of the Fiery Realm obey that man's commands."

Cold, controlled, Aiken goaded the man to make a move. "The smith has an uncanny way with iron. Should we test it here to see if what he said is true? If the hammer lifts from the ground your head will roll at my daughter's feet. I will take that as an acceptable compensation for your insults. I await the chance."

"All right then," the quarryman said. "I do not want to kill you. Nor do you want to kill me. I say we end the match, right here, in a draw." To test Aiken's resolve, he shuffled to the side. This time Aiken's blade stayed still.

Though the blade was still extended and pointed at the man's throat, it did not respond when the quarryman spat on the gravel, just barely missing Aiken's shoe. The quarryman was pushing his luck, but Aiken did not move.

The quarryman disparaged what he called the dainty blades, carving chisels, and mallets that Aiken used. He said a woodcarver's tools were no match for the power and strength that he, himself, wielded when he swung his mighty hammer. But Aiken's blade still did not move.

To get around the knife point, the quarryman took a side-ways, backward step, and pivoted on one foot. Laughing cruelly, he turned away and arrogantly dared Aiken to stab him in the back. "Come and get me, outlaw," he said, contemptuously. "Crackpot. Crackpot. Crackpot."

But Aiken refused to take the bait.

Casually swinging his hammer, the quarryman walked away without a backward glance, and yelled, "Pick up the stones, Pig-nose, and give them back to the slutty girl. Get a move on."

Wybert dropped to his knees. Hunched over the loose gravel, he scrabbled around in the quarry debris like a grubby beetle looking for the stones he had given Sunniva. Wybert jumped to his feet, dropped the pebbles into Sunniva's open palm and, after one last glance at Aiken's wrathful scowl, leapt down the terraces until he was, once again, at the bottom.

Aiken's knife still hung at his side in a loose fist. He sheathed Rushing Harm and, with a swipe of his arm, wiped the quarryman's spit off his face. He grabbed Sunniva's upper arm, pushed her around, and forced her to walk in front.

Though clearly shaken by the standoff that she had witnessed, Sunniva indignantly twitched her shoulder, and said, "Let go. You need not grab me so tightly. I can walk without your help."

Aiken answered her wordlessly with another forceful push.

III.

Back in the yard, Sunniva sulked in the shade beneath the tree. She still had not picked up the spinning that her mother had sent along. Aiken stood like a horse in the pasture who turns his back to the stormy weather, wind, and rain. Protective, yet so angry, he wanted nothing to do with his daughter until his rage subsided, he took a wide-spread stance and folded his arms across his chest. The threats of blood vengeance he had spoken to counteract the verbal assault upon her honor had left him with a foul aftertaste. To rid his mouth of the bitterness, he spat on the ground.

He put his hands to his head and grabbed fistfuls of hair. Growling deeply in his throat, he asked himself whether trouble would always follow him wherever he went. Did he endanger anyone to whom he came too close? He had thought his daughter's simple innocence would have staved off the frights and bad memories that had tormented him during the night. But instead they had come after him in the daytime, too, with even greater vengeance and, now, had threatened Sunniva.

There was no one but himself to blame for the foolish notion of bringing Sunniva to the quarry. The only excuse, which he could muster, for his poor decision-making was to blame it on the previous night's dreamtime events.

Aiken had crawled into bed but been unable to sleep. Instead, he had lain awake. Haunted by memories of the night that Egil was killed, he thought over all the ways that he had let his bench mate down. He wished he had been more vigilant. He should have seen the signs of trouble earlier in the day. The signs had been there, all along, but neither he nor anyone else had paid attention. If the men in the warband had known what was coming, Egil would still have been alive the following morning. But all regrets, both spoken and unspoken, between now and the Endtime, cannot bring a dead man back to life.

Back in the day, when Egil was known for the way he could cleverly cut a man down to size, Aiken and his companions had relished a good insult contest. Within their own brotherhood, they had met his challenges with humor. Because they expected the slurs they threw out would be met with equally clever slurs, the men in the warband had taken pride in giving it out as good as they got. They could go on like that all night long and at daybreak, on their way out the door, shake hands in friendship, slap each other on the arms and laugh. But common wisdom said that whenever an outsider attacks a man's dignity there is bound to be a fight.

According to the law-giver, bloodshed among one's kin was unlawful, but there were times when peace held no longer than the meadhall feasting. As soon as the men left the protective meadhall walls at dawn, they became adversaries again.

But, that night, even before the red gamecock crowed at dawn, when the doors were thrown open to the early morning light, more men than Egil lay dead on the meadhall floor.

From the very first moment that Chieftain Odel and his men had ridden into the inner stockade that day, Aiken's chieftain, Torwald, should have been alert to the danger. But instead, he had gamed and hunted with Odel, and remained out of touch with all that was going on around him.

Status-wise, the two chieftains had little but kinship ties in common. In those days, Torwald was one of the wealthiest in the clan. He had inherited rich farmland and collected hefty tolls on both river traffic and major roads leading between the market towns. He charged the merchants, who conducted business in his villages, a portion of their profits, and he collected tribute from the farmers who raised grain and meat on the lands he controlled. Torwald's prestigious warband was made up of men who could recount their esteemed warrior lineages for several generations.

In contrast, Odel had little more than the unsustainable presumption of a freeman's law-given right to lead a warband. Many of the men in his band had been hard-scrabble wanderers from outside the kindred and could find no one else to take them on. With so little farmland under his control, all Odel could offer his men was shelter in a sleeping hall and scanty amounts of food. Unless a man had his own holdings, he could not collect the grain, produce, or marketable items that were needed to support a wife. And because the men in Odel's warband had no families and lacked the requisite loyalty that men established through kinship ties, they were thought to be unreliable and no better than thieves. Men like that were often forced to resort to cruelty and underhanded coercion of the local farmers, just to keep clothing on their backs.

Odel should have given it up, sworn to serve another chieftain, and agreed to be his man. But instead he kept a tight grip on those unsustainable presumptions and a loose grip on his unreliable men.

As the serving girls went from table to table filling the men's cups with Torwald's abundant supplies of ale, Aiken saw how enviously Odel's men were eyeing the signs of his own chieftain's wealth. Yet, the ceremony proceeded as always: Torwald played the role of a gracious host; his wife took the cup around and, according to each man's rank, praised each one. However, it soon became apparent that some of Odel's men had taken slight.

Just as one man was at the top, one man was at the bottom, and that night Gerard was it. After he had been forced to accept as his betters those in Torwald's band, who were both younger and less experienced, but who ranked higher because they came from good families, he resented being seen as lowest in rank. He sat hunched over at the far end of the bench looking at the others with burning hatred and growling about being the last one to be offered the cup.

That was how the night had begun to play out, back then, in Torwald's meadhall.

And as Aiken lay beside Mildred, berating himself relentlessly, he once again rethought a strategy that might have saved Egil from his ignominious death. Aiken considered all the things he could have done differently. When a man is given the power to make others die, he also is given the power to keep others alive. What if he had spoken up and told his war companions to watch their backs that evening? What if he had said Odel's men could not be trusted? What if he had stopped Gerard the moment he had stood up from the bench, instead of watching him build his rage?

Finally, Aiken was unable to hold off sleep any longer. He rolled onto his side, tucked up his knees, got good and close to Mildred, and laid one arm across her shoulders and closed his eye. And as soon as he closed his one good eye, the swirling rainbow colors, which were visible only to his missing eye, lured him into the Iron-wood. There, in the muted dreamtime light, where the iron-rich waters ooze from the ground to fill a boggy pit with taint, Aiken was drawn to watch the oily sheen floating on the still water's surface. Throwing colors, the iron-slick swirls shifted from purple to red to orange to yellow. Though he tried, he could not resist its allure. He could not leave it. He had to watch the colors shift and shift again.

And, as always, the bogman rose from beneath the still waters. It broke through the ever-changing, colorful slick. Its long hairy arm, reddish-brown in color, lumpy and knobby as a tree root, reached out of the stagnant water. Aiken recoiled from the creature. But even then, it seemed like he was hobbled by ropes. Unable to move, he was unable to get away.

The bogman hoisted itself up and out of the pond. It scrabbled onto the bank, came up behind Aiken and grabbed him by the ankle. Repelled by the bogman's clammy touch upon his naked skin, Aiken opened his mouth in a soundless scream. But the bogman reached up to grab Aiken's shoulders, squeezed its talon-like fingers into his flesh, pulled itself up, bent its skinny legs in a crouch, gripped Aiken above the hips with its knees, and sat astride his back. Its arms wrapped around Aiken's neck so tightly, he gasped for breath. It poked at Aiken with long, claw-like nails. The bogman squeezed his mount hard in the midriff, whipped him into a frenzy of rage to get him going fast, and forced him to go to the place where dead men fight the night battles in the dreamtime.

But even in the dreamtime, Aiken repeated the same things that he had done before. He asked himself how to save Egil. But it never worked out. In the end, it always came out the same way as before. Even in the dreamtime, Odel and Torwald remained inattentive to the men on the benches, and Egil always died.

And just as Gerard had done that night, so many years before, he stalked like a predatory beast. Looming too closely behind the men's backs, he called attention to the sitting men's helplessness. Breathing heavily and narrowing his eyes, he tipped his head back, looked down his nose at them, and clenched his fists. All the men felt edgy. But no matter how often they yelled, "Sit down Gerard," he heedlessly prowled and threatened. Lest the evening turn into an all-out brawl, no one, including Aiken, wanted to force Gerard to go back to his low-ranking place on the bench. No one tried to take him on.

Then came the moment when Gerard bragged about an exploit so outrageous that Egil called him out on the laughable boast. That was when Aiken should have acted. But in the dreamtime, it always happened the same way that it had happened before. Gerard lost face, and everyone laughed at the slur.

And even in the dreamtime, though Aiken knew what was coming next, something always stopped him. Instead, he sat there, stupidly silent, sluggishly thinking: Egil, that was not a smart thing to say right now. You should not have said that.

Gerard's face swelled and changed color. Spit sprayed from his mouth. He snarled and stuttered so badly he could barely speak a cogent word. Finally, he got out two: "You lie."

He stalked up behind Egil, drew his side-arm, and stabbed Egil in the back. The wounded man jumped to his feet. For a moment he stood there arching his back. Then he fell forward, face down, flat across the table, and jerked twice. There he lay, arms splayed out to the sides, blood pooling around his unmoving body.

At first, everyone stared in disbelief.

By then it was too late, but Aiken and Alger jumped up, nevertheless. And all at once, Gerard's fellow companions were roused to his defense. When Aiken saw them coming at him from all sides, he did what he had been trained to do: he reached for his knife. But what happened next was always different in the dreamtime from the way it had happened before. He slapped his hip where his blade was supposed to be, but it had gone missing from its scabbard. He fell to his knees. His hands felt around on the floor. He crawled around beneath the table, searching blindly in the shadows. He called his knife by its name, over and over, but it was nowhere to be found. Where did it go? How could he have dropped it? You drop your knife, it is gone. Forever. Weaponless, he crouched like a cornered beast. Unable to move, he looked up and stared at five men. Ten eyes stared back. Five, drawn long-knives pointed at him. Aiken breathed hard and asked himself: what have I done?

His entire body jerked, and he awakened to the sounds of his own animal-like growls. The dreamtime memories had ended but the hurt had not. The throbbing in his head began and, as so often happened, the pain just knocked the wind right out of him.

Mildred awoke and got out of bed. Left alone to pull himself together, just the sight of his big, husky woman was a comfort. His wife was reliable. Nothing much troubled her nor threw her off her game. With her broad chest and shoulders and her well-filled-out arms and legs, she was solidly built, had her feet on the ground, and offered Aiken a steady hand-hold.

Mildred was known to challenge him and her brothers to arm wrestling contests and, though she rarely won, she always put up a good fight. Besides, winning was not the point. The point was to remind all the men in her family that she was a woman to be reckoned with. She was easily as tall as Aiken, and probably taller, but he was too proud to measure their heights. He only knew that she could look him straight in the eye whenever she had a good reason to, and frequently did. What would he do without her?

Mildred poured a cup of pennyroyal to counteract the invisible folk's harmful influences. Though Aiken did not think that sipping the broth did him much good, he sat up like an obedient child. She handed him the cup, but his hands shook so badly he was unable to hold it steady and gave it back. Mildred held it to his lips, but his teeth knocked against the rim. Refusing it, he said, "Put it on the table before you spill it into my beard. I will drink it later, after I settle down."

His wife folded a small cloth and soaked it in another warm, herbal broth that she kept near the hearth. Leaning over and touching him tenderly, she laid the compress over the scarred side of his face.

Though appreciative of Mildred's attentions, he knew there was nothing she could do to quell the ache. The pain went too deep. It seemed like the javelin that had taken him down was still lodged inside his skull. Unable to yank out that invisible, barbed, iron point, he was just as helpless that night as he had been that day when he had been hit and tried to rip it out of his face.

The heel of his palm pressed the warm compress into the sunken hole where his eye should have been. The searing pain in his head, the throbbing in his jaw, and the disgust he felt at his own appearance was nothing like the tests he had endured when he was young. Back then, pain had been a proof of his courage. But now, the pain and disgust were probing reminders of all that he had lost: his good looks, his honor, his friends and kinsmen, his former home, his worth as a fighting man, his luck, his high rank and his respectable place among men.

Mildred climbed back into bed. She gathered him in her arms and sang the charms that were supposed to keep him safe from the hidden folk who hounded him. Though her songs were no match for the bogman and never kept it away, her melodic tunes reminded him of the lullabies she had sung to quiet their babies. Just the sound of her voice soothed him. At times like these, Mildred's gentleness roused Aiken's sentiments to such an extent that his apparent weakness appalled him. Surely, he thought, only faint-hearted and shameful men need a woman's kindness as much as he did.

Over time, the sharp pain began to let up. By morning it would be a tolerable, dull ache. Day and night, pain was his companion. Sometimes it was nothing more than an acquaintance whose irksome habits he could ignore. At other times, when it turned against him and went on the attack, he wished that he were dead.

There he was, a former member of Torwald's honor guard, a champion fighter, clinging to his wife like a cowering child who, in the dead of night, sought his mother's protection because he feared an invisible creature who inhabited the Ironwood's gloomiest depths.

He kept his good eye open and lay there, clinging to life. Listening to Mildred's every breath he was comforted by the rise and fall of her chest. Only when the pale gray, dawn light seeped through the chinks in the walls and the holes in the thatch did he drift off to sleep.

With the loss of sight in one eye, sounds took on more meaning. Even the faintest noise might warn Aiken that something on his blind side forebode oncoming danger. And, as so often happened, when he was caught in that place between wakefulness and sleep, noises switched their true identity and masked themselves as something else.

A squeak of leather became the sounds men made when they hiked up their belts, hung heavily with long-knives and side-arms, hammers, steels, and throwing axes. They swung into their saddles, flicked the reins, kicked their horse's flanks, cried 'Yha-a-a-a' and were off. Aiken knew where they were headed and struggled against being there when they arrived. Yet he could not wake. Though he tried to find a way out of those long ago times, he was lost and unable to get his bearings. A sharp clang rent the air. And without fully grasping its true source, the noise became the clash of iron blades. Again, he was forced to live through the axe blow, the squeal of wood as it cracked, and the strike of flint against steel. Torches were thrown onto thatched roofs. Fire roared as it caught and sucked the air. Was this what his soul expected to live through time and again for one hundred lifetimes? The pungent smell of smoke, the thatch in flames, and to find himself in a house-afire? He must leap from the bed but cannot move. Unarmed against the attackers, he is helpless to save his children.

Aiken's whole body jerked.

Oh. It was Mildred chopping kindling. Her leather shoes squeaking. The iron pot swinging on the hook above the fire.

Though he was no longer trapped in memory nor dreamtime vision, his pain was real enough. To steel resistance against the throbbing in his head, he lifted an arm to stare at the blue designs that once had marked him as one of the warriors who fought in Torwald's warband. He tried to embody the strength of will he had cultivated back then, when the artist had stitched the outlines into his skin using a bone needle threaded with sinews soaked in berry juice and ashes. Back then, Aiken had gritted his teeth and said the needle-sting was nothing. Back then, when he had known nothing of what lay ahead, he had relished the pain. The ordeal had trained him to blunt the hurts a warrior was sure to suffer. It was an initiation he had had to endure. Back then, when he had been a good-looking, blameless youth, when his laughter had come so easily, so joyfully.

The window and door were open. Slanted sunbeams shone through the rising hearth smoke. Mildred was talking over the daily chores with Sunniva. Their young son sat on the floor, muttering to himself. After Bertolf had been taught recently to tie a bowknot, he now refused all offers of help. Instead, he insisted upon tying his shoes, "All by myself."

Other voices came to Aiken from outside the walls. Women left their houses, greeted one another, splashed water into their pails, gathered armloads of wood for their fires, and chatted as they walked to the pasture to milk the cows. Men yelled to their neighbors, sharpened their scythes, and jostled with their tools on their way to hay the fields.

Aiken settled into the straw-stuffed palette with a loud sigh. Mildred touched his hand and offered to refresh the warm cloth. But, in return for her affection, Aiken pressed his back against the wall and shoved her away.

"It is me, Aiken. I am not attacking you. I am offering to help you."

He was in no mood to beg her pardon. His wife should be used to him by now. When a man has learned combat readiness even his bed is not safe. He could never shed his vigilance. He was always on guard. He had been trained to snap to, to act fast and decisively. Without giving a second thought to what he was doing, any man who is trained for combat is always ready to come after a challenger with fists or weapons. He responds to imminent danger without thinking. He knew, all too well, how a man's life—his life—could change. It could happen in less time than it takes an eye to blink. Life was always at stake.

Mildred, unlike her husband, was slow to anger. She prided herself upon her patience. But that morning, Aiken's abrupt manner put her off. Severely tested and forced to defend herself, she was being given no choice but to go on the offensive. "Are you so above it all that you are content to lie abed all day? Did you forget you planned to take the oxcart to the quarry?"

She smoothed the creases wrinkling her apron with a self-satisfied air. And, after reminding her husband of his duty, she turned on Sunniva. "It is shameful to stare at your father like that when he is feeling so unwell. Go do your chores. Take the hog slops out to the pig pen and throw those left-over scraps on the table to the dogs."

Aiken felt his daughter's gaze and opened his one good eye. "Sunniva, tell your mother to stop her incessant hovering. No, wait. Do not go out yet. I have a riddle to ask you."

Each morning Aiken pulled himself away from that place of loss. Every morning he repeated the motto he lived by: show no fear or weakness. Every morning he struggled against drowning in the all-engulfing emptiness of guilt, shame and despair. Every morning he resurfaced, and every morning he drew a deep breath into his chest and set about repairing his life all over again. And every morning it was the same, and would always be the same, for as long as the three Matrones of the Becoming decreed he had one last breath, one last heartbeat, and one last thing to do. And not until that one last thing was done, would he be finished, too.

He pulled himself together, sat up stiffly, set his feet on the floor, leaned forward, rested his elbows on his knees and stared blankly in the direction of his feet. He did not want to harm those whom he loved. But when the listless moods and the tempers came over him, sometimes his wife and children just got in the way. Unable to control the immediate response, he lashed out in anger. And as a result, he spent a lot of time alone. And, yes, it hurt to be so lonely. He missed Alger and the other men who had been his companions in the warband.

If he gave in to the pain, the grief, the fear, and the disgust, he would only smother, beneath a layer of ash, the tender feelings he had for his family. Instead, he wanted to feel the happiness they gave him. Joy was like the sparks that burst from his flint when he struck it against the steel. He wanted to increase his happiness by fanning the tiny embers until they flamed. He wanted to tend it carefully, to feed the fire with kindling and sticks until its warmth made him feel keen about his family and work again.

He lifted his face to look at his daughter's. Ah, he thought, she is a gift of sunshine; what a fine young woman she is. Sunniva's two, sun-bleached braids were so long they fell to below her hips. When Aiken reached out to pull one of her plaits, his teasing made her giggle. He then devised a riddle, on the spot, just as a noble father would do, if he were a wealthy man-at-arms who lived in a longhouse, within the inner stockade, inside a chieftain's hill fort, and had a way with words. But as it was, he lived here in this small house, in a nameless hamlet, surrounded by an unprotected ox-road, and had nothing much to offer anyone but trouble.

Yet, he figured that if he could make a joke, then Sunniva would think of her father as a lighthearted man.

"Once I decorated my crown with flowers
But now I carry in my round belly
The fermented nectar that bees collect.
Tell me, who am I?"

"You made your riddle too easy. Ask a harder one."
"Tell me the answer anyway."

First, she gave the answer. "You described a pitcher filled with mead." She followed it with an explanation of her reasoning: "The wood from a flowering tree is carved to make a pitcher from which mead is poured."

She then told him that his description resembled a beautiful pitcher that he had turned recently on the lathe. He had carved the handle with pictures of flowers and bees and rubbed it with fat and beeswax until it was shiny. He had attached the handle to the pitcher with copper strips and rivets. Her mother, who was usually a practical woman, had been so jealous of the pitcher that she had wanted to keep it for herself. But because they all expected the pitcher to end up on a table in one of the warrior's longhouses, inside the inner stockade, she knew they could get a good price for it in the market. So, in the end, after it had sat in the middle of their table, where they could admire it for several days, Mildred had refrained from filling it with ale. She gave Aiken a downcast look and told him to keep it on a shelf in his work shed until market day.

Sunniva then added one final comment: "We never drink mead, anyhow. It would have been wrong to put ale in that pitcher. Besides, if we had, it would not have fit your riddle."

Aiken nodded in approval. Her answer, complete with added opinions and observations, brought a lopsided smile to his face. Cheered by her quick thinking, he asked himself how he could ever find fault with his life when his daughter was so clever and amusing.

At times like this, he treasured the resemblances between his girl and his mother. When Sunniva reminded him of Maida, the things she said and did brought his boyhood to mind. His mother, too, had been skillful with words. Whenever there had been a riddle contest, she could match wits with all the men in the warband. Though he had been but a child at the time, he remembered how proud he was of both his mother and his father, Eamon, whenever she counseled his actions and offered him the praise-and-promise cup to drink from. Perhaps she had even poured mead from a fine wooden pitcher, just like the one that he had carved, but he did not recall whether that was true or not.

Aiken had not seen Maida for many years and had heard recently that she had died a while back. So, here, where he was an outsider, his wife, daughter, and his son were all the kin he had left to him, not counting his half-brothers, who did not count at all. He had made his own kinship, which included all of four people. Or three, if he counted himself and those who were blood related.

Aiken stood and put his arm, proudly, around his daughter's shoulders. Sunniva was growing up to be a fine young woman. Big like her mother, and filling out in her arms and legs, she was almost as tall as he was. She would make any man proud who was lucky enough to marry her.

He told Sunniva to run out to the pasture and bring in the oxen. Her reward for answering his riddle was to go with him to the quarry to help him pick out a stone for Shipmaster Gevehard.

"You will do nothing of the sort," Mildred said.

But Aiken had insisted and, in the end, had gotten his way. And that was how the morning had begun.

IV.

Now, standing in the quarry yard, Aiken admitted that his wife had been right all along. From the very beginning, Mildred had been against his foolhardy plan. She had told her husband, in no uncertain terms, that to take a girl to the quarry, where she would be among those coarse men, was out of the question.

Mildred was right when she said the quarry was a rough place. Women and girls did not belong here. But had Aiken listened to his wife? No. Furthermore, he should have known better than to let his daughter out of sight. He had known the threats. It was his fault. He should have seen it coming. But he had done nothing to prevent it from happening. He was equally as guilty as he had been of Egil's death.

At first, after they had left home, things had gone so well. Maybe that was why he had let his guard down. He and Sunniva had enjoyed their pleasant companionship on the ride up to the quarry. Nearing the hilltop, Aiken had waved his arm out to his side and had urged her to first look at the fields and forests beneath them, and then to see how the rolling hills stretched all the way to the very edge of the earth.

Looking down at their miniaturized hamlet, shrouded by the smoke that was rising from each of the householder's rooftops, Sunniva pointed to the folks rushing about, and said, delightedly, "Look at them, they are small as ants."

Aiken had been amused by her shock and laughter but now regretted his decision. He had put his daughter in danger and had no one but himself to blame.

The men, who had been working beneath the lean-to, came toward Aiken. Walking rapidly across the yard, they carried iron levers and loops of rope slung across their shoulders. Aiken grabbed his own ropes from out of the cart and met them near the stone he had chosen. They lifted one end with their levers and wrapped ropes around it.

Next, the quarrymen brought the block and tackle and Aiken backed his cart up to the stone. Grunting loudly, they strung the ropes from a tripod of sturdy timbers, heaved it up slowly and loaded the stone onto the cart. Aiken picked up his tunic, threw it over his head and shoulders, stuck his arms through the sleeves and ordered Sunniva to take her seat on the bench. He flicked the goad over the oxen's backs, and the cart started to roll out of the quarry.

Swaying side to side, the cart was slowly descending the hill when he asked, "How did you get me into trouble like that? What started it off? I could have killed that man. If I had done that, they would have strung me up by the neck from the thickest branch in the quarry yard. That is what they do with outlaws, you know. If I were still a man-at-arms in Torwald's warband, a common quarry worker would never have dared confront me. But as it is now, I am an easy target. I have no rights before the law, no way to settle my grievances. You could be driving the cart alone and by yourself right now. Instead of a red stone laying in the back of the cart, my corpse would be laid-out."

Then, after he had given more thought to his ill-tempered accusations, he attempted to offset his anger by making light of the situation. "Here," he said, holding out the goad. "If you are going to be such a troublemaker, you had better learn how to handle a team of oxen yourself."

Sunniva gave her father a sidelong glance and refused to crack a smile. "I did nothing wrong. Right from the start, it was the quarryman's fault."

"You are not listening to me, Sunniva," Aiken said. "From the moment you took it into your head to flout my command, it went badly. I told you to stay near the cart. Your disobedience put us both at risk. When he called you a whore, I was forced to protect your womanly honor. What else was I supposed to do?"

"What is a whore?"

"A wanton woman."

"Well, for him to have said that, he deserved to be punished. I did nothing to give him that idea. Wybert may look like a man but he acts like a child. That awful man was the one who was so wicked. He hit me and threatened to give me a beating. I did nothing wrong. You were right to have threatened him."

"I want no more of your back-talk. You are being childish. Now, act like the grown woman you are. A dutiful father demands respectful treatment of his daughter's honor. I did what was expected of me. Now, you must do what is expected of you. A young woman's appointed role is to do as she is told. You must sit beside me in silence. When we get home, I will speak to your mother about a suitable punishment regarding your misbehavior."

V.

The ochre and blue-green colored stone now rests in the palm of one hand and the crystal ball in the other. Due to the additional meaning I have given the glyph that Nature drew on this little round bead, it has become a talisman. But that is where comparisons between Aiken and this stone come to an end. In contrast to the man with whom I now associate this stone, there is no need for second guessing, nor to reason out the stone's hidden motives. No, when all is said and done, a stone is exactly what it appears to be—a stone.

TWO

Red Jasper
If you will shield from attack.

Take this stone which is called Red Jasper and also called the Mother Stone. It is like the color of blood. It has shown to be good protection and to mitigate the peril of travel to other worlds. Bear it about with you and you shall overcome all causes and keep the body safe against your adversaries.

The Truth of Rocks, by Aluiss the Wise

I.

Here are two stone seascapes. The first depicts a calm, pale blue sea. Lying beneath an expansive, white, cloudless sky, it stretches all the way to the horizon where a pink line, so thin it is almost imperceptible, divides them.

The second stone is like an artist's ink wash. Drawn in gray and white tones, the lace-like design features a crashing wave curling in upon itself. Above the foamy water, white, pendulous storm clouds hang from a darkening sky. A Windbringer's eagle-like head and beak pierce the churning clouds. Feathered rosettes encircle its eyes to add to their size. I have heard it said that just to look into the Windbringer's eyes can be so frightening that, even from a distance, its prey becomes riveted to the spot, even as the monstrous bird comes swooping in for the kill.

Were a longship to come into the picture from the left and head into those crashing waves, I, too, would feel the oarsmen's terror when, in their struggle to survive, they hurl themselves against the Windbringer's and Lord Thunder's combined destructive forces.

If Nature is the artist here, she is telling me something about herself through these two opposing images. As much as the first stone owes its beauty to the serenity that comes to mind whenever I gaze upon a tranquil sea, Nature's raging power can, also, be terrifyingly beautiful. The sight of the storm is equally as fascinating or, perhaps, is even more captivating than the view of the motionless sea. There is a need, perhaps, as strong as hunger for food itself, to make even suffering into a thing of beauty, to make from tragedy a story, a picture, a carving that, also, expresses balance and harmonious design.

Surely, Nature has intended such beauty to be so eye-catching. I can see no other way for it to have happened, than for these two stones to have been created by deliberate thought. I cite for evidence of the ulterior awareness that went into the making of these stones, the way in which Nature repeatedly copies the workable motifs she invents, in the same way that a craftsman repeats the patterns he contrives.

I see the same natural forces at work in the creation of symmetrical, wave-like shapes wherever I look. A spiral begins at a point and moves steadily outward, around a central axis. Sometimes the curling spiral favors burgeoning growth, sometimes it favors the sublime, and sometimes the struggle to stay alive. I see it in water currents; in a snail's tightly curled shell; in a fern frond poking through the soil before it unfurls; in the bend of my finger; in a duck's tail feather that, embellished with a jaunty curl at its tip, is made to wiggle in a beguiling fashion for his mate's approval; and also, in the eagle's curved talons and beak, which are made with the intent to hook, grasp, and tear. I add to this list the whirlwind's rotation as it leaps across the land, spinning and curling, and furiously sucking into its center everything that lies in its path. Sometimes this abundant enthusiasm for beautiful, perfectly well-thought-out design increases the power of dangerous forces or a creature's chances for survival. But at other times it seems so utterly extravagant, so foolishly trivial, the design becomes unnecessarily wasteful.

A flower colors itself red. A bird covers itself with bright, yellow plumage. A father wren builds his small nest using matching twigs, each of which are broken to the same length. The bird lines it with spider's webbing and, to serve as tiny pillows, spider egg cases. From Nature's perspective, all things in this world are equally beautiful and part of her total design. I, too, am a product of Nature. I am not separate from her total creation, but am a single part. Unlike the trees and stones, however, I have arms and legs that allow me move about. Because I have eyes, I can see. Given a mind, I can think. Given feelings, I can respond to all that I encounter.

And, because I exist as one small part of Nature's worldly design, I participate in her expansive awareness, though in a more limited fashion than hers. It is for this reason that I am able to take in, to reflect upon, and to appreciate whatever is beautiful.

To create a well-balanced and symmetrically pleasing object that catches the observer's eye by copying Nature's orderly patterns and, to infuse it with meaning, has been one of men and women's talents for a long time. When a smith makes a bronze brooch, he embellishes it with intricate designs made of abstract faces, bird shapes, and copies of knotted cords. A woman embroiders a tapestry with pictures of flowers, trees, and birds. A weaver uses a combination of both contrasting and harmonious colors to make a geometric pattern on her loom. A carpenter builds a house, or a longship, or a storage chest, and decorates it with carved, stylized foliage. The desire to create something beautiful is rampant everywhere I look.

And, because people are, in themselves, products of Nature's design, the things they make are no different from the colorful flower, the tree's spreading crown, a thundercloud's roiling shape, or the tiniest piece of crystalline sand.

The knives that Berling makes, though objects of horror, are beautiful in a terrible way, though he says their pleasing design is merely accidental. The image of the snake lifting its head is simply a by-product of the material with which he works and the techniques that he uses when he welds the steel. He does not hide the knife's structure nor mask its interior. Its skin gives the onlooker a view of its skeleton. The way the twisted steel patterns catch the light and appear to bring the snake alive makes it beautiful, almost serenely so. Yet the design does not hide the violent forces that lie poised within the blade, nor the horror evoked by the strange, dream-like vision of a snake's sudden appearance at the very moment that its fangs target its victim.

This is the conundrum I face whenever I talk about beauty.

My hand naturally reaches toward another stone and picks up a figured land-scape. Holding it in my palm, I imagine I am standing upon a hillside from which I may gaze upon a series of shallow valleys and brown, shaded hills, which seem to diminish in height as they near the distant, pale gray skyline. Here and there, sketchy red streaks represent red-leaved shrubberies growing alongside a road. The sight of Nature spread out before my eyes like this, makes me feel as though I am feasting upon her abundant goodness.

Because the landscape pictured on this stone seems so similar to the view that Aiken and Sunniva enjoyed when their cart was traveling the high quarry road, I can easily imagine I am standing there on the hillside, looking into the distance, with an eagle-eyed view, after their cart has just passed by.

If I stare at the stone for a while, in uninterrupted silence, the picture of the hills and valleys becomes an after-image impressed upon the backs of my eyes. The vision overlays my sight of the stack of papers, the ink bottle, and the assorted quills arranged neatly on my writing table. The borders between me and my surroundings become vague and disappear. And when the landscape is all I see, my identification with this stone is complete.

Down below me, Aiken and Sunniva's small hamlet was organized around a series of increasingly larger concentric circles. At the center of the hamlet, Irmun's pole was erected like an axis on a wheel. Around this pole, there was a circular, open space called the commons. This was where the ashes of dead were buried and the living hamlet dwellers went about their daily activities. Crossing from one side of the hamlet to the other, they walked over the unmarked graves all day long, greeted one another and shared in the latest gossip. At times of celebration, they feasted, danced and stomped in rhythm on the ground where the ancestors' bones lay buried and, in that way, communicated with their deceased forebears who were never far away, and were, also, invited join in the festivities.

The houses built around the commons formed the first circle. Behind those hous-es, the second and third circles were made up of byres and storage sheds. Encircling all the buildings, the ox-road marked the hamlet's outer perimeter.

Out past the ox-road were grassy pastures and gardens. Beyond those gardens, there were cultivated grain fields and the low forests where carefully managed hazel, beech, and ash coppices grew. And out beyond the cultivated fields and low-forests, the wild forested regions lay, where outlaws, wolves, and wild boars were said to roam amidst the enfolding hills and valleys.

II.

Aiken's cart rumbled a quarter-way around the ox-road before he brought it to a halt beside his workshop. He unyoked the oxen and handed the ropes to Sunniva. On her way to the pasture, she passed through the central commons. Breathlessly greeting men and women whom she met, she eagerly described their trip to the quarry (with-out mentioning her part in the stand-off between the two men) and the stone that Shipmaster Gevehard had asked her father to carve.

Those who heard the news were eager to share it with their neighbors. And even before nightfall, every man, woman, and child in the hamlet knew that Mildred's husband had been asked to carve a picture stone for a shipmaster who crewed four longships that traveled the Merchant Sea. Early next spring, Aiken would cart the stone to the sea-people's village himself. It was a distance, the men in the hamlet reckoned, after they had paused a long while, and nodded their heads, reflectively, should take Aiken two weeks to travel, if not more.

III.

And, what if I were to speak with one of those gossips, who had been walking through the commons? She would, most likely, tell me how truly remarkable it was to think that one of their own was held in such high esteem by an important shipmaster who lived so far away. Especially when, here at home, most folks avoided Aiken if they could. Evidently, the shipmaster was unaware of Aiken's reputation for being a troublemaker.

Did I think, she wanted to know, whether someone should send word to the shipmaster and let him know?

I shrugged my shoulders noncommittally and urged her to continue.

The gossip would nod, take a breath and go on to say that Aiken's wife, Mildred, stood up for her husband, as any good wife should do. According to Mildred, he was a decent man and a hard worker. But if I asked anyone else for their opinion, I would hear that Aiken had a fearsome temper, did things differently and, in all the years that he had lived there, had never fit in.

How Aiken had been outlawed was one of those unanswerable questions that no one could figure out. And, because he never let on much about himself, his silence had increased everyone's curiosity and wild speculation about his affairs. Some folks claimed that he had been accused of something unspeakable at the chieftain's Assembly. But when they were questioned further on the subject, they admitted to uncertainty about what he had done to warrant the harshness of the punishment. Even Mildred seemed to be in the dark about the reasons.

Otherwise, it was a well-known fact that after Aiken and Mildred were wed—unlawfully, the gossip wanted me to know—they had begun to travel to the local villages to sell his lathe-turned cups, bowls, and spindles. That just went to show you how far he had fallen: he had gone from being a member of a prestigious chieftain's warband, where he had served in the honor guard, and was reputed to have been an unbeaten champion, to being a common woodcarver who made spoons and spindles for women, toy cows for children, and treasure boxes and high seats for the very same chieftains who had outlawed him.

How such a strange arrangement had come about was another one of those unanswerable questions. Some folks remembered a time when Aiken had threatened to curse a chieftain's steward during a confrontation, right here in the common yard. But, when pressed for more information, they were at a loss to recall just what, exactly, had happened. Whatever it was that he had said and done that day, it seems his shrewd bargaining skills had led to a tit-for-tat stand-off between him and local chieftains. Furthermore, it was said that no one wanted to mess with him because he usually came out the winner.

As for Mildred, as troublesome as it was to be married to an outlaw who went around starting fights and threatening to curse folks, her pride had known no bounds. Nor had her determination to make the best of a bad situation. Once she had figured out how the markets worked, she quickly discovered that the warrior's wives, who lived in the fort towns, were continually hard-pressed to supply the weavers in their loom-shops with enough yarn. And since she was a woman who knew how to get whatever she wanted, Mildred soon figured out how to turn that market shortage to her advantage. After she came home, she encouraged her kin to increase the number of sheep they bred each year. She then convinced the women to spin the extra wool into thread, which she sold at a good profit.

Most folks agreed that, because she had helped increase their wealth, Mildred deserved the powerful standing it gave her in the hamlet. But the way she put on airs and acted like one of the highborn warrior's wives, who dressed in fine garments and wore gold jewelry, annoyed them to no end. She seemed to have forgotten that the warrior, whom she had married had been outlawed and that she would never get any gold jewelry from him.

Besides, the women who spun for her resented the way she treated them. When she returned home and placed each woman's earnings into her hand, Mildred acted as though she was, out of the goodness of her own heart, bestowing the woman with gifts that were valued at more than she deserved to receive.

But, as irksome as it was to be treated so poorly, most folks did not blame Mildred for her uppity attitude. Instead they claimed that she had gotten the bad habit from her husband. It was not her fault, they said. Not one bit. It had simply gone to her head to have married that highborn warrior—though everyone knew that he was an outlaw, had lost his wealth, and had no claim to rank. And so, since Mildred was kin, and had a right to live in the hamlet, everyone put up with her arrogant ways and begrudgingly agreed to ignore her poor choice of a husband.

And now, I will bring this fanciful conversation to an end, part ways with the gossip, and pick up the story again.

IV.

After Sunniva and Aiken returned home from the quarry, it fell to Mildred to instruct their daughter in a young woman's proper behavior. The lack of respect that Sunniva had shown for her father's authority was both an affront to her mother's good training and, was shockingly unbecoming behavior for a young woman who was soon to be wed. There were certain things that Sunniva must learn before marriage. And if she had not picked them up yet, now was the time to learn them: "A proper woman does whatever the man to whom she is beholden tells her to do. Before marriage it is her father. After marriage it is her husband." This was Sunniva's place in the order of things, so she had better get used to it now.

Nonsense, Sunniva thought and was just cheeky enough to speak her mind on the matter. "I have noticed that you do as you please and make Father do as you tell him. Who is to say that I cannot do the same?"

Mildred cringed and nearly slapped Sunniva for her insolence. But, after a hasty glance over her shoulder convinced her that Aiken had not heard the disrespectful comment, she folded her arms across her chest, eyed her daughter distrustfully and hissed, "If you are so smart, you had better learn to hold your tongue and to think before you speak."

In contrast to Mildred, whose back was turned toward Aiken, Sunniva faced her father's seat at the table. Hunched over his bowl, with his elbows spread apart, he was spooning the last bites of his noonday supper into his mouth. She guessed that, because of the revealing way one corner of his mouth was curling in a sly smile, and his good eye was crinkling at the corner, he had, in fact, heard her comment and thought that her observation about who was foremost in his house was funny.

Because her father had been ostracized wherever he went and was barred from entry into the kin's close circle, he watched everyone with a wry amusement verging on bitterness. From his outsider's perspective, whenever he cast a cool eye on others' elevated opinions of themselves, he took note of the telling differences between a man or woman's actions and their pretensions of self-important pride.

Not that her father was not a proud man. He was a righteous man who was beholden to no one but himself. Sunniva had heard him say, on more than one occasion, that no man owned him. He owed allegiance to no one but his wife and children and took pride in his masterless status.

According to her father, to live a life of integrity meant that he was willing to put his life on the line in defense of truth. The highest honor should be accorded those who spoke honestly and who valued fairness and just treatment for all freemen before the law.

"And look where it got him," Sunniva's mother had said. Behind her father's back, that is. She would never have said it directly to his face.

According to Mildred, the honesty and integrity, which her father valued, were not as important as was her duty to obey her elders and the man to whom she was beholden. Because Sunniva must accept the authority of those men, whose dictates were meant to stand unquestioned, it was better to let those things that seemed to be unfair and dishonest go unnoticed. Nor should she point out those things that she was not supposed to see, even when she did see them, even if it was by accident. If you did not speak of something, it was not there, and never had been.

So, at times like this, when Sunniva believed that she had done nothing wrong, had not been allowed to fairly defend herself, and neither had she deserved the tongue-lashing, nor the punishment, which her mother was sure to hand down, it was difficult to assemble, from the two contrary standards by which she was being taught to live, one flawless ideal. In this case, because she admired her father's willingness to take a courageous stand in defense of the principles that he believed were decent and right, even though it had gotten him into trouble, Sunniva chose to follow her father's example. If marriage meant that she must dutifully follow a man, whose principals were of questionable merit, she would stand up for truth and justice and refuse to do whatever the man to whom she was beholden told her to do. Even if it got her into trouble.

"Perhaps, I will be my own woman and be beholden to no man. Instead of marriage, I will stay home with you and Father. I will take care of you when you get old, the way you took care of Harald."

"Sunniva, what has gotten into you today? Of course, you will marry."

With that statement Mildred meant, but did not say, that Sunniva had no choice in the matter. Her mother and father would decide to whom their daughter was wed, the value of her bride price, and when the marriage would be consummated.

"Now, listen to me, Sunniva. Because of the way you spurned your womanly work when you were at the quarry, you will spin a basketful of skeins." One quick jerk of Mildred's chin asserted the importance of her decision in regard to the punishment that Sunniva deserved. Then, she hastily corrected herself to add, "Nay, make that two basketsful. A second for your sassiness and for speaking out of turn. One basketful for each lesson that you must learn."

Until Sunniva was finished, she would neither be allowed to see her friends, nor to leave the proximity of the house, except when she did her chores. If she knew what was good for her, she would spend all her spare time in meditation upon her lessons.

"Now, get busy, or you will be stuck with that spindle in your hand, just like old Mother Necessity is."

Because the more thread that Sunniva spun the more her mother earned at the market, that fact alone riled Sunniva to no end. Some of the earnings should properly be hers, she thought. She was old enough to purchase items at the market for herself. Things that she would like to buy were a pretty bronze-wire pin and maybe some ribbons for her hair. But since Sunniva knew, from previous experience, that once her mother had handed down the verdict and the penalty had been set, additional arguments were pointless.

She also resented the fact that she had been deprived of an opportunity to defend herself. It was not hers and Wybert's fault that her father had been dragged into the fight at the quarry. The truth was that she and Wybert had only been looking at little pebbles. They had done nothing wrong. It was the horrid quarryman who had started the fight when he called her a whore and threatened to beat her.

When she had described the way that the quarryman mistreated Wybert, her mother had scoffed. Instead of showing any concern for his welfare, or even a small measure of suitable fellow-feeling for his suffering, Mildred told her not to waste her tears on someone whose life had so little value. Wybert's father had a right to gain from his foolish son's labor. It should be no concern of hers, her mother had said. Instead, Sunniva must attend to her own affairs and not lose sight of her work.

It was unfair, but then again, since there were so many unfair things in this world, she hardly knew where to begin counting them all. Her father, too, had been unfairly treated. Her mother, in an unusual moment of candor, had told Sunniva that Aiken would have died in the forest if it had not been for her. He had been a homeless wanderer, Mildred said, but she had taken him in. She had stood up for him when the other folks in the hamlet wanted to throw him out. But she had fought them off until, in the end, she and Aiken were wed. "So, then what were they going to do?" Mildred asked her daughter, "Make me an outlaw, too, and chase us both into the wild, forested regions?"

Sunniva's mother had kept her father alive. Just the thought of her father's bones moldering on the forest floor and covered with soggy leaves was too awful to imagine. Whenever it came to mind, Sunniva avoided thinking about it.

She added Wybert's bondage to her list of unfairnesses and, for the third unfairness, counted the fact that her mother took all her earnings from the thread she spun. The fourth was, of course, the unfairness of her punishment. But since she was given no choice but to accept her mother's judgment, Sunniva determined to stick with the work until she was finished.

V.

At times, she stood in the bright sunlight just outside the door. At other times, she spun by the dim firelight inside the house. She was so accustomed to twisting thread that her fingers could spin with her eyes closed.

On rare occasions, when Mildred was not there to oversee her daughter's spinning, Sunniva reached into the drawstring bag that hung from her belt. She secretly took out the little, red pebbles and clutched them in her fist. Because she had seen something beautiful in these stones, she was curious to see what other marvelous worlds awaited her discovery. Opening her hand, she fingered each one. She touched the stone on which she had seen the miniatured picture of the quarry with the red sky above it threaded with white clouds. On another she saw distant, rolling, black hills. There was another stone in which she could see a pond of clear water. Each stone was beautiful in its own way. She longed to leave behind this tedious world and to fly into each picture, just as she had done that day at the quarry.

But lest the pebble's hints of otherworldly adventure distract her from her work, she obediently slipped them back into her bag. She tucked the distaff under her left arm and set the whorl spinning. She pulled a few strands from the combed wool that was bundled around the narrow, oval-shaped basket at the top the long stick. She twisted the kinky fibers with her thumb and forefinger and, as the spindle twirled and the thread lengthened, she sang her spinning song:

"I long to fly like the pretty bird,
Oh, sing your song to me.
Oh, pretty bird,
Sing your song to me."

As she sung, the wheel continued to drop until it touched the ground. It stopped and tipped. Sunniva bent down to pick up the whorl. And, after she had wound the thread around the stick that formed its axis, she began again.

The smoke sifting through the thatch swirled to form a spiral, became a thin, wispy thread and trailed off to join the clouds high above Sunniva's head. Fascinated by the smoke curls, she became wholly absorbed in their beauty. Offered this opportunity to see beauty in the most ordinary things, she wished to grab hold of the wispy smoke strands and to make something beautiful from them. She would embroider the patterns she saw onto a dress. She would make it beautiful in the same way that her father made things of beauty from a simple block of wood. Like him, she would copy the leaves and vines that she saw in the meadows and the forest and capture the beauty that she saw all around her.

But instead, she was stuck spinning the thread that her mother planned to sell at the market. She had no time to make beautiful things. It hardly seemed fair that beauty was always beyond reach.

In time, the combination of warm, afternoon air, the repetitious tune she sang, and the spindle going around and around and around and around in a never-ending cycle, made her drowsy.

It was then that she heard a distant, melodic voice soughing in the wind. Though the words were different than her own, the tune harmonized with hers:

"Oh, pretty bird
Come spread your wings
Oh, pretty bird
Come fly to me."

And like the time that she had taken flight disguised in the form of a goshawk, Sunniva's outstretched, wing-like arms caught the breeze and lifted her up until she was floating upon those smoky threads. Gradually soaring higher and higher, she came, at last, to the one whose voice she had heard.

There was a Lady standing in the sky, spinning clouds. How wondrous was that?

Curious, Sunniva studied the Lady in the Clouds with her sharpened, hawk-like eyesight. The simply dressed woman had a pretty, round face surrounded by clouds of white hair. The distaff she crooked in her left elbow was tall as a walking stick and was made from metal so shiny it could have been forged from golden light. The basket at the top was wrapped with roiling mist.

Sunniva hovered on an updraft to watch the Lady in the clouds unfurl those beautiful threads. They were so fine, they floated on the gentle breeze and trailed into the distance until they disappeared.

Sunniva thought, I, too, should like to spin threads beautiful as those.

Apparently, the Lady heard Sunniva's thoughts as clearly as if she had spoken them aloud. She looked up at the bird-like girl who was circling above her head, and said, "These threads will be used to weave you a beautiful, new cloak. It will be breathlessly light and airy as the pink, feathered wisps of dawn. Now, settle here with me for a while, and I will show you how to spin the same as I do."

Sunniva slowly drifted toward the distaff. Her talons clutched the top of its basket and, once she had perched atop it, she tucked in her wings.

The Lady looked at Sunniva with a kindly, alluring smile and assured her that she had nothing to fear. "My affection is boundless as the sky. You will be cared for with an all-embracing love, if you agree to promise me just one thing."

The Lady pulled a bit of fleece from the distaff, rubbed it between her thumb and forefinger, and twisted a nearly invisible strand. Glistening like a wispy, silver wire, it was so fine that a spider could have spun it. Sunniva cocked her head to watch the Lady as she wrapped the cord around her bird-like leg and tie it in a knot.

"Because your wings are wind-bleached," the Lady in the Clouds said, "I shall name you Storm-pale. In this guise, you will have the wisdom the eagle needs. In time, you will sit between the great bird's eyes and will bring him knowledge of many things. You will have all this, and even more, if you agree to promise me just one thing."

It was in that trusting moment, when Sunniva was being honored for a wisdom, which her mother had so consistently deprived her of, that any mistrust she may have felt faded away to nothing. Sunniva, the hawk-girl, in her longing to be valued for her shrewdness and knowledge of what is just, right, and true, was eager to perch upon the Lady's wrist in the same way that a falconer holds a bird on her gloved fist.

But something held Sunniva back.

In response to Sunniva's apparent restraint, the Lady praised the merit of her offer. "Whenever you wear the dawn-colored cloak you will fly to otherworlds. You will be given second-sight, become a seer of the Becoming, and will bring about abundant harvests, peace between warring factions, and healing for those who suffer. How can you refuse this gracious offer? You can have all this, and even more, if you promise me just one thing."

Though the offer was enticing, Sunniva hesitated. "First of all," she said, "I need to know the name of the one to whom I am being asked to give my word."

"My followers call me Blessed," the Lady in the Clouds answered.

Sunniva knew her mother could vouch for Lady Blessed. Mildred had told Sunniva that, at the time of her greatest need, the Lady had brought Aiken into her life. Lady Blessed had given Sunniva's mother a gift from the dreamtime.

Sunniva had heard that Lady Blessed's followers never married nor were they beholden to any man. That in itself sounded like a good reason to give her word. But a gift meant that Sunniva would owe the Lady something in return. That afternoon, when she had spread her wings and taken flight, she had not expected to be asked to pledge her word. To make a promise is a serious matter. A vow should never be undertaken without careful deliberation. That was what her father had taught her. And he should know.

But, on the other hand, to become a wisewoman was an attractive idea. Figuring that, if she did become a seer of the Becoming and, if she could bring about abundance, peace and healing, she should, also, be able to alter a person's destiny in the same way that the three Matrones did. And if, by entwining someone's previously twisted life-threads with newer ones, it would become a thread that held a different sort of meaning from the one that had been twisted before, she could alter destiny just by spinning thread. How wondrous was that?

But she, also, knew that the thread that was tied around her ankle would curtail her freedom and lessen her choices. It would bind her to this promise until it was fulfilled. Recalling strategies that she had learned from her mother, whenever Mildred was bargaining with others at the market, Sunniva said, "Your proposal is generous. But first I would like to discuss some of the specific aspects of your offer. There are certain wrongs that I would like to make right. I would like to free Wybert from his bondage and to change my father's outlaw status. I want people to treat each other fairly and to listen to me when I speak the truth. If you agree, I will promise to be fully true to you."

Unfortunately, even I knew that Lady Blessed did not like to be toyed with in this fashion. She was not inclined to accept a sworn oath that included specific qualifications that encompassed so many far-reaching ramifications. To become one of the Lady's followers, a woman agreed to be fully true to her. There was no other way around it. Lady Blessed brooked no arguments. She expected her followers to obey her orders. She must never be challenged. Nor must her judgements be questioned. She must never be told what to do. She must never be interrupted. Nor must anyone ever outshine her.

Those who disagreed or questioned her authority were thrown out, left behind, and abandoned. Nor was she above the use of trickery in getting whatever she wanted. To hide the truthful meaning of her words, the Lady answered Sunniva in a slanted way. "Even now, as I speak, I create," she said. "If you will but promise me——."

It was during that momentary pause between the last spoken word and the next that Lady Blessed was interrupted. Mildred's pointy finger poked Sunniva in the arm. Sunniva's eyes blinked open, and the view of the Lady in the Clouds was gone. Gone, too, was the opportunity to see her new life-thread's many possibilities being spun before her eyes.

Sunniva glanced at her ankle but, when she saw no dangling silver thread wrapped around it and tied like hawk jesses in a knot, she shrugged off the vision's fanciful nature as nothing more than a make-believe daytrip to the dreamtime.

"Oh, Sunniva," Mildred said, "what am I going to do with you? I turn my back for just one moment and look what you have done. These threads are spun too loosely."

Intoning wisdom that she had learned from her own mother, who had learned it from her mother, who had handed it down from her mother, and all the other mothers who had gone before her, Mildred recited, "Only the butterfly is free to shed the cocoon it spins and to spread its wings. A woman's day to spread her wings is the day that her betrothed leads her to her new home."

She bent over Sunniva's basket and picked through the skeins. She pulled out those that were spun too loosely and demanded that Sunniva re-twist them. "A woman spins thread until the day she dies. Even when she is laid-out on the funeral pyre, she holds the whorl and distaff. She carries them with her to the land of the dead where she will spin until the Endtime. Such is a woman's fate."

Her mother was exaggerating. Not all the threads were spun so poorly—only some were. In response to being shamed so unfairly in this manner, Sunniva could not help but compare the common threads, which her Mother made her spin, to those that Lady Blessed unfurled.

If she were to become one of Lady Blessed's followers, her speech would go unquestioned. Whenever she encountered the many wrong things that she came across in this world, she would set things right. She would bring protection to those who lived within the bounds of her safe-keeping. She would spin a fate in which Wybert was neither blamed nor punished and would set him free from his bondage. The vicious quarryman would be repaid in kind for his cruelty. And she would make things right for her father, too, and change his outlaw status.

If she accepted the Lady's gifts of far-seeing, she would prophesy and reveal truths that were hidden from ordinary sight. She would become a counselor to a chieftain and sit at the high table during the grand feasts that were held in her honor. When he commanded she bring about rich harvests and success on the battlefield, she would walk between the worlds and forge otherworldly alliances. And, in turn, the chieftain and his beneficiaries would endow her with land, cattle, and wealth.

Though it was enticing to imagine a common girl becoming a woman of such stature, Sunniva knew that she could never hold such power. There was no truth in the beautifully uplifting dream-like vision of the Lady. According to her mother, that kind of nonsense was foolish. To believe in a beautiful world, where everything was good and true, was nothing but wishful thinking. Such idle, capricious daydreams should never be confused with the hard and fast things in this world.

Besides, if she told her friends that Lady Blessed had appeared to her in the clouds, no one would believe her. They would scoff and repeat the same malicious gossip they attributed to her mother and father. They would accuse her of putting herself forward, of having a haughty attitude, and of giving herself airs.

And so, in the end, Sunniva swore to never tell anyone that Lady Blessed had named her Storm-pale and had promised her a beautiful new cloak woven from the finest strands of dawn-colored light. Instead, she would stick to spinning ordinary threads, and be allowed to speak to her friends again.

VI.

Time passed. Soon it would be the darkest month of the year: Wolf's-month. And, every day that Lady Sun's shortened path appeared lower on the southern skyline, the hamlet-dweller's sense of unease increased. They had heard the tales describing the time of sorrow, when snow had fallen three seasons out of four. After all the crops had failed, men and women had survived the Terrible Winter by eating grubs they dug from rotten tree trunks, drinking soup they made from tree bark, and feasting on the sour crow's meat they roasted on spits over their flaming hearths.

Because it had happened before, everyone knew that it could happen again. If the long wintertime nights went on and on, they would never again be blessed with bright summertime days, abundantly growing crops, good harvests, or food enough to sustain them through the cold, wintertime months.

And though it was tempting to listen to the old, hunter's call in the blood that urged men and women to pick up their households and to follow the birds' flight south, folks resorted to faith in the knowable patterns they had observed since they were born. No matter what the elders told them about the time of famine, they trusted autumn to follow summer, winter to follow autumn, spring to follow winter, and summer to follow spring.

In preparation for outlasting the dark, wintertime months, they did what they had always done. Everyone took stock of their cold-weather gear, checked their food stores, chopped more wood, moved the cattle and sheep into the byres and nearby pastures, and settled down inside their homes. And for as long as men and women could draw together to share the pleasant moments their kinship offered, they sat together around their hearths and prized the warmth and spare light their fires gave off.

One evening, after the women's work was done for the day, several cousins and aunts crowded around the blaze in Mildred's home. They tucked their distaffs under their elbows, twirled their whorls, twisted their threads, and spun their tales.

"Tell us a story, Aunt Edith," one of the cousins said. And after much prodding, the eldest among the women agreed to tell the tale they all favored at that time of year.

There once was a time, in this world, when everything was dark and cold. Neither was there daylight, nor was there a progression of the seasons. This, then, is the story of how Mother Necessity balanced the darkness with light, and the coldness with warmth.

First, Mother Necessity took her place upon her high-seat, and Father Time took his place beside her. Together they summoned the ruling powers to stand before them. Mother Necessity welcomed them and told them that the time had come to assign their duties.

One by one, each Lord and Lady came forward to receive Mother Necessity's decree. To Lord Glory she gave rule over the army of star-warriors and the power to decide matters in regard to justice and the rule of law. To Lord Thunder she gave the power of storms and lighting bolts. To Lady Blessed, she gave the power of the seeds to lie down in the fields and to sprout with new life. To Lord Benevolent, she gave the virile force inherent in bulls, rams, and boars.

When Lady Sun stepped before Mother Necessity, she said, "Mother, just look at me. The truth is that my hair is golden and my face shines with brilliant light. Am I not the most beautiful of all the Ladies? Is it not right for me to stand above all others?"

"Who do you think you are?" Mother Necessity asked. "I am the one who hands out your gifts and duties. Not you. You are nothing but a jewel in my crown. No one, neither ruling power, nor mortal is free of my constraint."

"But, Mother, I want to be honored above all others," Lady Sun said.

"And what else do you want?"

"I want gifts befitting my high rank."

Mother Necessity then paused a long while. And after she had given much thought to this insolent request, she decided how to answer: "You shall have all that. Yes, you shall have everything that you have asked for. Look behind you, now."

Lady Sun turned around. A man was leading two white chargers who were pulling a wagon carrying a disk-shaped, flaming mirror. The first man was followed by a second man who carried a flaming long-knife. Behind him came a third man who carried a gold-ringed collar, a golden girdle, and a necklace that was made from gold and honey-colored stones. The fourth and last man carried a gold cup.

Mother Necessity said, "I decree that you shall wed the four craftsmen who made these gifts befitting your high rank. These morning-after gifts shall be the golden chains of your imprisonment. To consummate your marriage, once each year, you shall visit your four husbands where they dwell in the darkest tunnels that thread the mountain roots.

"For the rest of the year you will drive the wagon across the sky each day. Each night, after you have reached your destination, you shall cross the sea in your longboat, named Nightly, and return to the Gates of Dawn. The following morning, you will again drive your mirror-laden wagon. This, you will do each day and each night, repeatedly, until the Endtime."

Lady Sun, upon hearing Mother Necessity's ruling, broke down and wept bitter, golden tears.

"Why do you weep?" Mother Necessity asked, "Did I not give you all that you asked for? From now until the Endtime you will stand above all others and be honored for the light your flaming mirror gives off."

Yes, she had gotten what she asked for, but the gifts came with obligations greater than Lady Sun had expected. Henceforth, her bright rays would be bound to the four men who lived in darkness. Nonetheless, the beaming Lady had no choice but to mount the wagon. She took the reins in hand, cracked the whip, and the two chargers took off at high speed. She streaked across the sky, and along with the passage of time, light and warmth spread over the land. Each evening, she stepped aboard her longboat, Nightly, and rode it to the Gates of Dawn. Each morning, she again mounted the wagon. For half the year, each day her path took her further and further north, and for the other half of the year, her path took her further and further south.

When the time came, Lady Sun ordered her oarsmen to bring her to the mountainous island where her four husbands dwelt. After her ship came to the harbor, her oarsmen hauled it ashore. She walked up to the mountain entrance where a man stood outside the doorway. He welcomed her and told her that he would attend to her needs. She followed after him, and straightaway, the doors slammed shut behind her.

The four husbands welcomed Lady Sun. They sat her upon the high seat and ordered the feast to begin.

On the first night, they offered the beaming Lady a drink from the gold cup. Each man praised her with the appellation, The Brightest Light and Fire of Sky and Air. She took the cup, drank from it, and praised each of her husbands in return.

On the second night, they brought in a beautiful new cloak, embellished with colorful feathers and precious jewels, and laid it across her shoulders.

On the third night, her four husbands entertained her with stories.

On the fourth night, a lively dance started up and Lady Sun and her four husbands celebrated their marriage.

At the end of each evening's festivities, the attendant called out that it was bedtime. Each night, a different husband took her by the hand and led her to a smaller room where the walls were hung with tapestries, and the floor was covered with soft furs and rugs.

It was at this point in the tale that the aunts and cousins interrupted Aunt Edith. They slapped their thighs in anticipation and burst out all at once, "In return for the gifts they gave her, Lady Sun spends one night with each of her four husbands."

Relishing this opportunity to add more lusty details to the story, one cousin described how one of the Lady's husbands uncloaked her feathered cape each night. Another cousin described how each of her four husbands took his turn unbuckling her girdle and removing the fiery blade's scabbard. Another cousin described how each of her husbands unfastened the gold circlet that was set with honey-colored stones shaped like tears. Then, at last, came the moment all the women were most eagerly awaiting: when, each night, one of her four husbands would unpin the jewels that fastened her dress at the shoulders. After that happened, all the cousins and aunts knew what came next. Once Lady Sun's dress was undone, it slipped down over her breasts and lay heaped about her ankles.

"There she stood, shockingly naked before her husband."

The women laughed uproariously and made fun of the small, ugly creatures whom Lady Sun was forced to bed because of her self-important pride.

All except Mildred, that is, who thought that a man's appearance made no difference. Not as long as he was a hard worker and treated his wife decently, that is. According to her way of thinking, if her husband was a good man, that was all that mattered. First, she glanced at Aiken to see how he was taking the women's cruel jests, and then she glanced at her daughter.

Though Mildred still had faith in Sunniva's lack of exposure to worldly matters, she worried that such tales might burn her simple child's ears. She knew the signs of womanly awakening and feared this tale of uninhibited lust would increase Sunniva's interest in the local boys.

Mildred disavowed the belief that any woman, including Lady Sun, required more than one man to fulfill her duties in regard to child bearing. No woman's womb cried out so beseechingly for fruition. To require four husbands to satisfy her longings was downright greedy. It might leave another woman barren and lonely. Four husbands—just the thought of such a thing was outlandish.

She, also, disapproved of all suggestive references to acts performed in the privacy of a husband and his wife's marital bed. Worse yet, were those unlawful trysts that men and women, of lesser moral standards, were known to indulge in outside the boundaries of holy union. And worse yet, were the stories of the Lady Sun's assignations with men who lived in this world. People said that her husbands were so small and ugly that she was always on the look-out for more attractive men. Or, perhaps it was because the Lady was so lusty that she was forced to find men with whom she could lay abed on those nights of the year when she was unable to visit her husbands' realm.

Whatever was the reason, Mildred did not care to know. Nor did she approve. She only prayed that her blameless daughter would never hear those shameless tales. Said to give a woman the same rights that a man has when he picks his bedding partner, Mildred feared that such idle talk might stimulate her daughter's attraction to the young men in the hamlet and give her unwholesome ideas.

The youngest cousin wiggled on her stool and trilled, "Sunniva, would you not like to be given such wealth on your morning after? You would look lovely wearing a gold necklace and girdle. You could drink from a golden cup and look at your pretty face each morning in a flaming mirror."

How they all laughed at that idea. Though Mildred glared at the woman, it was no use—not after they were all worked up that way.

Finally, after the others had quieted down, Aunt Edith picked up the tale again.

Each of her husbands settled Lady Sun upon a fine bed and crawled in beneath the bedclothes with her. And, in this way they bound her in the darkness with soft, invisible ropes of sensual delights, flattery, abundant gifts, luxurious foods, and ever-lasting celebrations.

In time, Lady Sun became quite fond of her husbands. She wished to remain with them for a fifth night, a sixth night, and a seventh night. And so it went, on and on, night after night, until she forgot Mother Necessity's decree to drive the disk-laden wagon across the sky each day.

Listening dreamily to the tale, Sunniva wondered what it would be like to dress in fine garments and jewels as beautiful as the ones that Lady Sun wore. For comparison, she thought of the young men who were chosen each year to act out the story of Lady Sun's visit to her husbands' realm at Yuletide. The players dressed in fancy disguises that the women had sewn and wore masks that the men had made from leather, straw and scraps of cloth. Once they were dressed in their costumes, they pretended to speak like the Lady, her four husbands, and her twin brothers.

Yule began early in the morning following the longest night of the year. As the kinleader kindled the need-fire, the women in the hamlet sang mournful songs pleading with the ruling powers to help them in their time of greatest need. The kinleader then lit the Yule log from the need-fire's sparks and fed the flames until the bonfire was blazing.

That was when the pageant players made their grand entrance. The two men wearing horse-head masks, to stand-in for the Lady's white chargers, led the procession. Next came the Lady, accompanied by her standard bearer who carried the sun disk on a pole. Her twin brothers followed, each carrying a shield representing either the morning or evening star. And Lady Sun's four husbands came last. The people who lived in the hamlet followed the players around the ox-road, singing, drumming, and shaking rattles as they went.

Every day, men and youths from the hamlet competed against those who had come from other, nearby hamlets. They played games and held races in the fields, had tug of war contests, and wrestled. Lady Sun was always at the center of the festivities and handed out the prizes to the winners. Graciously seated upon her high seat, she was appreciative of all the attention that came her way. Mothers brought their children to her to bless with good fortune. Naturally, the smallest babies were terrified of the Lady's mask and cried. But the older ones liked the small, tasty treats she handed out. The little delights were made of dried fruit mixed with honey and toasted barley to represent the bountiful blessings that her mirror's golden rays gave off.

After sundown, the Lady, her brothers, her four husbands, and the others who made up her retinue, walked from house to house to share mulled ale and refreshments. The four husbands acted like the earth-dwellers who Sunniva's father had warned her about. Acting mischievously, they sang funny songs, talked in strange, silly voices, insulted folks, and made fun of the householders. They tried to trip people up, to push those who had drunk too much ale off their stools, and to kiss the women. Lady Sun's husbands were very naughty.

Finally, the time came for Lady Sun's twin brothers to restore order by pushing the four husbands out the door at the tips of their wooden long-knives. The Lady was always the last to leave. Before she went out, she pretended to lustily kiss the men, and everyone laughed.

Once they were all outside again, they were led by the two men, who were disguised as the Lady's white chargers, to the next, neighboring house. Of course, everyone in the hamlet wanted to watch their antics, so many of the folks followed the players and tried to crowd into each house when the door was opened.

Yuletide was a dream-like time. It seemed as though this world and the otherworld were one and the same. The men and youths, who wore the masks and acted-out the story, were no longer themselves but became one with those who belonged to another, everlasting time and place. This made it possible for all the folks in the hamlet to, once each year, temporarily inhabit that otherworldly space between the realms.

On the last night of Yuletide, the fire wheels were lit, and everyone cheered for sunlight's return. They feasted on the hog that had been fattened-up after it was fed the last harvested grain sheaf in late autumn. After the hog had been slaughtered several days before, as a blood-gift to the ruling powers, its flesh was cooked in a huge pot. There was always plenty of food to go around, so everyone ate their fill and danced around the bonfire. Then, at the end of the night, all the pageant players were given a good send-off. They would not return until the next Yuletide season.

Unless, that is, Sunniva pretended to play the Lady's role in the story, right now. After all, Lady Sun was Sunniva's namesake. Because she had the means right here, Sunniva thought it should be easy to visit that space between the worlds. She stuck her hand into the pouch that hung from her belt and rubbed the little pebbles hidden inside it.

Her memories of Yuletide mixed with her father's stories of the earth-dwellers and, before she even knew what had happened, a man appeared to come through a tiny fissure in one of the stones. Though his legs were still buried in the rock, from what she could see of him, half emerged as he was, he was not as small as she had expected him to be. Nor was he ugly. In fact, he was quite attractive, adorable, even. His full cheeks were ruddy, his shoulders were straight, his chest was broad, and his arms were well-filled out. His curly, dark hair fell to below his ears. He was dressed in a green tunic and wore a wide belt. A small, sheathed knife, with a red stone set into the pommel, hung from his belt.

His green eyes were sparkly and alight with mischief when he reached out from inside the little red stone. Sunniva took his hand and the earth-dweller pulled her through the crack.

At first, she felt queasy with fright. But this earth-dwelling man's gentle nature disabused her of any wicked intent and immediately put her at ease. If she were to act the part of her namesake, Sunniva should know these men intimately. After all, she was pretending they were her husbands. Upon entering their underground hall, she set about filling in their appearances. In time, her sense of them became so vivid, it seemed as though she could clearly see them in the flickering firelight.

The one who had brought her there picked up a necklace made from honey-colored, tear-shaped stones and fastened it around her neck. He then held up a mirror with which she could see how beautiful she was. A man who was inscribing the secret signs on a tablet had his back to her, but peeked at her, shyly, now and then, from over his shoulder. Another man, who was dressed in beautifully jeweled clothing, took her by the hand. He helped her sit upon a down-filled cushion, sat beside her, poured mead into her gold cup, and handed it to her. This was where beauty dwelt. She had found it at last.

A fourth man pumped the bellows until the fire in the forge glowed white-hot. His thick arms bulged with blue-veined muscle.

Entranced by the fire's allure, Sunniva stood and walked toward the forge. She watched the smith pick up a set of tongs with his left hand and use them to reach into the seething, white-hot embers. After he had grasped an iron blade by the tang, he placed it upon his anvil. He raised his hammer with his right arm and struck the blade several times. He then put the blade into the forge again. He laid the tongs on his work bench, but it took more effort to lay down his hammer.

He picked up the tongs again and used them to grip the knife by the tang. He pulled it from the seething coals and dipped it into a barrel. When he pulled it out, it was flaming. He rested the blade's tip against the iron spike that was poking out of his right wrist, where she would have expected a hand to be. He extended it toward her, and, along with the knife's presentation, invited her into this mysterious realm, saying, "This is where you will find whatever it is you seek."

Though enigmatic as a riddle, he spoke with such authority, she knew that what he said was true. One of the things she sought was beauty. And here, in this world beneath the earth's surface there was jeweled beauty in abundance. Truth was another thing she sought.

Though uncommonly shy of this man, she was drawn to his eyes. The smith looked at her with a penetrating fierceness she had never before encountered. Black as polished iron points, his glistening eyes reflected the red-yellow flames that were flashing across the skin of that brilliantly glowing knife.

Unable to turn away, she felt something deep inside her lower belly flutter and the place between her legs grow moist and warm.

The smith said, "This blade is named Right Truth. With this blade, you will bring light wherever there is darkness and cut down your enemy, Falsehood. Once I am finished, it will be yours."

Deeply lost in her imaginary world, Sunniva wished to never leave it.

Mildred, however, was increasingly worried by her daughter's rapt attention with Aunt Edith's tale. She glanced modestly at Sunniva, shook her head, tightened her lips, and pleaded for more restraint from the other women. "Sunniva is too young to understand those tales," she said in a hushed voice.

"Nonsense, Mildred. Just look at her. She is child-bearing age. She has a womanly figure. She is good-looking too—better than you were at that age. Surely, the young men have noticed by now. You cannot keep her at home with you forever."

To make fun of Mildred's simple reserve, another cousin chuckled, "Have you taught her yet about the difference between boys and girls? If not, you had better teach her now. Every woman must learn to put off men's advances until she is wed. After marriage, she must reverse her strategy. Then, she must give herself, willingly, to her husband whenever he wants to lay abed."

Things were getting increasingly out of hand. Now that they had begun to talk about Sunniva as though she was not even there, the crooked bent this conversation was taking had rendered Mildred speechless. For a change, she hardly knew what to say or do. She stopped just short of standing up, stepping behind Sunniva's back, and covering her child's ears with her hands.

Another of the aunts taunted, "A girl's mother must teach her daughter to fulfill that part of the bargain that she and her husband swore to observe on their wedding day. If you are not going to tell her, then, I will." And, looking directly at Sunniva, she asked, "Did you hear what I just said, young woman? You ask your mother to fill in the details."

Unable to put a stop to this dreadful conversation, Mildred directed her daughter to card and spin from up in the loft. "Mind you," she added, "a woman who lives in this world is unlike Lady Sun. Your dignity comes from your modesty, faithfulness and child bearing."

Sunniva snapped out of her reverie and nodded her head agreeably. Though still in a daze, she dutifully gathered her things and headed for the ladder.

Meanwhile, Aunt Edith refused to be outdone. Whenever standards concerning proper behavior needed to be upheld, she insisted upon having the final word. She dropped her thread, waggled her finger in the direction of Sunniva's retreating back, and in a deep and authoritative tone of voice, said, "Unlike Lady Sun, a woman must be humble and not set herself apart. Otherwise, Mother Necessity will come after her and punish her for her self-important pride."

Once she was satisfied that she had put an end, succinctly, to the other women's tasteless conversation and had reestablished her position as both the eldest in the community and, also, the one to whom all others deferred whenever the strict, moral standards were being enforced, Aunt Edith picked up the story again.

It was during this time of darkness, when Lady Sun was dancing and feasting each night, that the men and women who lived in this world feared the darkness would go on and on forever. In response to their terror, the people's kinleader rubbed two sticks together to spark the need-fire. And, to warn others of the danger they all were facing, he set the bonfires ablaze.

Lady Sun's twin brothers, Night-farer and Day-farer, upon seeing the people's beacons and hearing the women's sorrowful laments, vowed to release their sister from the hold that the four mountain dwellers had over her.

The two Lords of Battle made their preparations for the journey. Once they were ready, they stepped aboard their longships. Their crews rowed until they spotted the mountainous island. They quickly made for the harbor and, once they are there, drew anchor.

The Lady's twin brothers got ready to go ashore. Night-farer and Day-farer drew their flaming long-knives. First, they engaged the guardians who stood at the gateway to Lady Sun's husband's mountainous hold-out. Day-farer and Night-farer overcame the gatekeepers, opened the massive doors, and raced through the tunnels that threaded the mountain's roots. When they came, at last, to the door leading to the great hall, they threw it open.

The fight began. Night-farer and Day-farer attacked their sister's four hus-bands. And, though they fought long and hard, when the battle was over, the four husbands threw down their weaponry, and the Lords of Battle forced them to fall onto their knees.

It was then that Lady Sun remembered Mother Necessity's decree. She stood up from her high seat and, along with a promise to return at the same time the following year, kissed each of her four husbands and bid them farewell.

To prepare for her voyage, she ordered her followers to harness the two white chargers to the disk-laden wagon and to lead them onto her longboat, Nightly. Once she and her brothers were aboard their ships, their crews launched the boats, rowed out to sea, and headed for the Gates of Dawn.

And from that time forward, Lady Sun has driven her mirror-laden wagon across the sky each day until the time comes, once each year, to visit her four husbands. She then joins them in the roots of the mountain for four nights of celebration.

And this is where I end my story about Lady Sun the Brightest Light and Fire of Sky and Air.

VII.

Throughout the storytelling, Aiken had been sitting close to the fire, bent nearly double in an attempt to shed more light upon the small cow he was whittling. Nearly finished, he poked his son and asked quietly whether he would like the cow's horns to be long or short, and whether he would like the tail to be made from a piece of braid-ed twine. The boy jumped up, nodded enthusiastically, and stood at his father's knees. As the creature took shape before his eyes, he watched in wide-eyed astonishment. To Bertolf, it seemed as though his father was as powerful as Lord Benevolent, himself, the ruling power who gave them calves, piglets and lambs each spring.

Aiken looked at this son and smiled at the speechless awe he saw in Bertolf's face. His small son's admiration was worth more than all the coinage and the small measure of freedom that he received in return for the treasure boxes and high seats, which he was forced him to make for those despicable, back-stabbing, thieving chief-tains, who had outlawed him.

"Bertolf, someday soon, I will give you a small knife and teach you how to make wooden animals. We could start with a duck. Would you like that?"

In response, Bertolf cheered excitedly. Aiken laughed, pulled his son close to his chest, and hugged him tightly. "Shush," he whispered in Bertolf's ear. "Be a good boy and keep your voice low. You and me are the only men in the house right now. We are outnumbered by the women and must not disturb their storytelling." He lightly punched Bertolf in the arm, and added, "Eh, little buddy?"

Once Aiken had finished the cow, he dropped a bit of cheese glue into the hole that he had drilled in the cow's rear end and poked in a bit of twine. Handing it off to Bertolf, he whispered a warning in the boy's ear, "Be careful, now. Do not pull on the tail until the glue is dry."

Bertolf promptly led the animal to the cart, loaded it up, and drove it off to market. All evening long, he had been playing quietly on the rug at his mother's feet. First, he loaded his cart with the animals that his father had made him. Then, he drove them around the small house, under the table, and around the chairs. When the cart bumped into the stool legs, which were standing in for trees, it tipped over. It was a terrible accident. First the cart had to be gotten upright again. Then, because the cows and sheep had all run off, they had to be chased down. In the end, after Bertolf had loaded the animals back into the cart, he brushed off his hands, and said, "All in a day's work."

Quietly amused by watching his son, Aiken thought that he, too, would like to get into the wagon, along with the cows. To drive away and to disappear in the darkest corner of the house or, to be accidentally misplaced beneath the bed, was what he would like to do right now—if only he was small enough. And along with that thought came the idea of making a little man.

Somehow, Aiken had avoided calling attention to himself until then. But when he stood and wandered over to the shelf where he kept small pieces of basswood, he attracted the women's notice. After that, his game was up.

Aunt Edith asked, "Is that right Aiken? What do you have to say?"

Walking back to his stool, he stared at her with cold animosity, and said, "I did not catch what you were saying."

Aunt Edith repeated the admonishment that she had given Mildred: "A mother needs to teach a young woman about pleasing her husband in bed. She is your daughter, too. What are your thoughts on the matter?"

Now that all eyes were turned on him, Aiken sat heavily on his stool. He suspected people wondered how his wife could stand to kiss a man whose face was so ugly and whose mouth was so misshapen. He shrugged his shoulders to hide his annoyance and concentrated upon the chunk of wood. He did not like to be watched. He easily made mistakes when others, especially Aunt Edith, were scrutinizing whatever he did. To show Edith that he had other things on his mind, he exaggerated the way he first turned the block one way, then turned it another way before he lowered his head and began to make the first cuts.

Mildred shot sidelong glances in Aiken's direction. Well acquainted with her husband's moods, she knew how quickly he took offense. But, unfortunately, her aunts and cousins were neither as agreeable as she was, nor were they as cautious of his well-known, explosive temperament.

She also knew, from past experience, that once the women all got going, there was nothing she could do to hush them. That was especially applicable to Aunt Edith who was close to making herself unwelcome in their home, right now. If that crass woman did not stop pestering Aiken, Mildred feared that she would be on bad terms with her husband for the rest of the night.

Unfortunately, because of Edith's role as elder in the hamlet, she held a position that allowed her to claim the due respect that those who held such rank were automatically granted. Consequently, she readily took advantage of her unlimited freedom to do whatever she pleased. For her, Aiken was like an itch that cried out to be scratched. And, to get a rise out of him, to trip him up, to force him to spill out some of his closely guarded secrets, she habitually picked on him.

And, now, because of Aunt Edith's harassment, Mildred feared Aiken would become more unpredictable than ever. And, true to form, he stood, sheathed his whittling knife, put the roughed-out block of wood on the table, stepped behind Mildred's back, and rested his hands upon her shoulders.

It turned out, he did have something to say, after all. He bent over his wife, leant heavily into his hands, and hissed in her ear, "Take the women's word for it, Mildred. Sunniva knows more than you think she does. Are your eyes closed? Can you not see it? Sunniva is no simple-minded child. Evidently, I know our daughter better than you do. After all, she takes after my side of the family. Believe me, I can spot trouble coming when I see it."

Mildred nodded her head and rolled her eyes. Apparently, the subject of Sunniva's maturity had been on Aiken's mind for quite some time. And now that it had come up for discussion, thanks in part to Aunt Edith, he was taking this opportunity to get those concerns off his chest. But this was neither the time nor the place for that discussion. "Aiken," she said, "we need to talk about it later, in private."

Though she knew how impossible it was to hush her husband once he was all wound up, she nonetheless, gave it her best effort, and said, "Aiken keep your voice low."

"Listen, Mildred, if you continue to think that Sunniva is so childlike, she will fool you. She is headstrong and willful, and has a mind of her own. She is better suited to protecting her honor among a band of fierce fighting men, and matching wits with those who brandish weaponry, than to spinning thread amongst a herd of horny cows."

Patting Mildred's shoulders with a mixture of affection, stern authority, and loving concern for both his wife's and daughter's wellbeing, he said, "I sorely regret that Sunniva will never have a life among the highborn. That is the kind of life she deserves. I feel the grief so strongly, it is like a punch in the gut that can drive me to my knees and leave me gasping for breath. All because I was so unfairly treated, dragged out of the Assembly Hall, and nearly beaten to death." He pressed down hard and squeezed his wife's shoulders one more time to further stress his feelings on the matter.

Mildred, too, was unable to hold back from speaking her mind any longer. Until now, she had foregone any additional, opinionated comments about the bad habits their daughter had, evidently, gotten from his side of the family. And that included

Sunniva's tendency for idling away her time in fanciful thought.

She also knew that, before they were wed, her husband had had experience pleasing women in bed. Mildred had accepted his past and had chosen not to hold that blemish on his character against him. But his past mistakes now disqualified him from having an opinion on the virtues of chastity before marriage.

Looking up at her husband with a single, uplifted brow, she said, "No doubt, when you were her age, you were interested in the serving girls and invited them into your bed. Since she takes after your side of the family, I ask you, is that the kind of trouble you see coming our way? If you do, the sooner our daughter is wed, the better."

Aiken grunted in disgust. He hiked up his belt, squared his shoulders, and stood tall. "When I was Sunniva's age I trained every day. Girls were hardly on my mind. I slept with knives in my bed, not with girls. I was more interested in staying alive. Back then, I was on patrol with the older men. I had already fought in skirmishes and had proven my skill with weaponry. I was a tough young man at that age."

But, upon catching sight of the rapt attention Aunt Edith was giving his display of bravado, he lowered his voice, bent low, and whispered in Mildred's ear, "That is, I was tough in comparison to these women's soft mommy's-boys." With a tip of his head toward the aunts and cousins, he added, "I resent having to wed my daughter to one of their cowardly sons. Those flinching crybabies know nothing about what it takes to be a man, and they never will."

"Aiken, you are wasting your time making excuses. Now, begin discussion with Werther about Sunniva's bride price. The sooner you two men come to an agreement, the better."

"Yes, you are right. I am wasting my time. I am putting it off because of my aversion to Werther, and his blundering fool of a son, Wynn. But for now, I am not wasting anymore time talking to you. I am getting out of this house."

He picked up his heavy, outdoor tunic, threw it over his head, pulled the cloak and a cap off the hook near the door, grabbed his gloves, held the torch-plant stalk in the fire until it was flaming, left the house, and slammed the door.

Mildred's eyes followed Aiken on his way out. Stormy weather seemed to accompany him wherever he went. Just the thought of an entire eating hall filled with men like him was more than she cared to think about. And here, tonight, Aiken had said that Sunniva should live in a village filled with men like him. Whatever was he thinking?

Over the years that they had been together, he had been more trouble than she had ever anticipated. Back when she had been a young, simple-minded woman she had never guessed how hard it would be. The first time she had set eyes upon him he had looked so down-trodden, it had torn her heart out. The memory was still so vivid, it seemed like only yesterday, when she had been standing in her open doorway, idly wiping her hands on her apron, absently watching the men come in from the fields. Then, suddenly she was caught off guard by the sight of a stranger trailing sullenly behind her kin.

Clutching at her apron skirt, her fingers had begun to mindlessly ball the fabric into her fists as she thought long and hard about the man's unexpected appearance and what it meant. For months, she had begged Lady Blessed to send her a man of good heart whom she could wed. That was all she ever thought about. Even when she was asleep, she saw a man wandering through a woodland in the dreamtime. Then, when morning came, she had known that the dream-man was the one whom she was meant to wed. So, that evening when she saw Aiken, it was like being both asleep and awake at the same time. He had come straight out of the dreamtime woodland and walked right into her life. How wondrous was that?

There she stood, chewing it over, and mumbling to herself, "That is the man whom I will wed. That is the man. I know it is him." That night, her praise of Lady Blessed had known no bounds.

Then, upon noticing how frantically she was wringing the gathered apron fabric in her hands, she asked herself aloud, "Whatever am I doing?" She quit abruptly and, with wide sweeping gestures, smoothed out the wrinkled fabric, turned to go back inside the house, and finished making supper.

After seeing Aiken that first time, she was unable to think of anything else. She did not even know his name, yet was convinced that he was the one whom she would wed. Her women friends would have called it madness to have been swept away by thoughts of a man whom she had caught sight of only one time. But she had seen him in the dreamtime, after all, and that counted for something. Besides, Mildred told herself, she was simply being practical. She needed to find herself a husband. Wherever the stranger with the badly scarred face had come from, Mildred figured that if Lady Blessed had approved the match, he would simply have to do. It would be up to her to convince him to marry her and to make the marriage work.

Early in their courtship, Aiken told her that he would never strike a woman and had pledged his word to never hurt her. He said women deserved respectful treatment. But even that honorable promise had caused trouble in the hamlet whenever he tried to make the other men observe the same high standards by which he had chosen to live. More than once, Mildred had been forced to step in and to calm the air when he was enforcing whatever he thought was just and fair.

The first time that Aiken had seen a man hit a woman in the hamlet, he came up behind the man and, reaching around his torso from the back, had grabbed him by the wrists. Aiken pulled the man's hands behind him and held them hard in the small of his back. Aiken may have been a small man, but when he was angry, he was stronger than most of the men in the hamlet. After all, he had been wielding heavy long-knives and lifting shields, daily, since he was a child.

The man struggled to get loose and defended his actions, saying that he would do whatever he pleased with his wife. But Aiken replied, "Only cowards and weak-willed men hit women because they are afraid to strike a man."

He let go of the man's wrists, grabbed him by the shoulders and jerked him around. He stuck his battle-scarred face only a hand's breadth away from the other man's, and said, "Hit me, hit me, instead. Try to take me on, you cowardly weakling. You good-for-nothing dog turd, just try it. Come on."

Most of the men in the hamlet did not want to fight a man who had been trained to kill, and usually walked away. But one or two had agreed to Aiken's challenge. And, after they had been badly beaten, the other men in the hamlet had taken the hint. If a man planned to hit his woman, he did it where Aiken could neither see nor hear him.

Aiken was a good man. His heart was good. But sometimes he went about defending the things that he thought were right in the wrong way. Mildred had tried to convince Aiken that he did not need to be on constant patrol in the hamlet. But he argued that it was his duty. When he had been in the warband he had been a champion fighter who had taken on challenges for men and women who were too weak to protect themselves against their abusive attackers. Now it was too late to change him. He would never stop defending a man or woman's dignity. He knew how it felt to have no one come to his defense, and he had promised to do whatever he could to make it right for others.

Even when Mildred added up all of Aiken's good qualities, she had to admit that being married to him had been a lot of work. Though Aunt Edith had warned her, Mildred had refused to listen. Back then, even marriage to a battle-scarred outlaw had seemed better than the unfortunate life that she would have had living in her brothers' households.

Back then, because Mildred was the youngest in her family, the care of her elderly father had fallen to her. The years had added up and she was no longer the fresh-faced girl that she had been before. Instead, she was growing older and more wrinkled by the day. She was a woman whose time was running out. Harald was sickly, and everyone expected him to die soon. After he was gone, it was unlikely that any man would ask for her hand in marriage. Her best years for childbearing were over, and she feared she might never conceive. (Years later, Bertolf's conception had been a delightful surprise).

If she had remained unwed, everything that had been Harald's and hers, by default, would have become her brothers.' Without a husband, she would have had no way to replace the house in which she had lived all her life, the garden and the fields she worked, the sheep she sheared, and the cattle she pastured and milked.

She would have been told to pack up her belongings in a few baskets and satchels and would have moved back and forth between her brothers' households. Without children of her own, she would never have been called Mother, but would have been known as Aunt Mildred. She would have taken orders from each of her brothers' wives. Like a servant, she would have spun at their hearths, cared for their children, and rocked their baby's cradles. Whenever one wife grew tired of Mildred's presence in her home, she would have been packed off to another brother's hearth, where she would have been equally unwelcome. Just the thought of such a miserable life had been so distasteful that Mildred had known it would have meant her certain death.

Aiken had been her last hope of escape from a miserable fate, her last chance for survival. That evening, when she first laid eyes on him, dragging his feet and looking so downcast, she had never guessed how hot-tempered and headstrong he could be, once he got his strength back. And yet, there were times when he was so sweet, he was more like a puppy dog she allowed to follow her around and to get underfoot.

Even now, after all these years, there were times when she would catch sight of him striding across the common yard, and her longing would be rekindled. The way he carried himself in such a proud and erect manner, his arrogant strut and the little bounce in each step made her hunger for him all over again. Then, she would feel the same lusty desire that she had felt when they were young and newlywed. Yes, Aiken knew how to please a woman in bed. He was dearly loved. Yet she did not know whether all the love she gave him could ever make up for all the hurts that he had suffered. Sometimes she felt so helpless.

Driven by those thoughts to bow her head, she saw her empty hands resting in her lap, turned palm upright, as if asking for deliverance. She shook her head in wonderment and questioned the futility she often felt: how could she ever make, from this life she had chosen to share with Aiken, an orderly one? Sometimes she felt so helpless.

VIII.

In the meantime, Sunniva had dutifully carried her distaff, spindle, and a small rush lamp up the ladder to the loft. She gathered the fleece from the large bundle stored beneath the rafters, combed it with the carding combs, wrapped some around the basket atop her distaff, and sat on the hard, wood-planked floor. She hung the bottom half of her legs over the edge and swung them back and forth. And as her fingers twisted the thread, and the spindle twirled and slowly fell to the hard-packed earthen floor below, she got to thinking about her future husband—her real one, not her make-believe ones.

If she was forced to marry Wynn, she supposed he would make a decent husband. Hog breeding was something that Wynn and his father specialized in. Mildred had her eye on Wynn and wanted Sunniva to marry him because his father, Werther, was well off and would give her a generous bride-price, including one or two of his prize sows. That was what Sunniva figured, anyhow.

Early last summer, Sunniva and Wynn had stood, side-by-side at the fence around the hog pen, watching one of his father's boars mount a sow. Wynn had told her that he had to watch them mate because he might have to step in and pull them apart if the boar got too aggressive. At the time, it was thrilling to imagine Wynn leaping over the fence and wrestling the boar. If he were to do that, she figured, he would need to be strong and courageous. That was the kind of man she wanted to marry—if she had to marry someone, that is—a man who was brave and confident like her father.

Although she knew how piglets were made without being told, she pretended to be awed by Wynn's display of wisdom concerning the breeding of hogs. Because his father had increased the size of his hogs through careful breeding, both Wynn and Werther were proud of their hog's lineage. In exchange for barter, Werther let other men borrow his largest boar to mate with their sows. That way, everyone could have bigger pigs with more meat and fat on their bones. Werther said it was good for folks to eat more fatty meat.

But what had affected her most, that day, and still weighed most heavily upon her mind, was the way the hogs had bred so coarsely. Sunniva wondered whether her husband would drool and grunt the same way that the boar had snorted and followed the sow around. If she tried to get away, would her husband corner her and mate with her from the rear, the same way the boar had mounted the sow? She certainly hoped not. Although she had never seen her mother and father act that way, it reinforced her lack of interest in married life and in sharing her bed with a man.

No, if she was going to marry a man and to share her bed with him, she wanted something uplifting and beautiful to happen between them. She wanted something like her mother and father had between them. Though they had their differences, and often argued, they were also affectionate and truly respected and cared for one another.

She was unsure whether Wynn was the one with whom that would happen. That day, when she and Wynn had stood side-by-side at the fence around the hog pen, both their hands were grasping the top rail. His fingers edged closer and closer to hers as she edged her fingers away and slid her feet to the side. It was the same as the sow trying to get away from the boar.

The way Wynn's gaze lingered on her breasts, made her feel both awkward and tingly at the same time. She knew he wanted to touch her there, but she also knew where to draw the line. For the time being, anyhow, she would allow him to touch her there, but only with his eyes.

She was confident that she could protect her womanly honor without her mother or father's help. But the way that her father had humiliated her, only several days before, was still fresh in her memory and made her face burn scorching hot.

Because it was Blood Month, Wynn and his father were busy helping other folks with their butchering in exchange for a portion of the meat. Early that morning, he and Werther had come from their own neighboring hamlet to help Hrodwyn's father slaughter a hog. Sunniva remembered how Werther had boasted to all his listeners that it was the biggest hog the hamlet had ever seen (after all, his boar had sired it). If the beast had gotten loose and run riot, it could have torn all their houses down, he said. Of course, to say something like that was an extreme exaggeration, but nonetheless, Werther claimed to have handled everything just fine. He and his son had taken charge of the butchering for Hrodwyn's father and had kept them all safe from harm.

Meanwhile, Sunniva had seen her father standing off to the side, looking on with that same bemused, one-sided grin that she had seen on his face so many times before. When Aiken heard Werther's boasts, he seemed to think it was so funny, he held one closed fist up to his mouth to stifle his laughter. According to her father, only a fool brags about butchering a hog.

Later that day, however, her father's opinion had apparently changed. In fact, if there had been a bragging contest, her father's boasts would surely have won the prize. Although she hesitated to call her father a liar, because it was common in competitions of that kind to impress one's listeners by stretching the truth a bit, she suspected that he had embellished a few facts here and there by laying it on quite thick.

After the butchering was all wrapped up, Aiken had seen Sunniva and Wynn standing together. He walked right up to them, acting friendly. But Sunniva knew her father better than that. She, also, had taken note of the fact that he had strapped his combat knife onto his belt. That was something he rarely did, unless he was leaving home. She suspected he was up to something and doubted that friendliness was in his game plan. She had watched him humiliate people before and understood his tactics.

The first thing he would do was complement Wynn and show an interest in his work: "Quite a boar you and your father took down this morning."

To have been praised like that by the father of the girl, who he was sweet on, Wynn's chest swelled with pride. All the time that Aiken stood there, he let Wynn boast about the butchering. But Sunniva suspected her father was sizing him up, coaxing Wynn to let his guard down, just to make it easier to belittle him.

"Wynn, because I know how well you handle a blade, I would like to show you something," her father said, then surprised them both by unsheathing his combat knife. He laid the flat side of the blade across his left palm and held it out for Wynn's inspection.

No one in Sunniva's house was allowed to get near her father's knife. It was made for fighting—killing, really—not butchering. Because he kept the blade deathly sharp, it was extremely dangerous. He had told Mildred, Sunniva, and Bertolf that the blade had a will of its own. If you did not have a good grip on the hilt and absolute control of its length, from tip to base, the knife would know it. Without a firm hold on it, Rushing Harm would take advantage of your ignorance and strike out with an intent to hurt you. It was a mean knife.

Aiken made the knife sound so scary that everyone in the house was afraid to even take a sidelong peek at it. He rarely wore it but kept it in a box on a high shelf. He only took it out, now and then, to polish it or to strap it onto his belt when he traveled to the markets, or to places beyond the local hamlets, such as the quarry. No one ever challenged him or his right to bear arms when he wore it (except the foolish quarryman), even though everyone knew he was an outlaw. Aiken said that no one dared confront him. Evidently, he still had the nasty reputation that he had had before. Based upon his willingness to challenge other men to fight in one-on-one combat, she had heard it said that her father had been an undefeated champion until he was outlawed.

Tipping the blade back and forth he showed Wynn how the steel blade's herringbone patterns caught glints in the sunlight and made it flash. The design on its skin made it look like a snake slipping through water. Aiken told Wynn that the snake in the blade hid in the shadowy half-light and, before its victim saw it, would lunge at its prey unawares.

At first, she had thought her earlier mistrust of her father's motives had been mistaken. It seemed, instead, that her father wanted to invite the man, who might marry into their family, to engage in friendly, manly talk about a common interest. But it soon became apparent that no such congenial conversation had been his intention at all.

By comparing the creatures that each of their knives had taken down, Aiken contrasted this wondrous blade to the plain ones that Werther and Wynn used. "This blade's victim is neither tethered nor dazed by a knock on its head. When this blade meets a raging boar, nothing is done to make it easy for a man to slit its neck and to catch its blood in a basin. Courage is hardly needed to cut the throat of a lazy, old hog after it has been hobbled and tied up to a fence."

Her father told them that before he was Wynn's age, he had met wild boars head-on in the forest. Any young man, who wanted to become a member of a chieftain's warband, must first prove his valor with a successful boar-kill. The only weapons that he is allowed to take into the woods are one heavy boar spear and his gutting knife—a knife just like this one.

To make the boar's charge more lethal, it was trapped beforehand by the beaters and goaded to anger. The day that Aiken had stood there alone, holding the heavy boar spear, he had known that he needed to strike the boar's chest with certainty and deadly force. As he watched the beast's broad head and chest come surging toward him, he had known his timing had to be just right. There would be no second chance. Those tusks were sharp as a knife and could gore a man from his groin up to his neck.

Boasting about how he had passed the test and proven his courage, Aiken described how he speared the creature with just one thrust. After he gutted and skinned the boar, the head and hide were nailed over the door on his liege lord's hall to announce his brave deed to all who saw it. Aiken laughed when he recalled the marvelous night when they had feasted on the meat. They had celebrated the kill that night—his first big kill. That was the night that he had become a member of the warband.

Still a boy, in those days, green and untried at war, that night was the first time that he had been offered the praise-and-promise cup to drink from. When Torwald's wife had praised him, she had called him by his name and appellation: Aiken the Strength of Oak. She had invoked the name of his dead father, Eamon the Good Protector, who had been an esteemed fighting man, and she had recounted Aiken's warrior lineage.

Wynn stood there with his mouth hanging open, staring at Sunniva's father. Aiken had just pointed out the stark differences between the two men. The kinleader's wife would never praise Wynn after he had butchered one of his father's pigs. His father's hog lineage was more important than was his own. Even his own mother, Nelda, would do nothing more than give him a cursory nod that evening at the supper table. She would ask him how Hrodwyn's mother was doing, now that she had all that meat to salt and preserve. She would say, "I bet Arlett will be glad to have all that pork put away for the winter." That was the kind of praise that Wynn would get.

Aiken exaggerated the way that he looked Wynn over, from the top of his head down to his feet, and asked Wynn whether he wanted to be a warrior.

Wynn nodded agreeably, and said, "Sure." When put like that, what else could he say?

"You might be strong enough to kill a wild boar with a heavy boar spear," Aiken said. "Do you think that you could handle a blade like this one? This knife slashes through a moving target with such force that I can cut through flesh and bone as easily as I slice through butter when I am seated at the supper table."

Without a pause, Aiken drew attention to the fine gleam in the steel and pointed to each of the gold letters embedded in the blade's skin. Since Wynn was ignorant of the secret signs and could not read them, her father told him that they spelled Rushing Harm. When the fire in the smith's forge had fused the power of the blade's name with the steel, the unbreakable bond formed by the heat had increased the blade's deadliness.

"This blade is as fast as its name suggests. Men say it is invisible because no one can see it coming. That is how fast I can wield this knife. Sunniva saw me pull it once." Aiken held his thumb and forefinger so close together that only a thin ray of sunlight could be seen through the narrow gap between them. "I came this close to cutting a man's throat. Do you agree Sunniva?"

Without waiting for an answer, he boasted of the strength it takes to kill either an onrushing boar or a well-armed man who is coming straight at you. "This is the kind of knife that a man uses when he fights in a shield wall. Make no mistake about it, if a man is untrained, he is more dangerous to the man beside whom he is standing than he is to the enemy. Before you can use a knife like this one, you train with it for years. Otherwise, no one will trust you."

Although her father had encouraged Wynn to believe that he could join a prestigious warband, she knew that her father had no merit with the chieftains. He had no power to offer opinions regarding a young man's worth. The chieftains never even looked at her father. If they or their warriors wanted something from him, they sent a steward to talk to him, or told their wives to talk to Mildred. Sunniva knew this was true because she had seen him express his rage whenever one of the overlords or their men-at-arms rode past him in the markets, purposefully looking the other way to avoid seeing him. They knew who he was, but never spoke to him. They certainly would never hear him out. She had heard her father say, "I am too dangerous to mess with. No one wants to take me on."

Whether or not her father was as dangerous as he said he was, she did not know. But she had no doubt that he was clever enough to outsmart Wynn. Aware of her father's wry sense of mockery, his telling little smile, and the methods he used to cover his anger at having been left so powerless, she knew how he amused himself by ridiculing those people who he thought were beneath him. He watched for people's attempts to mask their motives behind thinly crafted disguises, and tried not to laugh out loud. She had seen him lead men and women, who he characterized as being beneath his dignity, into verbal traps, just to make fun of them later. He was a smart man and could easily outwit his prey.

Aiken pressed his palm against the flat side of the blade to demonstrate the metal's crucial flexibility. "A brittle blade becomes a dead man's weapon when it breaks. I have seen common butcher knives break inside the carcass when a man cuts it up. What can you do with a broken knife? Nothing. You can do nothing. It is useless. How will you finish your work for the day with a broken knife? The same is true in a fight. But when your life depends upon your blade in a fight, if it breaks, it is your life that is finished that day.

"This blade, though, is guaranteed not to break." He turned Rushing Harm's hilt toward Wynn and insisted he take it. "Go on, hold it. Feel the heft, the balance, and the weight in the steel."

"Can you feel the powerful luck in this knife?" Aiken asked and, pointing to the smith's mark, he tapped it several times. "It was made by a master craftsman. No man's blow can shatter this blade. It will stand the test against all others."

Wynn understood the honor he had been accorded and held the hilt with obvi-ous respect. The second test of a blade's worth depended upon whether a man used it. Otherwise, even the showiest knife had no merit. In search of a trace of bloodstain, Wynn looked Rushing Harm over and, upon identification of the telltale signs of tar-nish on the blade's surface, nodded meaningfully.

Wynn was staring at the woven patterns in the blade's skin when Sunniva's father told him to blow on it and to call it by its name. Wynn did as he was instruct-ed. The steel misted over, and when Wynn said, "Rushing Harm," the changeable hues flashed, and the knife came alive in his hands. Right there, before his eyes, the youth saw the snake in the blade rear its head and open its fanged jaw. At the sight of a snake's readiness to strike and to make the kill, a look of terror momentarily crossed Wynn's face, and he almost dropped the blade.

Aiken shook his head, regretfully, as if to say, this young man will never do. He would never make the cut. Unlike this blade, Wynn would never stand the test against all others. He would never meet the expectations that a chieftain demands of his warriors. "A man-at-arms must never flinch. He must never show fear or weak-ness. Never. Even when he runs heedlessly into a skirmish, even when he knows he is outnumbered, even when he knows he is about to die," Aiken said. "I did that."

But unfortunately, unless Wynn joined a warband he would never know the thrill of combat. He would never experience the trusted companionship that a man-at-arms shares with those whom he fights side-by-side. No, Wynn would never know how it feels to have honor bestowed upon him by his liege lord when his bravery is extolled in the meadhall.

"Wynn, when I was your age, I had already vowed to serve the long-knife. I had sworn to protect those who depended upon me for their safekeeping. And although I am no longer a member of a warband, I still observe that holy vow. I fought my first battle before I had even grown a beard."

The distance between the older man and the younger one was so great and so telling, Wynn had never experienced anything resembling what Aiken had described. The worlds that each man came from were so different, there was no way for Wynn to make sense of the life that Aiken had grown into manhood knowing. All he could do was gape at Sunniva's father, wondering, no doubt, whether that first battle was the one in which he had been so badly hurt in the face.

"I doubt that you have wedded your butcher knife the same way I wedded my combat knives," Aiken said. "Have you?"

Sunniva stood there, on the sidelines, watching the two men. Though, quite truthfully, there had never been much of a contest between them, she was the reason they were there, verbally squaring off. Yet, it seemed her presence had been entirely irrelevant. She was forgotten and invisible until Aiken told Wynn, "This knife stands for me and my daughter's bloodline. I slept with my blades beside me. This knife mothered Sunniva."

That was when her face turned bright red and burned with heat.

"This blade is my daughter's protector. If you so much as touch Sunniva before she is wed, this blade will come after you to defend her honor. And after you marry her, it will come for you if you ever hurt her. Do you understand what I am saying?"

Wynn eyed Aiken's blade. Indeed, this was a frightful-looking weapon. He had never held one like it before, and never again would he be entitled to such an honorary privilege. Only the highest-ranking chieftains and their warriors owned blades as fine as this one. He did not want it poking him in the gut and coming out his backside nor slicing him across the neck. No doubt it would do exactly what Aiken said it could.

He handed the blade back to Aiken and gave him a little nod. "I do Aiken, I understand." In an attempt to salvage a small measure of pride in his own self-worth, in front of the girl who he was sweet on and her intimidating father, he added, "My knife works hard and has bloodstain on it, too. My word is good. I promise to do what is right and honorable in regard to your daughter."

Aiken tapped Wynn on the shoulder in the same way that he would pat a dog on the head, and said, "Good boy."

Several days had passed since Wynn's hapless encounter with her father. But Sunniva still felt the burning humiliation, as much for her sake, as for his.

After the spindle struck the floor and toppled over, she left it lying still. Although she was hidden in the shadowy half-light, her mother's keen eyesight spotted her daughter's idleness. Mildred told her to come down and to wind the thread.

As Sunniva climbed down the ladder, her mother intoned her teachings: "Life is a struggle. Keep your eyes open. Remain vigilant against disorder. There is no time to indulge in pleasant thoughts. Mind the tasks before you. Fight distraction from your present work."

Sunniva wound the yarn around the spindle axis. Seething scornfully, she held a strand close to her mother's nose, and said, "Look. Find one flaw in it. It is perfect." And, after spitting out her invective, she added, resentfully, "You will get a good price for it in the market."

In response to her daughter's anger, Mildred acted like she did whenever Bertolf threw a temper tantrum. She brushed her daughter's hand aside, and said, "Go back to spinning in the loft."

Sunniva's sassy, disrespectful behavior had not, however, gone unnoticed by the other women. Reminded of yet another story that she had had half a mind to tell that night, Aunt Edith cleared her throat, smoothed her apron skirt, and looked around the small room. She grasped her knees, squeezed them tightly, took a deep breath, and with some sort of pent up need to express herself, asked, "Ready for another one?"

There was a young woman who lived with her mother. Called Rose Red because of her rosy cheeks and red lips, she was so beautiful that she often admired herself whenever she gazed at her reflection in the water pail. Though Rose Red had a suitor, she refused to wed him because she did not think that he was good enough to be her husband. Her mother, however, was eager to have the bride-price. So, she and the youth's father came to an agreement.

Rose Red's chores were to spin thread and to milk the cows each day. Early one morning, she set out for the pasture with her milk buckets. When she got there, she saw a woman seated on a rock, gazing in a bronze mirror. The woman said, "I have been waiting for you to come by."

Rose Red asked, "May I look in the mirror?"

The woman told her that she knew where mushrooms grew and asked Rose Red to gather some in the woods with her. The woman promised to show her the mirror afterward.

Rose Red and the woman set out for the forest. Once they were there, the woman picked a mushroom, handed it to the girl, and said, "Here, eat this one."

Rose Red took a bite, just as the woman had told her. But the mushroom lodged in her throat, and she began to choke. The woman held the mirror up to Rose Red's face. When Rose Red opened her mouth to cough, she saw the reflection of a small bird fly out. She collapsed and fell into a deep, death-like sleep. The woman with the mirror walked off. The little bird followed after her, and Rose Red was left alone in the woods.

Evening fell. When several men came through the dark forest, though they were surprised, at first, to see Rose Red lying just off the path, they picked her up and began to carry her home with them. When one man stumbled over a tree root, they dropped her. The blow to her back jarred Rose Red and she spit out the poisonous mushroom. The men picked her up and continued on their way. Once they were back in their underground rooms, they saw how deathly pale she was. After they built up a blazing fire to keep her warm, her soul returned, the color in her cheeks came back, her lips reddened, and her eyes blinked open.

The men told Rose Red to rest and not to leave, lest she become lost in the forest. They offered her the best food and drink if she would stay with them. But Rose Red was eager to get back home again and, the following morning, she set out.

When she came to the edge of the forest, there was a woman standing before a loom. Rose Red stopped to talk with her. The woman asked Rose Red to help her cut the cloth from the loom. "You will want for nothing," the woman said, "and no harm will come to you if you wear a cloak made from this cloth."

The beautiful fabric turned Rose Red's eye. The woman laid it across the girl's shoulders, wrapped it around her and bound the cloth with a heavy cord. She tied the cord so tightly that Rose Red could hardly breathe. The woman asked whether she would like to see how attractive she looked when she wore this cloth. The wicked woman then held up the mirror, and again, Rose Red saw the small bird fly out of her mouth. After that, she fell into a deep sleep.

That night, the same men as before came through the forest. When they saw Rose Red laying on the forest floor, they pulled their knives and cut her loose from the tightly bound cloth. Rose Red gasped and revived. After the men had carried her back to their underground rooms, they warned her not to leave the protection of their rooms again.

The following night, after the men had left, Rose Red heard a knock on the door. When she opened it, she saw a woman carrying an empty bird cage. She told Rose Red that she had been searching for a prized bird that had flown off, but she had become hopelessly lost and hungry.

Rose Red pitied the woman. She sat her down at the table and offered her refreshments. To show her gratitude for the kindness that the girl had shown her, the woman offered Rose Red a silver ribbon. She tied the silver ribbon around her neck, and the woman held up the mirror so that she could see how attractive she looked. The silver ribbon tightened of its own accord until it had strangled Rose Red and she fell into a deep swoon.

The men arrived home, but because the ribbon had slipped beneath the neckline on her dress, they did not see it and were unable to help her. They placed Rose Red in a box made of rock crystal. The men closed the lid and built up the fire in the forge to keep her warm, but she never wakened. Death was sure to follow unless her bird-like soul returned.

Meanwhile, Rose Red's mother thought that her daughter was surely dead by now and began to mourn her loss. But her betrothed still held out hope and swore to find her. He searched high and low, for many days and nights. One evening, he took shelter in a cave. He wrapped himself in his cloak and rested behind a large boulder. He awakened when he heard the men walk past him. On their way out, one man left a burning torch just inside the cave entrance.

Rose Red's betrothed decided to explore the cave. He took the torch and set out. When he came to a door, he opened it and was surprised to see that inside the room there was a blazing fire in a forge and an ironsmith's tools were laid out on a workbench. Near the forge, he saw his betrothed asleep in the crystal-sided box. Glad to find her, he opened the box lid, and saw the silver ribbon tied around her neck. He untied the ribbon and bent down to kiss her.

The captive little bird broke free of the wicked woman's cage and flew back to Rose Red. She awoke and her betrothed carried her home. They wed soon thereafter. Rose Red never again looked at her reflection in the water pail. She kept her eyes down and her mouth closed, tended the hearth, and bore her husband many fine children.

Sunniva understood, all too well, the meaning of Aunt Edith's tale. Unless she respects authority, acts agreeably, does as she is told, remains faithful to her kin, and marries the man her mother and father have chosen, so that they can claim your bride-price and increase their wealth, her life will not be spared. This much Sunniva knew.

Death threatened those who were different from the others, did not fit in, and had a mind of their own. If she refused to do whatever everyone else did and shirked those duties, which her mother said were expected of her, the consequences would be dire. If she heard voices that no one else heard and saw fearful, invisible things that others said were better left alone, she would be forced to live like an outcast in the wild, forested regions. Her protectors would be ironsmiths who wandered the woods at night and offered her a knife named Right Truth. But, in the end, even their iron knives could not help her. They could not save her from the wicked woman who uses a mirror to look for vain, simple-minded girls whose souls she can steal.

According to Aunt Edith's tale, the only way to save herself from such an unfortunate fate was to marry and to raise a houseful of children. This act alone was guaranteed to keep her in her proper place. Her husband would not allow her to wander off, to think thoughts that she was not supposed to think, nor to question those who told her what to believe.

If, however, she foolishly threw aside the promising life that her kin offered, and chose, instead, to follow the woman with the mirror, she would be as good as dead to them. After her soul had taken flight for otherworlds, her mother would not be there to poke her in the arm to wake her. Her father would ignore her because he was too busy carving a big red stone. Her bones would molder on the forest floor beneath a layer of soggy, rotting leaves and give rise to poisonous mushrooms.

Sunniva shuddered at the chilling thought of being so lost, so helpless, and so alone.

It was then that she heard another voice. This voice was not the one she had been listening to, the voice that was coming from deep inside her own heart. Nor was it Aunt Edith's voice, the one that came to her from the ground floor. This voice was coming from someplace else, from somewhere up above her head.

Sunniva was still seated on the edge of the floor. She pulled up her knees, scooted around, and looked behind her. It may have been too dark to see anything in the smoky haze, but she knew, somehow, that there was a woman seated in the rafters. The woman's back was bent, her head was bowed and, squeezed into the narrow confines beneath the thatch, she was sitting on the crossbeam, dangling her legs and spinning thread.

Sunniva's heart beat fast. She asked herself how could anyone have snuck into the house without being seen? How could someone climb up to the crossbeam without a ladder? The woman's whorl slowly dropped from the height of the crossbeam and, as the twisting woolen strand lengthened, Sunniva watched with rapt attention.

"Who are you?" Sunniva whispered, "What are you doing up there?"

In response to the question she sensed the woman's smile. "I could ask you the same," the woman said. "I know who I am. But do you know who you are?

"Oh, pretty bird
Come spread your wings
Oh, pretty bird
Come fly away with me."

Uncertain how to answer, Sunniva wondered whether she knew who she was. She answered to the name Sunniva but, otherwise, who was she? How would she know? It felt strange to be like the girl in the story that Aunt Edith had told. If, like Rose Red, she was given a dawn-colored cloak, what would her life be like if she flew away, like a little bird, with the woman in the rafters? Might the woman in the rafters be spinning a new thread to replace the one that had been spun for her before?

If the thread the Matrones spin is a story that she tells, both to herself and to others, to describe her life, will that story-thread determine who she is a meant to be by fixing in place who she is becoming?

If that were so, the woman in the rafters might be spinning a different storied thread for her, one that was different from the ones that her mother and Aunt Edith told about her future life with Wynn. And if that were true, it could determine another kind of life for her.

"What will happen to me if I go with you?"

"Sunniva what are you doing up there?" Mildred asked, "Who are you talking to?"

Sunniva stood, grabbed the small rush lamp and hurried to the place where she had heard the spindle touch the floor. "Do not go away," Sunniva said, softly. "Do not go yet. I want to talk with you."

Frantic to find the thread, she scanned the floor with her small lamp, but found nothing but rolling dust clumps. Otherwise, the spot was bare. Nor, when she lifted the light above her head, could she see anyone seated on the crossbeam in the rafters.

"No one. There is no one up here to talk to."

IX.

My curiosity about these creatures, whom we call men and women, is boundless. I want to learn everything there is to know about them. How it pains me to think of the many things that get away. I count among them their random thoughts and conversations that will never be recorded nor collected. Yet, with these written words I have salvaged a few, loose fragments of their lives. Unlike fleeting memories, the crystallization of this single night is now made hard and fast with ink and paper.

THREE

Sardonyx
If you will attract good fortune
And diminish hesitation and grant courage

Take this stone which is called Sardonyx, which is of a black color.
The best kind is one which is full of white veins. It gives a man
the strength of heart to overcome perils. hanged around the neck
it keeps a man's body against his enemies.
The Truth of Rocks, by Aluiss the Wise

I.

It seems so quiet just now. But lack of sound can be deceiving. Grerr, most likely, is attending to the two goats and his hillside garden. That is where he grows most of the food he cooks for us. A man of unique talents, Grerr is so quick, he can catch a trout bare-handed whenever he goes fishing in the streams. Another of his skills is the manufacture of automatons. Three of the toys, he recently invented, are copies of horses small enough to hold in one hand. Riding upon each of their backs are tall, skinny trees that either stand upright or tilt to one side. One of the trees sprouts palm-like branches from its trunk. The other two are topped with leafy-looking ball shapes. Beneath each of the trees is a small chair upon which a stack of books is resting.

He told us that he had seen these horses trotting through a dreamtime landscape. First, the trees jumped out of the earth like a rabbit and fell over. Then, because a dream, in which one sees a tree moving from its rooted spot will reveal the form that it wishes to take, he had seen the trees riding horseback. But where they were headed he did not say.

Grerr uses a small key to wind up the springs that he conceals inside the animals' miniaturized bodies. Then, as the mechanical devices unwind, they prance across the supper table. The night he showed us, we readily bought into his game. We laughingly told him that he could have fooled us into believing they were alive, had it not been for the way they repeated the same, stiff actions until they came to a halt when their springs wound down.

He offered me one of these horses for my collection. Though I readily accepted the gift, I suspect his shows of generosity are contrived the same way he invents his toys. There have been times, in the past, when Grerr acted so motherly, I trusted the sincerity of his feelings, implicitly. It was only after I discovered the ruse that I regretted not having been alerted earlier to his scheming.

Of the four of us, Allfrigg is the most enigmatic. He stays to himself most of the time, keeping busy with a variety of alchemical pursuits. He mixes potions in his laboratory and, through the cultivation of formulaic spells and arcane ritual, attempts to influence hidden, powerful forces which, in my opinion, are better left alone. Because he works without oversight by those who might, otherwise, question the integrity of what he does, several of Allfrigg's more dubious accomplishments have brought about grotesque results which, for the time being, anyhow, are better left unsaid. It is for these reasons that Allfrigg might seem to be the most dangerous of the men with whom I live.

But then there is Berling. Of the four of us, he is the one who has acquired the most fearsome powers. Because of the unholy alliance he formed with the Sons of the Fiery Realm, he has become privy to their most closely guarded secrets. Given the means to control fire at high heat, he changes the crumbly, bog-iron nuggets into the hardened steel with which he forges the exquisitely crafted weaponry that men favor for its proficiency in overpowering and killing other men.

Like the rest of us, Berling has secrets he refuses to disclose. But, otherwise, he is a man of surprisingly few unknowns. He is loyal to his friends, bold and forthright, shows his feelings readily, and is immediate in his responses. That is not to say he lacks a mean streak. Rather, he simply sees no reason to hide his meanness as others do.

As for me, now that the collection of these stories has become so demanding, I have been forced to set aside all other concerns. But before I took on this daunting and all-consuming project, it was my goal to collect all that humankind has ever written and to become proficient in all that people have ever known. I have a prodigious memory, am acquainted with most written languages, and read everything I get my hands onto.

It is my ambition to learn all that I can about the world that surrounds me. I practice self-control, have developed excellent observational skills, and have an innate ability for organization. Among the studies that I have mastered are arithmetic, astrology, cosmology, and Natural Philosophy. Grerr tells me that humility is not one of my strengths.

Though hampered by an inability to go out during the daytime, I do my best to document all that I discover by diligently recording my observations. In this way, I feel an intellectual kinship with Pliny the Elder, who was also preoccupied by his need to know and to record all that he learns. I have heard that whenever he moved through the streets of Rome, he rode in a palanquin and dictated his thoughts and observations to a scribe who followed alongside. Unfortunately, I do not have a scribe who will follow me around and write down every thought that passes through my head. But there appear to be other affinities that Pliny and I commonly share.

Paging through his book, Natural History, I find that he, too, collected stories the same way I do, to illustrate the variety of ways men and women have affected the natural order of things through their interactions with stone. Under the heading, "The First Use of Precious Stone," he includes tales about men and women who have adorned themselves with stones; drank from stone cups; used stones to cure their afflictions; and offered stones to the ruling powers in return for special favors.

In his discussion of Sardonyx, he tells the story of Polycrates of Samos who wished to ensure the continuity of his good fortune. It is a well-known fact that men and women have, over time, gone to great lengths to maintain their supply of luck. Some men have even been known to steal it from others. In the case of Polycrates, the day he chose to follow through with his intention to make a suitable gift to the powers, who were responsible for his good luck, he boarded a ship, put out to sea, and threw a signet ring into the water. The ring was made from a large, black sardonyx cabochon. On the top of the stone, there was a raised, intaglioed picture of three, pale brown and white bees flying around a stringed, musical instrument.

As it happened, after Polycrates had thrown the ring into the sea, a large fish, possibly a dolphin, swallowed it up. A fisherman caught the fish and brought it to Polycrates' kitchen. After the fish was cooked, Polycrates cut it open and pulled out the ring. Unfortunately, its return carried an ominous warning that his luck was about to run out. Shortly afterwards, Polycrates was lured into a trap and killed by an enemy.

One could say that, because the sea had spit out the ring in such a fashion it had refused to accept his gift. What I do not understand, however, is why Polycrates gave his ring to the sea in the first place. Perhaps, if he had been a fisherman who was hoping to bring in a good haul after he had cast his net, it would have made sense to have honored the sea in such a fashion. But the subsequent loss of Polycrates luck leads me to believe that the sea was not the most appropriate power to have been offered the signet ring.

What if, instead, Polycrates had given his gift to the three Matrones who were responsible for spinning his fate? Or, better yet, what if he had offered the ring to the very source of luck itself? I should think that if Polycrates had done so, he might have remained in the good graces of the powers who had favored him in the past.

Most learned men, with whom I have spoken, agree that the source of luck can be found in the very act of creation itself: Mother Necessity and Father Time's spinning dance around the egg from whence the earth's, the sky's, and the water's bounteous goodness comes when the eggshell fractures.

I include here a copy of a letter that was sent to me by a certain Natural Philosopher with whom I have corresponded. What follows is a narration describing, in greater detail, Mother Necessity and Father Time's dance around the egg.

He wrote:

These reflections are occasioned by a walk I took through a woods one dreary night, when, not too long ago, I was collecting luminous mushrooms and I lost my bearings entirely.

This woodland is renowned for being home to a variety of hidden folk who amuse themselves by playing tricks on ordinary men like me. The sky was overcast, my lantern was low on fuel, and I did not wish to remain afoot in a dangerous forest at night.

I presently came upon a small clearing where an old man was sitting beside a small fire, feeding it twigs. Behind him, at the edge of the clearing, several crows were perched on the lowest hanging branches. Each bird had tucked its head beneath a wing and appeared to be asleep. But when I approached, one of the crows fluffed its feathers and stretched out its head to look me over.

Explaining to the man how I had lost my bearings, I asked to share his fire till dawn. I told him I was certain I could find my way out of the forest once the sun had risen. He nodded his approval and gestured to the place where I should sit across from him.

The man was wearing a long, hooded cape that he kept tightly pulled around himself. It was so dark, that night, that the small fire shed little light and even less warmth. But to conserve our fuel we kept the blaze small.

Though I was staring into the fire, I could not help but sense his scrutiny. When I looked up to meet his gaze, my sensations were so strange that I shall try to explain them. Up until then, the hood he wore had cloaked his face in shadow. So it surprised me to see that one of his eyes was colored an opaque, yellowish white, and had neither a pupil nor an iris. For some reason, the sight, though unpleasant, made me return his stare. A scar ran jaggedly from one side of his forehead to the opposite cheek, and another crossed the bridge of his nose. The way his nose was flattened and twisted to the side gave it the appearance of having been broken at one time. Yes, I thought, he was once in a fight, got punched in the face, and was dreadfully cut up.

Presently, he suggested we tell stories to pass the time. I considered the matter a moment before I replied that since the idea was his, I should let him go first. He began by asking whether I had ever gone to the farthest reaches of the known worlds, and then beyond that, into the vast unknown.

I answered that I had not. "If I can get lost walking through a small woodland," I told him, "surely, I would lose my way entirely if I were to seek the farthest reaches of the known world, to say nothing of what lays beyond."

"As you can plainly see," the man said, "because I am sitting here before you now, I did not lose my way. I have gone and returned again to tell others what I saw. If you wish to go with me, figuratively speaking that is, we will find a place where there lurks, inside a seething smoke-cloud, bursting with sparks and filled with brightly colored, glowing gases, two beautiful, serpentine beings."

There we sat, staring at each other through the smoke. Looking into his one sighted eye, I saw an iris that was colored dark brown and the black pupil was so large it seemed as though its utter blackness absorbed my gaze entirely. Drawn into that blackness, I could just make out two tiny figures spinning together in a dance. At first, I did not know what to make of this unearthly vision, nor to what I could attribute it. But soon an inkling of the truth occurred to me. What this was, I thought, was something that the man had seen on his travels. It is the man's memory, I said to myself, of the time when he had seen the two dancers after he had ventured beyond the farthest reaches of the known worlds.

To be sure, I had the strongest notion that he was now letting me in on this uncanny vision. If such a thing were truly possible, that he could convey his thoughts and visions to me by just a look, it made sense that he would have hidden his gaze beneath the hood up until then. While these strange ideas were passing through my mind, I admit to being completely confounded but, also, equally fascinated.

Even as it was happening, I knew that I was sitting across from the man, with this small fire burning between us. Yet, it seemed, that at the same time that he was describing the place where he had been, we were standing together, side by side and far away, looking over a great chasm. I could see those dancing figures in the distance as clearly as if I were looking at them with my own two eyes. If I were to say that I was astonished by such a vision, it would be an extreme trivialization of how shocked I felt. There are no words to describe the curious sights I saw, but will do my best to relay them, nonetheless.

"The one being is shapely as a woman," the man said. "The stretch of her arms is so vast that they could wrap around the breadth of all the worlds and encompass them all at once. And even further than that, she reaches out to a nameless place beyond all known limitations.

"The other serpentine being is like a man. Although they have taken on human-like shapes, there is nothing earthly about them. The two beings are light and translucent as wisps of marsh gas exploding in surges, rising through an overlaying expansive, dust cloud.

"Mother Necessity's urge to both create and to destroy as she coils in Father Time's arms is what drives the rotation of the heavens."

And, just as he described it, I envisioned thousands of stars spinning around, leaving lingering traces of cycling multi-colored lights against the pitch-black sky. And in the very center of that black chasm were the two dancers.

"Father Time stands on one snake-wrapped leg, and tucks the other to his chest. He holds a small, round drum with one hand. A blue flame burns in the palm of the hand with which he beats a ferocious rhythm," the man said.

I heard the sound of that ancient drumbeat. Or perhaps it was the sound of my own heart beating increasingly louder until I thought my head would explode. I saw wrapped around each of the serpentine being's waists tattered orange, red, and yellow glowing filaments tied with bright, shining knots. These belts were being ripped apart, streaming on heated gusts that the man, who was seated across from me, called the four winds of change. The serpentine beings' crowns were adorned with sparkling rubies, topaz, and emeralds. Their combined four arms spun in a graceful spiral around the white-hot center where a glowing egg hung suspended between them.

Mother Necessity held a spindle in one hand. Flares like streaming torches came from the hand circling high above her head. Clouds of dust and flaming arcs streamed from Father Time's neck. Mother Necessity's bound plaits were strings of light whipping violently back and forth as the two went around and around.

"This expansion keeps edging towards forever," said my guide to this place beyond all known worlds. "It is greater than any reckoning."

From whence came the next thought, I do not know. Call it revealed knowledge if you will, but I knew that within that egg there were the smoking remains of an old dying star, inside of which new stars were being birthed and lit in continuous transformation.

The next thing I knew, I was wrapped in my cloak, lying curled up next to the spent, cold embers. It was just about daybreak. The spell, which had bound me, was over. The man and the crows were gone. Whether it was real or was a dream, I never have settled upon.

Inspired, perhaps, by this description of the emptiness of the chasm wherein Mother Necessity and Father Time dance, it occurs to me that the place where creation can be discovered is in the blackness lying dormant behind the writing on stones.

Unlike Polycrates' cabochon, the piece of Sardonyx I own is uncarved. Mine is nearly all black except for the series of white, parallel bands written upon it. When I look at it through the lens, I see that what had appeared, at first, to be one thick band is, actually, made up of a central wider one and three delicate bands bordering it on either side. Following the same curves, several narrower bands run alongside it. Near the right edge of the stone, Nature has finished her flamboyant signatory design with an additional grand, wave-like loop curving back upon itself with a flourish.

On the back side of the stone, I see the blackness behind the white writing. My desire to know what lies behind the writing on stones leads me to a speechless place. At first, it seems as unknowable as the bottomless chasm into which my correspondent had been staring. And, likewise, when I gaze at the blackness in this stone, I find, in its seemingly limitless depths, the pure, shapeless thoughts from which speechless thoughts give rise to words.

II.

Near the top edge of the stone, an additional thin, red line becomes the brief after-images a man traces with a torch when he is walking. Like a series of transitory arcs, the flame makes broad sweeps equal to the length of each of his footsteps before the moment-to-moment play of light disappears.

And as he did each night, before he settled in, he circled the ox-road one time. The sky was overcast, but his flaming torch-plant, along with the dim fire-glow spilling from the houses and the smoldering fire pits gave off enough light to illuminate his path.

Back at the house, he took his usual place on the bench beside the door, quenched the flame, and set the torch-stalk aside. He pulled his cap down over his ears, wrapped his cloak more tightly around himself, and tucked his gloved hands protectively inside its folds. He leaned back against the outer house wall, stretched out his legs, struggled to ignore the women's muffled voices coming from inside the house, and prepared to keep the night watch.

It was going to be a long night. He was shivering, and his teeth were chattering while, on the other side of the door, Mildred's aunts and cousins were seated comfortably around his cozy hearth, burning the wood he had chopped. But if things had worked out differently, if the three Matrones had spun his life-thread another way, that very same night, instead of taking refuge from the women inside his home, he would have been seated at Torwald's high table.

Living as befitted a man of high rank, a battle-hardened warrior who had made a name for himself by now, he and his companions would either be gaming or listening to the poet's praise-songs. They might have challenged each other to riddle contests, or matched wits exchanging insults. He would have betrothed his daughter to the best, young, fighting man in the warband. That was the kind of man she deserved, not the son of a hog butcher.

If nothing had changed, and if things were still the same as they had been before, his friend Alger would have been seated beside him, with his forearms resting upon his thighs, and his hands cradling an ale cup. Perhaps, the two men would have patrolled the roads earlier in the day. They might have seen a deer cross their path and given chase. Afterwards, they would have bantered back and forth about who had been in the lead and whose sharp aim had, in the end, taken the stag down. Boasting and arguing, in a joking way, they would have slapped each other on the arms and knocked their fists together and banged their ale cups on the table and laughed loudly. That was what they had done back then, when they were proud young men, in their prime, seated at the high table.

It had not been easy to earn a place at the high table. To work his way up through the ranks, he had to be tough. The competition for standing and treasure was fierce. And like all youths, he had begun at the bottom. Back in those days, men had mistaken him for an undersized youth with a pretty, boyish face, who was especially attractive to the serving girls. He was seen as a throwaway who would die young on the battlefield because of his small size and been made the brunt of men's jokes without fear of reprisal.

Seated near the lowest end of the bench, impatiently awaiting the day when he was confident enough in his skillful use of weaponry to defend his honor against those men's humiliating remarks, he had fumed and schemed about the ways he would show them what he could do with a knife. To console himself, he swore that, after he had proven himself, no one would ever mess with him again. Men would never forget his name.

When the day finally came, he stood and formally challenged the brutish man who had repeatedly dishonored him in the past, and had just done so again. "Your remark has slandered me," he said. "I, Aiken the Strength of Oak, challenge you to a meeting of the knives. Either take back your insult or accept my challenge. If you do not accept, you will be called a coward by everyone here today."

When his slanderer chose to shrug off the challenge with mocking laughter, Aiken replied, "All right then, we will spread a cloak on the ground and fight, fair and square. We will see who deserves to be so duly dishonored."

It was the height of summertime, and though it was evening, the sun had not yet set when the two opponents took their grievances out to the yard. The other men followed behind. Like roaring beasts on the trail of fresh meat, they shoved and pushed and wagered on their way out the doors. Even the serving girls, dutifully bearing pitchers of ale, came out to cheer for their favorite. And as Aiken, his opponent, and their seconds laid a cloak on the ground and marked off the perimeter, the bets were collected.

But as soon as the meeting of knives began, it became apparent, both to the on-lookers and to Aiken's opponent, that the two rivals were unevenly matched. None of the men in Torwald's band were surprised. After all, they had been practicing with Aiken daily. But the man, who had foolishly chosen to insult Aiken, soon discovered that the runty, little up-start in Torwald's warband was uncommonly good with a knife. This time, it was Aiken's opponent who was the mark, the easy-take down, the laughing stock who was in more trouble than he had bargained for.

Aiken was quick and light on his feet and proved to have the elegant grace that fighting within the small square required. If a man stepped outside the bounds, he would be deemed a surrendering coward who was giving up the fight. A man's reputation hinged upon how well he fought in one-on-one combat. Everyone watched each man's form, his confidence under pressure, his precise control of the blade, and his ability to contain his rage and to use it to his advantage.

Meanwhile, Aiken was watching for an opening in his rival's defenses. By forcing his heedless opponent to slash out with increasingly aimless cuts, Aiken quickly spotted what he was looking for. Then, all it took was one, perfectly aimed touch of the blade to draw the loser's single drop of blood. To prevent hurting his opponent too badly, Aiken pulled the cut and brought the fight to a halt.

Aiken bought a small roasted pig in the market to serve as an offering to Lord Glory, the ruling power who oversaw one-on-one combat. Both the winners and the losers enjoyed feasting on the pig meat. And those, who had placed their wagers on Aiken, shook their purses to show off the jingling sounds their winning coins made. As consolation to the loser, those who had watched from the sidelines reasoned that Aiken's uncanny ability derived from the fact that no one could see his blade coming. The hidden folk had made it invisible, they said. That spell, when added to his greater supply of luck, had made Aiken unbeatable. No one would mess with him again. Men would never forget his name.

Those were the days when luck had favored Aiken. He had been born to a good family, was strong and good-looking, clever and skillful with weaponry. Whenever others came up against him, whether they were gaming or fighting, they feared his greater supply of luck would lead to their inevitable loss.

After that first meeting of the knives, the men, who had seen Aiken dance between the blades, spread the word. And over the years, he was called upon to champion men and women who were too weak to defend themselves; he challenged men who had foolishly questioned his honor; and, at times, he had been asked to defend the truth when certain facts were being disputed.

Before he was outlawed, every man had wanted Aiken on his side. Back when he was on the high road, and the three Matrones had been good to him, little had he known what a cruel thread they were spinning. He had one challenge left in him, and that one would be his last.

After he had been robbed of half his sight, he could no longer see an opponent's blade coming at him from the right. Everything appeared flattened out. He had no sense of distance and was unsure of his aim. Although he knew there were things on his right side, whether he saw them there or not, he bumped his shins into benches, banged his head on low-hanging rafters, and knocked his shoulders against doorframes he had misjudged when walking through them. In contrast to the graceful movement he had prided himself upon before, he clumsily tripped over stools not in their rightful places, knocked tools off his work bench, and tipped over his ale cup. When turning bowls on the lathe, he made more mistakes than he would have, if he had had two good eyes.

Hurting and frustrated, he cursed and slapped and hit things. He threw the ruined lathe-turned bowl down on the ground, stomped on it and kicked at it, hurled it against the wall, or hit it with a hammer and broke it into splinters. He made a lot of noise slamming the door, kicking at broken shards, or picking up the stool and putting it upright again. Or, if whatever he had knocked off the table had not broken, he picked it up, and sharply banged it onto the table where it belonged.

Mildred would say, "Slow down, Aiken. Do not move so fast. If you moved more cautiously you would not get hurt and break things."

That was what she did to show her concern. Telling him what to do, how to act, and cleaning up his messes was all she could do—she could not get his eye back. In that way, Mildred was a lot like Alger. Just as his best friend had done before he got killed, Mildred looked out for him and tried to keep him from getting hurt. Though appreciative of her sincerity, caution had never been in his game plan. No, he had always thrown caution to the wind. All his life he had lived dangerously. The way he saw it, Mildred may as well have tried to convince a bird not to spread its wings and fly.

At other times, his sight played tricks on him. Then, he saw things and people with his missing eye that were not supposed to be there at all—like Alger. But if he turned his head to look with his good eye at what he saw with his missing one, what he thought was there disappeared. So that night, he was careful not to look directly at Alger.

Aiken had kept his best friend alive in his memory, even though he had not kept him alive the day they were ambushed on the bank of the Warring River. If he stopped thinking about Alger, or if he stopped talking to him, Aiken knew his friend would be dead and gone entirely. So, Aiken just kept talking, and Alger just kept being there, sitting beside him on his blind side.

Back when he had been a fighting man, they had sworn their pact in blood to never leave each other's side—not for as long as one of them was still standing. But, in the end, it was Aiken who remained. And here he was, pleading with Alger, the man who had gone down, not to leave his side.

But talking to his blood brother it was no longer the same as it had been before. Aiken sensed the way Alger's eyes bored into him with a narrowed, steely gaze. His friend goaded him with the same questions that he had asked repeatedly over the years, "When will you challenge the man who murdered me? When, Aiken? When?"

Aiken had no answer. He never did. What could he do but beg for Alger's tolerant forbearance. "I am no longer the man I was before. If I could have, I would have done things differently. I would have made Torwald listen to me that morning when we were camped alongside the river. I wish I could do it over again. If the men had heeded my warnings, you would still be alive tonight. I let you down. I accept your blame."

Feeling chilled, Aiken pulled his cloak more tightly around himself. He planned to stay the watch all night if he had to. To stay the watch was nothing new for him. Even when he was a child, even before his father, Eamon, was killed, Aiken had been ever-watchful. In those days, when his father was out patrolling the roads, visiting other chiefdoms, or taking part in a raid, Aiken had waited and watched for his father's return. He either sat on the bench in front of his mother and father's house or stood with the guardsmen at the gate. They taught him to watch for things that men and women who were coming through the gates might try to hide. Or if, at any given moment, they were suddenly under attack, he should be ready to engage in a fight. Aiken would stand beside them, grasp the hilt on his wooden long knife, sharpen his gaze, and stay the watch.

But whenever he saw his father coming, he got so excited, he jumped up and down, and ran in circles. The guardsmen teased him, good-naturedly, saying that he was not keeping the watch very well just then. And though they laughed at his antics, Aiken could not help himself. He was just too happy. Eamon rode through the gate, brought his horse to a sudden halt, leapt down, picked up Aiken, called him his little Acorn, and tightly squeezed his son in a big bear hug. Eamon swung him around until they were both dizzy and laughing. Then he lifted Aiken onto the horse's saddle and proudly led his son through the village until they reached the stables.

The day that his father did not return, Aiken was too young to fully grasp the meaning of Eamon's disappearance. Instead, he was concerned for his father's welfare. He told his mother that he planned to get on his mare and to search for his missing father.

Aiken still remembered the piteous look she gave him. When she saw her son's forthright attempt to be a grown man, she crouched down in front of him and explained that his father had gone to feast in the Victory Hall. Aiken asked whether his father would come home after he had left the hall. But his mother said, "No, Eamon will never come home again. He is never coming back. He joined Lord Glory's star-warrior Army of Ten Thousand Strong."

She held him on her lap and, rocking back and forth, they both cried for a long time.

Maida remarried, moved to her new husband's village, and left Aiken in the care of his uncle Otgar. A severe man, he told his nephew to never show signs of fear or weakness. After Aiken's father had gone missing, and his mother had left him, Aiken was no longer the trusting child he had been before. Along with understanding how things had changed, came the knowledge that it was time to shift his allegiance to someone who had not yet disappeared. He stopped crying for his mother and vowed to never let Uncle Otgar see any signs in him of fear or weakness.

Aiken watched for the things that men and women tried to hide, just as the guardsmen had taught him. Sometimes he pretended to be invisible. He kept the watch from places where he could spy on the grownups and the children with whom he played. He sharpened his gaze and listened for ways they might plot to threaten his safety. He was afraid of disappearing or of going missing like his mother and father had done.

The day he began training to be a fighting man, his childhood ended entirely. Under Otgar's tutelage, he was cut and scarred, slapped with the flat sides of blades, bruised and knocked hard with pommels, struck with spear staves, and butted by large men wearing helmets.

He was sent into the woods to stand alone with a spear pointed at an onrushing, wild boar. Though it takes only one, perfectly aimed thrust to the chest, to stop a boar when a fully-grown man lunges at it with a heavy boar spear and puts all his weight behind it, the animal had not gone down so easily for an undersized boy. The beast weighed more than twice as much as he did. If he had failed the test that day, he would never have grown to manhood. Instead, he would have been dead that day.

Aiken went at it again and again, hard, with the spear. Then he slashed at it with his combat knife. When he was finished, his hands had shaken so badly he could barely hold the knife steady. Gutting it, the bloody hilt kept slipping from his fingers, and he dropped it several times. The men who had been watching from behind the trees came out of hiding and laughed at his clumsiness.

That day, Aiken was more afraid of failing his uncle than of being hurt by the boar. So he was proud when Otgar affectionately slapped him on the side of the head, and said, "He is just a boy, after all. He is Eamon's son. He will grow up to be a good fighter. You just wait and see."

Though he had made a mess of that boar hide, they still hung it over the mead-hall door to mark his passage to manhood. Two nights later, they feasted on the boar he had killed and celebrated his entry into the warband.

Not long after that, he fought his first battle. After the fighting was over, those men, who had laughed at him before, were not laughing any more. That included Otgar, who was lying dead on the battlefield. Aiken had shown them what he could do. He had gained their respect. By sheer grit, he had toughed it out and hardened himself. Otgar had died knowing that his nephew had shown neither signs of fear nor weakness. And with his uncle's passing, the man who had been, up until then, standing-in for Aiken's missing father, also, disappeared. That made three.

Just as the guardsmen had taught him, Aiken knew, first hand, how unseen dangers, lurking in the shadows, threatened to turn his life upside down, at any given moment. As he matured, he became the very man the child had set out to be. He remained on guard and kept the watch night and day. Even when he was standing in full view, he hid his gaze. His scrutiny of others went along with his ability to spot an opening in a man's defenses.

Over time, he passed every test and became one of Torwald's toughest warriors. He was elevated in rank until he took his place among the honor guard and was seated at the high table. To protect Torwald's life became Aiken's duty. Ever-watchful, he saw and heard whatever men and women might say or do that hinted at unspoken truths, deceits, or betrayals. He drew conclusions from the simplest nod, shrug, off-hand comment, or seemingly innocent gesture.

But even when it was too late to change, Aiken wished he could have been more carefree and less suspicious. If he had been more trusting, like the men who accepted whatever they were told without questioning the leadership, he would never have been aware of the other chieftain's treacherous scheming. He would never have seen the baleful wolf's yellow eyes peering from the darkest corner, where it lurked, await-ing the time to pounce. To carry that kind of knowledge was a dreadful responsibility. It made him different from the others. His terrible forebodings set him apart.

If he had been more like the rest of them, if he had kept his eyes closed to what was going on, then he, too, would have been dead along with the others. But instead, because he had seen one too many things that he was not supposed to see, he believed that he had been aptly punished by the loss of sight in one eye.

Aiken first sensed the warning signs of treachery at the autumn Assembly, the meeting held twice yearly when all freemen in their kinship got together. Several of the younger chieftains wanted to put an end to the annual tribute payments that the rulers of the western lands demanded from them. But the older men had argued that both peaceful trade across their borders and the neighboring tribal leaders' promises not to invade their land was dependent upon the annual tribute. After they called the younger men's plan ill-advised, because it could lead to an all-out war, which they would surely lose, the older men soundly defeated the proposal.

But even as Torwald and the men, who were seated at the high table, gamed and congratulated themselves upon their victory, the aggrieved, younger chieftains, whose proposal had been defeated, began to collect in the shadows and to speak in hushed voices late at night. And even as their conspiratorial plotting began to play out, the men in Torwald's warband remained blithely unaware of the danger. No one had guessed that the angry chieftains would retaliate by murdering one of their most prestigious clan leaders. The idea was so outrageous that no one but Aiken had questioned whether something underhanded might have been going on.

No one wanted to suspect an ally, a fellow kinsman, someone whom they trusted and relied upon for protection. No one wanted to believe that a close relative would betray them. Everyone refused to even consider the possibility. As a result, though the signs were clearly visible, they chose, instead, to ignore them. When the Assembly was over, Torwald and his men rode home and forgot about the dispute over the younger men's proposal.

And even as the devious scheme was set in motion, not even Aiken had suspected that a common cattle raid would lead, within days, to Torwald's downfall. But, begin it did. And shortly after they returned home, the headman from a hamlet, which was located within Torwald's holdings, asked them to find a missing cattle herd.

If the herd had wandered off, Torwald claimed they would find the missing cattle. Or, if they had been stolen in a raid, he and the men in the warband would chase down the thieves and return the cattle to their rightful owners. But to the men in the warband it was a nuisance to chase down the culprits at that time of year. The raiding season was over. The weather was inclement. They were eager to be done with it and to get home again. They wanted to pick up the games where they had left off, to drink more ale, to spend more time lazing about in the hall, and laying abed with their wives and unwed consorts.

Instead, they were searching aimlessly for missing cattle and sleeping in tents on hard, frozen soil. They asked repeatedly how an entire herd could have gone missing without leaving a trace? As the days went by, the aggrieved farmers, whose animals had disappeared, said that it was bad for the cows to go so long without a milking. The headman became increasingly outspoken and belligerent in his accusations, calling Torwald and his men lazy, incompetent, good-for-nothings.

The Warring River flowed between Torwald's and Oswald's holdings. Naturally, whenever a warband was on the move and approaching their borders, even if they were fellow kinsmen, the suspicious chieftain, whose holdings were on the opposite side, would increase the number of his patrols.

Though it was unlikely for an entire herd to have crossed the river without leaving a few stragglers behind, Torwald's men asked permission to search for the missing cattle inside Oswald's jurisdiction. At that point, no accusations had been made, but the other chieftain's men were unfriendly and blocked their path. They told Torwald that they had sent for their chieftain and expected him to arrive soon. Torwald and his men would be allowed to cross only after Oswald had granted permission.

But Oswald was taking his time in coming, and Torwald was unwilling to wait any longer for his arrival. When he and his men tried to force their way across, they were held off at spear point. Aiken interpreted their unfriendliness as a sign of dangerous hostility, but no one else took it that way. The other men in Torwald's warband just brushed it off, saying Oswald's men had misunderstood their orders.

Misunderstanding or not, Torwald was irate. He refused to be put-off by the low-ranking men in Oswald's warband. But to have fought their way past Oswald's guards would have been perceived as an unlawful attack because of the law against fighting fellow clansmen.

Torwald's hands were tied. His only remaining option was to tell a couple of men, who were good at tracking across enemy lines, to ford the river and search. The ground was frozen, and a recent snowfall had obscured any prints that the herd might have cut into the soil. Yet, upon their return, the two men swore they had successfully tracked the cattle. They had seen them grazing in a field and, had also seen, watching over the cattle, some of Oswald's men seated on horseback, along with a few of the farmers who lived in the near-by hamlet within Oswald's jurisdiction.

Up until then, no suspicions had fallen on Oswald. If a kinsman attacked another, or stole land or property from a fellow clansman, he would be accused of an intolerable act of war. Since the scouts' report would lead to a criminal accusation against Oswald and his men, the charges would have been brought to the Assembly in the springtime. If the scouts swore an oath to tell the truth, they would have placed the blame upon either Oswald or the farmers who lived across the river from the missing cattle's home pasture.

The chieftains who sat at the high table, one of whom was Torwald himself, would hear the sworn testimony. The evidence would be weighed, and judgement would be brought to a vote by those in attendance. There would be a condemnation, and reprisals levied against the lawbreakers. The punishments often amounted to stiff fines and a loss of standing among the kin. The law was clear. But, no one wanted to wait until springtime, least of all the farmers whose livelihood depended upon getting the cattle back.

Torwald's men had sat around for days with nothing to do but go on aimless searches. They did not want to wait any longer for Oswald to arrive and to defend himself against their allegations. There were differing opinions about what they should do next. The younger, more bellicose men became impatient. They talked among themselves and wanted to resolve the problem their own way. As a result, the older men became increasingly wary of the grousing among the young bucks.

Keeping control of a band of erstwhile fighters was dangerously unpredictable. When men depended upon nothing more than sworn oaths and loyalty to one another to bind them together, discipline within the line of command was loose. Sigmund, one of Torwald's counselors, wanted to give the younger men something to do. He picked those who, like Aiken, were loudest in questioning the leadership's decision-making. Along with ordering the men to find the missing herd, Sigmund egged them on with hints that Torwald would reward them well if they found the cattle and herded them back to the home pasture.

And if they were unable to find the cattle? Sigmund encouraged them to take measures against those who had stolen the herd.

That night, Sigmund led the small band of men whom he had picked. Following the scouts they lit their way with torches. After they had forded the river, they rode around, but never found the herd. The snow was falling in big, fluffy flakes and covering any tracks the cattle may have made. After the scouts had led the men in circles, Aiken and the others became increasingly hot tempered over their poor intelligence.

The accusations put the scouts on the defensive. Equally flummoxed, they boldly leveled a charge against someone within their own ranks. They said that a traitor had known the cattle had been spotted and had passed the information on to Oswald's men. The scouts claimed that since Oswald's men knew that Torwald's men had located the herd, they had moved the cattle and hidden them elsewhere.

Once the devious suggestion was made that one of their own fellow companions might be gaming both sides, they all began to eye each other, distrustfully. Wondering who amongst them was taking payment from Oswald for information about the goings-on inside their camp, each man tried to out-do the others to prove his loyalty to the group.

After that, things got increasingly out of hand. Aiken and his fellow war companions headed for the nearby hamlet within Oswald's holdings. Upon arrival, they lit the additional torches they had brought along. And after whooping and hollering and racing around the ox-road with the flames streaming out behind their backs, they threw their torches onto the householders' roofs.

After Aiken had thrown his torch onto one of the thatched houses, he stopped to watch the fire take hold. The flames crackled and roared as the air was sucked into the blazing conflagration. Mayhem erupted as men and women ran screaming from their homes.

Aiken did not see the man approach, but only became aware of him when he grabbed the horse bridle. The man gave Aiken the evil eye and shouted, "I know who you are, Aiken the Strength of Oak. To call you by your name gives me the power to demand the Sons of the Fiery Realm avenge this injustice."

Enraged that a common farmer would speak to him like that, Aiken drew his knife and stabbed the man.

And as he slumped to the ground, he leveled his curse:

"I, a dying man,
Will haunt your dreams
And follow your bloodline.

For a hundred lifetimes
I will curse your children
To fiery punishment."

The man's knees buckled and, before he collapsed, he called upon Mother Necessity to take her bitter revenge:

"What must come,
Shall come to be."

The man fell in a heap with his legs bent at strange angles. Aiken stared at the lifeless body lying on the snow-covered earth, his disgust tinged with the terror of having been cursed.

Early the following morning, the missing cattle were found grazing in the home pasture. Whereas the other men removed themselves from blame, Aiken felt queasy. He was sickened by the thought that they had killed innocent farmers and their families.

But Sigmund and the others accused the farmers of having stolen the cattle. The thieving farmers had deserved the punishment, they said. "You see, the cattle came home after we killed the men who had hidden them. The cows knew where they belonged."

Aiken did not see it that way. "We killed unarmed farmers," he screamed. "They were innocent of any wrong-doing. We should have protected them from Oswald's men, not killed them. Oswald's men were the ones who took the cattle."

"No, Aiken, you got it wrong. Now, get it straight. We got back at Oswald for stealing the cattle by torching his hamlet."

"No, you are the ones who have it wrong," Aiken said. "We got back at the wrong men."

Somehow, it had not occurred to them that, whereas Oswald now appeared to be the blameless victim, Torwald and his men would be accused of crimes against the kin.

Up until then, the two chieftain's intermediaries had met without either side having leveled any accusations against the other warband. Nor had they made any progress. All Torwald's men had done was to request permission to search Oswald's holdings. Though their appeals had been repeatedly rebuffed, day after day, Torwald's men had taken the high road. But now that the cattle had been returned and Torwald's men had torched the hamlet, their position in the negotiations had worsened. Oswald's charges against them could turn lethal.

Yet, Torwald had seen no reason to mistrust the other chieftain or his men. After all, he and Oswald were kinsmen, and kinsmen kept the peace during negotiations. When he sent two counselors to Oswald's camp with an offer to work out a settlement agreeable to both sides, Torwald believed that the other chieftain would be true to his word and honor the truce.

If Aiken's chieftain and the other men in the warband had suspected Oswald of the underhanded cruelty that he later proved he was capable of committing, they would never have let their guard down. They would never have gone hunting on the banks of the Warring River. But Torwald's lack of distrust had put them all in jeopardy. The following morning, they had ridden foolishly into the trap that had been set for them within a stone's toss or, as Aiken knew all too well, a well-aimed javelin-throw across from Oswald's holdings.

III.

Seated on the bench in front of Mildred's house, with only ghostly Alger sitting there beside him, out of all those men who had been on his side of the conflict, Aiken was the only one still alive. If he had gone hunting that day, he would have died alongside his fellow war companions. He would not have been forced to bear the shame of outliving his chieftain and the other men. But as things now stood, he alone had promised to see justice was meted out and the murderers were punished.

Looking at the black, starless sky, Aiken begged whatever ruling powers were out there to expose the truth and to prove him right. He was certain that Oswald was the one who had set them up and done the dirty work, but he believed that Leofar was the one who had planned the ambush. After all these years, he still wanted to bring charges for his companions' murders before the full Assembly. Aiken knew men who could lay the blame for both the planning and the execution of the murders upon Leofar and Oswald. But no one would agree to accuse the two men. The chieftains had walled off the truth behind a conspiracy of silence.

Of two minds, whenever he thought about shouldering the blame, Aiken continued to fault himself for outliving the others, but also believed that he and the other men had been misled. If Sigmund and Torwald had sent spies to watch Oswald's camp, they would have known who was double-crossing them. But, instead, the lack of decent leadership and the poor decision-making, along with the two men's misplaced trust in Oswald, had betrayed Aiken and the others. Each blunder had added to the mistakes they had previously made and, in the end, all the men had been killed—all but him.

"Alger say my worry that morning was justified. Stealing the herd was in the murderer's game plan. It was their first move. They baited us, and we fell into their trap. Tell me that I was right. Just tell me."

But instead of a response to his demand that Alger acknowledge the accuracy of his scrutiny, the faint echo of taunting accusations, which he had heard repeatedly over the years, continued to linger somewhere in that space between the worlds of both the living and the dead. "If you were so smart and saw it coming, why did you not speak out?"

Aiken shook his head, remorsefully. How many times had he heard this harsh rebuke? How many times had he answered, "I did speak up. But no one listened. Do you not remember, Alger? I told you. But, no—you, too, refused to heed my warnings."

Alger was no better than the rest of them. Instead of backing Aiken, that morning, after he had accused Leofar and Oswald of plotting to harm them, Alger had, nonetheless, taken Torwald's side. He had only come to Aiken's defense when the others began to accuse him of treasonously gaming both sides.

And, Torwald, instead of listening to Aiken, had treated him like a misbehaving child. Because of the doubts he had raised about Oswald's innocence, Torwald accused Aiken of being overly suspicious, and reproached him for unfairly blaming his fellow war companions for the unnecessary killings.

To be a warrior meant that a man lived daily with an ever-present threat of his own inevitable death. All the men in the warband had accepted the risk. They had, also, accepted as common knowledge that, along with the damage and the destruction of the commoners' homes, byres, cropland, and livestock, there would be deaths and injuries among the unarmed population. Deaths were unavoidable whenever men were at war. And men were always at war.

Nevertheless, no one liked to be accused of killing unarmed men, women and children. Except for the most brutal men amongst them, each of the men felt bad about it in his own way. Killing unarmed commoners was just something that fighting men never talked about, except for the times when they used cruel mockery to cover their regrets.

The distrust between them continued to escalate until all the men were shouting at one another.

One man asked, "Who suggested we burn down the hamlet?"

Another man asked, "Who lit the first torch?"

Another asked, "Who started the race around the ox-road?"

But no one was willing to own up. Everyone denied responsibility for torching the hamlet. Now that Aiken's accusations had broken their unspoken rule of silence, he had brought their shame into the daylight, and they hated him for it.

It was Sigmund who took their denunciations to the next level: "Aiken, since you are the one who sympathizes with the cattle thieves in Oswald's hamlet, I think you are the one who was gaming both sides."

"No, I am not a traitor."

But they began to crowd around him. Turning against him, they pointed their fingers, raised their fists, accused him of betrayal, heaped him with scorn, called him a backstabbing double-crosser, and a snake in the grass, until Alger stepped into the center of the conflict.

He drew the line right there and dared no one to step across it. "Aiken is loyal," Alger said. "He would never do such a thing. Now shut your mouth, or you will answer to me."

Alger's willingness to raise their divisiveness to the level of fighting calmed the air immediately, and the crowd around Aiken began to disperse. Each man knew that whenever their hostility rose to that level, it dangerously weakened their ability to fight off an attack from another warband. They were already on shaky ground. To leave it alone and to forget about the dispute was in each man's self-interest, and so they walked away.

Erwin came up to Aiken, stretched out his hand, and said, "I regret my assault upon your honor. You are a stand-up man, Aiken. You did not deserve to be treated that way."

Aiken agreed, begrudgingly, to accept his apology. He took Erwin's hand and they shook.

Erwin slapped Aiken on the arm and asked, "Are we friends again?"

"Yes, we are friends."

That was when the headman strode into the camp. He told Torwald's men that a wild boar had been spotted and some of the farmers had it trapped. The farmers would act as the beaters if the men wanted to hunt. Since everyone wanted to forget about the conflict, they began to saddle up.

But as Aiken was preparing to ride out, Torwald stomped up to him and said, "Not you. You stay here to guard the camp. And while I am gone," he scolded, "I advise you to think about your actions and your speech. You think too much about the wrong things. By the time I get back, you had better have straightened out your thinking. Do you understand what I am saying?"

"Yes, I understand."

Aiken understood quite clearly. By singling him out to be the fall guy, Torwald was deflecting the blame from himself. Though he held Aiken responsible for the bickering within the group, the true cause of bad blood between them was Torwald and Sigmund's lack of decent leadership. The reason that everyone felt on edge were the mistakes they had made repeatedly, and that had worsened their position in the negotiations with Oswald. Aiken could figure it out, but no one else could.

When Alger heard that Aiken had been ordered to stay behind, he told Torwald that he, too, would stay back to watch the encampment.

The other men gave the headman a horse to ride so that he could lead them to the boar. Torwald and the others mounted their horses and, laughing mockingly at Aiken and Alger, rode off.

Alger's most admirable traits were loyalty, unswerving trust in his leaders, and obedience to their orders. Whether or not he agreed with their actions, thought they were right or wrong, or their motives were honorable or dishonorable, was no concern of his. No, Alger did whatever his superiors told him to do. It was Torwald's and Sigmund's job to do the thinking. After they had thought things through and come up with a plan, Alger obeyed their orders.

Likewise, Alger figured that sticking by his blood-brother was the same. Alger might have thought that Aiken's suspicions were unfounded, but conformity to the other men's charges against his blood brother ended right there and went no further. Whether he agreed with Aiken's accusations did not matter. What mattered was the oath they had sworn. Alger never questioned whether they should stick together. No matter the consequences, they remained inseparable. Ever since they had been small boys playing together, their devotion to one another had been unshakable. It had always been that way and always would be.

The two men spread a hide on the dried, flattened grasses near the river where they could sit. Off to the side, they lit a small fire for warmth. The frigid water flowed past, sluggishly. There was a thin skin of ice near the shoreline. The sky was overcast. Occasional snowflakes floated down, landed on their shoulders and hair, and stuck in their beards.

At the edge of the camp, their three attendants sat around another fire beneath the lean-to where the men's war-gear, horse tackle, food, and other supplies were stored. Their horses were tethered in the scrub behind the lean-to.

Aiken sat with his legs folded. Idly throwing a short knife, he raised the tip to his shoulder and threw. The knife spun half-way around and came down point-first to stick upright in the frozen soil. Aiken reached out, grabbed the knife by the handle, pulled it from the dirt, and tossed again.

Once he had seen two men in a heated dispute. Seated across from each other at a table, one man was a wealthy warrior who had a large estate, and the other was his steward. Both men's forearms rested straight out in front of them on the tabletop. The warrior leaned heavily into his arms and stuck his face into the other man's. He accused his steward of cheating him of the full amount that he was due after the autumn tribute had been collected from the farmers within his jurisdiction. The steward pulled back and denied the accusation.

He was about to stand up and to walk away in a huff when, without a warning, the warrior stood rapidly, whipped out a short knife and smoothly flipped the blade. The lethal knife was in and out of his hand so fast and so precisely that, before anyone saw it coming, it struck the steward's forearm, right above the wrist, between the two bones. Stuck fast to the table, the man who had been hit just stared at the blade for a moment before he screamed. Now, that was good knife-work.

It was so unexpected. No one had seen it fly through the air. No one had known where it came from. But there it was, a slim blade with two cutting edges and a sharply tapered point. The warrior had made his position in the argument clear: the steward was beholden to him and would go nowhere without his permission.

Aiken guessed the man had hidden the knife inside his left sleeve. As he rose from his seat, the knife dropped, and his right hand grabbed the hilt. He raised his arm and let go of the blade before anyone saw it coming.

It was just weighty enough to carry momentum and to drive the thrust, deeply, into its target. The knife was shorter than a man's forearm and had a narrow crossguard. The shape made it easy to conceal. No doubt, that was the purpose of the design.

No hidden folk had spelled it with invisibility. No indeed, it had taken months of practice to throw a blade with that kind of cunning accuracy and speed.

And like the man who had concealed his knife, Aiken was doing his best to conceal his seething rage beneath a well-contrived, calm exterior. Lest his anger flare up at any given moment, he spoke in a flat and subdued, mumbling drone between each of his well-controlled knife throws.

"How can they believe that I would double cross them?" Aiken said, threw the blade, and pulled it from the soil.

"What have I done to give them that idea?" he said, threw the blade, and pulled it from the soil.

"I pointed out the way that Leofar has endangered the peace with his scheming, and now has gotten Oswald to do his bidding," Aiken said, threw the blade, and pulled it from the soil.

"Aiken, it is offensive to think that way. Leofar is Torwald's nephew," Alger argued.

"It is not offensive to draw attention to someone else's offensive actions," Aiken said and threw the blade.

"You are already in trouble. You cannot accuse his nephew. Torwald will not stand for it. What has gotten into you?"

Aiken pulled the blade from the soil, slipped it into its sheath, shrugged and slumped down over his folded legs. "Why does no one else see that Oswald's men were ordered to steal the cattle herd and then to move them back to the home pasture? The farmers were innocent. They had to follow Oswald's orders, or they would have been punished for refusing to obey their liege lord's commands."

"Torwald does not see it that way."

"Why not? We were set up. Why does no one else see it? They can think it through, just the same as I do."

"Aiken, you need to trust Torwald to make the peace with Oswald. He knows what he is doing."

"No, he does not. He knows nothing. Nor does Sigmund. He was the one who urged us to torch the hamlet. And now he is blaming me."

"No one likes to be accused of killing the commoners."

"Well it was dead wrong. That was how I was raised. But, that is not the point that I want to make. Oswald's men are to blame. Oswald and Leofar cannot be trusted. I saw the two men conspiring at the Assembly. They are angry at the older chieftains who rebuffed their proposal. I am trying to protect Torwald and the rest of us. I was taught to watch out for danger. That is why you and me are in the honor guard. It is our duty to speak out. If I cannot prove my innocence, you know what that means."

"Aiken, you worry too much. Just wait and see. It will blow over."

"Sigmund should man up and take the blame upon himself."

"It was all a mistake. Oswald had no reason to steal the cattle."

"But if he did raid the cattle, we need to ask what he hoped to accomplish? Why did he set us up? We need to figure out his game plan. What is his next move?"

"Aiken, you must stop thinking that way. You are being overly suspicious."

"You do not like it, either, when I raise suspicions and ask questions."

"I know what will stop your brooding." Alger said. He stood and began to walk off.

"I am not brooding," Aiken yelled at his backside. "I am thinking."

Alger turned his head to look over his shoulder, and replied, "Well you think too much. What you call thinking, I call brooding."

Returning with his satchel strap casually draped over one shoulder, Alger sat across from Aiken. He dug around inside his bag and pulled out the pouch in which he kept a small wooden cup and four sheep hocks. "Let us not argue anymore."

"All right."

Alger dropped the gaming pieces into the cup and, grinning broadly, attempted to lure Aiken into a match by rattling the cup close to his ear. "Do you want to throw the knuckle-bones to test your luck?"

Thinking quietly over his situation, Aiken said, distractedly, "I am undecided." Fearful of the dead man's shade who had cursed him two nights before, he reached beneath his clothing to pull out a small, silver talisman cast in the shape of a woman's profile. It hung from a long, braided sinew cord that he wore looped around his neck. This little silver woman was a stand-in for his luck-woman, his feminine guardian and otherworldly protective power who was tied so closely to his warrior lineage, she was said to be an aspect of his soul. And now, he questioned whether his luck-woman could be trusted to protect him. Would she remain loyal? Was she powerful enough to withstand an assault by the Sons of the Fiery Realm. Or would she back down? Would she surrender?

Aiken admired the silver woman's beauty. To indicate the abundance, she brought with her wherever she walked, she wore a cloak and a long trailing skirt, both of which were lavished with border trims richly woven in geometric patterns. Her single, long plait was pinned in a knot at the nape of her neck. The rest of its length hung down her back as a sign of her bounteous goodness.

Most importantly, the silver woman held a drinking horn filled to overflowing with the sweet tasting mead of luck. Whenever Aiken's luck-woman offered him the drinking horn, she held it to his lips so that he might drink his fill. Supping the mead of luck, he took in the power he needed to shape events according to his wishes—whether it was to win a game of lots; to be the victor in a challenge; or to come through pitched battle alive.

If he compared his luck-woman to the women, whom he knew, neither the mother who had abandoned him, nor the aunt who ignored him, nor the meadhall serving girls who teased, flattered, and flirted, but who had little else to offer but fleeting pleasures, had shown the kind of loyalty and strength he now required.

And if his luck-woman were to leave him, as so many of the women in his life had done, Aiken's luck-given protection would be gone. Left susceptible to the dangers that the shade of the dead man posed, the cursed man would blame Aiken for the suffering that he and the other men in the warband had brought upon the innocent men, women, and children who were living in the hamlet when it was torched. From his place in the otherworlds, the man's shade would invoke the Sons of the Fiery Realm's wrath. He would claim that Aiken deserved to suffer the same fiery punishment that he and his kin had suffered. And furthermore, he would demand that his vengeful curse be bound to Aiken's family for the span of one hundred lifetimes.

And, if those ruling powers heard the dead man's plea and agreed to avenge the dishonor that Aiken had shown by his malicious use of fire, all those luckless men and women in Aiken's bloodline, the children of his children, and the children of their children, all of whom were as yet unborn and were as innocent of any wrong-doing as the children who were living in the torched hamlet had been, they, too, would be at risk of fiery revenge. This was the fate that Aiken feared most of all.

"Aiken are you listening to me?" Alger asked. "Now, stop your brooding. Do you want to throw the bones or not?"

A better question would have asked whether he preferred to learn the truth than to continue with his useless speculation upon the unknown outcome of the curse.

Aiken's answer was an unenthusiastic shrug of one shoulder.

Interpreting his friend's gesture in the affirmative, Alger dumped out the bones. He picked one up, tossed it into the round-bottomed cup, covered it with one hand, shook, and turned the cup over onto the hide. When he picked up the cup, the two men saw that the rectangular, roughly shaped bone had landed with the side called dog upright. It was worth one point. He handed the cup to Aiken who did the same. The only difference between their throws was that this time the bone landed belly side up to indicate its worth was four points.

Aiken was glad to see that his luck-woman was beside him on the first throw.

"So, what shall we wager?" Alger asked, and held out a handful of coppers.

Aiken dug into the pouch that hung from his belt but brought out a smaller number. He held the coins in his palm. Feigning a self-assurance he did not feel, he said brashly with a cocky jerk of his head, "This is all I have. But if I am lucky I will have all these and yours by the end of the game." He then dumped his paltry pile in front of his folded legs.

They agreed to wager one copper each throw. The men put their coins in the ante pile. The first to shake, Aiken picked up the four bones, tossed them into the cup, shook, and turned it over onto the hide. He saw two dogs, a back, and a belly. The bones added up to a total of nine points.

Next it was Alger's turn. He tossed the bones into the cup, shook, and turned it over. He counted three narrow sides, and one back. The bones added up to twenty-one points.

Alger brushed away the few snowflakes had fallen onto the ante pile with his fingertips, scooped up the coppers, and said, "Better luck next time."

Aiken kissed his lucky token on the cheek. To replenish his sense of well-being, he imagined his luck-woman was kneeling on the hide beside him where she could hold the drinking horn to his lips. He drank his fill and, once again, is place in the world was restored.

He tucked the silver woman inside his tunic. In a place where she was closest to his heart, the cool, silver talisman touched his skin. Like long, delicate fingers, it caressed his chest, and his worry left him. Things would work out for the better. Oswald and Torwald would reach an agreement. He and the other men would go back home. Torwald's wife would oversee the roasting of the boar they brought back from the hunt. They would feast on the meat, dripping with grease. They would lick their fingers and feel content. His favorite serving girl would smile and flirt and offer to come to his bed that night. The ordeal would be over at last.

Anticipating the celebration, Aiken pulled out the token. He kissed his silver woman, doubled the ante and heard his luck-woman clap her hands and mew with pleasure.

Over the course of the game one man lost a throw, then the other. But rather than the confidence, which his luck-woman usually inspired, he imagined her sulky voice was asking whether he trusted her protection. Why else would he question her ability to keep him safe? Why would he test her loyalty by throwing the bones? If he no longer trusted her protection, his luck-woman asked, why should she stick by him? Trust went both ways. Why should she promise to take on the Sons of the Fiery Realm if he had lost his faith in her ability to come out the victor?

After he lost over half his tosses, he knew for certain that his fears were justified. He sensed his luck-woman's simmering resentment and suspected she was not doting on him the way she had done before.

Aiken rubbed the token between his fingers. He lifted the small silver figure to his lips and kissed her. Fondling the token with one hand, he shook the round-bottomed cup with the other. And as the bones rattled against the sides of the cup, he imagined he was cupping a woman's breast while droning a litany beneath his breath: "I need your luck. Fill your cup. I need your luck. Fill your cup."

But his pleading did no good. Filled with apprehension, he suspected that the bonds that tied him to his luck-woman were loosening.

After he had lost toss after toss, Aiken knew it for certain. He wanted to lash out and to say: what is wrong with you? How can you doubt my affections? I am good to you. I keep you near my heart. Do not go. Do not leave me.

The end of the game was looming. He had one coin left. One chance remained to win the ante pile and to turn the game in his favor. But the outcome depended upon more than a few coins. Aiken and the warband were in a precarious position. His future bloodline was at stake. He wanted assurance that his luck-woman would protect him and all his descendants for a hundred lifetimes.

He held his hands close to the fire and rubbed them together. He lifted them to his mouth and blew to warm them. He picked up the last copper and, snapping it between his thumb and forefinger, flipped it carelessly onto the hide.

He shook the cup, fitfully tossed the bones, and when he saw that he had thrown four narrow sides, his confidence was restored. He pounded his fist into the opposite hand's open palm. He squeezed his fingertips together, kissed them, and blew into the air to send an affectionate gesture to his luck-woman. "We did it. You and me are still in the game."

"Sorry to disappoint you," Alger said, "but I still have one toss left."

This time, Alger cast one of each—a vulture, a back, a belly and a narrow—the highest possible score. He scooped up his coppers, punched Aiken in the arm and said, "Want to play another game?"

"I have nothing left to wager."

"In lieu of coins, I will accept your promise to repay me later."

"No. I do not trust my luck today. I will lose for certain," Aiken said. "My luck is bad." Aiken pulled the sinew cord over his head, looked at it with scowling displeasure, said, "What good is this useless piece of silver, anyway? It is just a worthless piece of junk," and angrily tossed the token aside.

The silver woman landed in the soft, new-fallen snow and lay there buried. Like any real woman who might have stumbled if he had angrily shoved her aside, his luck-woman cried out in alarm and indignation. Grievously suffering from that last, intolerable insult to her pride and dignity, she pushed herself up and stood. Her fingertips flailed at her skirts and irritably brushed away the snow.

The empty drinking horn lay on its side, half-buried in the snow. She bent down to pick it up, turned her back to Aiken, and walked off. Carrying the snow-encrusted horn in one hand, she carelessly swung it back and forth dripping the last remaining drops of luck's bounteous goodness in the snow. At the edge of the river, Aiken's luck-woman twisted her neck to look back at him from over her shoulder. And, after she had given him one last, ill-tempered glance, she tossed her head and walked directly into the water.

Left alone, a luckless man seated on the riverbank, a place from which he could not follow her, Aiken wanted to call out: No. Wait. Come back. I did not mean to hurt you. Do not go. Do not leave me.

Scrambling onto his hands and knees, he frantically crawled to the place where he had thrown her. Desperate to find her, his open-handed fists shoveled away the thin layer of snow. His fingers raked through the dried, matted gasses. But she was gone. He could not find her. His protection was lost. His guard was down. A crow passed overhead. Its ominous shadow swiped across him like a sign of doom. And Aiken was no longer the Strength of Oak. He was Aiken, weak and helpless as a babe.

His run of luck was over. Now that the Matrones had taken back their gifts, all it would take to push him over the steel-edged, narrow path he walked, daily, between life and sudden death was one aggressive shove. Then he would fall, just like his luck-woman had fallen. And his bloodline would surely suffer from fire's wrath for a hundred lifetimes.

"Torwald is cornered at the river." The local headman's boy came riding towards them on Sigmund's galloping horse, looking scared and screaming, "Torwald is cornered at the river."

There was nothing to do but jump to his feet and run to the lean-to. Aiken yelled at the attendants to saddle the horses. He and Alger threw their leather jerkins over their heads, slipped the baldrics holding their long-knives over one shoulder, tightened the heavy belts, hung with shorter combat knives and side arms, and fastened the buckles. They stuck the war-hammer and throwing-axe handles through the belt rings. They put on their leather and bronze helmets to protect their heads and ears. They grabbed their shields and spears.

Now, Oswald had done it. This was the day their bickering turned into openly ruthless warfare. Oswald's promise to keep the peace between them was broken. Everything was set in motion and now it was too late to stop.

Aiken repeatedly asked himself why he had not made Torwald listen. Even after he had been punished for speaking out, even after Torwald had refused to listen, he blamed himself. Even as Aiken grabbed the reins from the attendants and hopped aboard his mount, he asked why he had not been more convincing? What if he, too, had gone hunting? Might he have persuaded them not to hunt so close to the river? Maybe he could have turned them away. But now it was too late.

The two men kicked their heels into the horses' flanks and bounded off. The camp was not far from the place where the other men were hunting. They rode recklessly, hard and fast. Aiken's shield banged against his back. His scabbard, axe and hammer flapped and smacked his thighs. Big snowflakes flew into his eyes, stuck to his lashes and wetted his face. The slush coated his arms, legs, and helmet, and lodged in his horse's mane.

Skirting the edge of the woods, they followed a cow path leading toward the sounds of combat. Seeing the other men's horses herded together in a grove up ahead, the two men peeled off to the right and came to the top of a bluff overlooking the river. Aiken hauled back on the reins. He looked down through the blowing snow and saw the killing field. Torwald's men were trapped in a bowl-like depression. Scrubby brush and closely packed, spindly trees grew on three sides of the steep bluffs and, on the fourth side, they were hemmed in by the river. Several huge cottonwoods grew at the river edge. Packed into the tight space were twice, or even three times, the number of men attacking as there were in Torwald's defending band.

A gust of wind briefly cleared the air of falling snow. From his place on the bluff, in a single fleeting moment Aiken saw, down below, on the right, an additional warband partially hidden in the scrub and reeds growing alongside the marshy riverbank. There were more men than he could count. Aiken knew it then: We will all be killed. This is where I die.

The curse would be invalid. He would die and leave no offspring. No children would be threatened by the Sons of the Fiery Realm.

IV.

But he was not dead. He was alive. Nor had he left this world without siring offspring. Now there were two children to protect from fire's deadly wrath. It was chilling to think that the fiery curse might be the reason that he was still alive and had fathered children: to think that his life had been spared for the ghastly reason that the curse must be fulfilled was too horrid to consider. He pulled the cloak more tightly and, in an attempt to distract himself, Aiken stood up from the bench.

But memories continued to pursue him, nonetheless. He could never get away from the curse of fire. It would follow him wherever he went. Already, the dead man's curse had threatened to play out on more than one occasion. When Sunniva was a small child, Mildred had been preparing to make the torch-plant stalks. After she had put a jar of melted tallow on the edge of the hearth, she had gone out the door, only for a moment, but little Sunniva was left in the house alone. When Aiken walked in, he saw his little daughter holding a torch-plant stalk that she had dipped into the tallow and then had stuck into the fire. Sunniva was standing there, unmoving, as if she had turned to stone. Holding the flaming stalk, she was staring, wide-eyed, into the blazing fire. The liquid tallow was dripping in small flames. It could easily have spread to her clothing and caught her hair on fire. Aiken rushed over, grabbed it from her hand, and quenched it in the water pail. It was a narrow miss. He swore he heard the shade's distant laughter: "Almost got you that time."

After that, Aiken was doubly wary of keeping his small children safely distant from the hearth. He was so fearful of fire that he had encouraged both Sunniva and Bertolf to hold small flaming sticks. To be certain that they, too, were as fearful of fire as he was, and to teach them to keep a safe distance from the flames, he had let them burn their fingers, so they would know about the pain that fire causes. Mildred was furious. But to keep them safe he had to hurt them. That was how he had been raised.

A crying fox was answered by a barking dog. Thinking it was best to check on the chickens, just in case the fox was snooping around the byres, Aiken stomped his feet and took a short walk around the house, feeling his way as he went.

After he returned to his place by the door, he planted his feet firmly on the ground and stood a while.

Left with a terrible unknowing, recall had come to him, over the years, only in bits and pieces. The one thing he could never forget was the moment he had said, "We will all be killed. This is where I die."

He asked Alger, "Did you see Oswald or Leofar? Were those their men?" Unfortunately, he knew the answer already. Their attacker's faces were hidden by helmets, their bodies heavily padded with leather jerkins. To conceal the warbands' identities, the shield markings had been painted over with char.

"We will all be killed. This is where I die."

The last time Aiken saw Alger alive was when he yelled, "Our reinforcement will turn the skirmish our way. Go. Go. Go."

But they both knew it was a lie. "We will all be killed. This is where I die."

They could never win. Though outnumbered three to one, four to one, Aiken vowed to retaliate against as many men as possible before they took him down. "We will all be killed. This is where I die."

He leapt from his horse, pulled the shield from his back and drew his long-knife. Coming from its scabbard, he heard it hiss. It was good to have the hilt in his hand. He hefted its weight and made the connection with his killing arm. Anger flooded over him and he roared, "Oswald broke the peace. He will pay for this."

Aiken took a step. He followed with another, and another, all the time thinking, "Now, they have done it. Now, they will get their comeuppance."

He ran through the thickly grown brushwood covering the side of the bluff. He hit level ground, reeled, staggered backward, lost his balance, and stepped forward to regain it. Stunned by his awkwardness, he explained the blundering action to having struck his head against a low-hanging branch. Ashamed to have done something so foolish that a child might have done it, he attributed the lack of vision on the right to his helmet having slipped to the side. He threw his forearm up to straighten it, but the fist holding his hilt rammed a long, wooden haft.

It was then, when he dislodged the point and twisted it in the wound, that he felt the pain and screamed. Blood gushed from his eye and cheek. He threw down his shield and let go of the blade. He reached up to his face and felt the javelin's barbed head. The small, deadly point was buried in his cheek. In a fit of terrible pain, he grabbed the wooden haft and pulled on it with both hands. Angry that a man would use a cruel ranging weapon, he cursed the coward. What kind of man stands on a riverbank and throws a barbed spear from a safe distance to thin the ranks? It had given Aiken no time to react. None to defend himself. He cursed the man who would stand there and, with cold indifference, estimate how to aim at a moving target, in a strong wind, his vision obscured by falling snow, and to hit the mark spot-on without putting himself at risk.

Aiken's knees buckled. Though he pulled on the haft with all his might, he was unable to dislodge the barbed point, so he pushed instead. But it would not budge. He had never expected to die this way. After all the years that he had practiced fighting in hand-to-hand combat, what ultimately was taking him down was a ranging spear, thrown from a distance.

The pain was so great he feared falling into a faint. Lest the haft drag on the ground and twist the barbed head in the flesh, he held it with his right hand and crept along the ground on his knees. He wanted to die with his blade in hand. Blinded by his own gore, his left hand felt for the weapon he had dropped. Calling it by its name, he crawled, sightless, through the drifting snow.

"But not Endbringer. No, no, no." He begged the Matrones to forego the use of their blade named Endbringer. "No. No. No. Keep Endbringer away. Keep it away. I do not want to die. "

After that, he remembered nothing.

V.

Chilled to the bone, he rocked back and forth, hugging his chest. When the savage memories came over him like this, there was no way to stop the agony. It was impossible to shove aside the dreadful thoughts. It was useless to try. He would never be rid of what had happened. He would never be done with it.

The fateful moment had been inscribed forever upon his soul. He had relived each cruel moment so many times, it was like guiding a chisel along the same lines that he had previously carved. Each time the memory of how he had been hurt came to mind, his attention followed and deepened the grooves until he feared he might punch a hole right through to the backside.

All he remembered after he had blacked out, was awakening to a strange face peering down at him through a foggy blur. The man asked, "Are you awake?"

All Aiken could do was grunt in reply.

The man answered, "Good, good, good. You have been insensible for so long, we feared we were giving you too much poppy."

Aiken did not know why he was laying insensible in a strange bed. He reached up to feel the painful side of his face and touched the herbal compresses that were bound to his head with cloth. His entire face was swollen. His mouth hurt too much to speak, and it did not work right, anyhow. The man held a spoonful of softened mush and encouraged him to eat. After Aiken had mouthed a few bites, he fell into a doze, but was encouraged to waken again. It was too painful to open his mouth, but the man insisted he eat. He told Aiken that he needed to restore the blood he had lost so that he could regain his strength. The man held a cup to his mouth and Aiken sipped bone broth through a straw cut from a horsetail plant.

Uncertain about the blood loss, and too groggy to understand, Aiken did not know why his head was wrapped, or why was he there at all. But his mouth did not work well enough to ask. All he could do was grunt.

Another time, when Aiken awakened, a man, whom he did not recall having seen before, was changing the compresses. Aiken prodded the edges of his puffy cheek. Although the man discouraged him, Aiken continued to probe the uncovered wound. His fingertips sunk into the empty socket where his eye had been. When he felt the stitched threads and the puckered skin covering the hole, the sudden, horrible shock made him retch.

The man who was attending him was kindly and sympathized so deeply, he seemed to feel Aiken's pain as if the hurts were his own. Shedding tears alongside Aiken, the two men sobbed together. Aiken tossed side to side, and though the man petted his head to soothe him and called him the sweet names that a mother calls her boy, nothing the man said quieted him.

Forced to strictly admonish Aiken, the man said, "You must lie still," and told him, in no uncertain terms, "You must remain calm. You must not rip out the stitches, or you will really make a mess of your face. The flesh was so badly torn, we might never be able to repair it again. You do not want a big hole in the middle of your cheek, now do you?"

Aiken was spent. So weak, he had to give in, he only knew one thing: that he was grievously disfigured, and half his sight was gone. What lay beyond that simple truth was the vast unknown and the spare uncertainty of what would become of his life from then on. He stared into the vastness of that unknown, certain only of living a terrible dream from which he would never waken.

Later, when Aiken was able to mumble a few garbled sentences, he told the men that if they wanted to deal for ransom, Torwald would give them whatever they asked. But they, in turn, assured him that he was not their prisoner. He urged the men to bring him his clothing, weaponry, and horse, so he could get back home. But they, in turn, just clucked their tongues, shook their heads, and advised him to lie still. He had almost bled dry, they said. He was too weak to leave their care. They were not his enemy. They would not kill or torture him. He could trust them. He was in good hands, they said.

He only knew that he lay abed, in a dark room, lit by small flames that were tucked into niches in the walls. His needs were taken care of by four men whose names were Dvalinn, Allfrigg, Grerr and Berling. They identified themselves as, a scholar, an alchemist, a craftsman, and a metal smith, all of whom were highly skilled and well respected in their chosen fields.

One day, Aiken was convinced that Torwald was on the riverbank and needed his help. He threw his legs over the side of the bed and stood but was so weak he became light-headed. His knees gave out and he fell. Two of the men picked him up and laid him in the bed.

Up until then, the men had chosen to withhold the truth about his companions' deaths. They feared that he would become despondent if he knew and would lose his will to live. But after Aiken had tried to rise from the bed and had fallen several times, they had no choice. One of the men was forced to tell him that his war companions had all been killed. All were dead but him.

At first, Aiken did not understand. "No, that cannot be," he said. "I hear Torwald's voice. He stands here and calls me a lazy good-for-nothing. He tells me to get out of bed. He says he needs my help on the Warring riverbank."

It was then that the man was forced to explain that it was Torwald's shade who was appearing before him. Regrettably, the only way to prevent his chieftain's soul from wandering was to bury his bones. To light the pyres and to bury his bones was what Torwald was asking Aiken to do.

VI.

The day I came across him, I cannot say for certain whether it was by chance or by design that I found him. But I do recall having been drawn, on a whim, to take a walk.

Now, in hindsight, I suspect it may have been his luck-woman who had taken me by the hand and led me to the place where he lay stricken and in need of help. Perhaps, if otherworldly women feel the same as earthly women do, she felt remorseful after she had deserted him, and found, in me, a way to make up for her earlier pique of ill humor.

Lighting my way through the tunnels with only a small, flaming torch-plant, I could barely see a thing. When I stumbled over his body, I nearly fell. At first, I thought the obstruction in my path was an animal carcass. But when I took a closer look at the heap of bloody rags, I could see they clothed a man's body.

It was not until I glanced at the tunnel ceiling and saw pale, slanting sunrays shining through the ragged, root-lined edges of the sinkhole through which he had plainly fallen, that I understood how he had come to be there at all. Because the hole was quite some distance from where he was laying, I concluded that he had crawled that far before collapsing.

Unsure, at first, whether he was alive or dead I crouched beside him. Passing the torch back and forth to shed more light on the man, I saw that he was curled up on his side with his back to me. His knees were pulled up to his chest, and his hands were pressed to his face. Blood welled through the gaps between his fingers with each of his heartbeats.

When I heard him groan, I knew he was not only alive, but awake, aware of my presence, and trying to speak with me. The sight of the long javelin shaft, the business end of which lay beneath him, convinced me that the wicked ranging spear was protruding from his face. Immediately stricken with horror, a fit of shivers wracked my body.

Filled with pity for the man, I could only guess at his dreadful pain. If I had not found him, there would have been no help for him. He could never have gotten out of the tunnel alone.

Right then and there, I could have walked away and left him to his fate. But if I had, he would have become a corpse. Several days later we would have had to clear the tunnel of his stinking remains. So either way, whether he was alive or dead, the wounded man was on our hands. I figured we had no choice but to offer him our aid.

Not knowing how long he had lain there, I hated to leave him alone. I tore some strips of fabric from his clothing to make a pad and told him to place it over the wound to slow the bleeding. Before I took off, I patted his shoulder and told him I would return soon.

Without giving a second thought to what we were doing, we hurriedly organized a rescue party. There was no time to throw the staves—those long, Hazelwood sticks carved with secret signs that we use for questioning what the Matrones have decreed—nor to consider how complicated the consequences of our actions would become. As a result of acting so swiftly and with such single-minded purpose, it had not occurred to us that our goodwill gesture would start a long and enduring conflict concerning the possession of his unborn daughter's soul.

How were we to know that we would be tied to his future generations, as well as to Lady Blessed and Lord Fury? At the time, the coming dispute over who had first lain a claim against his daughter in payment for a debt, which he was about to incur, never crossed our minds. (Well, allow me to qualify that statement by saying that it had not occurred to three of us. There was one amongst us who had seen an opportunity to acquire an ingredient that he needed for one of his potions.) As for the other three of us who had no hidden motives, because our immediate inclination was to save his life, we went ahead, at full tilt, without a full grasp of the troubled mess we were getting ourselves into. It was not until later that the complications arose, and the finger-pointing began.

Allfrigg brought dried herbs to stop the bleeding and a tincture made from poppy juice. Because the injured man was unable to mumble more than a few, meaningless words, we were unsure of his name. Berling, Grerr, and I did our best to comfort him while Allfrigg gave him several drops of the tincture upon his tongue.

After Berling had wiped some of the blood from the man's face, he said, "Look how young he is."

Knowing his youth increased the sadness we felt. Although we did our best to steady his head and limbs, the man trembled, writhed and fought against us.

The slender, javelin point was about the length of a man's hand, and its barbs made it impossible to pull from his flesh. The long, iron socket made it equally impossible to push through to the opposite side. Apparently, the man had been in a state of confused desperation and had forcibly tried alternatively to both push and to pull it from his flesh. But, unfortunately, his attempts to rid himself of the wicked ranging weapon had shoved it more deeply into the wound. Nor could the long wooden haft have been easily snapped off. It is for these reasons that such a wicked ranging weapon, though small, will incapacitate anyone it strikes. Apparently, the barbed point had come at him from a steep angle and struck him with a sideways blow. The thin, sharp edge had grazed his eye and the barbs stuck in his cheek. The poor man was caught like a fish on a hook and was equally as helpless.

I held the torch while Grerr and Berling held the man steady. He was strong, and it was difficult to keep him still. Allfrigg used small blades, jeweler's saws, and other tools to cut out the point. Lodged in tightly and hooked under the cheekbone, there was no easy way to remove it. The young man's dreadful screams echoed through the tunnels and caused a terrible ringing in our ears. After Allfrigg finished the awful job, he packed the wound with yarrow to stop the bleeding.

Clearly, if we had gotten to him, immediately, after he had been hit, the damage would have been less severe. But the combination of wrenching on the haft as the young man had crept along the ground and through the tunnel, the hard landing he had taken when he fell, plus the way he had mangled his flesh when he tried to rip out the barbed point, along with the trouble we had removing it, meant that there was a hole where his eye had been and, from the tip of his eyebrow to his chin, a ragged gash zig-zagged across the right side of his face.

When we were ready to move him, Grerr first climbed into the goat-cart that he had brought along. After we lifted the man in, Grerr cradled his head and applied pressure to the injury to slow the bleeding. Even with three of us pushing, the weight of the two men made a heavy load for the goats to haul. The march through the tunnels and back to our rooms went slowly.

Throughout the ordeal, the man remained awake. Though he was in dreadful pain, he continued to mumble incoherently. In an attempt to throw himself from the cart, he tried to roll over and to push himself onto his knees. He was a tough fighter, all right, and we struggled to contain him. Lest we increase his unease, we did not want to rope him down. But after we had been forced to halt our progress through the tunnel several times, such drastic measures seemed inevitable.

Allfrigg made one, final attempt to settle the man. He leaned over him, placed his mouth close to his ear, and whispered very quietly. Allfrigg's style was so different from Berling and Grerr's strong-armed approach to doing things that we simply scoffed at first. Yet, whatever Allfrigg had said, the avid attention he had given to the injured man's needs seemed to distract him from his immediate desire to return to the battlefield.

We had to piece together the meaning of his garbled speech, but after we had figured it out, we understood what he was trying to tell us: he wanted to get back at the ones who were responsible for the attack on their warband.

Allfrigg asked, "What will you promise us in return for the help we give you?"

I realize this will sound like a weak excuse for our deplorable actions, but we were in shock and giddy. Desperate to divert ourselves from the blood and gore that we had witnessed, when we realized that the young man was apparently distracted by word games, each of us devised riddles to disguise the ridiculous things we wanted in return for our efforts to save his life, and to help him get back at those who had wronged him. Eventually, our riddling seemed to settle him down. He rolled onto his side, curled up, and fell asleep.

At the time, we praised Allfrigg's clever spellbinding skills. But after all was said and done, I am repelled by the persuasiveness of his scheming. There is no other way to say it: Allfrigg took advantage of us—not only of Aiken, but of the rest of us as well. The total assault upon our senses had left us vulnerable and Allfrigg tampered with our trust. As far as I am concerned, his behavior was inexcusable.

What had begun as a way to distract a wounded man from the ugliness of his suffering later took on far-reaching significance. We had concluded a bargain after which he owed us.

For some of us, it was a mere riddle contest, a diversion, a simple word game. But of course, there were bound to be repercussions. Though, at first, some of us gave it little thought, Aiken's daughter was always at the back of our minds. In our private, nightly musings, she became a solution to our loneliness, along with the other problems we faced. Over time, we became increasingly attached to the fulfillment of Aiken's obligation.

Years later, each of us remembered differently the hazy, peculiar conversation that we had had on that slow walk home. Recall is an imperfect faculty, an unreliable trickster when engaged in a search for truth. Yet memory's ability to evoke certainty in all that it chooses to show and tell us, enlists our absolute trust. But this much I know for certain: that ambiguous word game led to the eventual forging of the long-knife that, even now, as I write, lays on the far edge of my table.

As for Aiken, the poppy's spell bestowed a blessed forgetfulness upon him, and he remembered nothing. It was not until he awakened and had gained lucidity that we explained how he had been to the land of the dead. But, we told him, we had managed to pull him back just in time, before he had crossed the Venom-Cold River. To console myself, I believe there was a small measure of truth in our explanation. Surely, he would have died if I had not found him.

After we got him back to our rooms, we cleaned the wound. Allfrigg, who is skillful with a needle, stitched the gash, and drew the eyelids together. Unfortunately, because so much of the flesh had been badly torn, it was a hard and grueling task—to say nothing of all the blood we had to staunch.

After all was said and done, it did seem fitting to have asked for compensation. Nothing comes free in this world. Mother Necessity and her three daughters, the Matrones, are most insistent that every action results in consequences. Such is the law of the cosmos, which is dutifully maintained by the three sisters: what must come, shall come to be.

Because Aiken's care consumed us for so long, and since he was forced to winter here, we resented the imposition, at times. But after we had gotten to know him better, we became quite fond of the man. Berling and Aiken often talked about weaponry. Grerr noticed the little items that Aiken whittled and showed him how to make more complex designs using saws, drills and other small tools. And, because Aiken's curiosity was boundless, I taught him to read and to write the secret signs and shared a few of our secret teachings.

With the approach of springtime, the ground began to thaw and, after Aiken's wounds had healed, he became increasingly restless. One day he set out to attend to the gruesome task of burying his dead companion's bones. Usually, when a well-respected man or chieftain's body is lain on the fires, others come from near and far to honor his memory and to celebrate his passage to the everlasting hereafter. But Aiken's war companions' bodies had been left to rot on the riverbank.

Because we were unable to help Aiken with the grisly task, it was his duty to build the funeral pyres alone. When he returned three days later, he was so riled up, he insisted upon setting out immediately. Driven by his need to prove who had been behind the murder of his companions and to seek justice in their names, he left our underground rooms against our gravest concerns for his welfare.

VII.

Aiken crouched on his haunches to start a small fire with the flint and steel. Once it was flaming, he lit the torch-plant stalk, and left the little fire to burn itself out while he walked the ox-road one more time.

He wanted to strike out against those men who had hurt him and had killed his war companions. But since there was no one to hit, he was forced to swallow the anger he felt toward those who had looked the other way when the murderers had all gone free.

Like the rest of us, he had believed that whatever happened in this world made sense, events had meaning, and conflicts worked out the way they should. To have run into the conspiracy of silence, which the chieftains had agreed to enforce, had gone against all his expectations.

He had learned that those who were in service to Torwald, including the men who had remained in his fort town when he and the others had traveled to the War-ring River, had either been killed or been forced to swear oaths to other chieftains. Yet and even so, on the day that Aiken had set out in pursuit of justice, he had been unusually trusting. He had grown to manhood believing in fair and impartial justice and had expected the law to punish the guilty for their crimes.

Because he had been a witness to the crime, he expected men to respectfully listen to his testimony. He believed that men wanted to know the truth as much as he did, and would punish those who had murdered Torwald and the other men in his warband. He believed that those who were called upon to speak would uphold the truth, and the guilty would be brought to justice for their crimes. He still had had faith in the rule of law.

And it was with this belief in the inherent dignity of each freeman, and his sim-ple trust that all men felt the same way he did, that Aiken set out for a hill fort where his cousin, Gordon, was chieftain.

Back in the day when Aiken had been a member of Torwald's honor guard, he would have been accompanied by his companions, all of whom would have been well-attired in their war gear. They would have caught everyone's eye as they rode through the village astride their well-groomed horses. After they entered the inner stockade, they would have been shown to his cousin's private chambers, invited in, and generously served food and drink.

But because he had no horse to ride and was dressed in nothing better than the hand-me-down clothing we had given him, Aiken was treated like a man of no dis-tinction and was turned away. No amount of arguing could convince the gatekeeper that he was the chieftain's cousin. He was told to wait until the appointed day when Chieftain Gordon heard grievances and requests. Until then, he was forced to sleep in the fields and to eat whatever he could hunt in the woods or fish from the streams.

When the day arrived, he was allowed to enter the meadhall. Surrounded by his cousin's guardsmen, he joined the crowd of merchants, farmers, and craftsmen awaiting their turn. Gordon was elevated on the dais above them all, seated on his high seat.

When Aiken was called upon to speak, he strode forward and greeted his cousin, "I honor you, Kinsman Gordon, and ask you to hear me out. I need to bring the case of Chieftain Torwald's murder to the Assembly. To learn who was behind the crime, I require a kinsman who will back me and swear an oath to speak the truth."

Since his appearance was no surprise to Gordon, Aiken assumed that his cousin had been forewarned of his immanent arrival. And, apparently, he had devised several excuses with which to defend his inaction. Unfortunately, for Gordon, he was a poor liar.

"I do not know you," Gordon said. "Whoever you are, you are no kinsman of mine."

"You do not recognize me?" Aiken asked. Astonished by Gordon's blatant refusal to acknowledge their close family ties, he sought to enlighten Gordon. "I am Aiken, the Strength of Oak, son of Eamon the Good Protector. Our fathers were cousins."

Gordon rested his elbows on the chair arms, laced his finger together at the level of his upper chest and, alternately straightening and curling them in a fretful manner, said, "You are mistaken. My cousin Aiken died alongside Torwald. You are no relative of mine. Whatever happened to Torwald and his men was unfortunate. But no one knows whose chiefdom was to blame for the attack."

Gordon dropped his left hand, laid it in his lap, lifted his right hand to his chin, and began to fondle his beard. "Everyone suspects a warband from another clan was forced to defend itself against Torwald's misguided raid into their territory."

Left momentarily speechless by such an outrageous claim, Aiken stared at Gordon in disbelief. He suspected his hapless cousin was attempting to save his own skin by lying, but was doing a very poor job of it. To challenge Gordon's false claims with the truth, Aiken said, "No, you heard it wrong. I was there. I was hurt in the attack. It took me this long to get my strength back. I am the only survivor. There was no raid. It was an ambush. We were lured out of our stockade under false pretenses to find a missing cattle herd. They were not stolen by an outside clan. Instead, they were purposely hidden by our own kinsmen. The theft and the attack were unlawful acts of war."

Feigning disinterest, Gordon refused to discuss Aiken's charges. Instead, he stared blankly into the middle distance and tapped his fingertips on the chair arm.

Gordon's apparent disinterest in his cousin's claim was making Aiken increasingly irate. "I, myself, saw their bodies. The dead were on Torwald's land, on the bank of the Warring River, across from Oswald's holdings. To say any different is a lie. I was there during the attack. I burned their bodies myself, months after they had been brutally slaughtered. At least their kin could have honored them at the burial site."

Nonchalantly shrugging his shoulders, Gordon gave the impression of feeling no remorse. None whatsoever. The failure to respect his dead kinsmen seemed not to bother him in the least. "If what you say is true, it is slanderous. But this is the first time I have heard of it."

"Have you so little regard for your own kinsmen?" Aiken said, heatedly lashing out at Gordon for his coldness. "All men are entitled to respectful treatment after death. You dishonored my chieftain and war companions when you left them hanging from the trees where their murderers hung them. You refused to care for their bodies and insulted your own kin. What is wrong with you? How can you care so little for your fellow kinsmen?"

"Me? One of the leaders of my clan?" Gordon asked, self-righteously taken aback by Aiken's charges. Abandoning his well-contrived disinterest, he said, defensively, "What gives you the right to shame me here, inside of my own meadhall?"

Gordon glanced toward his guardsman and, with a simple hand gesture, indicated that Aiken should be escorted from the hall.

Dumbfounded by Gordon's meaningless attempts to throw the blame on him, Aiken asked, "Why has no one taken revenge for their murders? Your disrespectful behavior will cause the Matrones to curse your bloodline."

"How dare you threaten me with curses," Gordon shouted, and repeated what he had said before. "I do not know you. You have no right to demand this from me." Drawing each word out for emphasis, he repeated, "You—are—not—my—kin. It is contemptible for you to walk in here and to accuse one kinsman of attacking another."

Gordon then paused a moment, after which his side of the conversation took a strange turn. First, he ordered the approaching guard to stand down and to await further orders. Then, he waved Aiken over and, bending forward, rested his elbows on his knees. Lowering his voice, Gordon spoke in a confidential tone, "Look, Ai—," he said, before stopping himself from speaking Aiken's name aloud. "You already have a reputation for being a troublesome brawler, and now you are becoming a nuisance," he said, stabbing the air with his finger for emphasis.

"So this is how I plan to deal with you. The charges you want to bring to the Assembly could start a blood feud. I will not allow that to happen. If you walk out of here and forget about it, I will, also, forget your charges. But if you persist, I will have you outlawed."

"How can you can outlaw me? I did nothing wrong. I did not break the law."

"I will say that you are want to stir up trouble within our kinship by weakening our alliances. To maintain the peace within the kinship is of primary importance. You know how difficult it is. Men hold onto their grievances and pass them on to their sons and daughters.

"They complain that others made them look foolish; insulted them or cheated them in a game. They say they were not paid back on time for a debt incurred or were not backed in a conflict. They accuse others of not pulling their weight or of giving gifts unequal in value to the ones they received in the ceremonial exchanges. They even complain they were given gifts they did not like or complain that their kin refused to attend a feast to which they were invited. Even such trivial grievances can smolder for years and years—for generations.

"You must not make this claim upon my kinship nor involve me in a damaging and needless blood feud. Do you not see, Ai—," Gordon said and, once again stopped short of speaking Aiken's name aloud before he continued, "If you and others of Torwald's kin feel compelled to wreak a bloody vengeance against Oswald and Leofar, their closest kin will, in turn, raid those who attacked their family members.

"We are all related through birth and marriage. A blood feud will suck us all in. The killing and burning of villages and meadhalls could escalate until the violence was completely out of hand. It would be impossible to stop. Our entire kinship could be weakened. If that were to happen, we would become vulnerable to an attack from another clan."

"No, you have it wrong," Aiken said. Shocked by Gordon's line of reasoning, he disputed his cousin's weak defense. "I do not intend to engage in unremitting blood feud. Fear of each other does not make for lasting peace. What matters is trust and fairness. What I propose will not weaken the clan. This is the reason that disputes are brought before the Assembly. Instead of two factions within a single bloodline coming to blows and wiping out entire families, two men fight to settle the score. This is the way men keep the trust between them. It will strengthen our alliances."

"Do not lecture me. Nor may you address me in that tone of voice. I owe you nothing."

"Gordon, I insist that you listen to me. If you—."

"I am Chieftain Gordon to you."

"As I was saying—Cousin Gordon—if you do not agree to stand up for me, I will be forced to bring my charges to the Assembly without you. Now that you have told me the names of Torwald's murderers, I will demand that you, Oswald, and Leofar swear oaths to speak the truth. If you three refuse, I will challenge each of you to single combat."

If Gordon's purpose had been to goad Aiken into revealing his intentions, he seemed to have achieved the effect he wanted to provoke. Gordon stood, shook his finger at Aiken, and yelled. "No, you will do no such thing. Your accusation of my complicity in Torwald's murder has gone too far."

He called his guards and told them to remove Aiken from the hall. "Never show your face again, neither here, nor at the Assembly. If you do, you will be refused entry. Remember, I can have you outlawed. Just go away and forget this ever happened."

Affronted by the lack of respect he had been shown by a fellow kinsman, Aiken said, loudly enough for everyone in the hall to hear, "Gordon, you fool, how can I walk away? How can I forget Torwald and my war companions were murdered? Where do you think I will go?"

"You have slandered me. Now get out of my sight."

The guards stepped forward to escort Aiken out, but he elbowed his way past, saying, "I will walk out by myself."

Humiliated in front of the villagers and farmers, who were staring at him as he passed through the crowd, he shook off the guards when they tried to apprehend him. He walked through the commons and took off for the gate.

He knew the guardsmen whom he passed. He had joked and feasted with these men. He had fought beside them. They had sworn oaths together and had promised to back each other whenever they fought common enemies. All his life, he had been protected by his fellow kinsmen and by the law's guarantee of fairness. But now that he had been called a nameless nobody, he was invisible. The guardsmen stared over Aiken's head and refused to even acknowledge his presence.

VIII.

Shortly after his visit to Gordon's hill fort, Aiken went to the village where the springtime Assembly was held. As a freeman, he had a right to bear arms, to attend the meeting, and to take an active part in expressing his approval or disapproval on all matters that were brought up for discussion.

But when Aiken appeared at the hall, the doorkeepers would not let him enter. He was certain they recognized him and were responding to Gordon's orders to keep him out. After he was refused entry, he brazenly tried to push his way inside but was forcibly barred. Norton, the chieftain in charge of maintaining order during the meetings, was called to the door. A big, hulking man, he stepped out of the hall and stood between the open doorway and Aiken.

Asked to explain himself, Aiken said that he had come to attend the meeting. But Norton claimed that Torwald's man, Aiken, had died in a raid. Choosing to dismiss him as an unwelcome imposter who had no right to be there, Norton ended his rebuke with a warning, "If you attempt to enter again, you will be forcibly removed."

"But what you heard is wrong. I am not dead. As you can plainly see, I am very much alive. To prove my right to enter the hall, allow me to stand before the lawgiver and recite my lineage."

Chieftain Norton partially acquiesced to Aiken's request, saying, "All right, but, until you have proven your right to enter the hall as a freeman you will be deprived of your weaponry. Only after you have been granted the right to bear arms will they be returned."

Trusting Chieftain Norton to be true to his word, Aiken handed his knives, spear, and axe to one of the guardsmen. Norton then ordered two of his men to take Aiken by the arms and to lead him into the hall. Norton preceded the three men as they walked down the narrow aisle in the center of the hall.

Aiken was brought forward, like a captive enemy, to stand before the high table. The hall was crowded with standing men holding spears and shields. Aiken spotted Leofar, the man whom he loathed with a vengeance, seated on the chair where his former chieftain, Torwald, once had sat.

Leofar jumped to his feet. In shock, he slapped his hands flat on the table and leaned heavily into his arms to stare at the man who was entering the hall, the one man whom Leofar knew could accuse him of his uncle's murder.

"This man requests admittance to the Assembly," Norton said, "but his claim to be a freeman is in dispute. He says he is Aiken, a member of Torwald's chiefdom, but I have heard, from trustworthy sources, that all the men in Torwald's warband are now deceased or have sworn to serve other chieftains."

At the sound of the two men's names being spoken aloud, each man in the hall looked to the one beside whom he stood and asked uneasily what this strange and unexpected appearance forebode.

The lawgiver walked to the center of the dais, struck his shield with his hammer to quiet the murmuring din, and yelled, "It is unlawful for a man to enter the Assembly unless he is accompanied by his chieftain. If you claim to be a freeman, I ask you to name the chieftain whom you serve."

"I am Aiken, the Strength of Oak. Torwald was my chieftain. He is dead but I am here on his account."

"Then do you claim to be a masterless man?"

"No. I serve Torwald. It was he who ordered me to come here and to seek redress for his murder."

"A freeman swears to serve the higher good when he recognizes his chieftain's authority," the lawgiver said. "Only by vowing to respect his chieftain, and to observe the rule of law, with an all-abiding loyalty, can a man live the exemplary life, which he has been taught and trained to observe. Under his chieftain's tutelage a man offers devotion to the law's higher authority, gives generous blood gifts to Lord Glory and Mother Necessity, promises to speak the truth and to maintain his respect for the laws, which she, in her wisdom, calls upon mankind to observe. Only then can there be order in this world."

The lawgiver paused a moment, breathed deeply, looked over the assembled men and continued to recite with wholehearted conviction, "Our Assembly is made up of righteous people who recognize the true nature of man and call upon Lord Glory for guidance. It is when the Lord's rule of law is abandoned that order is chased from the commons and the ensuing chaos results in grim lawlessness.

"I see this happening even now. Unless we put a stop to its spread, wickedness will gain ground. It is only through devout observation of Lord Glory's standards and his rules for conduct by good and honorable men that the common order will prevail. We observe the freemen's right to bear arms. We respect and honor the freemen's superiority over women, unarmed commoners, and those who are held in bondage.

"Unless each man commits to filling his heart with an abiding respect for the truth and justice, which Lord Glory stands for, and abandons the unholy wickedness of this world, will he be able to live an honorable life."

The lawgiver looked down at Aiken from his perch on the dais, and said, "Have you sworn to uphold the law and to honor and respect Lord Glory?"

"Yes, I stand before you now, Aiken the Strength of Oak, and agree to honor Lord Glory and the rule of law. I denounce Spider the Entangler and the chaos he brings with him into this world. My chieftain, Torwald the Thunderous Fighter, and all his men, but me, were killed unfairly in an attack. To discover who planned the ambush, in which my chieftain was killed, I have come here, today, to learn the truth."

"Before I can acknowledge your right to attend the Assembly and allow you to level your charges you, who claim to be Aiken, a member of the deceased Chieftain Torwald's warband, must recite your lineage."

"I am Aiken the Strength of Oak, son of Eamon the Good Protector and nephew of Otgar the Spear-bearer, both of whom were sons of Chad the Battle-proud, who was a son of Dunstan the Dark Stone, who was a son of Heard the Brave, who was son of my namesake, Aiken the Strength of Oak. I have come here, today, to learn the truth and to challenge the men who were complicit in the murder of Chieftain Torwald."

"Who will you call upon to guarantee the truth of your claim to be a freeman? And what is the name of the kinsman who will witness the truth of your charges?"

"I call upon my cousin, Chieftain Gordon the Power of Rule, whose father was a son of Dunstan the Dark Stone."

"I now ask Chieftain Gordon to come forward."

Gordon angrily pushed his way through the crowd and, thrusting out his jaw, stood defiantly before the lawgiver to announce himself. "I am Gordon the Power of Rule."

"Chieftain Gordon, will you agree to act as a witness to these charges? If you do not speak the truth, you forfeit your honor and your authority to be a leader of men."

Gordon leant to the side and, after exaggerating the way he looked Aiken over from his head to his feet, said with evident disgust, "No. I denounce this man. I have never seen him before. He is no kinsman of mine."

"Liar. You are a liar," Aiken said loudly.

"You can see how this man has come here to incite violence. His slanders are proof. He insults our laws and speaks disrespectfully of the honorable men who are here today. He does not deserve to be shown the honor that is reserved for freemen, exclusively."

After he said his piece, Gordon ducked into the crowd and disappeared.

The lawgiver addressed Aiken, saying, "According to your witness, you, who claim to be one of Torwald's men, have come here with a shameless lack of concern for the opinion of others. Because you did not present yourself according to the rules of the Assembly, your request is refused. You are not who you claim to be, nor have you offered the proper supplication and offerings, which are deemed necessary to uphold your honorable intent. You have, by this very act, shown disrespect for Lord Glory and his rule of law which states that only freemen may speak at the Assembly."

"I agree that no man should stand above the law," Aiken said in his defense. "I have come here today to challenge Chieftain Torwald's murderers and to ask Lord Glory to decide the truth in this matter."

"You are speaking out of turn. You cannot contradict me." The lawgiver thundered. "Only the lawgiver knows the wishes of Lord Glory and speaks for him. I, alone, stand for the ultimate truth. Devotion to Lord Glory is indispensable to the sustenance of our free system of government. If anyone were to claim to be a freeman, order would be replaced by chaos. Even now, I see how the rule of law is falling by the wayside. The justice that Lord Glory, in his infinite wisdom, gave mankind, and the order that was built upon an honorable respect for what is right and wrong is being trampled in the dust."

"That is why I am here today. I ask to uphold the rule of law."

"You are not allowed to speak. If a man no longer observes the principles of righteous behavior, he no longer acts in a way that discriminates right from wrong but instead pursues his own unbridled appetites, pursuit of vengeance, and a lack of respect for the common good. An abandonment of these upstanding values will lead to shameful chaos."

"No one is above the law," Aiken countered. "I ask only for this much, to be allowed to put my life on the line in defense of truth.

"Shut him up," Leofar yelled. "I can take no more of this. We should not be forced to listen to his demand to mete out justice in Torwald's name. Everything he says is like a knife in my heart."

"If I am proven wrong in my stance before Lord Glory," Aiken screamed. "I ask to die honorably in a meeting of the blades."

"Look at this monster, will you?" Leofar yelled, pointing at Aiken. He stuck out his chin, and said, "He thinks he can stir up trouble by claiming to be a fellow kinsman but he has no right to be here."

"I am a freeman the same as you."

Leofar gave Aiken a long, hard look of sneering distaste and, poking his finger in Aiken's direction, said, "This despicable man deserves only our scorn. He is not one of Torwald's men. I knew all of my uncle's men and loved them dearly as I love my brothers. This display of false self-righteousness pains me greatly.

"And, now, let me tell you this," Leofar continued, "my father and Torwald were great chieftains, two of the finest men who have ever led their warbands. I aim to follow in their footsteps. You can trust me when I tell you that I will be one of the Assembly leaders for a long time, just as Torwald was.

"After my uncle was so viciously attacked—horribly attacked—I grieved his death for a long time." He paused briefly to exaggerate the way he wiped his tearless eyes and to show how deeply moved he was by his own speech. "You can trust me when I tell you this. There is no need for an investigation into his murder. I am my uncle's closest kinsman, and I alone will take care of it. This much I know: my uncle was attacked viciously by a chiefdom from a clan in the western lands."

"That is a lie."

"I promise to learn the truth. This imposter deserves only our scornful abuse. Even now, I have men scouting in enemy territory. Infiltrating other chiefdoms, including those who claim to be my allies, they have been given orders to buy information that will lead to accusations against those who were behind my uncle's death.

"No one will get away with it," Leofar yelled. His mouth opened wide as a ravenous beast's and his narrowed eyes scrutinized all the men in the hall. "No one wants to cross me," he said with a raised fist. "Anyone who disagrees will start a feud with me."

He pointed to several in the crowd and then to himself, and said, "I know my suspicions are unfounded. I know you are all behind me, every one of you. I promise to lead a full army against those tribes in the western lands who attacked my uncle and his warband. Because they broke the peace, I refuse to pay the annual tribute."

Leofar spread his arms out to the side and looked around. "Are you all with me? Will we retaliate for this murder against our kinsman?"

The men who were standing in the crowd beneath the dais had just been warned. Fearful of harboring possible spies within their own bands, lest suspicion fall upon them, they had no choice but to wholeheartedly agree with Leofar—or to share Torwald's fate. To show their support, all the men beat raucously on their shields.

"We will wipe them out," Leofar shouted above the din. "We will set fire to their meadhalls and villages. Every guilty man will pay-up with his life. Leave the leader to me. I want his blood. To honor my uncle's memory and the memories of his fellow war companions in the manner they deserve, I insist they return their bones."

A groundswell of cheers followed Leofar's shameless bragging.

"Ask me to show you where they are buried," Aiken yelled above the shouting voices. "I buried them myself. You, too, know where they are buried. Their graves are on the bank of the Warring River, where you murdered them."

"Who let this man in? Leofar said, stabbing his finger in Aiken's direction. He opened his mouth, pulled back his lips to show his teeth, and growled loudly, "This man disgusts me. Look at him. He is a filthy wanderer. Get him out of here."

Leofar glanced hatefully at Norton, and said, deep in his throat, "You will learn not to cross me, Norton. If you do, what happened to Torwald will, also, happen to you."

Raising his voice, Leofar yelled, "I say, we outlaw him."

Aiken had never felt so helpless. Standing in the very same hall, in which he had attended Assemblies since he was a youth, he was being threatened with expulsion. Deprived of his rights, his merit, his name, he silently pleaded for recognition from those men, whom he knew. Desperate to be acknowledged, he turned his head to look over his shoulder, but no one would meet his gaze. He tugged at the man holding his arm and tried to lift a hand to cover the scarred side of face, crying, "You know me. I am Aiken, Eamon's son, Otgar's nephew. Look at me."

Those who stood closest recoiled and backed away. No one wanted to cross the man who was standing on the dais, issuing threats. Shamed by their unwillingness to face up to Leofar's bullying, the men below the dais were surrendering. In return for saving their skins, they were willing to turn their backs on the one man who was exposing their cowardice.

Everything Leofar said was a blatant lie. Everything he said was meaningless and twisted. Leofar had turned the charges, which Aiken was prepared to level against Torwald's killers, against the accuser himself. But all the men in the hall struck the floor with the butts of their spears and voiced agreement with the intimidator who stood on the platform leering at them.

The man on the dais had told them that the rules did not matter and they agreed. Instead, they were willing do whatever it took to avoid admitting the truth, as each man became increasingly aggressive in defense of the lies he was so blatantly endorsing.

The more obvious was the truth, the more loudly did they chant, "Outlaw. Outlaw. Outlaw."

The Lawgiver stepped forward and raised his arms. Once the hall was quiet, he outlawed Aiken without naming him. "You, who have come here with your ill-advised statements, lack of respect for the rule of law and, I will add, your well-known habit of engaging in violent challenges, now stand accused of slander."

He looked down at the men who stood on the floor beneath the dais, and said, "This man's impurities have been deemed potentially harmful to himself and to others. His subsequent loss of both honor and respect demands a suitable punishment. Similarly, when he fails to meet the prevailing standards by casting out such impurities, he is expected to accept ostracism and thus to bear his shame humbly and alone. One of the best ways to relieve himself of this burden, which shame has cast upon him, is to denounce, continuously and with hostility, these same outside influences which chaos engenders. The more shameful he feels, the greater is his hatred for his own improper actions, and the less threatening will they be to his soul. Every man must follow the commands which Mother Necessity and Father Time decree and, most of all, every freeman must become a fighter in Lord Glory's warband. A single person is nothing without the whole. What counts most is a man's devotion to Lord Glory's rule of law."

Leofar broke in to add, "The very forces of darkness, which his man represents, pose a fundamental threat to all the freeman who stand here today. I pledge to lead the fight against those forces of darkness myself."

And again the men in the hall cheered.

"Though this man, who stands before me now," the Lawgiver said loudly, "claims to be a righteous man, it has been proven that he has no rights before the law. If we were to let this man into our Assembly, we would further weaken the standards upon which this gathering of freemen was built, and the natural law that Mother Necessity decreed we follow. For as long as I am the lawgiver, I will resist the forces of chaos that seek to impinge upon our freedom. All freemen must take to the battlefield and enter the struggle to support our laws. The warrior will save the world from disorder in the name of Lord Glory."

He looked directly at Aiken and, without addressing him by name, said, "You have been dishonored. It is therefore unlawful for you to claim to be a freeman and to speak here at the Assembly. Men like you are a threat to the traditional order upon which the knowledge of right and wrong is built. You exemplify the undermining and destruction of our freedom because you lack discrimination. We all are under siege by the loose standards by which you have chosen to live.

"Therefore, to sustain the purity of the Assembly of freemen, this man, who stands before you now, shall, from this moment on, go unprotected by fellow kinsmen."

The men in the hall erupted in cheers.

"I did nothing wrong," Aiken cried. In answer to this unfair expulsion from their midst, he said, "I broke no laws. You are the ones who have broken the rules. You cannot outlaw me. The facts stand against you. The truth stands against you. The law stands against you. Mother Necessity stands against you. Not a single one of you will get away with this injustice."

But no one heard him. Aiken had shown each of these men their own desperate weakness and they, in turn, hated him for it. Their fear was so strong that it had overcome their sense of right and wrong. Instead, they had made their hatred lawful.

"I am Aiken the Strength of Oak, son of Eamon. I am a freeman. Name the charges. I will not leave until I have answered to the charges."

Everything was turned upside down and inside out. His appeal for justice had become its very opposite: loathsome, rank unfairness. Aiken was one man alone, facing down a hall full of armed men, each of whom were voting for his own self-preservation. Given no chance to defend himself against their denunciations, Aiken became one silenced voice pitted against the other men's fears. And the loudest voices won.

Nevertheless, Aiken screamed, defiantly, "Leofar, I accuse you of Torwald's murder."

"You have slandered a man in good standing," the lawgiver said, sharply. "All the assembled freemen here today have honored Chieftain Leofar the Most Agreeable Leader. For as long as he continues to maintain his goodwill toward us, everything that we can devise will be done to show him the honor he deserves. We offer him gratitude for his service and generosity."

"Look at me, Leofar," Aiken yelled, "and remember me. I promise to challenge you, someday."

"Get this despicable worm out of here," Leofar yowled. "I cannot stand the sight of him. Get him out of here. Punch him in the face. Crush him."

"Next time I see you, I will take you down," Aiken screamed. "I will send your soul to Mother Torment's lowest land of the dead where the oath-breakers dwell. That is your just deserts."

To put an end to their captive's contemptuous display of self-righteous anger, Norton called one of his guardsmen forward. The two men, who were holding Aiken's arms, forcibly stretched them out to the sides and pulled back hard, while the third guard punched Aiken in the gut. That silenced him. Once the air was knocked out of him, Aiken folded at the waist. His knees buckled and, unable to support his own weight, he hung limply by his arms between his persecutors.

The men in the crowd stood by, coldly staring with smug indifference at his expulsion from their midst. By allowing this blatant abuse of what the law stood for, instead of coming to the defense of an innocent man, the men in the hall were hoping to keep the ravenous monster, who stood on the dais, from coming after them instead. In their place, they threw Aiken, like a piece of bloody meat, into the gaping maw of their own fears. To relish the feel of ultimate power, those who otherwise felt so helpless, were protecting the smallness of their self-important pride by excluding the truth-teller from their midst.

Those who stood in the center drew apart just enough to make a narrow path through which Aiken and his captors could pass. Dragged by the arms, Aiken's feet trailed across the hard-packed, earthen floor, as Leofar yelled defiantly, "He should never have been let in the door. Let him creep back under the rock from which he came. No, better yet, crush the worm beneath your heel."

Out in the yard, Chieftain Norton oversaw the beating. His guardsmen punched and kicked Aiken until Norton yelled at them to stop, "Hurt him, I said. Not kill him." Thumbing toward the forested regions beyond the stockade wall, he said, "Let him die out there in the woods."

They picked up Aiken by the arms and legs and carried him through the village as far as the open, outer stockade gates. The men who held him by the limbs swung him back and forth between themselves and, on the count of three, threw him out. He hit the ground hard on his back. Then they tossed out his weaponry. His spear, axe and knife hit the ground with dull, ringing thuds.

Instead of killing him outright, they had seen fit to cast him out beyond the reaches of their kinship. Had they truly believed that he was an imposter, they would have hung him.

But they had not hung him. They had outlawed him and allowed him to keep his weaponry. Aiken figured their actions were an admission that they had known him and had outlawed him, unlawfully.

By decreeing a death by wandering, they had freed themselves from threats of blood vengeance that might, otherwise, be brought against them, sometime in the future. It was against the law for others to take him in, to shelter him, or to show him any form of kindness. He would be shunned from all society, lose all affection and respect. There could be no contact with those who had befriended him in the past. Expulsion from the kinship meant death was inevitable. But because they had not killed him outright, no fellow kinsmen could be accused of Aiken's murder.

He had to get out of there before they changed their minds. Creeping on hands and knees, Aiken grabbed at his weaponry. He sheathed the knife and stuck the axe handle into his belt. He used his spear as a prop to pull himself up. Because the pain was too great to stand upright, or even to catch his breath, he limped down the road, hunched and bleeding and headed toward the small encampment that he had made for himself in the woods.

IX.

Seated before the small fire in the woods, Aiken wrapped his arms around himself and rocked back and forth. He had nowhere to go. There was no one to whom he could turn. He was now fair game to all those who might want to get back at him for any grievances they may have held against him, including simmering resentment over those challenges, which Aiken had won, when he had showed-up each of his opponents as blustering, incompetent fools.

Convinced that, by some quirk of fate, the Matrones and the ruling powers had singled him out for their amusement, he feared they had contrived a means by which to play a cruel prank on him, just to make a point. Though he had abided by the law and done what was expected of him, the glaring truth of his predicament became a clear warning to others: any man who puts himself forward and stands out from the rest of the crowd will be mocked for his arrogant pride.

To avoid this dreadful fate, Aiken had learned, too late, that it was better to remain hidden in the crowd and to fit in with the others. It was better to never ask a question for which there were no ready answers, nor to look too closely when rooting out a threat. It was better to never seek the truth, to never ask why, nor to ask the meaning of the things that he saw happening all around him. For, if such a seeker strove too hard in his search for knowledge, he ventured into the darkest regions where those otherworldly forces would spare no effort in their pursuit to take him down.

If even the ruling powers had formed a united front against him, Aiken felt the chilling terror of being more alone than he had ever been before.

Several days later, Aiken went looking for his mother. He had visited her, occasionally, over the years but had never felt welcome in her home. Her husband, Seaver, had never liked him, and his half-brothers were resentful and unfriendly. Bruised and hurting, Aiken made his way to the village where Maida lived. Unable to get inside the inner stockade, he hung around the market until he saw one of her women.

Shortly afterward, Maida found him at the edge of the woods. She caught at him and, clutching him tightly to her chest, wept for all that had befallen her son.

"Stop. You are hurting me. I am bruised," he said. "I did nothing wrong."

"I know, I know. I am just grateful that you are alive," his mother said, stroking his head.

"What? What did I do? Why do I deserve this?"

Maida begged for understanding. She, too, was helpless to change things in his favor. Her husband, Seaver, was only a single warrior who held a lesser rank. He had no power to sway the chiefdoms. Instead, Seaver had been forced, at the tip of a spear, to swear an oath to the powerful men who had absconded with Torwald's wealth. In defense of her husband's actions, she said, "Naturally, he promised them his unquestioning allegiance. What else could he do? Otherwise, they would have killed him, along with me and our children."

Maida described how Leofar had distributed his uncle's holdings among several of his cousins because Torwald had died without siring any sons. Leofar had made his own brother chieftain of the village where Aiken and she once had made their homes. He married off the widows to his own allies, and kept the bonded men and women for himself, his brothers, and his cousins. He threatened death to those of Torwald's men, who were still alive, unless they swore allegiance to him. Everything had happened very swiftly. Obviously, it had been planned well in advance. Leofar's men had swooped in like a victorious army.

The thought of such despicable men living in his house; of going through his goods; of keeping some things and throwing out others; of feasting at the same tables and of sitting on the same benches and chairs on which he had once sat alongside Alger, threw Aiken into a fit of anguish. He wanted to hit someone hard. But, since he had no one to strike, he took out his anger on the very man who should have seen it coming, the man who should have protected him and offered him guidance. "Torwald. That old fool."

"Aiken, do not blame Torwald. He did what was right. No one suspected his own nephew would turn against him."

"I did."

"Torwald's greatest flaw was his trust in others. He was a wise and judicious man. When he rejected the younger men's proposal, he made the right decision. If we stop paying tribute to the rulers in the western lands it will lead to an all-out war that we cannot win. He trusted the younger men to accept the Assembly's decision. That was the honorable thing to do. But now it is obvious that some of the younger chieftains resent the older men's hold on the Assembly. This is how they plan to challenge the old guard. And since the older men can see how Leofar turned against his uncle, they are afraid of him and are willing to do his bidding."

"You are certain that it was Leofar? And other men know it too? You are certain of that?"

"Yes," Maida said, "and now that everyone knows that Leofar was behind the ambush, they are willing to go along with him, just to keep him off their backs.

"Aiken, I carry the blame for all that has happened to you. If only Eamon had not died—I should never have gone off without you. You were such a clever child. I still have the little duck you carved for me. I cry whenever I see it. Oh, Aiken, you were so sweet. I adored you. I remember how you played with Alger. He was such a simple child. Following you around, the way he did, he obeyed whatever you told him to do. What happened to Alger?"

"Mother, you do not understand, he is dead."

"Oh, Aiken, Alger too?" Hugging herself, she rocked back and forth, barely able to contain her grief. "After Eamon died I should have gone back to my father's house. I should have taken you with me. I should have protected you." She touched his ragged scars and caressed his cheek. "This never would have happened if I had not remarried and left you with Otgar."

"Otgar was good to me."

"Living in Otgar's house was not the same as being raised by your own father and mother. No one looked after you properly. They let you run wild. But after Eamon was gone something died inside of me. I did things I later regretted. Do not hold it against me or think that I did not love you and your father. He was the dearest man I have ever known. I wish I had never remarried."

"Mother, I hold no grudges against you. Believe me."

But whatever has happened in the past is impossible to alter. Her empty regrets meant little when confronted with the heart-rending failure to protect her son from what had happened in the past, and what was happening now. Yes, Aiken had run wild. He had lost his father and, afterwards, because his mother's new husband resented the time she spent with a child another man had sired, she had left him in someone else's care. Nor did Otgar and his wife have time and patience for the small boy who was living in their household. Their own sons were grown, and Aiken's uncle had other things on his mind. From an early age, because no one had truly cared about him, Aiken had been forced to watch out for himself. There had been good reasons to mistrust the grown-ups and to hide from them.

No, there was no way to make up for having left him. There was nothing his mother could do but offer her son a purse full of coins and jewelry and a tied-up rag filled with bread, cheese, and cured meats.

Aiken took the food but refused to take the jewelry. Even though she had abandoned him, he still loved her. After all, she was his mother. Aiken told her that he feared she would become the butt of Seaver's wrath if he ever found out that she had given the jewelry to her outlawed son. When she insisted his needs were greater than hers, he took two silver coins and gave back the rest. Maida pulled her son to her chest, laid her head against his shoulder, pressed her face into his neck, and wept. Aiken held her and smoothed her head and back. He had never seen her so cowed and befuddled. "You are scared. Does Seaver hurt you?"

When Maida refused to answer, Aiken was struck by how powerless he felt to protect even his own mother.

He made her a single promise. He vowed to stay alive, to remain a masterless man, and to be answerable to no one but himself. He swore to get back at the thieving, lying, murdering curs who had outlawed him. He finished by leveling a curse against himself. As with any well-stated oath, he swore that if he were to break his promise, he would send his soul to Mother Torment's lowest land of the dead where the oath-breakers dwell. That was where he would find his enemies. His soul would never rest until he had gotten back at them for what they had done.

Even while living under a sentence of certain death, Aiken made it his ambition to prove the guilt of the chieftains who had been complicit in Torwald's murder and to retaliate against those despicable men who had banded together and threatened him like a pack of wild dogs. That was the only way he could repair his honor and keep his soul safe.

However, and unfortunately, the Matrones seldom heed a man's preferences or his well-laid plans. The threads, they twist, snarl in ways that make the entangled cords impossible to unravel.

It could be said that the situation in which Aiken found himself was like the picture of the deer and the cat that the tattooist's needle had engraved upon his skin. Innocent as the blue deer, he had observed the law, but the law had, in turn, unfairly punished him. And like the blue cat in pursuit of the blue deer, Aiken was perpetually caught in a forward flying leap. Hungering for the pure feelings that truth and justice called to mind, his arms were forever grasping for that innocent deer. But, regrettably, his faith in goodness would remain out of reach, until both the innocent deer and the cat's hunger for justice were consumed by the fire that, in the end, would eat him, flesh, skin, and bone.

Those who had outlawed Aiken had no need to chase him down, to corner him, nor to force him into a trap. After wandering for a while, he forgot his promise and lost ambition. Though he had learnt the name of the man who he needed to challenge, there was no way to get to Leofar.

Aiken had nothing. He had no plan. He had no pride. He had no honor worthy of defense. His attempts to be his own man had failed him.

The beating that Norton's men had given him had left him with more than one broken rib. The pain made it impossible to hunt. At times, his ribs hurt so badly he could barely stand. Time and again he was forced to lean against a tree, just to catch a breath. He had no food and nothing to drink. He refused to return to the men who had taken him in, and to plead with them to feed and shelter him again. He could not humble himself that way and admit to his failure. If he could not make a go of it on his own, it was better to die. He would simply sit down, lean back against a tree, and never get up again.

When the day came to quit his wandering, he set out to find that place in the woods where he could leave his bones beneath a tree's wide-spread canopy. But instead of walking into the center of the forest, he lost his bearings and came to the edge of the woodland. Doing his best to keep out of sight, he skirted a field where several men were sowing a field. Careful to walk without making a sound, Aiken was stepping on his tiptoes. In light of this self-observation, he realized how ashamed he was of the man he had become: a man so fearful of others that he had to sneak and hide.

A ghost of a man whose heart still beat but, otherwise, was dead enough to haunt the living, Aiken stood there a long time, just out of sight, watching the group of farmers. They walked across the plowed field in a straight line. Like dancers synchronizing their movements, they reached into baskets full of seeds and swung their arms in arcs in such an orderly fashion, it was somehow calming just to watch them walk, turn, then walk, then turn again, over and over.

Riveted to the spot, he could not turn away. How did the farmer's ordinary lives keep going from one day to the next? Each of their days were the same as they had always been, whereas nothing in his own life was the same as it had been before. The farmers were unaware of his tragedy. Unaware of everything and everyone whom he had lost. For them, nothing had happened. Their lives had not been cut short the way his had been. How would he ever forget the moment that he had seen those men standing on the river bank and said, "This is where I die."

Peering between the leaves and branches, he remembered how he had felt when he had been a child hiding behind a large storage trunk in his uncle's house. From there he had spied on Otgar and the other men in the warband, who frightened him. He had listened to them tell their tales, plan raids and feasts and hunts. And he had set his sights on being as tough as those big, strong men. Someday, he promised himself, when he was old enough to fight, he would never let another man see him as an easy mark. He would never let anyone see him as an easy take down. He would not be scared. Men would never forget his name. And now they had.

After a while, several women and children appeared. The women were chatting noisily and carrying jugs of ale and baskets filled with food. The boys and girls ran around, chasing each other. The women called to the men and waved their arms in greeting. They laid out the noon-day supper on the edge of the field. The men quit their work and joined them. They joked and laughed and passed the jugs and baskets around, grabbed at the bread, and speared hunks of meat with their knives.

And Aiken was hungry.

That was all he knew. He was hungry. Nor would he be scared. Without giving it another thought, he just walked out of the brush and aimed straight for those men, women, and children, and their food.

When the farmers saw his approach they all stopped talking and stared. One of the men stood up and, picking up his small knife, brandished it as he walked toward Aiken, yelling, "Stop right there. Do not come another step closer."

Aiken lifted his arms out to the sides and held his open palms out to the front to show the man he came in peace. He was surrendering. "I do not want to hurt you. See? I will put down my weaponry right here. I am hungry and thirsty. I want to help with the fieldwork. If you will give me food and something to drink in exchange."

The man told him to wait right there and walked back to the group. Some of the men said they did not like the looks of him, but others were willing to give it a try. The one thing they all agreed upon was that, at this time of year, they were always short-handed. It was early springtime and already they were getting behind with the fieldwork. The men made Aiken disarm before they would give him something to eat. They waved their arms to shoo him away and pointed to a place far enough from where they sat. That was the only way they felt comfortable about having an armed, battle-scarred, monstrous-looking, scavenging stranger, wearing stained and torn clothing in their midst.

After they finished eating, one man handed him a wide, narrow basket full of seeds and showed him how to rest it against his hip and to hang the attached leather strap across his body. "What happened to you? Uhh?" The man said, laughing in Aiken's face, "You probably never sowed seeds before. It is pretty hard. Let me see if you can do it."

No doubt they all felt smug about having an outlawed warrior asking them for a handout. Ready to avenge every slight they had ever suffered at the hands of the chieftain's men, they were eager to kick around someone who had always used rank, prestige and weaponry to tell farmers like them what to do.

After they finished, they moved to another field. They first cleared it of rocks and then seeded that one too. Aiken begged off from lifting the heaviest rocks and found the men were surprisingly accommodating when he described how he had been beaten at the Assembly. Maybe just the knowledge of how badly the chieftains' men had hurt him was enough to encourage a small measure of fellow-feeling for his predicament.

It was not until evening began to settle-in that they called it quits for the day. The man who had brandished his small knife showed Aiken to a storage shed. He pushed the door open and told him to sleep inside. A short time later, another man opened the door a crack. With the same cautious regard that he would have shown a stray dog, he reached in, set a bowl of food on the dirt floor, pushed it forward with his fingertips and slammed the door shut.

That night, when the rain began to puddle inside the shed, Aiken found a dry corner where he could sit with his legs tucked up. Wrapped in his cloak and bedroll, he spent the first night with the things that mattered most to him: a bowl of food and a meager shelter with a leaky roof.

He had nowhere to go, no friends, no kin. His place in the order of things had shifted so drastically beneath his feet, he had no sense of where he stood. He had gone from being a wealthy man-at-arms, and a champion fighter, who had made a good name for himself, to a nameless, ragged wanderer, begging for a bowl of food.

Though the chieftains and their men had done all they could to break him—they had cut him, chased him, and beaten him—they had not gotten to him all the way. So far, he had held them off. He was not dead. Not yet, anyhow. And he intended to stay that way.

That night, after he had gotten enough food in his belly to restore some vague resemblance to his former ambition, he planned to stay in the hamlet only for as long as it took to get his bearings—maybe another day or two. Once he had figured it out, he reckoned he would move on again.

And he would have, too, had it not been for the woman who was soon to become his wife. That night, she, too, had lain awake till dawn, but making other plans for him.

X.

Years later, he was still there, in the same hamlet, sitting on the bench outside Mildred's door. The sky was clearing, leaving a few scattered clouds, and the moon was making its nightly crossing, the same as Aiken had seen it do so many times before.

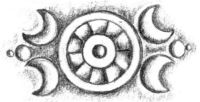

FOUR

ᏟhᎯᏞᏟᎬᎠᎾᏁᏉ

Ᏻf you will protect against night terrors.

Take the stone which is called Chalcedony, which comes from Chalcedon, the port on the Sea of Marmara. It is good against madness and dangerous invasions of fantasy.

The Truth of Rocks, by Alviss the Wise

I.

Last night, when I was visiting with Grerr in his garden, he pointed out a curious kind of insect that has turned itself into a walking stick. By copying the trees in which it lives, the color of its carapace and its long, thin shape so perfectly match its surroundings that I was easily fooled by its disguise. It was only when I noticed that the twig, at which I was looking, had six legs that I spotted the singular flaw in its concealment.

"Now, Dvalinn," said Grerr, "tell the walking stick that you are lost, and ask it to point out the direction you should take to get back home."

Though I gave Grerr a querulous look, I did as he directed. And, sure enough, the clever little creature lifted its right, front leg and pointed its finger toward the tunnel opening through which I had come.

On my way back home, I continued to think about additional examples of mimicry, which Nature has contrived, besides the walking stick's disguise. The first, which came to mind, was a mother deer's collaboration with Nature. By giving birth to a fawn who is covered with spots that mimic the surrounding foliage's play of shadow and light, her baby can hide in plain sight wherever it lies resting.

Another example that comes to mind is a type of crab, who is known to decorate its shell with debris it scrounges from the sea floor. When finished dressing, the little creature becomes so at-one with its surroundings, it is almost impossible to spot. How this obsessive little crab manages to pick each item, when there are so many things from which to choose, I do not know but can easily sympathize with its dilemma.

An aggressive, rather than a passive disguise, which moths and butterflies commonly share, is meant to stand out rather than to disappear amidst the surrounding background. Through advantageous use of its wing's symmetry, the insect copies the eyes of a moth-hunter's own worst enemy to design a costume that resembles an animal face. To mimic the eyes' sparkling glints of reflected light, the moth has given the two eye-spots additional touches of realism by crossing each of the two, central, concentric circles with a narrow, white, diagonal line. This disguise turns the moth into what appears to be a predatory animal scary enough to frighten the small, unsuspecting birds who might, otherwise, want to eat it.

I have, also, heard of a plant that came up with a particularly unique manner of

fitting into its landscape. Growing in a hot and arid land, where few bees and butterflies make their home but, rather, where there is a plethora of flies, the plant has made
its flower look and stink like rotten carrion. The large, five-petaled, star-shaped flower
is buff colored, textured with red squiggly lines, and is covered sparsely with red hairs.
To a man like me, the blossom is not particularly attractive, but to a fly the bloom
must be quite appealing.

Somehow, this plant has made for itself a deception that takes advantage of the
insects, which are found most abundantly within its environs. The flower's uncanny
aptitude for copying carrion, right down to the color and stink of its blossoms, en-
tices the flies to lay their eggs upon the blooming imitation. The maggots then crawl
around on its petals and do whatever the flower has tricked them into doing to ensure
its own survival.

How the stinky plant or the walking stick have managed to dream up these new
realities by mimicking the natural world in which they live remains unproven. But,
however it came about, the plant, the deer, the crab, the moth, and the insect have
devised clever solutions to the problems they faced when living in, otherwise, inhospi-
table places.

Though each are successful in their knack for mimicry, there is a singular draw-
back to these imitations. Once the plant has reached its most exquisite perfection
of likeness to its surroundings, its blossom will forever mimic carrion; the moth will
always bear an image of two eyes upon its wings; the insect is trapped in its imitation
of a stick; and the little crab will forever obsess over the decorations it adds to its shell.

None can remove the costume and the mask they devised. Somehow, the time
of shapeless malleability, when anything was possible, has come to an end. There
were limits to the natural powers that had granted the moth, the plant, and the crab
their wishes to become whatever they wanted to be. To put it simply: their progeny
have no choice. Their descendants must live forever in the landscapes in which their
disguises are best suited. By and large, the plants and creatures are born without the
options that men and women have been granted, which allow them to create their
own costumes and masks. In this respect, humans differ from Nature's myriad of
plants, animals, insects, birds, and fishes.

Unlike the creatures, who are born with their disguises intact, men and women
are born naked. Though they have inherited little from their ancestors with which to
disguise themselves, it is men and women to whom Nature has given the most freedom to participate in their own creation.

Nature has endowed humans with a unique inner resourcefulness. Their talent
for calling to mind memories of what they have done and seen in the past, makes men
and women different from all other creatures. This endowment of memory empowers
a man or a woman to see something with their mind's eye and to give it substance by
copying Nature's patterns, shapes, and colors. It is from this interior knowledge that
men and women draw when they imagine something that has never been seen nor
done before. By picturing an image in their mind's eye, men and women can then set
out to make real whatever they imagine.

In this way, because they were born lacking fur, they have created clothing. Because they were unable to swim like a fish, they have made boats. Because they were born without the shelter, which clams, turtles, crabs, and snails were born with, they have made houses. And, unlike a bird who knows only one architectural design for building its nest, people have built their houses in all shapes and sizes. Furthermore, because men and women lack the teeth, claws, talons, and beaks with which to hunt and fight, they have invented spears, arrows, and knives, all of which look, disarmingly, like elaborate copies of pointy teeth, claws, talons, and beaks.

Once a man or woman's mind has unleashed this power of inventiveness, they are set apart from those creatures who are born repeating whatever their ancestors devised. Though other creatures have tapped into Nature's imagination, a man or woman is unlike the others, for their abilities are far-ranging and nearly unlimited.

To reshape the world according to whatever can be imagined is the force that has driven humankind's successful survival in this world. Over time, people have traversed the earth. And in each place they have chosen to live, whether it was a desert, a forest, or the grasslands, they have ensured their survival by changing the way they do things.

In this way, a man or a woman may call upon the same ingenious power of mimicry that runs rampant throughout Nature's creation. The urge to copy Nature, and to give additional depth and meaning to whatever they create, is so compelling that nothing a man or woman makes or builds will be designed without elaborate decoration. A man or woman cannot help but copy the things they remember they saw in their environs.

And likewise, because a man may, also, make-up a story, and give it whatever meaning strikes his fancy, I have chosen two of stones that are laying here on my table to see what kind of scenario I can come up with. The first is an unevenly shaped, pale blue shard, and the second is a misshapen, circular, white one.

If Nature were to cup these two stones in the palm of her hand and to offer them up for my inspection, she might ask, "What can you make of these?"

And if I were to pluck the stones from Nature's palm and to hold them in the lamplight, after I have turned them this way and that, I might answer, "This stone resembles an artist's rendering of a cloud that was painted with a watery blue pigment."

"And what do you make of the other one?" Nature would ask.

"I see in the translucent, white one, a lustrous quality that is reminiscent of the moon."

Under the pretense that it is nighttime and everything in this small, moonlit world lies in partial shadow, I playfully move the pretend cloud from left to right. It slowly covers the pretend moon and becomes brilliantly backlit in the process. And as the cloud's soft and wispy trailing threads slowly drift along, the moon's full contour becomes slowly visible again.

After the imitation cloud has moved into the distance, I lay it down upon my desk. I lift the crystal ball to one eye and pretend the lens is a seaman's looking glass. With childlike glee, I scan the distant horizon and see a man seated upon a bench in front of a house.

For as long as the women were telling stories that night, he would not be going back inside his house anytime soon. He pulled his cloak more tightly around himself, tucked his hands beneath his arms and leant back against the wall. He reminded himself that he had the night watch and, if he intended to keep the bogman away, would need to stay alert.

Across the common yard, a door opened. A long block of light was shed on the ground by the blazing hearth inside the house. A woman stepped out and went around the corner. A short time later, she returned from her errand and went back inside. She closed the door and the yard went dark.

An owl hooted, a stick cracked. There was a rustle. In the distance wolves began to howl. He heard Plodder lowing and commiserated with his oxen. They were as wary of sleep as he was, now that wolves were howling out in the hills. Along with the approach of Wolf's Month, he and the other farmers were more protective of their sheep and cattle and kept them in close to their homes. Back in the day when he had had an eye for high-spirited stallions, he would never have given more than a passing thought to a team of oxen. But these days, he was more protective of Plodder and Smart-one than he had ever been of his horses. And just the thought of his oxen naturally led to reminiscences of Harald.

It was Mildred's father who had taught him everything he knew about a well-trained team of draft animals. He sure did miss the old man. As hard as it was to believe that a sickly old farmer could have understood a young fighting man, who had been in the prime of his life until he was hurt, Harald was the only one who had truly known him. Harald understood pain. He understood how it felt to be unable to do the things that you had done so well before. He understood how it felt to have those men and women, whom you had trusted and truly cared about, turn their backs on you.

Though Harald no longer sat on this bench, spreading goodness, it still offered a kind of solace only he could have given Aiken. Now aglow in the moonlight with a faint, blue-black luster, this bench was worn smooth and shiny by folks who had rested here over the years. Aiken took off his glove and, rubbing his bare hand over the planks hewed from a maple tree, he felt the grain's subtly raised lines.

He never sat where Harald used to sit, though other people did. Whenever he saw someone sitting there, even Sunniva or Bertolf, who did not know any better because they had been born after Harald's death, he had to stop himself from shooing them away, saying, "That is Harald's spot. I keep it open for him." But unlike Alger, Harald never came for a visit.

After his arrival in Harald and Mildred's hamlet, this bench was the place where he had sat each day to await his daily handout. Looking back upon that time, he recalled just how aimless he had been. Broken, hungry, and gaunt, he was almost frail. He had been so thin his bones' contours could be seen beneath his skin.

He held his hands close to his face. They were steadier now, most of the time, anyhow. And thanks to Mildred he was no longer hungry. She was always shoving food in his direction, always feeding him, and always asking whether he wanted more to eat.

Even the first time he had seen her, she was bringing him a bowl of food. Coming straight at him, hitting the hard-packed dirt with her heels, if she had been carrying a stick he would have turned and run. That was how determined she looked. Without ever halting, not even once to pass the time of day with anyone else whose path she crossed, Mildred came right up to him, pushed the bowl and a piece of bread into his hands, and asked, "What is your name?"

"Aiken."

"All right, Aiken," she said, "My name is Mildred." She pointed to the bowl. "I ladled an extra spoonful of my good, rich gravy over the stewed meat. I am sure that you will like it."

He looked at the food and then at her, and said, "I am sure I will, Mildred."

After they stared uncomfortably at each other for what seemed like a very long time, she pointed to the bench outside her house. She told him to bring the bowl back in the morning. If he wanted to start the day off right, she would give him a bowl of gruel with an egg cracked into it, along with a bit of bread and meat.

"Yes, yes, I will do that," he said.

"Well then, you do that," she said, turned and walked away.

The following morning, Aiken dragged his feet to her door, hunched down on the bench, set the empty bowl beside himself and waited. Still in the daze brought on by hunger, pain, and lack of sleep, he questioned how he had come to be there at all. His memory was vague about the details. Too dull-witted to think it through, he only knew one thing: that he had somehow lost his bearings and ended up in this small hamlet where everyone but him was kin.

Weary and broken, he felt as numb as an arm or a leg that has gone to sleep. He felt so chilled, even the hottest fire could not have driven away the cold. Yet, some-how, he was still alive. Desperate to conceal the shameful weakness he recognized within himself, he feared the men in the hamlet would see him as he saw himself—a deeply flawed man. If he could not work because the pain in his side was too great, or could not stop the trembling in his hands, they would find him lacking. Then they, too, would beat him and chase him away, just like the chieftain's men had done. If he was forced to wander off again, he would head for that tree in the woods and give in to its beckoning offer to leave his bones in everlasting slumber beneath its canopy.

Mildred opened the door and handed him the bowl of gruel. She had not changed her mind overnight, as he feared she might. No, in fact she had cracked an egg into it, just as she had said she would. After he had become a danger to anyone to whom he came too close, when not even his own mother would offer him shelter, here was a stranger, and a woman at that, who was kind enough to feed him. He was so grateful, he nearly cried.

When she handed him the piece of bread, spread with butter and topped with a chunk of cured meat, their fingers touched briefly. Thankful for even that small contact with womanly warmth, Aiken remembered it fondly throughout the rest of the day.

Whenever the men asked for help, Aiken stepped up and did whatever he could, given the pain he was in. And they, in turn, avoided speaking with him, or even looking at him directly. If they could have, they would have pretended he was not there at all. He was a nameless outsider, an invisible nobody who had come from out of nowhere, hardly worth the trouble.

That evening, after his work was done for the day, Aiken found Mildred's father, Harald, seated on the bench. Aiken dipped his head in greeting and sat beside him.

Staring straight ahead at nothing, Aiken asked, "Do you, do you mind, if I—," but the rest of the words failed him. Aiken balled-up his fists and squeezed so tightly his knuckles turned white. He dared not let on about this weakness—not if he wanted to stay alive—and he thought he did—want to stay alive, that is—but was uncertain even of that much, just then. He waited until words sufficient enough to get across his meaning came to him. "If my hands get restless," he said, opening his fingers and clenching again, "Alger gets annoyed."

Harald said, "A man never needs an excuse for the work he does," and asked, "Who is Alger?"

"A friend," Aiken said. He bowed his head, unsheathed his whittling knife, unfastened his whetstone from his belt, and began to sharpen the blade. He then picked up the scrap of wood he had found, earlier in the day, and began to make the first cuts.

"You have good hands. What are you making?"

When Aiken replied with nothing more than a shoulder shrug, Harald understood that he would need to carry on both sides of the conversation himself. "You must think me lazy," he began. "But believe me when I tell you this: it is not my nature to sit all day. When I was young, I even worked in the quarry for a time. But after I worked so hard all my life, my knees gave out, and I was forced to walk with a stick. Then this misery came upon me next. Now my hands have stiffened-up so badly, I cannot hold the stick. I can hardly hold a cup or spoon to feed myself. Instead, I sit and tend the fire. The warmth eases the pain in my joints."

Harald described the horror of watching, over a span of several months, his fingers twist into the shapes of claws. Now that he was confined to the house, he missed being included in activities he had once been a part of and complained bitterly about his helplessness.

"Would you believe that I was once the headman of this hamlet? And now all I do is sit and stare at the folks coming and going across the common yard." And though he understood that men were too busy to stop and pass the time of day—or he tried to understand, anyhow—he felt forgotten and covered his grievances, poorly.

After brooding silently for a while, he perked up, and said, "Aiken, tell you what. You can be my eyes and ears. You can tell me what you see and hear when you are working in the fields and helping the men with their chores. Mildred gossips about the women, but you can tell me what the men are up to."

Aiken shook his head and muttered, "No, no, no." Though stumbling and grasping for whatever words he could muster, the attempt had failed him. Worrying him further, he questioned whether he would ever speak a complete thought again. Not only had he lost an eye, his family, his home, his standing, and his strength, he had lost everything inside himself as well, everything that made him him.

Here he was, seated alongside a kindly old man, in this peaceful hamlet, surrounded by folks who simply did their chores each day, yet all he could see were men's bodies, turned to bones and haggard flesh, hanging from ropes and twisting in the wind, clothed only in the remaining sun-bleached fragments of what they had worn the day they were killed. Aiken wanted to weep.

"Take your time, son," Harald said, patting Aiken's knee. "You were badly hurt. I can see that much." And, with astonishing awareness of Aiken's tongue-tied predicament, he added, "The words come back in time. I know."

"You do?"

"Yes, I fought too, and I got hurt. I know it takes time to heal."

To hear a man speak in such a kindly fashion, Aiken's throat tightened so much he thought he might choke. Here he was, seated on the bench, facing the common yard, where everyone could see him. So scared of the dangerous storm-clouds raging deep inside him, he dreaded what might happen if he were to let his guard down, for even a single moment. For, if he did, if the threatened unstoppable torrent was unleashed, he would be exposed as a weak and weeping no-good failure of a man. And then the men who lived in the hamlet would beat him and chase him away, just like Norton's men had done.

Everything seemed so pointless. Aiken hunched down and looked in the direction of his feet. Still clutching the block of wood in one hand and the small knife in the other, he crossed his arms at the wrists, pressed them tightly into his lower belly at the level of his hips, and rocked back and forth.

In time, he shook his head side to side, and said, "It all went wrong. I tried to warn them." Looking up at Harald, he added, "But no one listened. You see? It does no good to talk. If what I say gets anyone in trouble, they will beat me again. If they do, it will kill me."

He stopped rocking, pulled himself together, dropped his arms to his sides, and after he had sat there for a while, forcefully dug his knife into the chunk of wood and shaved off a long piece. He shaved another. And then another, another, and another, until he had shaved the entire chunk down to nothing. He threw the last sliver on the ground, stood up, walked away, and did without supper that night.

The next day, by the time evening had rolled around, Aiken was so hungry he had no choice but to join Harald on the bench. Not if he wanted to eat Mildred's food, that is.

And sure enough, as soon as Harald saw Aiken coming toward him, he asked, pointedly, "How was your day?"

When Aiken sat down and answered with nothing more than an unenthusiastic shoulder shrug, Harald let Aiken know that his weak excuse for lack of speech was unacceptable. If Aiken intended to share the bench, Harald demanded he talk.

Since most folks either turned away or stared past him whenever they saw Aiken's ruined face, the sight of Harald's warm, inviting smile, persuaded Aiken to be more convivial. He took his time. Talking slowly, though he stumbled over his words and stuttered, he described what he and the other men had done that day. Though their chores had seemed insignificant, at least to a former fighting man, even that bit of gossip was enough to satisfy Aiken's new bench mate. Besides, there was something comforting about these ordinary, but purposeful daily tasks. To gaze at a newly seeded field at the end of the day had offered him a sense of accomplishment he had never known before. It settled him.

From then on, Aiken found Mildred's father seated on the bench outside his house each evening to welcome him. Eager to hear about Aiken's day, Harald praised the work he did. Over time, the delight that Aiken saw in his new friend's face whenever he told a good story encouraged him to speak more boldly. He began to look forward to each evening when he could sit alongside Harald and talk about his day. He asked Harald about the crops they grew and where all those rocks came from. Did they grow over the winter from little pebbles, he wanted to know, and Harald always answered his questions as well as he could. "Well, that is hard to say," Harald said. "I only know that there are always more stones in the field in the springtime than there were the previous autumn."

Compared to the life and death struggles Aiken had dealt with all his life, there was something pleasingly substantial about picking rocks out of a field, sowing seeds, chopping wood, clearing stumps, and digging and filling holes. And then, the next day he and the other men started all over again to pick more rocks out of the fields, sow seeds, chop wood, fill holes, and the next day to do the same. The repetition was comforting. Routine became his refuge, Harald and Mildred his sanctuary.

To keep himself from getting tongue-tied or stumbling over the words too badly, he practiced telling himself a story while he was working. And, over time, he increasingly embellished his tales with his own wry observations. To make Harald laugh, he imitated the other men's speech and exaggerated their descriptions.

"Here, I have one for you Harald. You know that man—Otto? Well, today he spent half the morning inspecting the holes in the ox-road. And headman Lyn, he told some of the men to fill them. I helped."

"Glad to hear he is keeping up the road. Good roads are important. If the holes get too deep a man can twist an ankle or break his cart wheels."

"Well, he, Lyn, that is, assigned the work. We did a good job of it. Leastways, I think we did. I never filled holes before. Where I come from, the bonded men do it. Anyhow, Otto got ahold of the headman's elbow, and he would not let him go. Otto walked around with Lyn and pointed out each hole. None were done right, he said. He found fault with each and every hole and explained how the men should fill it better. When one of the men, with whom I was working, saw them coming, I heard him say, 'What is Otto doing here? If he is working with us, I am leaving.'

"I know Otto wanted Lyn to say, 'Otto, you are so clever about filling holes, I will put you in charge of the road up-keep.' Instead, the headman looked like he was hurting badly because he could not shake Otto's grip. If that know-it-all, Otto, started to work alongside the other men, Headman Lyn knew that each and every one of them would come up with an excuse and walk off. After that, Otto would be left to do it alone. Then he would complain because no one else was helping. It would never get done that way. Not if he was in charge. He just angers men. He does not understand that the more he tells folks what he knows, the less anyone wants to be around him."

Harald nodded his head. "Hey, hey, son, you got that right." And his twisted fingers poked Aiken in the knee as he said, "That is Otto. I heard that about him before. He is peculiar."

So, there they were, two outsiders, Harald and Aiken, both in pain, sharing the simplest, most commonplace stories, gossiping about the foolish men who had chosen to ignore them.

How simple his life had become. When he helped the men with their fieldwork, he struggled silently to hide the sharp pains in his side each time he took a breath or moved. And every evening he told Harald about his day, ate supper on the bench, and fell onto a pile of straw to await a sleep, which never came. Then each morning he rose again and sat on the bench to await his daily hand-out.

One evening, after the rain had been coming down by the bucketsful all day and still was coming down hard as evening was settling in, Aiken was seated on the bench, alone, soaking wet and shivering, awaiting his daily hand-out. And Harald was, apparently, sitting inside the house missing Aiken's manly company.

When Mildred came to the door, instead of handing him a bowl, as she usually did, she said, "Harald says you should come inside."

Shy about walking into their house, Aiken closed the door and stood there. Unable to recall ever having been inside a farmer's house before, he thought to himself: So, this is how they live. In contrast to the longhouses, in which he had lived his entire life, it was small and built in the shape of a square. The furnishings were inelegant. There were two narrow beds, a table near the central hearth and another narrow one pushed up against the wall, a few shelves, some wooden storage boxes, two benches, and a couple stools.

After he had been living outdoors for so long, it felt cramped inside. The space was too tight. The walls were too close. The roof was too low. The air was too smoky.

"I will get more wood," he said and turned to go outside again, where he could have more open space around him.

"There is plenty of wood," Mildred said curtly, "Harald does not want you to eat outside. He wants to talk with you." She pointed to the bench near the hearth and said, "Sit there and dry yourself out."

Mildred was acting like Aiken was a stranger whom she had never before laid eyes upon. She looked him up and down, clucked her tongue, shook her head, and mumbled beneath her breath, "This will never do."

She walked over to one of the storage trunks, lifted the lid and dug around until she found a tunic and a pair of Harald's trousers, lying neatly folded near the bottom. She handed them to Aiken, and said, "You are so wet you could catch the death of a cold," and insisted he change before she would let him eat.

Well, that was a kindly thing to say. Evidently, there was one other person in this world, besides Harald, who did not want to see him dead. Aiken walked over to a corner, turned his back and, huddling in the shadows, changed his clothing. When Mildred saw him walking toward the door, carrying his dripping wet clothes, and trailing muddy water across her well-swept, earthen floor and fur rugs, she told him to leave them near the wood pile. She would try to clean and mend them later. But if they were too far gone, she would tear them into rags. He could keep the clothing she had given him.

Mildred finished her supper preparations and invited Aiken to sit at the table. After she served the men, she sat on a stool at the end. Throughout the meal, although she kept her eyes down, as was proper for an unmarried woman, now and then Aiken caught sight of her peeking up at him.

When he told her that her pickled roots were the best tasting he had ever eaten, she smiled so broadly, and with such kindly eyes, he took her reaction to mean that he had not lost his touch with women, entirely. To know that, given a face as ugly as his was, he could still make a woman smile, encouraged him to do whatever he could do to make her look happy like that again.

At the end of the evening, that lingering desire to see Mildred smile led Aiken to offer to help her with the chores the following morning. He told her that the work he did would be in exchange for the food she gave him and her offer to clean and mend his clothes. "I will do whatever you tell me. I can chop wood, carry water, or work in your garden."

On his way out the door, he stopped, looked back over his shoulder, and said, "I am especially good at butchering hogs." Well, the unspoken truth was that he had never chopped much wood, carried water, or planted or weeded crops. The bonded men did that. But he did know how to skin and cut up wild game.

After that first supper, Aiken was invited to join them every evening. Sometimes, Aiken fed the old man because Harald's painfully curled fingers could not pick up or grasp a spoon. Lifting a cup to Harald's lips, Aiken was mildly surprised by the contrast, he observed, between the man he had been before, and the man he was becoming. Back when he had been one of Torwald's men, to have fed an old farmer would have been beneath his dignity. But here he was, seated in a small house in some out-of-the-way hamlet, feeding Harald. Occasionally, Aiken was asked to dress him and to help him in ways that a woman should never have to help a man. Yet the more he did for Harald, the more attached he became to the man.

After supper, when they sat together near the hearth, Aiken was seldom without his whittling knife and a chunk of wood. Back when he had been a boy, whenever he was idle, he would sharpen his blade and pick up a scrap of wood. Mostly, he had made toy horses, cows, and wooden knives. But if he saw an attractive design on one of the women's brooches, or on a man's belt buckle, he would make a copy using the technique called chip-carving. As he grew older, it became second nature for Aiken to make spoons with funny looking heads on the handles, combs, and other small ornaments that he could decorate with those same clever, chip-carved designs worked into the wood.

Before he left their house for the night, Aiken waited until Mildred had turned her back, then he would set the little things that he had made on her table. The next day, when she appeared to be surprised and questioned him about the little carvings, he pretended to know nothing about them. Instead, he suggested the spoon or figure had been a secret gift from the hidden folk.

Mildred, however, refused to play along or to smile. Instead, she demanded he admit to having carved the little items. But each time Mildred insisted that Aiken own up to making them, he dug in and increasingly enjoyed poking fun at her.

One day, after Mildred had been acting broody for several days, Aiken asked whether she felt unwell. When she replied sharply that she felt just fine, he asked, "Well, then, is something worrying you?"

Apparently, that was the moment she had been waiting for. "Aiken, I am worried about you. You pretend not to have made the things you gave me, but I saw you carve them. What do you take me for? A fool? I know you better than that. I worry because you do not take your talents seriously enough. But I can see, in your skillful carving, an ability to make bowls, cups and spinning whorls on an old wood-turning lathe that is sitting unused in one of the storage sheds."

Obviously, Mildred had thought the matter through. But the sudden news was a shock to Aiken. They walked to the shed, she pulled off the tarp, and he, in turn, unenthusiastically looked over the old turning lathe.

"I guess I could repair it and make it work," he told her. "But after that, I would need to get the tools and to learn how to cut a chunk of spinning wood. That, is the hard part. Turning bowls is not like whittling a scrap I pulled out of the wood pile. Turning on a lathe is no idle pastime that I pick up after my work is done for the day. It is the work. It will take time and practice before I can master the skills. Nor can I do it without the tools. Just cover it up and forget about it."

But her silent answer to that suggestion was a look so drastic that Aiken was reminded of the day he had seen her coming straight at him in the common yard. And, likewise, her cold, hard eyes were convincing proof of her determination.

"All right then," he said, "I will see what I can do."

The rotating part of the lathe was built into a wooden frame similar to a narrow table standing about waist high. Above the frame, a long, thin pole, made from a sapling, extended across its entire length. One end of the pole was fastened to the rafters overhead and the free end was knotted with a rope. The other end of the rope was tied to the treadle beneath the frame. The rope was frayed, chewed apart by mice, most likely, and would need to be replaced.

Aiken told Mildred that by attaching the pole to the frame it could be moved outside. He had seen men use machines like these in the markets. By moving the pedal up and down with his foot, the wood-turner pulled the cord that was wrapped around the spindle onto which the piece of wood, which was being turned, was stuck between two iron spikes.

There was still a piece of wood there, set crossways between the two rusty spikes. Pumping the treadle, Aiken rested his wrists on a long, lengthwise plank to show Mildred how the wood turner would hold a chisel against the spinning wood and cut on the down-stroke. When he lifted his foot, the spring in the pole returned the treadle to the raised position to make it ready for his foot's next down-stroke. It was a clever machine. This pole, though, was dry and had no spring in it. It would need to be replaced.

When a man worked with a sharp tool pressed against a spinning target, it was important to keep his hands steady, he told her. But he neglected to confess to the inherent weakness that accompanied his partial blindness. It would be hard to judge the exact connection between the tool and the spinning wood. When everything looked flattened out, it was hard to judge where something started, and the other thing left off. He doubted whether he could do it.

Besides, he had begun to fear sharp tools and weaponry. They made him cringe. One stray chip or sharp tool striking him in his good eye would turn his entire world dark forever. Never before had he feared being hurt this way. But now he did. Never before had he experienced fear with such gut-wrenching acuity. It was no good. He wanted to be rid of it. But this fear stopped him dead in his tracks and made him feel like he was bound with ropes.

He wanted to throw the tarp over the lathe, to turn his back on it, to walk away, and to be done with it for good. But Mildred was standing beside him on his right. And on his left a pile of rubbish blocked his path. To get past Mildred on the right, he would need to shove her aside and to take off running. Cornered, Aiken had no choice but to explain how, if the turner lost control, the tool could slip, fly off and strike either him or someone who was standing nearby. Maybe that was what had happened to the wood-turner, and maybe that was why he had never finished turning the bowl.

Mildred stepped behind Aiken's back, laid one hand upon his shoulder, and said, "You must be careful, Aiken. I do not want you to get hurt."

Was she giving him permission to cover the lathe and to walk away? Did he take her up on the offer?

No. The way that Mildred had stepped behind his back and touched him made him feel protective—not of himself but of her. Though his ribs were still on the mend, and he was often short of breath, felt weak and tired, Mildred's touch upon his shoulder made him feel strong—strong in a way that he had not felt for a long time. Not since the morning of the day when he had fallen on the bank of the Warring River. He wished that Mildred would never move her hand. She could keep it there forever.

Uncle Otgar had never let him make excuses for a weakness or a failure. Aiken had outwitted his fears and overcome his weaknesses before. Maybe, he could teach himself to rely upon the feel of the wood beneath the cutting tool and, simultaneously, overcome his fear. "Mildred," he said, to her as much as to himself, "if I can handle a heavy long-knife with precision, surely, I can handle a small chisel."

Aiken removed the partially turned bowl and handed it to Mildred. "Burn it. The wood you cut on a turning lathe must be green. I know that much, at least."

He asked her to look around and to see whether she could find a chisel. They both searched but were unable to find any tools. Anything made of iron was too valuable to leave in a storage shed. The iron would have been melted down by now and put to other uses. Or, if it was still here, it would have turned to rust by now and been useless.

Returning to his study of the simple mechanism, Aiken pumped the treadle to watch its moving parts. When the rope broke, he crouched down, cut it loose, and held the dangling length out to Mildred. "I will need another rope. Can you get me one?"

He was sitting on his heels, picking at the knot with the tip of his knife and cutting through the tag-end where it was attached to the foot peddle. Mildred was standing beside him, praising his dexterity and cleverness with tools and mechanical things, when somehow, whatever she said just naturally led her to tell Aiken that she wanted an oxcart for her morning-after gift so they could take the things he made to market.

The day was full of surprises. At first Aiken was unsure whether he had heard her right. Had she just proposed they marry? He stopped, looked up at her from his hunched position, and said, "Did you just say you want a morning-after gift?"

She shrugged her shoulders and nodded bashfully.

"I thought that was what you said. Might you not be getting ahead of yourself?"

Aiken had been living day to day. He had given no thought to the future. He may have wanted to keep Mildred close, for the time being, anyhow, but had not followed through on that line of thinking. He had gone no further than a plan to fix the lathe for the simple purpose of making Mildred smile. He had not planned to stay here, in her hamlet. To settle down with Mildred had never crossed his mind. Not even once.

"Then you will need to find another man. I cannot give you an oxcart. I have nothing to offer Harald in the way of bride-price and no means to support a wife. I have no fields to work and no cattle. I have nothing. Nothing. I lost everything I ever owned. I have no kin. People—my people that is—claim that I am dead. I have not even got a name. They took even that from me."

"But, Aiken, it will not always be that way."

He stood up and looked at her in the eye. He wished he could have been the man she saw standing there before her. He truly did. But she was sadly mistaken. "Answer me this: how could I give you an oxcart? Now who is acting like a simpleton? To suggest we marry is just plain foolish."

"Aiken, I cannot be so easily put off. Everyone in the hamlet talks about the way we spend so much time together. According to the gossips, apparently, we spend too much time together. If it goes on like this much longer things will appear unseemly." And that would never do. Mildred would never allow suggestions of unseemliness to tarnish her well-regarded reputation.

Aiken shook his head in wonderment. All this time, he had thought of Mildred like a sister, the sister he had never had. He had thought of Harald like another father, a third father to make up for those whom he had lost, both his real father, and the uncle who had been the next best thing. Somehow, without drawing the connections, he had fancied Mildred and Harald as a second family. For a man who prided himself on being ever-watchful, he had foolishly misread the signs and had come to believe in a fanciful delusion. Up until then, things had been so simple. From one day to the next, he had done whatever Mildred told him to do, without giving a second thought to what came next. And this was it. Marriage came next.

Now that Mildred had spoken her mind, it was impossible to return to the way things had been before. Her suggestion had just changed everything in regard to how they stood with one another. He could no longer pretend to be the younger brother who liked to poke fun at his older sister whenever she chided him and told him what to do. Whatever was he thinking? He and Mildred were not brother and sister. He was an unmarried man and she was an unmarried woman. To any observant outsider, most of the time they acted like husband and wife, except for one thing.

Admittedly, Mildred had a point. He could hardly eat at her table, indefinitely, without making his intentions known. But what were his intentions? She was no serving girl. As much as he had liked the feel of Mildred's hand upon his shoulder, he could not coerce her into bringing him his ale and crawling into his bed when the night was over, and then, the following evening, ignore her in favor of another woman's charms. How could he? He did not even own a bed. If he wanted to stick around, he would need to dispense with those old habits.

He would need to start acting like other people did. Though his world had come to a halt, and his uncertain future held no meaning, other people's lives moved on with foreseeable results. Other people fell asleep at night and woke up in the morning. Other people married, slept together, and raised children—together. They grew older, and their children married and had children. Time never stops, not even for an aimless man.

He knew that no chieftain would ever take him into his warband. His fighting life was over. He could never return to the way things had been before. He would never have his old life back again.

No, Mildred had given him little choice. It was summertime now, but winter was soon to follow. If he took the easy way out and simply walked away, he would, no doubt, die of cold and hunger. This was all there was. This was it.

III.

A burst of shrill laughter came from the other side of the wall against which Aiken was leaning. Shaken from his reverie, he sat up, looked around and leaned back again. He pulled the cloak around himself more tightly and thought over what had happened after they had gotten through that long, awkward day. Mildred was right when she had said, "It will not always be this way."

After he had replaced the old pole with a sapling, sharpened and polished the rusty spikes, greased the hole inside of which the iron spindle rotated, and tied a new rope to the pole and treadle, he was hardly clear of all the difficulties he faced.

Before he could begin to turn bowls, the little building, which was to become his workshop, was stuffed with broken-down rubbish that needed to be hauled away or burned. Drifts of mouse droppings were piled in the corners. The thatched roof needed to be patched, and the spaces between the wall planks needed to be chinked with moss. But before he could do that, the moss needed to be collected from the forest floor and fresh thatching materials needed to be cut. He did not even know how to repair a thatched roof. Though Harald said he would teach him, everything that Aiken did felt so hard. Everything was so much trouble. All those tasks had been done by the servants. He had seldom chopped and stacked wood, or thought about a leaky roof, or questioned whether there were holes in the walls, or the hay needed to be stacked, or trees needed to be felled and hewed, or the hogs butchered, and their meat salted and smoked, or a field cleared of overgrown brush. No, he wanted to say, let the servants do it.

He wanted his old life back again. He wanted to sit down to a meal with Alger and his chieftain. He wanted to jump on a horse and to ride away, to chase down a deer and to celebrate the hunt in the meadhall. He wanted to play a game with Alger, to listen to the poets sing their praise songs, and to be honored for his service with gold and treasure. He wanted a serving girl to fill his cup with mead, to bring him bread and cheese and meat, and to crawl into his bed at the end of the night and to please him, with none of the attendant responsibilities a wife entailed.

Instead, he had nothing. But then, he remembered there was Mildred. But whenever Aiken looked at her, and wanted to lay abed with her, she insisted they marry first. Unlike the serving girls, whom he had easily coerced, when Mildred refused his affection, she became impossibly cold and distant. If he had used his strength to force himself upon her, her brothers would have turned him out of the hamlet.

There was nowhere else to go, but if he continued to live here, he would be buried alive in meaningless tasks. The only way to make a go of it was by turning bowls. His life depended upon a lathe-turned bowl.

Where was the honor in that? Where was the proof of his valor? After he had figured out how to turn a bowl, even after he had been brutally robbed of half his sight, no chieftain's wife would offer him the cup and praise his lathe-turned bowl. Where were the poets who sang praise songs about a wood-turner who had deftly attacked a block of spinning wood with a chisel?

He did not even own a chisel. Though Mildred had promised to get him one, somehow, after he had the chisel in hand, but before he could use it, he would need to go into the forest to cut fresh wood. Forced to do these ordinary tasks alone, his shameful destitution reminded him of the humiliation he had felt that day when he had stood in his cousin's meadhall, and then again at the Assembly, and Gordon had claimed to never before have set eyes upon him. From his privileged place of honor on the high-seat, he had looked down at Aiken with evident disgust. His eyes had switched uneasily from side to side, as though he feared that even a cursory glance at Aiken's torn-up face would surely taint him.

Twice, Aiken had pleaded to be called by his given name. Twice. "Do you not know me? Do you not know me?"

No, Gordon's blatant refusal to acknowledge that he had known a man whose father was his own father's cousin, a man with whom he had played when they were young, a man whom he had seen countless times over the years, had been more demeaning than anything that Aiken had ever before encountered.

Not to acknowledge a man by calling him respectfully by the name that his mother and father had given him, a name that had been passed down through the generations, a name that resonated in his bloodline and reflected the family soul, a name made famous by the great warriors in the past who were present in Aiken's very make-up and who still lived-on at the very core of his being. No, no, no. There was no greater insult to a man's very personhood than denial of his rightful name. Aiken had challenged men for lesser slights. But, when he had come up against that greater offense, he had been helpless to defend his own good name.

Aiken and Mildred were working inside the shed. He was sweeping up the mouse droppings, and she was bent nearly double, digging through the rubbish and tossing things out the door. But when he glanced up at the wall, he became so caught up in his frustrations that the mildew stains and texture patterns on the wooden planks began to reassemble themselves into Gordon's face. Aiken did not know what came over him. He only knew that he could not stop himself from reacting to what he saw there: Gordon's face. He was right there.

Aiken dropped the broom and slammed his fists into the wall. The loathsome man did not deserve to sit on a high seat. Aiken's former chieftain should have been seated on that chair. Aiming at Gordon's chin, Aiken punched the wall. His cousin was a man of questionable honor, and lesser prestige. Aiken hit Gordon on the nose. His cousin should have been seated at the far end of the bench, amongst the lowest ranking men. Aiken punched the wall again, and again, but Gordon refused to go down.

"Stop. Aiken. Stop," Mildred screamed shrilly, and grabbed him by the arm. "What are you doing? Stop."

Ready to grapple with her, he turned to elbow her roughly in the chest and to shake her off. But seeing the terror in her face, he stopped. The spell, cast by his anger, broke. He slowly lifted his hands and looked at his scraped and bleeding knuckles. He shook his head in disbelief. "I do not know. I do not know what I am doing. Fighting, I guess."

Wrapping his arms around her, he held her close. "I feel so bad. Believe me, Mildred. I will never hurt you. Do not fear me. I am not a monster. Will you ever trust me again? Can we be friends? Can we be the same as we were before? I beg you."

Mercifully, Mildred took him by the arm and led him to the house. First she set Aiken down on the bench outside the door. Then she grabbed a stool from inside the house for herself, along with a basin of water, a small jar of salve, and a handful of rags.

Harald poked his head out the door, looked them over, shrugged, and went back inside.

In preparation for washing and bandaging his bruised and bleeding fingers, she carefully inspected each one. She poked, pinched, and gently moved them back and forth before concluding, "Nothing is broken."

Seated knee to knee, his arms lay stretched across his lap while she tore strips of cloth to bind his fingers. Embarrassed by the surge of anger that she had witnessed, Aiken could not bear to look her in the eye. "I am good for nothing but fighting and cannot do even that anymore."

"That is not true, Aiken. You are clever and can figure things out."

"Being too clever is what got me into trouble in the first place."

"It can also be your saving grace when you apply your skills to making things of value. I know that you can do whatever you put your mind to."

"My mother said the same thing."

"Well, then, there can be no argument. Your mother and I both agree upon your talents. Look, you have two good hands. Your palms are broad, and your fingers are well-formed. You have a craftsman's hands. You are strong and hit hard. You are lucky you did not break any of the bones in your fingers. Put your strength toward making things instead of hitting things."

"No," he said, staring down at his lap and shaking his head side-to-side. "You have me wrong. I am a luckless man. Even my own mother refused to take me in."

"Aiken, you can trust me. I promise I will never turn you away."

"How can you stand to look at me? I hate the way I am. Once I was good-looking and now I look like some wretched creature who crept out from under the rotten leaf mold in the forest. Mildred, I will only bring you harm. I am unfit to live among men and women. I am worthless. Find another man, Mildred." He began to stand up but she grabbed him by the hand. "Leave me be," he said, shaking his hand half-heartedly and, without quite meaning it, added, "I will go away."

"No, Aiken. You are the one who is wrong. I see in you a clever man who is determined to make a good life for himself. That is the way I see you. Whoever hurt you and forced you to become a wanderer, did not crush you all the way. You still have your pride. Sometimes I sneak a peek at you because I like to look at you. I like to see the sparkle in your eye, and the way the corner of your mouth turns up in a clever little smile whenever something amuses you.

"I remember the day you told me that the hidden folk had left me secret gifts. You had meant to tease me and grinned when I told you to stop your foolishness. But I wish I had never said it. I want you to poke fun at me. I want you to grin and act silly. I should have shown you, then, how much you mean to me. You are a dear, and tender man. The day you walked into the hamlet was the luckiest day of my life."

"Mildred, if I am lucky at all, it is because I have you to watch out for me."

"Then, I will share my luck with you. Between the two of us, there is enough luck to spare. Promise me that you will stay. I cannot go on without you." She lowered her voice to a whisper, and said, "Harald needs you too. I cannot care for him much longer without your help. To see the way you treat him so tenderly does my heart good. Promise me that I can count on you."

Mildred was sitting on the stool, still clutching his bandaged hand tightly in her fists. She had a strong grip and was not about to let him go. From where he stood, he looked down and saw, in her face, more affection than he deserved, mixed with the grief and fear that he had brought upon her by his threat to leave her. Who was he fooling? Never again would he find a woman with such sincere simplicity. Add to that, he trusted her.

They could have argued over who was right, and who was wrong until the Endtime. But it would have done no good. Mildred was as stubborn as they came. Mildred won the argument, easily. And Aiken said simply, "I will stay."

If he were to contain his rage, to stopper it up in a bottle and to let it out, only in small drops, he would need to funnel the hostility, driving his rage, into something of greater value. To make things women used for cooking and serving food meant little. Aiken needed to make things men valued, things men treasured, something he could truly be proud of having made.

He had sworn an oath to Torwald and could not break it. Nor could he break his hands. He needed to keep his hands intact, or he would never bring the guilty men to justice. If he broke all the bones in his hand, he could not hold a knife hilt or fight the man who had hurt him and killed his war companions.

If he intended to accuse the guilty chieftain, to confront those who were responsible for the cover-up, and to make them accountable for their actions, he needed to stay fit. He would need to take care of his hands so that he could practice his cuts and defenses. A combat knife was a tool, and so was a whittling knife, and so was a chisel, and so was a saw and an axe. They were all made of iron and all of them cut.

These thoughts then led naturally to the next. If he wanted to protect his hands he should never hit the wall again. What kind of aimless fool does that? If he had to hit something, it was better to strike a chisel with a mallet. If he could not cut down his enemies, he could cut down a tree and hew it into planks. Since Gordon did not deserve to sit on a high seat, Aiken would cut the promise, which he had sworn, onto the back of a chair that he would make for Torwald.

It had been Aiken's duty to protect his chieftain and to warn him of the danger he was in. Torwald had chosen not to listen. Instead he had foolishly ridden into a trap. But Torwald's bad decision-making had not negated Aiken's duty. The design that Aiken cut into the wood would honor his promise to see that the guilty were brought to justice for their crimes.

To set his resolve, he stood in his workshop in front of the wall upon which he had pictured Gordon's face. He held a piece of charcoal that he had picked out of the hearth and, on that same, exact spot, drew a picture to cover his cousin's face. Just as Gordon and the other chieftains had erased Aiken from their kinship, erased his name, erased his life in the warband, erased all recognizable features from one side of his face, and had left him with nothing but a blur of scarred flesh, Aiken, in turn, erased his cousin's face. To replace Gordon's betrayal, he drew a picture of what he saw in his mind's eye—a man who, like himself, was kneeling before his chieftain. A chieftain who was presenting the kneeling man with an arm ring as a token of the holy and unbreakable trust that two men share when they promise to be fully true to one another.

But before he could find the time to turn that roughed-out sketch into a wooden chair, and before he could cut the wood from which he would make the chair and the turned bowls, there was the field-work, the harvest, and the trees he needed to hew and chop that would keep Mildred and Harald's hearth fire burning throughout the upcoming, wintertime months. And once he had cut down the trees, they would need to be skidded out of the forest, and into the yard. And for that he needed to use Harald's oxen.

Harald told Aiken that because they had been the last team he had ever trained, he did not have the heart to slaughter them. And, because it had been a long while since the oxen had been given much work to do, they had led an easy life munching grass in the pasture and chewing their cuds all day. At first, when Harald began to teach Aiken how to drive the team, the two, fat and lazy oxen had chosen to ignore him. But, over time, the two animals became familiar with Aiken and agreed, begrudgingly, to respond to the goad and to obey his voice commands.

Aiken gave the oxen a warning. He told them to get used to working hard. Once he had figured out how to buy a cart for Mildred, they would be put to work more often. He often talked to the oxen like that when he was alone with them, skidding timbers into the hamlet, loading hay and straw onto their backs, hauling rocks that he had cleared from the fields on skids, or was doing other kinds of field-work.

It was restful to be around their big, sturdy bodies, and he often patted their rumps. The oxen's powerful haunches and their simple needs helped Aiken feel more settled. He had begun to give his life a different kind of meaning than the one it had before.

And evidently, Harald had also given a different kind of meaning to Aiken's daily presence in his home. Though no words regarding marriage plans had, as yet, passed between the two men, Harald began to treat Aiken the same way he would have treated Mildred's suitor.

One evening, over supper, Harald said, "Come springtime, you and Mildred will want to start a new team. It takes four years to train a young steer to be a good draft animal that hauls and plows dependably." With a forward tip his head, he added a second admonishment, "After that, you will need to train a new team every other year."

To train a steer to respond to verbal commands and the light touch of a goad was hardly the same as breaking a proud and lively stallion to a saddle. Up until then, Aiken had thought ahead only as far as springtime. But now he needed to plan ahead four years. Instead of looking back with that long, lingering glance at yesterday, he began to look ahead to the farmers' off-season when he could take up carving and wood-turning.

What Mildred had said about his capable, craftsman's hands was true. To work with his hands had always been easy for Aiken. After he had outgrown the simple whittling he had done as a boy, he had picked up techniques and a few tools whenever he talked with woodworkers in the market towns. He asked them what tools they used for making different kinds of cuts and which woods were best for carving. When he asked how to make a clever item, such as a small ball rolling around inside a hollow shape, or how to carve a wooden chain, some craftsmen had refused to let him in on their secrets. They would ask, "Why do you want to know?" But other men were proud to teach their skills to a highborn man and would gladly accept a coin or two in exchange for a bit of learning.

Though a wooden chain was useless, it was a clever way to show-off his deftness with a small knife. He enjoyed seeing the awe in people's faces when they said, "It is a puzzle." After they had inspected each link in the chain more closely, they remarked upon the fact that they could find no seams in it. When they asked, "How did you make it?" Aiken would smile enigmatically and refuse to let them in on his secrets.

Back when he had been a man-at-arms, he had often admired the carved furnishings in the longhouses and the chieftain's meadhalls. But to understand how the craftsmen had put together the pieces that made up the boxes, chairs and benches, he had been equally as flummoxed as those folks whom he had fooled with his wooden chain. The hidden joinery was hard to figure out unless a man had a certain kind of secret know-how.

As the days shortened, and the nights lengthened, and the harvest season trailed off, Aiken figured the time had come to make his way back to the underground rooms where he had been nursed back to health. That was where he could get the secret know-how which he lacked.

IV.

The men were surprised to hear about his interest in woodcraft and the mechanics driving a turning-lathe. Because Berling was the man with whom Aiken had shared the greatest brotherly affection before, the smith felt rebuffed by his reduced interest in fine weaponry.

But Grerr responded to Aiken effusively. He told Aiken that he believed in his artisan soul, one which was more akin to his own. Dvalinn teased Aiken, saying that he suspected the change was due to a woman's influence. That forced Aiken to confide in the four men and to describe his growing attachment to Mildred. They all gave him funny, mischievous looks, and asked, "So are you planning to marry and raise a family?"

Though he only stayed with them for a day or two each time he visited, he learned how to use Grerr's pole lathe and the techniques for assembling chairs, boxes, and benches. Dvalinn answered most of his questions regarding the secret signs, and the influences one could bring about by spelling out the words he planned to carve into the chair back.

Because he had no wood-working tools of his own, Berling displayed a turn of heart when he offered to make the set of the tools, which Aiken needed for carving and turning wood. His first project had been to turn the wooden handles into which they would fit the iron tools that Berling was forging. Once the tools were finished, Berling and Grerr presented him with the complete set. It included: several chisels he could use for turning and carving; gouges, along with a wooden mallet he could use for carving; three small hammers and axes of different sizes; an adze, and a large broadax; augers he could use for drilling holes; a saw, a hacksaw, and blades; a set of rasps, files, and a drawknife for fine shaping; a bradawl for making small indentations in the wood; clamps for holding the wooden pieces in place when he was either carving or gluing; and a hand plane for smoothing the flat surfaces.

Once Aiken understood the woodworking basics and had the tools, he set to work. He used the large broadax to cut the trees he needed to make the chair. With the help of Harald's oxen, he skidded the logs into the yard. To scrape the bark, Aiken used the axe Berling had forged. He hung a plumb line and used a straight edge to mark the width of the panels on the end of each log. A charcoal snap-line marked the line lengthwise. He scored the timber by chopping notches along the topside, and took each one down to the marked line. The remaining wood pieces were removed with a smaller axe.

The blade bit, the chunks gave way, the chips flipped to the side, and fell at his feet. Now that he was cutting with a sharp iron blade, he was coming back to himself. Overcoming caution, he once again became the fearless man he had been before. Sometimes he ripped at the wood until he heard it scream. It felt good to hit something hard, to feel the strength in his arms, legs, and back, and to hear that high-pitched squeal. By then, his ribs had mended, and he could breathe without it hurting. It felt good to drink in the air whenever he filled his chest. It was so good to be alive and to breathe freely once again. He could not get enough of life.

When he was finished, he had a flat, broad surface, flush with the marked line.

To smooth it further, he carefully aimed each blow with the adze. In the end, he had a pile of planks stacked neatly in front of the small building that had become his workshop. Proud of what he had accomplished, he stood there with his feet apart, and his fists loosely resting on his hips. After he admired his work, he took a deep breath, turned, and headed toward Mildred's house. Thirsty and eager to pour himself a cup of ale, he was ready to quit for the rest of the day and to relish his sense of accomplishment.

Over the following days, he smoothed each plank with the hand plane, drilled holes along the edges using the template he had made, and pegged them together with cheese glue. Once the glue was dry, he had four, good-sized panels from which to cut the sides, back, and seat. The hand plane was a good tool for smoothing the joins and flattening the surfaces. In the end, the planks were so smooth that he could rub his hands over them without feeling any bumps or rough spots.

After all the years that he had looked at the high seats in the chieftain's mead-halls, he knew what they should look like. Just as Grerr had shown him, he drew the shape of the side piece with charcoal. It included the front and back legs and the curved armrest. He used a small saw and an adze to cut it out according to the lines he had drawn. It was like whittling, but used bigger tools to shape a piece of wood about a hundred times larger than the little chunks from which he whittled spoons. He then used the first piece as a pattern. He laid it on top of the second, uncut side piece, and traced around the lines. He then cut the back and seat in the same manner.

To make certain the pieces fit snugly in the joints, he held them together and adjusted each surface until it made a tight bond. He induced Mildred to hold one side piece and the back, while he propped the other side against the workshop outer wall. He held the seat with one hand, and stretching out his arm, he leaned back as far as he could without letting it drop. Both he and Mildred admired his work. Even in its roughed-out state, it was thrilling to envision the completed chair. At Mildred's urging, he explained how, after he was finished carving the designs, he would use pegs to attach the side pieces to the back. Then, he would fasten the bottom to the side-pieces with a join called a mortice and through-tenon and lock it in place with a wedge. After that, the chair would be fully assembled.

The one secret he kept from her, the one thing that he would never disclose and that would always go unspoken between them, was that he would leave some cuts unfinished until the justice, which he sought for Torwald's murder, had been meted out, and the score was settled.

Over time, although there were days when he had ambition and a brief sense of accomplishment after he had overcome each obstacle, there was no lasting satisfaction. Some days he felt so hopeless, he would just as soon give up and die. It would have been easy to force another man to take him down. He could just strap his knife onto his belt and take off for Leofar's fort town. Aiken would be cut down before he got as far as the meadhall door.

On days like that, when he felt half-dead, he went through the motions that kept him alive. He did the things that he had promised to do for Mildred and Harald. Though his mind was far away, he prepared the wood for carving and turning, ate and rested. But the day that he set the chisel against the wood and struck it with the mallet was the day that his life took a more lasting turn for the better.

Aiken laid a side piece across the two trestles that he had set up in the yard and secured it with clamps to prevent it from slipping. This chair was meant to keep alive his faith in the fulfillment of the promise he had made to Torwald. That was the meaning he thought he was giving it, anyway. But hidden and unspoken, even to himself, the chair was also memorializing that part of him that had, also, died that day, alongside Torwald, on the bank of the Warring River.

To show the way plants struggle to break free from the shadowy underground darkness where things rot, and the dead are buried, the pictures he drew of scrolling, intertwined leaves and tendrils were meant to stand in for living plants. Made from green wood, these make-believe leaves would look like greenery had grown from the earth to make a seat for his dead chieftain. When Aiken thought of Torwald, he pictured a robust man whose life had been cut too short, too soon. The way Aiken saw it in his mind's eye, because the soil, in which Torwald's bones were resting, was fertile and full of life, he would keep Torwald alive in his memory. When the chair was finished, his chieftain would remain as alive as the grass and trees and vines that Aiken had seen growing around Torwald's grave.

Following the lines he had drawn, as he tapped the mallet against the chisel, the grooves deepened, and the curved shapes began to take on a well-rounded appearance. The plants he was picturing were fanciful and unlike anything that anyone had ever seen growing in the forest or the meadow. But beneath his hands they became believable as living vegetation.

Aiken stopped to inspect the work he had done. His hands and tools had pulled the full shapes from the plain, flat wood to create an illusion of life. And as the vines and leaves took on depth and form, his passing thoughts became something lasting, something he could touch. Something to hold on to.

He wanted no more of death. He wanted a life with Mildred. He wanted children. This was what the stems and foliage were meant to represent. From his partial death on the bank of the Warring River, a new life would emerge. These make-believe, living plants would reach up in a sinuous manner to take in the glorious, life-giving sunlight. That was when he decided, then and there, to name his first-born daughter after all these marvelous gifts from the sun.

It was a beautiful thing to be a part of creation in this way. He put down his tools to stroke the wood. It was pleasing to trace the smooth, curling lines with his fingers. The feel of the soft-surfaced wood reminded him of those times when he had run his hands over the skin of those softly curving women with whom he had lain abed when he was an attractive man-at-arms.

After he was hurt, it had shamed and wounded him deeply to think that no woman would ever again want him for a bedmate and would never kiss him on the mouth. He had thrown down those feelings of attraction for women and ground them beneath his heel. He had twisted his foot over and over, and angrily driven them into the dirt. Under the pretense that he and Mildred were brother and sister, he had continually pushed away those lusty feelings when the two of them were working side by side. Not until the day that she proposed they marry did his feelings begin to change. It was then that he had, once again, begun to see himself as an attractive man. Attractive, at least, to one woman.

Sometimes when he looked at her, he felt the same desire he had felt when he had watched the meadhall girls pour his drink. Mildred was older and not as pretty as some of those young girls had been. But she had so much more to offer him. And just as he had done when he had enjoyed those women who had crawled so willingly into his bed, he wanted to smooth his hands over Mildred's full-figured bosom, her waist and her hips, and to feel her soft skin beneath his hands.

He was so fond of Mildred that even to be apart from her for half a day gave him heartache. Along with his attraction to her, he was certain that she, too, wanted to lay abed with him. Come springtime, once they were wed, he would redeem the affection that a man has for a woman when they come together and wrap each other in their arms.

Aiken sighed with longing. He could hardly wait that long. He wanted to feel Mildred's every curve. To stroke the length of her strong legs all the way from the bushy triangle between her thighs down to her feet. He wanted to cup her heel in the palm of his hand, and to stroke her leg, and to circle her lower belly, soft and round as an overturned bowl, and to sink his hand into the enticing space between her open thighs. He wanted to unbraid her plait and to comb her hair with his fingers, and to pull her toward himself, and to kiss her hard on the lips. He wanted to lay atop her, to enter her, to push himself up with his arms, and to thrust his hips, and to please her.

Ever-watchful and attuned to sound as he was, he had not heard a woman's approaching footsteps, yet he knew that someone was standing at his right elbow. Mildred never snuck-up on him that way. Lest he startle and jump, she always greeted him whenever she came near. But whoever was there, on his blind side, had not made a sound. Eager to see her, Aiken turned sideways, only to be disappointed when he discovered that no one was there.

Yet, he felt a woman's slender hand touch his. The uncanny feeling that something strange was happening made his skin crawl and prickle. At a loss for words to explain something that he could only sense without understanding how he came to know it, he felt a womanly presence wrap her fingers around his fists. He held his tools very still. He breathed in deeply and began to tap the chisel with his mallet.

Up until then, the world had appeared shadowy and gray. But now, when he lifted his face to absorb the sun's warmth, the flaming disk shone more brightly than it had before. It seemed as though a southern wind had blown away the clouds that made his world so bleak. The sparkling water in a nearby pail reflected numerous small, glittering suns, each of which were dancing to the same rhythm he was tapping with his mallet. The sky was a deeper blue. All the colors brightened. Every autumn-colored leaf and sun-bleached grass blade trembled with inherent life. Something had changed.

Then he knew. It was his luck-woman who stood beside him. She held the drinking horn she had dipped into the source of luck and raised it to his lips. Brimful of the sweet-tasting mead of luck, it splashed over the rim as he supped, and he felt the luck sustain him. He was certain this wood was alive, alert, aware, awake. And so was the water, the soil, and the rocks. And so was the sunlight. And so was the grass, and so was the wind that gave trembling movement to the trees. He breathed in the air that gave him life, and his breath became his soul passing on wings through his nostrils to fill his lungs with luck. All material things in this world responded in the same way as did flesh-and-blood men and women. He was surrounded with luck. He was surrounded with soul. Luck was the soul of the worlds. Mingling with everything, luck was present in everything. This world was a living being, filled with soul. He took it in and absorbed that luck.

Reminded of a time when he was drawn into a game of dice with a merchant who came from a faraway land in the southern regions, the man had shaken the cup while beseeching his luck-woman, "Oh, Fortuna, oh, Fortuna."

And because Aiken fancied the name, he, too, called his luck-woman Fortuna. And ever since that day, whenever Aiken clasped his tools, Fortuna wrapped her hands around his fists and, as they worked together, the luck flowed between them.

So that was how it happened that Aiken's luck came back. His luck-woman, Fortuna, gave him more than the power to win a game. The spring-fed waters from which she draws the mead of luck are located high atop the mountain and are hard to reach without a luck-woman's otherworldly help. Yet, once a man or woman imbibes those waters, their workmanship is endowed with beauty enough to wash away both theirs and other's sorrows.

V.

At that time, Aiken had yet to grasp the dormant talents that lay, like seeds in his inner darkness where they awaited the warmth and early springtime rains to nudge them into sprouting. Because we figured our teachings were part of the deal that we had struck with him, over time and many subsequent visits to our rooms beneath the ground, Grerr, Berling, and I taught Aiken all he needed to know.

In the end, it was what we taught him about harnessing binding words and letters that gave him the power to influence Necessity's laws and that allowed him to settle the score with the man who was behind Torwald's murder.

I often wondered whether Aiken understood the abilities he had residing in his hands. He may have, but at the time had not fully grasped their significance. Mistaken as he was, in those days he still believed his manly powers were best displayed when he was forcefully holding a knife hilt in his hand.

Instead, it was his skill with chisels and mallets that would, someday, give him the power he needed to sway both his and other men's fates. Over time, Aiken became increasingly adept at weaving spelled signs together with spoken words and actions. Given that knowledge, he could either awaken the pleasure of the ruling powers and bring blessings to a man's kin and allies, or awaken those powers' anger and bring down otherworldly wrath upon his enemies. The signs he carved gave men confidence, guided them in the best way to go, and named their destination. Such was the power of signs and written words that Aiken had residing in his hands.

FIVE

Fluorite
If you will kindle
The mind of any man and make his wits sharp.

Take this stone which is called Fluorite. Its diverse colors are often seen in bands of green, purple, blue and red. If any man will bear this stone, it gives him good understanding in many things that may be understood. It shall drive away your adversaries and make your enemy meek.

The Truth of Rocks, by Aluiss the Wise

I.

Like a chieftain seated on his high seat, the long-knife now holds the place of honor on my table. And like the man, who once wore this blade strapped proudly on his belt whilst overlooking the men and women who were seated below his dais in the meadhall, this blade is now elevated above the stones, each of which are standing-in for one of those who were seated on the benches. There is a piece of dark blue, star-embedded lapis lazuli, a polished slice of spring-green serpentine, and a naturally formed, multi-hued, hexagonally-shaped, fluorite crystal. Tonight, in celebration of the long-knife's birth in Berling's forge, one stone will come forward with an offer to entertain us.

Yet, as I gaze upon this peacefully laid-out tableau mimicking a joyful, celebratory meadhall feast, I cannot avoid the threat implied by the long-knife's deadly presence. A knife as long as this one has but a single purpose—for making war.

This seeming paradox reminds me of a piece of writing I recently acquired. I found the document amidst assorted papers and other items, which I picked up when I was visiting an acquaintance. In trade for a book, of which I had two copies, he offered me a pile of seemingly unrelated books and papers, stacked and tied with twine.

As for the name of the man whose writings were included amongst the papers, unfortunately, it has been lost. When I asked about the bundle's provenance, my friend could only tell me that he had acquired it from another collector of oddities and figured stones.

Reasoning that even things that, at first glance, may appear to be worthless scrap can have value in a collection like mine that seeks to trace an idea's development over time, I accepted the bundle. It was only after had I reached home that I sorted through the papers and was delighted to find this anonymous man's provocative perspective on war and celebration.

He wrote:

I should like to explain how, behind these two constants in men and women's lives—both to celebrate and to make war—lie their needs to gather, to eat, to belong amongst their own kind, and to protect the things they have gathered from those whom they fear will take it all away.

If I were to weigh these two seemingly dissimilar urges on a scale—celebration and war-making—I would place on one end of the balance beam men and women's desire to celebrate the continuity of a prosperous and abundant life. And on the other end I would place their urge to bring about the death of a common enemy. On one end is life and on the other, death. Yet neither is as dissimilar nor as opposed to the other as it appears to be at first sight. For, when both are equal in value, each counters the power of the other at the very center of the balance beam.

To present an example of the way that celebration and war shift from one to the other, I offer for consideration the darkest night of the year when the powers who rule both life and death open their otherworldly doors to that space between the worlds. To bring back life-giving sunlight, and to experience that moment when life and death, light and darkness, creation and destruction are held in perfect abeyance, men and women are urged to reenact the Yuletide story.

Their mimicry of Lady Sun and her four husbands' indulgence in pleasurable activities encourages men and women to abandon the rules that ordinarily guide their day-to-day conduct. Counter to the standards, which they uphold and observe throughout the rest of year, the celebrants are persuaded to eat gluttonously, to drink immense amounts of ale, to stay up all night dancing around the bonfire, and to flirt openly with those who are not their spouses.

Whilst the daytime racing and wrestling competitions are held in the fields in lieu of wartime fighting, the veneer of friendly relations often sunders. The balance beam tips and, as it weighs more heavily toward the side of war, violent brawls break out amongst the celebrants.

Then the knives come out. When on the fourth, and last night of the Yuletide celebration, Lady Sun's twin brothers, the Lords of Battle, pretend to force an end to the festivities at the tips of their wooden blades, the hardship that men and women connect with wintertime darkness, is overcome. The celebrants' hope for a plentiful growing season is renewed. The sun returns to its orderly pattern. And everyone goes home to awaken the following morning to the daily toil associated with their orderly lives.

Until war breaks out. With the addition of iron weaponry, the stakes get higher. Instead of men jostling in the fields for sport and participating in the reenactment of Lady Sun's story, each man on the battlefield reenacts the hero's defeat of the monster. Whereas the masked monsters in the story are little men who live in the roots of the mountains, the wartime monsters are ordinary men who are no different from the aggressors, but become inflated to monstrous proportions by fear and hatred. Instead of the jubilant celebration that is meant to ensure abundant growth, participation in war brings about sorrowful destruction and starvation. Instead of the affection that men and women feel for those whom they include within their kinship, the warriors are attracted to those outsiders whom they fear. Instead of an outpouring of love followed by new life, the out-pouring of rage and hatred leads to an enemy's death.

Whilst, on one end of the balance beam, the combatant experiences the horror of wartime fighting and, on the other end, the promised celebration, he feels most empowered when he is living from one moment to the next in the center of the perfectly balanced scale. To give weight to the combatant's need to avoid those open doors that lead to the land of death, is his desire to stay alive. To turn the fight in his favor, to overcome deadly darkness, to make it to the end of the balance beam, to feast among the victors, and to awaken the following morning to sunlight's warmth, life's continuity becomes his sole purpose.

As for those who do not make it home, but who die in the conflict, before the otherworldly doors slam shut, the Lady of the Slain and her husband sort through the fallen. Those who fell are guided to the land where the dead go. Where, upon their arrival, they celebrate their entry to the realm of the ruling powers and, like seeds lying dormant in the soil, will feast and drink forever to life's renewal in the everlasting hereafter.

Now, as I look over each of the stones on my desk, I ask which amongst them is most appealing? Immediately my attention is drawn to the transparent colors in the eight-sided fluorite crystal. The bottom half, tinted a blue-green color, shades to a darker tone near the crystal's mid-section. A nearly straight-line cuts across its center. Above the line a deep purple gradually fades to pale blue, then deepens to dark blue at the crystal's very tip.

Reminded, by these pure and brilliant colors, of the times when I have seen the Northern Lights appear, I raise the lens to one eye and look more closely at the fluorite. After I have stared at it for a while, my eye loses its focus. And, in time, I make out the shadow of a man staring at the torch-lit stars, each of which is a watch station manned by a slain warrior in Lord Glory's Army of Ten Thousand Strong.

And then the show of lights begins.

II.

His attention was drawn to what appeared to be the wispy edges of a tattered cloak hanging in midair. Coming and going, the swirling streams of greenish light looked like wind-blown, shredded fabric. The ever-shifting colors first appeared in one corner of the sky, then quickly moved to another. Eventually the colored lights grew so strong they outshone the stars from one horizon to the other.

It seemed as though the star-warriors had quenched their torches, all at once, jumped upon their horses' backs, and galloped off, at great speed, with their brilliantly colored cloaks streaming out behind them. Shimmering and flaming, the star-warrior's cloaks, along with several of the banners that signified each of the warbands making up the army, flashed red, green, and purple.

A rider decked out in his war gear came from the right, racing on a white charger with his purple cloak flapping out behind his back. And keeping pace beside him, seated upon a second horse, the Lord's standard bearer carried the flag that represented Lord Glory's power: a monstrous wolf bound by ropes and flanked by two spear-bearing warriors.

The Lords of Battle, Day-farer and Night-farer, led their warbands. Both carried identical circular shields decorated with a spiral in each of its four quadrants. A banner with an elaborately decorated hammer-head signified Lord Thunder's warband. The Lady of the Slain drove her leopard-pulled cart. Streaming overhead, her banner pictured a gold-bristled boar. Keeping pace beside her on her right was her son, White Fire the Bold, and on her left was her husband, the Lord of the Whirlwind. And beside him, his standard bearer held aloft the banner emblazoned with a triskelion: three interlocking bird heads with a whorl in the center.

Another army was coming from the direction they were headed. This one, too, was led by a great Lord whose standard bearer carried a flag. Contrived to look like a knotted snare, a series of crossed diagonal lines with a small circle at each intersection signified Spider the Entangler's army. The Lord of Thieves and Tricksters was riding one of his own monstrous progeny, the wolf named Treachery. Together they brought with them the chaos of the battlefield.

The armies met. The flags began to wave about confusedly in great swirling bursts of brilliant red, green, and purple. The clashing went on for a long time. Then, as though it were seemingly coming from out of nowhere, a great bird-like creature swooped down upon the wolf and rider. A fight ensued between the Wind-bringer and the wolf. In the tumult, Spider's standard bearer fell from his horse. After the flag went down, one of Lord Glory's men grabbed it up and raised the captured flag aloft to show everyone that he had won the prize.

The Wind-bringer's sudden attack had turned the battle in Lord Glory's favor. Spider and Treachery called the retreat. His army turned and headed in the direction from which they had come. Lord Glory, the Lords of Battle, Lord Thunder, the Lady of the Slain, her son, White Fire the Bold, and the Lord of the Whirlwind were on the chase, followed by their bands of followers and the Wind-bringer.

In time, the colorful banners trailed off to the left, and the star torches were once again lit by the ten thousand star-warriors who would stay the watch against Treachery's return to chaos.

The gradually dimming colorful lights had nearly vanished when four of the star-warriors peeled off from the rear of the army. Though the horsemen were coming from a great distance, they were apparently headed in the direction of Mildred's house. Galloping over the tops of the trees, the four horsemen rode at great speed and grew in size with their approach.

Then, there they were: his Uncle Otgar and three of his former war companions. The horsemen reined-in to an abrupt halt in front of Mildred's house.

He stood up from the bench and walked toward the men to greet them.

And, even as the skittish horses were tossing their heads and rearing, pinning back their ears, striking the ground hard with their front hooves, squealing, and snorting, the horsemen struggled to contain their mounts and assaulted him with their grievances.

"Aiken, what kind of a man are you?"

"Weakling."

"You should have died the same way we did."

"Coward."

"Sweat blood you good for nothing, weak-willed runaway."

"You double-crosser should never get away with what you did."

"You snake-in-the grass swore an oath to Torwald. Now make good on it."

"You made a promise and we hold you to it."

"Challenge the man who killed us to a meeting of the blades."

The aggressiveness of their stance forced him to back away from the men and their horses. His legs bumped against the bench, and he fell onto the seat. He rested his elbows on his knees, tipped his head and, like an overturned bowl, cupped it in his slayed-out fingers.

"No, no, no. Go away," he mumbled repeatedly, shaking his head side to side. "Get out of here."

He wanted to push away the disturbing sights and sounds of war and death. But the torments arose from the dreamtime and came after him no matter what he did. If he could have, he would have shaken out the terrible memories and been left only with the good ones. But he could not stop the hectoring voices. Nor did it do any good to cover his ears. The ghosts of dead men had gotten inside his head, it seemed.

"You dishonored yourself."

"Coward."

"You owe us."

"You swore an oath to Torwald."

"Now make good on it."

They were speaking so loudly, all at once, it was impossible to discriminate one voice from the other.

"Stop ganging up on me," Aiken screamed, just to drown them out. "It is wrong for you to accuse me of your deaths. I tried to warn you, but you refused to listen. Stop talking. Stop talking. Stop talking. You have it wrong. It was not me who double-crossed you. Before I die, I promise to prove who turned against us. I promise. I am not a cheater. Nor am I a coward. I will set things right. I will prove who was behind your murders."

For a man who had so avidly challenged others, who had never backed down, was notoriously combative and known for his recklessness on the battlefield, Aiken had out-lasted all those men in Torwald's warband who had predicted his youthful death. They had mocked his prescient insights, called his warnings overly-suspicious, and accused him of traitorously gaming both sides. Yet here he was. Still alive.

Aiken yelled at the top of his lungs, "All of you are dead. You are the good-for-nothing run-aways. Compared to what I must do, just to stay alive each day and to keep my family safe, you have it easy. Now get out of here."

Mildred stuck her head out the door. "Are you all right Aiken?"

"Yes. I am all right."

"I heard you yelling."

"I was yelling. But the men who were ganging up on me are gone now."

"Oh."

Mildred knew better than to ask who had been harassing him. Even if he tried to explain, she would never have understood that there were dead men, men who had once been members of Torwald's warband, men who had been his friends and close companions, men whom he had trusted, with whom he had gamed, and whom he had fought beside, who now wanted to see him dead—as dead as they were—and would do anything to take him down.

"Well," she said, "I came out to check on you. Are you sure you are all right? Should I tell the women to go home now?"

"No. I told you. I am all right. Enjoy your night of storytelling."

"Well then, are you warm enough?"

"No."

Mildred ducked back inside and shortly afterward came out again. Carrying a cup of mulled ale, she handed it to him, and said, "You are a good man, Aiken."

She tucked a fleece hide around his legs and muttered, "Easy now. Settle down. Settle down. The women will be gone soon. I promise."

Embarrassed by his wife's attentiveness, he poked fun at her, saying, "You will make me soft, Mildred. Just let me be. Go back inside."

By now, all the folks who lived in the hamlet were accustomed to Aiken's screaming in the night. The loss of control he displayed whenever he was caught in the grip of the dreamtime specters, who assaulted him so relentlessly with their grievances, no longer shamed him. But his need for Mildred had never gotten past him. No matter how much trouble he caused her, no matter how stormy the weather had been, she had always been there for him, had always looked out for him, and had always backed him up, just as Alger had done until the day he died.

Though Aiken reckoned a man expected loyalty from his wife, he regretted the many times he had sorely tried her patience. Overwhelmed, just then, by the warmth of his affection, he grabbed her by the hand and pulled her down. He kissed her hard on the mouth and laughed. "There, now I made you blush. Go back inside with that pink flush blooming on your cheeks. You look ten years younger—like a bride. See what Aunt Edith makes of that."

Mildred punched him in the arm, said, "Aiken, you are such a joker," and slipped inside the house.

Regardless of what Mildred said, he knew the women would not be leaving anytime soon. They were just getting started and would be there half the night. Still shaky, Aiken held the cup with both hands. He carefully lifted the mulled ale to his lips and, sipping slowly, felt it warm him from the inside out. When Mildred offered him the cup her praise was spare and unembellished—he was a good man and a joker—but he never doubted her sincerity. He trusted her honesty through and through.

The life he had led in the meadhalls had been replaced by a life spent in a work shed. His seat at a chieftain's high table, where he had sat alongside Alger and been surrounded by his companions, had been replaced by a lonesome bench outside of his wife's door. Of all the men with whom he now lived, he would never have a friendship of the kind that he had had with Alger. There was no way to replace him.

Though his memories of Alger had changed for the worse, and his friend's shade was no longer the dependable and kindly man he had been before, but had become hostile and defiant, Aiken could neither get rid of Alger's shade, nor did he want to.

But now that Alger had left along with the others, Aiken was alone.

On lonely nights like this, he wished that Harald was still here, seated beside him, spreading goodness, just as he had done that first winter when Aiken had begun to live in the hamlet. Back then, Harald's pain was often so great that he could not sleep. And since that made two sleepless men between them, Aiken sat up with Harald to keep him company during the long, wintertime nights.

One night, Harald asked Aiken to tell him what his fighting life was like. At first, Aiken refused to open up. But Harald had lain abed, propped up on pillows, and stared at him, waiting. Though Aiken wanted to stand up and to walk out of the house, instead, he pleaded for Harald's patient forbearance. "Once a man sees how frayed the fabric is that holds men and women together, it is impossible to repair the damage. After that happens, no one can believe in the rightness of the world. It changes him forever." That was what had happened to him, he said. Since he had lost his trust in goodness, he could no longer be right with this world.

Harald told Aiken that he, too, had fought when he was young, and added, "You have seen the scars when you helped me dress."

He and his oxen had been levied by the chieftain's men to drive wagonloads of food, water, and war gear onto the battlefield. Not that he was given much choice, but because he thought it was his duty, he had agreed willingly. However, he had not expected to be handed a shield and spear. Forced to fight in the shield wall, he had been just another body to toss in front the enemy in hopes of slowing their rival's forward assault.

There were several battles and Harald fought in each one until he was too badly hurt to get up and fight any more. A couple men picked him up by the arms and legs and tossed him into a wagon. But since they needed to make room for plunder and captives, every now and then they stopped to throw off those who were expected to die, along with the corpses. After that, they just kept going. Somehow, Harald had managed to stay alive and to make it home again. But he had lost his oxen and wagon.

Harald ended his story saying, "I never did get another wagon, and it took four years to train another good team. War is a terrible waste of strong men's lives and productive farmland. It is no good to go to war. It is better to put in a good crop in the springtime and to harvest it in the autumn."

Aiken, however, was unwilling to accept Harald's simple-minded trust in goodness. "As much as I have seen of death and suffering, I still believe that men need to go to war. Men need to patrol the roads. If no one fights to protect your land and homes, someone else will come and take it away." Aiken had been taught to act honorably and to favor loyalty to his leaders and his war companions above all else. He valued the act of putting his life on the line of attack. He had fought to keep safe those men and women whom he had sworn to protect.

The stories that the poets told in the meadhalls celebrated the great fighting men who had lived, fought, and died in the past. Aiken and his companions had measured themselves against those heroes. They, too, wanted to be honored like the great men who had lived in the past and been emulated for their bravery. He had striven to be known and remembered for his courage, just like the rest.

But Harald was steadfast in his belief. "I believe that you are wrong but accept your right to have a different opinion, Aiken."

"Tell me then, does your soul go out at night when your body is asleep, looking for your wagon and oxen? Do you still fight in that shield wall? Do you still want to get back at your enemies?"

"Yes, I fought the night battles. After I got hurt, I worked hard to get my strength back. I chopped and hauled wood, plowed fields, dug holes in the dirt, pulled weeds, cut and stacked hay, hewed trees, and butchered hogs and cattle. I had my family around me. Together we worked in all kinds of weather. We celebrated the changing of the seasons, the weddings and the births. Over time, the sight of swaying barley stalks replaced my memories of those killing fields, and I began to forget what had happened there. That was when I stopped fighting the night battles."

Unlike Harald, Aiken had not had a home and family to return to. After everything had been taken away from him, he had been left with nothing. Instead of growing up close to the earth, learning to plant and harvest barley, his elders had assumed that he would become a member of the warband. They had begun training him at an early age. No one questioned whether it was right for children to go to war. Boys and youths were the strongest and most aggressive fighters on the battlefield. They were eager to get up close to their rivals, to look them in the eye, and to test their skills against seasoned warriors. Because they were too young to know the risks, they unwisely put themselves in danger. They fought recklessly, because they had not yet lost a dear friend and had never been badly hurt, nor had they seen the ravages of war.

"My father and uncle raised me to be a killer. Even when I was a boy, I sat on my father's knee, listening to the men tell their war stories. I never knew anything but death and killing. My father was killed. My uncle was killed. My friends were killed. My chieftain was killed. Killing was my life. Killing is part of who I am. Death made me. War made me."

Aiken confessed to the terrible things that he had seen and done—unspeakably cruel things that made him feel like he was no longer a man but a monster. He put into words the shameful, ugly things that he had done, things that even the other men in the warband had refused to call to mind because they were so unspeakable. It was hard to object to what the other men in the group did when everyone else went along. When a man is told that it is all right to be cruel, it is hard to remember that other people think those same ways of acting are wrong. The men in the warband wanted to win. If they had to do horrible things to benefit their strategy and to acquire more plundered goods, they did whatever was necessary to come out the victor.

"This cruelty is also who I am," Aiken said. "This is how death made me. I regret what I did. But I return to the horror night after night. Maybe now that you know what kind of man I am, you will not want me to marry your daughter."

"Aiken, you are a good man. All men have inside themselves a potential for cruelty. You did what was expected of you. I know what it is like to be in the midst of battle. I know the risks a man must take and the hurried decisions he must make when there is no time for second guessing. Now that you have spoken so honestly, I respect you more than I did before, not less. My mind has not changed. I believe that you are an honorable man and I will bless your marriage to Mildred."

"I am grateful," Aiken said. He did not believe that he had always acted honorably, but hesitated to question Harald's judgment. He would accept whatever uplifting praise he could get.

"A man just responds to some kind of horrid fascination with ripped apart bodies, spilled blood, and broken bones. I was born that way. I hate it, but I cannot leave it alone. I would go back to fighting if I could. I have never felt more alive than when I was on the battlefield. An elation comes over a man when he is fighting. Time slows. Every moment counts. Nothing is more important than coming out the victor. Nothing could ever match the thrill and danger I lived with daily. It makes no sense, does it, Harald?"

"Aiken, whenever you despair, think of Lord Glory. Remember that even after the wolf mauled his right hand, he never gave up hope. He still believed that he could take on his rival and capture Treachery. It was Lord Glory's victory that brought an end to the Terrible Winter."

But Aiken did not see it that way. After Lord Glory's blood was tainted by Treachery, he became untrustworthy. When Aiken had seen how Lord Glory's rule of law, and the peace he had once enforced, had fallen by the wayside, how could he keep his faith in those ideal principles? Ever since Aiken had been unfairly outlawed, he had held a grudge against Lord Glory.

That day at the Assembly, he had asked the Lord to have the final say. He had pleaded for a chance to prove his charge of murder with single combat—the form of judgment by arms that fell within the Lord's oversight. But Lord Glory had done nothing to bring about the peaceful resolution of his grievances. Nor had Lord Glory proclaimed a fair and just punishment against those who broke the law. No, after the Lord's right hand went missing, so too, had evenhanded justice. The Assembly had become nothing but mob rule. The wolf may have been defeated, but treachery had won the contest.

"Now we have everlasting war. After the hamlets and the villages began to increase in size, men needed more pasture and farmland to feed their growing families, and the warlords became increasingly greedy for land and riches. Things are worse now than they were before. The stronger tribal chieftains overtake the weaker ones and make war a constant."

Aiken had always been an observant man who thought things through for himself. And now that he was an outsider, he had a lot of time to think. He could see how the conflicting grabs for power between the warlords benefitted the men who sat at the high table. The leaders used rage and hatred to bring men together, to instill a common purpose, and to arm themselves against the others. But it was the men who sat on the benches who fought and got hurt. They were the ones who suffered for the sakes of the leaders who were unwilling to put themselves on the line of attack.

"Their rivalry increases as each chieftain seeks to show-off the powerful status he has achieved by gathering more followers and acquiring more goods for himself and his tribal allies. The more those leaders seek to garner greater prestige, the more they need to assert their status. They keep control through violence and fear, and they strengthen their alliances with gifts and celebrations. The more men lust for wealthy goods, the more willing they are to engage in war. The leaders attract followers by promising war booty, and the cruelest men rise to the top of the ranks."

From this distance, Aiken could see the shallowness of the chieftain's bluster and the name-calling of their rivals. If he had learned one thing, it was what happens when people allow power to go unchecked. The most powerful men, like Leofar, were shrewd. They cleverly achieved their aims with underhanded scheming and found ways to survive by deceitful means. Their shows of wealth and strength all rang hollow.

But over time, Harald had worn Aiken down. And though Aiken only felt it when he was in Harald's presence, some of his faith in the rightness of the world came back. In those days, it seemed as though he could breathe in the goodness that surrounded Harald like a sweet scent of roses.

But when Harald was no longer there, Aiken's faith in goodness just disappeared. Like the first warm day in early springtime when Mildred opened the house to air it out, before Aiken could catch hold of Harald's lingering trust in goodness, the wind just blew it all away. Belief in truth and goodness was illusory as air.

Without a leader or companions to rely upon, Aiken trusted no one but Mildred to back him up. He had made mistakes he regretted. He had been abandoned by his kin and been left to navigate the unpredictability of life alone. He had been a homeless wanderer but had made a home and a family to replace the ones he lost. Still, it was not enough.

III.

The wind was picking up and Aiken felt chilled. He pulled off the fleece that Mildred had wrapped around his legs and dropped it onto the bench. He stood and, with the moon lighting his way, took a brisk walk to get his blood moving fast. And as he walked, he heard the talk and laughter coming from Alf's house. The man had a houseful of cousins, a pot full of ale, and was telling stories that night.

Aiken avoided spending much time with the men in the hamlet. If he had intended to join the men in Alf's house, when he walked in the door, they would have stopped talking, turned, and stared at him. He was unwelcome among them, and he knew it.

One time, when he had seen a man hit his wife, Aiken had stepped in between them. The sight of the cowering woman had reminded him of his own mother, Maida, the last time he had seen her. Aiken turned on the man and threatened him. But, unlike the time when he was unable to protect his own mother from her abusive husband, Seaver, Aiken could have hit the man right then and there. Shaking with rage and clenching his fists, Aiken had wanted to punch the man in the face and to see blood spurt from his nose, but the man backed off.

Mildred said that that kind of rage did not belong here in the hamlet. This was not the place to express the kind of wrath that he experienced when he was on the battlefield.

That was one of the reasons that the men in the hamlet had not taken kindly to him. They did not like someone telling them how to treat their women. But there were other reasons too.

When he had first wandered into the hamlet, the men, who had agreed to take him on as a field-hand, had not expected him to stick around past the growing season. After he had served his purpose, they had assumed he would wander off again. It was one thing to be seen as an itinerant wanderer who was working for his keep. That was acceptable. But when Aiken had presumed to marry into their kinship, his presence in the hamlet had gone too far.

The trouble began when Harald called a family gathering to announce Mildred's betrothal. Mildred's brothers had spoken out against the marriage, saying that they did not know where he came from nor who his forebears were. Then, when Harald said he planned to give his daughter and her future husband a share of his fields, her brothers objected. "The way we see it, we have been working those fields and giving a share of the produce to you and Mildred all these years. Those fields should rightfully be ours. We earned them."

The brothers shouting got louder, and Harald likewise raised his voice in disagreement. "Mildred and Aiken plan to wed in the springtime. They need to plant and harvest those fields. How else can they feed their family?"

Mildred's brothers claimed that it was unlawful for a highborn man to marry a common woman and threatened to run Aiken off. Harald, deeply hurt by his own son's lack of respect, began to cry. He groused about the years that he had been headman and had worked so hard to promote the wellbeing of their kinship. "This is how they thank me," he said over and over. "Aiken is not even my own kin, yet he shows me more kindness than my own sons do."

Mildred laid her hand upon her father's shoulder, bent to kiss the top of his head, stepped into the middle of the argument, and stood nose to nose with her eldest brother.

Mildred was tough. If she had been a man, she would have made a good warrior. She looked her brother directly in the eye, and said, "So are you going to run me off, too, then?" She took a step forward and pushed her chest so forcibly into her eldest brother's chest, it was like the clashing of two shield walls.

The brothers stood crowded together between a bed and the table to present a united front. So when her eldest brother took a step backward to catch his balance, he stepped on the brother's toes who was standing right behind him, and they both nearly fell over. They never did recover their dignity. And, after that bumbling, laughable show of united, brotherly strength they had no choice but to back down on their threats.

In the end, Harald got Headman Lyn to agree with him. And since the headman handed out the rights to work each field, the brothers had to accept his decision. To save face, they claimed that they had wanted things to work out that way, all along. Since Mildred and Aiken were now working those fields, the brothers said, it was a good thing because they were no longer responsible for keeping Harald and Mildred's larder full.

After that problem was taken care of, the next obstacle to their marriage presented itself. Although Aiken lived outside the law, the law still decreed who he could wed. It was unlawful for a highborn man to marry a common woman, but a highborn man could keep an unwed common woman for a consort. However, when Aiken suggested that simple solution to the problem, Mildred broke into tears. She insisted they bind their holy union with a ceremony. So, in the end, Aiken and Mildred got around what was forbidden by speaking their vows in secret. Otherwise, everything was had been done according to tradition. Aiken gave Harald several coins for Mildred's bride price, and Lady Blessed sanctified their marriage.

Foregoing the usual crowd of celebrants, they stood, hand-in-hand, inside Mildred's house, in Harald's presence to speak their vows. Aiken told Mildred that she meant more to him than all the jewels and gold in the entire world. Mildred gazed lovingly at Aiken and told him that he was a beautiful, precious gift from Lady Blessed. And he, in turn, humbly accepted the honor but knew that he was nothing of the sort. He was neither good-looking nor a treasure. He was an ugly troublemaker, but accepted her praise nonetheless.

Back when he had been a member of a chieftain's warband, it had been assumed that he would have had enough wealth to keep, for a bedmate, an unmarried woman who was beneath his freeborn status, in addition to a wife. But as it happened, the woman of low birth, whom he wed, was the one who kept him.

That evening, Aiken began to sleep in Mildred's bed. The marriage was consummated and the following morning he presented his new wife with a morning-after gift. After they had yoked it to her father's oxen, she made a big show of her fine new cart. She handled the goad herself and drove it around the ox-road, telling everyone, proudly, that it was her morning-after gift. The cart was proof enough.

Although most of the men in the hamlet had taken the brother's side and disapproved of Aiken and Mildred's unlawful marriage, folks who lived so closely together were accustomed to overlooking the obvious when it came to keeping the peace. Because everyone had secrets, they all agreed that, sometimes, it was better not to get too curious about what their neighbors were up to. And though folks concocted all sorts of stories about Aiken's past, only half of which were true, he saw no reason to disabuse them of their faulty notions.

He just kept walking past Alf's house and headed in the direction of his workshop. That was the only place where he could feel at ease enough to let his guard down.

He lifted the latch and opened the door. It was dark inside but for the faint moonlight spilling in from the open doorway and a few pale blue, slanting moonbeams leaking in through random cracks in the walls and spaces between the thatch. He held his hands out to the front and stepped inside. He turned to the left and felt around the way that he would have done if he were blind in both eyes.

When he came upon Torwald's chair in the nearby corner he ran his hands over the carved grooves. Touching one of the two finials, his thumbs and fingers sensed the carved animal's wolfish shape. He followed its upright, pointy ears to the very tips, then let his fingers sense the eyes and the wolf's long snout. He slipped one finger into the beast's open mouth. Its lips were pulled back in a threatening grimace to show off its sharp teeth.

Until the day that Torwald had made his fatal mistake, he had been renowned for his balanced judgment and his strength in the face of an enemy. The honors that others bestowed upon him were well deserved. The men in his honor guard respected his decision-making. Although he slipped up now and then, as all man did, they admired his judgment, and obeyed his commands, up until the very end, when he took them all, but Aiken, to the grave. But even after the breech between him and his chieftain had driven them apart, Aiken continued to honor Torwald's memory.

He recalled the time when Torwald had restored the peace between two hamlets located within his holdings. It had been early springtime, right before men began to sow their crops, when the farmers who lived in the two hamlets were unable to agree upon a disputed boundary between two fields.

Upon hearing of the dispute, Torwald and about ten of his men, including Aiken, had ridden first to one hamlet and then to the other. The farmers were so at odds they refused to set foot in each other's hamlet to talk the matter over. Torwald divided his guardsmen in half and told each group to direct the farmers in each hamlet to meet at the disputed border. If they were unwilling to meet, Torwald said, the men in the warband should sway them to his point of view at the tips of their spears. After they had threatened the recalcitrant farmers in that manner, the men in both hamlets were more willing to meet at the disputed border between their two grain fields.

Torwald told the farmers to stand where they believed their borders lay. After the men had walked into the fields and taken their places, the fields, which they claimed were theirs to plant, overlapped by a considerable distance. The men in the warband were forced to break up fights between the men. Each group accused Torwald of siding with the other, because, they said, he had kin living there. But Torwald answered, "I have kin in all the hamlets. And so do you. We are all blood related. We are one tribe and need to stand together to solve this problem peaceably."

The hostile farmers paced back and forth. Forming small groups, they continued to air their grievances and to devise further arguments to support their claims. Finally, Torwald paced off the distance between the disputed lines and set the boundary midway between them. He ordered the men from both hamlets to come to where he stood. He posted some of his guardsmen at the outer edge of the circle. Yet the arguing farmers continued to punch and push each other. Aiken had been forced to step in between fighting men and to stop their blows with his spear haft.

Other men were ordered to bring hammers, spades and posts with which to position the new boundary. Once the border was set, Torwald and his men rode home.

Yet, that autumn they heard complaints from the two headmen. Each accused the farmers from the other hamlet of moving the posts. The summer had been dry, and the farmers feared their scanty stores would not last them through the winter. Again, Torwald settled the dispute. He told his guardsmen to take shifts, day and night, to watch the posts until the fields were harvested. That winter, he invited the two headmen and the leading farmers from each of the hamlets to feast with him in the meadhall and to settle their grievances. The following spring, Torwald sent some of his own household men to plant a living fence. From then on, a permanent hedge grew along the boundary line. That settled it.

That situation had proven Torwald's well-regarded decision-making. Aiken was proud to have dutifully served him. If their weapons had not enforced the fairness, someone could have been hurt.

Knives and spears can carry enough might to enforce the peace. But a decision to go to war is a different matter. Then the agreement to set and protect boundaries, prevent fights and save lives, became its opposite—belligerent aggression. To declare war against the tribes in the western lands was dangerously provocative. Leofar insisted that it was more honorable to put an end to the annual tribute. He had attempted to convince the other chieftains for years, but they were hesitant to provoke a war. The tribute was the price they paid to govern themselves. If they lost, the upheaval could end governance by the freemen who met at the Assembly. It would put an end to the rule of law as they knew it. Instead, they would lose their freedom and be forced to obey other men's laws. The amount of tribute they would be forced to pay would increase along with double-dealing. It would mean the men and women in his tribe could no longer offer allegiance to the ruling powers they revered but would be forced to bow down to the ruling powers the men in the western lands worshipped. Many men feared they might be forced into bondage and driven from their homes if they lost the war.

The danger of the ensuing chaos had been Torwald's greatest fear. His concern was the reason that he had ruled against Leofar's proposal at the Assembly. And because Torwald had defended what he believed was a deliberate and thoughtful decision, he had been brutally murdered in an ambush. Aiken's knowledge that Leofar, the man whom he had sworn to challenge, could provoke such irredeemable destruction was more weight than he could possibly bear alone.

Aiken stood in the open workshop doorway and looked both ways down the narrow alleyway running between the sheds and byres. Longing for his chieftain's guidance, Aiken watched, as he often did, to await his chieftain's entrance. The vacant chair in the corner was ready for Torwald. But the trouble was that Torwald never came, and he never would.

But who was this? Caught off guard momentarily, Aiken looked again. Alger was coming toward him through the narrow alleyway. Aiken recognized his friend's square jaw and well-trimmed beard. The long, yellow hair that grew to a peak in the center of his broad forehead was combed straight back and fell to his shoulders—his beautiful friend. They embraced, clapped each other on the shoulders, and held each other at arms-length.

"Let us not fight any more, Aiken."

"I need you to back me, Alger. Say you will."

For a moment, Aiken saw in Alger's eyes the full restoration of all that he had lost and all that he still longed for. Alger. His very best friend, his trustworthy blood-brother was once again the very same man he remembered. Not a day older, undamaged by war, he was the same man that he had been that fateful morning when they had thrown the bones on the riverbank, before everything had fallen apart, before Aiken had been left to burn Alger's bones on the funeral pyre, and before he had sworn to settle the score.

Aiken turned around to look inside his workshop. To his surprise, while his back was turned, it had been prepared for a feast. To celebrate Alger's return, the walls were hung with weavings and embroidered tapestries. The tables around the sides were covered with woven runners, bronze platters, gold cups, and silver pitchers, filled to their brims with mead and ale. The polished tableware shimmered in the light cast by the torches, rush lights, and blazing hearths.

Aiken took his friend by the elbow and led him inside. He showed his friend the many chairs and benches, ale bowls, trenchers, and treasure boxes that he had carved over the years. "I am no longer the man I was before," he said. "These are the signs of the man I am now."

He led his friend onto the dais where he had set Torwald's chair at the center of the table. The boxy high seat had a straight, tall back, and the two sides formed its legs and armrests. Aiken told Alger that when their chieftain takes his seat, the two finials decorating the chair's tall back are carved in likenesses of wolf heads to convey Torwald's ruthless leadership. The two armrests, formed in graceful curves to match the robust lines of the man's well filled-out forearms, each end with a bearded man's carved head.

"When Torwald sits upon this chair, he will rest his hands upon these two heads and will be filled with the power to send his killers, Oswald and Leofar, to Mother Torment's lowest land of the dead. That is where they belong—among the oath-breakers."

The back of the chair was carved with a design commemorating the moment when Aiken had kissed Torwald's hand and promised to be his man. The great surrounding knot interlaced the two men like a braid. Ribbons and rich foliage linked them with their war companions, their families, and the lands they had promised to keep safe from encroachment by intruders.

Aiken rubbed his finger over the letters that he had carved into the scrolling ribbon at the top and read aloud the words, "'This promise shall endure until the Endtime.'

"Someday, when Torwald sits upon this chair, he will take in the signs of power that are pictured in the wood. The force of the designs will sink into his bones and strengthen the heart of his command with luck."

Alger complimented Aiken on the way the high seat graced his hall. All the items that Aiken had carved pictured a warrior's life and raised his ideals to the most heroic heights.

"All but one," Aiken said, with the typical, dry humor that he used to mask how painfully weak, powerless, and helpless he often felt. He picked up the treasure box that he had made to illustrate Wayland's story, and said, "This is a reminder. Its sole purpose is to let the chieftains know that I have not forgotten their treachery."

The pictures Aiken had carved on the box elevated the skills of a craftsman, not a man-at-arms. It illustrated the threat he posed whenever he turned against the man for whom he worked and infused whatever he made with curses rather than with luck. "Do not think that I cannot do it, either, because I can, and I will."

Aiken led Alger to a chair at the high table and, after he had pulled up another, sat beside his friend. Apologetic about the lack of serving girls in his meadhall, Aiken said, "Tonight, the women are all seated around the hearth in their own hall, telling stories amongst themselves."

Since Aiken was host and had no serving girls to pour the ale that night, he reached across the table to pick up a lathe-turned pitcher full of ale, and two empty wooden drinking bowls that he had carved himself. About the size and shape of the upper half of a man's skull, each drinking bowl was beautifully embellished with two elaborate handles that mimicked a horse's curved neck and head. Aiken filled one and handed it to Alger. He then filled another for himself. Each man hooked his hands under the two horses' necks and wrapped his palms and fingers around the bowl. Cradling them, they both raised the ale bowls, said, "To our brotherhood," and took a sip.

"Alger, would you like to hear a story?"

Upon seeing Alger nod agreeably, Aiken set his bowl down, opened the lid on the box illustrating Wayland's story, peeked inside, clapped his hands and called for Giles.

The storyteller walked into the meadhall. He was dressed in a long coat woven from woolen cloth dyed dark yellow and richly trimmed along the borders. It was open down the front and closed near the neckline with two bowed brooches. The coat was cut in a style worn by both men and women who lived in the southwestern lands.

"Greetings Aiken," Giles said. "I am honored to be present in your meadhall tonight. What pleases you?"

"My good friend Alger and I would like to hear the story of Wayland the Smith."

"Ahhh, that is a story I know it well and will gladly entertain you. I was living in Nathen's hill fort when Wayland was the foremost smith in the land. You may have heard other's tales about Wayland, but they are all of ill repute. You see, stories are like gossip. They change direction as readily as does the wind. Sometimes a flight of fancy will lead a storyteller to go one way and, at other times, to go another way. To make his mark upon the tale, with no regard for truth, a man may choose to add some clever detail just to make a point or to impress his listeners with his talents. But you may trust me to relay the facts, for I was the poet in Nathen's meadhall when these events occurred."

Wayland was a big, strong man who was born from a union between a water sprite and a cunning man who had come from the land where the ice never melts. When he was a youth, he apprenticed to become a smith. Once he had come of age, he set up his forge in the village under Chieftain Durbin's domain. That was where Wayland first became known for his well-crafted weaponry, jewelry, and tableware.

One summer, Chieftain Nathen attacked Chieftain Durbin's hill fort. Nathen burned the village and put all the people who lived there in bondage. He treated them cruelly and sold many captives. But Wayland was singled out and taken to Chieftain Nathen's hill fort. Once he was there, he was ordered to make weaponry for Nathen's warriors. But Wayland refused to make knives and spears for such a cruel man and ran away instead.

Fearing the weaponry that Wayland made could be used against him,

Chieftain Nathen said the smith should work for no one but him and those who served in his warband. He sent his men to chase down the smith. When Nathen's men found Wayland in another town, they came upon him in the night while he slept, bound him with ropes, and took him away.

When the smith was brought to stand before Nathen, the chieftain said, "Wayland, I am a wealthy man, and I get whatever I go after. I offered you jewels, gold, silver, bog iron, copper, and tin with which to make fine tableware, jewelry, and weaponry. I gave you men to work the forges under your direction, but instead you insulted me by running off. Now you will never run again." The chieftain told Wayland's captors to hamstring the smith. And so, it was done, just as Nathen ordered.

Soon afterwards, Wayland propped himself on sticks, and hobbled into the deep forest. He came to the banks of the fast-running brook where his mother, the water sprite, dwelt. He told her his troubles and she, in turn, told her son to gather wisdom from the hidden folk, for their teachings would become a boon to him and help ease his pain. Each day thereafter, he walked lamely over the hillside fields and through the meadows. He studied the flowers, the trees, and the wild creatures. In this way, Wayland came to learn the secret teachings from the hidden folk.

One day, Nathen's daughter, Hilda, went hunting with her falcon. Her bird flew off and Hilda followed. Soon she lost touch with the others with whom she was hunting and became lost deep in the woods. She wandered about until she came upon the brook where Wayland sat. He was watching the fish, frogs, and other small creatures. Studying their movements and their patterns he was learning secret things from them.

When Wayland saw her looking at him he smiled and spoke gently. Since she saw no reason to fear him, Hilda walked up boldly, greeted him and sat beside him. He pointed out the many hidden things he had discovered about the flowers and the trees, the fish and the other small creatures that lived in the forest. And since Wayland was a man who understood the power of beauty and the seductive quality of pleasure, he cast his wiles as he spoke.

Immediately smitten with Wayland, Hilda asked the smith to make her necklaces and brooches, cups and platters, all designed with these hidden things in mind. In this way, she told him, she would remember the enchanted time she had spent seated there beside him. Wayland forgot his anger and hatred for all things having to do with Nathen and agreed to do as she requested. When her companions appeared, Wayland said goodbye to Hilda and told her to come and see him whenever she wanted.

Wayland made beautiful things again, and Hilda came to see him often. One day he showed her a necklace he had finished. He stood behind her and fastened the clasp. When he bent to kiss her on the back of the neck, she turned to face him and returned his affection.

Shortly afterward Hilda stopped coming to the smithy. And, since Wayland was a man who refused to be put off, he made up his mind to go to Hilda. He packed the necklaces, brooches, and arm rings, which he had completed, and took them to her chambers.

When he arrived, however, Hilda would neither open the door, nor speak with him. Wayland had not counted upon being rebuffed in this fashion. He refused to leave, pounded loudly, and demanded entrance to her chamber.

To put a stop to the trouble he was causing, Hilda's serving woman opened the door. Though she told him to go away, Wayland pushed the door open and forced his way inside.

He found Hilda hidden in the shadows holding a cloth over her head. When he pulled the cloth away, he saw her cheek was bruised. When he asked what had happened, she said that her brother, Rand, had beaten her. Although she pleaded with Wayland to go away, he refused to leave. Hilda began to cry. She tried to turn away from him. But he grabbed her by the wrist and asked why she cried so hard. He wanted to know what she was not telling him.

Hilda told Wayland that Rand was jealous because he knew how fond she was of him. She feared her brother would kill them both. Finally, she told Wayland her shameful secret. Her brother came into her bed at night. Because Spider the Entangler had promised Rand an uncanny protection if he agreed to violate the forbidden act, her brother's ugly deed had made him unbeatable on the battlefield. These were the forces that Hilda and Wayland were up against.

When Wayland understood how wickedly Rand had mistreated his sister, he was enraged. He told Hilda that it was not her fault. He would not hold against her what her brother did. But for the sake of both their lives they must hide their fondness for each other. Whatever he did next would be done to make things right. And so, they parted ways for a while.

Wayland set out to make a short knife for Rand. First he made a visit to the hidden folk whom he had befriended in the forest. They told him how to craft a blade and to bind it with a spell. The words he wrote with secret signs would counteract the otherworldly powers that Rand had acquired and would guarantee that the knife killed no one but its owner.

After the blade was forged, Wayland inscribed it with secret signs and filled the grooves with gold. When he was finished, the blade read, 'Wayland made me for Rand.' It was in this way that the spelled signs became self-cursing to its owner. Wayland crafted a fine gold hilt with a red stone in the pommel and sheathed the knife in a jeweled scabbard.

When it was finished, Wayland carried the blade to Nathen's meadhall. There was a feast that night, so he brought it inside. Hilda sat between her father and her brother. Wayland stood before Nathen's son. Propped up on his sticks, he held the sheathed blade in his hands, and lowered his head humbly. He extended his arms to present Rand with the knife. Hilda's brother was all eyes for the beautiful blade's hilt and the sheath encasing it. He grabbed the knife and scabbard away from Wayland and told the smith to go away. He said that craftsmen were not allowed inside the meadhall on feast nights unless they were there to serve food and to tend the fires.

Wayland turned away and made his way out of the hall.

Rand held the sheath with his left hand and, as he drew the knife with his right, it turned against its owner. With deadly vengeance hidden beneath its beauty, the blade sliced Rand across the thumb pad. Rand stuck his thumb into his mouth, touched the drop of blood to his tongue, and gave no further thought to the injury.

It did not occur to him that Spider, as was his wont, had deceived him with false promises of invincibility. Rand was not fighting on the battlefield, where he was unbeatable but, rather, he was feasting, unprotected, in the meadhall.

Throughout the evening, Rand was ashamed to have hurt himself unsheathing his own knife and tried to hide the cut. But by the end of the night his thumb was festering and swollen to twice its size. Still, Rand continued to believe that he was invulnerable to harm and gave no thought to the injured thumb.

Laying abed, he was overcome with chills and fever and began to shake. He saw the terrible haunts of men whom he had killed in the cruelest fashion and was frightened for his life. By morning, the thumb had turned black and, by afternoon, Rand lay dead.

Nathen was immediately suspicious. He took the knife to Wayland, and said, "Now, cut yourself with this blade and die of poison the same way my son did."

Wayland drew the blade from the sheath and sliced his inner wrist. As his blood pooled in small droplets along the slash, Wayland looked coldly at Nathen and said, "There was no poison except for the wickedness Rand had within himself. What killed your son was his own depravity."

Nathen assigned a man to watch over Wayland. He was told to make certain that the smith did nothing to the wound that would offset the poisonous effect of the blade. But Wayland went back to work and showed no sign of weakening.

Hilda visited Wayland the very next day, and together they plotted their escape. Because Wayland had studied the bird's movements, he knew how to design wings with which to fly.

Hilda's mother's kin lived on the banks of a river that joined the brook that was home to Wayland's mother, the water sprite. Hilda told the smith that she would go there to visit her uncle. Her serving women would accompany her, along with the men-at-arms who were loyal to her. Once she was at the place where the brook and the river converged, she would await Wayland's arrival.

Hilda sent her falcon hunting, and Wayland set traps. They collected birds and attached the feathers, they had gathered, to the mechanical wings that Wayland had contrived.

When everything was ready, Hilda left for her uncle's hill-fort. Several nights later, the moon was full. Wayland made his way to the top of the highest hill and buckled on the harness. He spread his wings, left the sticks behind, let the wind gusts lift him, and began to pump his arms. And as he soared over the land, with his mother's guidance, he followed her watery moonlit reflections like a chain of open, silver links.

Wayland flew as far as the place where the brook joined the river. When he saw Hilda standing on the river bank, he stopped pumping and, trusting to his wide-spread wings, floated down and landed. She wrapped her arms around him in a loving greeting. Her men helped Wayland into the horse-drawn wagon. Hilda sat beside Wayland as he rested and swore to never again leave his side.

Once the order was given to move on, her group of followers and the wagon carrying Wayland the Smith and Hilda the daughter of Nathen made its way toward a life free of her father's cruelties.

Wayland and Hilda came to her uncle's hill fort and, in return for their allegiance, they fell under his protection. They set up their household on an island in the river. Wayland made jewelry for Hilda and weaponry for her uncle's kin.

That is how Wayland got even with the cruel man who had killed his friends and hobbled him. Wayland had convinced Nathen's daughter to shift her loyalties and to attach herself to him. He had brought about the man's son's death. But unlike Wayland, who fathered a son who became a great hero, Nathen died hated and alone. It was a fitting punishment for a cruel man.

And so, this is where I end my story of Wayland the Smith.

IV.

Aiken heard the dogs making noise again and shook himself alert. Still holding the treasure box that illustrated Wayland's story, he was pleased to know that it did what the signs and figures were meant to do: it got his message across. Aiken set the box down on his work bench and closed the lid. He admired it's good, tight fit, lightly tapped the top with his fingertips, and said, "Goodnight, Giles."

The box was almost finished. After it was rubbed with another coat of bee's wax, the polished wood would glow in any meadhall whose chieftain was lucky enough to own it.

Arms extended, Aiken shuffled toward the open doorway. He pulled his cloak tight, stepped outside his work shed, and latched the door. Aware that wolves, foxes, or even hard-scrabble outlaws might attempt to sneak in past the ox-road, he set out to take another look around the hamlet before he returned to his place on the bench.

Wayland had lived at the behest of the chieftains, just as Aiken did, but in the end, the smith had come through the worst of it alive. By outwitting his enemy, he had regained his freedom and had built his reputation. And though Wayland had not been a fighting man, he had kept his pride and self-esteem after he was hobbled. For Aiken the story was important to keeping his faith in justice alive.

His own battle of wits had begun the day that he had fought over his right to keep Torwald's chair inside of his own work shed. And ever since that first confrontation with the chieftains' men, every encounter had been another battle to stay alive and to hang onto his status as a freeman.

It happened that first autumn after he had begun to live in Mildred's hamlet but before they were wed. Up until then, no one but the local hamlet dwellers had known that Aiken was living there. Though the chieftains would have found his presence in the hamlet unlawful, it had been a mark of Aiken's pride in his own self-worth to refuse to cower or to hide.

There had been several, recent light dustings of snow that had quickly melted. But the day of the encounter with the chieftain's men, the heavy, snow-laden clouds looked like dark gray pillows stuffed with downy goose feathers. Everyone was watching the sky that day, saying, ominously, that Old Mother Frost was about to shake out her pillows and to bury them beneath heaps of snow.

The overlord's steward and tribute collector, Edberg, had been late in coming that year and was in a hurry to beat the on-coming storm. Though everyone could hear his entourage coming from a distance, one man rode ahead to announce the steward's arrival. Escorted by several mounted men-at-arms, their horses' hooves clattered on the frozen soil, and the heavily laden wagon wheels creaked beneath the weight of tribute that the steward and his men had gathered from the other nearby hamlets.

Those men and women, who were inside their houses, threw on their heavy coats and outdoor tunics. Men pulled on their caps. Women covered their heads and shoulders with their shawls and wrapped the ends around their necks. They rushed out their doors, ready to haul the tribute out of the storage sheds, and to load it onto the chieftain's wagons. There was a lot of hand clapping, shouting, and scurrying back and forth. And Headman Lyn, after he grabbed his knotted cords, and ran out his door, was trying, against all odds, to take charge of the ensuing confusion.

V.

I have heard it said that there once was a time when no man owned the land or demanded tribute from another. Elders, like Aunt Edith, described a pleasurable, well-watered garden centered around a fruit tree. The first people were said to have lived there in blissful harmony. According to the stories, sickness, death, and warfare had been unknown until men and women disturbed the order, which Mother Necessity had established. When their claims to have powers equal to her own challenged her rulership, she angrily bade them ousted at the tips of flaming long-knives. And so it was Lord Glory the Shining Firmament, the one who governed the progression of the seasons, stood for the orderly movement of the stars, the sun, and the moon and who, because of his enforcement of Necessity's decrees, brought an end to men and women's sojourn in the peaceable garden.

To be sure, the thought of a pleasant garden, from which men and women were banished, envisions an interesting, cautionary tale. But I have lived a long time and my recollection of those events differs in the details. According to my memory, the troubles began when men and women ceased hunting and gathering their foods. Instead, they planted fields and gardens and tamed the animals they had previously hunted. Some settled on black, fertile soil, and others settled on rocky soil. Some found valuable stones and metals, and others found none.

Those who had settled on poor soil were unable to grow the food they needed and acquired less goods. They elected kinleaders to lead them on raids. Arming themselves with the same knives, arrows, and spears, with which they had previously hunted animals, the raiders then set out to hunt and to kill those of their own kind.

The attackers plundered the losers' hoarded goods, and took for themselves the rich farmland, mines, and quarries from which the valuable stones and precious metals were dug.

Those who were under attack fought to protect their land and property. They built fences, walls, stockades, and piled earthen berms. They learned to make better weaponry and tactically developed the shield wall.

At first, all the men were required to arm themselves with weaponry. But forcing those men, who were in the prime of their lives, to leave their homes and to join the raiding parties, or to man the defenses when the fields needed to be planted and harvested, and the stock animals required care, became too great a burden. Those who refused to follow the kinleader were forced to give up their weaponry along with their freedom.

The kinleaders, who refused to give up the power that they had been elected to hold, became the chieftains. By placing themselves above the men and women who had less might, they drew into their service other men who wanted to keep both their freedom and their weaponry. Those who gathered around the chieftains promised to fight, year in, year out and formed well-armed warbands. And since the warriors had the means to fight, they were able to take more of the things they wanted from everybody else.

As for the farmers who had been left without the means to defend themselves, they were forced to rely upon the chieftains' bands of warriors to assure their safety. In return for their protection, the farmers gave the chieftains regular payments, including stock animals, produce harvested from their farms, and other forms of wealth.

VI.

And so it was, that day in Mildred's hamlet, that Chieftain Garvin's steward was coming to collect the annual tribute. Dressed in the kind of finery that a man of high rank wore to show-off his status, he wore a knee-length, heavy woolen tunic, dyed with rare, blue woad. His sleeves were tight at the wrists and trimmed with a narrow border. The tunic hem was trimmed with a wider, matching border woven from threads dyed yellow, green, and red. His cloak, woven in a multi-hued chevron pattern, was draped across his right shoulder and pinned on the left with a fine brooch. Several gold arm rings clinked whenever he moved. His belt was closed with a shiny bronze buckle inset with thin sheets of garnet. His long-knife was sheathed in a scabbard decorated with silver plates.

Since the knife's jeweled, gold hilt looked too elegant to wear in combat, most likely his weaponry was worn for show. If he fought with a blade like that, men would fall all over themselves in an attempt to kill him, to strip him of his weaponry and jewelry, and to plunder it for themselves. During the chaos of battle, even an ally might find it hard to resist the temptation to gain so many riches from such an obvious weakling.

In marked contrast to the steward, no one doubted the guardsmen's readiness to fight. To make a suitable show of the Chieftain's might, they were dressed in their war gear, wore heavily padded leather jerkins, and covered their shins with leather guards riveted with bronze plates. Their spear points, helmets, and shield bosses had been polished until they shone. The long-knives, axes, combat knifes, hammers, and other kinds of assorted hardware that hung from their belts clattered whenever they moved. Strapped onto their backs were shields painted with Chieftain Garvin's insignia, two red stags reared up in conflict.

To present a suitable threat to any insolence that the unarmed farmers might pose, it was the guardsmen's duty to thwart all attempts to cheat Chieftain Garvin of his fair share of the harvest. After all, he and his men put their lives on the line of attack to protect these men and women who worked the fields and herded cattle and flocks of sheep. In exchange for their protection from the ever-present threat of robbers and hostile clansmen, their Chieftain and the members of his warband expected to be well compensated for their trouble.

The farmers acted suitably humble, fearfully bowed their heads and bent their backs as they brought out the annual, year-end tribute payment. They laid out the baskets of grain, cheeses, root crops, cured meats, bundles of tanned hides and sheepskins, bags of fleece, jars containing honey, and foods preserved in brine and sealed with bees wax. The tribute piled higher as men, women, and children all ran frantically back and forth. Meanwhile, in the midst of all the hubbub, Headman Lyn counted the knots he had tied in strings to account for all they owed Chieftain Garvin.

In contrast to the hamlet-dwellers' shows of humility, Aiken held himself apart. Early that morning, he had lain Torwald's chair back across two trestles and begun to carve the secret signs at the top of the design. Envious of the guardsmen who were dressed in all their war-gear, he had chosen to ignore the steward and his men by showing them his back. Their appearance had been unexpected but, had Aiken known that they were coming, he would have refused to hide. Though his presence in the hamlet was unlawful, he had promised to never cower, nor to show any form of fear or weakness. If he was challenged, he would go down fighting.

For a man who kept the watch constantly, it took a lot out of him to turn away from a pack of armed killers who might, at any moment, decide to pounce on him and to take him captive. Fighting against his need to keep them in his sights, he struggled to keep his rage and resentment over the unfair treatment, to which he had been subjected, bottled-up, corked, and under pressure.

Tapping the chisel with his hammer he carved a long, neat ribbon of wood.

The two wagons, along with the guardsmen and the tribute collector had come into the hamlet and had drawn to a halt on Aiken's left. The steward dismounted, and on his way to examine the pile of tribute building up on Aiken's right, he walked past the wood carver. At the point that curiosity got the better of him, he stopped mid-stride, turned, retraced his steps, and stood behind Aiken's back to watch him.

After the steward had seen him carve for a while, he walked over to the two, chair side pieces that Aiken had leant against a third trestle, on his left. He bent from the waist and propped his hands on his knees to examine the designs. Once he figured out what Aiken was carving, he asked, "Is that a high seat you are making?"

Back in the days when Aiken had been a man-at-arms, Torwald's household steward ranked lower than the warriors in the chieftain's honor guard and barely merited more than a cursory greeting. But now that Aiken was a masterless man who was neither beholden, nor answerable to anyone but himself, the reasons not to humble himself had doubled.

"If you know what I am making," he replied testily, "why ask?"

"I will claim it as part of the tribute."

"No, you will not. I do not intend to let it go," he said in a low rumbling growl.

"Do you fancy it for yourself then? Do you plan to make yourself the headman of this hamlet and to hold sway over your followers, here in the central yard?"

"I warn you not to toy with me," Aiken said. "No one will sit upon this chair."

The steward folded his arms across his chest, and said, "Do not threaten me—not if you know what is good for you. No one in this hamlet makes a high seat for any over-lord other than the one to whom he owes allegiance. And that is Chieftain Garvin."

"I owe allegiance to another chieftain, and this will be his high seat."

The tribute collector stared at Aiken who, in turn, refused to return the man's gaze. Every sinew in Aiken's neck and jaw tightened as he tapped the chisel in a perfectly steady, methodical rhythm. Aiken knew the tribute collector was looking him over. He could sense the man's disgust at the sight of someone who was dressed so shabbily in rags. No doubt the steward would ask himself why a common farmer was carving a scene portraying a man's holy honor to his liege lord—a man who, apparently, because the woodcarver had challenged his right to take the chair, was not Chieftain Garvin.

The overlord's man might not have been too clever but, sooner or later, he was bound to put it all together. Because the markings on Aiken's arms were plainly visible, the steward would conclude that Aiken was not, in fact, a farmer. Nor was he a common woodcarver. The tell-tale signs of Aiken's warrior identity were staring the steward in the face.

And once the man had figured out that much, the conclusions he drew could lead to trouble. Inevitably, the tribute collector would ask himself how a warrior, who was loyal to another chieftain, had come to be living here amongst the swine herders. He might think that Aiken was either a run-away, or an outlaw who was being hidden by the men and women in the hamlet. For farmers to capture a warrior and to hold him hostage was unheard of but, nonetheless, a possibility. A threatening situation could develop if the tribute collector concluded that Aiken was a spy, was being held for ransom, or was an outlaw hiding out. In any case, the farmers would be forced to hand Aiken over to the chieftain.

The tribute collector said, "I have a right to demand the high seat."

Aiken stopped tapping and turned to face the man. Up until then, the man had seen only the back of his head and the left side of his face. But when Aiken showed him the disfigured side the steward jerked his head and looked away. He swallowed hard before he could force himself to look again.

The youthful steward was good-looking. His eyes were grey-green, his face was long and narrow. He had a strong jawline, ruddy cheeks, red lips, and a straight, well-proportioned nose. His chestnut-brown beard and mustache were well-trimmed, and his curly hair fell to the length of his chin. These features, when added up, gave the man the grace that a lucky man is said to have.

In contrast to this man, who was confident in his knowledge that all men and women who looked upon him felt warmth when they were in his presence because of his pleasingly good looks, Aiken wore painful woundedness on his face. The reddened scars were freshly knitted together. The skin looked pale, stretched taut and thin. The obviousness of his suffering suggested the fears that any man would harbor about being either savagely hurt or killed. Some saw in Aiken the uncomfortable warning of what could happen to a man who put himself on the line of attack.

Since Aiken knew how alarming his appearance was, he had picked up a habit, which he found particularly annoying but, also, found equally hard to control. By tipping his head protectively to the side and down, he would try to hide the ugly side of his face and the shameful sign of weakness that partial blindness revealed. In addition to the horror of his injury, he felt vulnerable because of the chieftains' accusations and the shame they had cast upon him.

Unable to answer to the false charges, which had been brought against him, he was powerless to clear his good name and to restore his reputation. Instead, he had been forced to carry other men's shame for the rest of his life. And though the shame he carried was not his own, but was theirs, to remind himself that he had nothing to be ashamed of did him little good.

Whenever others stared at him, the equally weighted shame of being ugly, partially blind, and a disgraced outlaw, made him feel as though he was standing before an accuser. His head would tremble, and he would look down in submission before his anger and pride rose up to counter the impulse. After Aiken had waged the inner battle, he had to go through every time, he would clamp his jaw and push his face forward to meet others' stares head-on.

Those who did not know Aiken believed his antagonistic challenge was meant to curse them with the envious evil eye, and for that reason they reacted fearfully to his defiant stance. Aiken figured he had two options: either to hide his gaze, or to return the stare. But either way, he knew he could never win. This time, he chose to look the tribute collector in the eye, and said, "This carving is destined to become another man's chair. It is not for you to take."

Aiken reckoned the tribute collector might try to take him captive, bring him to the chieftain's fort town and, because the high seat was not yet finished, force him to complete the chair. After that, he would order his men to hang Aiken and to be done with him for good.

But if they took him captive, they would need to hobble him the same way Chieftain Nathen had lamed Wayland, or he would run away. And since Aiken had no intention of being hung, hobbled, or imprisoned the way Wayland had been, the steward was left with only one option: to order him killed. But if they killed him, the chair would never be completed. The tribute collector was caught in a double-bind.

Aiken may have been an outlaw and fair game to all comers but, in this situation, he guessed he held the upper hand. Aiken had caught sight of the steward from the corner of his eye when he was studying the quality of the carved designs. That observation led Aiken to believe that the tribute collector lusted badly for the high seat.

Aiken's haughty posture and protective stance threw down the challenge. Silently, he asked himself who would be the first to draw a weapon. If he and the other man squared off, and if he could stay one step ahead of the game, the contest was certain to come out in his favor.

"I will not let go of this chair," he said, "nor will I allow you to take me captive. If you try, I will fight you to the death."

But as soon as he had stated his position, Aiken recognized the singular problem working against his favor in this competition: he and his opponent were poorly matched. A long-knife hung from the steward's belt, and he had a band of warriors at his back. Aiken had a chisel in his left hand and a mallet in his right. Carving tools were hardly suitable weaponry. Nor did he have any back-up. Standing off to his side, there were a bunch of unarmed farmers who would do nothing to protect him. In fact, they would be glad to see him tied up and hauled away in the back of a tribute wagon.

The tribute collector began to ask Aiken's name, paused, thought better of it, and turned his head to look back over his shoulder. Aiken realized that the man was about to call his guardsmen. His head twitched in that slight tremor to the side, and he dropped his gaze. He cursed himself just then, for when everything depended upon a bold display of bravado, he had humbly responded with a shameful show of weakness.

It was during that fitful, sideways twitch that Aiken caught sight of Mildred standing in amongst her kin. Huddled off to his right, across from the trestles, the farmers were watching the standoff unfold between the two men. Mildred's eyes were huge, and her fisted knuckles were stuck in her mouth. When Aiken saw her, he realized that Mildred mattered more to him than either his safety or his pride. He may have put his life on the line, but he had not meant to put her life on the line as well.

Accordingly, his need to protect the chair was unimportant. Rather, it was his duty to protect Mildred. After he had let Alger run to his death, Aiken had felt so remorseful that the immediate need to take care of Mildred now appeased the shame. Aiken promised, then and there, to never let any harm come to her.

It was unlawful to live amongst her kin, and they would suffer for having sheltered him. Blazes lighting up the sky, and the aftermath, a heap of ashes where their homes had been, would be poor payment to the men and women who had given him refuge.

Before their homes were torched in punishment for hiding an outlaw who had challenged Chieftain Garvin's tribute collector, it was up to Aiken to turn the situation around. He prided himself on being a decent man. He had sworn an oath that stated no more good men would die on his watch.

Nor would he let them take him captive.

It was foolish to think that he could stand up to a band of well-armed men with only a mallet and a chisel in his hands. To be chopped to bits by the man's guards would be an ignoble way to die. Clearly, he had made a mistake. Aiken laid the tools down on the carved panel. Stiff and tight as a rope holding back a spooked stallion, no slack remained with which to make a second mistake. He pulled the rope tighter.

He looked the man straight in the face and said, "If you want this high seat so much that you would kill me for it, let me get my blade. We will spread a cloak right here, on the ground. You and me will fight for it, to the death, fair and square. Either accept my challenge or be called a coward by everyone who is here today."

Aiken may have been an outlaw, but when two men agreed to single combat, it became just those two men, equal in rank—and their blades. On rare occasions, when the stakes were highest, challenges to fight each other to the death were spoken and accepted. When a man could defeat another man by no other means, he could pit himself against his enemy and, depending upon nothing more than his skill in weaponry, either win or lose. And since Aiken had lost everything, including his own name, all he had left to wager was his life.

The tribute collector, however, had more to lose—much more. Due to rank, prestige, and wealth, he had a comfortable life and did not care to lose it. Aiken had known other cowardly men who, like the tribute collector, were greedy for approval and treasure, but were unwilling to fight for it. He could see it in the man's soft features.

All this time, the steward had seen only a scrappy wanderer spoiling for a fight. But now the tribute collector slowly put two and two together. Aiken could almost hear the man's thoughts. At first, it took a while to get much traction. The steward's thoughts creaked and groaned before they moved forward, slowly. It was only after they picked up speed that he suddenly realized that this woodcarver was not a nameless wanderer. No, he was not the man who he appeared to be.

Aiken's challenge of single combat was all it took to make the connection. Aiken could see the spark of recognition in the man's eyes. Now, the steward knew that the man, who stood there before him, was one of the men who had died a year ago on the bank of the Warring River. Here, then, was the problem: Aiken was neither as dead as he was supposed to be, nor was he an imposter. He was the real thing.

People may have dismissed Aiken as a well-known brawler who took slight easily and readily challenged men, but more significantly, he usually won. The tribute collector obviously knew that if he agreed to fight Aiken without stepping outside the roped perimeter around a square cloak, his challenger would surely come out the victor.

The guardsmen knew it too. One man stepped forward with an offer to champion Chieftain Garvin's steward by taking his place in single combat. But instead of accepting the humiliating overture, the steward raised his hand and ordered his man to stand down.

He then directed his attention to Aiken. He tipped his head back arrogantly, looked down his nose to address him in a nasal tone of voice, and said contemptuously, "I know who you are. You are an outlaw. And for that reason, I am not required to accept your challenge of single combat."

Unmasked and desperate, Aiken tucked a thumb into his belt and rested his other closed fist on the wooden chair back beside which he was standing. He leaned into it, composed himself, and displayed the authority of a man who owes allegiance to no one but himself.

Confident that a reputation, for the kind of cunning that a man possesses when he knows how to spell out words, will go a long way and make him an opponent whom no one wants to mess with, Aiken devised a threat that relied upon the skill he displayed by carving the secret signs right here, beneath the fist that was leaning into the back of the chair.

When so few men and women could read or write, written words were believed to hold within them powerful forces that, otherwise, remained hidden from ordinary sight. Written words were said to carry meanings that could open the space between the worlds and make things that were invisible visible. Spoken utterances lasted for as long as the object upon which the equivalent written words survived. Of course, all these beliefs were neither unfounded nor were they delusional. They were true.

A spoken word was light as breath and disappeared. But a written word made it hard and fast. The man who could spell out the sounds that composed words could capture time and convey the past to the present. Even a dead man's words could last for many years into the future without an audible voice. Once words were written they bore thoughts that, by the mere act of writing them down, became equal to powerful, influential forces. No one would doubt Aiken's mastery of those forces. Proof of his persuasive argument was right there, on the chair back, where anyone could see the strangely branching letters.

Though Aiken had formerly scoffed at those who threatened to call down curses, it was not because he did not believe a man or woman could bring down misfortune upon one's enemy's head. He did. He knew first-hand what it felt like to be cursed. But back when he had been a fighting man, he had judged such men and women no better than helpless cowards. He had seen in them inferior, faint-hearted folk who were unwilling to fight. Never before had Aiken seen himself as weak and vulnerable. But, now that he had placed himself in the same category as those whom he had previously judged so harshly, he understood that they had possessed no other recourse for getting back at others who held more might. When a man cannot fight his enemy, he will curse his enemy.

He breathed in deeply and filled himself with the complete and certain authority of a man who has nothing left to lose. First, he looked around meaningfully at the crowd of hamlet dwellers and then, he looked at the guardsmen. Finally, he turned his menacing gaze upon the steward, and said, "If you intend to kill me before you take this chair, I will call as witness everyone who can hear my last, dying words." He paused just long enough to let his words sink in before he continued, "Then, I will curse doubly anyone who sits upon this chair."

He gave each of the farmers and the guardsmen a grim, hard look, and said, "I will curse both anyone and everyone who touches this carving."

To take advantage of the way that folks thought he gave them the evil eye, his one-eyed piercing gaze became an asset in his arsenal. "Each and every one of you will be cursed if you so much as touch this chair when you pick up the pieces to pack them into the wagon."

Stripped of the power that he had possessed before, when the men, whom he had challenged, had quailed before his knife, he now picked words as his choice of weaponry. Aiken had always possessed a knack for seeking out other's weaknesses and for anticipating their moves. Quick to respond and to strategize on the fly, all it had taken was a brief exchange, amounting of little more than a cut and a parry to assess another man's fighting habits. From those simple observations he had analyzed how they would use their weaponry and had gotten a feel for where they would go next. To cut and parry with words was the next best thing.

He laid out exactly what he meant to do: "Believe me, Edberg, I know your name and how to load my words with menacing intent. By naming you a breaker of the law I will incur the wrath of the Matrones, the Three Cruel Ladies of Retribution who spin men's fates and take vengeance upon those who have sworn false oaths."

Edberg's sudden realization of the scope of Aiken's threat became a rousing terror. In a futile attempt to find a way out of the foolish predicament, into which he had so unwittingly gotten himself, his eyes darted rapidly side to side.

As always, Aiken was one step ahead and was quick to see the openings in the man's defenses. He knew how easy it would be to cast doubt upon Edberg's honor. "Do you remember how we attended the Assembly together, feasted, and swore our oaths? Do you remember how we promised to come to each other's aid?"

And, furthermore, to hint at accusations of collusion among the chieftains and their underlings who had refused to punish those who were guilty of Torwald's murder, he said, with stinging malice, "Do you remember? Do you remember how no one came to Torwald's aid when he was ambushed?"

Since he saw no reason to limit the threats to this world, he threatened to see Edberg's soul punished in the after-life as well. "Do you know what comes of men who break their oaths? Since I was denied rightful justice, I plan, instead, to take rightful vengeance. You can tell my enemies that I will be coming for them next. I have been to the place where the dead go and have returned with the sole purpose of dragging the lot of you, who betrayed Torwald, down to Mother Torment's lowest land of the dead, where the oath breakers dwell. There, I will fight each and every one of you until the Endtime. If you kill me now, I will take my accusations to the Victory Hall and will call upon both Lord Glory and the Matrones to mete out the punishment."

Then, after he had alluded to his uncanny ability to do exactly as he threatened, Aiken graciously offered Edberg a way out. "But if you want to avoid the curse, offer to make an honorable exchange. This chair stays here, but I will make another one just like it. After I finish it, the copy will be yours. I know you will please your liege lord when you present him with a replica of this high-seat. No doubt, you will be well rewarded."

By this single act of appealing to the man's desire for promotion and increased prestige in the meadhall, Aiken had made his offer sound generous. Holding up his hands and splaying out his fingers, he said, "These hands have been touched by luck. I am giving you a choice. You can either present Chieftain Garvin with a chair that is infused with luck or one that holds a curse. Which do you prefer?"

Right from the beginning, this encounter had not gone well for the tribute collector. Now Aiken could see the fear in his eyes. No doubt Edberg was as frightened of Aiken as he was of the shades who return nightly from the land of the dead to wander this world and haunt the living.

Aiken knew how this worked. He had seen the way men in the meadhalls gossiped and humiliated men like Edberg who were afraid to fight. This encounter had shamed Edberg in front of his men. His refusal to accept a challenge from a half-blind, ragged outcast had proven his unmanliness. If he had relied upon a champion to act on his behalf, he would have doubly disgraced himself and become the talk of the meadhall. Only women and weak old men relied upon champions to stand-in for them.

Nor could Edberg walk away without the chair. If he did, he would lose face entirely. He would never regain his men's respect. They would laugh at him behind his back and call him a fearful, strutting dandy who was too cowardly to protect his honor. He might lose his rank and position as tribute collector if his chieftain discovered his failure.

This situation had become painfully embarrassing for the man. Not only did the guardsmen know this outlaw was one of Torwald's men, they were also well acquainted with Aiken's reputation. Now that it was clear that he had outlived his chieftain, they also understood that he was no nameless imposter as Leofar, Gordon, and Oswald had claimed. No, he was Aiken, Torwald's man, and was very much alive. Worse yet, Edberg's guardsmen had heard him swear to wreak vengeance against the men who had ambushed Torwald on the bank of the Warring River. If word of this encounter ever got back to Edberg's liege lord or became gossip in the meadhall, there could be unpleasant repercussions. Most likely, Edberg would have to bribe his men and swear them to secrecy. Plainly, Edberg could not refuse Aiken's offer.

It was obvious to Aiken that this tongue-tied, strutting dandy was uncertain how to proceed and was in need of help. Speaking with the conviction of a man who has cornered and disarmed his enemy, Aiken lowered his voice until it was no louder than a whisper, and said, "This is how we play the game, Edberg. It is your move next. You go ahead and bargain. And, by the way, in case you cannot read the signs that I am carving, they say, 'This promise shall last until the Endtime.' It refers to the justice that I intend to mete out against Torwald's killers and their accomplices." Then Aiken waited for his opponent to decide. Not that he had given him much choice.

Most likely, if Edberg had known ahead of time how much would be at stake, he never would have tried to take the chair. He would have pretended to never have seen the outlaw and would have walked right past him. But now it was too late to ignore him. He could hardly walk away without the chair. There were a couple of ways to end the standoff. On one hand, since an outlaw's life was worthless, if his men killed someone, who everyone thought was dead already, they would be free of blame. But on the other hand, this particular outlaw would be unable to benefit Edberg if he were dead. It would be a shame if the chair was never completed. The gift of this chair to Chieftain Garvin could be used to raise his prestige in the eyes of his liege lord. And then, too, there was that curse.

But if he made a grand show of giving it to Garvin, Edberg would, no doubt, be richly compensated.

The sight of Edberg's eyes glazing over, made it easy to imagine what he might be picturing. No doubt, he could imagine the meadhall on feast night. Edberg would make a grand appearance when he stepped inside the doors. He would walk down the center, followed by two men who carried the well-draped chair. Upon reaching the dais, he would whip off the cloak that covered the high seat and present it with a flourish. Pleased by the surprise, Chieftain Garvin would throw his arms out to the sides. And, in jovial wonderment, he would step down from the dais, grasp Edberg and hold him to his chest in a tight embrace.

Then his chieftain would say something clever, such as, "I must try it out."

Aiken knew that simple statement was the best that Garvin could come up with. Most likely, the man had never, ever, not even once in his entire lifetime, come up with one, single clever thought. Everyone knew that he was an easily manipulated freeloader who lived off the other chieftains' good graces in return for his votes at the Assembly.

Once Garvin had set his amble backside on the seat, Edberg would drop down on one knee before his chieftain. Like the man who was pictured in the carving, he would pledge his lifelong fidelity. And because neither Chieftain Garvin nor the steward could read the secret signs he would say the words that were carved onto the back, exactly as Aiken had spoken them—but with a different meaning, of course—to seal his everlasting loyalty to his chieftain.

Garvin would be pleased by his devoted steward's gift. He would ceremoniously command an attendant to bring him his treasure box He would open the lid and graciously show his gratitude with a gold arm ring or a jeweled brooch. Edberg would humbly accept it and kiss his liege lord's hand. After he had received Garvin's display of affection, Edberg would become the envy of everyone in the hall. There would be no ugly gossip calling him a coward or a strutting dandy. No one would dare malign him.

Edberg simply had to have the chair. But one quick, sidelong glance at this coveted high seat reaffirmed just how protective Aiken was of the chair that Edberg wanted so desperately. If Edberg ordered his guardsmen to make a show of strength, there would be a nasty struggle. Aiken was prepared to put up a fight—or at least he looked like he was. His feet were spread wide apart and his knees were bent in a crouch. His arms were cocked out to the sides. His appearance was designed to show just how relentlessly threatening, fearless, and unstoppable he would be if he were forced to protect the chair.

To increase the threat that his posture presented, and to frighten Edberg into thinking about what he might do if he got ahold of his knife, Aiken eyed it and made a slight lunge.

Edberg took a step backward. Afraid that the outlaw might make a grab for the long-knife that hung from his belt, unsheathe it and attack them all in a frenzied display of rage, he reached with his right hand across his front and grasped the knife hilt on his left. When Aiken saw Edberg's terrified reaction, he forced himself to keep from giving himself away with a smirk.

Clearly, the tribute collector had only one option left: to compensate Aiken fairly. The man reached into the bag at his hip. Without taking his eyes off Aiken, his fingertips felt around inside it. He pulled out a handful of silver coins and at least one gold one. Without counting them out, he held them on his flattened palm, extended his hand toward Aiken, and said, "Here."

"Done," Aiken said. "I will take it."

Once the bargaining was over, if one could call it that, what with a challenge to fight each other to the death and the threatened curses, Edberg and Aiken settled upon the terms of their agreement. Since the chair was still unfinished and was meant to sit in another man's hall, Aiken said he would deliver the second, identical one in the springtime. He planned to carry it in the cart that he would buy with some of the coins that he was clutching tightly in his fist, and would give the rest to Harald for Mildred's bride-price. As part of the arrangement, Aiken demanded safe passage on the roads and protection in the market.

If Edberg reneged in any way, Aiken threatened to level that curse. He would smash the chair to bits with a hatchet and burn it on a bonfire, even if he was forced to set fire to the meadhall in which it was housed.

"Remember, Edberg," Aiken said, "what happens to men who break their oaths. For now, you appear to be a lucky man, but that could change in no time." And the two men shook on the agreement.

To have taken on a thin-skinned weakling like Edberg might have seemed insignificant to others, but Aiken counted their battle of wits among the first of his successes in his seemingly endless battle against the chieftains.

After he had worked on the two chairs all winter long, he delivered the second identical one in the springtime. It was placed upon the dais in Chieftain Garvin's meadhall where it's remarkable design caught the eye of everyone who saw it. After Edberg was forced to tell his chieftain the name of the man from whom he had gotten the chair, the word got out. When the other chieftains discovered that the woodcarver who had made Garvin's new high seat was, in truth, Torwald's man, they understood the double bind that Aiken had caught them in.

Rumors spread about the ominous likenesses between recent events and the cautionary tale, which the old women told, about a pleasurable garden from which men and women had been driven by Lord Glory the Shining Firmament, after they had transgressed the might of the ruling powers and had challenged Necessity's laws which stated that there must be consequences for every action. And, furthermore, since Leofar had begun to assail Lord Glory's standards of justice in favor of Lord Thunder's unprincipled might, the subsequent turmoil that Spider the Entangler could evince with his penchant for unleashed chaos carried with it the potential for far-reaching and unbearable suffering among the commoners whose fields, herds, produce, and lives were at stake whenever feuds, raids, retaliation, and war wreaked destruction in their wake.

Any ensuing unrest among the farmers, merchants, and craftsmen was sure to affect the chieftains' rule. Powerful men feared lawless instability and the double-dealing that threatened their alliances. To find their way through the entangled landscape that governed their affairs, each man needed all the luck he could get—even if he had to buy it.

Their uncertainty had been set in motion because Leofar had unsettled the order by murdering his uncle. After Aiken had been outlawed and the chieftains had covered up the murder, men had lost respect for the Assembly and no longer trusted the freemen to make lawful decisions. Though the chieftains feared the repercussions that Leofar's dominance over the Assembly might cause, they were also equally fearful for their lives if they crossed him.

They also feared Aiken. Because they had all been complicit in outlawing him, men knew that it was better to keep their distance. Aiken's threatened curses only partially worried them. The chieftains, also, believed that after Aiken had escaped from the otherworldly forces, who ruled the land of the dead, he had acquired an uncanny strength. Even before he had died and returned, he was reputed to be an uncanny fighter, a testy, defiant man, even a dangerous man who no one wanted cross. And now that he was endowed with an even greater cunning, no one wanted to find out what he might do if he was threatened. To the chieftains, Aiken was a slumbering, venomous snake who was better left to sun itself on a rock lest his anger be provoked. It was better to tiptoe past so as not to wake him.

Though to let him to live was risky, when chieftains' fortunes were so precariously balanced between prosperity and disaster, and luck was such a valued commodity, they believed that if Aiken had received cooperation from the otherworldly powers from whom he had escaped and had the ability to pass on luck because of his uncanny ability to spell out words, they were willing to wager that his carvings could shield them from the treacherous chaos that threatened to unseat them.

To own such power made Aiken untouchable.

Though aware of his true identity, the chieftains publicly maintained the lie that the real Aiken was dead, and that the man with whom they traded had been accused of slander. Because they never agreed to lift the onus of his outlaw status, Aiken had been left with little choice but to abide by their decision. He continued to live boldly as an outlaw in full view, while they continued to maintain the uneasy truce by giving him safe passage on the roads between his home and their villages.

His choice of weaponry had changed but his approach was still the same. The way he saw it, he was simply making different cuts with different tools. Whenever the high-ranking warriors' or the chieftains' stewards, with whom he bargained, made their request for a high seat, treasure box, or other, smaller item, Aiken always treated their negotiations as a challenge. His outlawed status may have made him masterless, yet he had taken on the role of the craftsman who carved the chieftain's high seats. By elevating their placement above all others who were seated beneath them in their halls, he had raised the distinction of their leadership inside the very buildings from which he was excluded.

He may have discovered how to make the items that men valued, but the satisfaction could never make up for what the chieftains had done to him. Between himself and each of the men with whom he bargained, he always left an open threat hanging. Lest they neglect to keep their end of the agreement, Aiken continued to be that testy, defiant man the chieftains feared. And like the proverbial sword of Damocles, he became a suspended, drawn blade, hanging above them, ready to drop and to strike a man's head from his shoulders.

Although Aiken knew how fragile were the ideals of truth, honor, justice, and loyalty that governed men's actions whenever they assembled, he needed to believe in their timeless, upstanding qualities, just to get through each day. He saw in his carvings a form of signage. Through pictures and secret signs, he could point imperfect, cowardly, and dishonest men in the direction they should go. In this way, he believed that men could become just and honest, upright men of stature.

He became a silent voice to remind them of the goodness that flowed between the worlds whenever men treated each other respectfully. But Aiken also knew how easy it was to forget the goodness that Lord Glory stood for, and how imperfect he was when he tried to live up to the ideals that Harald had stood for.

If the luck were to flow unimpeded through his hands, he could give no thought to the man whose meadhall his carving would grace. Otherwise, whatever he made would come out wrong; he would need to scrap his efforts and begin afresh.

When he began to work on each chair, bench, or treasure box, he took pride in what he could achieve with his hands. Each day, before he picked up his tools, he set aside his angry resentment and overcame his desire to curse each man for whom he had been asked to make the chair or bench or box. Yet, he could not help but taste the sourness of his own rising bile. He would just as soon say, "Spit on them all," and cleanse his mouth of the foul disgust he had for them and, also, for himself. But what good would it do?

Instead, he did his best to act as Mildred saw him. In her eyes, he was an upright man who was determined to make a good life for himself. He could have asked, "Who me?" and looked over his shoulder, thinking that she was describing someone who was standing right behind him. That was how far he felt from the mark. Yet, he made peace with himself so that he and his family could live within the chieftains' domains.

Aiken had made peace with the circumstances of his life.

VII.

Mildred's aunts and cousins came out the door, said good night and thanked her for her gracious and generous hospitality. As they walked off, Aiken and Mildred listened to the women's chatter until the last door slammed shut. She picked up his empty cup, laid her hand upon his shoulder, and invited him to come to bed.

"If it is all the same to you, I will sit outside a while longer to watch the moon," he said.

Mildred knew how often Aiken sat up most of the night. To pretend it was his duty to watch the moon, as if some danger would befall it if his attention strayed, broke her heart. To offer it as an excuse for staying awake, when that was the only way he could keep away the monsters that populated the dreamtime, made her sad. Yes, it was sad to see a man of such indefatigable courage be afraid of sleep, the very thing that most men and women yearn for because they find it is so restful.

But for Aiken, sleep meant that he had to let his guard down. That was when the invisible folk snuck up on him, captured him and rode him onto the battlefields where he was forced to relive the horrors that he had experienced so long ago. Aiken had never talked to Mildred about the bad things he had done back then, but she knew how heavily his past weighed upon his heart.

Back when Harald was alive, Mildred had woken one night and, upon hearing the two men talking, she had gotten out of bed. Dressed only in her night shift, she had stood just beyond the dim circle, the hearth light cast, to listen with horrified fascination to the two men speaking.

When Harald glanced over and caught sight of his daughter standing there at the edge of the shadows, with her eyes open in a wide, unblinking stare, he had scolded her as if she was a child. He shamed her for showing herself, only half-dressed, to a man to whom she was neither related, nor, as yet, wed. These stories were unfit for her ears, he told her. To hear them recount the gruesomeness of war would unsettle her sensitive nature.

A woman must protect her sense of safety, Harald told her. To be a loving mother to her children, she needed to be soft and gentle. To raise them properly, she needed to believe there was goodness in the world. "To hear about the way men kill each other will terrify you," Harald said. "Now go back to bed and cover your ears with a pillow."

Harold then lowered his voice and told Aiken, "Never tell her these stories or she will give up hope."

"Yes," Aiken responded, "that is what happened to me. I gave up hope."

Mildred had crawled back in bed but had not covered her head with a pillow. Instead, she had lain there thinking of ways to restore Aiken's hope.

Now, here she was, years later, unsure whether she had accomplished what she had set out to do. She seated herself on the bench beside Aiken, pulled her shawl more tightly around herself and said, "I will sit here and join you for a while."

Aiken took the sheepskin off his knees and draped it across her legs. He opened his cloak and, to keep her warm, spread his arm out wide to enfold her in his embrace. He reached across with his other hand and, taking her hand in his, tucked them into the cloak folds. They sat together, snuggling up close, holding hands and watching the crescent moon's slow progress across the sky.

Eventually, Mildred broke the silence. "Aiken, when you go north, I want to send Sunniva along with you. It will give her practice in the proper way to serve a man his meals and to care for his clothing. Since attention to a man's care seems to be a duty Sunniva is deficient in and does not fully grasp the meaning of, it will teach our daughter a woman's work. You must understand that your daughter's upbringing in this matter is just as much your responsibility as it is mine."

It was not until Aiken had raised objections to her child-rearing practices earlier in the evening that Mildred had seen fit to bring this subject up with him. "You must not pamper Sunniva. You need to be strict with her. You must insist that she help the women who live in the sea people's village with their work."

"It will be good to have Sunniva along," Aiken said. "She can see a part of the world that those men and women, who live inland, rarely visit. Do not worry," he said, squeezing her hand. "I will watch out for her and keep her out of trouble."

If father and daughter were keeping each other out of trouble, that would be a good thing. Mildred's decision to send their daughter along to serve her father was an excuse that she had contrived to cover her actual motives. The truth was that Sunniva would be ordered to bring her father home again. She was to prevent him from following through on any whimsical notions to which he might fall prey while visiting those peculiar sea people.

Mildred had not liked the look of Shipmaster Gevehard, not one bit. She did not trust that man in the least. Nor did she like the way that Aiken had been so attracted to the man and wished to please him. Her worst fear was that Aiken might take off and swear an oath to follow the man in the same way that he had sworn to follow his chieftain so many years ago. He had even made a chair commemorating his pledge to follow Torwald. And look where it had gotten him.

How Aiken thought that he could stay so long in a village with folks, whom he did not know, was beyond all comprehension. Her kinsmen were the only folks he could bear to be around. And even then, whenever they gathered for a celebration, something would usually set him off. Someone would cross him, speak a word he took the wrong way, or blindside him if they accidentally bumped his right elbow and made him spill his drink. Then, he would become enraged and walk off in a huff before he got into a fight. At least he knew, by now, that it was better to walk away. He would use as an excuse for his absence from the festivities his need to chop wood, carve, or turn bowls on the lathe outside his work shed. And there he would hide, for the remainder of the day, while she and the other folks breathed sighs of relief because he was not among them making trouble. That, too, made her sad.

Whenever they went to market, he fared better if he left everything to her. She took care of the bartering while he spent his time sitting on his stool, leaning back against the cart. To be seen with a small knife or carving tool in one hand and a block of wood in the other, was not unnatural for a woodcarver.

But she knew. She recognized that same wide-eyed stare he would get sometimes. If he was around too many people at any given time he would get uncommonly restless. Although he tried to hide it from her, she could see how his hands began to tremble if too many people were crowding around him.

He would act as though the men and women in the market were coming at him from all sides, grimacing and threatening, and looking like the same sinister enemies he had fought when he was young. But it was when he began to yell at people and to tell them to go away, that Mildred would graciously act as though there was nothing peculiar about her husband's strange behavior. She would step in, take him by the elbow, and hustle him back to his stool near the cart. Then, once she had gotten him seated, he would look up at her and tell her how he feared for his heart. She would lay her hand on his chest and sense how fast his heart was racing and skipping beats. She would tell him to settle down, hold his hand, pat him on the shoulder, assure him that he was going to be all right, kiss the top of his head, and convince him that she could take care of everything without his help.

If she had left things up to him, he would have pulled everything off the table, packed up the cart and headed home. Only a woman who was as confident, strong-willed, and capable as she was, could have handled him. If he had married a weak, subservient woman who obeyed his every whim, they would have suffered dreadfully. In fact, they probably would have both been dead by now.

"I do not understand why the escorts are coming next spring to lead you north," Mildred said. "Can they not bring their own cart and take the stone themselves, like the chieftain's steward does when he collects the annual tribute?"

"Mildred, it means a lot to me to deliver this stone myself. Gevehard wants me there until the ships set out. For me to be with him and to explain the meaning of the signs I carved is important to their success. He wants me to commemorate the stone at dawn on the morning they leave." Aiken squeezed her tightly and kissed her on the cheek. "Rest assured, Mildred, I will miss you every day that I am gone."

Yes, her husband was a charmer. She just hoped that he could hold himself together without her presence. "Aiken, I expect you to get home in time to help me with the planting. Since you plan to take my best team of oxen, it will be harder for me."

"Plodder and Smart-one are my team too. I am the one who trained them, you know."

"Yes, I know. You will take good care of them, too." Whenever Aiken acted like a sulking child, he stretched Mildred's patience thin—too thin, too often.

She was too busy to give in to the sort of nonsense that her husband consistently indulged in. Yet, she seemed to have no choice. She knew that Aiken heard voices when no one was there and conversed with dead people. He woke the other folks in the hamlet with his yelling and screaming in the night. She was grateful that those who heard him were no longer alarmed by the noises he made. They would simply mumble, "There goes Crackpot Aiken. Off his head as usual," roll over and go back to sleep.

Nor did she understand why carving this stone was any different from all the other things that Aiken made. But for him, it was different. He had begun to talk to the big red stone in the same way that a child plays with his toy animals and dolls. But in this case, the doll was a large, pretend-woman in the shape of a rectangular, stone slab. Ever since he had brought the stone home from the quarry, he had increasingly closed himself off behind a wall of silence. He was absent, even when they sat together at the supper table. Mildred was jealous of the attention that he gave the stone and had begun to think of the slab as another woman whose company he preferred to keep more than hers. Even to think about how much it hurt her, brought her close to tears.

Yet, she indulged Aiken's every whim the same way folks pampered their children. Of course, she tried to keep him within bounds, but there were limits to what she could do. He was not a small boy who could be picked up, carried into the corner and set on a stool whenever he threw a tantrum. No, he was a strong and willful man who did whatever he pleased.

The day after the shipmaster had asked Aiken to make the stone, he had spoken of nothing but Gevehard on their way home from market. Her own, grown husband had acted like a young, unmarried woman whose suitor was the shipmaster. That was how smitten he was.

Since no amount of tearful pleading or cajoling had made a difference, she had had no choice but to accept her husband's foolish wish to deliver the stone himself. It was just the same as all the other times when she had been forced to put up with his peculiar, nonsensical demands, fears, and rages.

Years ago, Aunt Edith had tried to dissuade her from marrying Aiken. "Now, you listen to me, Mildred," Edith had said. "Your mother and I were sisters. When she was laying on her deathbed, I promised to look after you. You need to understand that the man who you are sweet on is a fighting man. You have never known a man like him before. He is not like your father and your brothers. He does not fit in among the other men in the hamlet, and he never will.

"Aiken lived his whole life in the market towns and villages," Aunt Edith told her. "When most folks who live here rarely walk any farther than the closest, neighboring hamlets, Aiken rode the roads between the chiefdoms on horseback. He cele-brated in the chieftain's meadhalls and had servants who took care of his every need. They chopped his wood, carried his water, and thatched his roof while he gamed and hunted. He wanted to acquire wealth and treasure. He does not know how cows and pigs are bred, nor how to plow fields and plant grain. Sons learn those skills from their fathers. They are born with the good, black soil under their nails. But a fighting man is born with blood on his hands. Ever since Aiken was a child he was taught to make war. For Aiken, challenging men to fight in single combat was the way he built his reputation, not by breeding the largest hog or raising the biggest turnip in his garden. He was trained to be a killer. What does he know about living peaceably among our kin? Open your eyes, Mildred. Even the things he holds most dear are different from the things we value."

"He holds me dear," Mildred told Aunt Edith.

After she had waited for so long to make a home for a husband and their babies, Mildred had been too caught up in her youthful enthusiasm to listen to Aunt Edith's dire warnings.

Instead, she had taken Harald's advice. "Nothing gets past that man," he told her. "He will make you a good husband."

But now that her husband was trying her patience every day, Mildred agreed that things had turned out the way that Aunt Edith had predicted. Yet, Mildred had no regrets. Her marriage was just different from what she had anticipated, back when the bloom of youth was still on her cheeks.

Sighing deeply, Mildred stood, patted Aiken on the shoulder, and stooped to kiss him on the cheek. "Good night then. I will see you in the morning. Try to get some sleep." She walked inside the house and closed the door.

VIII.

A thin and misty backlit cloud swept breezily across the sky and scudded beneath the luminous white, round-bottomed moon. Lent the appearance of a longship pitched at a high angle, it split the rolling swells and trailed a white-flecked spume in its wake. Aiken was reminded of the men who pulled a total of thirty oars, fifteen to a side and looked to Shipmaster Gevehard who stood in the prow, guiding his crescent ship, Wave Crestar, home to safe harbor.

What Aiken was making this time was different from the treasure boxes, ale bowls, benches, and high seats that he carved to grace the chieftains' meadhalls. Each of those carvings was meant to increase a man's prestige—something that Aiken cared not one whit about. Why should he care about those despicable men?

This carving was meant to guarantee safe passage for Shipmaster Gevehard and his men whenever crossed the Merchant Sea's dangerous waters. Men's lives were at stake with this carving. Aiken had made a promise that no more good men would die on his watch. He was doing important work.

This was the first time that he had made a carving for a man who treated him respectfully. The day that he had met the shipmaster, Gevehard had honored Aiken as a man in good standing. He treated Aiken as a man of rank. Gevehard had not been afraid to speak with him openly. Nor had he acted squeamish when he looked Aiken directly in the face. Gevehard had firmly shaken his hand. He had not shunned him. He had seen no reason to rely upon others to protect his reputation, nor to deal with him through an attendant or a steward. In fact, Gevehard told Aiken that he would seat him at his high table. He said he wanted Aiken to be there when they consecrated the memorial standing-stone. Gevehard intended to praise a simple woodcarver, a man who was a craftsman like Wayland.

"I would be honored," Aiken replied.

And three days later, he went to the quarry, and carried the stone home in the cart. He and several men, who wanted to boast about moving a stone that was about to go as far as the Merchant Sea, unloaded it from the cart and propped it against the workshop's outer north wall. After the men had left, Aiken stood there, looking at the stone for a long time.

Over the years, his appreciation of fine craftsmanship had deepened. Now raw wood and stone aroused his wonder and curiosity. He was awed by the patterns that the grain formed in the wooden chunks and planks he worked with. He relished the tiny circles in bird's eye maple and the way some wood grains formed waves like flowing water.

The day he had seen this rock slab in the quarry yard, he had known this was the one he wanted. It had spoken to him that day when he picked it out from amongst the others that lay randomly in the yard. Aiken had been crouched down beside it, tracing his finger along a red line that ran through a pale-yellow patch. When he saw the way the line curved and split into two he was reminded of the blood veins on the back of a woman's hand. It was then that the prized spark, which he always waited for, came to him unexpectedly. To see the stone that way made him think that it was not inert at all. The stone was a living being. He knew, then, he could make, from this slab, a battle-savvy weave-woman. She would be a fighting-man's wife: a woman who, by weaving the fabric on her loom while her husband, Gevehard, was gone from home, assured his safety and, with each passage of her shuttle, gave him victory whenever he fought pirates and sea monsters.

As he expanded upon the possibilities, Aiken built up this imaginary woman and named her Hild. When he was finished carving she would be the same as he was, cut, scarred, and marked with the signs of her identity and her purpose. Over time, Hild's uncanny weaving skills would assure Gevehard and his men of the fortitude they needed to fight the terrible forces of unknowable risk that lurked beneath their longships' hulls.

Maybe Wayland was the only man who could have understood the amount of time and thought that Aiken put into his designs. He first worked out the rough ideas by drawing a stick through a box of sand that he had collected. He smoothed it out and drew the pictures several times before he was satisfied that all the elements worked well together. Then he picked up a chunk of lime and copied the design onto the stone. He rubbed it off and drew it several times until he was certain the figures and the signs would serve his purpose well.

When he was ready, he placed his hammers, mallets and chisels on the small wooden table that he had nailed together from rough planks. Looking over his tools, he checked to see whether each was well-hafted. He repaired those that were loose in the socket with pitch. After that, he sharpened the chisels with his files and whetstones. Once he was content that the tools were all laid out parallel to one another in an orderly manner, he brushed his fingertips across the handles and was ready to begin.

He picked up the smallest mallet and the tracing-chisel. Holding the cutting tool in his left hand and the mallet in his right, he began. With the well-tempered and rhythmic hammer blows of an experienced and confident carver, he followed the white line that he had drawn. When he was finished he had defined a shallow groove.

Aiken commanded his tools with the same precision that he had demanded from his knife when he had fought either a challenger or a foe on the battlefield. Each stroke protected those men, whom he had sworn to save from harm, and assured their safe passage. With each strike of the hammer, the meaning of the pictures and the secret signs were being twisted into the men's life-threads. The three Matrones' gifts would ensure the men's souls of an anchor point. Their return would be successful. Gevehard and his men would carry home wealth in their cargo hulls. No more good men would die on his watch. Aiken was making sure of it.

On the days when he could see Lady Sun driving her solar wagon low across the southern skyline, he stood with his back to her for warmth. With sunlight beaming down upon Hild's flat surface, Aiken told her about the men who pulled the oars and of Shipmaster Gevehard. He told her how the sea lapped against Wave Crestar's hull. When he described the serpents that lived beneath the waves, he was confident that this battle-proud weave-woman was determined to do everything in her power to make Gevehard's boats invincible. If one of the monsters, who lurked beneath the longboats hulls, lifted its head above the waves and lashed out with its poisoned tongue, Hild would drive it off before the creature's tail smashed the boats to splinters.

When she heard the story that she would, in time, come to stand for, Hild softened and Aiken's iron tools needed to exert less effort to enter her stony hardness. Aiken held his chisel nearly perpendicular to the red stone's surface. He swung the mallet with all his might. A small chip broke free, arced and fell to the ground at his feet. Again, and again he swung and hit the chisel. He was engraving without a struggle. And the chips fell away with ease.

After he had finished carving a line, Aiken dropped down on his haunches and warmed his numb fingers over the small fire he kept burning nearby. His breath clouded around his face as he spoke his pledge aloud, "No more good men will die. It will not happen, not on this stone's watch."

On days when the weather allowed him to work, Aiken was out in the yard carving Hild. Now that the days were so short, he was already laying out his tools before dawn, and he did not quit till dusk. Whenever he was carving, or even thinking about the designs, he would get so lost in his work that he seemed to be living in a pleasant dreamtime landscape. He forgot to eat and drink, and sometimes kept working until Mildred was forced to send Bertolf to drag him home. Then, he would nap before supper and look forward to carving the next day.

The dogs began to bark again and Aiken's attention returned to where he was seated on the bench. He put a hand down and pushed himself up. His legs were stiff after he had sat all night in the cold. Heading toward Mildred's chicken coop, he walked noiselessly between the sheds and byres before he stopped to listen. When the chickens began to squawk, he opened the door and surprised the fox. The little fellow snuck out in a low crouch with a chicken held captive in its mouth. Once it got past Aiken and was in the clear, the fox nimbly pranced off. Aiken chased after it and threw stones until the little sneak was forced to drop the bird and flee.

The hen shook herself out and clucked with salvaged pride. Aiken picked her up and felt her wings. Sensing no damage, he carried her back to the coop. He would tell Mildred to check the red hen more closely in the morning. The fox would be back again on another night. But tonight, they each had had an opportunity to meet up with their adversary. He might need to lay a snare for the creature. A fox pelt that Mildred could wrap around her neck would make a pleasingly warm collar. But, being so practical, she would probably save it and sell it in the market come springtime.

Once he was back at the bench, he tucked the hide around his legs and settled in to watch the moon-boat float effortlessly across the sky.

It continued on its way to safe harbor in the west, eventually went behind the tree branches and the nearby hills and disappeared. Aiken stood up from the bench, said, "Good night Alger," opened the door to his house and went inside. He had stayed the watch. He had held off the bogman for one more night. Now, he would get in a quick nap before another day began. When he awoke, he would agree to be Mildred's husband and a father to his two children for one more day and get back to carving Hild.

Part Two

SIX

Brown Onyx
It will provoke sorrow, fear, and terrible fantasies.

Take the stone which is called onyx. It is also called worry stone and sadness.
And if it be kept in a man's treasury, it will stir up trouble, cause
misfortune, and fearful dreams. And also, it will torment a man with
self-doubt, and bring about contention between friends. And this has been
proved by men of late times.
The Truth of Rocks, by Alwiss the Wise

I.

I recently acquired this relic from a shopkeeper who deals in hard-to-find rarities. How he came to own it he would not say. And though I asked to purchase it, the man would not part with it. To plead my case I explained the lengths to which I have gone to preserve specimens as fine as this one and asked him to respect my stewardship of history by allowing me to acquire it.

Unfortunately I was unable to sway him to my line of thinking. But because I had convinced him of my knowledge of old textual forms, he asked me to decipher the meaning of the inscription engraved upon its surface. Although there was a time when I had been more intimate with those who lived in Babylonia and could fluently speak their tongue, now that there are none with whom to converse, I have gotten a bit rusty. I nonetheless agreed to sort out the meaning of the inscription as best I could and, before I left his shop, copied out the characters.

Most likely, the rectangular object should be called a hammerhead. Carved from brown onyx, it is about the length of my hand and is half as wide. Thicker than my thumb in the center, both ends taper to dull edges. The inscription was engraved upon the wide, level surface on the left side of a centrally drilled hole through which a wooden handle had been inserted at one time. The three rows of individual characters that make up the text are enclosed within a small, rectangular box divided by two lines. Each character is formed by a combination of short horizontal and vertical lines, and an occasional diagonal one.

Stone hammers, such as this one, were Babylonian fighting men's favorite weapon. But, clearly, this was not an ordinary hammerhead. Rather, it was made to serve a purpose other than fighting.

With these thoughts in mind, I settled upon the most sensible meaning I could give the text. The following evening I returned to the merchant's shop with the translation in hand. On my approach to the shopkeeper's building, I was surprised to see that during my absence it had been seriously damaged by fire. The man, along with a few of his neighbors, were digging through the charred rubble. Lit by candles and oil lamps, he was pulling out whatever he could salvage. He told me there had been a dreadful thunderstorm the night before, during which the roof covering his building had caught fire when it was struck by a lightning bolt.

Fortunately, the onyx hammerhead had survived and lay in a box along with several small trinkets. However, I could see, from its appearance, that it had suffered from the heat. Marring its surface were several white, splotchy spots that had not been there before. But, otherwise, the hammerhead seemed to have come through the fire undamaged.

The merchant was grateful for my efforts until I explained the meaning of the inscription:

This stone in defense of our village,
To the Lord of Thunder,
We dedicate this gift.

The shopkeeper drew a breath, his eyes grew round as saucers, and his face blanched in horror. Fearful he would fall into a faint, I reached out to steady him. He hastily picked up the box in which the hammerhead lay and thrust it into my hands. He told me to take it away. It was bad luck, he said. If the stone had been a gift to Lord Thunder, the man feared that the Lord had known he possessed it and had sought to punish him.

To mistakenly own something so dangerous now terrified the man. If I wanted it so badly, he said, I would accept the risks involved. He believed that to make a profit, or even to retrieve his original cost, would prolong his current streak of bad luck, and refused to accept my offer of what I considered a reasonable payment. I gladly took it away, but, upon further reflection began to question my previous assumption that the lightning strike had been a random, chance occurrence that carried no meaning.

It could be said that all phenomenon hold meaning and will frequently correspond to important matters. When two events occur at the same time, it is natural to infer the coincidence has meaning. And if this is so, it is possible to observe in any event an encoded sign that conveys important information that can explain consequential matters, such as lightning bolts striking hapless shopkeeper's buildings. And if it were true that the lightning strike had been a sign that held an important message, now that the hammerhead was in my possession, I would need to decode it.

The characters that spell out the text are complex and demand a working knowledge of the meaning that the combined lines, which make up each of the signs, stand for. But there are simpler signs from which a man or woman may frequently draw meaning. Men and women have been reading the signs since long before they had devised the means to write their thoughts with glyphs and letters.

To think of this world as a three dimensionally written text, one can draw conclusions by linking the most commonly known associations between events. Our memories serve, in this respect, to connect these relationships by grouping associations together. For example, if a man sees dark clouds on the western horizon and hears the distant sounds of thunder, he will remember other times when these observations led to rain and, because of this association, will learn to seek shelter from the oncoming storm.

Other signs I watch for are those that are conveyed by the flight and song of birds; fortuitous meetings; the sight of a falling star; strange appearances of certain animals; or the discovery of either unusual or long sought-after objects, such as books and figured stones that have come into my possession in a timely fashion.

To catch sight of the signs I must stay ever-watchful. Though some signs may seem to be unrelated to the event with which it coincides, and may have a different relationship with time, even such seemingly illogical and unrelated correspondences may, also, connect with one another.

The observation of these correspondences allow a man to infer meanings that can shed light upon many of the questions that he might be pondering. And, furthermore, when the meaning itself, to which he has assigned an object or an event, is what connects them, he will, quite naturally, come to believe that he can influence his fate by manipulating the meaning that he lends it. He will then ask himself how his future actions may be guided by the knowledge that he has gained through the meaningful interpretation of the signage he has observed.

In the case of the merchant, after he had reasoned that his shop had caught fire in punishment for displaying the hammerhead in a trivial manner, he solved his problem by passing on the dreaded object to me.

To follow this line of reasoning with another then leads me to the believe that I may shape reality by using the power of my mind to imagine something that I wish for by controlling the signs in a thoughtful manner.

The imagination is one of the most powerful, creative forces on earth. Beliefs that arise from our thoughts are what drive all men and women's lives. The belief that one can shape reality by controlling the power of one's mind is not a fallacy but a truth. Such a belief is not delusional. I see the proof of this belief everywhere I look. I am surrounded by the objects that men and women have made, the fields they have planted, and the roads they paved. I eat the bread that Grerr bakes and wear the clothing that someone sewed. If I were to suddenly strip myself of everything that, at one time, originated as an image in someone's mind, I would find myself in a wild state, bare naked.

Because men and women have, from the very earliest times, understood that what they saw in their mind's eye could be made manifest with their hands, it took but one small leap of the imagination to believe that there was little difference between the manufacture of a hammerhead with tools and hands, to accept as truth the belief that thunderclouds could be manifested by thought and desire alone.

It is for this reason that the kinleader, who offered this gift of a hand-made hammerhead to Lord Thunder, had hoped to reshape the world according to the way he wished it to be. And if the signs, which he had instructed the craftsman to inscribe upon the stone, were a stand-in for the imagined thunderstorms, by writing the characters and controlling the signage in a skillful manner the kinleader would come to believe that he could influence the very things that the signs stood for.

Possibly, the local farmers were suffering from a devastating drought, and the villagers feared an imminent attack by their rivals. And though the kinleader may have, otherwise, felt helpless to turn events in his favor, by holding this hammerhead in his hand while he was looking up at the sky, and offering the Lord this carved, onyx hammerhead in exchange for rain enough to soak the grain fields and a promise of victory in the case of war, he was envisioning the world, not as it was, but as he wished it to be. In this way, the hammerhead, which had been made from a stone that was conveniently similar in color to the imagined thunderclouds, became a vessel for the man's hope, both through the signs that were written upon it and through the embodiment of the hand-carved stone itself. And because he was acting faithfully in accordance with his beliefs, it seems this predilection, which all men and women have for hope, arose from an innate part of his make-up and led him to believe that he could bring about the desired change that he hoped to achieve just by wishing it into being.

The assumption that events that happen in this world will reflect events that occur in the otherworlds is due to Mother Necessity's indisputable laws governing causation and effect. For, just as the famous alchemist Thrice-greatest Hermes wrote so succinctly in his Emerald Tablets:

That which is below is like that which is above
And that which is above is like that which is below.

That is to say, that according to Hermes's thesis, the same way that spoken and written words form links between two or more people, so too, written words and pictures may link the visible with the invisible. It is through this power of the imagination that the visible images and the audible words that can be seen and heard in this world will become links to that which exists in the otherworlds.

Likewise, the kinleader would have believed that, by picturing with his mind's eye something that he and his people wanted and needed, he could manifest whatever they desired. To accomplish this goal would depend upon his request being audibly and strongly stated. It needed to be held in a pure enough state to be uncorrupted by doubt. And if he were successful, he would bring about a manifestation of the higher authority, namely Lord Thunder, and along with the Lord's appearance, the guarantee of rain and victory in the time of war.

Defeat was not an option. The successful manifestation of the kinleader's desire would only occur if his belief in its attainment was stamped indelibly upon his mind. If he wished it to come true, the demand that he was making upon the ruling powers could never fade from his mind. Failure must never come to mind, only the successful achievement of what he was wishing for. This was the path to truth and goodness: the belief that his thoughts could create whatever he needed. To summon rain through his force of will was the same as making reality conform to what he saw in his mind's eye: the appearance of massive thunder clouds on the western horizon.

And what else, I ask, but a stone hammerhead could represent the kinleader's willfulness so forcefully? When he has seen, with his own eyes, how his hammer blows shatter the bones of his enemies? And when he has seen blood spray like red rain and soak into the soil, and through this action bring about the prosperity and the wealth that he wished to attain through victory over his enemies? What else could represent a man's willfulness better than a stone hammerhead? What could be more persuasive? Here then is the perfect vessel for the kinleader's willfulness when conjuring the image of rain and victory.

I harbored no doubts regarding the hammerhead's power. Convinced, as I was, that the merchant's fears had been correct, I concluded that the Lord had, indeed, wreaked a vengeful justice against the man by punishing him with the thunderbolt.

But what, I asked, should I to do with such a dangerous object?

Now that all obvious signs pointed to the Lord's jealousy of anyone who would display his hammerhead, along with a variety of trinkets and collectibles of dubious worth, without having offered it the deferential respect it should have garnered, I was caught in a dilemma. I did not want to part with the remarkable specimen. Yet, I feared Lord Thunder's wrath. In itself, the large piece of onyx was especially fine and the writing on it made it quite unique. And now that I had been forewarned of the dangers that accompanied ownership of the hammerhead, it was crucial to make a decision before disaster struck.

Thus, to discourage the Lord's temper, I have set the onyx hammerhead alongside the long-knife. And now that it is seated at the high table, like a splendidly attired visiting chieftain, after it has been accorded the honors it deserves, I hope these two allies will agree to protect each other's homes and borders instead of ravaging them with fire.

To study the inscription on the onyx hammerhead more closely, I look at it through the crystal ball. As my inner awareness sinks into the brown, translucent stone's depths, I recall a time when I was surrounded by dense fog mixed with smoke. I am overcome by a dream-like state of wonderment. And after I lose my bearings, lest I stumble and fall, I become very still.

II.

Here, then, was a land where Lord Thunder held sway. A broad hand came through the thickened smog to pull back a heavy drapery from a doorway. A tall, lean man stepped through the entrance. He was well-groomed in a dark green, woolen tunic and brown trousers. His lower legs were wrapped tightly with intricately patterned, yellow, woven bands. A cloak woven in brown and green squares was thrown across his shoulders and pinned in the center of chest. His yellow, sun-bleached hair was combed straight back and fell to his shoulders. His red beard was shorn close to his narrow cheeks and pointed chin. His deeply set, pale blue eyes were shaded by a sloping brow and focused with an eagle-like intensity.

Torn shreds of brown-colored fog-trails slithered across the ground and curled around his feet. The sound of his footsteps squelching through the muddy puddles suggested a hard, drenching rain had fallen overnight.

As he made his way through the dense curtain of mist, he could hear his crew members' muffled voices down on the strand. Working alongside the master shipbuilder, they were finishing the repairs and caulking the seams between the planks with a combination of pine pitch and sheep's wool. On the first sunny day, the master shipmaster planned to varnish the boats to make them fully seaworthy. Other men on his crew would be checking and waxing their oars.

Familiar with the way that fog distorts sound, he knew their closeness was but a deception. To get his bearings, he called out with a booming voice, "The winter has dragged on too long. It is time we go to sea."

In response, each man called back, "Hey, Gevehard."

Listening hard to the men's voices, he scanned the white, soupy fog. When he saw their faint shadows cast upon it like a curtain, he set out again. Feeling his way as he went, he headed toward the place on the shoreline where Wave Crestar rested in the slipway, along with the three other ships that made up his fleet this year.

From among the four, Wave Crestar was the largest, and Gevehard was its sole owner. A couple of boats were owned collectively by several brothers who split the take, and the fourth was owned by two cousins who were said to never leave home without the other.

Gevehard had begun to ride the longboats with his father, Garr, when he was a boy. After the first time he had gone to sea, it had drawn him back year after year. The sea held an allure neither he nor the men on his crew could live without. Once a man had gotten a taste for life at sea, once the thrill and excitement had captivated a man, it could be gotten no other way. He had been on the water so many times, he was more confident when finding his way by the position of the sun and stars and reading the waves and currents, was more enlivened by the feel of the wind in his face, and was more at ease adjusting to the rocking motion of the boat's floorboards beneath his feet, than whenever he walked on land. And it was Wave Crestar, his mother ship who carried him and his men in her belly

Wave Crestar's serpent-headed prow loomed toward him from out of the murk, and his heart leapt in his chest. Ah, there she is, he said to himself with a sigh—his greatest love. Yes, to be Wave Crestar's shipmaster was his greatest pleasure. He stopped mid-stride and stood there. He slowly shook his head side to side, equally in awe of both her beauty, and of the master shipbuilder's remarkable skill in putting her together with such grace.

Gevehard strode up to his boat and placed his hands upon the strakes that formed Wave Crestar's hull. He took in her wide, flat belly and the graceful lines that extended from her high serpent head at one end, to her spiral tail at the other. And just as his boat was made from oak planks and had the strength of that mighty tree, Gevehard's hands were sun-browned as oak bark and broad enough to have been carved from an oak trunk. They were twice too large for the length of his arms and his thick fingers were gnarled from years of grasping the oars and handling the steering oar.

At that moment, his ship so filled him with pride that he believed he could slip his huge hands beneath her shallow, flat bottomed hull and, with a mighty roar, raise all thirty men, who would be seated on the benches, high above his head and hold them there. That was the kind of uncanny strength he needed whenever he led his men.

Once he had heard a tall tale describing the way the waves had threatened to swamp the boat and to drown them all. But he and his men had never wavered. They had no fear of a storm-lashed sea. Nor had Gevehard cowered, the storyteller said. He stood in the prow scanning the waves, watching expectantly for that fateful moment when he would spot the sea serpent's gold-ringed collar rising from the roiling depths. And when he saw the dreadful serpent rear up as high as the ship's peaked prow, Gevehard fearlessly urged his men to row harder. Wave Crestar's shallow belly skimmed the tops of the waves until they came so close to the serpent that the shipmaster could look right into that fearsome creature's mouth. With its black, forked tongue flicking back and forth, the serpent and Gevehard faced each other down, head-to-head. And, scenting no fear on the shipmaster's breath, the serpent slipped beneath the surface, and the water became smooth as shimmering glass.

The night the shipmaster first heard the tale, he had laughed heartily. But there had been no truth in either the description of the serpent nor of his courage. Poets were known to make the real into the imaginary with a turn of a phrase. And though the story impressed his wife, Adelheide, the unspoken truth was this: he admitted the risks and he placed his bets accordingly. Each year, before he left, he wagered everything he had. And then, when everything was on the line, he had one of two options from which to choose: he could either win or lose. If standing fast against defeat sounded like a man placing his feet squarely in the prow and staring into a sea monster's gaping maw, then, he would accept the poet's description.

But, truly, he was nothing without his men. They were the ones who were the heroes. When he yelled, "Pull," he was confident that each of his men would pull the oars with more vigor than any one of them believed he had in his arms, back, shoulders, and legs. It was only when all thirty men were working together that they became a formidable force to reckon with. When they were under attack and he yelled, "Let's go," the men leapt the gunwales with their shields and axes in hand and boarded the enemy ship. Indomitable together, each man, alone, knew he might be leaping to his death, and still he jumped into the conflict and gave the fight everything he had.

And so, this year Gevehard would challenge the Matrones, and once again he would throw the lots. Whenever he guessed wrong and lost the wager, he carried the blame for their failures. As in previous years, Wave Crestar would be out front, making him the leader responsible for the wellbeing of over one hundred and twenty men, and for all the trade goods they carried in their longships' hulls. It was up to him to bring them safely home again with stores enough to make it through another winter. If they were to remain here in this village, on the shores of the Merchant Sea, they depended upon trade in amber nuggets, furs, salt, and their wives' fine weavings to make up for everything they otherwise lacked.

Gevehard looked out toward the sea and his men followed his gaze. Soon they would stand on the backs of their serpent-headed longships. They would look into the black, bottomless depths beneath the swells and feel both the excitement and the dreadful knowledge that anything could happen. Each man would reach deep down inside himself and touch the confidence that he had in his own strength and would courageously take on whatever the Matrones chose to fling at him that day.

Gevehard went from one man to the next, greeting each one. He clapped him on the shoulder, grasped his arm and squeezed.

"Hey, Arnold, it is good to have you with us. Your father and uncle were great seamen. I know you are equal to their reputations."

"Hey, Rolf, it is good to have you along with us again this year."

When he came to his nephew, Gevehard recalled the day when, four years earlier, he had told his brother's widow that Rodger was old enough to join the crew. Gevehard recalled how young and fresh he had looked back then, with his round face, bright pink cheeks, and sparkly green eyes. His mother, Innis, had looked Gevehard straight in the eye and said, "If you must, then take him. But promise me that you will watch out for him. He is my darling boy. Rodger is all that I have left to me in this world."

"You know, Innis, every man is important," he had replied. "I cannot promise to treat him any differently from the others. But now is the time for him to learn the ways of the sea. I should have taken him before now but allowed you to dissuade me. It is time you let him prove himself."

Four years later, her baby boy was fully grown and newly married. Rodger had handled himself well and already showed the mettle it takes to be a leader. Enraptured with life at sea, Rodger, along with four other men had agreed to pool their resources. If the trading was good this year, they might get ahead enough to build a ship. They would take out a smaller boat after they got home and head northeast to the forested regions where they would begin collecting timber. Taking the master shipbuilder with them, they would look for trees that had grown into the shapes they needed to construct the boat. If they found enough of both the straight trees and the branching trees they needed to make the keelson, stem, and stern posts, they would spend the winter making a ship they could take out the following season.

Rodger would then begin collecting his crew from among the eager young men who were growing into manhood. With the addition of Rodger's boat, they would increase the size of the fleet to five, assuming none were lost this year on the voyage.

When Gevehard joked, "Rodger, do you plan to build a boat bigger than Wave Crestar?" everyone laughed.

Rodger answered cheekily, "No, it will be shorter by two men."

Gevehard slapped him on the shoulder. "Did I hear you say longer by two men? Rodger, you are just cocky enough to replace me and to lead the fleet someday. I can feel it in my bones."

In acceptance of the mock respect, with which his uncle had honored him, Rodger gave Gevehard a teasing, toothy, ear-to-ear grin, and humbly tipped his head.

Already, Gevehard missed the one man whom he had always depended upon, but who would never again join them in the boats. Edmund and Gevehard had been best friends all their lives and had gone everywhere together till now.

Blaming himself for Edmund's injury, after he got home last year, Gevehard had taken to his house and refused to leave it. Lest anyone see how red and swollen his eyes were, Adelheide had covered for him, telling those who came to the door that he was sick abed with a stomach ache. Gevehard had promised Edmund that he and his family would always be well taken care of, even though he could no longer work as hard as a man who had two arms.

Walking toward the outlying barren fields and rugged pastureland, Gevehard headed away from the village. Though a fine mist still hung in the near distance, the fog was breaking up and floating across the land in thick, swirling strands. He passed windblown dunes and patches where sharp-edged sedges and pale green grass spears had begun to poke up from beneath last year's rotten, matted vegetation. He called a greeting to a boy, who, along with one of the village dogs, were watching several of his black and white spotted heifers, and a mother cow and her calf. Becalmed by the sight of the peaceable cattle muzzling the tender grass blades, Gevehard walked up to the cow, called her by her name, patted her haunches, and admired her calf.

Out across the fields, a thin layer of gray ash covered the dun colored soil—all that was left after the farmers had put a torch to the dried garden waste and stubble in preparation for planting this year's crop. The people who lived here could grow little in their soggy fields during the cold summertime months. Gevehard paused to talk to a woman who was digging in a small garden patch she had previously mulched with seaweed. Now that most of the fields were sprouting, the men would be leaving. Then they would be back again in time to shear the sheep, oversee the butchering, hay the fields, and bring in the meager harvest.

He paced beside a narrow stream, thinking about his men and how stretched apart they were by their fear. They were always scared before they left, but this year their unease seemed to forebode something worse might be in store. Their trepidation was so contagious that even he had begun to feel their terror.

Gossipers foretold the tragic loss of the all the boats and men this year. They claimed that he and his men had been cursed by the ancestors. Though Gevehard had tried to stop the rumors' spread, he had been unable to root out its origins. Like a seven-headed monster, which if you cut off one head, two more grew back, festering resentment continued to feed into the belief that their forebears had turned against them. And, since men and women responded more readily to their fears than to any facts with which he could present them, nothing he said nor did could allay their concerns.

Folks were angry with the gale winds, the heartless sea, the raging rivers, the cold air, the snow and frost, the dark nights, and the gloomy days that made their lives so hard. When things did not go right, men and women sought to blame all their troubles on someone. To make sense of their suffering, to stave off the dreadful loneliness that resided at the bottom of each man and woman's soul, they needed someone to whom they could point as the cause of all their problems.

And Gevehard was the man to whom they pointed. When things went wrong, men and women took out their anger on the man out front. And since he was the man out front, his every word and action was scrutinized by the villagers for hidden meanings until they had managed to describe whatever they feared the most.

If things did not get better, all the villagers would turn against him, not just the servants and the grudge-holders, but also the men who crewed the ships. He understood that everyone needed something from which to hang their hope, some assurance that there was a purpose to every gainful benefit or set-back. It was each person's nature to point to a tangible reason for the underlying unease with which they lived each day. Yet his knowledge of human weakness did not make it easier to deflect their worry.

He had pointed to each boat's construction. He had praised each man's preparation. He had shown them the good weaponry and shields with which each crewmember was outfitted. He could tell them that he was the one who knew the markets, the coves, the shorelines, the currents and the winds better than anyone else. But aside from those assurances, there were no solid facts. There was only the vast unknown that lay before them. And, naturally, the worst that the villagers could imagine had grown in size until their fears and resentments had become overwhelmingly and unde-niably as monstrous as that seven-headed beast.

To counter the villagers' suspicions, to set their minds at ease, and to encourage their belief that he could carry on and lead them for another year, he had staked ev-erything he had on Aiken's standing stone. He had sent four men to escort the stone carver and had expected them back before now. It had been over a month since they had left and tonight, the moon would be new. He planned to leave before the moon was full.

Gevehard scanned the fog bank and asked himself: Where are they? Had some-thing gone wrong? Had they run into trouble on the roads or been waylaid by out-laws? Had the rivers washed out the roads? Had the stone carver not finished on time? Had Aiken kept the coins that he had been given to seal their trust and then reneged on their agreement?

The only time that Gevehard had spoken to the stone carver was the day they met. He had judged Aiken from what he had seen of him and from what others said of his reputation. He and Aiken had bargained and had made their promises with a handshake. That was all he had—that and his baseless trust in a man whom he did not know.

In the end, Gevehard knew only one thing—he had placed his wager on a man who had sworn oaths to a chieftain and carried the scars to prove that he had fought courageously. Yet the man was a stranger. Gevehard did not know his kin, nor where he came from. And, though he had asked around whenever he talked to the other chieftains with whom he traded, and they had assured him that the woodcarver had never cheated anyone, whenever he asked about the man's past they became peculiar-ly tight-lipped.

What assurance did Gevehard have that he had not placed his bets on the wrong man? He was relying upon a man whom he did not know, yet trusted him to be true to his word. That was all he had—just his word, sworn before Lord Glory. That, and a bold belief in fair trade in the marketplace and respect for the law to back it up. When all you could rely upon was trust in a man's honorable intentions and faith that he would be true to his word, a handshake was holy and sacred. But of course, Geve-hard knew that men lied and would attempt to take advantage of his willingness to believe them. Men were notorious for spinning out tales of deceit just to get whatever they wanted. He had to be ever watchful and to read the signs constantly. So, what had happened? Had he been duped?

The thick, misty air began to thin out. And as the distant haze was lifting, the air began to brighten, and Gevehard could just make out four horsemen and a team of oxen pulling a cart coming his way on the road. The shipmaster took off immediately, bellowing and waving his arms.

The riders whooped from the backs of their trotting horses and reined-in to a stop beside Gevehard. They told him that the roads running alongside the Linden River had been good. But after they had followed it to the Alder and then to the Mire, the roads had turned to mud. The cart had been stuck so many times they had lost count. "That man Aiken, you can depend on him. He is a good man."

"There is nothing soft about him. I thought that someone who spent his days carving toys for children and spoons and bowls for women's supper tables might not be much of a man. But he pitched right in and we got the cart moving whenever it was stuck."

"Good to hear it. What else have you got to tell me?"

"He brought a girl with him. Made her cook for us," the man added with a chuckle. "She was half-decent at skinning and spitting a hare, but her father spent more time teaching her how to do it, than it would have taken him to cook it himself."

"It turns out he was a fighting man once."

"I knew that."

"He likes to cook game over a campfire."

"I tell you, we were hungry that night, but our supper sure tasted good in the end."

"Right, what was left of it after it fell into the fire."

"We got one bite each."

The men were so happy to be home again, even talk of their hunger and troubles on the road made them cheerful.

"The ford across the Mire was deep and rough going. I feared, more than once, that the waters would swallow us up. But no matter how the water raged, it was not going to sweep that heavy stone away."

"We hung onto the cart and oxen when we were crossing and used them as break-waters."

"After that, we came to the Gray and followed it to the big Muddy. At times, we had to diverge from where it was flooded but picked it up again. That is why it took us so long to get home."

"The roads were so bad not even the outlaws were out."

"You did good," Gevehard said, swatted one of horses on its haunch, and added, "Now, get home and greet your wives. They have been asking about you daily."

Gevehard took off in wide, loping strides, yelling, "Hey, hey, hey."

Aiken drew the oxen to a halt, jumped down, and the two men grasped each other by the forearms, grunted, "Yeah," and shared a big, boisterous hug.

"Am I glad to see you."

"Believe me. I am equally glad to be here." Aiken waved his arm in Sunniva's direction, and said, "This is my daughter, Sunniva the Gifts of the Sun."

Gevehard nodded and welcomed them both to his village. Aiken jumped excitedly into the back of the cart, pulled off the tarps covering the stone and introduced Hild the Battle Maid. Gevehard leapt into the cart to stand alongside Aiken. There she was, the big red stone. The slab lay flat, roped down securely on a bed of smoothed, tightly spaced saplings. Aiken dropped down into a crouch and, running his fingers over her surface, followed the lines he had carved.

Immediately, Gevehard made out Wave Crestar's flat-bottomed silhouette.

Awed by the likeness to his ship, he wanted to trace the grooves in the stone himself. He nudged up close to Aiken and felt his ship's long, lean belly and her high, peaked serpent head and tail. He pressed both hands onto her picture, and said, "My ship is right here where I can hold her in my hands. How did you do it?"

Aiken answered with a shoulder shrug, and asked, "Did I get her right?"

"Oh, yes."

Gevehard stroked the little stick-figure men and lines standing-in for their oars. And as he did so, he took an oath, right then and there, to see that each man came home alive and in one piece.

Aiken pointed out the winding sea serpent beneath Wave Crestar's hull. Above the boat, he had carved a picture of the blazing sun-wheel that Lady Sun carried in her wagon. Below and to each side, two circles represented the shields, which the Lords of Battle carried. As he ran his fingers around the winding border, Aiken described the ribbon upon which he had written the secret signs and read aloud, "I, Aiken carved this stone for Gevehard, son of Garr, son of Gerard, son of Glenn who brought us to this land. Help us now, Lord of Rich Waters."

Aiken patted the stone, and said convincingly, "Here is the hard proof that these men's descendants remember their courage and their fortitude." He followed the con-tiguous looping, which made up the complex knot, with his fingers to show Gevehard how the ribbon wove in, out, and through to bind all the generations together in never-ending, bounteous continuity.

"Your name, spelled out in secret signs and carved in stone, along with the names of your forebears assures you and the villagers of their protection and the unbroken line of family luck. No one who sees this stone will fear their ancestors have been forgotten. No one will believe that these three men have turned against their ungrate-ful descendants. If the souls of these three men are sufficiently satisfied that they have been remembered for their bravery, the villagers can rest assured that their forebears will put in a good word for them with the Lord of Rich-Waters whenever they ask for good harvests, bountiful fishing, and successful sea journeys."

Anyone who knew Gevehard would tell you that he was rarely left speechless. But on this one occasion he could find no words with which to express his gratitude. All he could do was reach toward Aiken, pull him to his chest and clap him hard on the back. "You understood. You understood what I wanted, and now you have given it to me." How could he have doubted this man? He liked and trusted Aiken entirely. "You understood exactly what I needed. I am so grateful."

The two men walked alongside the oxen until they came to a place on the road where they could unyoke the team from the cart. Then Gevehard, Aiken, Sunniva, Plodder and Smart-one continued to make their way between the mounds that formed this village. Atop each man-made hill was a house and its attendant sheds. After the earliest settlers had chosen to live so close to the shoreline, here, where the land is so flat, men and women had, over countless lifetimes, built up these mounds with layers of clay and dung to raise their sod-brick homes above the watermarks.

Gevehard explained how the river's swollen channels overflowed their banks and flooded the land each spring with snow melt. Whenever the water was high, anyone who lived here needed to be well suited to paddling a boat just to get between their homes and outbuildings.

Aiken, in turn, voiced amazement at the effort it had taken to build these numerous hills as a precaution against the risk. Gevehard added that, between early spring and late autumn, flooding could happen, without warning, at any time. A man or woman must always be prepared for the worst, because it will inevitably happen.

The shipmaster led the way up the largest mound's slope. From there, Aiken could see the many mounds and buildings surrounding them in all directions. On this one mound alone, he counted one large building and several smaller ones, all made of stacked sod bricks, additionally coated with daub. Any timbers they used came either overland or oversea. Gevehard pointed out his longhouse, the outdoors cook-house and an open, roofed eating area. There were also smaller sheds and byres, and the working men and women's sleeping halls. Gevehard held the paddock gate open so Aiken could lead Plodder and Smart-one in and, after he called a boy over, told him to take good care of their guest's oxen.

Gevehard greeted the man who was overseeing the boys who were mucking out the paddock with pitchforks and shovels. He introduced Aiken to Edmund and explained that, because Edmund no longer rowed the boats, he was both the steward who managed his household affairs and was the commander in charge of mustering men to protect the village whenever Gevehard was away. Edmund's right sleeve hung loose and empty, its end tucked into his belt. Gevehard warmly placed his arm across Edmund's shoulders and recounted the story of how, on their last voyage, his friend's arm had been severed. They had been skirmishing against sea-raiders who were coming over the gunwales when Gevehard stumbled. If he had fallen, he would have been cut down. But Edmund jumped in front of his shipmaster and took the strike that would, otherwise, have sliced Gevehard in two. After that, Edmund shielded Gevehard as he gave the enemy the fatal blow.

In an attempt to deflect Gevehard's praise of his selfless courage, Edmund asked, "What else could I have done? We depended upon you to get back home again. No one knows the sea and shorelines better than you do, Gevehard. We would have been lost without you."

Gevehard gave Edmund a mournful expression, shook his head and looked his friend in the eye. "No. I am the one who will be lost without you, Edmund. No one can take your place." Gevehard heartily clapped his friend on the back and claimed that no one jumped the gunwales as well as Edmund.

After they took care of the oxen, Gevehard led Aiken and Sunniva toward his home. Walking in the door, they were both astonished by its size. The narrow longhouse was furnished with numerous benches and tables. Beyond the high, steeped roof beams and rafters, the uppermost peak was so blackened from smoke, it disappeared in the shadows. This home was so unlike the one where Aiken and Sunniva lived, in comparison, it made their house look small as a storage shed.

At the far end, a doorway, which was hung with fabric, led to the room where Gevehard's family lived in their private quarters. When a woman parted the curtain to look out, Gevehard urged her to join them with a wave of his hand.

Walking toward them was a tall, good-looking woman, wearing a dress sewn from soft wool, dyed dark green. An embroidered leather purse, a sheathed short knife and several chains from which small tools dangled hung from her belt. Two large, shield-like gold brooches, set with clear and honey-colored stones, were pinned at her shoulders. Draped between them, were four strands of glass, silver, and gold beads.

Gevehard presented Adelheide the Most Noble of Women. He referred to his wife as the other commander, even when he was at home. He could always count on her to kick him out of bed in the morning, he told his guests, and to push him out the door after he had eaten his morning porridge.

Whereas Adelheide gave her husband a kindly, patiently knowing look, Aiken and Sunniva shared his joke with polite laughter. The respect and deep affection with which Gevehard and Adelheide held one another was apparent in that briefly exchanged glance.

Adelheide greeted Aiken, welcomed him and his daughter to their village and offered them anything they needed to make their visit comfortable. Sunniva would stay with Rodger's family, and Aiken would be the guest of one of the men who patrolled the outlying farms and roads.

Aware of the way that his well-dressed hosts were looking him over, Aiken brushed at his dusty tunic and picked at his mud-caked trousers. It had been so many years since he had set foot in a longhouse of such grand dimensions and had spoken so casually, on equal terms, with men and women of such highly ranked stature that he hardly knew what to do with himself. Adelheide noticed his discomfort and suggested they let their guests change out of their road-worn garments before they ate. She slipped her hand inside Sunniva's elbow, leaned in to speak with her, and the two women walked off arm in arm.

Gevehard made a wry comment about women's priorities, and said, "Come along then, Aiken, and get cleaned up before we eat."

Gevehard grabbed a couple boys from the paddock and they walked back to the cart. All together, they carried Aiken's bags to the house where he would be sleeping.

III.

When Aiken returned to the longhouse, women were setting the table with bronze and silver platters, cups and jugs. Edmund had already arrived. The three men walked around the hall. Aiken admired the carved benches, but Gevehard passed off his compliments. None matched Aiken's skill, he said, and listed several items he wanted Aiken to make for him, including a set of carved doors for the longhouse.

Women brought basins of water and offered men linen towels with which to wipe their hands and faces. Another man walked in the door to join them. Gevehard introduced Aiken to Jerold, the newly appointed commander. Whenever they were in the boats, Jerold would rank second to Gevehard.

Aiken was coldly sized up. As he was shaking Jerold's hand, he was scanned from his feet up to his face. The commander took note of the breadth of his shoulders and the circumference around his arms and neck. He seemed more interested in the stone carver's hands than curious about Aiken's scarred face. No doubt, Jerold knew what sharp, steel blades did to a man's flesh. He had seen it all before, probably worse.

Gevehard took his place at the center of the table, indicated where Aiken should take a place on his right, seated Edmund on his left, and assigned Jerold to the place at Aiken's right.

Adelheide entered, carrying an extravagant gold cup. She walked toward the place where Gevehard stood and faced him from across the table. From his vantage point, Aiken admired the jeweled designs on the beautiful cup. Each of the four, large, honey-colored stones, with which it was decorated, were surrounded by three inter-locking, concentric circles that seemed to represent spreading ripples disturbing a still, watery surface. A delicate pattern of spiraling hearts filled the spaces between the arcs and the third circle. The spaces formed by the arcs were filled with a texture of minute, gold grains, like sand on the beach.

To honor the wealth, which the sea-stone gave the men and women who lived along the shoreline, the design seemed to tell a story in pictures of the honey-colored stone's origin. An elaborate border was carved with secret signs. As the cup passed between Adelheide and the men, Aiken tried to read what they spelled but was unable to get the gist of the text. Because there were several letters that he had never seen before, he reckoned the signs spelled words in a dialect he was unfamiliar with. Aware that the shipmaster visited markets that were located on the Tin Islands, Aiken guessed the cup may have come from there. He had heard that the craftsmen who lived in the Tin Islands were highly skilled and if, indeed, the cup had come from there, Aiken agreed their reputations were well deserved.

Adelheide lifted the cup to shoulder height to greet her husband, and said, "Gevehard the Brave Heart, Wave Crestar's shipmaster and gracious kinleader of this village, all the men and women who live here celebrate your indomitable wisdom and honor your fortitude. I bid you eat well, here, in the company of these men who are so important to your successful voyage."

After she had spoken, Gevehard took the cup, turned to look at each man, and praised him. "With such heroic men of stature, we are certain of success." He drank from the cup and handed it back to his wife.

Next, she stepped in front of Aiken and lifted her cup. "Aiken, the Strength of Oak, I praise the memorial stone you carved. Your excellent craftsmanship will be a comfort to both the fighting men who pull the oars and to those men and women in our village who benefit from their heroic actions. I am grateful, Aiken, for the strength of heart you bring with you today and will share with us for many days hereafter."

Aiken breathed in deeply, took the cup with both hands and drank. The passing of the praise-and-promise cup offered a man an opportunity to show off his skill in creating word-pictures. To impress his listeners, Aiken said, "Shipmaster Gevehard and Adelheide, I am honored to sit here, in your wealthy hall. I am grateful to have been accorded this opportunity to serve all the men and women who live here in your village. Indeed, I have made the blood-red stone into a sentry who will protect the sea-faring men who row the oars. Hild the Battle Maid will stand the watch and weave their victory. Just as the rope ties a ship to its anchor, she will knot the cords that tie the men to their homes and will bring them back to their families. When the great serpent-ships return to their home harbor, their bellies will be filled with wealth."

If Adelheide had chosen to follow the proper ceremonial standards, she would next have served the cup to Jerold who was the second in command. However, he was seated not on Gevehard's left, the direction in which she would next turn, but rather, was seated on Aiken's right, a position of lesser rank than the one where Edmund sat.

Although the household steward held a position, which was usually deemed inferior in status, the men appeared to have worked out another ranking system between themselves. The affection between the two men was apparent and reminded Aiken of the feelings that he had had for Alger. His sense of Gevehard's grief at having to leave for the shipping season without Edmund's presence aboard the boat, was a sign that the shipmaster's affection for men went deep.

At the same time, Aiken thought the unusual ranking indicated that Jerold's position was uncertain. Upon meeting the man, Aiken had not found him particularly likeable. Perhaps Gevehard kept Jerold at a distance because of some personal distaste. Aiken wondered whether Jerold would need to earn his rank on the upcoming voyage before he was permanently granted the status that was usually conferred upon a commander.

After the men had all been offered the cup, the shipmaster lifted his arms to shoulder height and spread them out to the sides to indicate the men should take their seats. Women brought loaves of bread and crocks of butter, platters of cured meats, smoked fish, cheese, and bowls of pickled roots. Aiken was pleasantly surprised to see that the serving spoon, set into a bowl of pickles, was one which he had carved.

Gevehard had purchased it from Mildred on the day that he and Gevehard had met in the market. After the shipmaster had given her a coin for it, he held the tip of its handle between his thumb and forefinger and, tapping the spoon's bowl against his cupped palm like a tiny oar slapping the waves, had said, "When I get home, I will give it to my wife, Adelheide. We will both treasure this spoon as a reminder of the standing stone that Aiken will deliver next spring."

That was the first time that Mildred had heard of the arrangement, which Aiken and Gevehard had worked out earlier in the day. Although she graciously held her tongue, as soon as Gevehard had set off to rejoin his companions, she turned and glared at Aiken.

He had been more settled and content than he had for a long time. His mind was far away, already making plans to take the cart up to the quarry as soon as they got home. Then, there she was, coming at him, mad as a wet hen.

"What is this I hear about you leaving next spring during the planting season? You know I cannot leave then."

"You will not need to ride along."

Mildred frowned and shook her head. "How can you take the cart so far north? You cannot even go to market without me riding along to ward off the throngs of people who you think are out to get you."

For her to have pointed out his weakness so bluntly, right there, where other folks were standing around them, had hurt Aiken deeply. But he was too proud to let on, and said, "I am my own man, Mildred." He may have said it aloud but, silently acknowledged his own underlying uncertainty. He needed to prove, if only to himself, that he could be a man without leaning on a woman. "Early next spring, four men will come to accompany me. We are likely to run into outlaws on those roads. You will only get in the way if we are attacked."

"I need your help at home during the planting season."

Never, in all the years that he had known her, had Mildred ever backed down. And so, as if to prove her point, she had shown him just how long she could carry on.

But Aiken calmly explained how his plans were set in place. He had already accepted the shipmaster's coinage in exchange for a promise to deliver the stone. He had assured Gevehard that he would remain in the village, both to celebrate its importance and to honor the memory of the villager's forebears. No matter what Mildred said, nor for how long she carried on, he would not, and could not, back out of the agreement. He was a man of his word. She needed to understand that this commission was more important than all the boxes and chairs that he had made for the thieving chieftains who he despised so much.

"The shipmaster said that his life and the wellbeing of his village depend upon what I can do to help him out with a stone I carve. He wants me to back him up, Mildred. The man is in urgent need. I promised to do whatever I could to help him. No man of such importance has ever before regarded my craftsmanship this highly."

But Mildred remained unconvinced. Tears filled her eyes, overflowed and streaked her cheeks. "I need you, too, Aiken. Do my needs count for nothing? Am I so unimportant?"

"How can you ask me such a thing? Of course, you are important."

So, there he was, on a busy market day, with his arms wrapped around his wife. He did his best to comfort her, pulled her close, patted her head, and told her how much he cared for her. And then, when Bertolf saw his mother weeping, he left the boys with whom he was playing, came running, grabbed her skirts, and started wailing too. Aiken was forced to herd them both over to the cart and to sit Mildred upon the stool. He picked up Bertolf, hugged him tightly and placed him on his mother's lap.

Aiken then drew back, set his fists on his hips, and told them both to pull themselves together. "Save your tears until we are on the road back home, Mildred. Right now, we are in the market. This is not a good place for your snuffling."

Aiken walked over to the trestle table upon which his carvings were displayed and took care of those women who wanted to bargain for a bowl, spoon, toy cow, or spindle. Shortly afterwards, a red-eyed, sniffling Mildred elbowed him aside and took her place again behind the table.

"Go on then, you will just make a mess of things and give them away for nothing."

After he had been forced to put up with his wife's withering tirades for quite some time, in the end, he had convinced Mildred to accept his plans. And now, here he was, seated at Gevehard's table, ladling pickles with the spoon he had carved.

The men ate and talked of the trade in amber, woven fabric, salt and furs. Although the sea presented dangers, it also gave them riches. The tear-shaped bits of honey-colored stone were scooped from the shallows; seawater was evaporated in salt pans; and the fish they caught, dried, and salted sustained them on their voyages. It was for these reasons that to remain in the good graces of the Lord of Rich-Waters was of the gravest importance.

Gevehard described how the seafarers traveled along the coastlines, bargaining their trade goods for the food, grain, and raw materials they needed to survive here. Additional goods that made their profits highly lucrative included the items they found in the overseas markets, which they traded in the inland markets closer to home. The chieftains needed precious metal ingots, wine, oil, and other items such as decorative glass, jewelry, and even high-quality whetstones to show off their wealth and status and to exchange with other chieftains whenever they formed alliances.

For the men who lived here, rowing their boats to market was in their blood. Their earliest forebears had lived along the Belts coastline. Since the beginning of time, they had scooped the amber nuggets from the sea and carried those precious stones in their boats to the Tin Islands and to harbors along the western coastline. They had traveled the sea for so long that poets recalled the times when those heroic men had fought sea monsters with their bronze-cast weaponry. Though the winters were hard and grueling in those northern lands, the ancestors had made their homes there until the Terrible Winter had taken its toll.

When their ancestors could take no more of the devastation that the Devourers' and Wind-bringers' had brought upon them, Lady Sun had shown Glenn the way to this village on the shore of the Merchant Sea. They had loaded their ships with the few cattle, sheep and horses they still had left and, under Glenn's leadership, had struck out for the south.

When they arrived, the original inhabitants had been decimated by the pestilence, which had come inland from the sea on the serpent's poisonous breath. Most of the homes and farms had been abandoned. The few remaining survivors were so weakened by illness and starvation that when Glenn's ships pulled ashore they were easily overcome and forced into servitude.

At that time, the village had become a hornet's nest sheltering pirates. The sea-raiders had used the village as a base from which to attack the merchant boats that plied the waters throughout the region. All that changed when Glenn and his people moved into the village.

"Piracy worries us all, "Gevehard said. "We all fear for our lives. Whenever we are at sea, we are constantly on the lookout for bands of sea-raiders. The previous kin-leader, Erol, was condemned by many people, so when Glenn came, he approached the men who lived along the coastline and promised to keep this harbor safe from attacks by sea-raiders. The descendants of those men are now our crucial allies."

"After Glenn's death, his loss was mourned for a long time," Edmund said. "Even before he died, the villagers worried about their future. When a man, who was as revered as Glenn had been, was about to leave for the everlasting hereafter, they feared that his experience and savvy ability to guide his men would be lost to future generations. To alleviate the villager's worry, Gevehard's father, Garr, had asked the wizened old man to lay his hands upon his tiny son. Though Gevehard had been a mere babe at the time, when he was set upon Glenn's lap, his father had hoped that, by the means of such a gesture, his great grandfather would pass on some of his ineffable wisdom before he died. And, in that way, Garr had meant to remove the villagers' doubts and fears that the qualities of leadership, which Glenn embodied, would be lost. And to reassure them that his son, Gevehard, would be graced with the family luck."

Gevehard said he was uncertain whether he had been gifted by the old man that day, "But" he added with bemused regret, "it is certain that I have not inherited my great grandfather's beautiful voice."

Even to that day, every man looked longingly at the sky and wished Lady Sun would find him as attractive as she had found Glenn. It was said that she gave men extraordinary gifts and pleasure. Yet, try as they might, no man could pitch his voice as high as Gevehard's great grandfather's. It was said that Glenn had sung in a high tenor so unlike any other man's that it had been bestowed upon him by the hidden folk. There was no other way to have acquired such a beautiful voice.

Gevehard leaned in toward Edmund and whispered in his ear. The steward left the table and slipped quietly through the door to the family's quarters. Upon his return, he set a bronze platter in front of the shipmaster. All the men eyed the rich gifts laid upon it.

First, Gevehard picked up a gold arm ring forged in a twisting, braided design. Holding it out to Aiken, he thanked him for his service on behalf of their village. "I treasure our friendship, Aiken the Strength of Oak. Now, before Lord Glory the Shining Firmament, ruler of men's oaths, I promise to be fair and trustworthy."

Aiken accepted the ring and answered, "Gevehard the Brave Heart, I am honored to have been chosen by so great a liege lord to carry out the work you requested. Before Lord Glory the Shining Firmament, I promise to serve you, dutifully."

Both men closed their oaths, saying, "May the Lords treat me favorably if I tell the truth. May they be offended if I lie or break our trust."

Aiken slipped the circlet over his hand and, marveling at the honor that Gevehard had bestowed upon him, displayed it on his wrist. To be given a gold arm band had been beyond his wildest expectations.

"Aiken, I am always on the lookout for battle hardened men and can find places for them in my household or on the crew. Your craft with signs and binding words can make us powerful enough to never know defeat. I want you to conjure favorable winds by twisting wind-knots to settle a rough headwind or to give us a tailwind by untying the knots."

Aiken shook his head, and demurred. "I am better at carving pictures of knots than at tying them. To learn those uncanny knot-tying tricks, I would need to become an ally of the Lord of Rich-Waters, the Old Man of the Winds. It is he who masters the air's movement and—."

"What would it take?" Gevehard bluntly interrupted. Impatient with Aiken's excuses, he said, "I will pay you well. If a man tamed the Wind-bringer, we could tie ropes to the creature and be pulled across the water with such ease, my men would turn soft and lazy. I need you, Aiken. What will it take to get you on board?"

"Although I am grateful for your praise, and the fanciful notion is appealing, I am afraid you have me wrong. I am not a cunning man. I am little more than a common woodcarver." Aiken shook his head, looked down at his hands and, raising an eyebrow, honored the well-known wisdom that a woman's reputation is derived from the knot-tying and weaving skills she uses to protect her husband and sons whenever they are gone from home. "It is a woman who braids sinew threads, but it is a man's strong sinews that lift his weapons in the fight."

"Well, I can hardly have a woman on my boat, even if she has the power to tie wind-knots. You think it over Aiken."

Gevehard picked up a small knife from the platter and handed it to Aiken. It was sheathed in a piece of folded leather that was sewn down the blunt side of the blade and was stiffened with a riveted piece of engraved sheet bronze. Aiken slipped the small knife from the sheath to admire it. The blade was as long as a man's hand span when measured from the tip of his outstretched thumb to the tip of his little finger. Broad and heavy, it had one sharp edge and a thick, broke-back, blunt edge that angled in a straight line toward the point. To decorate the blade, an intricate knot pattern was inlaid with beaten gold and silver wires that had been set with the heat of the forge into the shallow grooves engraved in the steel. The grip was made from a bone-like material and the pommel was made from a pointed, oval shaped piece of amber.

"The amber gives a warrior luck and protection and assures him of Lady Sun's blessings," Gevehard explained. Tapping the handle with his finger, he said, "The animal from which this came is a great beast that lives far to the north where the ice never melts. This was cut from its tusk. The beast's toothy weapon carries strength and endurance. I recognize these invincible traits in you, Aiken. You must carry it with you always."

"I am flattered to receive such a splendid gift," Aiken said but did not say that he was additionally grateful to have been identified as a warrior of merit.

One last item remained on the platter. Gevehard untied the strings closing a small leather pouch and poured the silver and gold coins contained inside it into Aiken's open palm. After he had counted them out, the shipmaster explained how the coins had been minted in his own village using ingots, which he had acquired from the silver and gold traders who live in the land of the long-haired kings. He picked up one coin to show Aiken the face that represented Lord Glory who ensured trust in the marketplace. Turning it over, Gevehard pointed to a lizard-like creature with clawed feet and a tail, curled high above its back. He handed Aiken the coin and the leather pouch, saying, "I am grateful for your fine workmanship."

Gevehard abruptly pushed back his chair, stood, and said, "Now it is time to show you my boat. Come on. Let's go."

IV.

Down on the strand, Aiken had never seen a ship of such magnificent size. Though he had seen similar, smaller boats plying the rivers, he was pleased to have pictured Wave Crestar's graceful lines so well. Introduced to the master shipbuilder, Aiken showed his high regard for the man's remarkable know-how. Awed not only by the skill that it takes to fit together something so large, he was equally impressed by the shipbuilder's ability to manage the number of men that it had taken to hew the timbers, to build the hull by overlapping the strakes and riveting them together with iron, and then, to build and put the frame inside the hull once it was finished. He did not know how else to compliment the shipbuilder on the fine boat that he and his crew had built, but did what came naturally. He admired the well-made scarf joints that had been roved together with iron rivets and affectionately rubbed his hands over the wood grain.

As Gevehard and Aiken continued to walk along the shoreline, the shipmaster told him what it was like to live so close to the Muddy River. Said to be a river leading no-where, it was both a curse and a blessing. It was so shallow further inland that it was not deep enough to float even the shallowest boats. For that reason, the Muddy offered the villagers protection from raiders, who lived further inland and might want to wage war or pillage by boat. But, of course that also meant that they were unable to take their own boats to the inland markets. The greatest advantage to living so close to the river was the fresh, potable water it provided, though at this time of year it was necessary to let the sand and mud settle in the pail before the water could be used. Whenever the river flooded, the roads running through the river's mud flats and the delta marsh became impassable. For the rest of the year, the few roads were easily patrolled.

Gevehard pointed to the numerous small, rocky islands and sand bars farther out in the bay. The people who lived here liked to say that the islands hid entry to their village by moving about in the night to confuse any outsiders who might want to at-tack them by sea. When the tide was low, the sand bars could ground an unsuspecting shipmaster. Those men who had honest reasons to find their way through the bay had gained their knowledge of the harbor from their fathers. All summer long, merchants arrived on smaller boats. Men who traded furs and amber nuggets came from the northern shores of the Belts and the Merchant Sea. Some fur-traders even came from the land where the ice never melts and the sun never shines throughout the long wintertime months.

Out in the bay, several small fishing boats bobbed about on the waves, while up above, swallows flew past on wide-spread, slender wings. The bird's wire-thin tail feathers streamed out behind as they dipped, twisted, and turned in midair, cheerily calling vit vit vit.

Gevehard pointed to a distant osprey tracing graceful circles against the sky. In time, it came so close to the shore, the two men could plainly see the bird's white head, marked only with a thin, black line drawn back from the corner of each eye. The feathers on its under-wings and tail were colored a pale, grey-brown at the blunt tips.

Five swallows broke away from their loopy play. In an attempt to chase and harass the larger bird, they called flit-flitt, flit-flitt and challenged one another to see who amongst them could come closest to the bigger bird's long, narrow wings and to peck at the tips of its feathers. One bird came closest, then, at the last moment, veered away and, chirping gamely, vit vit vit, seemed to laugh at its success.

To get beyond the reach of the determined, little birds, the osprey lazily spiraled on an updraft, whistling, u-eelp, u-eelp, u-eelp as it rose increasingly higher.

Both men, watching the osprey closely, were ready to parse the meaning of the bird's appearance. If they judged the bird's flight and song bore a message, they would tease apart the significance of this moment.

The osprey halted its forward movement and, as if it were suspended on a string, hovered effortlessly in midair. When it deemed the moment was right, the bird dove feet first into the water and skillfully snatched a fish with its talons. Flapping its wings, it splashed at the water several times before it regained loft.

For Gevehard the message was clear at once. Just as this bird had remained undeterred by the swallows, the boats in his fleet would be safe from harassment by pirates who manned smaller, lesser boats. And just as the osprey had grabbed a fish from the waters, he and his crew would pluck wealth from the harbors wherever they pulled ashore.

"Aiken, the Lord of Rich-Waters has sent us an important message," Gevehard said with an excited slap on Aiken's shoulder. "He is pleased with the pictures on the stone. You have brought us luck. I knew you would."

Aiken accepted Gevehard's approval humbly and returned the praise. "Gevehard, no doubt you have caught the Lady's eye, and she, too, has sent you a message. You are perhaps more like Glenn than you admit."

Convinced by the show of wealth in Gevehard's longhouse, Aiken had deduced that the shipmaster had been well-favored by the ruling powers. "Lady Sun is pleased that you have honored the memory of the earthly man she loved so dearly. No doubt she will watch over your trade routes from her vantage point, high above the earth, and will bless you with good fortune."

"I want to believe that what you say is true," Gevehard said, and nodded approvingly. He shrugged one shoulder and, turning to go inland, said, "Come along, then. Let us find a place to set the stone."

On their way inland, the two men climbed a steep, ragged embankment. Once they were on higher ground, they came to a large dune where grass blades poked up sparsely and a stand of twiggy shrubs had begun to leaf out. The tiny, new leaves lent the air around the branches an appearance of a floating, pale green, misty cloud.

At the edge of the holy grove, Gevehard bowed his head and slowed his pace out of respect for this place where their forebear's bones lay buried. In the center there was a pile of heaped-up stones, colored dark brown by the blood stains that had been left there along with men and women's gifts. Boat-shaped outlines were laid out with white, lime-painted stones. Each marked a gravesite beneath which their forebears' bones lay buried.

The two men paced back and forth in search the likeliest place to stand the stone. Aiken carried the digging spade he had grabbed from out of his cart. Talking it over, they agreed upon the most suitable location. Aiken found two sticks in the grove, laid them crosswise on the spot and, looking up at the shipmaster for final confirmation, asked, "Here?"

Gevehard nodded his final approval and left to get his men and the cart.

Aiken set his spade in the soil, put his foot on its topmost edge and neatly sliced straight down. As the sandy soil began to pile up, the gold ring on his wrist slipped up and down his forearm. After all the years living as an invisible, despicable outlaw, he had been seated at the right-hand of the shipmaster. He had been praised for the stone he had carved, been offered the cup to drink from, and been given a gold arm ring. Aiken was so moved, he could barely contain his joy.

Yet certain questions remained and continued to nag at him. Just what, exactly, had he sworn to do when he had accepted the ring? There were no ready answers. Beyond Gevehard's vague reference to being on the lookout for well-trained fighting men, what did it mean to be the shipmaster's man? He questioned whether their descriptions of wealthy trade goods had been intended to whet his appetite. Maybe all the talk about wind-knots had not been a joke.

Last autumn, the meeting with Gevehard had seemed, at first, like a chance encounter. But since then, it had taken on greater significance. It had been so unexpected and, yet, somehow, he believed that it had been meant to happen for a reason.

Late last summer, without suspecting the good fortune that was soon to come his way, he and Mildred had left home at dawn, and after spending the day on the road, had arrived at the market town just before sundown. The following morning, Aiken had hoisted onto his back the high seat that he had carved for the local chieftain. Nearly doubled over, he had carried it to the inner stockade gates. Waiting to deliver the chair to the steward, he had seen eight men arrive on horseback leading additional packhorses. To judge from the bronze trappings on their horse bridles and the quality of their clothing and weaponry, Aiken identified them as men of standing who traded goods that had come from the overseas markets. They would not need to set up in the commons like ordinary folk but would have private audiences with the chieftains and the warriors in each of the fort towns they visited.

To set himself apart from the commoners in the crowd, Aiken pushed up his sleeves. One of the men dismounted, walked up to Aiken and asked when the steward would arrive. After they had exchanged a few pleasantries about the weather and conditions on the roads, the man asked Aiken what he had wrapped up in the tarp. Since it was clear that Gevehard could pay well for his carvings, Aiken untied the ropes and pulled off the hides covering the chair.

Carved into the chair back was a picture of Irmun's pillar. Crowned with leaves and entwined with vines, the pole was centered within a border formed by two snakes. Above the pillar he had written the name of the man for whom he had made it.

Gevehard knelt before the chair and, as he skimmed the snakes with his fingertips, told Aiken how much he would like to own a chair like this someday, but there were more important matters that he needed to attend to first. Because he wanted to offer tribute to the dead forebears to whom he and his people owed their lives, he asked Aiken whether he could carve a memorial stone that would recognize the many struggles the men in his bloodline had overcome.

Naturally, Aiken had readily agreed.

And now, here he was, about to set the stone in the holy grove where Gevehard's forebear's bones lay buried. To have achieved a strong presence on this land had taken four generations. Glenn had been the founder of this village. Garr and Gerard were the men who had strengthened the kin's position on the headland, had established the trade routes, and had built their reputation as trustworthy traders in the markets. It was Gevehard, the fourth in their lineage who, by standing solidly upon his forebears' shoulders, had brought increased wealth and a more comfortable lifestyle to his people. Now that the village had become a large and successful market town, the time had come to honor those men for their grit, fortitude, and determination. If Glenn, Garr, and Gerard's souls were sufficiently satisfied with the stone, those men and women, who now lived comfortably on this land, would be assured that their ancestors were watching out for them from their place in the everlasting hereafter.

Gevehard's bearing and his respectful treatment of the men with whom he worked reminded Aiken of his own father, Eamon. Some of his fondest memories of Eamon were of the times when he had climbed onto his father's knee and had listened to the older men recount the stories of the battles they had fought.

One night, his mother, Maida, had said, "Do not let him listen to those tales. They will stir up monstrous creatures in the dreamtime. Then he will cry and wake us."

But Eamon had replied, "It is better to hear about the fighting now. That way our little son will become a brave man when he grows up. He will not cry." His father patted Aiken on the shoulder, and said, "Not with me here to take care of you. My little Acorn, you may trust me to protect you from the scary monsters."

"Do you promise?"

"I swear an oath before Lord Glory to take care of my little Acorn. From here on out, you will not run into any monsters in the dreamtime."

Unfortunately, his father's assurances had not lasted. Shortly after his mother had told him why Eamon was never coming home again, Aiken had been playing with a golden ball in the dreamtime forest. Tossing it in the air and catching it, he accidentally dropped the ball. It began to roll downhill, and though he had run after it as fast as he could, the ball had gotten away from him. Unable to catch it before it plunged into a deep pit, he knelt beside the edge and dipped his arm into the filthy, red water all the way up to his shoulder. He felt around on the muddy bottom of pit but could not get hold of it.

Though he was startled when the bogman stuck its head up from beneath the water, Aiken asked the creature to return his gold ball. But it just laughed at him. It took ahold of Aiken's wrist, poked him with its long, sharp claws and refused to let him go.

Aiken had tried, night after night, to get his gold ball back. But, before he could catch hold of it, he always awakened as soon as he felt the bogman's claws poke and scratch his skin.

Sounds of Gevehard and several men coming along the path that led from the road alerted Aiken to their approach. The crew members appeared to be so accustomed to working together, they barely needed to speak. Some pulled the cart by the tongue and others pushed against the sides and back. They maneuvered the cart back and forth until the back end was lined up with the trench that Aiken had dug. Two men stuck the wedge-shaped logs, which Aiken kept in the cart, beneath the wheels to keep it from rolling and carefully tipped the cart back until the rear-end rested on the ground. Aiken left the ropes wound around the stone, but untied the ones that held the stone to the cart floor. He gave them to the five men who stood nearest the trench. Two men climbed into the cart to join Aiken and they rolled the stone over the row of smooth ash trunks that formed its bed. As it slipped down toward the cart edge, the other men pulled on the ropes to carefully guide it into the hole. The men pulled, heaved, shoved, and pressed their shoulders against the stone until it was upright in the trench.

They held the slab steady while Aiken first filled the hole with stones and then shoveled in the soil he had dug. He mounded it at the base of the stone and tamped it down hard.

When he was finished, Aiken explained how the stone honored their forebears with the pictures and the words that were spelled out in secret signs.

After the men had all cleared out, hastily pushing and pulling the cart, Aiken saw Sunniva standing a ways off, staring at him. She walked up to him and handed him a basket filled with offerings for the hidden folk. He threw his arm around her shoulders and told her that she brought him more than a basket—she brought him luck. He kissed her on the forehead and sent her back to the village, along with a reminder to help the women with their chores.

Aiken spread his arms out to his sides and filled his chest with the sharp, salt-scented air. As he scanned the dunes and thickets, he compared this empty place to the dense woodlands where he and his family lived. Day after day, as he and Sunniva had traveled through the forests, they had seen how the good black soil turned to sand, and the trees were replaced by scrubby little shrubs. These poor cousins of the inland trees, diminished in height and breadth, were like outcasts whose seeds had been tricked into putting down roots on the windblown dunes.

The way the twisted shrubs grew in the rocky sand, leaning away from the wind that blew so unrelentingly from the sea, their spindly trunks and gnarly branches looked as though they were slowly creeping inland, clawing their way toward the rich soil where the forests were thick, and men and women planted grain crops and pastured large herds of cattle. Here, where each dwarfed shrub should be proud to have endured in such a forbidding land, Aiken felt a kinship with the poor outliers. He asked himself whether a man, who was an outlaw with a twisted face, might, like these shrubs, set down roots here and become one of Gevehard's men.

Inside the basket of holy offerings, he found a wooden bowl filled with curdled milk, a crock of butter, and one round, flat bread. He laid the small linen towel, with which the basket had been covered, at the edge of the grove amidst the shrubs. On top of it he arranged the gifts that were meant to honor the hidden folk who inhabited the shoreline and the forebears who were buried there. He had heard it said that the dead leave behind parts of their souls along with their bones and, as their bones turn to earth, they become one with the hidden folk.

Edmund had warned Aiken that some folks claimed to have seen a man and a woman who had been the original inhabitants of the village before the Terrible Winter's pestilence came upon them. Because their descendants had been forced into servitude by those who came from the north, folks said that the original inhabitants held grudges against Glenn's descendants. To reduce any animosity they might hold against Glenn, the very man whom they despised because he had overcome them, taken their land, and forced them into bondage, Edmund explained the importance of honoring those forebears, too, and to beg for their forbearance when they saw the stone being set there in Glenn's memory.

Aiken kept these thoughts in mind as he told the many hidden folk and ances-tors, whose bones rested here, that he did not want to offend them. He asked them to regard his and the shipmaster's efforts favorably. Addressing the original inhabitant's forebears, he told them how he sympathized with their plight. For he, too, had lost the land he had inherited, his rank, and his wealth, and was now beholden to the chieftains for whom he carved.

Alerted by a persistent movement at the edge of his vision, Aiken jerked his head around just in time to catch sight of a man and a woman seated in a stone-outlined boat. The man was dressed in light-yellow tunic and tan trousers, and the woman wore a pale green dress. Their knees were tucked up to their chins and their arms were wrapped around their legs. Then, just as quickly as they had appeared, his sight of them dissolved, and they were gone.

Though he had lost the ability to trust whatever he saw, years ago, he continued to stare at the outlined boat and dared the shades to reappear. But they never did. Struck by the horrible thought that, if he was careless, he might disturb the dead, he promised to never step inside the boats where the bottomless layers of dead men and women's bones lay buried. He begged them to forgive any carelessness that he and the other men may have been guilty of when they placed the memorial stone in the trench. And, from then on, whenever he visited Hild in the holy grove, Aiken walked carefully around the edges of the small, white-painted stones outlining the boats. And if he saw a stone out of place, he set it back where it belonged.

V.

The following morning, Aiken wandered around the village. First he checked on Plod-der and Smart-one. Then he headed toward the shoreline where the longships rested in the slipways. Originally, he had planned to offer to help the master shipbuilder with the boat repair. But once he was down on the strand, he stopped and stood off to the side to watch Jerold put the men through their paces. Each man wore a helmet and padded jerkin and held a shield and a long, wooden knife weighted with lead ingots.

Jerold walked with a heavy gait. His hands were clenched in fists and his jaw was thrust forward as he threw his weight onto his forward foot, and followed with his shoulders. Brusquely calling out the fighting positions, cuts, and guards, everything the man did was meant to garner the men's respect and fear, but he did nothing to earn their affection.

After he paired the men off, Jerold occasionally jumped in when a man required more instruction. Some of the men were young, a few were old as Aiken, but most were somewhere in between. It took no time at all to judge these men's combat skills. They were definitely not up to Aiken's expectations.

Back when he had been in Torwald's warband, he and his brothers-in-arms had practiced daily, year in, year out. He had begun training when he was eight years old and by the time he was fifteen, had been admitted to the warband. War was a con-stant threat and a fighting man owed his life to being in top form. But these farmers and fishermen became fighting-men according to the seasons. Between planting and harvesting, they set aside their hoes and spades, harpoons and fishing nets, and picked up and sharpened their long-blades and axes.

Jerold sauntered up to Aiken, planted his feet squarely, tucked his thumbs into his belt, and said, "These men are nothing like the ones you fought, are they?"

Aiken answered with his own wry observation, "Nor do you act like a farmer or a fisherman."

"You got that right," Jerold replied. Both men knew it was different inland. There, men sought riches and prestige. To increase their holdings of good farmland, the chieftains raided enemy clans during the summertime months. The most powerful among them fought hard to control the mines and quarries from which valuable stones and minerals were mined, and to take ownership of the bogs where iron nuggets grew. In contrast, here along the shoreline, there was nothing worth protecting but sod houses and flocks of sheep. "The farmers here cannot even grow a good grain crop," Jerold said and spat on the sand in disgust, as if to implicate the very ground upon which he stood.

These men were good enough fighters for what they had to do, Jerold said. They only needed to hold off a small band of pirates. But, if these men were forced to fight enemies who were as fierce as the ones whom he and Aiken had fought, all these men would be dead in no time.

Aiken asked Jerold where he came from, but the commander answered vaguely. Though he claimed to have served in a warband farther south, he neither named his tribe, nor the chieftain whom he had served.

Aiken guessed that Jerold had run off and broken his oath. Not that it mattered. He could hardly hold such an indiscretion against Jerold. Nor did his own reputation appear blameless at first. To defend himself against the unfairly imposed outlaw status that he had been forced to endure all these years, always took a long, round-about explanation. And just like Jerold, he did not care to get into it just then.

Nonetheless, Aiken could not abandon his curiosity. He would have liked to have learned what the man was hiding beneath the grim expression he had contrived to give nothing of his thoughts away. The man's speech pattern was consistent with a dialect that was spoken by the tribal people who lived far to the south. How much did Jerold know, first hand, of the vicious struggles between the warlords who lived in that rich, agricultural region? Might Jerold's chieftain have been one of the weak men who had been unable to retain their leadership against the crushing odds? If Jerold had known the game was up, might he have turned his back on his liege lord and looked for another chieftain whom he could serve?

Most likely Gevehard would know why Jerold had traveled so far north from his original homeland but had agreed not to mention it. To maintain the other men's respect for their commander if, in truth, the man had been untrustworthy in the past, Gevehard would want to keep Jerold's past a secret. Since Gevehard now relied upon Jerold to present a show of unwavering loyalty, how could the shipmaster trust someone who had once treasonously turned his back on a chieftain to whom he had sworn protection? A chieftain or a shipmaster would suspect a man, who had broken his oath, of being more interested in saving his own neck when the going got rough. And if that were so, it would easily explain why Gevehard seemed to distance himself from the commander. A disloyal man would not throw his body in front of his shipmaster and take the blow that was meant to kill him the way Edmund had done.

Aiken was proud to have suffered no such disgrace. Unlike a man who had abandoned his oath, he had not sunk so low. Although he had fallen in status because he had been treated maliciously, it was no secret that he had sworn to prove who had murdered his liege lord.

In time, Jerold's pride in his designated status loosened his tongue. He crowed proudly, "Gevehard sought me out," and, rocking back and forth between his heels and toes, grunted "Yup. Yup, he did," emphasizing every guttural sound for good measure, and added one decisive nod at the end. "He always keeps an eye out for hardened fighters who have trained in a warband. He offers good compensation to those who agree to join his household men."

But after having spoken so enthusiastically, Jerold took a step back and changed his tone. To counter any presumptions that Aiken might have about being offered a place on the crew, Jerold added, "Make no mistake about it. Rowing a boat is hard work. Everyone takes a turn at the oars. Even the shipmaster rows. No one is spared. No one has special status. Everyone on the boat is equal when it comes to manning the oars."

Intent upon Aiken's hands, Jerold observed the broad palms and the strong, straight fingers. If Aiken wanted to protect those hands because of the fine tool-work he did, he had better think twice about wanting a place on the boat. "Look around and see what rowing does to a man. His hands get so gnarled and frozen-up they turn to claws. Once that happens, a man is good for nothing else."

It had not occurred to Aiken to want a place on the boat but, if he did, the commander would not want a man on the crew who might compete for second highest in rank. Undoubtedly, Jerold had noticed how easily Aiken had gained Gevehard's confidence.

It was obvious the two competing impulses were fighting for dominance in the commander's thoughts and speech. Did he see in Aiken a potential rival, or did he see in him a well-trained, dependable fighter? Every man on the crew made a difference when fate decided whether they had the strength and endurance to make it home again with all four boats and their cargo intact.

Yet Jerold's pride in his new authority could not be contained. He praised the shipmaster for being an honorable kinleader who took care of his own. Jerold used Edmund as an example to describe how men, who had been hurt, were not cast off when their fighting careers were over. It went without saying that a man who was maimed in battle was still respectable here. Given whatever work he could do, he was not forced to wander off alone. Jerold stared at Aiken's face, raised an eyebrow, and left the unspoken hang between them like an unanswered question.

Aiken clenched his jaw and stared back. A chill descended over their conversation. And, for a while, they watched the other men's fighting techniques, occasionally commenting coldly on a good guard or cut. Jerold finally broke the stony silence by asking Aiken whether he still fought.

Aiken answered bluntly, "I am rusty in combat, but still practice the cuts. I have found ways to compensate for my blind side."

"Well, given your evident weakness, these men will be a good match for you."

Jerold offered to let Aiken practice, if he wanted to jump in. "We will be practicing with wooden knives for a couple more days before the men use their steel blades, so you should not get hurt. After that, the men get more ruthless and the injuries begin to winnow out those who are unfit. You would not want to jump in then."

The commander walked over to the pile of wooden blades that lay on a leather tarp and picked one up. He lifted a shield from another pile and handed them both to Aiken. "Here try these out."

Aiken picked through the worn leather helmets, poor as they were. Fuming beneath his breath, he repeated Jerold's words in a low rumbling growl, "Given your blindness, you cannot match men who can really fight. Given your weakness, you should not get hurt fighting with a wooden knife. You would not want to jump in when men are practicing with real weaponry." Aiken would have liked to have shown Jerold what he could do, back when he was young. Back when he was a champion. Back when he had had two good eyes.

Aiken tried on several helmets before he found one that fit. He looped the ragged, banged-up shield over his left arm and held the wooden knife hilt in his right hand. He hefted it, placed his feet closer together, positioned one in back and one in front, bent his knees and centered his weight.

To get his initial, angry reaction under control, Aiken took Jerold's round-about attack on his dignity as a new form of challenge, similar but different from those that he once had relished.

The memory in his arms and legs began to take over, and he pretended to have a confidence, he did not feel. He held the hilt above the shoulder that corresponded with his rear foot, took his starting position, and followed with several cuts in midair. He ended the final stroke with the pommel at his belt line and held the nearly horizontal blade pointed down at a slight angle.

Letting it all come back, he began to feel the excitement of meeting an opponent in one-on-one combat. He had not met a man in combat, even in practice, since the day before he had fallen on the Warring riverbank. Though he had not wanted to admit the truth, even to himself, this was the moment he had been waiting for. This would be the proof. He would either match the man against whom he was paired off against, or the unspoken qualms that he had been harboring for years, in the darkest regions of his soul, would prove to have been justified.

If Aiken was unable to match his opponent, Jerold would have succeeded in asserting his position as second in rank. He would not need to worry about being shown up by another former warrior who had come from the inland regions. It would also put a decisive end to Aiken's practice. He would take off the helmet, toss the wooden knife and shield back in their respective piles, walk down to the shoreline, and offer to help the master shipmaster with the boat repairs.

The commander called over one of his best men. He was younger than Aiken by at least ten years. After they shook hands and squared off, they exchanged a few good cuts and banged on each other's shields, but remained in a close draw until Jerold called a halt to the mock combat.

Aiken stood there, breathing hard. It was not until he glanced to the side, that he realized some of the other men had stopped their practice to check out the newcomer in their midst. No doubt, they had heard that he was a man who had fought in a warband in the south. And now that they had seen what he could do, they elbowed each other and returned to their practice.

Aiken and his opponent shook hands again. He playfully clapped the man on the arm and complimented his skill, saying, "I am grateful you did not make me look like an old fool in front of the other men."

Aiken's rival shook his head, and said in disagreement, "You are good. You stood your ground, and challenged me, all right. I could learn something from you, Aiken. If you are willing to teach me, that is."

Aiken shrugged off the praise.

The man went back to practice with his previous partner and Aiken stood alone, holding his wooden knife loosely in his fist. He admitted to feeling more competent than he had expected. Maybe the wooden knife carried with it pleasant memories of his youth, when he and Alger had practiced together. And, as if that thought alone was enough to evoke his friend's voice, Aiken heard, as if it came from out of nowhere, "You can do it. One last fight against the one who murdered me. That is all it will take. Just one last fight."

Aiken sighed grimly. He was not as alone as he had thought.

He practiced with several other men, until, at the end of the day, he was certain that Jerold had put him to the test and would report back to Gevehard. Aiken cocked his head to the side, turned the knife hilt toward Jerold, and handed it back. "I know I am rusty but am confident my former skills will come back in time."

"There is never enough time."

Aiken thanked the commander for the opportunity, turned and walked off. Although, that morning, when he had first wandered down to the strand, he had never given so much as a passing thought to joining the crew, he now was toying with the possibility.

VI.

On the day of his arrival, Aiken had been invited to eat supper with Gevehard in his longhouse as the shipmaster's honored guest. The first evening, when he walked into the shipmaster's longhouse, Aiken was taken aback by the men's rowdy lack of rank. Though the shipmaster towered above everyone in the village, when he joined in their banter, he acted as though the men in his household all shared equally in his dignity.

No doubt, when men lived so closely together on the boats, the barriers, which rank usually imposed, had broken down the divisions that were common to those men who lived in more settled conditions. Yet, Aiken sensed that beneath the casual exterior, if a man were to cross the shipmaster he would be shown out the door and never invited in again. The ranking was there but hidden.

When Aiken walked in the door, one of the horsemen, who had accompanied him on their journey north, waved him over toward a cluster of benches. Aiken greeted the men in a friendly manner but, as always, felt like an outsider among the others and did not have much to say. He kept to his old habits and after a while moved to the bench closest to the hearth. He pulled out his small whittling knife and a piece of wood that he had brought with him from home.

A few of the men gathered around Aiken, seemingly expecting the notable stone carver to bring about some marvel right before their very eyes. Aiken, however, became increasingly uncomfortable with the way they were crowding around him. Wanting them to back off, he demonstrated how he planned to rough out the shape of a toy cow. He held the wood block out for their inspection and showed it to them from all angles. With the tip of his knife, he pointed out how he planned to make the head, legs, and rear, and added that he would give it to Gevehard's boys when he was finished.

The man, with whom he had ridden north, took the hint, patted Aiken's shoulder and wandered back to the clustered benches. The others followed and, after they were seated again, picked up the conversation where they had left off.

When Gevehard's two youngest boys ran in from outside they showed no interest at all in the toy cow Aiken was making. Unable to sit still and to act like grown men, they ran around the hall, tumbled, and jumped and did whatever they could to get the seated men's attention. Two of the men reached out to grab the teasing boys by their wrists. They stood and, lifting the children by their arms, swung them out to the sides and twirled them around until the boys were shrieking in delight.

Someday, Aiken thought, one or both of those boys will be a shipmaster. They will sit at the high table, and possibly, if those men, who are spinning them around, live long enough, they will be seated on the benches, looking up respectfully at those same boys and will acknowledge their authority as either kinleader of the village or shipmaster of the fleet.

Gevehard walked into the long house, touched Aiken on the shoulder, gave it a squeeze, and said, "Jerold tells me that you impressed him. He said that you are a bit rusty, but you know the cuts. As I said before, I am always on the look-out for seasoned fighters. You and I will talk later."

VII.

After that first day in the village, Aiken practiced daily with the men down on the strand and, every evening, joined the shipmaster at the table along with the guardsmen and those who commanded Gevehard's household men. Frequently, Gevehard asked Aiken about the markets and the chieftains for whom he carved. Impressed by Aiken's astute observations, Gevehard was curious to know how a woodcarver had acquired so great an understanding of the warlords' constant maneuvering between themselves.

Aiken explained that, although he appeared to be an outsider, he had known many of the chieftains back in the day when he had been a member of a warband, and he liked to keep up with the gossip. He wanted to know who was outsmarting whom and who would come out on top. "I may be invisible to them, but I have my reasons for keeping abreast of their affairs. I know inside men who will talk to me when I offer them a cup of ale, a toy for their children, or a spoon for their wives. We sit behind my cart while Mildred keeps up with the women's gossip out front. The warriors rarely speak to me, but their wives talk to Mildred. She encourages both the common and the highborn women to spill their secrets about their men's home lives, and she passes on whatever she learns to me."

Gevehard was equally interested in Aiken's assessment of the men with whom he practiced each day. After they had finished eating, Gevehard would draw Aiken aside and ask him to judge the men's fighting skills. Whenever he shared his observations, Gevehard would nod and add, "I know what you are saying. You are confirming my estimations. I like having you there as a third man, someone who can recognize skillful fighting when he sees it and will either contradict or agree with Jerold's and my assessments. Keep it up."

One evening, when Aiken was seated directly opposite the shipmaster at the table, he was cutting his meat with the knife that Gevehard had given him. The shipmaster stretched out his arm, tapped the blade with his longest finger and declared, "That knife is but a token. If you swear to be my man and agree to join us in the boat, I will have your name written in gold on a well-crafted long-blade. It was made by a master smith who lives near the western sea. The knife will be a good gift."

At times like that, the shipmaster's casual demeanor fell away and his listeners came to attention. Because his word carried the authority his leadership demanded, when he said, "I want you with us," Aiken took it as a command.

But a sidelong glance at Jerold suggested otherwise. Avoiding Aiken's gaze, he stared straight ahead. His face looked hard and stiff. No enthusiasm there.

Aiken had no doubts about whether he would be welcomed aboard the boat. He would not. As time went on, Jerold became increasingly resentful of the attention that Gevehard gave Aiken's comments whenever he was asked to weigh in on which of the men he thought could hold their own in a fight. Aware that such a judgement should rightfully be issued by the commander, Aiken was being drawn into a conflict that he had never intended to engage in. The commander would be protective of his rank, would rightfully defend his position if he were challenged, and would be a tough opponent.

VIII.

The following day, Aiken was practicing on the strand when one of Gevehard's household men walked up to him and pulled him aside. "Gevehard wants to speak with you," he said. "Come with me.' He offered no reason for the shipmaster's command, walked ahead of Aiken, led him to the door of Gevehard's private chambers, and left.

Gevehard greeted Aiken at the door, shook his hand, and showed him inside. Adelheide poured red wine into a cup. This fermented grape beverage, Gevehard said, was brought from the coastline far to the south. He served it only on rare occasions when he wished to honor a guest with whom he had important matters to discuss. Adelheide first offered the cup to her husband and praised his discerning leadership and then offered the cup to Aiken and praised his loyalty and skill.

After she poured wine into a second cup, she left the pitcher and cups on a nearby table and left the room. The men picked up their cups and Gevehard pulled up a bench for Aiken, seated himself on a stool and, sitting not at the table, but across from each other, he pulled his stool so close that their knees were nearly touching.

"Aiken, I prize loyalty, and I trust you feel the same as I do. I am confident that you will stand up for a leader to whom you have sworn allegiance, whether or not you question his judgment. But I also know that you are not afraid to speak up, even when it challenges another man's opinion. You are a perceptive man. You read the signs, ask questions and draw connections between the things you observe. You are willing to change your assumptions according to what you see, even if it does not fit into the set of beliefs with which you started. Or, if it contrasts with your previous assessments, you are willing to change your beliefs according to what you observe at any given moment and will speak out boldly when you present an argument. This is what I like about you."

Aiken shrugged off Gevehard's flattery, but the shipmaster held fast to his favorable appraisal. Insisting that Aiken was too humble, the shipmaster explained, "I notice how closely you watch everything that goes on around you. You see numerous layers in all their depth and understand men's motivations. You question and think through what, at first glance, seems to be unrelated, yet you fit your observations together in meaningful patterns that aid your understanding of the surroundings. When you put those connections into your carvings, your unique point of view is what people recognize in your work. This is the quality that people bargain for when they ask you to carve a chair, a box, or even an ale bowl.

"Same as you," Gevehard continued, "I am always alert, always on the watch. And, just like you, I read the signs. I want to know what is up ahead, so that when I get there I am not surprised.

"Aiken, you are honest and forthright. You feel strongly about what is right and will put your life on the line in defense of what you believe in. You do not hold back, nor do you mince words, but you express what you see. This is why, when we face strangers in the markets and must decide who to trust and who might cheat us, or attack us later in an attempt to steal our goods, I want you at my side."

It was so unexpected, Aiken was stunned speechless by Gevehard's confessed need for his communication and observational skills. Apparently, Gevehard had not wanted Aiken's fighting arm at all. Instead he wanted the very aptitude that had so annoyed his former chieftain. As it turned out, the qualities that had been, in one man's sight, a sign of Aiken's foolish distrust of others, had become, in another man's eyes, recognizable signs of intelligent discernment. Gevehard trusted Aiken's judgments as no man had ever trusted them before.

Turning Gevehard's offer around in his mind like a piece of wood he was about to carve, Aiken studied the possibility of joining the crew from all sides. "I am honored to serve you and am grateful for your generous offer. I understand that you have taken my weakness into account and am grateful that you have overlooked my partial blindness. But I am not a cunning man, nor am I the man I was before. These days, I am only a common woodcarver."

Gevehard's nature was to watch and listen. Rather than offer a hasty response, he remained silent, tipped his head to the side, lifted an eyebrow, shrugged his shoulders and gave Aiken his full attention.

Gevehard's pale blue eyes were so colorless they seemed to be made from sea ice. Meeting his uncanny stare, Aiken said, "I see and admire the same qualities in you. I respect your powers of discernment. You are a thoughtful man who never acts foolishly. But if, on the morrow, you feel that you have spoken too effusively, I will understand and lend you a graceful means of retreat when you take back the offer."

Gevehard shook his head, and answered, "My mind is made up. I will not rescind the offer. I want you on the crew. What will it take to convince you?"

"Before I can either accept or decline," Aiken answered bluntly, "I want to know how informed you are of my past," but gave Gevehard no time to reply. Instead he listed the superficial, telling features of his appearance that were impossible to hide, the things that everyone took note of immediately when they first met. "From the markings on my arms you identified me as a former warrior who had once served in a chieftain's warband. And, as anyone can see, I was hurt fighting and am blind in one eye.

"But it would surprise me if you had not asked the men, with whom you traded, what they knew of me after you had asked me to carve the stone. Would you not have asked others how they judged a man with whom you had entrusted such an important task? Surely, you would have wanted to know why I no longer serve a chieftain. Might what you had learned not have influenced your offer to join the crew?" He looked Gevehard squarely in the face and demanded to know: "What have men told you about my reputation?"

A man, who was less confident than Gevehard, might have been put off by Aiken's overtly stated challenge. He screwed up his mouth, tipped his head to one side and shrugged his shoulders. "I admit to having asked the men with whom I traded if they knew Aiken the woodcarver. Men who knew you by name told me that you have a lucky way with the things you make. The chieftains and the warriors, with whom I spoke, in fact, displayed an unconcealed envy. They congratulated me on playing a good game and told me that your chairs and boxes are rare and difficult to come by because you make only one or two large pieces per year. They were dumbfounded by the idea that such a fussy woodcarver would acquiesce to my request to carve a stone. They were all of the same opinion that I had scored well when I procured your agreement."

"Well, yes, wood is easier to carve and to cart around. But for permanence, stone has no match."

"As you know, I am grateful you agreed. Those men who own one of the high seats or treasure boxes, you carved, invited me inside their meadhalls or private chambers and proudly showed them off. They claimed your chairs and chests carry more prestige than those made by other craftsmen. Men who did not own one of your larger pieces but had seen your workmanship, or who owned a special trencher that you had carved with a knotted design integrating the secret signs, or even an ale bowl with carved handles, all spoke highly of your skill.

"It seems your character is also well known. I heard stories of your intractable stubbornness. You may be reputed to be a man who never backs down, but they all agreed that you are trustworthy, have never cheated anyone, or reneged on an agreement."

"If they know my name and that my word is good, they also know that I plan to carry out an oath I swore to fulfill."

"Yes, they implied something dangerous about you, something that made men keep their distance. But now that I know you, Aiken, I have trouble connecting the quiet and thoughtful man, who is seated here before me, with the man they described. When I pressed the chieftains for more information, they alluded to a shameful circumstance in your past. They said it was better not to ask and refused to tell me what happened. That fact alone indicates that something dishonorable occurred."

Gevehard then hastened to add, "The way I see it, their silence on the matter reflects badly upon the chieftains. It does not indicate that you were in the wrong. But," he added, turning his statement into a question, "could it be you who were wronged?"

Upon hearing this reference to the very crux of the matter they needed to discuss, Aiken nodded gravely. "Unlike the times in the past when I instilled fear in those men whom I faced on the battlefield, or who I challenged to one-on-one combat, I am dangerous now because powerful men fear the underhanded treachery I can expose. Something happened that they feel deeply ashamed of having been a party to."

"Clearly, each man I spoke with was unwilling to admit to his own complicity in the matter," Gevehard said with a nod to convey his understanding. "They all maintained the silence. To a man, each and every one of them told me that it was something no one talked about. They warned me off and told me, to my face, that if I and my men kept poking around, I would stir up resentment and make myself unwelcome in their meadhalls and village markets. They said, 'If you value your trade with me, do not ask questions about the woodcarver Aiken.'"

Gevehard bent low and, speaking with barely concealed hostility, said, "One man even threatened me outright. He told me that a small band of traders is easily disposed of on the roads. Whatever they fear, I will not touch it."

"It is too late." Aiken said, glancing down at the way they sat knee to knee. "You have already gotten too close."

"Aiken do not worry on my behalf. From now on, we will give that chieftain's hill fort a wide clearance. I do not need his trade. But, tell me, what do you know about that man? His name is Leofar."

Horror-struck at the thought that he may have unwittingly contributed to Gevehard's murder on the roads, Aiken swallowed hard and asked himself whether bad luck would always follow him wherever he went. Did he imperil any man to whom he got too close? Powerful men had branded Aiken a nameless woodcarver so as to dissociate their own names from his, yet any carving that was associated with his name was suggestive of the prestigious displays of wealth and privilege they all craved. There was no sensible way to explain the dissembling the chieftains engaged in.

"Why are those men afraid of you?"

"They fear what I might do."

"Is it because you are a cunning man, and they fear the spells you put into your carvings?"

"No. Once I threatened to curse a man, but that is not the reason men fear me. I am not a cunning man. There is nothing special about the words I spell in secret signs.

The chieftains for whom I carve speak from both sides of their mouths. They think my carving is lucky because I returned from the land of the dead, while at the same time they claim that I died on the bank of the Warring River alongside my chieftain. Obviously, they cannot have it both ways. I cannot be both alive and dead at the same time. They drag my reputation through the mud and pretend the man who carves their high seats is an unknown man with the same name as the one who died on the riverbank. There is no end to the lengths they will go to protect their fragile reputations."

"What makes you so dangerous? Have they all schemed to wipe something shameful from their memories?" Looking hard at Aiken and, spitting out his words in a tone of contempt for all the men with whom he had spoken, Gevehard asked, "But, you have not forgotten, have you?"

Aiken pulled his elbows in close to his sides, folded his arms across his chest, and paused a moment before he went on. "Of all the men who made had up an entire warband, I am the only one who is left." He looked down at the floor and shook his head. How could he ever begin to explain? He rested one elbow on the opposite fist, lifted the other hand to his forehead and squeezed. He wanted the weight of this burden to lift from his shoulders but knew it never would lighten. Even this far north, the chieftains had slipped into every corner of his life. They would never stop hounding him. Would there never be an end to it?

Aiken looked up, dropped his arms and, curling his fingers around his belt, clenched his fists. "One of those men murdered my chieftain and the men in our warband. He was one of our own kinsmen. No doubt, they would never have told you how they divvied up Torwald's estates and took his wealth as war booty after they had covered up the murders. They refused to let me speak at the Assembly. Instead of being given a fair hearing, I was thrown out and nearly beaten to death.

"They would not have told you that I have sworn to bring the guilty men to justice for their

crimes," Aiken said, and scoffed at the strange condition in which he lived each day and night. "I live as an outlaw, in full view of the those who cast me out. I am indeed their kinsman, though they do not admit it. I can trace my warrior lineage back many generations." He tipped his head to one side, as if questioning their peculiar, unspoken agreement. "If I do not make trouble, they let me be. I have a wife, Mildred—you met her—and two children, Sunniva and the little boy back home whose name is Bertolf. My first responsibility is to my family, so I comply with the demands the chieftains impose upon me. I swallow my pride and anger and refrain from making trouble."

He drew back from Gevehard, hunched down and, resting his arms on his upper thighs, dangled his hands loosely between his knees. "I do not live as comfortably as you do, although I did at one time," he said and, picking up and raising his cup, he added, "I do not drink grape wine and mead." He shrugged his shoulders and added in a flat tone, "I make do. As it turns out, carving suits me. I owe that good fortune to my wife. It was Mildred's idea."

Gevehard crooked a finger to his lower lip, shook his head slowly side to side and added his own perspective on all that Aiken had said. "Those from whom you expected justice gave you none. The chieftains get what they want but you get nothing. No one told me that you had been outlawed. I do not believe the disgrace is yours."

"No, the men who outlawed me disgraced themselves."

Gevehard stood up from his seat on the stool, and slid onto the bench beside Aiken. He put his arm around Aiken's shoulders and pulled him in close. "You need not live as an outlaw any longer. Not here. I want you to bring your wife and settle amongst us. I will give you land to farm and men to work it. You can betroth Sunniva to the son of a well-regarded man. I want you on the crew. Will you join me? Say you will. Your knowledge makes you powerful, Aiken. Land, gold, whatever you want, it will be yours—I value your expertise that highly."

Aiken took several breaths to loosen the knot in his throat. He twisted the gold band at his wrist. Yes, he still longed for the thrill and excitement of walking the blade's sharp edge, to once again balance, precariously, from one moment to the next. Those days when he had danced between the knives and come through safely on the other side were the times when he had felt most fully alive. All winter long, when he was working on Hild, his outsider status in the hamlet had not mattered any longer. He had believed that he was fated, through the stone, to be together with men who lived by the law of the long-knife.

And now that an opportunity to have that life back again was within arm's reach, a nod, a handshake, a simple 'yes,' was all it would take. He could smell and taste all that he had lost. He could see it dangling there. It was so close he could easily grab hold of it and have it back again. All that was required was to stretch out his hand.

But Aiken was not sure whether the wealth, prestige, and all the trappings that came along with it—a fine house, a good horse, the gold and bronze brooches, the jeweled hilt on a well-crafted long-knife inscribed with his name spelled in secret signs inlaid with gold—mattered all that much anymore. Only one thing mattered.

He leaned back, pressed his neck into Gevehard's arm where it lay draped across his shoulders and tipped up his head. To look for strength up there in the darkness, he stared into the ceiling rafters but saw only the one thing that prevented acceptance of Gevehard's offer. The burdensome weight of his decision to see it through to the end left him no choice but to explain the whole, rotten truth of the binding situation he was in.

Aiken shrugged off the shipmaster's arm and turned to face Gevehard. "The night I burned my war companions' bones, I made a promise. Without knowing who was behind the ambush that had resulted in my war companion's murders and partially blinded me, I vowed to champion justice. Someday, I must fulfill my oath to clear my name and to restore my war companion's honor. If I am proven unsuccessful in the attempt, at least I will die trying. Necessity has ordained it and there is no way to get around what I must do."

Gevehard nudged in closer to Aiken and, looking at him with deep sadness, said, "But, you were wronged."

"My dead chieftain and my dead brothers are the ones who were wronged."

Although there were times when he resented this promise with a burning hatred, there were other times when the need to restore justice was all that mattered.

Sometimes it was all that kept him alive. From one day to the next, the need to defend the truth grumbled in his gut like an insatiable hunger. It went on and on with its grinding purpose to retaliate for his losses. The need for justice was lodged so deeply inside him, there was no way to get away from it. The sight of his dead war companions' bones hanging from tree branches could never be erased from his memory.

Gevehard asked, "But, what if an opportunity to challenge the guilty man never presents itself?"

"There will come a time when the need to satisfy my craving to see the guilty brought to justice is so great that I can no longer contain it. Even though the well-being of my wife and children is all that truly matters, when I am given no choice but to answer for my soul's redemption, I will say goodbye to Mildred, Sunniva and Bertolf and take off. I will force a judgment by arms or will die in the attempt. I will assault the guilty chieftain's hill fort single handedly if I have to. In the end, the only way that I can go on living is to accept my own inevitable death. The only way to maintain my self-respect is to make peace with the oath I swore to fulfill."

Gevehard folded his hands in his lap and shook his head. "It will be a travesty if the life of such a talented man ends in a terrible death." He turned to face Aiken, and asked, "What is the name of the man you suspect? Join with me. We will pick a fight and take him on."

"No, I refuse to name the man I must challenge. The dispute is mine and mine alone."

"Then you will leave me guessing."

"That is how it must be."

"Is it Leofar?"

Aiken shook his head. He refused to let Gevehard's rank pry the truth from him. Nor would he encourage the shipmaster and his men to wage war on his behalf. Living where they did, on the shores of the Merchant Sea, the shipmaster and his men had no reason to engage the rogue in a fight. If Gevehard met up with Leofar again, he would only have a few men at his side. If he chose to raid or to attack his enemy's fort town, Gevehard and his men would never make it home. Aiken had sworn no more good men would die on his watch. Never again did he want to see trees hung with the corpses of men whom Leofar had killed. He had seen it once and one time was enough to last a lifetime. He could not live another day with the knowledge that he had allowed them to ride into a death trap.

"Aiken, you show remarkable resolve and fortitude. Few men are so steadfast. To believe that you must bring a wrong-doer to justice, when all the odds are stacked against you, is a terrible weight to carry. It is one under which an ordinary man would crumble. I admire your courageous loyalty. But you should not carry the burden alone."

Gevehard grabbed Aiken's shoulder, squeezed it tightly, and gave it a shake. "In the meantime, before Mother Necessity ordains the time that you must act, I want you to be my man."

"I am grateful for the trust you have shown me. But I must plead for time to think it over."

While they had spoken, Aiken had turned the gold arm ring around and around in a fretful manner. He now began to slip it over his hand.

But Gevehard refused to take it back. "No, I want you to keep the ring. Do not say no just yet. I will grant you all the time you need." And to reassure Aiken that he had given him the ring in return for the trust that he had shown when had he carved the stone, he said, "No matter your decision, you should keep the arm ring. But you must come with us. I need you beside me.

"I want to tell you this in strict confidence: I cried for days after Edmund was hurt. From the moment he was injured, I never left his side. I stanched the bleeding, cauterized and dressed the wound, and held him in my arms to comfort him.

"I trust no one more than Edmund. I need one man with whom I can speak in confidence. But there is no one to whom I can turn. Edmund and I grew up together. And, although his family had been in service to our family for three generations, he and I went everywhere together. After my father died, I made Edmund a freedman. And now that he will no longer be at my side, folks doubt whether I can hold up to the strain. There are no men on my crew who can take Edmund's place. None but you. I am loyal to those who stand by me. I want you to come with me."

"You do not know me. How can you say such a thing?"

"I know you well enough to recognize a rare quality in you, Aiken." And with those words, Gevehard rose from the place where he was seated beside Aiken. Un-masked and vulnerable after he had opened the door to his heart, now was the time to close it. He took back the role of shipmaster and village kinleader. The audience was over.

Aiken stood. He hardly knew what to say. "Gevehard, there is no other man whom I would rather serve. You have high standards. You treat people right. The gracious respect with which you honor your men reminds me of my father, Eamon. Although he died when I was small, I recall how fairly he treated other men."

Walking Aiken to door, Gevehard said, "It saddens me to never have met your father, Eamon. I can see by the way you speak of him that he was an admirable man of character. It humbles me to think that you compare me so favorably to your father. You have given me the most gracious praise in doing so. When we first met, I knew nothing about you but I trusted you implicitly because of your demeanor. I guessed that you had come from a long line of honorable men.

"Now, just as you are becoming acquainted with my father, grandfather and great grandfather through the stories you hear describing their lives, I also know something about the ground from which you sprang. I am grateful you told me. I bid you now, go with the grace of the Matrones."

Gevehard watched Aiken walk off. Then, a sudden idea seemed to present itself and he called out, "The wisewoman will arrive tomorrow and will perform a ceremo-ny the following evening." And, to additionally tempt this recalcitrant woodcarver with the prestige, which only he could grant, Gevehard said, "I plan to seat you beside me at the high table. On my right."

IX.

Later that night, Aiken undressed and prepared for sleep. He folded his tunic and trousers, placed them beside him in an orderly pile, laid down, pulled the bedding covers up to his chin, and thought about the promise that he had made to Torwald. His conversation with Gevehard had forced him to confront the truth: his commitment to challenge Leofar was nothing but a way to salvage pride in his own self-worth.

How he planned to force Leofar to admit to the men's murders or to face him in one-on-one combat still remained the sticking point in his scheme. Unless he was a member of a warband, he would never get inside Leofar's stockade. He would never feast in the rogue's meadhall and would never confront the man face to face.

The way the shipmaster's arm had draped across his shoulders like a yoke, still weighed heavily upon him. If he were to offer his service to Gevehard and to take his place beside him in the role of the shipmaster's confidante, he would follow the men on the crew at dawn as they splash through the shallow surf. He walks up the plank ramped against the gunwales. The last two men to board each ship pull the anchor stones, and shove the boat away from shore.

The steersmen place their hands upon the steering oars in the sterns and the oarsmen slip their oars through the bung holes in the planks. Oars extended, the men silently draw the wing-like oars against the sullen water. Given life-like motion, the ships float so lightly they barely touch the water.

Like winged serpents, they glide like grease on water. The ships wedged prows cut soundlessly through the waves with grace and ease. A man in each of the four boats lifts a curved, bronze war-horn to his lips and together they sound a sonorous harmony.

Afloat in the gray morning mist, one by one, each steersman pulls his boat close to the others, and the men lock their ships together with grappling hooks. Those oarsmen, who are unable to contain their joy at being at sea, leap across the gunwales. Like flying swallows the men twist and flip through the air. The Lord of Rich-Waters' gentle winds shred the drizzled mist and caresses Aiken's cheeks. The clouds break, and Lady Sun brightens the vaporous morning.

In time, the seamen leave behind the calm waters in the bay. Under the oaken planks beneath their feet they sense the black, bottomless depths.

Adrift in the pleasant daydream landscape, he watched the water throw rainbow colors from its greasy surface. Soothed by the shifting red and yellow, blue-green, ever-swirling, ever-changing, never-repeating designs, he wished to remain enchanted there forever.

The creature's head broke the surface and rose from the red-tinged water. First came its sparse hair, tangled with rusty, iron grains. Then came its face, lined and welted with unshapely lumps. Water dripped from its scrawny torso.

Arms thin as bones, knobby at the elbows and wrists, reached out to him. It called him affectionate names, told him how lovely he was, how it could never get enough of him. "All fighting men are beholden to me. I give them the iron they need to forge their weaponry. My steel is what gives a man the edge in a fight."

Aiken felt the cold, clammy hands upon his skin. He fought against dissolution, struggled hard against the pull that would take him beneath the water's surface where he would drown in the bogman's clutching embrace.

The bogman scrabbled out of the pond and hoisted itself onto the bank. Naked but for the long hair hanging in clumps, its lumpy skin was stained the same color as the reddish-brown water. Its shortened torso, bent in a crouch, came after Aiken. It crawled like a four-legged spider on its long skinny arms and legs. The bogman stretched out to grab Aiken's arm and pulled itself upright.

Aiken recoiled, tossed his head and tried to pull away, but the bogman grabbed his wrist, hung on tightly and pulled against him hard, "You cannot get away from me. You never will. You will never forget."

From where it stood, high as Aiken's chest, it reached up to stroke his cheek with its long fingers and to admire his scarred face, "I can never get enough of men's blood. How pretty are the injuries iron makes. Steel is so sharp, it cuts so well and makes such a fine mess of a man's flesh."

Before mounting its ride, the bogman sang to gentle him:

"Like to like, from blood, to bog, to steel.
The unbreakable, iron circle
Dissolves a man's soul from his flesh so well.
Like to like, from blood, to bog, to steel."

It grabbed Aiken's shoulders from the rear, hoisted itself up, wrapped its thin legs around Aiken's waist, squeezed its arms around his chest, kneed him hard in the side, and slapped Aiken in the back of the head. "You were wronged. You were wronged. You were wronged. Now, get even."

And there he was, standing outside Leofar's hall. Aiken walked through the open, double-wide doorway. Standing inside the entrance he looked around. The doors slammed shut behind him.

A feast was in progress to celebrate an alliance between Leofar and another chieftain. The two warlords were giving each other gifts while the men on the benches were boasting of their prowess and sealing their brotherhood with pledges.

Aiken took a seat. Speaking in low, guarded tones, he told the men seated beside him that he had secrets to share. Everyone likes a secret and those who were closest leaned in. Aiken lifted a fine silver cup, and said, "I know this cup. I drank from it before, when I was in Torwald's service." He asked pointedly where these fellows thought the burnished cups and plates, bowls and other tableware came from. He told them that the wealth this man displayed in his meadhall had once belonged to his uncle, Torwald, the same man who had been Aiken's chieftain. He described how Torwald and his war companions had all been brutally cut down by the man who now sat across from them in this very hall.

"This chieftain cannot be trusted. He is a thief, a liar, and a swindler. He offers to let you in on his schemes. But I am here to warn you. Do not to be taken in by his hollow shows of prosperity. He stole this wealth from fools like you who took him at his word. Men like you, who ask only to obey, without asking questions, follow his leadership, blindly. Men like you, who never question, cannot discriminate between their foes and friends. Men like you hold onto whatever your leader tells you and willingly wage war against those whom he accuses.

"But I, for one, have never believed Leofar's lies. In retaliation for asking questions, he threatened a small band of merchants. He told them that they could easily be disposed of on the road. That is the punishment, as everyone knows, for asking questions. It is better never to ask. Rather it is better to do as you are told.

"While Leofar murders and plunders, the other chieftains fear that they will be the next to fall. They turn their backs and look away. They ask no questions."

"Even now, I suspect the man is boasting about the murders he plans to execute before the night is over." And, in a low, throaty whisper, he asked, "Will you, too, look the other way when his men stab you and your bench mates in the back?"

No one questioned Aiken. The only thing they knew was fear. Men beholden to Mother Necessity and Father Time look for someone to blame, someone to attack, someone to get even with. Each man wants to quench the dissatisfaction that threatens to unravel at the very core of his being. And Aiken asked, "Is that not each and every one of you?"

The men who were listening to Aiken glanced warily at Leofar and his men. The two warbands sat lengthwise on opposite sides of the two blazing hearths, eyeing each other distrustfully.

Aiken stood and declared, "I promise to see justice restored by a meeting of the knives. Who will back my defense of truth?"

Aiken was the man whom others feared and hated. He was the man against whom everyone had turned because he spoke the truth. But now he was about to turn the tables. He was about to challenge their belief in Leofar's authority. He was about to challenge the man's carefully contrived image. He was about to disprove that Leofar was the only one who could lead his followers to victory and acquire the wealth that comes from overwhelming, successful achievement.

But even more astonishing than their mindless, unquestioning adherence to their leaders' cause, was the ease with which a man's hatred could rise to the level of incendiary violence. How easily a man's sworn allegiance can turn whenever his doubts begin to tarnish his positive beliefs. When seething resentment over having been misled is turned and, when he is presented with a less risky and more convenient opportunity to come out the victor, who can refuse the offer?

One word was all it would take to kindle their underlying resentment. These fearful men craved the chance to get even whenever they felt threatened. When a spark is thrown into the tinderbox, a man's urge to protect himself flares up and makes him shamelessly small and mean.

And one by one, each of Aiken's bench mates rose to his feet. Across the central fires the men on the opposite side eyed them, distrustfully. The men on both sides waited for someone to make the first move and Aiken obliged. He pressed his hands flat against the table, straightened his elbows and hurtled across.

He strode up to Leofar and, from across the table, challenged him. "I, Aiken the Strength of Oak, accuse you, Leofar the Mighty Leader, of murdering Torwald, your own uncle, in an ambush. Because you broke the family bond of trust and peace, I now deem you a luckless man. I hereby swear an oath to speak the truth. My testimony is true. I was there. I saw it happen. I alone survived."

Leofar stood. Pushing hard against the table, he leaned into his arms. His lips puckered in disgust as he stared at Aiken. His eyes narrowed with glaring hatred. Pointing his finger, he jabbed the air. "Liar. You are an outlaw who deserves to be hung." Spewing spit in his accuser's face, he said, "I deny the charges. I claim innocence."

"I refuse to accept your testimony," Aiken said. "I hereby call upon Lord Glory and the Matrones. Let the Lord take his rightful place upon the high seat. After he consults with the three sisters, let him proclaim me victor. Let the truth be known."

Aiken's voice rose in a crescendo until it echoed from the walls and rafters. "Leofar, the man, who now stands before me broke the peace. I hereby invoke the ruling powers' wrath."

The doors opened wide and slammed back hard against the walls. Startled by the noise, the men jumped and looked, wide-eyed in the direction of the doorway. There it stood, open to the black sky and still air. There was no hint of wind.

To dismiss the naughty, childish troublemaker he saw before him, Leofar sought to rebuke Aiken. "I know this man's reputation for challenging men." And with a wave of his arm, he swung it in an all-encompassing gesture that was meant to move his men. "Get him. Grab him."

But his men remained seated. No one was willing to break the uncanny spell that had entered the hall through the double-wide open doorway. There was something otherworldly in the hall that had not been there only moments before. Leofar's men remained seated and stared blankly ahead at nothing, as though they were frozen stiff.

Thwarted by their refusal to obey his command, Leofar stalked behind his seated men. He slapped each one hard on the side of the head, tagging him for this infraction against his authority with a promised punishment for refusing to do as he was told. Leofar came around the far end of the table and strode heavily up to Aiken.

Leofar looked around, scanned the benches where his men were seated, and raised his voice heartily. "Now that Aiken has thrown his tantrum and willfully imposed this distracting entertainment upon an evening that is meant for celebration, who amongst you will act as my champion? Who will stand-in for me against this one-eyed outlaw, this good for nothing braggart?"

But no one moved. Who would be willing to die championing a duplicitous man for whom they had so little regard?

"My cause is just. I, Aiken the Strength of Oak, stand ready to defend the truth."

His bench mates crowded around him, brandishing spears.

"We meet as equals, Leofar. You and me. We will fight to the death, fair and square on level ground. May the one who is right prevail in a judgement by arms."

He unpinned his cloak, whipped it off his shoulders with a flourish and laid it flat on the floor in the space between the two blazing hearths. He took his time neatening the edges until all four sides were lined up parallel with the surrounding walls. Another man ran up to him carrying wooden stakes, a hammer, and a rope. Aiken paced off three feet on the diagonal from one corner. The other man drove a stake into the dirt floor at the place where Aiken's toes pointed. They paced off each of the three remaining corners and drove the stakes. They wrapped the rope around the stakes and tied a knot to make a square perimeter. After he had looked it over, Aiken was satisfied. He picked up his cloak, handed it off to the man who was acting as his second, and looked at Leofar.

"Let us live by the truth. We stand here before Lord Glory and the Matrones. I answer for myself. Leofar, you must now answer for your actions. I choose side-arms. Unsheathe your weapon."

X.

Aiken sat up, breathing hard. He looked around in the surrounding darkness, but it was impossible to see a thing. He threw off the bed covers, stood and fumbled around for his trousers. He stepped into each leg, tightened his belt, pulled on his tunic, and stuck his bare toes into his shoes. He grabbed his cloak, tossed it over his shoulders and felt his way, cautiously, past the other sleepers. He reached the door, opened it quietly and slipped outside. There, he stayed for the rest of the night. He did not go back inside the house until the first signs of steely gray light began to spread across the eastern horizon.

Amber
If you will overcome perils
And all terrible things and open the eyes to second sight.

Take the stone which is called Amber, and it is a yellow color and is found in
the sea called the Belts. Bear it about with you and it will be good against cruel
men and chiding and will protect against bad luck and keep the body safe against
your adversaries.

The Truth of Rocks, by Alviss the Wise

I.

Grerr's amber specimen measured about the length of my little finger and was twice as wide as my thumb. To magnify whatever was embedded inside the stone, we used a variety of crystal lenses.

A large, bulbous shape appeared to be an insect's abdomen and a small, ball-shape its head. I guessed it was a spider, but for further proof, we counted the number of its legs. There were four on the side, which we were looking at. But, when we turned the stone over, its remaining legs were too badly entangled to arrive at an accurate count. Nonetheless, we convinced ourselves that there were a total of eight, and concluded that we were looking at the fossilized remains as an ancestral spider.

Another, tiny, long-bodied insect appeared to have two wings. Though it's shape resembled an emerald green insect called a lacewing, unfortunately, after it had been trapped inside the amber it had lost its brilliant, jewel-like tone and was now the same dark brown color as the spider. The other pieces suspended in the amber teardrop resembled bits of straw.

We congratulated ourselves upon establishing the identity of the little creatures, but when Grerr began to sing the praises of Lady Sun's tears, my inherent, skeptical turn of mind was immediately aroused. To refresh my memory of a description of amber, which I had read some time ago, I pulled The Histories of Tacitus from a shelf and, after paging through the copied text, found the citation.

According to the Roman historian, precious amber nuggets and drops of common tree sap are, in fact, one and the same substance. To back his claim, Tacitus drew upon his observation of the insects, which he had seen, suspended inside amber nuggets. He proposed a scenario in which the insects were caught in sticky, liquid tree sap and, as it hardened, became permanently encased inside it. He believed that the exuded tree juices were then buried in the forest floor debris and hardened, over time. The stone-like drops of sap were then washed into the sea and collected after they had floated ashore. For further proof, he recommended holding a chunk of amber in a flame to see whether it burned like pitch or resin.

As I was reading the entry aloud, I noticed that Grerr was becoming increasingly distraught. In fact, to suggest that a piece of amber should be submitted to a test horrified him. Opposed to burning even a small scrap, he accused me of seeing no mystery in the teardrop.

"If you believe amber is nothing more than common tree sap," he said, "then what meaning do you attribute to the story of Lady Sun's amber tears?"

What his question had to do with my pursuit of knowledge I could not fathom, and asked, "Grerr, do you truly believe that this piece of amber was a tear she wept? According to Pliny the Elder, several stories explain amber's origins. In one tale, there were three sisters who, after they were turned into poplar trees and rooted to a riverbank, shed amber tears whilst grieving the death of their brother, Phaëthon. According to another story Meleager's sisters shed amber tears after they were turned into birds."

"How will I know which of those women cried this amber teardrop?"

"Grerr, surely, you are not serious. Are you? First of all, how can you claim a woman cried this teardrop when you were the one who cut the nugget into its current shape?

"Secondly," I continued, "aside from these make-believe explanations of amber's origins, perhaps the greatest historical truths may be found in the story's portrayal of women's sorrows. However, that argument is neither here nor there, but is a distraction from the more important question that will be answered by holding a scrap of amber to a flame and, through comparison to burnt pinesap, prove whether the two are one and the same."

"If the test destroys the mystery surrounding amber's origins I do not care to know the outcome."

"Nonsense. The true origin and composition of amber presents an intriguing enigma worthy of discovery. I would like to solve the problem it poses. To hang onto mystery with no regard for truth is a futile and meaningless activity, Grerr. I can think of no viable reason to resist further exploration. Sooner or later, you will need to recognize the truth for what it is.

"According to the Natural Philosophers, the only way to solve a question is to base one's knowledge upon first-hand observation."

"I do not agree," Grerr said, sulkily. "To give it such meaning would turn something wondrous into something commonplace and ordinary. To approach this question in such a trivial manner betrays amber's extraordinary qualities. It limits the sense of the wonder I experience when I admire its beauty. Amber is a distinctive material, which requires special treatment. It invites one to imagine the sublime."

He then smiled mischievously, and said, "I should like to find Lady Sun or one those women who were turned into trees and birds. To spy on them, preferably if they were scantily dressed, would be quite splendid. Perhaps, if I comforted the grieving sisters, they would repay me with kiss. What do you think? Would you like to accompany me?"

Uncertain whether he was jesting or seriously considering such an outrageously voyeuristic pleasure, I said, "No, of course not."

"You do not wish to spy on those women?"

"No."

"Well then, I can tell by your tone of voice that you scorn my confessed weakness for women."

"That is not true. What you do with women is your business. But when I am in the presence of a woman, I prefer to cultivate reserve rather than to give in to lust."

Grerr scoffed at that defense and, furthermore, insulted my manliness by saying, "Ideas hold more interest for you than women do."

"That is not true," I said, embarrassed and annoyed by his accusation. Forced to defend myself and to prove my manliness, I showed him the figured stone on which the picture of a naked woman is depicted. "You see, I, too, take pleasure in the sight of a woman's body."

But, even so, he refused to credit the ownership of a picture of a naked woman depicted on a stone as proof of my manly proclivities. "She has no breasts, Dvalinn. How do you know this is a picture of a woman? Now you are the one who is talking nonsense."

"Well, anyway," I said, "you can see her if you squint your eyes. Try it. Do you see how seductively she is dancing before the fire?"

"Dvalinn, if you believe this a picture of a naked woman, I can tell you now that this stone is as close as you will ever get to a woman without her clothes."

Though Grerr's assault upon my honor had shockingly crossed the line, I was, nonetheless, willing to forgive his lapse in common courtesy and attempted to turn the conversation back to the topic of mystery, which we had previously been discussing.

"The same holds true for the times when I have asked to see the inside of your toys. Then, too, you told me that if I knew how they worked it would spoil the overall mysterious effect they have on the viewer. But, I am neither a fool, nor a child, Grerr. I know your mechanized creatures are not alive. If I knew how ingeniously you had fitted all the parts together, it would increase my sense of wonder."

"But what about the designs?" he asked.

Well, that was another topic of discussion upon which we had previously disagreed. One of his hybrid creatures has the head of a blue bird with a duck bill, a round collar splayed out around its neck, a dog's rear legs and feet, and a tail that ends in a trailing vine that sprouts four flowers and a large palmate leaf. Another toy would resemble a chicken, if it were not for the long neck which curves more like a heron's. And yet, its head is topped with a comb like a rooster's and its long tail is more like a dog's.

Though the sight of his creatures may delight some who see them, they leave me in a state of bewilderment. The figure I find most disgusting is a human-like creature who lacks a torso and a neck. Its unshapely head is attached at the creature's waist. Sticking out from the bottom of its spine, there is a curly tail, like a pig's, and it wears pointy, red shoes on its little, piggy feet. And, lest I forget, there is also the little naked man whose nose is shaped like a long trumpet.

When Grerr winds up the creatures with his key, he plays a jaunty tune on a small pipe to accompany their performance. The chicken-like creature wags its dog-like tail, the duck-like creature waddles on its dog-like legs, and the creature with pig-feet spins around as if it were dancing to a song that the little naked man is pretending to play on his nose.

"What meaning can you possibly give those monstrous creatures?" I asked.

"Are you calling me a monstrosity?"

"No, of course not. I am simply curious. Explain it to me. I did not mean to judge you."

"Yes you did."

Things were getting increasingly heated between us. "The meaning of the toys you invent is completely lost on me," I said.

Our disagreement then turned into a shouting match when Grerr raised his voice to a high pitch, and screeched, "Well, you called me a monstrosity. Take it back."

"I did not. There is nothing to take back," I practically screamed.

I had not meant to ridicule him but, apparently, he identifies with his bizarre assemblages more than I realized. In an attempt to calm myself, I paraphrased an argument that the Roman orator, Cicero, had used: "It is better to avoid references to something that is so far-fetched that the description is beyond all meaningful recognition.

"And, furthermore, Grerr," I added, "by drawing so exclusively upon your own little world, your wild ideas for strange mechanical devices becomes untethered from the everyday world in which the rest of us live. Though the designs may be shockingly unexpected, I find your uninhibited expression merely bizarre. They do nothing for me."

"The monstrous, is where Nature hides her secrets."

"Does she hide them because she is ashamed of them?"

"No-o-o-o-o," he squealed. "I see these creatures in the dreamtime when my soul visits the places where they dwell. It is by making the dreamtime real, that I reveal the mysterious, creative forces that are otherwise hidden beneath the surface of everyday living. And, for that reason, the things I make are commendable.

"Dvalinn, you hang onto simplistic reasons to explain away the complexity of your nighttime visions because they frighten you. You try to hold the dreamtime within small, manageable boundaries, and then you congratulate yourself because you give your vision meaning according to the rules you follow. Furthermore, you are hostile to anyone who questions your simplistic reasoning. The dreamtime's logic is so unfathomable that you will never gain understanding of its complexity by such futile references to the practical, first-hand observations you espouse."

"The way I see it," I argued, "to combine the everyday truth with the dreamtime truth may be commendable, for sure, but to leave out the former, and to be left only with the latter is like building a house of sand. Without a foundation in logical, and provable truth, it will be swamped at the next high tide. It will not hold up to investigation nor to an attribution of something meaningful to all of humankind.

"Things I do not know, nor understand, fascinate me," I continued. "I am, by nature, a skeptic. Before I can accept simple hearsay, I seek proof. Because these mysterious things elicit my curiosity and stretch my mind, their wondrousness urges me to ask questions. The danger of preserving wondrousness for its own sake would mean that whatever intrigues me most will result in the invention of the wildest possibilities that I can imagine. If, in my desire to hold onto the feelings of wonderment, I turn away from an honest regard for facts, I will cease to desire knowledge but will, instead divert from the truth and be lost in distortions of reality. If I were to grab onto, and to insist upon the maintenance of only the most intriguingly glamorous and outlandish claims, my curiosity would be channeled in false directions and I would be led into hopelessly dead ends."

"Dvalinn, you think too much. You would be happier if you did not ask so many questions. If you simply accepted of the way things are, instead of asking what they mean, you would be more satisfied with what you do know. Would you have believed that the walking stick was, in fact, a real insect if I had made an exact, mechanical re-production of it? Would you then have accused me of creating a meaningless, fanciful, or even monstrous delusion? If you had not seen the living walking stick, and known that you were awake and not asleep, would you have refused belief in it, too?"

He had me there. I did not know how to answer. It was true, the sight of the walk-ing stick had defied my previously held expectations of an insect's typical appearance. Here, then, was another mystery I would need to solve. "Do you think, perhaps, that the walking stick escaped from Nature's dreamtime?" I asked, expecting no answer.

"I think that because my mechanical devices frighten you," Grerr answered, "you need to categorize their maker and put me in a little box labelled, 'Overly Inventive Monstrosity,' and 'Voyeur Who Has a Confessed Weakness for Women.' I think you treat me like one of your more bizarre collectibles."

Well, that did it. I refused to engage any further with his outlandish attacks and insinuations. But, nevertheless, as I gathered up the things I needed for collecting pine samples, I continued to defend my stance. "I believe all knowledge should be open to dispute and investigation. The only way I can set my mind at ease is to explore the mysterious in ways that do not fear knowledge but that thrive on it. If, by my discov-eries, I learn that amber is, indeed, the hardened juice of trees I will have increased my passion for learning and exploration. To answer one question will spark ten more. I will not rest until I have discovered amber's true origins."

"You will never burn this precious piece of amber," Grerr said. He grabbed his teardrop and, clutching it protectively in his fist, left my reading room.

Though shortly afterward, he apparently had changed his mind, I suspect his true motive for returning was to further disparage my exploratory pursuits of truth. He threw a tiny chunk onto my table and said, "Here. You can burn this little scrap." But on his way out the door, he turned back to say, "I hardly know you, Dvalinn. You evidently live in a world other than the one in which I live. How can you question whether Lady Sun shed this amber teardrop?"

Dismayed by his utterance of angry imprecations and his unwillingness to have absorbed anything that I had said about amber's true origins, I threw up my hands, but remained unworried. Though I had hoped our positions on the matter would not be so divided, I believed they were, actually, not all that divergent.

I truly value those strange and amazing stories of amber's origins, for they give shape to common truths that all men and women share. By offering meaningful sig-nificance to their struggles, joys, and sorrows, no matter whether the women in these tales live in this world or in other worlds, the feature they all share are the tears they shed. And through this comparison to amber, men and women's common, saltwater tears, also, become precious.

Walking through the pine grove, I found several specimens worthy of my study: a few pine needles, all of which were sticky, and a large drop of pinesap wedged into a cracked piece of lichen-covered bark.

After I returned to my reading room, I removed one of my own amber specimens from my cabinet and set it upon my table. I then picked up the crystal ball. I first studied the amber nugget and then the sticky droplet. By moving the lens back and forth between the two, I could detect an unmistakable resemblance—both were similar in color and equally translucent. For further proof of their likeness, I used a pair of tweezers to pick up the tiny scrap that Grerr had thrown onto my table. Holding it in the lamp flame, I watched it bubble and melt and caught a whiff of pine. I then picked up one of the pinesap droplets and observed how it responded in a similar fashion.

So there you have it. My observations have confirmed the correctness of Tacitus's premise. Somehow, the liquid pinesap had lost its stickiness as it hardened and, over time, had turned to stone. But how it got into the sea, was yet another mystery I would like to explore.

I hold this piece of amber before the lamp, to examine it further. There is a bit of white, fluffy, cloud-like stuff inside it, and three, pale golden, circular bubbles that must have formed when the sap was liquid. Because the light lends a golden-tinge to the four fingers against which the amber rests, I question whether the sun also casts this same golden sheen to whatever its light falls upon.

In spite of having searched through the Natural Philosophers' writings, I have found no references to sunlight's color. Though I have heard it said that light is colorless, since we live from night to night rather than from day to day, I have no way to answer my question by direct observation.

As to whether this piece of amber is indeed a tear that Lady Sun shed does not really matter. Even if it is hardened pinesap, it nonetheless makes a fitting talisman for the life I long to live but can never know first-hand. In fact, to accept it as a substance a tree made from sunshine better suits the purpose of my analogy. For just as this drop of amber is akin to hardened light itself, I and those of my own kind will turn to stone if we chance to stray within the presence of the light the Lady's mirror casts. And, so too, just as Lady Sun drives her wagon across the sky each day in lonely exile from her lover, we are exiled from the world above our heads and are forced to hole-up in these lonely caverns after daybreak.

To see sunlight second-hand through other's eyes is the only way to solve the mystery and to discover whether sunlight's true color is golden as an amber teardrop or is clear as rock crystal.

I hold the lens-like crystal ball above the stone and allow some time to pass. My imagination comes to the fore and, with the approach of Lady Sun's wagon, the eastern skyline slowly brightens. Her two white chargers first appear. And, as the hazy disc begins to breach the skyline, the surrounding air floods with a golden light.

The solar mirror comes more fully into view along with two bright, blurry spots accompanying the sun disk on either side. At first, the two circles keep pace with the mirror as it rises. The Lady pulls her fiery long-knife from its scabbard and attacks the low-hanging fog that threatens to enshroud her wagon. She vigorously swipes her knife side to side and the accompanying circles vanish.

My view expands to include the shallow, man-made hills, scrub-covered dunes, and the wide, tawny-colored beach. A scattering of long-necked birds walk past on spindly legs and poke their slender beaks into the sand. Several screeching gulls dive into the small, white-fringed surf as it splashes the shoreline.

II.

From her place atop a mound in Gevehard's village, the sight of the sun breaking through the low-hanging clouds, and the steam rising from the sparkling pink-hued waters in the bay evoked a calm and peaceful feeling, almost soothing enough to counteract her underlying worry.

After she had been given strict instructions to watch her father closely, her observations that morning had added to her concerns for his welfare. Her mother had warned her that he might act in ways, which were contrary to thoughtful deliberation. And, if he did, Mildred had said that she must put an end to any foolish notions to which he might fall prey. And now that she was picking him out from among the men who were beginning their daily practice down on the strand, she questioned whether the improvement of his fighting skills was one of the things her mother might look upon with suspicion and disfavor.

She wished she could report back to her mother. For if she could, perhaps Mildred would agree that her father's behavior presaged participation in yet more troublesome and dangerous activities. But since she was neither as confident as her mother, nor as courageous, when it came to be telling her father what to do, she stopped short of going down on the strand and chewing him out the way her mother would do.

The times when she had seen her father, he had greeted her warmly, given her a kiss on the forehead, reminded her to help with the women's chores, and had looked content. Once again, he was living as he had done when he was a young man. He was treated with the respect he deserved, ate each evening along with the shipmaster in the longhouse, and practiced daily with the other men.

Over the years, her father had celebrated the good life that he had had, back when he and the other fighting men had spent their leisurely evenings gaming and telling stories in the meadhall. She had listened avidly to the life he described and imagined it would have been a wonderful way to live. But now she understood that he had neglected to mention the women who were unwelcome in the hall unless they were there to praise and honor the men and to pour their ale. Women, like her, had no time to play games, hunt, or celebrate in the meadhall. They were too busy raising children, cooking meals, running the household, milking cows, spinning thread, and weaving the fabric, which their men sold in the markets along the sea coast.

Her father had, also, neglected to describe the harsh lives of the men and women who lived in servitude. While the freeborn men gamed and hunted, the bonded men and women were forced, against their will, to prepare and to bring the men their meals, to keep the hearth fires burning, and everything else running smoothly.

Up until now, she had given little thought to the differences between a highborn freeman, a farmer, or a servant. But here, the distinction stared her in the face all day long. At first, after her arrival, she had been unsure of where she fit in. But, because she reckoned that a woman was beholden to a man, her place in the order of things depended upon where the man, to whom she was beholden, was ranked. And since her father was one of the men who was invited to sit with Gevehard every evening, it meant that her rank was equal to that of the freeborn women. Therefore, she was expected to act as self-importantly as Frida did, and not as humbly as the serving-girl, Mila did.

She had been visiting Gevehard's village now for three days and this was the morning of the fourth. She had risen early and, because she had had a few moments to spare, had stepped outside to watch the sunrise and to think things over before she would be called upon to help the women in Rodger's household milk the cows and attend to the other, daily chores.

Upon her arrival, Adelheide had welcomed her to their village and led her to the outdoors cookhouse. The household girls had set her a place at the end of a table and a stool to sit upon. One of the girls gave her a platter generously covered with but-tered bread, cheese, smoked fish, cured meats, and pickles. When, in accordance with her mother's strict admonitions, she had offered to help, Adelheide said, "You are our guest, Sunniva. You need not help with the meal. Sit down and eat. I have sent a girl to fetch Frida, Rodger's wife. When she arrives, she will help you settle in."

Because the people who lived here accented their words differently and spoke in ways that she had seldom heard before, she occasionally had trouble understanding what they said. Her father had warned her this might happen. When the escorts had first arrived in their hamlet and then, when they had traveled on the road to Geve-hard's village it had taken some time to parse the meaning of their speech. But, eventu-ally, she had begun to catch on. Her father, though, had no trouble understanding their unusual speech patterns. He told her that he had grown up playing hide and seek with his friend Alger in the markets. And, because he had heard so many dialects, he had learned how to figure out what people meant. And though Sunniva spent time in the markets helping her mother sell her father's carvings, she had not picked up the many dialects as readily as her father had. She occasionally asked people to repeat what they said and to speak more slowly.

The shipmaster's wife asked how she might best praise Aiken and the memorial stone when she offered him the cup to drink from. But Sunniva had explained, along with appropriate hand gestures and shakes of her head, how foolishly ignorant she was of her father's ways. Because her father kept to himself most of the time, he never talked about his work.

Although she hardly knew what to tell Gevehard's wife, she was assured that it was easy to praise a man. Adelheide cracked a mischievous smile, and said, "A man will believe just about anything a woman tells him if she embroiders his qualities lavishly enough. This is especially true if she can stitch a few gold threads into the design." Though Sunniva hardly knew how to react, the other women giggled at Adelheide's comment.

Apparently, the same principal held true for the times when a woman offered a man a drink from a golden cup. Adelheide poured mead into a beautiful gold cup, smoothed her skirts and apron, cradled the cup between her hands, and asked one of the girls to carry an additional pitcher full of mead. After she returned, she clapped her hands and ordered the household girls to serve the men their noon-day supper.

When one of the girls lifted a dish from the cookhouse table, Sunniva saw, tucked in amongst the pickles, a spoon that her father had carved with a wolf head on the handle. She smiled, greeted it as if it were a friend, and said, "I saw my father carve that spoon."

"Oh, that is my favorite. You are so lucky. My father never did anything but cast a fishing net each day. He died when his boat overturned in a bad storm. We all talk about the stone your father carved and hope it will give the seamen and the fishermen luck."

To hear someone speak of her father and his workmanship that way surprised Sunniva. Though she knew that he was clever at carving spoons and making chairs and boxes, she had never thought that being his daughter made her very lucky. Where she came from, people did not like him very much and said nasty things about him. Her mother had even been forced, at times, to defend his right to live in their hamlet. And, furthermore, some people's negative opinions about her father had rubbed off on her.

But now, Sunniva discovered that people in Gevehard's village thought different-ly about her father than did the folks back home. To them he was the man who would bring their sons, husbands, and brothers home again with food enough to see them through the winter. Because of her father's skill with words and signs, people called him a cunning man, though she had never thought of him like that before. She had always thought of him as a common, one-eyed woodcarver, except for the uncommon distinction of having served in a warband before she was born.

Whenever people questioned her about him, they seemed both eager and wary of whatever she might have to say. Sunniva would shrug her shoulders, lift an eye-brow, tip her head to the side, and say, "My father is just an ordinary woodcarver who keeps to himself most of the time." She thought that was all there was to say. But since cunning men were said to visit with the hidden folk and to spend their time alone using word-craft to cast spells and curses, whatever she said unwittingly reinforced their opinions. And if she added, "He also enjoys engaging folks in riddle contests," people's eyebrows shot up and they nodded in a telling manner.

After the household girls had served the men their noonday supper in the longhouse, Frida showed up along with the family's serving girl, Mila. They helped Sunniva unload her satchels, bags, and baskets from the cart and carried them to Fri-da's house. On their walk through the village, Sunniva noticed how the houses were built with gutters and pipes to catch the rainwater and to channel it into cisterns. Frida explained how rare and precious fresh water was, here where they lived so close to the sea. Up until now, Sunniva had always taken fresh water for granted. At home, the well water was sweet and sparkling clear, but here the river water was muddy colored, and tasted brackish.

They climbed the mound atop which Frida, Rodger, his mother Innis, and his two sisters, Agata and Ainsley lived. Inside, Frida explained how very crowded their house was. She showed Sunniva the bed where she and Rodger slept and the one that Innis and her two daughters shared. Unlike Adelheide and Gevehard, who lived in the longhouse and had room enough to spare, Frida said Innis, her three children, and now her daughter-in-law, all lived in this little house, where there was barely enough room to breathe. That made five people living in a small house.

Sunniva noticed that Frida had forgotten to count Mila. If she had, that would have made six. But, apparently, the serving girl did not count as one of the residents of the house. Mila slept on a pallet in the storage area, above the attached byre where the cows, chickens, ducks, and pigs were kept. Frida showed Sunniva the ladder she would climb and hoped that she would not mind sharing the pallet with the serving girl.

Mila warmly offered to help Sunniva pile her baskets and bags in a corner. She told Sunniva that she would sleep on the floor and let their guest have the pallet all to herself. But Sunniva refused the offer, saying, "It is your bed. I will not take it away from you." She sat upon it, patted the thin, straw-stuffed mattress, and said, "Look, there is plenty of room for both of us."

Though the serving girl seemed more generous than the others, Sunniva soon figured out that it was Mila's role to serve, for, after all, she was the serving girl. Though all the women in the household spun wool, wove fabric on their looms, milked the cows, cared for the garden, prepared food for supper, made the cheeses, and dried and salted the fish that Rodger and his man-servant caught, it was Mila who did the heavy lifting and the dirty work, the things that no one else wanted to do. She carried the water, ground the grain for making the bread, took the slops to the pigs, collected and dried the dung they burned in the hearth, swept the floor, dug and weeded the gardens, cleaned out the byre, started the fire in the morning and dampfered it at night, disposed of the night-soil, filled holes in the mound with a mixture of clay and dung, and washed up after meals.

In the evenings, when Rodger appeared at the door, his mother and two sisters crowded around him. Pampering him with the same attentiveness one would give a baby, they elbowed Frida out of the way as they brought him ale and slices of bread, chunks of cheese and small bowls of pickles to tide him over until supper was served. To see how Frida was often left to look on from behind their backs, Sunniva questioned whether Frida was ever alone with her husband.

After they had eaten supper, Rodger left to spend time with his friends in Gevehard's longhouse, and the women spun by the hearth. Then, when everyone started yawning sleepily, Mila dampfered the fire and, carrying a small rush light, led Sunniva up the ladder.

The first night, after Sunniva and Mila had crawled into the narrow bed they shared, they had lain so close together their noses were nearly touching.

Mila seemed to enjoy having someone from afar to gossip with, and said, "If we are going to share a bed, we should get to know each other. Tell me, what is it like where you come from?"

"I do not live in a market town like this but in a small hamlet. All the people there are my cousins, aunts and uncles. The land is hilly and the trees are big. We milk cows and herd sheep the same as you do. The house I live in is smaller than this one. I sleep in the loft back home too, just like you. I travel to the markets with my mother and father where my mother sells the thread that the women who live in our hamlet spin and the bowls and spindles that my father carves."

"You can do that? You are free to come and go as you please? And you get to keep your earnings?"

"My father says that he gets to do whatever he pleases so long as he makes no trouble. That is what he says, anyhow. I am a common woman like my mother, but my father was a freeborn man before he was outlawed."

"Outlawed?"

"Perhaps you have not seen my father. But when you do, you will see that he was badly hurt one time—he could have died—and the markings on his arms, chest and back identify him as a former member of a chieftain's warband. My father owned several horses and servants back then. He had land and lived in a fine house. The village where he was born was one of the wealthiest trading centers in the region, until—." Sunniva stopped, right there.

She had already said too much about her father's past, her present home life and, by implication, her mother and father's unlawful marriage. No one in her family talked about those things. If the shameful subject of his masterless status ever came up, her father became over-wrought. It was for that reason that she and her mother always sidestepped talk about anything that might send him into a rage. Whenever he started to pace the floor and hit things they tactfully changed whatever subject they had been discussing to something less volatile. And if the subject of her parent's secretive marriage ever came up, her mother began to cry.

"Forget what I said just now."

"I will. I can keep a secret," Mila said. "All the servants can," and after she had readjusted to a more comfortable position, she asked, "Does your father and mother get to keep what they grow in their fields too?"

"Well, not all of it. The chieftain's man collects tribute every autumn. Where I live, none of the farmers hold the land. The chieftains do. They grant the farmers the right to farm the lands they hold within their jurisdictions. The kinleader decides which family gets to work which fields. My mother tells me that it is important to remain on the kinleader's good side."

"Will your father be forced to give away the gold and silver coins that Gevehard gave him in return for carving the memorial stone?"

"How do you know about those coins?"

"The girls who served the men their noonday supper in the longhouse saw Gevehard count them out before he gave them to your father in exchange for the stone. There were lots of coins."

"Well, you know more about it than I do. I thought you said that the servants can keep a secret."

"Whatever happens in the longhouse is not a secret."

"Well, I told you a secret, now you have to tell me one."

"If I had a choice, I would like to work in the loom shops."

"That does not sound like a secret."

"Yes it is. It is one of my secret thoughts. Do not tell Innis or Frida what I said or they will be angry."

"All right, I promise. I have secret thoughts too."

"If I worked with wool all day my hands would be soft, and weaving on a loom is not as backbreaking as the work that I must do. But I have no choice. Innis reminds me that things could be worse, but I like to daydream about the things I would rather do."

"Me too. I would like to embroider pretty pictures with colorfully dyed threads rather than spin them."

"Living here is not so bad. Innis is kind. At times, she even treats me like a daughter. But she is quick to slap me when I do not do things the way she wants me to."

"My mother slaps me too."

"Even though the loft is the darkest corner in the house, sleeping above the animals is warmer in the wintertime than it is on the ground floor. Some folks are forced to sleep in the byres along with the pigs and the chickens. That would be awful."

"That hardly seems fair. My father says that all men and women should be treated with respect and dignity."

"Your father sounds like a good man."

"My mother says he is. But not everyone agrees with her. Have you lived with Innis for a long time?"

"I came here to work for Innis four years ago. She says she likes to start her girls young. That way she can teach them how to do things her way. Being a child also made it easier to trade me for a batch of young hogs. That was what I was worth back then—a litter of weaned piglets. I am worth more now. Other than my brother, the rest of my family live on farms further inland. I have not seen them since I came here."

"Do you miss your family?"

"Yes. Before Glenn and his tribe settled here, my family held the land we worked and we owned our own cows and sheep. It was after the Terrible Winter that the forebears of those folks, who now are the landholders and the freemen, took possession of our land. Glenn and his tribal people moved into the vacant buildings and gave the few, starving survivors, like my great grandparents, food in exchange for work. Glenn's people are no better than thieves. They took our homes, our farms and our freedom."

"That is not what I heard," Sunniva said. Questioning the accuracy of Mila's account, she repeated the version of events that she had heard from the men who had escorted her and her father north. "The escorts told us your forebears could not have fed themselves. They would have starved had it not been for Glenn's arrival and his tribe's repopulation of the land. They told us that Erol plotted with Lord Spider, sold-out his people to the pirates, and then turned to piracy himself. Though people who feared an attack, paid him off, he still sent out his sea-raiders to chase them down and to steal their goods."

"That may be," Mila spat out, "But, some people dispute your account."

"Well the escorts told us that Lady Sun showed Glenn this land because he helped bring about the end of the Terrible Winter. But when the ships, carrying his tribal people, landed here, Erol's men attacked Glenn's men. So, in the end, Glenn had no choice but to treat them as antagonistic foes."

"Well," Mila countered, "I heard that Glenn made-up the story about Lady Sun's affection for him. My people say that Erol defended our homes heroically. Our forebears were the ones who settled this land and built these mounds. Yet, ever since Glenn's arrival, we cannot hold the land ourselves. All that we produce is kept by the landholders.

"It is unfair to make the women in the cookhouse chop the meat, cut the roots, stir the huge iron pots, grind the flour with which they bake the flat bread, and toast the grain to make the ale. They cannot come and go as they please but are forced, against their will, to do twice the amount of work the freeborn women do. The workers are overseen by the freeloading masters who increase their wealth at their expense. While those who care for the cows, do the fieldwork, and labor in the smithy work hard and put in long days suffering in the heat and smoke, they want us to forget who we are. They want us to forget that we, too, are a tribe. Edmund is one of us. He could be our kinleader. Many people would get behind him. Have you seen Edmund yet? He is the one-armed man who works in Gevehard's household."

"Yes, I met him when my father put our oxen into the paddock."

"Edmund was the ship's commander before he got hurt. So now those gossips, who claim to speak for the dead, say that, because Edmund is more thoughtful than Gevehard, and always weighs his actions carefully before he makes a move, was the one who was behind the shipmaster's success."

"Is that true?"

"Well, that is what the gossips say. He and Gevehard are half-brothers. Did you know that?"

"Is that a secret?"

"No, everyone knows it. Both men had the same father but, because Edmund's mother was a servant in Garr's household, he took her to bed with him. He figured that it was his right to bed any woman who was beholden to him."

"Can a landholder do that?"

"Well, of course he can, Sunniva. Where do you come from, anyway? Your father probably did that too, when he was one of the chieftain's men."

"No. He would never have done that."

"All men do it if they are given half a chance."

"Maybe that is one of the things that my mother does not want me to know about."

"Well, she did a good job keeping you pure. The landholders make the laws and do as they please with the women. If you lived in a market town like this one, you would learn about all sorts of seedy things that your mother would disapprove of."

"Would Rodger take you to bed?"

"Well, no, not Rodger. He looks straight through me. Nor does he have any time for Frida. He would rather spend his nights gaming and wrestling with the men in the longhouse.

"But, anyway, Edmund's mother was a servant and that made her son a servant, too. Garr could have given him freedom but refused. How cruel is that? Not to give your own son freedom? It was not until after Garr died that Gevehard made Edmund a freedman and his second in command on the boats.

"The dead are spiteful and know things. When they are forgotten, they get angry and feed the gossips' rumors. They say that because Edmund will not be aboard the ships this season to counsel Gevehard's actions, the shipmaster will bring down the entire fleet. Edmund makes smarter decisions. He can foresee what might happen even if it never happened that way before. But because Gevehard gets stuck in his ways, he thinks things will always be the same as they were before. Thinking like that, he could make a fatal mistake when he is leading the men."

"It would be horrible if the ships were lost and all the men died."

"I am of two minds. On one hand, it would be right for those, who keep us in bondage, to suffer for their wicked deeds. But on the other hand, I worry for the sake of my brother. He serves in another household and will accompany the man to whom he is beholden. Although he is not yet a freedman he is allowed to carry a knife and is practicing with the men down on the strand each day. Of course, he will still have to serve his master, even on the boat. But if they have a good year, in exchange for the coinage Gevehard gives him for rowing, his master will make my brother a freedman when they come home. That is almost as good as being free, even though he will have no land to farm and will continue to work for his current master. But I say that he should be given more. No one should have to buy his freedom."

"The landholders plundered our land and our houses after the pestilence killed so many. They could not keep things running smoothly without us. Not when so many of their men take off on the trade ships every year. They owe us. My brother should be given land, cattle, and sheep. He should be paid for all the work he did but instead his master will make him pay for his freedom with his work on the boat. Sometimes the way the masters and landholders make all the laws and give us nothing in return makes me so angry I could scream.

"But my brother says he does not care. He does not want to be a farmer but would rather be a merchant. The first thing he plans to do is to buy his wife's free-dom. That way their children's children will be freemen and not beholden to anyone. I asked him to buy my freedom, too."

"Then would you live with your brother and his wife?"

"I would rather live with the man I want to marry. How about you, Sunniva? Are you betrothed?"

"No. I would rather become a wisewoman. I have seen the Lady in the Clouds several times, mostly when I spin thread or feel drowsy. Sometimes I disguise myself as a bird and fly up to see her."

"Sometimes, I imagine clouds look like sheep or cows, but I have never seen a lady in the clouds."

"I do. If I close my eyes and make believe that I am flying, sometimes I can see her spinning clouds. I talk to the Lady in the Rafters, too. I like to think that she listens to me because no one else does. The Lady in the Rafters and the Lady in the Clouds are really Lady Blessed in disguise."

"You are lucky to have seen Lady Blessed. What does she look like? Is she pretty?"

"Oh, very pretty. She has a big bosom and braids her hair in a long plait. And even though she is married, she does not cover her head with a scarf. She has a distaff made of gold. She told me that she would weave me a dawn-colored cloak if I promise to serve her."

"Will you?"

"I do not know. Mostly, I pretend she is my friend. I pretend she is seated in the rafters when I go to sleep. Sometimes she sits beside me on my bed."

"Maybe she is up there now."

"Maybe. But I do not see her there tonight. She disappears whenever someone else is speaking. It mostly happens when I spin fleece or go to sleep at night. The first time I saw her seated in the rafters, my mother would not let me sit down below with the other women. They were telling stories about Lady Sun and her four husbands. Sleeping with her four husbands was one of the things that my mother did not want me to learn about before I marry."

"Sunniva," Mila giggled, "I think you are confusing make-believe with what you want to believe. Are you sure you do you not want to marry?"

"No, but, like you, I have no choice. Besides, a common girl like me could never be a wisewoman. Now I told you two secrets, so you have to tell me one more."

"All right," Mila said. "The man who I am sweet on works in the smithy. Will you promise to keep my secret? Absolutely?"

"I promise to keep your secret, absolutely. Tell me."

"I might be carrying his child. Do not tell anyone."

"I will lock my lips shut," Sunniva said, and twisted them closed with her fingers. "See? Will the baby's father marry you?"

"We need permission from both Innis and the ironsmith. But if a baby is coming, most likely they will let us marry. Of course, Innis will be angry if I have a baby. An infant strapped onto my back will make it hard to keep up with the work. But I am strong and can do it. Or, maybe the ironsmith will trade me for something that Innis wants. If the ships bring back iron ingots, they will make the rivets and the hardware that the shipbuilder needs to use to make Rodger's boat. So maybe she would trade me for iron rivets. Then I could live in the smithy with my husband and work in the smith's household. That way, when the child is older, he will become an additional servant in the ironsmith's workshop. Ironmongery is a good craft for a man to learn. If I stayed here with Innis, she would make me leave the baby with one of the old women who spin all day. She would rock the cradle when I am working. Then I would see my baby only when I need to feed him. But when the child is older, he could feed the chickens and herd the sheep.

"The smith lets my betrothed make things from scrap iron that he finds and melts down when he has the time. He sells the things that he makes in the markets. He told me that he will save his earnings and someday will buy both his freedom and mine. He is learning how to forge knives and could sell those too. We will both work twice as hard as the landholders do. And, whatever we make will be ours. I could help him sell what he makes in the market."

"That is what my mother does. She sells my father's carvings."

"If I had my own house I could weave and keep my baby all to myself. I would not give it away to someone else to care for in the daytime. Or, maybe I could be a wet-nurse for one of the freeborn women who do not want a baby pulling on their tits all day. But I would not mind. I would happily nurse two babies. Then I could keep my baby all to myself."

"Mila, my mother wanted a house, a husband, and a baby, too. She asked Lady Blessed to grace her with those things. You, too, should ask her for a house. If my father had never walked into our hamlet, I would never have been born. So she got both a husband and a baby—me. She already had a house but would have lost it to her brothers if she had not married. My mother told me that Lady Blessed brought my father to her so that she could marry him. She even saw my father walking through the dreamtime woodland. Do you ever see the house you want to live in when you visit the dreamtime?

"Yes. I see the child too. He will have hair so pale it looks almost white."

"My mother wants me to marry Wynn, but I never see him in the dreamtime."

"Do you love him?"

"I do not know. What is it like to love a man?"

"Oh, you think about him all the time, and miss him when he is not there with you. See? Even now, I am talking about him and wishing that I was with him."

"I do not feel that way about Wynn. But my mother tells me that he will be a good match because his father raises hogs. Lady Blessed has a husband, but she is also a wisewoman. She was never beholden to any man until she was certain of the man whom she chose to wed."

"I have heard it said that an ordinary woman cannot be married to an ordinary man and also be a wisewoman," Mila said. "Instead, she would need to marry a man who lives in the otherworlds and have a secret husband."

"Well, that sounds perfect. Then I would not need to share my bed with him or cook his supper."

"I think your head is in the clouds, Sunniva. That is what I think."

"Well, I would be in the clouds if I was flying like a goshawk."

"Girls," Innis yelled from down below, "stop talking now and go to sleep."

Drifting off, Sunniva whispered quietly, "The Lady in the Clouds calls me Storm-pale."

Floating in that place between, where no clear lines distinguished wakefulness from dreaming, she saw, high above her head, in this house where the roof was pitched at so high an angle, Lady Blessed sitting in the rafters. Though she looked very small and far away, Sunniva could plainly see her there, and spoke of her wish to fly in the guise of a goshawk, and to have a secret husband.

III.

Each day began before sunrise. Wakening to the sound of Mila greeting the hearth with a song, Sunniva knew that the serving girl would first stir the last of the glowing embers. Then, before she fanned the flames to awaken the fire, she would offer the hearth a gift of kindling. And then she would thank the Hearth Mother for cooking their food, heating their homes, lighting the darkness, and giving them hope for another good day.

It was a comfort to know that, no matter where she was or how different things appeared to be, here among the sea people, all the women did the same tasks in the same order that her mother was doing them back home. That morning, Sunniva had almost believed that she was in her own bed, in her own house, until she opened her eyes.

After she had dressed and combed and plaited her hair, she stepped outside the house to watch the sunrise. And now, upon hearing her name being called, she regrettably turned away from the pleasing sight of the sea.

"Sunniva, we are leaving for the pasture to milk the cows," Frida said. "Come grab your milk pails. Do not forget your stool the way you did yesterday."

Yesterday, because Mila had gotten a late start, she had begged Sunniva to help her get the fire going so that she could run outside to fill the water pail. But Frida overheard their conversation and instructed Sunniva, in no uncertain terms, to never, ever help Mila with her chores. If Mila was behind in her work, it was her own fault that she had over-slept, and she deserved a beating.

Sunniva was so flustered by the harshness of Frida's rebuke that she forgot to carry her stool out to the pasture. She only remembered when Frida mockingly asked whether she planned to kneel beside the cow when she was milking that morning. After that, Sunniva had run back to the house to get it. And then she, too, along with Mila, had gotten a late start doing her chores. But Sunniva was not beaten. Nor was Mila. It had been an empty threat.

So today, Sunniva grabbed two pails, balanced them on the shoulder yoke with one hand and, grasping the stool with the other, took off for the pasture along with Frida, Innis and Rodger's two sisters.

The blue sky brightened and the tiny, white, springtime flowers, dotting the green meadow, turned their faces to the sun. To fully delight in the sun's warmth as it took off the morning chill in the air, Sunniva and Frida each set their stools beside a cow and sat with their backs to sun. As usual, Innis and the two sisters had chosen to sit apart from Frida. Sunniva pulled on the cow's teats, listened to the rhythmic splashes filling the pail, breathed in the scent of warm milk, took pleasure in the big warm body eating the freshly sprouted, dew-soaked grasses, and was extra careful to milk the cow exactly as Frida had taught her two days ago.

After her arrival, when she had helped the women with their milking chores, according to Frida, Sunniva was milking the cow all wrong. How ridiculous, Sunniva thought. How many ways are there to milk a cow? She had been milking cows since she was a child. But here, in this village, there was only one way to do something and, apparently, that was Frida's way.

Unable to act like the agreeable, well-mannered, and humble guest that her mother and father had told her to be, the words just came tumbling out of her mouth, "This is how my mother taught me to grasp the cow's teats and pull." But her ill-tempered outburst only succeeded in making things worse for both herself and her mother. And, in the end, the increased negative appraisal of her training at the hands of her mother also forced Sunniva to defend Mildred.

Though she continued to argue that she had always milked the cows this way back home, Frida countered with a stern warning: this particular cow would kick her in the head if she did not get milked exactly as Frida demanded. "A cow can kill you with a good kick to the head, you know," she said. And haughtily citing Innis as the final authority in the matter, Frida finished the discussion by saying, "Well, this is how we do things here. If you refuse to do things right, I will tell Rodger's mother that you are doing them wrong."

Frida halted her milking and stood up from her stool. To imply that humiliation, punishment, and loss of privileges would ensue if Sunniva did not do exactly as she was told, Frida stood behind Sunniva's shoulder and watched her closely until she got it right.

"All right then, is this what you want me to do?" Sunniva asked. Clearly, Frida would not give up until she had taken control of every portion of the work they shared. In the end, Sunniva did her best to accommodate Frida's every demand. That included how to pick fresh greens, to make the cheeses, and how to speak to Mila in a self-important and bossy manner.

So, today, when Sunniva and Frida were seated side by side milking the cows, Sunniva listened meekly to Frida brag about her new husband. Because Frida was proud to have married into a prominent family, she often boasted about Rodger's prowess. Born from Glenn's bloodline, his father, Ryce, had been the shipmaster who led the fleet until he had been killed fighting a band of pirates. After that, his wife's plans for a good life had been ruined, and Innis had been left to care for their three, small children, alone.

"Sunniva, do you think that Ryce's early death means that Rodger's family is unlucky?"

"No, but Ryce and Innis were certainly unlucky."

"I worry that Rodger might be unlucky, too."

"I doubt it," Sunniva said. "He is such a jovial, good natured man. It seems, rather, that lucky things have always come his way." She then added in a sing-song tone of voice, "After all, he was lucky to have married you."

Apparently, the mockery went right past Frida, who simply answered, "No matter what you say, I do not think that he should test his luck this way but should stay home with me. Now that Rodger is so intent upon building his own boat, Gevehard plans to entrust the entire fleet to his leadership someday. That is what Rodger told me, anyhow.

"If Rodger's father had not died, he would be the next in line to become the kinleader of the village. Then we would live in the longhouse. But instead, the day that Gevehard saw his older brother go down, right in the midst of fighting pirates, he claimed to outrank the commander and took charge. He acted as though there could be no question of his birthright. Imagine how the older men must have felt when they were forced to entrust their safety to a man who was only half their age."

"It sounds like Gevehard is the luckiest man of all."

"Well, that was what he did. That night, after they had fought off the pirates, the crew members credited their successful victory to Gevehard's leadership and agreed to put him in charge of their boat. People say that his pale-blue eyes are the cause of his cunning. Once he sees something it sticks in his head and he never forgets it. He just knows things and remembers things that no one else does. He stores them away. That is the reason men claim that Gevehard knows more about the sea currents and the lay of the shorelines than any other man on the boat. And, even though he was only Rodger's age at the time, the following year they put him in charge of the entire fleet."

"Oh my. He sounds like a very capable man."

"He is. Then, when he returned home, he took Ryce's place as kinleader. He already was living in the longhouse, along with his brother and Innis. But when he married Adelheide, she forced Innis to move into the little house we live in now. Imagine the amount of prestige that would follow," Frida said, dreamily, "if someday Rodger led the fleet. Then I would live in the longhouse and would have an entire household of servants to oversee, not just Mila."

"Would you kick out Adelheide?"

"Maybe. I could have my own loom shop, too. Just like Adelheide's."

Of two minds, apparently, Frida seemed to be unable to recognize that prestige and risk went hand in hand. Though she was worried about the dangers that could befall her husband, she had conveniently overlooked the fact that she could only have the wealth and status, which were accorded the kinleader's wife, if Rodger had proven his ability to lead the men when they were rowing the longships to the overseas markets.

"Are you sure Rodger is lucky?"

"Oh, he must be. How dangerous is it to crew the boats? Ever since my arrival, the fishing boats have bobbed about in the bay so placidly it hardly seems possible for any danger to befall the men. This morning, the sight of the sun reflecting off the sea gave me so much pleasure, I wished to float around in a boat myself."

"Any fool will tell you that the sea is an untrustworthy ally," Frida countered. "You must never rely upon what appears to be a calm sea. Storms arise so swiftly, they take everyone by surprise. There have been times when the winds coming from the northwest raged so furiously that the roofs blew right off our houses. We all crawled beneath our beds and tables to shelter from the storm and pleaded with Lord Thunder not to take our lives."

Frida recalled a time when the Muddy River had overflown its banks and flooded their fields. "Our cows, sheep, and horses were drowned," she said, looking as though she might cry. "Oh, Sunniva, it was horrible to see their bloated bodies floating in the stinky water."

Frida's descriptions of the cold, sodden winds and the times when the river had overflowed its banks so swamped the delightful quality with which Sunniva's morning had begun, it seemed as though many days had passed since she had watched the waves roll peacefully ashore. Warned of the dreadful terrors, which might befall them, Sunniva stared at the blue sky, knowing that, at any given moment, it could turn dark and threatening.

"But," Frida said, in an attempt to turn her attention away from the horrors she had witnessed, "I must not bring my fears to mind. That kind of talk sours the milk and causes the men's luck to leave them. Innis says it is better to think about the gold and jewels the men bring home. That is what she told me, anyhow."

"Rodger's mother should know. After all, her husband's luck deserted him when he was fighting pirates."

"Innis says the men believe their women spin cords to pull them home again. So, whenever I am spinning thread while Rodger is away, I will think of the moment he will greet me and pin the brooch, which he promised to bring me with a red stone in its center, onto my dress."

But as soon as she stopped describing the brooch with the red stone in its center, Frida lost track of the good luck it represented and was overcome, once again, with gloomy foreboding. Her lips quivered and tears filled her eyes. "The truth is that the gold brooch that Rodger promised to bring me is more like the gold in the storyteller's song," Frida said. "The gold-colored tears that Lady Sun cries when she grieves the death of the man she loved is the storyteller's gold. If Rodger does not come home, I will have neither gold, nor a husband. Only Lady Sun cries precious tears. A common woman cries salty tears when her man does not come home. Oh, Sunniva, what will I do? I will miss Rodger so much. We want a baby so badly. But am not even carrying a child yet and now he is leaving."

Sunniva attempted to turn Frida's thoughts away from her grim reflections upon the impermanence of life and, instead, encouraged her to think lucky thoughts again, by asking, "Will Rodger give you a brooch as beautiful as the ones that Adelheide wears? On the day of my arrival, I was unable to stop staring at her jewelry. Did Gevehard bring Adelheide those brooches and beads from the markets he visited? They are unlike anything I have ever seen. The large honey-colored stones that jut out from the center of her brooches are especially beautiful."

"Adelheide dresses in her finery because she is the kinleader's wife," Frida said, gamely attempting to forget her worries. "It is the mark of her prestige to wear her wealth every day and to show off the abundance that her husband promises to bring the village with his leadership. The other village women only wear their brooches on special occasions, such as wedding feasts, celebrations, ceremonies, and Yuletide. But if I become the kinleader's wife, someday I, too, will dress so richly."

To show Sunniva a stone like the one that was set into Adelheide's brooch, Frida pulled on a cord she wore looped around her neck and held out a bead. She stood and walked over to the stool upon which Sunniva sat, lifted the cord over her head and, holding it out with both hands, ceremoniously passed the string over Sunniva's head. "You must keep this amber bead as a sign of our friendship. Now, whenever you look at it, you will feel bound to the men and women who live here in our village and will remember the time you spent with us."

Sunniva humbly accepted the round bead. It was the same color as a droplet of honey, was larger in diameter than a thumbnail, and was drilled with a hole through which the cord was threaded. Holding it in the early morning sunlight to admire its beauty, she said, "I brought some small gifts from home. There are several spinning whorls that my father turned on the lathe and a few lengths of woven trim. But this is more valuable than anything I can offer in exchange."

"That is not true. The memorial stone your father carved is more valuable than all the honey-colored stones that anyone can ever pull from the sea. This bead's true worth is a mark of our friendship. But," she added, "A spinning whorl your father turned on the lathe would certainly be appreciated. Threads spun with one, he made, would carry more luck than those that are spun with ordinary spindles. It would give me additional confidence in Rodger's safe return."

Sunniva first licked the translucent stone to test whether it tasted sweet like honey. Though only mildly disappointed by its lack of flavor, Sunniva was so fascinated by the sparks it threw from deep inside that she had not been listening very closely to what Frida was saying but simply nodded politely. But when Frida paused, bit her lower lip, and asked, "Is what Gevehard says true?" Sunniva was forced to ask, "What did he say?"

"Sunniva, you were not listening to me, were you? I asked you whether your father is a cunning man. Gevehard told the villagers that Aiken can read and write the secret signs. He says your father has worked a spell on the stone to assure the men's safety. You would not lie to me, would you, Sunniva? Is it true?"

Sunniva stopped rubbing the stone between her fingers and turned to face Frida. Up until their arrival, she had given little thought to the purpose of the red stone. But, when she saw the fear and uncertainty in Frida's face, after she had worked up her courage to ask whether what the shipmaster claimed was true or was only a deceitful exaggeration, Sunniva felt obliged to say something just to make it so. "Yes, I give you my word, it is true."

Though she said it, she was uncertain whether what she promised was indeed the truth. Mildred had taught her to mask a fact with a falsehood whenever circumstances required. And since Sunniva did not know whether the descriptions of her father's cunning abilities were truthful or were simply wishful thinking, this seemed like a time when such a lie was called for.

But then again, she thought, perhaps there was a grain of truth to the belief that her father could make things happen by carving signs and words. She wished so much to tell Frida what had happened on the day of her arrival when she had visited the holy grove. But because she had no way to speak of things so strange, she remained silent.

IV.

Now that it was suppertime, it was hard to believe how quickly the day had passed. After they had milked the cows, curdled the milk to make the cheese, picked fresh greens in the pasture, and spent time in the garden pulling weeds, Frida had woven some cloth on her loom, Sunniva had spun fleece, and then they had milked the cows again before they prepared supper.

After they had eaten, Mila was washing up while the family members were sitting around the supper table. They were leisurely enjoying the early evening twilight when Adelheide appeared in their open doorway. She politely refused their offer to join them because, she said, she had to go from house to house to round up more help.

Edwina, the wisewoman, was expected to arrive tomorrow, and now that Adelheide and the household servants were struggling to keep up with the fieldwork and all the other springtime duties, in addition to stocking the boats, the preparation for the upcoming ceremonial feast that was to be held in Edwina's honor was more work than they could manage alone.

"Innis, can you spare Frida and Sunniva on the day of the feast? I would like Frida to oversee the decoration of the longhouse."

Innis assured her sister-in-law that, of course, she and the girls could fill in for Frida here at home. She also offered to send Mila along.

Adelheide glanced directly at Frida, and asked, "Do you remember how it looked at Yuletide?"

Frida beamed and nodded so enthusiastically, Sunniva thought her head would surely loosen and fall right off.

"Yes. I remember. I helped decorate it then, too. I am honored to have been asked."

When Innis directed a questioning glance at Sunniva, she replied excitedly, "Yes. I will be happy to help in any way I can."

After Adelheide was gone, the conversation turned to discussion of Sunniva's father. Rodger looked meaningfully at her with his wide, toothy grin, and said, "Geve-hard told me that he might ask your father to join the crew."

It was such a shock that Sunniva replied, "No," more loudly than she meant to.

Rodger ignored her immediate response and, since he was surrounded by admir-ing women, pushed out his chest and continued to brag about the private conversation that he had had with his uncle. "Gevehard asked me what I thought of Aiken. He wanted to know whether he could hold his own in a fight. I told him that Aiken is a good fighter. He really knows how to handle a blade. And, on my recommendation, Gevehard has agreed to offer your father a place on the boats."

This was the first time that Sunniva had heard the news that her father might become one of the crew members. But it confirmed her earlier suspicions that prac-ticing his fighting skills was something that her mother would have disapproved of. She thrust her head forward, stared at him in wide-eyed disbelief, and said, "No, he cannot go." Grabbing hold of the first reason that came to mind, she attempted to take on some of her mother's authority when she explained why her father would be unable to join the crew. "He does not know how to row a boat."

"Any fool can row a boat," Rodger answered with a hearty guffaw and a simple shrug of his shoulders. And, to further back his statement that such a ridiculous argu-ment held no merit, he added, "Sometimes we take captives who know nothing about life at sea. They row just fine."

"My father and I need to go home," she said, hoping to cut off any more discussion of the matter by saying loudly and defiantly, "My mother expects us to get back home in time to help with the fieldwork." And, giving her final words special emphasis and weight, she demanded, "You must tell Gevehard that my father cannot join the crew."

Rodger laughed at the thought, "No one tells Gevehard what to do, except may-be Adelheide."

The other women may have tittered quietly at the thought, but Sunniva did not think his little joke was very funny. Never before had the springtime, back-breaking fieldwork felt so beckoning. "We do not have servants, you know. We do the work ourselves. Mother depends upon my father and me to plow and plant the gardens and the fields."

"Your father is a skillful fighter," Rodger said contemptuously, "he should not have to plow grain fields. He practices with us daily. All the men agree that he is a good fighter even though he is blind on one side. I heard someone say that he was a champion, back when he served in a warband that was led by one of the foremost chieftains in his tribe before he was hurt. Is that true?"

"Well, yes." Momentarily and unwittingly so filled with pride that she was unable to hold off her wish to boast of her father's prowess any longer, she said, "Once I saw him pull his knife on a man who had threatened to hurt me. My father moved so fast, I did not even see the blade coming." She pointed to her neck to emphasize the danger the man had been in. "The knife stopped right here, below his ear. If my father had not pulled the cut, the man's head would have been severed from his body."

In response, all four women gasped. They appeared to be both envious and excited at the thought that Rodger might, also, pull a knife on someone who was threatening to hurt them, just as Sunniva's father had done. And along with their increased eagerness to see Rodger fight on their behalf, all fears for his safety were momentarily forgotten. Their previous worry was ushered out the door, and in its stead, the women's thirst for blood vengeance was invited inside to join them here, where they had been seated so pleasantly around the supper table just prior to its mention.

In an attempt to bring a note of caution back to the conversation, Sunniva said, "My father could have been killed, you know."

But after Rodger had grown so highly in the women's eyes, he took on the full authority that his status as protector of their household warranted, to say, "I doubt that. He is fast, for an old man. And his aim is true for someone who is blind on one side."

Sunniva then regretted her description of how her father had come to her defense. She realized, too late, that she had inadvertently added to her father's seemingly legendary reputation. And now, in addition to the effect that her reminiscence had had on the women, it also had increased Rodger's excitement.

To persuade him otherwise, she could hardly have described the less than exemplary behaviors her father showed in the privacy of his own home—his angry outbursts over the most trivial matters and the times when he awoke screaming in the night. When he was forced to be alone so often, just to keep from starting fights and threatening to strangle other men in the hamlet, she asked herself, how he could live so closely with over a hundred men for several months before one of his own bench mates pulled a knife and killed him out of spite?

In contrast to Sunniva's silent misgivings, Rodger was spilling over with enthusiasm at the prospect of fighting alongside her father. "Will he join us? He would be a good man to have along. Besides his fighting skills, Gevehard told us that he is a cunning man who can work spells to protect us when we are away at sea."

The thought of her father floating away on the longboat, so filled her with dread that a shrill, "No," burst from her mouth, followed with a frantic-sounding, high-pitched, assertion, "Well, I do not know. I think that he would have told me if he had plans to leave me here."

Yet, as much as she wanted to strengthen the other men's nonexistent resistance to their plans for her father, and to build her insistence that she must not be left standing on the shoreline alone, she also knew that she could hardly speak for her father. He would make his own decisions. And that was the problem that her mother had warned her about.

How could she ever return to her mother's household without her father? After she had been blamed for starting the fight between her father and the quarryman, she had been forced to spin two basketsful of fleece. That punishment for something, which she had been falsely accused of, had been bad enough. What would her mother say if she came home without her father? How could she explain It? She could hardly say that she had, somehow, lost sight of him on the road. Then she realized, with a start, that she would never get as far as the road. She could not even yoke the oxen to the cart.

To counter Sunniva's downcast appearance, Innis sought to reassure her. She grinned slyly, and said, "Well, you would not be left alone for long. You are an attractive girl. We could easily find you a husband."

Sunniva did not want to live here. The silence at the table sucked all the air out of the house. It went on for far too long. As she glanced from face to face, their blank expressions seemed to say they were puzzled by her reticence. After all, a man's family owed its prestige and wealth to trade in the overseas markets. To be granted this chance to join the crew, her father should feel honored, and his daughter excited at the prospect of increased family wealth and the possibility of a better marriage. To Sunniva, it seemed that each of them was silently asking: Are you daft, girl? Are you unable to grasp that this is how things are done here in this village?

V.

The following day, Sunniva was crouched beside the bundle of fleece that her mother had packed for her—along with strict instructions to have it all spun by the time she returned home—and was sticking handfuls of the wool into her basket. She needed some time alone to think things through—without Frida, Mila, and Innis telling her what to think and what to do.

On the first day of her arrival, Sunniva had dutifully gathered her spinning things together and had offered to keep Frida company while she wove fabric on her loom. Frida reached toward Sunniva's distaff to pinch the unspun fleece. Rubbing it between her thumb and fingers, she crinkled her nose with evident disgust and asked, "What kind of an animal is this from, anyhow? Did you shear a pig or wild goat? Compared to our sheep's fleece it is very coarse and scratchy."

After that, because it was so coarse and scratchy when compared to the soft fleece that the women in this village sheared from the sheep they raised, she was ashamed to spin it in their presence. Instead, she sought places where she could sit at a distance from other's prying fingers.

Because it was unlikely that any of the women, who might say nasty things about her mother's fleece, would be out in the meadow where she and Frida had picked fresh greens the day before, she headed in that direction.

And, on her way to the pasture, she had half a mind to stop at the holy grove. After Adelheide, Frida, and the women in the cookhouse had spoken so respectfully of the big red stone, Sunniva thought she should take a second look. Confused about what she had seen there on her previous visit, she thought that if she were to spend some additional time gazing at the stone, it's full meaning might become apparent.

Previous to their arrival in Gevehard's village, she had known only one thing about the stone: to both hers and her mother's annoyance, her father had been so engrossed in carving it all winter long that he had completely ignored them. But now she understood why he had been so intolerant of distractions. For her to have ridden in the cart with the red stone behind her back, without having given it the due respect it should have garnered, if what the women said was true, she would be reluctantly humbled.

That first day, when Adelheide had sent Sunniva to the holy grove with the basketful of offerings for the hidden folk, she had come upon Gevehard and his men just moments after they had finished setting the stone upright in the soil. The men were crowded around her father where he stood beside the stone. He traced the grooves with his fingers and, as he named each of the secret signs, threw light upon its most significant meaning. He explained how the letters, when spelled altogether, along with the pictures he had carved, honored Glenn and asked him to put in a good word for them with the Lord of Rich-Waters. Because their plea was carved in stone, which was permanent and enduring, her father assured the men that their request for safe and prosperous voyages would last for as long as the stone stood in this holy grove.

Attempting to catch a glimpse of the stone from behind the men's backs, she stood on her tiptoes and peered over, around, and in between the men's shoulders and heads. And as her father spoke, his description of the secret world pictured on the stone had a profound effect on her. Her sight contracted to such a small size, she seemed to be peeking through a pinhole from a great distance.

It was then something strange began to happen.

First, the green snake uncurled from its nest and slid into the blue water. Seeing how it undulated atop the surface of the waves so absorbed her attention that she could neither look away nor even blink her eyes. The Lady Sun's twin brothers, the Lords of Battle, carried their bright star-shields and brandished their flaming long-knives. Escorting their sister on her progression across the sky, Day-farer led the way and Night-farer followed. And meanwhile, the mirror, which Lady Sun carried in her wagon, was spinning around in a brilliant, yellow swirl, the same way the fiery wheels did after they had been lit at the end of the Yuletide celebrations. The brilliant, noon-day light, which the flaming disk cast, reflected from the blue water's faceted surface and fractured into thousands of sparkling pieces.

And while all this was going on, those men, who were seated on the benches in the boat that her father had carved, no longer looked like little stick-figure men, but seemed real enough to be the very same men who were standing alongside Gevehard. Lady Sun brandished her flaming blade. And as it cut through the air it threw off gold-colored sparkles. And as the sparks showered the men seated in the boat, each man dropped his handhold on his oar and reached up to pluck a falling gold coin from midair.

The dazzling vision then broke apart and fell away in shards. Left with just the sight of a dazzling, white trace, Sunniva was blinded for a moment. Everything went dark the way it did whenever she walked into a house after she had been outside on a bright, sunny day. Awed by what she had seen, Sunniva stood there for a while and stared straight ahead until her eyes adjusted to the shadows. When one of the men jostled her, she blinked several times and her vision returned.

Meanwhile, Gevehard's men were in a whirl of activity. None of them had seen what she had seen. If they had, they would have been equally as dumbstruck as she was. Instead, they excitedly congratulated themselves for their neat and hasty work, clapped each other on the back, praised her father's skill, shook hands with Gevehard, and thanked him for honoring their founding-father's memory. A couple of the men picked up the cart's tongue and others pressed their shoulders and hands to its sides and back. They worked together to turn it around and pushed it along the narrow path that led to the place on the road where her father had first parked it.

The vision was like those that she had seen when she looked at the pictures on the little, red gravel pieces that Wybert had given her. But this time, because of the intention her father had given the picture, he had shown her the world she was meant to enter. It seemed as though the stone was an open doorway surrounded by a frame. The ribbon that bordered the picture separated the dream-like world from the familiar world that she inhabited in the daytime. Though she had only seen it for a moment, somehow, she had been granted a sight of that otherworld. Convinced that what she had seen was equally as real as the everyday, familiar world, which she inhabited whenever she was awake, she concluded that the otherworld was there all the time, hidden beneath the surface. But it remained out of view except to those who were granted the sight with which to see it.

In the past, whenever her mother had caught her staring vacantly into the middle distance, Sunniva had been scolded. After she had learnt this hard lesson from her mother, lest she be reprimanded and excluded from the company of others (as had happened on the night when the women were telling stories), she knew that it was better to keep her private reveries hidden and to herself. To safeguard what she had seen, she told herself that the vision was hers and hers alone, and she would choose with whom she wished to share it.

As the sound of the men's voices faded away, Sunniva looked at her father as though he were a stranger whom she had never before laid eyes upon. Who was this man who stood beside the stone, smiling at her with his crooked grin? How could he have called forth the dreamtime with the pictures and secret signs he had carved?

After she had been ignorant of his skills all her life, she was suddenly tongue-tied in her father's presence. All the time that she had lived with him, in the very same house, he had kept his secret talents hidden. And since there were no words with which to describe what she had seen, she wordlessly handed him the basket that Adelheide had given her.

And though he had thrown his arm around her shoulders and affectionately told her that she brought him luck, she was too stunned to speak. Instead, she asked herself, how does one talk to a man who has such cunning skills?

But now, on her second visit to the holy grove, her doubts resurfaced. Her father was not a cunning man. No, he was the same man whom she had always known. Besides, he had given her no attention since their arrival. That, too, was the same as the way he had ignored her all winter long. He was the exact same man that her mother said he was: a childish man who did whatever he pleased. And now, his senseless behavior was about to get her into trouble with her mother.

Sunniva would need to put the stone to a test. If she were to renew her awe of her father's cunning skills, and to remain confident in the stone's power, and to regain her certainty that Lady Sun would fill the four ships' hulls with wealth, and to know whether she could trust the Lords of Battle to assure the men's safety, the pictures would need to come alive again, in the same way that she had witnessed them before. Only then would she believe that the women in the cookhouse were right. To see the vision a second time would be her proof.

"Hild the Battle Maid," she asked politely, "will you kindly show me the hidden world that lies hidden beneath your skin?"

But nothing happened.

Again, she pressured the stone to reveal its secrets: "If the door, which has been mysteriously pulled shut to otherworldly visions, were opened again, might I be allowed, once again, to see the green snake undulate atop the sparkling blue water and Lady Sun's flaming knife throw off sparks like lucky gold coins?"

But when nothing happened the second time, she became increasingly adamant in her demand. Yet, the more resolute Sunniva became, the more stubbornly Hild resisted.

Put off, in this way, by the stone's aloof unwillingness to respond to her commands, Sunniva was reminded of the freeborn women who, from their lofty positions, looked down upon her mother whenever she sold the yarn the women living in the hamlet had spun. In the eyes of the warrior's wives,' Mildred was a common woman who was unlawfully wed to an outlawed highborn man. To the freeborn women, Sunniva's mother represented the threat that their warrior husbands' unwed, lowborn consorts presented. And just to prove their status, the highborn women frequently forced Mildred to demean herself before they would agree to buy the skeins. The sight of her proud mother lowering herself so humbly before those highborn women angered Sunniva to no end. And now she was equally angry with Hild. And, to stifle her urge to throw a rock at the stone, she turned away.

It was then that she caught sight of the holy offerings. Though several days had passed since she had brought them to her father, they were still here. The wooden bowls had been licked clean and lay tipped onto their sides. A few remaining scraps of bread crumbs looked unappealingly soggy. She walked over and, after she inspected them more closely, was sure that the hidden folk would never eat them. Perhaps she should pick up the bowls and scraps of bread, tie them up in the towel, and bring them back to Adelheide. But after she gave it more thought, she concluded that because of her lack of familiarity with the ways of those hidden folk, who lived here in the holy grove, she should leave them where they were.

If, instead, she fixed the offerings and made them look tidier, perhaps her respectful actions would convince the stone to respond to her request. Sunniva pulled on the linen towel's corners to straighten it until it lay flat. She turned the bowls upright again and arranged the bread crumbs in a neat and orderly pile.

After she concluded these small, purposeful attentions to the offerings, she apologized for her momentary pique of ill-humor, and asked respectfully to see the vision again. Though uncertain where the words came from, she was stirred to speak with an authority and conviction she had rarely given voice to before.

"Hild the Battle-woman,
   I, Sunniva the Gifts of the Sun,
   Daughter of the one who made you,
      Aiken the Strength of Oak,
   Now make this request:
      Show how Lady Sun
         Will bless Gevehard and his men
         With a safe voyage
         And will shower the sun's rays
         Upon the men like gold coins."

It is said that locales, such as the holy grove, where the blood gifts are made and the dead are buried, become places where the separation between the worlds is thinnest. In places, such as these, it is easier to move between the ordinary world, where men and women dwell, and the invisible, secret places that are inhabited by the ancestors and the hidden folk.

Whether or not Sunniva could see the hidden folk, she did not know for certain. She had never seen them before but, somehow, she suspected that they were there with her. She became very still and attributed the sounds of the soughing wind, the rattling rushes, and the surf splashing on the stones at the shoreline to the hidden folk's whispers.

She sat before the stone again, wrapped her arms around her tucked-up knees, and allowed the comforting dreaminess to come over her. It was then she knew that someone was watching her. Might it be Lady Blessed? In response to the peculiar sensation, Sunniva turned slowly in the direction from which she sensed the gaze. But, instead of the familiar sight of the Lady, she was startled to see a woman standing in the thicket, behind the offerings.

She was dressed in a sleeveless gown, woven from green shimmery fabric, light and fine as the tiny, new leaves that were budding from the branches in the thicket right behind where she stood. The woman's light brown hair hung loosely to the length of her waist. She was so beautiful that just the sight of her took Sunniva's breath away. The woman raised a hand to the neckline of her bodice and touched a brooch set with a large, honey-colored stone in its center.

"May this sea-stone offer protection
   From the wickedness I see
   Set here before me, here in this place
   Which is most holy to me.

May this sea-stone keep watch
  From invasion by those who would steal from me.
May this stone guard me
  From the wicked words cast by the envious.

By the powers who make this world,
  I evoke he who is my power,
    Let him weaken the words written
    On the red stone.
  Erol the Brave, oh Steadfast Strength,
    Leave the place wherein you dwell.
    Now come forth.

I welcome you.
  Act to render powerless what I see before me now,
    That which so insults my vision."

A tall, thin man then stepped out from behind the woman. Dressed in light-yellow tunic and tan trousers, his skin was pale as birch bark and his eyes were translucent as moonlight. His white, sun-bleached hair was pulled back from his face and knotted above one ear. At the side of his left leg he wore a jeweled scabbard that housed a blade with a fancy hilt. He carried himself with the confident bearing of a young chieftain who routinely promised danger to those who overstepped and did not know their place.

He walked past the offerings, and without a halt in his step, picked up a soggy bread crumb and threw it into the dirt. He stepped on it with the ball of his shoed foot and, after twisting it back and forth several times to grind the bread into the soil, he said, "Compared to what Glenn and his kin took from us, these paltry offerings are an insult."

He walked up to the red stone and glared at it for a while, then turned and walked straight toward Sunniva. He crouched before her and cupped his hands over his knees. The way he gazed so deeply into her eyes, she was unable to look away.

"Why should I make the pictures come alive?" he asked.

"Because to see them again will prove the stone can protect Gevehard and his crew."

"Where," he asked, with barely contained hostility, "is my name written on that stone?"

Intimidated by his forcefulness, Sunniva shrunk back. "I do not know. I cannot read the signs."

"It is not because of your ignorance that you do not know. The reason is that my name is not written there. Gevehard's name is there along with my enemy, Glenn's. But my name is not. Tell me, how can you defend a man who came into so much land, power, and wealth, only for one reason: because his great grandfather came here and took it all away from me—me. What does a young woman like you know of suffering, you who have the freedom to move about at will? My children suffer daily because their land was forcibly taken from them by Glenn and his tribe. Now my descendants are shackled by invisible chains and forced to do whatever their masters tell them. They are treated like inferiors, no better than cattle. At times, they are treated worse than animals.

"And now, you want to see the stone make a pretty picture? But I have more important demands. I want my children freed from servitude. I and my people should be seated at the high table and offered the cup to drink from. If my demand is not met, I vow to repay with hatred those who keep my children's children bound in servitude."

"There is nothing I can do," Sunniva said, "I am only a visitor here and do not know how to help you."

He turned his head to the side and spat a great wad of saliva in the direction of the stone. "I will curse their voyage. Their fleet will be destroyed. They will die the same way we did when Glenn came here—by the knife."

Panic welling, Sunniva forced herself to overcome her initial fear of the man, and said, "No. You must not curse the voyage. That will be cruel. It will betray all your people. There will be bonded men aboard the boats who have been promised their freedom in exchange for their service."

"Glenn stabbed me in the heart and bound my kin. And, now, you expect me to forget what he did?"

"No, you do not understand what I am saying," Sunniva said.

"No. It is you who do not understand."

"But there will be bonded men as well as freedmen on the boats. You do not want them to get hurt, do you? Do you feel no kindness for your own people?"

"Underlings, like them, who continue to thwart my endeavors, tire me."

"But if you curse the voyage and the ships are lost, everyone will suffer. Everyone depends upon the food and raw materials the men bring home. I know how much your children suffer. I am sad for Mila and for the women who work in the cookhouse. But Mila's brother will be rowing the oars because he serves one of the men who will be aboard the ship and, in return, he will be made a freedman. Mila wants to marry a man who plans to forge the iron they bring home. He has promised to buy her freedom with his earnings."

"Your argument has no merit. Nor are freedmen like Edmund any better. He slavers over Gevehard and gave his arm to protect his master."

"They are brothers."

"Only by half. I am embarrassed to call Edmund one of my kin. He is tainted by Glenn's bloodline and I refuse to acknowledge him. He has nothing to show for his obedience to Gevehard but an empty sleeve dangling from his shoulder. Instead of being a freedman he is more dependent upon Gevehard's favors than he was before. I only favor those who are bred from my tribal lineage. I will call upon the Lord of Thieves to attack their boats and bring this mixing of the blood to an end. Let the sea-raiders steal from those who plundered our land, homes, and wealth."

"No, you must not do that. My father may be aboard the boat."

"Why should I care?"

"My father also lost his wealth, his land, and even his name after he was outlawed."

"I know about your father, Aiken. Being a masterless man gives him more freedom, not less."

"No, that is not true, he is only free for as long as the powerful men, who want his carvings, agree to grant him freedom. He has no rights before the law. He lives at the chieftains' whims. Any moment they might come after him and no one will protect him."

"Aiken was free to carve this stone," the pale man said and glanced distastefully in Hild's direction. "He chose to make it for the thieves who stole this land from me. That alone deserves Lord Spider's punishment."

The pale man backed away, sat on his heels, and began to claw at the ground. "I, Erol the Steadfast, call upon Lord Spider the Entangler to turn against those who plundered our land and homes. The good life cannot reach us. We are left without. I seek the wealth that was stolen from us. I say, take it all back. Take back all they took from us. I call for a time of reckoning. The thieves need to account for what they did."

"No, you must stop."

"No, it is you who must stop. Listen to me."

He scraped together two piles of sand and pebbles and picked up the two hand-fuls. He stood, spread his arms out to his sides and, as he turned in a slow circle, he sprinkled the sand around himself as he leveled his curse:

"Spider the Entangler, Lord of Thieves,
    Son of the Devourers, Weather and Mist,
    Loop a snare, tie a knot.
        Entrap the longboats
        Led by Gevehard, son of Garr."

And before Sunniva even knew what was happening, the curse that Erol was calling forth began to evoke a picture from the dreamtime. Fed by the fear and hatred that grew in men and women's hearts, it seemed as though both those worlds, which were visible to the sleeping and to the waking, mingled in that place between. The world she saw when her eyes were open, overlapped with the world of the murky dreamtime. Subtle strands separated from the evoked fog, whipped about, and began to tie themselves into hundreds of knots. The misty cords looped under, over, and around and, in no time at all, they had created a huge net with which the Lord of Thieves could capture the ships.

"No, stop. You must stop," Sunniva tried to scream. But her attempts to pitch her voice loud enough to alarm the villagers and to bring them running were muted. Unable to match the pale man's strength when she said, "It is wrong for you to think that it does not matter. It is the women who bear the greatest burden," the wind sucked her voice right away and the words came out of her mouth in breathless whispers. "I speak for them," died out.

"Stop interrupting me," the man screamed. "Gevehard's men are hardly pure. They are killers like everyone else. I wish them luck." He snapped his head to the side, and with that single gesture, the green-clad woman left her place near the holy offerings.

She came toward Sunniva and knelt behind her back. Intending to silence and mollify Sunniva, the woman bent forward until their cheeks were nearly touching. She laid her arms across Sunniva's shoulders, bent her arms at the elbows and, with her hands pressed against Sunniva's heart, uttered her own binding curse:

"You, who are ensnared,
Will be caught by your
Attraction to feckless men."

"No, you have it wrong," Sunniva tried to say, "you know nothing about me," but the words got lost, somehow, before they could make it out of her mouth.

"Oh, but I do know. The dead know everything. I know that attraction is a trap. It is a net woven by your sentiments."

The green-clad woman's spoken words became unseen hands plaiting strands of invisible ropes. The cords whipped about in midair and wrapped around Sunniva's arms and legs to hobble her.

"Your sentiments will capture you and lead you toward Lord Spider's chaos—do you not feel it?" the pale woman asked. "Can you not see it? Can you not feel how compelling he is?"

And, as if the very act of saying the words aloud had made it so, a faint picture came and went fleetingly from the dreamtime. Her mirror image lay trapped inside a bubble. In a place where the surrounding allure of beauty had tempted her to enter, its confines held her soul captive. The bubble popped. The beauty vanished. And, surrounded by a ruin of broken shards, she was left alone to grieve its loss.

"You see?" the green-clad woman said, "It is impossible to release yourself from men's illusory, treacherous allure."

The more Sunniva tried to move, the more she became aware of her bondage. How, then, had she fallen into this invisible trap? Unable to move, unable to speak, she had been caught in the green-clad woman's snare. Clearly frightened of her helplessness, she was defenseless as Mila. Defenseless as all the women in the cookhouse. Defenseless as the bonded women who were bedded against their will by freeborn men.

"The harder women struggle to free themselves," the woman said, "the more the web tightens. It is impossible to get away from fraudulent men."

Try as she might, Sunniva could not dispel the hold this pale woman had cast. Nor could she free herself from the woman's powers of suggestion. Although the woman's touch was light as air, Sunniva was unable to break free of the bondage. For just the briefest moment, Sunniva caught sight of a man, an ironmonger who stood before his forge and pumped the bellows. She was about to plead with him to save her and to cut her free from these invisible cords with his invisible blade, but before she could call out to him for help, her sight of him was gone.

"He cannot help you either. It is only Lord Spider to whom you must look, and in whose embrace you must lay. He is the one who protects those who have no other recourse."

"No, you have it wrong," Sunniva wanted to say, but she had lost the voice with which to speak it. She had never been attracted to feckless or fraudulent men. Uncertain of whether this was really happening, she asked herself whether she was stuck in the dreamtime. Was she unable to wake, or was she trapped somewhere, by this ghostly woman's arms, in a region between those places where the dead go and the living spend their days? Though Sunniva tried to loosen herself from the woman's soft and gentle hold, she was unable to move.

Nor could she stop the deceitful web that the pale man was calling forth. Raging on and on, he was turning in a slow circle and calling out loudly:

"I, protector of the lowest of the lowly,
     Urge my children to wage war
          Against the thieves who stole their freedom.
               Lord Spider the Entangler
Son of Cruel Striker and Needle,
Father of Mother Torment, Anguish,
               Corpse, and Treachery,
     I call upon you to
Assail those who
          Brought despair unto my children.
Take revenge against
          Those who spit upon your heritage,
          Those who forget to hail you,
          Those who neglect to seat you at the high table,
          Those who are most worthy of your punishment.
Arise, vaporous steam-raiser,
          Shimmering air,
          Teasing creature of the night,
          Sly originator of deceits.
I call upon you to
Knot a snare to
          Entrap Gevehard's ships,
          Fool him with false beliefs.
               Let him seek shelter
               Where the enemy awaits.
Cunningly loop thick strands of fog."

Unable to burst free, Sunniva was both in the holy grove and not there at the same time. Along with her perception of time whipping back and forth, her wish to see the pictures on the stone come alive was granted. But, instead of a beautiful and uplifting sight, her vision became its opposite: a distorted and monstrous massacre. Her sight of the sand and the small white, outlined boats in the holy grove, was crowded out by a single picture of the longship that her father had carved. It became dimensional and multiplied four-fold. Four heavily laden ships were lying low in the water, headed toward a shoreline.

The beautiful, beneficent vision she had seen before became something that her father had never intended. The little stick-figure men seated on the benches came alive. Gevehard stood in Wave Crestar's prow and pointed to a shoreline enshrouded by the strangely conjured fog. Sunniva heard the shipmaster's faint voice. But it came from so great a distance that it was impossible to discern his words. She wanted to scream: Stop. Stop. Stop. Turn around. Turn around but she was helpless to do so.

Instead, she heard, clearly and distinctly, the pale man's curse:

"Lure the seamen.
Deceitful curtains,
Woven from strands of mist,
Create a web.
Delude my enemy's sight and hearing.
Offer a false promise of safety
Where pirates hide along the shorelines.
Trick my enemy.
Mistake things for what they seem to be
Not for what they are.
Loosen the ships of death.
Attack.
Spare no one."

The vision she had seen before became horribly twisted by the pale man's curse. Pirate boats were slipping through the mist, silent and unseen. Unobserved by the seamen who were manning the four trade ships' oars, the pirate ships snuck up on the longships. From her distance of time and space, the horror tightened Sunniva's stomach. A scream lodged in her throat.

Hidden by the conjured, deceitful mist, the pirates were stealthily surrounding Gevehard's ships. It was only when the small boats broke through the draped, curtain-like haze that the men who were seated on the longships' benches became aware of the attack. They dropped their handholds on the oars and hastily grabbed their shields and weaponry. But it was too late. Given no time to prepare, they were swiftly cut down, one man after another.

Left with no way to stop the bloodletting but to call, "Retreat," those, who were able, abandoned the three ships in the forefront. They used grappling hooks to pull their ships together, ran across the benches and leapt the gunwales to take refuge on the fourth. They manned the oars and rowed away to regroup from a distance.

The pirates who were left to plunder the spoils undisturbed, tied their smaller boats to the larger trade ships and spilled over the sides. Like ants crawling over a piece of meat after it had fallen on the floor, they ravaged the ships. Carelessly tossing aside the corpses and wounded men, the pirates wreaked havoc on the three longships. They formed lines to pass the crates, bags, and crockery, in which the trade goods were stored, from one man to the other and packed them onto their own, smaller boats. To work with such speed, it was clear that they were well-practiced at this form of thievery.

"Father of Misfortune,
Kindle the flames of revenge."

But whimsical Lord Spider is partial to no one and has no favorites. He has no desire to attack and conquer, but delights only in turmoil. Underhanded in everything he does, whenever he is in the midst of playing his cruel and crooked games, he destroys alliances and changes sides more readily than it takes an eye to blink. To keep his power intact, to make a show of his might, he pleasures in pushing antagonistic forces to the brink of chaos.

Gevehard's men regrouped. They manned the oars of the single longship and circled the pirate boats. It was Gevehard who threw the flaming brands to engulf the pirate's boats in flames. Those thieves who were still aboard the three longships jumped into the water. And those, who were in the smaller boats that had not yet gone up in flames, rowed back and sought cover in the river estuary in which they had originally hidden before the attack.

At the end of the battle, Gevehard's crew had set afire, or lost to thievery almost all their trade goods—almost their entire stock was gone. After the pirates fled, Gevehard's men leapt onto their three remaining ships. They untied the burning pirate boats, put out small fires, manned the oars and rowed out to sea. There, they went through the bodies of those who had fallen, dressed the injured men's wounds, and stacked the dead in Wave Crestar's hull.

Erol's contrived vision left Sunniva exhausted. Her stomach was turned inside out. Her chest was so tight she could barely breathe. But she was given no reprieve from the assault.

"A woman is placed in a difficult plight," the green-clad woman lamented. "To protect herself and her children, she is forced to compromise. She, too, can be equally clever and cruel as her oppressor. If you doubt me, you have not yet fallen prey to a man's treachery and deceitful ways. Though you are still young, I see it in your face. I know war is in your heart. Do not judge me. It is only when you recognize, within yourself, the same dark qualities, which you find so attractive in the man of your desire, that you will free yourself from his allure. Know this:

"You, too,
    Will become love-crazed for a man
        Who rends your heart
            In two.
You, too,
    Will be helpless to keep
        From following him
            Into the darkness."

A vision came and went as though from somewhere outside herself and, in a flash of brilliant light, Sunniva saw herself running after a man. Unable to see his face, she saw him only from the backside. Then, just as quickly as he had appeared, he disappeared. And yet she followed after him. And even as she ran into a great, black hole in the earth, though she feared it was her open grave, yet she chased him, and the sun's brilliant light turned pitch black.

"It is a woman's curse
    To rely upon the man
        Who is her enemy.
  When she deals with her heart's demands
      There is no clarity.
Can you not feel its treachery?
    Do you not feel
        The way that you, too,
          Are ensnared?"

A passing movement caught Sunniva's eye. Though still bound by invisible cords and unable to twist her head to the side to catch sight, directly, of what she had seen briefly with her side-eyed view, she located the source. Somewhere in the distance, out beyond the edge of the big red stone, the shape of woman was striding towards them. From out beyond the edge of the stone, the small figure disappeared and reappeared and grew in size until her head and shoulders were fully visible. Sunniva recognized her at once.

Lady Blessed stepped around the edge of the stone. She wore a brown dress and a plainly woven shawl of muted colors tossed across her shoulders. With each of her steps she struck the earth with the tall, black distaff she carried. An elaborate gold ring encircled her neck and a sheathed short-knife hung over her stomach from a thick belt fastened with a large gold buckle, set with colored stones.

Forced by the Lady's sudden appearance to stop the recitation of his spell, Erol stepped outside the circle of sand and faced Lady Blessed. Pointing his finger, he spat out, "You come too late, you man-crazed woman."

"Erol, you turned your back on me long ago," Lady Blessed said. "It was you who failed to protect those men and women who had relied upon you for their safe-keeping. It was not me who turned a back on them. It was you. You begrudge those living men and women who survived you and their forebears. And now, you want to bring ruin to your children's children because you resent those who are alive.

"When you call upon Lord Spider, you play a dangerous game. His presence will only increase the suffering. You may get what you want when you deal with Spider the Entangler, but in the end he will ruin you. The time of pestilence, which was your final undoing, was brought about by Spider's progeny. But long before that, you abused your power and put yourself above the law. Without regard for what was just or fair, you used your role as village kinleader to gain more wealth for yourself. You forced your men to engage in piracy and took captives to row the oars. You forced merchants to pay you off in return for your guarantee of safety from attack. And then you sent your men out to ambush them when they were in open water."

"Lady, go back to spinning the clouds. Leave this for the men to sort out."

"You need me, you foolish man," Lady Blessed said, "but because of your penchant for constant gaming, useless baubles and fleshly delights, you are the one who lost your gold. You were the one who had no time for the men and women who relied upon your leadership. Instead you chose to become a sea-raider. You put yourself and your personal needs above the others. You have no one to blame for the tragedy that befell you and your people but yourself."

"Lady, I did no wrong," Erol screamed. "I am the one who decides who belongs here, so get out. It is my right to decide who gets what. Only those who follow me can be included. I have the right to decide who stays. If they do not do what I want, I have tremendous power. All others are cursed and thrown to the dogs."

"To believe that only those who fit your tribal birthrights," Lady Blessed argued, "are allowed to remain is ultimately destructive. It cannot be done. All men and women are subject to my mercy. I tell you, it is important to remove the seeming differences between those who are born to one tribe and those who are born to another. For as long as you promote this separation between men and women you only strengthen the status of the highborn."

"As the kinleader of this village," Erol spat out, "I have the absolute right, perhaps even the duty to call for an uprising. I will only rest when all those who live here have destroyed one another. Then this cursed village will be abandoned forever. Only the dead will be left to rule this land."

He spread his arms wide enough to include within his reach all the white, lime-painted, stone-outlined boats, and said, with smug satisfaction, "Lord Spider is my friend. And these are my followers. The more men and women who die, the more followers I will bring to Lord Spider and Mother Torment's hall."

"You foolish man," Lady Blessed said, "now that you have turned to Spider, you will be eternally beholden to him:

"From now until the endtime
    You will know no other pleasure
        Than to drink
        The bitter mead
        Of your resentment
        In Spider the Entangler's hall."

"Go away, Lady," Erol said, and turned away from Lady Blessed. He retreated to the center of his sand-sprinkled circle, a place from which he could continue to spew out his hatred:

"I call upon the protector of pirates,
    Wily and deceitful shipmaster
        Of Nail-ship,

Destroyer and disrupter.
I command all wisewomen in Lord Spider's grip:
　　By my order,
　　Deceive Gevehard and his crew."

Lady Blessed walked up to him, looked him in the face, and used the butt end of her distaff to break up and scratch out the circle that Erol had sprinkled around himself. His arms fell to his sides in helpless dismay.

She stared coldly at the green-clad woman, and said to Erol, "I see how, even in death, you make use of women as you please."

Lady Blessed turned away from Erol, charged up to the green-clad woman, flapped her apron, waved her distaff, and screeched, "Shew, shew, shew. Get away, get away. Shew, shew, shew. Get away. Shew. You have mistakenly chosen to align yourself with my enemy. Now, get out of my sight. Return to Mother Torment's Hall."

The pale woman dropped her arms, straightened her back, stood, and glided so effortlessly, her feet barely touched the earth. The woman gave Lady Blessed a condescending glance as she passed her, walked up to Erol, held a hand to his face, caressed his cheek, took his hand in hers and led him to the place behind the offerings at the edge of the thicket.

Lady Blessed stood beside Sunniva, and clutching the black distaff in her right hand, rested its butt end on the soil. Using the distaff as a prop, she leaned over to smooth Sunniva's hair, and said, "My wind-bleached Storm-pale, you have so much to learn. When one is granted second sight, the world can be a confusing place, at first. The vision of the stone you sought was but a mere deception, a diversion, a simple form of artistry. Though it took on dimension, it is incapable of all that I need from you, right now.

"Instead, I need you to pass the cup between Erol and Glenn. To restore honor to all those involved is vital to bringing together all the men and women who live in this village. It is when people are disrespected that they resort to fighting and calling down curses upon their enemies. The restoration of honor is the best way to save face for all those who are involved. That will be the way to end hostilities and to promote peace. In this way, those who are now held in bondage will be integrated into the larger community on equal terms. Talk of what is good and bad must defer to talk of respectful recognition."

"But how?" Sunniva cried. "How can that be done?"

"Unfortunately, Erol is the one who must speak for his people." Lady Blessed touched Sunniva in the center of her brow. And at her touch, Sunniva saw, in a flash of insight, the inside of a longhouse. It was so huge, both ends extended far into the deep shadows. Tables were set up lengthwise along both walls. On one side, the living men and women from Erol's tribe sat and, on the other side, sat Glenn's tribe.

The longhouse was swamped by the forebears, many of whom had been enemies when they were alive. Men who had fought each other, killed each other, all milled about. Among them were also the original inhabitant's forebears who had disapproved of Erol's turn to piracy.

What would they all talk about at the tables? Would those who had been held in bondage recall those who had restrained their freedom and kept them down? Would those who had kept others in bondage recognize and admit to the cruelty they had used to restrain the others? Would they promise to honor and respect the dignity that was inherent in each man and woman's humanity? Or would the landholders refuse?

Among the living there were men and women who, like Edmund, carried both ancestral families within themselves. When it came time to honor his ancestors who did Edmund honor? The man who had raped his mother and refused to free him from servitude? Or the man who refused to acknowledge his birthright? On which side of the hall would he sit? It seemed those men and women who, like Edmund, had both factions within themselves, were the ones who were best suited to mending the divisiveness between the ancestors and to bind them together. Their very lives were the result of the conflict. Many of those men and women's births had been the result of men's domination of the women whose lives they controlled. Either an enforced peace was required or a perpetual war would wage inside such a person.

And seated at the high table on the dais, Glenn and Erol were awaiting Sunniva's approach. Yes, her approach, because she, too, had been born by a mixing of the blood, by the coming together of a highborn man and a common woman who were unlawfully wed.

Sunniva was overwhelmed by such a vision of the two enemies seated side by side at the high table, and of those who were seated on the benches below, where the men and women of the tribes had come together to make peace.

This, then, was what Lady Blessed wanted her to do: to pass the cup between Erol and Glenn, and to offer the cup to each of the men and women who sat across the divide, deep as a bottomless chasm, staring hatefully at each other. To ask each of them to promise to honor and respect each other's humanity, to tolerate their differences rather than to exclude those whose beliefs or talents were different from their own, and to allow them to have an equal say in how things should be done. That was the only way to truly strengthen this community.

And, after the cup had passed between them, they would await the entrance of the storyteller who would tell their stories tenderheartedly, show sympathy for their suffering, and tolerance for their differences with thoughtful benevolence.

It was an impossible task. It could never be done. "No. No. No," Sunniva cried. "Take this request away from me. Take it away. Take it away."

"For as long as men and women have walked this earth," Lady Blessed said, "they have crossed the seas, the mountains, the forests and the plains, looking for better places to live. All these people are my people. It hurts me to see the antagonism between them and the suffering that one group brings upon the others. It is better to celebrate the differences than to maintain conformity and impose restraints through violence. The guilty must be held accountable, understand the consequences of their actions, be given an opportunity to make amends, and be allowed to seek redemption."

"But how can any penance be equal to all that the wicked have done?"

"I have confidence in your strength, Sunniva," Lady Blessed said "Do not let others shame you."

Lady Blessed then cocked her head and became very still. listening music, coming from far away. "Do you hear that?"

"Yes."

Coming from the direction of the village were several women's high-pitched voices raised in song.

"Across the five rainbows,
Across the six dawns,
Across the red daylight."

"Run along now, Sunniva. Go," Lady Blessed said.

Turning away to further assault her rival, she took off in long, loping strides. Pointing her distaff at Erol, she made stabbing motions in midair. With lips pulled back from her teeth, she spat out her invective: "You foolish man, you still have a chance. Either make peace with your enemy or you will be beholden to the Lord of Thieves from now until the Endtime.

"May you, who thirst for blood,
    Become the fly
        Who seeds the maggots
        That eat you from within."

Sunniva pressed her free hand flat against the ground to steady herself and reached out for her basket. Slowly, cautiously she got to her feet. She stumbled and nearly lost her balance before she had regained enough of her former composure to stand upright. She took several steps before she paused to glance back over her shoulder. The woman in the pale green dress turned and stepped into the thicket. The man followed. He and the woman then dissolved into fine strands of mist and disappeared, along with Lady Blessed.

VI.

If this was what it meant to be granted the sight of things that no one else could see; if this was what it meant to be favored by Lady Blessed; and if this was what it meant to fly on a goshawk's wings; Sunniva wanted nothing more to do with it. She would rip the feathers from her wing-like arms and tear them into shreds before she agreed to be a wisewoman. Never would she run after feckless men who led her into dark places.

No, she would do what her mother told her to do: she would marry the man who had been chosen for her. Mildred knew what was best. That was what her father always told her. Wynn was so dependable he was boring. How could she possibly take down Lady Blessed's enemy, Spider the Entangler or carry the cup between Erol and Glenn?

"I go to the house
Belonging to the wind.
I go to the grassy fields

Belonging to the sun."

The song's description of a beautiful place where she could lose herself in soothing serenity offered to counteract the horrors she had witnessed. Following the sounds
of the women's sweet voices she was led to walk between the mounds until she came
upon a cluster of singers gathered near the longhouse door. Sunniva stood off to the
side and swayed in time to the rhythm of their singing. Some of the women's half-
closed eyes lent a look of dreaminess to their faces. Others sang with wide-eyed expressions that could best be described as utter terror.

A woman stood before the group. Most likely, she was the wisewoman, Edwina. To lead the women with a consistent beat, she tapped the hard-packed soil with
a black distaff. Similar to the one that Lady Blessed had carried, it appeared to have
been forged from iron and was almost as tall as the woman herself. There was a ring
at the top of the basket from which a wooden spindle hung. Sunniva had never seen
distaffs like these before. What kind of cord the wisewoman might spin with an iron
distaff and a wooden spindle, Sunniva was uncertain. Such a distaff would be impracti-
cal. It was too heavy to carry around and to use every day.

The wisewoman's grey hair was plaited, but not too neatly, since it had failed to
capture many of the loose strands messily sticking out around her deeply creased face.
Along with a touch of out-of-control derangement, her disheveled appearance empha-
sized her grim outlook on the world. She wore a simple dress. Her shawl was pinned
together haphazardly in the center of her chest. Hanging around her neck were several
cords from which were hung small bags, beads, and other oddments that Sunniva
assumed were amulets worn for protection from her otherworldly enemies.

She turned, looked at Sunniva directly, and said, "You are tardy. Where have
you been?" She jerked her head to the side and indicated, with a quick nod, that Sunniva should join them. "But leave the basket behind."

Had Edwina confused her with someone else? Since the wisewoman did not
appear to be someone with whom she could argue, Sunniva set her basket on the
ground. The singers shuffled to either side to make space for her in the center, and
Sunniva eased in amongst them.

Since the tune was simple and repeated, Sunniva found it easy to sing along once
she had figured out the words.

"Across the five rainbows,
Across the six dawns,
Across the red daylight,
I go to the house
Belonging to the wind.
I go to the grassy fields
Belonging to the sun.
I go to the yew tree
Where the Matrones spin."

Striking the ground with increasing vigor, Edwina shuffled her feet in time with the beat and, as she turned in small mincing steps, began to take on the appearance of a slowly spinning whorl. The singing went on for a long time. The women repeated the tune until, without warning Edwina lifted the distaff high above her head and brought it down, swiftly, to forcefully strike the earth one final time. The women all stopped singing. All but Sunniva, that is.

Sunniva flushed and, fearful that another sound might escape her lips without consent, raised both hands to cover her mouth.

Edwina stomped up to her, reached toward Sunniva's chin, squeezed her jaw between her thumb and forefinger, and shook it. "Do you plan to sing all by yourself? To show-off your lovely voice?"

"No," Sunniva said. And, to excuse her blunder, added, "But no one explained what I am supposed to do."

"Well then, I will explain it to you now. When I raise my distaff overhead, everyone stops singing. Is that clear?"

Edwina searched Sunniva's eyes with a penetrating glare cold as ice. But what she hoped to find, Sunniva did not know. "Tell me what you saw," Edwina said. "Your eyes are aglitter with the brightness of one who has seen the hidden folk. I know the signs. What did you see?"

Sunniva's eyes grew big and round. How did she know? She blurted out, "I saw two of the hidden folks in the holy grove just now curse the voyage."

The other women gasped in horror.

"You are a liar," Edwina said. "What foolish make-believe."

Immediately remorseful, Sunniva strove to take back what she had said, "Yes, you are right, I saw nothing of the sort. It was childish of me to say such a thing."

Edwina flapped her hand at the other women and dismissed them with a curt, "Leave us. The girl is a spoiled child. She knows nothing. Leave her to me. I will reprimand her myself. You will gather tomorrow at noon. Kendra will lead you then. Go away."

Sunniva ducked low enough to scoot beneath the woman's outstretched arm and took a step.

"No, not you," Edwina said and lowered her arm to block her path. "You cannot leave until you tell me what you saw."

When Sunniva was a small child, she had been scolded for what she had seen and done. She had meant no harm. First, she closed one eye and held a hand up to hide the hurt side of her father's face, so that she would see only the handsome side. Then she moved her hand to cover the pleasing side of his face and peered at the other one. How could one person, depending upon which side of his face you saw, look so different? She repeatedly switched her hands back and forth, first to peer at one side and then at the other. Of course, she knew, all along, that he was the same man. He was her father and was not scary or frightening. Nor was he monstrous, as some folks said. He was a loving, affectionate man, except when he was angry.

And her mother looked scary, too, whenever she was angry—just as she was right then. When Mildred saw how Sunniva was amusing herself, she grabbed her daughter by the back of her dress and pulled her away. She leaned down and, breathily hissed in Sunniva's ear, "Your father is a good-looking man."

For his wife to say such a thing, when everyone knew it was so false, confused Aiken momentarily. He gave his wife a look of shocked puzzlement, followed by one of gratitude. "Mildred, you know, and I know how I look. Do not be so harsh. Leave Sunniva alone. She meant no harm. We were playing a peek-a-boo game. I was making silly faces at her."

Mildred glanced angrily over her shoulder and glared at Aiken with a look that was hot enough to scorch. "You stay out of this," she said, rapidly dismissing his opinion as one that did not count.

Mildred dragged Sunniva out the door and pulled her around the corner of the house. Out of the sight of others, where she could shame her little daughter in private, Mildred told Sunniva that, for as long as she never peered at her father in that way again, or commented upon his looks, or referred to the scarring on his face, it was as if she had never noticed. Therefore, for as long as she never spoke of it, in truth, he was a good-looking man.

Untaught in the ways of the world, Sunniva pleaded with her mother. She knew her father was good-looking and loved him dearly with all her heart, but preferred to see the handsome side of his face and not the ugly side. Unfortunately, her pleas for understanding only made things worse. In response to having spoken the forbidden word aloud, she so evoked Mildred's ire that her mother slapped her little daughter's cheek. Sunniva whimpered and cowered beneath her mother's fierce gaze.

"It is more honorable to lie at times," Mildred insisted. "If something is never spoken of, it does not exist, nor did it ever happen."

"Now," Mildred said, "go tell your father how sorry you are."

Sunniva's father stood in the center of the open doorway. With his left hand pressed against the doorframe and his straightened arm extended high across the opening, he leant his right arm and shoulder against the opposite side. There he stood, staring thoughtfully across the common yard.

Too scared to look at her father, Sunniva hunched her shoulders and squeezed through the space between the edge of the doorframe and his legs. She whispered, "I am sorry," and sneaked back inside.

"You did nothing wrong, Sunniva," he said.

Hidden in a corner with her dolls, Sunniva harshly scolded them for peeking at forbidden things. Too afraid to come out of the corner, she snuck a peek at her father now and then. But he just stood there for a long time, staring across the yard. Finally, he dropped his arm and walked off. Then it was safe to come out again.

Sunniva never forgot the lesson. Her father would say the words had been spelled out in secret signs and scratched into her bones. She had learned her lesson well and, from that day forward, had hidden the truth whenever there was a good reason.

Now, it was Edwina who was staring into Sunniva's face and challenging her to speak about what she had seen.

They stood in the center of the village where everyone could see the older one continue to demean the younger one. But Sunniva was not a small child. She was a grown woman and Edwina was not her mother. The wisewoman had no right to shame her here, in front of others.

Increasingly irate at the treatment she was being forced to endure, Sunniva straightened her shoulders and made up her mind. The more Edwina tried to pry the information from her, the stronger became Sunniva's determination not to speak another word.

What she had seen was so frightful and forbidden that she must never speak of it. If she did, it would cause a panic among the villagers. It could decrease trust in both her father's workmanship and in Gevehard's ability to lead the men. Fearful of some unknown, terrible consequence if she exposed the truth, Sunniva locked her lips. It consoled her to think that if she never spoke of what she had seen, it would never happen.

Because Edwina's approach had gotten her nowhere, she changed her tactics. She asked why she had never seen Sunniva before. "What is your name," she asked, "and where do you come from?"

But after having resolved not to speak, Sunniva refused to answer.

"You do have a name, do you not?" Edwina said mockingly. "Do you know that much at least?"

To convince Sunniva that she had done nothing wrong, Edwina changed her tone to one of kindly reassurance. "There is no need to be frightened. But if you saw something, now is the time to tell me. Whenever someone catches sight of the otherworlds, it is the wisewoman's right to know. This is a privilege inherent in my position. Even when blameless, simple-minded girls see something connected to the invisible realms, the wisewoman owns them, not the child who saw them. The invisibles can show themselves in uncommon ways. Even an ignorant child may carry an important message from the otherworlds. You are required to tell me."

But there, Edwina was wrong. Though Sunniva was uncertain of what meaning she should lend to that which she had seen, Edwina did not own her experience. Besides, she had no words with which to describe the pale man and the green-clad woman. She could not have spoken of it, even if she had wanted to. But she did not want to.

To offer Edwina something that would throw her off the track, Sunniva thought she might tell her about the Lady in the Clouds' promise to give her a cloak of many colors. But even her visions of the Lady were hers and hers alone, so she resolved not to speak of them. However, because the Lady had described the mysterious vision of the stone as nothing more than a distraction, Sunniva told Edwina what she had seen when the pictures, which her father had carved on the stone, came alive.

There was nothing secretive or forbidden in her descriptions of the spinning flaming disk and of the snake swimming over the surface of the sparkling blue water. And, because Sunniva had heard it said that a wisewoman could tease out the hidden significance of dreams, she asked, "What did the vision mean?"

"Oh, so you are the insolent daughter of that ugly man who carved the stone I have heard so much about? And now you have come here with a far-fetched story to prove its worth? Well," she said in a proud and demeaning manner, "he can only plead with the forebears."

The way her mouth twisted as she spewed out her scornful mockery of Sunniva's father, made her look as though the words she spoke were so bitter she must spit on the ground to rid herself of their disgusting taste. "What your father does has little value. I see all the influences from which Mother Necessity and the Matrones spin their threads. It is by my actions alone that the best choices will come about."

Not only had Edwina spoken aloud the forbidden word describing her father's appearance, but Sunniva felt she must stand up for the stone and her father's skill. "My father is famous for his craftsmanship. Many chieftains admire his work. He spent all winter carving the stone. His use of the secret signs will assure the men of a successful voyage and will overcome the curses that were spoken against it."

"What do you mean by curses? There are no curses against the voyage. Your father only carves pictures and spells out words in signs. Can he bring about successful voyages and bountiful harvests by spinning destiny? I weave fate. Can your father do that?"

This conversation, if one could call it that, had riled Sunniva to no end. She did not like to be challenged in such a demeaning manner, nor did she like to be treated like an ignorant child. "My father's stone will anchor the men to their homes. It has the Lord of Rich-Waters and Lady Sun's blessings. My father's words and pictures are engraved in stone and that is everlasting."

"So," Edwina countered, "do you think that Lady Sun favors you and your father? To win the Lords' and Lady's favor is not an easy task. Just carving a picture and writing words is not enough. Not if he wants those ruling power's blessings. He will need to move between the worlds and to speak with them the way I do." She lifted one eyebrow, and asked, "Can he do that? Can he read the thread the Matrones spun and change men's fates?"

Her thin lips curled into a small smile so miniscule it seemed difficult for her mouth to form. Perhaps, her inexcusable behavior derived from her need to be a forceful and domineering figure. In the process of making herself into a woman who can wield such power in a hall filled with dangerous men, had she forgotten how to smile and, over time, become unfamiliar with such pleasing expressions of joy?

Before she turned to walk away, the wisewoman taunted Sunniva with one last command, "Bring the stone's luck with you to the spinning ceremony when you come tomorrow night. And, remember, I plan to keep my eyes on you. Do not try to play any tricks on me because you will not get away with it."

Sunniva bent low to pick up her basket of fleece. As she straightened, she yelled loudly at the woman's retreating back, "I am not lying. I saw how the stone will protect the men and fill their ships with wealth."

The wisewoman turned and, walking back, fiercely tapped the ground with that black, iron distaff every step of the way. Edwina looked Sunniva up and down with undisguised loathing, poked her fingers into the handfuls of fleece, and picked out the whorl. "I see you spin ordinary threads. Well, they are of little value."

Embarrassed by the fleece she had brought from home, Sunniva said, "I know it is coarse. It can never compare to the soft fleece that the women in this village spin, but we do not breed the same kind of sheep."

Edwina's mouth twitched in that quick, mocking smile, and she snorted, "It is not the sheep and the softness of ordinary thread that I speak of, you silly girl. What I want to know is this—can you spin victory and wealth as I do? Can you, girl? Be forewarned: I plan to keep my eyes on you."

After she had dropped that hint of power derived from the hidden knowledge she wielded, Edwina turned on her heel and walked off, tapping the ground with that black, iron distaff.

Both awestruck and annoyed by Edwina's superior manner, Sunniva mumbled angrily to herself about the smug, self-important woman. The wisewoman had not explained what she meant by spinning victory. She had neither described how she accomplished these marvelous outcomes, nor had she explained how to influence a man or woman's destiny. It was despicable for an esteemed woman to taunt an innocent, young woman for her own personal amusement. Its pettiness only showed the smallness of her character.

At loose ends, Sunniva wandered aimlessly in the direction of the outdoors cookhouse. In preparation for tomorrow night's feast, a couple of the stalwart, older women stirred huge iron pots. Others made bread, churned butter, or toasted the grain with which they brewed the ale. Their arms were thick as tree trunks, their hands were veined and gnarled. Their torsos were thick, and their breasts hung flat like empty sacks bulging above their beltlines. It was hard to believe that these women, too, had been young, fresh-faced, and shapely as Mila and Frida. Yet, when one woman glanced up at Sunniva and smiled, she saw in the woman's eyes a look of kindly pity, a recognition of the familiar worry that she could see in Sunniva's youthful face. Certainly, the older woman remembered a time when she had been young and hopeful. A time when she had believed that she could make and keep a happy family home, complete with a husband and their children.

Each day a woman lives with the knowledge that a time will come when she will experience the first, most terrible, insensible sorrow: the death of a child or a husband. And, yet, she continues to feed the fire each morning and sings her song of gratitude to the Hearth Mother.

Women are taught to weep and to dry their eyes and to get on with whatever needs to be done each day. They express their grim determination with thin, tight lips and heavily creased faces. They bake the bread and brew the ale—that is, if there is grain enough in the larder after the hardship and rigors that winter or famine impose.

These women tend the master's gardens, milk the master's cows, find fuel, and keep the master's fires burning. They carry the water, which in this land, so close to the sea, is rare and precious. They spin the wool, weave, and dye the cloth that the men trade for the grain they cannot grow themselves. And if their men die at sea, the women are left to care for sons, daughters, nephews, and nieces. A woman might be left without even a brother to look after her. And if they live long enough, they care for the children of their own grown sons and daughters, along with their master's children.

Does a woman ever come to a time when she can outlive grief? Or, does each woman hide it away out of necessity? Must each woman keep it tucked beneath her dress, in a safe spot near her heart, like the amber bead that hung threaded on the cord around Sunniva's neck.

EIGHT

Yellow Jasper
If you will expound all
Dreams and prophesy of things to come

Take the stone which is called Jasper, and it is a pale yellow in color. And it makes a man to overcome his adversaries and gives prophesying through interpretation of all dreams and makes a man to understand dark questions hard to understand.

The Truth of Rocks, by Alviss the Wise

I.

Whilst digging through the wooden box, which the merchant had shoved into my hands and told me to take away, I found, buried beneath a pile of ashes, another relic to add to my collection. After I cleaned it of the smoky grime, with which it was encrusted, I could see it was an engraved, yellow jasper cylinder seal.

I asked Grerr for a handful of the clay he uses for casting bronze, flattened it with my palm, pushed a stick lengthwise through the hole in the cylinder, and after several attempts, made a good relief impression. Considering its small size (it is about the length my thumb), the figures engraved upon its surface are remarkably well-detailed.

Upon closer examination of the clay impression, I identified the figure on the right as the Lady of Bountiful Harvests. She wears a striped gown with long, full sleeves, and an elaborate headdress, decorated with wheat sheaves, encircles he head. She stands with her arms upraised, facing a naked woman on the left who holds a large basket filled with assorted fruits and garden produce. To the side of each figure there are palm trees and resting rams whose legs are folded beneath them.

I rinsed the jasper bead to rid it of the clay film adhering to it, raised the crystal ball to my eye and the yellow color flooded my vision.

II.

That morning, two women were commenting upon how yellow the sky looked. After the rain had fallen hard all night, the storm was moving off to the southeast, but the air was still heavily laden with water.

"The sky often turns yellow after a storm has passed, Sunniva. It is nothing to be alarmed at."

Sunniva was less alarmed by the color of the sky and more alarmed by what she had seen the night before when, upon her visit to the dreamtime, she had seen a tall, lean man crouched down before her. Dressed in a long black coat, he had a narrow face and dark, curly hair. He told her that he was the one who had given her the knife that she had inadvisably thrown into a puddle of water.

Yellow Jasper · 307

Upon awakening, she was unsettled by the nonsensical meaning of her nighttime vision. And, even as she was walking between the mounds with Frida that morning, avoiding the deepest mud puddles, her sense of unease continued to trouble her. There was no one with whom she could talk about the dreamtime vision, nor discuss what she had seen in the holy grove the day before, nor give voice to her humiliating encounter with Edwina. And, now, rather than eager anticipation of the upcoming day and the ceremonial feast that evening, she was absorbed in her failure to have lived up to the trust that her mother had bestowed upon her regarding her father's safety.

Inside the longhouse, Frida explained how very crowded it would be that evening. She paced off the places where the two rows of tables with benches on both sides would be lined up parallel to the long sides of the hall. The men, whom Gevehard had invited to attend the ceremony, were those who crewed the boats, prominent farmers who had large sheep and cattle herds, men whose wives managed productive loom shops, and merchants whose furs, amber, and salt were traded in the markets. Each man would be accompanied by a woman from his family. Altogether, there would be more than two hundred and fifty men and women in attendance.

The permanent tables and chairs on the dais extended to the full width of the longhouse. Those who would be seated there included Gevehard, Adelheide, Edwina, and thirty of the men who were responsible for the success of the voyage.

"Now that Adelheide has put me in charge of the longhouse decoration," Frida said, "it just goes to show that she and Gevehard expect me to take on the duties of the kinleader's wife someday."

Sunniva however, was unsure whether she agreed. Gevehard's wife appeared to be an ambitious woman who would not readily give up her control of the longhouse and the status it implied. Instead, it seemed that all the women who had shown up that morning, with brooms and bundles of cleaning rags in hand, could easily have taken care of the decorations on their own. They had, no doubt, assembled to clean and decorate the longhouse many times over the years, long before Frida had come to live in the village. But, by entrusting the duty to Frida, Adelheide had made it an honorary privilege to oversee the decoration of the hall because of her marriage to Gevehard's nephew.

The household boys brought in basketsful of dried dung and built fires in the two central hearths. Men carried in armloads of torches and set them in the iron brackets nailed to the wooden studs in the walls. Some of the women wrapped rags around their brooms and, after they had leant ladders against the walls, climbed up and stretched as high as they could to dust away the spider webs that had accumulated over the wintertime months.

When Mila showed up, she and Sunniva lifted a long, woven runner from one of the trunks, unfolded it, and laid it lengthwise across the high table. Elegant tableware was taken from another chest that two of the boys had carried in from the family's private quarters. The two young women opened it and carefully took out the silver and bronze plates, and the iron forged spoons and forks. They set them at each of thirty places at the high table, along with the finest platters and pitchers.

Mila and Sunniva formed a team to set up the long rows of tables. They hefted the trestles that had been stacked against the walls and carried them to the places where they would line up in rows. Then, they lifted the stacks of planks that leaned against the walls and carried them to the trestles and laid them flat.

Later that morning, women lifted textiles from the trunks stacked in the storage sheds. They shook out the sweet-smelling herbs with which they had been packed to keep moths from eating holes in the wool, and carried them by the armloads into the longhouse. To hang the decoratively woven and embroidered cloths, they stood on benches or climbed ladders and looped the attached cords over sharpened wooden pegs that were pounded into the sod-brick walls. Those that were long and narrow, and hung lengthwise on the walls, were embroidered with pictures telling entire stories.

Entranced by their beauty, Sunniva imagined how the women had threaded their needles with colorfully dyed woolen strands. For months on end, they had made each tiny outline and stem stitch by patiently poking the needles into the linen to memorialize the lives of the men and women who were the predecessors of those who would be gathered in the hall that night.

The men and women's stories seemed to begin on the left with the Windbringer and the Frost Devourers' scourging of the land where Glenn and his people had lived before they came to this village. Embroidered, curling blue lines portrayed the howling winds, which the Windbringer's flapping, widespread wings had set in motion. The Frost Devourers looked large enough to stomp their big feet on top of the little, snow-covered houses and to smash them flat. They wore long, white, skirted garments and their white hair and beards formed storm clouds around their heads.

The next picture showed Glenn and the men, women, and children of his tribe loading their boats with horses, sheep, cattle, and household goods. The men were clothed in their tunics and trousers. Embroidered cross-hatched lines indicated the tightly bound, woven bands they wore wrapped around their lower legs. The women wore colorfully patterned shawls over their dresses.

The following section depicted several boats afloat on the embroidered black, wavy lines that stood-in for the sea. Above them, Lady Sun was driving the two white chargers that were pulling her mirror-laden wagon. The round, golden mirror was flaming brightly with yellow, wavy spikes.

To indicate their new home in this village, on the southern shoreline of the Merchant Sea, several small buildings with steeply pitched roofs were set atop three mounds. Men led their horses and animals off the boats. The men in Glenn's warband were dressed in their leather jerkins and helmets. Long-knives hung from their belts and they carried spears and shields.

The next segment of the story portrayed the battle between Glenn's and Erol's men. Spears were flying through the air, and several wounded men lay on the ground in skewed positions.

Mila jumped onto the bench to stand beside Sunniva. "See, this is a picture of Erol and Glenn," Mila said, naming the two men who were facing off and pointing their long-knives at each other.

The next scene showed Erol lying flat on the ground with a long-knife stuck upright in his chest. Red embroidered threads showed the blood streaming from his heart.

"I saw Erol in the holy grove yesterday. He was a bad man and a pirate," Sunniva said. "No matter what you say, he deserved to die."

"You saw Erol?" Mila said in wide-eyed disbelief.

"There was also a woman dressed in green. I do not see her in any of these pictures. Who was she?"

"The woman dressed in green was wisewoman to this village before Glenn and his tribe came. Her name is Mila, too.

"She invoked Erol's presence and cursed me."

"She did? How about Erol? What did he say? Is he angry about the memorial stone?"

"Erol cursed the ships."

Mila, throwing-off the humble bearing she had possessed only moments before, said, greedily, "He cursed the voyage?"

Immediately regretting her simple statement, Sunniva jumped down from the bench. Now what should she do? This was the second time she had opened her big mouth when she should have remained silent. Lest she be punished for this infraction against the secrecy, which she should have maintained, she must never say another word about it. The frightening possibility that she had become a mouthpiece for Lord Spider, terrified her, and she swore to sew her lips shut.

Mila jumped down from the bench and, looking at Sunniva squarely in the face, asked, "Will Erol's curse take down the entire fleet?"

Panicking at the horrible thought, Sunniva, cried, "No, you misunderstood me."

But for Mila, the fantasies of getting back at her masters were rapidly overtaking any sense of propriety and self-preservation. Unable to keep from speaking her mind, forthrightly, she said, "You know, Edmund will be left in charge if Gevehard never returns. Adelheide prefers him to Gevehard and invites him into her bed whenever the shipmaster is gone. She knows how to play both sides of the game. She will do whatever it takes to keep herself in the longhouse no matter who is kinleader."

"But he cannot fight. He has no right arm."

"What does that matter? He can still be our kinleader. After all, he, too, is Garr's son. Adelheide's father was a second-generation freedman. She, too, is one of our tribe. Garr was angry when Gevehard married her. He believed the bloodlines should never mix, though he was guilty of doing that himself. Some folks say that Gevehard's sons will never become kinleader for that reason. It is more likely that Rodger will, if he outlives Gevehard. Just watch and see how Adelheide acts when she is around Edmund. One way or another, after the ships go down, Adelheide will make sure her boys become kinleader. Then it will be a new day for all of us."

Sunniva's eyes got big and round—just to think of Adelheide in bed with Gevehard's half-brother was too outrageous to consider. "No, Mila, now who is indulging in mindless make-believe? Say nothing more about this to anyone. No one at all. It did not happen like that."

"Sunniva, you did see them. You asked me about the woman who was dressed in green. You cannot get out of it so easily. You will need to pick sides. There can be no middle ground. Those who are caught between both sides will be crushed in the onslaught. You are either with us or against us."

"Mila stop it. You are frightening me. You misunderstood."

If she said anything more about Erol's curse, it would be akin to throwing sparks into a heap of dry straw. Anything might ignite the servants' desire for retribution.

Like an extension of the linen tapestry pictured in embroidered threads, Sunniva imagined an uprising would begin with the rumor that Erol had cursed the voyage. The servant's anger would explode like a cauldron of liquid fat thrown onto an already raging fire. And after it had spread rapidly among them all, by nightfall, just when the feast was about to begin, everyone would know about Erol's vengeful curse. The servants might be inspired to take up arms, or even to set the longhouse ablaze.

Horror-struck at the thought, she recalled her vision of that endless longhouse where opposing sides sat facing each other, and the two tribal leaders were seated at the high table. And there she stood, in the center of the hall cradling the cup that Lady Blessed had handed her.

Frida caught sight of the two idle women and walked over to remind them to get back to work. Unaware of the miniature battle into which she was inadvertently walking, she asked, innocently, "What are you two talking about?"

Mila, inappropriately beset with her prematurely imagined freedom mouthed off, "Oh Frida, let us be. We were looking at the embroideries."

Frida slapped the serving girl's cheek, and reproved her for her insolences, saying, "Mila, hold your tongue. Do as you are told, or I will tell Rodger to beat you till your skin is raw."

Mila held her hand to her cheek and glared so hatefully at Frida that it made Sunniva's skin crawl.

After Frida walked away, Mila gave Sunniva a blank, cold stare and turned her back. Sunniva stepped behind Mila, touched her on the shoulder and whispered, "I thought that we were friends."

Mila's lips curled in a sneer, and said, "I am only friends with those who stand up for me."

They walked together over to one of the benches. But neither looked at the other nor did they speak another word. They each lifted an end and carried it to a place beside a table. Setting it down, Sunniva broke the silence to ask, "But what about your brother? Do you not worry that he will be among the dead if the ships are lost at sea? His children would be orphaned."

"It will serve him right for siding with the enemy."

"Mila how can you be so cold?"

Mila straightened and glared at Sunniva. "You know nothing." Her eyes, coldly distant, seemed to see, not a friend, but a faceless enemy. "You need to pick. Whose side are you on?"

The threat was nothing new to Sunniva. She had been stuck between two sides all her life. Since she was a small child, whenever her mother and father argued she had sought out the best places to hide. But, sadly, Lady Blessed had not offered her the option of hiding. "Can both sides come together peaceably? You know, sit down and talk things over?"

"That is idle daydreaming. The time for negotiation is over. I want justice. Nor are you entirely blameless," she said, spitting out disdainfully, "your father is one of them."

Equally conflicted about taking a position, Sunniva understood the ambivalent tension between the landholders and the bonded men and women. Was she in favor of abundant goodness, even when distribution was unequal, or was she in favor of the destruction and death that accompanied war? How did she define goodness when the chaos that Spider engendered carried with it an opportunity that could, possibly, result in change for the better?

On one hand, Sunniva thought of the men her father had pictured on the red stone. Those little stick-figure men, who represented the fully-dimensional men who would be seated in the longhouse tonight, were the men who, someday, in the near future, would struggle to free themselves from Spider the Entangler's fog-woven net unless something was done to put a stop to the curse.

And, on the other hand, it saddened her to think that, because the servants were unable to protect themselves, they were forced to build and wear masks whenever they were around the men and women who had the power to hurt them. But, unlike the false-faces that men wore at Yuletide, which endowed the wearer with other-worldly power, and stood for increased abundance and loving ties between the kin, these false-faces hid the true intentions and hatreds of those who wore them. These masks were meant to protect a man or woman from those who controlled their lives.

The men and women, who were kept in bondage, withdrew into the only places they felt safe. Familiarity with their master's lives allowed them to disguise their secret powers over those who, otherwise, controlled them. They learned to eke out the hidden meanings of what was said and done. And by fitting together the many disparate bits of information, which they picked up about their masters' private lives, the servants exchanged promises of secrecy for small freedoms. And it was with those deceptions that they created the hoaxes around which they built their own lives.

Could a response to injustice ever be free of violence? Is it ever right to hurt others? There were no guarantees that those who were held in bondage would gain their freedom if they took up arms against the landholders. In fact, they were outnumbered and untrained in the use of weaponry. They would need to arm themselves with hatchets, scythes, and cooking knives. Common household tools could not stand up to the long-knives, spears, hammers, and axes that were made to overwhelm an armed adversary.

This is what men and women do to one another. Men like Erol and Glenn, and women like the green-glad woman who, rather than showing kindness for another woman's plight had, instead, turned against her. People choose sides as readily as they take a breath.

Perhaps she should follow the green-clad woman's suggestion. Perhaps she should take refuge in Spider the Entangler's embrace, just to be on the safe side. And with that thought, Sunniva caught sight, briefly, of that tall, thin man, dressed in the black coat who she had seen the night before. He smiled broadly and raised his arms in a victorious salute.

And for just the briefest moment she felt as though she was wrapped in a soft, comforting blanket. A soothing calmness came over her, and she began to cry in gratitude. Her tears were like the raindrops that fall after a long, hot, dry-spell. When even the sun-bleached grasses threaten to become tinder and start wild fires, the downpour comes. And the leaves feel the wetness. And the fields and meadows soak up the water. And the earth sighs and praises the stormy rain clouds. This was what goodness felt like. Gratitude.

When Frida saw Sunniva in tears, she walked over, and angrily demanded to know what she and Mila had been arguing about.

"It was just a small disagreement between two friends." Sunniva said, in defense of Mila. She turned her back on Frida, wiped her eyes, and began to walk away.

But Frida grabbed her arm and pulled her aside. "You are getting too friendly with the serving girls."

"What do you expect? You make me sleep beside her in the storage loft. Or do you think that I am one of your servants too? I will have you know that my father is a freeborn man and I can come and go as I please. Now let go of me."

"Listen, Sunniva. We do not treat the servants as poorly as Mila claims. Do not be taken in by her lies. All her people lie. Mila and her people eat just as well as we do."

"Stop speaking to me so harshly. I am not one of your servants, Frida. Stop telling me what to do, what to think, and how to manage my life."

"How do you want me to talk to you?"

"Respectfully."

"Well. if you do not act like the rest of us, you will wear out your welcome here."

"You mean I should act like one of the self-important, highborn landholders?"

"You are not one of us. You do not belong here. You do not fit in. Unless you change your ways, I will report back to Innis and tell her how wicked you have become."

"Then what will she do? Tell Rodger to beat some sense into me? Let me go, Frida. Stop telling me what to do. I can be friends with whomever I please."

The two women turned their backs and stayed apart. And though they avoided each other for a while, by mid-afternoon they had agreed to forget their harshly spoken words, put aside their grievances, and called a truce. Sunniva reckoned that since she was, apparently, going to be stuck with Frida for as long as she and her father remained in Gevehard's village, she may as well save herself the trouble of being disagreeable. Instead, she would try to make the best of a bad situation. That was what her father always told her to do. Compared to the threats that her father had staved off, this argument was trivial. However, acting agreeably was not a skill that her father had taught her. Rather, it was just the opposite. And, like her father, she seemed to habitually poke at other people's hidden soft spots just to get a rise out of them. But, nonetheless, she decided to give agreeableness a try.

After the women had finished the preparations for the evening, Sunniva and Frida stood together to admire how glorious the longhouse looked. "You did a great job today, Frida."

"Do you really think so?"

"Oh, yes," Sunniva lied. Her mother would be proud. "Gevehard and Adelheide will be very pleased when they see how beautifully you managed the longhouse decoration."

On their way back to Innis's house, the rain began to come down hard. They covered their heads with their shawls, grabbed each other's hands and, trying not to slip and fall in the muck, ran, laughing, between the mounds.

They each gathered their dresses, aprons, shawls and scarves, along with their men's clothing. Sunniva showed Frida the new tunic and trousers that she and her mother had sewn for her father. Because he usually dressed in rags whenever he carved, cut wood, and worked in the fields, he had refused her mother's offer to make him a new set of clothing. But when Mildred insisted that it would put her to shame if he did not take more pride in his appearance and, instead, continued to look like a wandering beggar, he agreed to let her make the clothing he would wear to the ceremonial feasts.

The night that she and her mother had finished sewing, he tried them on, and said, "I wish you could be there too, Mildred."

And, likewise, Sunniva also wished her mother was there. But, unfortunately, she was on her own.

She and Frida laid the clothing on the beds and took turns pressing the clothing flat with hot, smooth stones. After it stopped raining, Sunniva carried her father's clothing to the house where he slept. She carefully laid them out flat atop his bedroll and satchels to keep the tunic, trousers and new cloak from wrinkling.

Both Frida and Sunniva put on their best dresses and aprons and combed their hair. Since Frida was married and wore a head scarf, she told Sunniva how much she missed fixing her hair in pretty styles and asked whether she could arrange Sunniva's hair.

Sunniva was delighted and readily agreed with the suggestion. Frida braided two plaits, and as she wound them in spirals and pinned them above each of Sunniva's ears, she passed on a tidy bit of gossip. "I overheard Adelheide speaking to Innis about you."

Sunniva's eyes opened wide in disbelief. She shook her head, and asked, "Why would they talk about me? What did Adelheide say?"

"Keep still, Sunniva. Do not move your head or I will stick you with a hairpin. Can you keep a secret? Aart's parents are in town for tonight's ceremony. They were my neighbors before I married Rodger. Adelheide discussed a match between you and Aart. Adelheide told Innis that Aart's mother showed interest and wants to meet you and your father before they go back home—oh, no," Frida said, and though she clapped both hands over her mouth, she was unable to hide the gleeful look in her eyes. "I cannot say another word about it. I already said too much. But, Aart's father has one of the largest farms in the area and his mother has a big loom shop.

"If you married Aart, it would be a good match for you. Gevehard plans to make him a steersman. Just think, whenever I go home to visit my family, I could come and see you, too. You would be my next-door neighbor. Our children could be best friends."

"What? How can that be?" Sunniva asked, stifling the need to cry. "My mother plans to betroth me to Wynn."

Being next-door neighbors to Frida was the last thing that Sunniva wanted, and the second last thing was to marry Aart. How was this possible? How could people, who she did not even know, think they could plan her life for her? Not only was it assumed that her father would be leaving with Gevehard, but now they, also, had be-gun to plan her betrothal. She did not like to be told what to do, but in this situation, after she had been stripped of a mind of her own, she felt so helpless, she knew the green-clad woman was right.

A woman has no choice but to stifle her anger. She must stuff it into her mouth whole, chew it up, and swallow. Her rage would then eat away at her insides like feasting maggots until she, too, became one of the cursing shades who were buried in the holy grove. And when she opened her mouth, instead of words, a cloud of buzzing flies would burst free to harass those who had told her what to do and who to marry and how to live her life. And like the shades in the holy grove who, after they had been left with nothing but self-defeating, sour malice, she would call upon Lord Spider the Entangler for revenge.

III.

That afternoon, everyone had been tracking the position of Lady Sun's wagon as she drove it across the sky. And, along with the lengthening shadows, those who had been invited to the feast impatiently awaited the doorkeeper's call to assemble in the yard outside the longhouse doors. Finally, when the sun was low enough on the skyline, but before it had set entirely, the doorkeeper blew his horn, and Sunniva was among the first to arrive.

Adelheide had told her to accompany her father when he entered the hall and to sit beside him. And now, here she was, about to sit beside her father in Shipmaster Gevehard's hall on the eve of their voyage.

She idly looked around but her mind was far away. Weighing the dreadful out-come of the curse, which she had witnessed being spoken the day before, against her eager anticipation of seeing Edwina overpower it, she silently uttered pleas and repeat-edly begged Lady Blessed to assure the men's safety. Leaning her weight first into one foot and then into the other, she clasped and unclasped her hands and swayed side to side as she reconsidered the task that the Lady had given her.

Men and women walked into the yard, clothed in their finest. Just as Frida and she had done, the other village women had, also, dug their best dresses, shawls, scarves, and jewelry from the bottoms of their storage trunks. The guests called to one another, gathered in small groups in front of the closed longhouse doors, and talked ex-citedly. The men clapped each other on the back, and the women grabbed each other by the hands and kissed cheeks.

At last, the doorkeeper opened the large, double doors and allowed the men and women to enter. Sunniva stood outside the doors, looking inside while impatiently await-ing her father's tardy arrival. When she heard him call her name, she nearly jumped with excitement and turned to see him waving. He wore his new cloak draped across his right shoulder and pinned in place with a simple bronze pin on his left. His lower legs were wrapped with the new bands that she had woven especially for this occasion.

She was so proud of seeing her father dressed so well that she had to stop herself from pulling the cloak out to its full width to admire its spread. Awed by the gold arm ring that Gevehard had given him, she was dazzled by the way it caught the setting sun's rosy light.

Sunniva pointed to the old, scuffed belt her father had fastened with the plain bronze buckle he had worn for years, and said, "Father, you need a shiny new buckle to wear with your new clothes."

"This one does the job just fine. It holds everything up that it needs to."

Aiken looked her up and down and, after he tucked a loose strand of hair behind her ear, kissed her on the forehead to show how pleased he was with her appearance.

Unable to hold her tongue any longer, Sunniva blurted out, "Are you leaving with Gevehard? Rodger said you might be offered a place on the crew."

"I have yet to make a promise," he said, frowning and shaking his head side to side. "It is too soon to tell." He put his arm around her shoulders, and added, "We had better get inside."

Gevehard stood near the door greeting each man as he entered. Those who were wealthy merchants and farmers, and the men who would be manning the boats stood at their places behind the benches. Each man's wife, sister, or mother stood beside him. Gevehard escorted Aiken to the high table and tapped the place where he would sit at his right, in the seat reserved for the evening's most honored guest. The other men and their wives, all of whom were already standing in place at the high table included Jerold, Edmund, the four steersmen, the owners of the three other ships, and the master shipbuilder. Three open places remained at the center of the table.

Edwina the Friend of Prosperity appeared at the door. Dressed in a manner befitting her name, her gown was dyed the color of dark forest trees and her cloak was blue as gentian flowers. The hems were finished lavishly with layers upon layers of trim. Long gold and silver chains and strings of colorful beads hung around her neck and looped to the level of her belt. Her single plait, neatly braided with red ribbons and wound into a single knot, was pinned at the nape. The rest of its length hung like a rope down the center of her back.

Gevehard bowed graciously and offered her his elbow.

The many gold rings that Edwina wore on her wrist jingled when she lifted her arm and laid her hand upon Gevehard's arm. As the shipmaster and the wisewoman walked slowly toward the high table, each of their steps were accompanied by the sound of that black, iron distaff striking the earthen floor. Her two helpers, Tate and Kendra, followed. One carried a silver pitcher and the other carried two bags, one of which was noticeably larger than the other. Gevehard escorted Edwina to her seat at the high table, on his left, and her helpers took their places behind her. The shipmaster then took his place at the center.

No doubt, Edwina had noticed that she had been seated, not on the shipmaster's right but, rather, on his left. It was the stone carver and his daughter who were seated in the place of greatest honor.

Once they had all taken their rightful places, Adelheide entered. Carrying the gold cup, she walked up the center aisle and faced her husband. The shipmaster's wife then spoke her words of greeting and praised Gevehard's leadership.

She next offered the cup to Aiken. Signs had been observed, Adelheide said, that proved the Lord of Rich-Waters, the Lords of Battle, and Lady Sun were pleased with the words and pictures that Aiken had carved on the memorial stone. And now that the upcoming voyage had clearly been favored to receive their otherworldly blessings, all the villagers were confident of its success.

Sunniva watched Adelheide astutely as she praised Edwina, Jerold, Edmund, and the other men who were seated at the high table. If this was what Lady Blessed expected her to do, she would need to study Adelheide's carefully chosen words and phrasing.

Adelheide stepped down from the dais and carried the cup to the men who had taken their places at the long rows of tables. She stood before each of the landholders and merchants and praised him for his stewardship of the land and for all that he did to increase the wealth of their community. She praised each of the crew members for his courage and strength. As each man accepted her cup and drank from it, he swore to be Gevehard's man, to fight valiantly, and to dutifully serve all the men and women in the village. He then vowed to send his soul to Mother Torment's lowest land of the dead if he ever broke his promise.

This night was one of the most important celebratory feasts of the year and was expected to last till shortly before dawn. Though it took a long time for each man to get his due, each man and woman shared in this celebration of their community and listened attentively. They were all content and happy to hear each man named, thanked, and honored for his service. It reinforced their feelings of importance, the bonds between them all, their history and their friendship, the roles each person filled within the group, and their need for one another. It was like saying: we are a community; we are a group; we are important to one another; and we respect each person for what he does for all of us.

After Adelheide had finished greeting each man, she returned to the high table and offered Gevehard the cup again. Once she had taken her place at the table, Gevehard cradled the gold cup in both hands and, raising it to shoulder height, he extended it to the assembled host. Each man lifted his cup in unison and together they honored the Lord of Rich-Waters and their forebears.

Gevehard then said, loudly, "Let us eat well."

Everyone sat and, immediately, women, men, boys, and girls hurried in, carrying trenchers full of pork and roots, platters covered with round breads, bowls of pickled foods, and crocks filled with butter and cheeses. Each man's wife, mother, or daughter served her man before she served herself. She ladled stew onto his plate, gave him pickles, butter, and bread, and kept his cup full. Those men who, during the shipping off-season, rowed fishing boats, plowed fields, tended cattle and sheared sheep, became fierce fighting men overnight. The hall was noisy with their voices as they grabbed food and speared hunks of meat with their knives and yelled at one another.

Sunniva was both excited and intimidated by their barely contained rowdiness. But, she also suspected that, although it had been many years since her father had been in a hall as large as this one and had heard the roar of so many men's voices, this was where he wanted to be most of all.

Sunniva caught sight of the desperate look on Frida's face. Though she longed for Rodger's undivided attention, she was forced to lean back from the table so that he could jostle over a joke with the friend who was seated on Frida's opposite side. In this house full of men, Frida's husband, with the faraway look in his eyes, was gone already. Rodger was no longer hers. He was now Gevehard's man.

This observation then reminded Sunniva that the shipmaster might, also, own her father. She reached over and, because she knew how guarded he was of his blind side, she was careful not to startle him when she touched him on his elbow.

He looked at her, smiled and said, "I trust you have my back, Sunniva."

Yes, I have my father's back, she said proudly to herself. If only she could hang onto him and not let go until she got him home again—but how likely was that?

In time, the men's hunger was sated. Gevehard stood, and his guests followed his lead. Those who had missed the signal were nudged in the sides and stood, shame-faced. Gevehard escorted Edwina and Adelheide to the door, and the others left the hall in his wake.

The woman who managed Adelheide's household took over. Standing at the front she ordered those who were in her service to prepare for the wisewoman's cer-emony. Women cleared the tables of the tableware. Men broke down the tables and piled the trestles and planks against the back wall. The benches were set parallel to the dais in the front with a wide aisle was left open down the center.

Up at the front of the longhouse, the permanent high table on the dais remained and several of the tables at both ends were moved and placed behind the ones in the center to make a double-wide platform. Rugs were laid on top and a step-stool was set beside it. Two grunting men lifted a heavy log chair, which had been carved from a single stump of wood, and set it in the center, close to the front edge.

Tate busied herself with the items she had carried into the longhouse. She took several items from the bags and set them in place on the table that had now become the wisewoman's high platform.

Kendra waved her arms, called to the singers in the women's chorus, and hurried them into their places. Because several of the singers still lingered in the center of the hall, she had to clap her hands and chase them down. Eventually, all the singers were clustered off to right side of the high platform and turned toward it at a slight angle. Torches were refreshed, the hearths were stoked, and men and women were allowed back inside.

A thick and heavy feeling of anticipation, combined with unease, spread like waves pouring in from the sea. Those men, who had been boisterous before, were hushed, and their silence was tense. The combination of everyone's hopes and fears felt so strong that the sum total of their mass expectancy threatened to overwhelm them all.

Among the chorus singers were women who believed that everything must be perfect. Fearful of making a mistake, lest a lapse occur and doom the men to failure, they hummed the tune quietly and repeated the words to themselves.

To hide from Edwina's gaze, Sunniva had taken a place at the far end of the back row. Moving her head side-to-side, she spotted her father in a row near the back. He was seated beside one of the men with whom he had become friendly during their practice sessions down on the strand. Frida and Rodger sat close to the front, near the center. Innis sat beside Rodger on his left and Frida sat on his right. Sunniva was moved by the obvious affection the newly-weds had for one another. Rodger held Frida's hand, patted it, and looked lovingly into her face. Frida squeezed their hands together and looked happy to share this brief moment with her husband before he went back to being Gevehard's man.

Outside the longhouse, numerous burning torches lit the yard. More men and women were crowded outside the doors, and those who could find room to stand against the walls squeezed inside. The fates of the men who had been chosen to row the boats would impact the lives of the all the farmers, merchants, field workers, cattle herders, fishermen, servants, those who tended the salt pans, and the women who wove in the loom shops. Failure meant a hard winter, even death from sickness and starvation. Loss of even one shipload of trade-goods could set some farmers, craftsmen, and merchants back for years.

Last to enter, Gevehard took his place at the front of the benches and turned to face the assembled crowd. Once everyone was quiet, Edwina walked through the doors.

Her pace was slow, her demeanor stately, as she progressed down the central aisle. Like a boat cleaving worried waters with her prow, she rode the surface of their expectant waiting and left behind a glittering wake. To fill herself with the force she required for her cord-spinning, she soaked up the strength of all those in the building, pulled their eyes, their soul-stuff, the power of their luck, and focused it to a pinpoint.

The reverence, the fear, and the awe with which the wisewoman approaches the powers, who control abundance and weather, is cautious. Like the song with which a woman greets the hearth each morning to constrain fire's deadly wrath, the only times when connection with the otherworldly forces is deemed harmless enough for contact, is when the contrived orderliness of ceremony transforms its power into something steady enough to hold it safely.

During ceremony rules govern the participant's safety, and barriers are erected between those who live in this world and those who live in otherworlds. Ceremony transfers the otherworldly power to a person or to an object. Few can handle it, but the wisewoman who leads the ceremony has learned how to control the dreadful powers. Through invocation of those mysterious, otherworldly presences, a wisewoman fills herself with the individual power she needs to walk between the worlds. For these reasons, she is granted the strength she needs to take on and do battle with the devastating forces of drought, sickness, floods, wind storms, and human enemies who threaten those who look to her for their safe-keeping.

The greater is the wisewoman's desired effect, the greater is her peril. Her greatest enemy is chaos. She desires, above all else, the power to influence others and the course of events. Her need to fill herself with individual power, her craving for the intoxication of her rapture, and the fervor and ecstasy that accompanies the experience of sending her soul to otherworlds is balanced by the fear that she may be unable to force those otherworldly powers to do as she commands.

To traverse that boundary into the unknown, the wisewoman becomes part of the creative forces. By identification with the powers of the creator, she makes things happen by swaying the otherworldly powers to do her bidding. Akin to Mother

Necessity, Father Time, and the egg around which they spin, she makes meaningful order from the, otherwise, chaotic forces of the abyss that threaten to devour them all. Truly, it is a fearsome strength.

Whenever she ventures into the otherworlds, she knowingly risks falling prey to those same destructive powers against whom she must pit herself. For fear of other-worldly contagion, anything or anyone who touches or embodies this power must reside in the margins, live in the liminal places where they will be set apart from those whom they serve.

Edwina stopped directly in front of Gevehard.

The shipmaster spread his arms and greeted her by name and appellation. "Edwina the Friend of Prosperity, I command you, now, to see what is yet to come. Spin our fates with your words. Give our esteemed seamen the glory of success."

The wisewoman accepted his demand with a serious nod of her head.

Gevehard looked at all those who were seated, stood against the walls, or were crowded in the yard outside the doors and addressed them, saying, "Edwina the wisewoman will now draw wealth to our village on the thread she spins and give us a victorious voyage."

He held Edwina' elbow to help her step onto the stool, and from there, onto the high platform. He then took his seat on Adelheide's left, at the center of the hall.

Holding her distaff in her right hand, the wisewoman lifted her arms overhead and called out in a loud voice, "Lord of Rich-Waters the Bountiful, Lady Sun the Brightest Light and Fire of Air and Sky, and Lords of Battle the Protectors of Seaman, grace us with your presence. Make the longships swift and quicken their journey. Rejoice in the men's victories whenever they come up against their foes. Promise the seafarers fruitful gains in the markets. Keep the men and their families safe from sick-ness and from harm. Assure their safe return. Lords and Ladies, we depend upon your good will. Let those who dwell in this village receive your bounteous goodness."

Spreading her arms out to the sides like wings, Edwina flapped her wide sleeves several times. She then struck her iron distaff on the tabletop in a loud and insistent rhythm. Like the beat of an enormous, sonorous drum, the rhythm swelled to fill the space inside the longhouse. And as the men and women who sat on the benches and who stood against the walls felt the vibrations inside their chests, the increasingly expectant fervor Edwina was building among them grew in strength.

When the time was right, Edwina nodded to Kendra to begin the singing. At first, the women's voices sounded soft and shy. But as the chorus singers' confidence increased, they felt the beat reverberate inside their chests, drank in the air and filled their lungs. Their breaths rose in their throats and they pumped out the music until it filled the hall.

In time, the wisewoman sat on the chair made from a tree trunk, placed the dis-taff between her knees, pulled fleece from its top, twisted it into a thread, and wound it onto her whorl. She twirled the spindle and began to spin a length of thread. Every eye in the room watched it drop. And as the lengthening thread neared the floor, some of the onlookers stood up from their seats to get a good view of the dangling whorl's descent.

Edwina allowed it to fall all the way to the floor where it tipped. Tate picked it up and handed it back to Edwina. She then wound the thread around the axis and spun another length. After Tate had handed it to Edwina a second time, the wise-woman fingered the thread's full length to silently read the entire voyage the men would take. All those who were assembled held their breaths as she studied it with meticulous care.

Edwina came to the end, carefully wound the thread around the whorl's axis and hooked it onto the ring at the top. She stood up from the chair, and the two burly men discretely lifted it down from the platform.

She turned her back to the audience. When she turned around again, everyone gasped. A large sea eagle stood before them. The bird's hooked, yellow ochre beak was almost the height and width of the mask's black head. Its large, round eyes were pointedly terrifying.

Barely shuffling her feet, Edwina began to turn in a small circle, like a whorl spinning on an invisible thread. Gradually picking up speed, she lifted her arms out to her sides with the distaff tilted at an angle. Her braid lifted until was nearly horizontal. Her sleeves flapped like wings, and her skirts filled and bloomed at the hem. And her increasingly frenzied spinning gave flight to the sea eagle.

Both Kendra and Tate jumped onto the high platform and held their arms out to their sides. Though forced to avoid that spinning, iron missile, they both were ready to ease the wisewoman away from the table edges or to catch her in case she began to tip and fall.

Sunniva understood what Edwina was doing. What she had merely imagined, was being given material, tangible presence, right before her eyes. For, she, too, had become a bird when she had spun thread. But in this case, the bird and the spindle were one and same. To complete the totality of her transformation, Edwina's spinning whorl-like, bodily form had become the sea eagle.

In time, Sunniva stopped watching the distaff carrier's dance. Her eyes closed, her head tipped forward and, though she had forgotten the words, she continued to hum the tune quietly, beneath her breath.

It was then that Lady Blessed walked in through the open doorway. Unremarked by anyone in the longhouse, she shuffled alongside the wall, came up to Sunniva, stood directly behind her, touched her on the shoulder, leaned in close, and whispered, "Come along with me."

Sunniva sensed the Lady's breath upon her skin, felt the pressure on her shoulder, and heard the intimately spoken voice. She jerked her head to the side and nodded agreeably. Lady Blessed carried the same iron distaff with a spinning whorl hooked onto the ring at the top that she had carried the day before. Sunniva took the Lady's hand and followed her out the door. Walking hand in hand, the two women passed unnoticed through the crowd gathered outside, went around the corner and came upon a ladder leaning against the longhouse eaves.

The Lady climbed to the top of the ladder. She first lifted one foot onto the steeply slanted roof and then the other. Sunniva followed her up the ladder. The Lady extended her hand and pulled Sunniva onto the thatch. Lady Blessed crept toward the peak. Poking the distaff into the thatch to steady herself before she took each step, she looked back now and then to affectionately encourage Sunniva along.

At that height, Sunniva was not as confident as was Lady Blessed. With each halting step she took, she bent so low to grasp and hang onto the thatch, she was nearly crawling.

Although the moon's pale, blue light lent the two women a whitish, faintly translucent appearance, no one in the yard seemed to notice them climb onto the roof. When Lady Blessed and Sunniva reached the topmost peak, they straddled it to position themselves upon a platform from which they could work their spinning from a more expansive view than was Edwina's. The Lady unhooked the whorl from the ring at the top of the distaff, handed both to Sunniva, and told her to spin the thread.

Eager to see Edwina battle Lord Spider in the guise of a sea eagle, Sunniva held the distaff between her crooked elbow and her waist. She twisted the fleece and wound it around the whorl to get it started. She twirled the axis with her thumb and fingers, and as the spindle dropped slowly, she listened to the muffled women's voices coming from down below.

There were other sounds too. Less like voices, the music sounded more like the bronze war-horns she had heard the village men blow. The horns were made from long tubes shaped in a half-circle. A man blew into the smallest end and the sound came out the wide, funnel-shaped end. Frida had told Sunniva that, whenever the men were out to sea or passing through a fog bank, the longships talked to one another through their war-horns.

Speaking in a wordless language all their own, the horns' long, deep, mournful notes occasionally broke into short, joyful, high-pitched yips. Like strange birds calling back and forth to one another with their low and high-pitched harmonics, the tones slipped up and down to make simple melodies. At first, the haunting music was too faint to ascertain from which direction it came. But, in time, the songs became increasingly, aggressively, louder.

Sunniva was certain the sounds were not coming from anywhere in the village. Once she had located the direction from which they came, she turned her gaze out past the mounds and buildings. From where she stood, she could see the shoreline, and the numerous small islands and sand bars in the bay surrounded by the sparkling, moon-reflected water.

It was then that her sight of the star-lit sky and the reflective sea split apart like a drawn curtain. Out beyond the opening, the sky was colored bright yellow. From the height at which Sunniva stood, she could see distant longships heading toward the shoreline. They passed in between, behind, and in front of the small, rocky islands in the bay. As the horns alerted those who lived in the village of the ship's immanent arrival, men and women ran to greet them. And as they ran they counted: One, two, three. One, two, three. One, two, three. Jamming their fists, worriedly, into their mouths, the men and women asked, "Do you see a fourth?"

"No, I see only three."

The increasingly frantic women cried in high pitched voices, "Where is the fourth ship?"

The men and women stood expectantly at the edge of the sea listening to the long, mournful tones sliding up and down and breaking, now and then, into excited yips. The three longships came straight at them and stopped when their prows struck the sandy beach. A charred, wood stump was all that remained of a serpent head on one of the boats.

Some of the men and women ran through the surf to help pull the boats ashore. Men inside the ships threw out the anchors and leapt into the splashing surf. They set the planks against the gunwales. The weary seamen clambered down the steep ramps and trounced through the shallow waves. Those who were able to, carried on their backs the men who were too weak or too badly wounded to walk on their own. Some men fell face down and spread their arms to embrace the earth. Others ran to wives, fathers, mothers, and children, and hugged their families close.

From her distance atop the high-pitched roof, Sunniva could see herself, running frantically from one seaman to the next, looking into every man's face. If her father had joined the crew, as Rodger said he would, he was neither among those men who were standing upright, nor was he among the wounded.

The shipmaster was the last to climb from the boats. Gevehard lifted one leg over the gunwale and halted. It took too great an effort to lift his second leg. Four men took him by the arms and lifted him down. He shook them off and, leaning heavily on an oar, limped through the surf, dragging the thickly bandaged leg behind him. He looked not at all like the vital man who was feasting that night in his longhouse, but weary and beaten.

Stately Adelheide never lost her composure. She walked up to her husband, offered him the cup and greeted him. After Gevehard had supped, he spread his arms out wide enough to gather all the men and women to him at once.

Gevehard told the villagers how they had had only a few days remaining before they reached the harbor. Believing they were in friendly waters, their heavily laden ships had approached shorelines that had always been held by men whom they trusted and with whom they had never been at war. Surprised by unknown sea-raiders, who were sheltered in an estuary, which their allies had always protected in the past, he and his men had fought hard and overcome the pirates. But, in the end, they had lost most of their trade goods in the fighting. They filled the three ships with the wounded. Those who were still fit to row had taken seats on the benches. But because there were not enough men to row the fourth ship, they had been forced to leave Wave Crestar behind. They filled her belly with their dead, towed her out to sea, and set her aflame with a torch.

Those women, whose worst fears were now confirmed, began to howl. Gevehard walked from one wailing woman to the next, held her tightly and praised the man who was never coming home again. He said her husband, brother, father, or son had fought valiantly and rowed with enduring strength. "But so many men were killed," he said. And repeatedly mumbling the refrain, he seemed to be unable to take it in, but needed to convince himself of the truth, "So many men were killed. So many were killed."

The sounds of the women and children's cries were deafening.

Tears were streaming down Sunniva's cheeks. How could all the men and women, who were, even now, seated inside the longhouse, not hear the dreadful keening?

Lady Blessed took back her distaff and, as she wound the thread onto the spindle axis, addressed Sunniva, saying, "Storm-pale, I need intermediaries in this world. You have seen what can happen. I have shown you the natural progression of events that will follow the curse that Erol evoked. A foretelling is a vision of the forces at work and how they will bring about events in the future.

"But through your interference you can alter this course of events and bring the curse to a halt. What you have seen can be prevented by riding the Lord of Rich-Waters' winds in the guise of a goshawk."

"Edwina will fight off the threats," Sunniva said, frantically.

"No, Edwina is playing both sides. It is now up to you."

"But how can I change the course of events?"

"Sunniva, I favor those who praise goodness and benevolence and turn my back on those who forget me or prefer the discord that Spider offers. I stand for connections between people. Rather than favoring those who rise above all others, and the achievements of single, heroic figures, I encourage men and women to work together for the good of all. I represent the power of voices that, when raised in song, move people's sentiments to rapture together. I stand for respectful, patient negotiation. Change happens slowly when people work together and show kindness to one another. To comfort the brokenhearted who mourn, to free the bound, to treat the wounded and those in pain, to respect others, to neither steal nor bring about harm: this is what I stand for. I dismiss my enemies and welcome my allies. Anyone who serves me, does so at my pleasure. I am the one who puts them in a place of power, and I will put them out if they displease me. I decide how power works and, also, who is allowed to exercise it. Now, Sunniva, I order you to spin the men's fates another way."

"But how?"

"Gevehard will know from the song and flight of birds how to avoid the pirates who will be hiding in an estuary."

"But what will I do?"

"I will show you. Who is better suited to this task than you? Your father's life may be at stake in the outcome."

"No. It is unfair of you to ask this of me. I cannot wage war against the Lord of Thieves. You are stronger than me. You do it."

"Sunniva, I cannot do this alone. What I showed you can be averted. Though the vision of three ships coming ashore foretells the natural progression of events the curse evoked, a strong act of willfulness can halt the dark forces that Erol has set in motion. I, alone, cannot do it. To challenge the curse lies beyond the realm I govern. I must have intermediaries in this world. It is not Spider the Entangler himself, but she who does his bidding who you must battle. I have confidence in your abilities to go head to head against the sea eagle in the guise of a goshawk. I know you can do it Sunniva."

"Edwina? You want me to fight Edwina?" Sunniva cried in a choked screech, "No."

"Sunniva, I ask you to wage war on my account. Only you can take Edwina down."

"No. I will do nothing of the sort. I did not expect this."

"The secrets of otherworldly flight are not given out to dabblers. If you want to keep your own little world controllable and contained, and to fly through soft, pretty, clouds, then you are wasting my time. The otherworlds are not more beautiful than this world is. They, too, are hard and fast as iron and equally conflicted."

"Then I do not want to be a wisewoman. One world of trouble is enough. Find someone else to wage war against the Lord of Thieves on your behalf."

It was then that a loud crack resounded so forcefully that the entire building seemed to shake, and the connection between Lady Blessed and Sunniva was severed.

Sunniva looked around. There was no sign of Lady Blessed. The sea was placidly reflecting the brilliant, white moon, just as it had before. Near the shoreline, the four, unmanned, freshly varnished longships were resting in their slipways. Only now did Sunniva become aware that, somehow, she was standing atop the longhouse roof. Momentarily uncertain how she had gotten there, she was confused and did not understand what had possessed her to climb onto the roof.

She bent low, crept down the steep incline, and jumped the short distance between the eaves and the ground. She ran around the corner and snuck inside the door. She shuffled around the inside walls and joined the clustered singers. Wiping the tears wetting her cheeks, she looked at the expectant men's faces, fearful that many of them were as good as dead already. First she had been asked to broker peace and had refused the task. Then she had been asked to pick sides and had failed to accept what Lady Blessed had requested. Did it mean that she had sided with Spider the Entangler and would be the cause of her father's inevitable death? Were the events, which she had seen, both in the holy grove and then from atop the rooftop, similar in horror to those that her father saw whenever he awoke screaming in the night after his visits to the dreamtime? If so, she now understood his terror.

The wisewoman no longer wore her mask. She opened her arms expansively, and as she spoke, her words took flight, as if on wings, to pass above the men and women's heads. "In the guise of a sea eagle, I ventured to the Lord of Rich-Waters' home. I carried the cup and praised him. I promised him your gifts and asked him to favor the men's sea passage. He assured me of his gracious blessing in return for your offerings. He promises to fill your boats with wealth."

Wives squeezed their husband's hands, and the men and women looked at each other with joy in their hearts.

Edwina unsheathed her knife. She cut the thread from the fleece atop her distaff and walked slowly to the far, left edge of the platform. She laid the loose end on the table and, as she walked backwards, unwound the whorl and laid the cord flat on the rugs covering the tables. "In the markets to the east," she said, "you will fill your boat with grain. In the markets to the south you will find fruits, dyes, precious metals, colored stones and jugs filled with oil. From the markets to the west you will bring home copper and tin."

When she came to the end of the thread, she turned to face all the men and women and said, "I tell you this: you will give wing to the serpent-headed longships. With Shipmaster Gevehard the Brave-heart's leadership you will joyfully skim the billowing waves. Never will you falter. The Lord of Rich-Waters will dispel the stormy, rain-driven breakers and bless you with favorable breezes, calm seas, and wealth."

Edwina picked up the end that lay at the right end of the platform and, as she pulled it, wound it around her fingers to make a small ball. "This is the thread of your voyage. I now draw the ships home again. They will meet the waves and return the seamen to their families."

Tate and Kendra each took one of Edwina's arms and helped her step down from the platform. She handed the thread to Adelheide and told her to weave the blessed thread into her textiles. Gevehard and Adelheide gave Edwina a purse filled with coins. A young woman came forward, carrying an armload of fine fabrics, and another woman brought her a beautiful necklace strung with colorful beads. Men and women stood up from the benches and, swarming around the wisewoman, praised her and showered her with additional gifts.

Standing off to the side, Sunniva questioned why Edwina had said nothing about fighting pirates. Whose ships had she filled with wealth? The sea-raiders'? The wise-woman had done nothing to keep the men safe from the frightful fate that she, herself, had seen befall them. No, Edwina had lied. The wisewoman had not pulled all four of the ships home. She had led the men to believe they were safe when, instead, they were rowing their ships into a trap. Edwina had woven a spell of deception.

If the wisewoman had become smitten with those forces that Spider the Entangler embodied who, in his desire to challenge the very forces of creation, had made a mockery of Nature by monstrously copying her creations when he fathered the children with whom he set chaos in motion, then Edwina too, like Sider, after she had fallen under his sway, had made a mockery of truth and had set the forces of chaos in motion with her lies.

In Sunniva's dream-like vision, Gevehard's demeanor had been so unlike the enthusiastic man Edwina described. Now that Sunniva had seen both the vision of the men who fought the pirates and those who came home in tatters, she was uncertain what to do. Truth was a slippery thing. If the wisewoman had hidden the truth, where had it gone? If by never saying something she could make it untrue, though she knew it was true, what was she supposed to believe?

Sunniva knew the answer: She was the holder of truth. She was the truth-speaker. And if that was so, she had been given a frightful responsibility.

Now, when so many lives were at stake, the weakened connection between Sunniva and Lady Blessed had broken under the pressure. And just as Erol had done in the holy grove, Sunniva took out her fear and anger on Lady Blessed. To excuse her failure, Sunniva blamed the Lady for dragging her into this hopelessly entangled situation. What if she had been given more time, might she have spun their fates another way? What if she had been given an iron distaff? But now it was too late. There was no time to find out.

Men and women were milling about inside the hall and wandering leisurely out the doors. Sunniva found her father speaking with several men. When he saw her, he threw his arm around her shoulders, and pushed her forward in front of the others to proudly extol the addition of her voice to the women's chorus.

Sunniva, in turn, was shy of the men's gazes. She wiped her eyes and cheeks with her fingers, pulled away, and tried to hide behind her father's back.

Lifting her lips close to his ear, she whispered "What will happen if Edwina did not spin the cord right? What if she serves two masters and only three ships make it home? What will happen if the servants curse the voyage and plan to wage war against Gevehard's kin?"

Aiken looked bewildered and squeezed her tightly. "Sunniva," he said in a low voice, "where did you get those ideas?"

Scared to speak of what she had seen, had neither agreed to do, nor had had the time to fix, she feared that her own cowardice would make her guilty of all the men's deaths, including her own father's. Sunniva stared in horror at the bleak possibility that she might be cursed to go to Mother Torment's lowest land of the dead, where she would suffer everlastingly along with the oath-breakers. She pressed her balled fists into her eyes and stifled a sob.

When Aiken saw how disturbed she was, he said, "Surely, you are all worked up by the feasting ceremony. But you must not fall prey to wild notions."

He eased her away from the others and led her through the doorway. The yard was lit by flaming torches, the waxing moon, and the star-warrior's torch-lit sky.

Aiken caught Sunniva's hand in his and remarked upon how brightly the star-torches shone that night. From where they stood, at the southern edge of the Merchant Sea, the stars sparkled more brilliantly than they ever did back home. "Think how they would look," he said, "if I were to observe them from Wave Cre-star's deck. I would have an expansive view from one skyline to the other."

Sunniva gasped, squeezed his hand between hers and held on tightly, wishing to pull him away from his fate with the strength of her arms alone. Though she feared the truth might come out and cause something dreadful to happen, she said, nonetheless, "No, you must not leave me here. You will not come back. I did not see you on the shore. You will die at sea. I know you will." She pleaded, "You must not go. You will be killed."

Confused, Aiken asked what she meant. But when he got no answer, he said, "Surely, you are speaking gibberish. Show the men and women you have confidence in me. I swear my stone is good as a shield. The signs I carved arouse protection from the Lord of Rich-Waters, Lady Sun and the Lords of Battle. Words are as good as anything that a man or woman can contrive. I am satisfied with the communication I use. The secret signs and pictures I carved are powerful enough to guarantee the men of a successful voyage. I put little store in visions like those that wisewomen are said to have. Dreamtime experiences only plague a man and remind him of remorse. There is no truth to be found in them, only wild make-believe and terrible memories that haunt and disturb one's sleep."

But Sunniva was unpersuaded by his confessed terror of the dreamtime and demanded he listen to what she had to say. "Edwina claims she can read the threads the Matrones spin. She says she can move between the worlds and change what is yet to come. But I fear Edwina has done something wrong, something terribly wrong. I am certain of it. Something dreadful will happen unless I fix it."

Aiken shook his head in frustration, and asked, "Where did you come up with these foolish notions, Sunniva? You cannot fix something that the Matrones have destined. The wisewoman's spinning means nothing. No one can change fate by spinning a man's life thread a second time. There is only one thread and that is the one the three sisters spin. No woman living in this world can change it. It is fixed forever."

In an attempt to explain what he had done when he carved the stone, he said, "The act of writing secret signs uses of the power of words to appeal to the Lords and Ladies who sit at the high tables in their otherworldly halls. It asks them to look with favor upon men and women's endeavors. Because it asks the forebears to speak on behalf of their descendants, it becomes the means by which a man or woman can influence the Matrones. These actions become part of the thread and start further actions. But once the thread is spun, all that went before will affect what is yet to come. One may neither go back in time nor change the future. It is only one's actions now, in the present, that can influence what is yet to come."

Unsure of whether she followed his argument, Sunniva asked, "But then, how can one affect things that happened in the past before they become the future? What if the ships were cursed? Is it possible to spin a thread in the present that will affect what is yet to come and, in this way, counteract the curse?"

Her sighing father shook his head in irritation. Stymied by his inability to answer his daughter's questions, he sought escape by drawing attention to the great bridge spanning the nighttime sky. Aiken raised his arm and, with broad, sweeping motions, indicated the full arc that connected the worlds. He pointed to the southern skyline where the brightest star in the sky flashed red and blue. That was where the gatekeeper guarded the entrance to the sky-bridge. Unlike back home, where trees and hills blocked their sight, here one could see the entire span, from one skyline to the other.

How Sunniva's father thought to reassure his unhappy daughter by drawing attention to the full breadth and magnitude of the sky was unclear. For, in contrast to feeling uplifted, she thought only of how small and inconsequential this world would look to the Lords of Battle, Lady Sun, or the Lord of Rich-Waters when they stood up there and looked down. According to her father, she could plead for their favor. But, in comparison to their might, she would seem smaller than an ant. Why should they care?

She doubted whether anyone could have an impact on how things came about. In her experience, she had only been tormented by the fruitless promises that Lady Blessed had, as of yet, never made good on. And now that she was expected to wage war on the Lady's behalf, Sunniva's loss of faith had led her to conclude that to sway those mighty powers to one's cause is not simple, but rather, is an arduous and dangerous task.

She buried her face in her hands, and cried, "I want to go home tomorrow."

"No, Sunniva. Before we can leave for home, we will be here for several more days. I promised Gevehard that I would be here on the morning the men leave. I must lead them in a ceremony in the holy grove that will honor the stone and venerate their ancestors."

Fearing that her father would then leap onto the boat and float away to his inevitable death, Sunniva cried, "No, we must go home right now. I promised mother we would help with the fieldwork."

Aiken gently held her face between his rough, calloused hands. Her skin was soft, clear, and unblemished. If he could, he would treat Sunniva with the same care he gave to a delicate, thin-walled, wooden vessel that he had turned on the lathe from burled maple. Too beautiful to use, he would never take it to market. Instead, he would wax it, put it on a high shelf in his work shed to prevent it from cracking and would take it down, only now and then, to admire. No, he did not want Sunniva to feel the strife that threatened their lives. He wanted to protect her from the misfortunes and conflict in this world, the suffering and the trials that life provoked.

Though he wanted to open his heart to her, the barriers he had erected between them were not that easily broken down. He could not tell a young woman about a fighting man's life. Men do not tell women how threatened they feel. Only another fighting man understands the fear he lives with daily. He is scared all the time but never talks about it. When a man acts bravely, it does not mean that he is unafraid but, rather, that he is willing to put his life on the line for something of greater importance, something he truly believes in—the welfare of his home, his family, his village, and the men to whom he has sworn allegiance. After that, he needs to keep his faith. He needs to believe that he will come through to the other side of danger alive.

A story, such as the one that Edwina had given them, offered hope. But when its promises fail to come true, people turn to despair. They bitterly resent those who have offered unfounded beliefs in wishes. He, too, felt the pressure of the villager's hope. It was a heavy burden to bear.

If Aiken could have spoken these thoughts aloud, he would have given his daughter the totality of all that he had learned. To live is to suffer from strife. Pleasure is momentary and elusive. Yet, it is good to wake each day. One can either fall prey to trouble or face it head-on. One by one, each choice leaves him with less freedom. And when there are no choices left, Endbringer cuts his life thread.

Unless a man is certain of his luck, fear will bring even the strongest man to a halt. Aiken knew. War had made him. Death had made him. War had killed his father. War had killed his uncle. War had killed his chieftain. War had killed his friends. After he had seen all those good men die, men who had been so dear to him, how could he live? He fought death off every day.

But because he could not speak such thoughts aloud, he said instead, "Tonight Edwina did what Gevehard commanded. She assured the men of success. Whether or not she spoke the truth does not matter. She gave men and women hope."

If any man understood what it was like to see Treachery looking out through the eyes of those whom you thought were your friends and allies, he was the one. But, although his daughter had also seen treachery, Aiken was as deaf to her entreaties as his own chieftain had been to his warnings when he had tried to caution Torwald to watch his back. Nobody wanted to listen to a doomsayer. Aiken did not understand what Sunniva had seen. He did not listen to what she had to say. Nor did he understand that war had made his daughter, too.

There was only one way to answer Sunniva's distraught questions. "It would have been wrong for the wisewoman to have pointed to one man and to have said, 'You will die on the voyage, but your bench mate will return.' What matters is the faith that men have in Shipmaster Gevehard and their belief that they will make it home again. That is all that truly matters. That is the only way a man or a woman can live each day."

IV.

Before he parted from her at the door to Innis's house, Aiken commanded his daughter to stand firm. Be resolute. Be loyal. Watch and learn from Adelheide. "She is a woman of fortitude. When Gevehard is gone, the villagers look to her for guidance. Even when pitted against the worst imaginable conditions, people trust her to hold them together. And, you too, Sunniva, must be strong. Learn to make the best from whatever you are given. However you draw the lots, serve others dutifully. Stand tall and show me that you are the steadfast daughter of a former fighting man. Make me proud, Sunniva. Show your faith in the memorial stone I carved."

Sunniva looked into her father's face, so aglow in the blue, long-shadowed moonlight, and knew that what her mother had said was true—her father was a beautiful man.

Sunniva opened the door and walked inside. Rodger's two sisters were asleep. She lit a small rush lamp from the glowing embers in the hearth, climbed the ladder, and sat on the edge of the straw-filled pallet. She was proud of her father and wanted him to be equally proud of his daughter. She was born from a bloodline of warriors. The knife had mothered her. She would be as fearless as the men and women who had gone before her. Those men had shed their blood protecting the home where she was born. That was what her father had taught her.

Be fierce and resolute, her father had said. Show loyalty, he had said. Be like Adelheide, he had said. But Sunniva knew about another, secretive, side of the shipmaster's wife. She knew what happened when Gevehard was gone from home. She knew some of the secrets that the servants shared with one another—the secrets they held like knives to their master's throats along with threats to let the whole truth out unless their silence was bartered in exchange for small, appropriately valued freedoms.

Frida, Roger, and Innis came in, acting giddy. His mother quietly left the newly-weds alone. She crawled into the bed that she shared with her sleeping daughters and, no doubt, covered her ears with a pillow. Sunniva heard Frida and Roger kiss, grunt, pant, and moan one more time before circumstances forced them both to sleep alone for the duration of the voyage. Maybe tonight would be their lucky night. Maybe tonight they would make the baby that Rodger, Frida, and Innis wanted so badly. But thoughts of Frida carrying a child who might be born an orphan, and of Rodger, who might never see his child, made Sunniva start to cry all over again.

Shortly afterward, Mila climbed the ladder and, as she prepared for sleep, asked guardedly, "Can we be friends again?"

But after Sunniva had seen how swiftly Mila could turn from friend to enemy, she did not trust her. How could she? Yet, because they shared the same bed, she had no alternative but to say, "Perhaps we can agree to call a truce."

"I was wrong about you Sunniva, you did stand up for me. I heard the way you spoke to Frida. You are more like me than like the landholders. When war breaks out we will need people like you who are acceptable to both sides."

Though Sunniva nodded silently, she was sharp with her answer. "I will only sue for peace. I will not act as a spy. My father is an honorable man who taught me to hate people who game both sides."

Mila sensed she had gotten off on the wrong foot again, changed her line of questioning to a more neutral topic, and asked, "What was it like to sing for the wisewoman?" But when Sunniva did not reply, Mila added, "You and me make a good team, Sunniva—say something."

But when Sunniva refused to face her, Mila finished undressing, slipped beneath the covers, turned away from Sunniva, and curled up on her side.

Since she had no option but to sleep beside Mila, Sunniva held it off for as long as she could. She sat on the edge of the mattress, slowly unpinned her hair, combed and loosely plaited it, pulled off her dress, neatly folded it, and packed it inside her satchel.

She blew out the flame on the small rush lamp, crawled in beneath the bedclothes and sheepskins, pulled the covers up to her chin and stared into the darkness. Though she longed for Lady Blessed's comfort, she did not see her seated in the rafters that night. Sunniva felt lost and alone. To console herself, she pulled her elbows in tightly and hugged herself. As much as she admired her father, he had given her little reassurance. Even tonight, his red stone had drawn all his attention, just as it had for the last several months. Hild was all he had spoken of.

In search of a reason not to have seen her father disembark from the boat, she convinced herself that he had never left. He had never gone to sea. She and her father would go home. He would ask her a riddle and poke fun at her and make her laugh. They would be safe from harm when Wave Crestar went up in flames.

But just the thought of the boat in flames was more than she could bear. Her ribs tightened around her heart. She feared it would burst from the pressure, and a squeezed cry rose in her throat.

Was it true that she only wanted to see pretty pictures? According to the Lady, it was wrong to believe that, if she became a wisewoman, she would fly unconstrained in the guise of a goshawk to a place where she could seek an otherworldly husband and indulge in pleasant adventures.

When Lady Blessed demanded that she act as an intermediary in this world, and travel to otherworlds on her behalf, because Sunniva had misunderstood the full scope of a wisewoman's practice, she had flinched. She had not built up her strength.

When her father was young, he had practiced daily to build up his strength. He told her a fighter must never flinch but willingly run into a skirmish knowing that he could die. And now she had failed him and everyone in the village. She had not understood that a wisewoman's duty demanded she confront the treachery and horror that underlay men and women's lives.

Like the story that Aunt Edith told about the girl named Rose Red who had let her soul escape in exchange for a glance in the mirror, a pretty cloak, and a silver ribbon, if Sunniva, too, fell prey to otherworldly enemies, she would be shut up in a crystal-sided box.

The distant sound of thunder announced Lord Thunderer's and his warband's immanent arrival. Amassing strength in the northwest, they were raising the clouds, stirring the air, and beating hammers and axes on their shields.

And, Sunniva, too, became caught up in their raging. Her anger pounded like a small creature drumming inside her chest. To put storm-words to her way of thinking, she announced her refusal to be shouldered with the weight Lady Blessed had placed upon her. The true meaning of the promised cloak, though woven with threads light and misty as clouds and dyed the true colors of dawn, she now understood, would be lined with leaden ingots.

Once the cloak was placed upon her shoulders, she would know how dark and heavy was the burden she bore for others. The lives of Gevehard and his men were just the first of the weights she would carry. If she swore to be fully true to the Lady, all the wealth the chieftains lavished upon their wisewoman could never compensate for the amount of sorrow and fear that she would take upon herself when she agreed to wage war, in the otherworlds, on behalf of other's.

She did not want the villagers to suffer. Nor did she want to be the one who un-burdened them of their pain. To know that she could alter the fated course of events, but had chosen not to, was an unfair demand to place upon her.

Angry the Lady had misled her, Sunniva was ready sever all ties.

Her fists clutched at the blankets. Her hands felt empty. She regretted having left her little red stones at home. The little pebbles would offer her protection. She was certain of it. Dug from the same vein in the earth that her father's red stone had come from, the red stones carried with them the same strange powers that had allowed her to have waking dreams and to enter otherworlds. Without the little red stones, she doubted whether she could find her way back to the earth-dwelling men's hidden chambers and the protection they offered.

When she had last visited the four earth-dwelling men, she had felt as formidable as Lady Sun herself. Shown a flaming knife and a golden mirror, she had sworn to stand up for truth and to fight deceit. But, now, she could not bear to look herself in the eye and to see, in the mirror, a coward. She had chosen the easy way out. She had become a liar.

Wishing to be freed from the daily constraints this world placed upon her, she closed her eyes, and as sleep overtook her, she left behind the rules that govern the familiar and the ordinary and sought, instead, the place where she had gone before.

Her future and her present collided and she knew, even then, to whom she would turn. Though she had intended to head back to the place where her soul had gone before, she ended up in a meadow. In Aunt Edith's tale, the morning sun had shone, but now it was nighttime. Nor did she see the Lady with a mirror seated on a rock. No, Sunniva was looking for one of the ironmongers who had saved Red Rose from the Lady with a mirror. She would ask him to cut her free from the cord Lady Blessed had tied around her ankle. He was the one who, because of his massive strength, forceful gaze, and powerful control of fire and iron, was the most compelling of the four earth-dwelling men. He was the one she knew for certain would protect her from what endangered her.

Yes, it was the iron-monger who, with astonishingly prescient foreknowledge, had understood exactly what was needed. Using thought-bricks to build a forge, he had set himself up in the strange, dreamtime landscape.

And that was where Sunniva came upon him, dragging the worrisome cord that Lady Blessed had tied, like jesses, to her ankle, back when she had been a carefree hawk-girl. She approached the grimy, ash-covered man where he stood beside the small, charcoal-burning forge in the meadow. His skin was blackened by the iron dust and the cinders with which he worked. Neither good-looking nor heroic in stature, rather, he was a one-handed, common ironmonger. Yet, something about his demeanor conveyed his utter fearlessness.

At first, he seemed to be unaware of her. He worked the bellows until the coals glowed white hot. The fire cast a flickering patchy light upon the dense, black shadows darkening his face. His tongs grasped the tang of a short, herringbone patterned knife blade. It was the same one that he had shown her before, after she had been pulled through a crack in the little red stone. Then, the ironmonger had told her that he would give her this blade. Now, he pulled it from the radiant embers and studied the yellow-red, rippling flames that crept in throbbing waves across the iron's red-hot skin.

Only then did he look up and seem to see her for the first time. Eyes like searing, black, iron points stared at her, flashing with the knife's small, red-yellow flame's reflective bursts. Lit only by the fire in the brick forge, the ironmonger and Sunniva stood together in the blackness of the night.

Thunderclouds built around them. Roiling with the moist, risen air, the black and bloated clouds hung ominously pendulous above the place where they stood and pressed down upon them with their foggy weight. Thunder rumbled. Lord Thunderer threw his flare across the massive cloud's interior to light it from within. Sunniva's chest throbbed with each booming hammer-strike on his shield.

"Are you sure?" the ironmonger asked.

"Yes," Sunniva said. She was angry to have been led unwittingly into this dreadful situation. Lady Blessed had enticed her with promises she had never made good on. Until now, she had been a simple girl, but the Lady had changed the rules mid-game. Now, in exchange for that dawn-colored cloak, Sunniva had been told to wage war against the Lord of Thieves' follower, Edwina, the wisewoman who did his bidding. She had been charged with the duty to offer the cup to both Glenn and Erol and to sue for peace between them. The Lady had broken her word twice. And now there was more at stake than a pretty, dawn-colored cloak. Men's lives were at stake. The burden was too great to bear alone. Sunniva did not believe she was strong enough to carry the weight.

The ironmonger repeated his question, "You are sure?"

"Yes." Unbending in her decision as is Lord Thunderer whenever he threatens to wage war against those who overstep his bounds, Sunniva drew the line and firmly held her ground. Determined to make this choice, she raged until her target was well-defined. Like a flash of brilliant light, her words burst forth in one, simple, angry statement. Sunniva the Gifts of the Sun growled, "I want Lady Blessed to go away and to leave me alone." The echoes of what she said rolled across the sky like an air-rending thunderclap.

Permission granted, the ironmonger approached the cord that bound Sunniva to

Lady Blessed. Though it looked deceptively thin and delicate as a ray of light, a mere spider's thread draped between two thistles growing in the field, he knew better. This strand was strong and hard as tempered steel. The iron spike, sticking out from his wrist, reached into the empty air. He hooked the thin cord and teased it in closer. Raindrops, like tiny, sparkling, crystal beads strung along its length, glittered reflectively with each of the lightning flashes. He pulled the cord taut with the tip of his spike, lowered the searing-hot knife, pressed the blade against the tension, and sliced it through. Accompanied by a thunder clap, the cord that had bound Lady Blessed to Sunniva was severed. Its frayed ends snapped loose and untwisted in a sudden gust. There, she had done it.

The Lady Who Spun the Clouds wept with furious indignation and grief. Rain came down in a sobbing downpour. Raindrops pounded the earth. The cloudburst quenched the fire in the forge. The embers sizzled and the night turned pitch black.

Sunniva stood alone in the field. Drenched and soaking wet, she trembled in the cold. Each thunderclap reverberated inside her chest. She had expected to feel exultant but, instead, she felt its opposite. The release from service to Lady Blessed did not give Sunniva the relief she had hoped for. The wind lashed her vehemently, punishingly. Her foothold on the earth was tenuous.

In time, a colorful dawn cloaked the dreamtime meadow. Early morning breezes bounced her in the air like a thistle seed. Uplifted and twirled about, dizziness overtook her. She floated here and there until even the frail weight of her soul pulled her toward the earth. Tossed on a cloak woven from the colors of dawn until its threads unraveled, she fell through the holes in the torn cloak. She was falling, falling, falling through the tattered lavender, pink, and golden light. No one was there to catch her. As she fell through the gaps in the shredded, dawn-colored cloth, no one was there to pull her to safety.

And as she fell, an emptiness brought upon her by an insatiable hunger in the blood growled deep inside her. What was this need that has no name? An overwhelming sadness soaked every part of her being and filled her with lonesome remorse. Would she never again take flight in the guise of a goshawk and feel that joyful freedom? Was she to be the cause of her father's death? What has she done? In a fit of anger, she had thrown away her promise.

Awakening to Mila's early morning greeting to the Hearth Mother, slowly loosening herself free from the grip of sleep, her bed seemed to be floating above the earth. Though the straw-filled mattress was at her back, it tipped so erratically from side-to-side and from back-to-front she feared she would slip right off and land on the hard floor. She grasped the fabric cover and held on tightly until her firm hold on the earth, to which her body would always be attracted, settled.

Sunniva pulled the amber bead from beneath the neckline on her shift. She rubbed the tear that Lady Sun had shed, in her grief, for the man she loved. This little, honey-colored pebble carried memory of death and loss. Warmed by Sunniva's body heat, the bead felt soft as skin and alive. Assured by this single drop of sorrow that the pain she suffered was common to all of womankind, she knew she was not alone in her sadness. When seen that way, the bead's understanding became a comfort.

The vision of Gevehard limping ashore, the groans she had heard from the wounded men, and the sounds of the mournful women were, also, held within this honey-colored teardrop. Yet, as much as this destiny seemed fated, another possibility nagged at her. Like all men and women who live at the mercy of forces, which will do with them whatever they want, she knew that the duty, which Lady Blessed had imposed upon her, was not through with her yet. These pictures in her mind, of the wounded and dying men and the sorrowful women, were strung on the cord that Frida had slipped over her head. And there they would remain to remind her of her duty: to fly in the form of a goshawk over the land like a plea for peace; and to pass the cup between men or women who are no longer beholden to each other.

Though the bead itself was light as a feather, the memories that were held within it added to its weight. So heavy, it would hang about her neck and drag her down until she was hunched as an old woman. The fear of the losses she had seen would surely haunt her with its niggling ferocity. It would go on and on until she had somehow changed the four longships' course on their fateful voyage. Not until then, not until she had put it right again, would she be able to put to rest this demand that had been lain upon her.

But for now, Sunniva's only recourse was to keep the fated sights safe and hidden. Her fallback was hope. Hope that, just as her mother had taught her, if she never spoke of something, it was not real and would never happen. She would keep the bead, and all that was held inside it, hidden beneath her dress. If it never saw daylight, it would never happen. This was the hope she clung to, the hope that was hanging around her neck on a cord.

V.

After it had been raining for the last two days and nights, many of the shallow holes atop the mounds were filled with rainwater. And now that the sun had broken through the clouds, scattered, reflective puddles embellished the clay and dung mounds like shimmering blue jewels. The village was aglitter in the sunlight, but Sunniva took no pleasure in the sight.

The questions Mila had asked repeatedly taunted her. In the end, because she feared for her father's safety, he was the one to whom she remained most loyal. She would side with Gevehard and was determined to warn him of the danger.

Compellingly attractive, Shipmaster Gevehard, with his red beard, blonde, swept-back hair, and cloak billowing out to the sides, strode vigorously across the flat-topped mound. His blue eyes were so pale that just to look at him could be peculiarly chilling. Yet, and even so, they added to his appeal and to his reputation for having a cunning way about him. The shipmaster spoke with the folks he met, squeezed their arms, slapped their shoulders, asked after their families, and called their children by name.

Unlike the villagers, for whom Gevehard was their kinleader, Sunniva had never had a reason to speak with him except for occasional greetings. She stood off to the side, wrung her hands, and sucked in her thin, worried lips. That morning, she had woken with the strange notion that Gevehard had seen her face in the cup from which he drank and would know she had a message to give him.

To stoke her courage, she convinced herself to walk up to him. And then, without even knowing how she had gotten there, she found herself standing right before him. She looked directly into those cool, blue eyes that sent shivers down her spine, and told him, "It is my duty to warn you that there will be pirates waiting to attack you. You must change course."

Nodding thoughtfully, he said, "I assure you, it goes without saying that there will be pirates. I have fought them many times. And of course, I am careful. Every man on my crew is important. I do not intend to lose even one. Your worry is justified. It is no different from any woman's concerns. All mothers, wives, daughters, and sisters are anxious for the sake of their men."

"But these pirates will hide in an estuary you believe is safely held by men whom you have never fought before. You will think that the place in which you seek shelter is held by allies when, instead, they are your enemies."

Though his attempts to calm her were sincere, whatever he said only further convinced her that he was taking her warnings too lightly. He was not listening properly. When he asked whether she was sweet on that young man, Aart, Sunniva was certain of it. No, the shipmaster was not taking her concerns the least bit seriously. Though horrified at the thought that Gevehard would think she might have a crush on that arrogant boy, she swallowed hard and dared not speak her opinion aloud. She did not want to tell the shipmaster that, now that everyone knew of his plans to train Aart to be a steersman, he was too cocky for his own good.

Aart had tried to catch her attention, on more than one occasion, even though she had looked the other way. Though she had done her best to ignore him, as was proper for a young woman who was soon to be betrothed to another, he had consistently shown off in front of her. Did Gevehard think that she was just another silly girl whose only thoughts were about the boys she was sweet on? Her concerns were of greater importance. Far greater. She carried the weight of all the men who would be sitting on the four longships' benches. And it was too great a burden to bear alone.

Apparently, this attempt by Gevehard to change the subject of their conversation meant that she had no choice but to let the story out. Although she feared that to do so would increase the risk, if she were to convince Gevehard of the danger he faced, she needed to describe what she knew about the attack on the boats. "I have seen the signs and know only this much—three boats will return, and Wave Crestar will not be among them." Just to say it aloud made Sunniva's voice crack.

"I know sea-raiders hide in coves and river mouths. Being shipmaster and foremost leader of all the men carries with it the responsibility of avoiding those pirates who lay in wait for us. Can you tell me when and where the attack will come from?"

"It will happen on the return voyage, when your ships are most heavily laden."

"Sunniva, I respect your father's ability to see things in their entirety. If you, too, have the gift, I am all ears and am willing to listen to whatever you can tell me. But, unless you can give me an indication of an attack, a clear sign of the danger, something that I can watch for, my itinerary is set, and I cannot change course. There is only one way to get back home."

Sunniva shook her head and turned her gaze away. She wrung her hands, looked down at her feet, and kicked the dirt. Gevehard needed a sign, something he could watch for, and she had nothing to offer. If she had done what Lady Blessed had asked her to do, she would have been able to answer his question with a clearly stated prophecy and a description of the omen he should watch for. She felt so small, so empty, so poor, and helpless. She had nothing to give him.

Then, she remembered something Lady Blessed had said. She had told Sunniva that an intermediary could pass on important information. The Lady had said the men would see a sign and know from the song and flight of birds how to avoid the last fight against the pirates who were hiding in a river estuary. The Lady had wanted Sunniva to observe a sign that she could pass on to Gevehard, some portent of danger that she could tell him to watch for and to recognize. It now became clear as day. "Yes, you must be alert to the song and flight of birds. That is how you will know that there is danger up ahead. That is when you will know that those whom you trust will deceive you."

"Well, then," Gevehard said with a shrug of his shoulder, "I shall remain vigilant and watch the sky at all times." He chuckled, squeezed her arm in a friendly way and said, "I will do my best. I always use whatever knowledge I have at hand. Rest assured, I will see that no harm comes to my men."

"No, you do not understand. The threat will be greatest when your guard is down, when you believe that you are in safe waters."

Gevehard ignored her last warning and adopted the same light-hearted tone with which he had gossiped with all the men and women whom he had met that morning. "Sunniva, I constantly weigh men's trust. I know you are friends with Frida. She is quite a fine young woman. You need not fear for her and her husband's safety. Rodger is a strong and capable young man who will be rowing the oars for many years to come. Next year he may have a ship of his own. I promise to take care of Rodger and your father, Sunniva. Your concerns are the reason that I want Aiken to come along with me on the boat. He knows how to read the signs. He is a very clever man. You have good reasons to be proud of him.

"You might want to help the other women with their work. They express their worries by throwing themselves wholeheartedly into the preparations for the upcoming feast. The men will be honoring their ancestors in the longhouse just before we leave. Adelheide told me how hard you worked before, when you helped decorate the longhouse walls with the women's weavings and embroideries. Some of the tapestries are very old, you know. The women weave the men's safe return with each passage of their shuttles. Every time the woof crosses the warp, the men gain confidence and their courage increases. When they see the women's tapestries on the walls, they are reminded of past, successful voyages."

His suggestion, however, only reminded Sunniva of the embroidered picture of Glenn and Erol battling it out for supremacy over this land, and she gasped in horror. The curse of servitude had been stitched forever into the fateful legacy of this village. "To prevent the attack," she said, "it is important to make close allies with those men and women who are kept in bondage. The best way to accomplish that is to free them."

"I made my best friend a freedman" Gevehard said. "I married the daughter of a freedman. I believe that all men and women should be free. But to convince the other landholders takes time."

"It is wrong to keep men and women in bondage. You might start by freeing the women in the cookhouse. There will not be enough time to stop the curse unless you act immediately."

"What do you mean by curses, Sunniva?" Gevehard asked sharply. "Do not threaten me. It is not your place to speak to me this way. Nor is it your right to tell me what to do or to order me about. You are a guest here. It is better to remain silent on matters that have nothing to do with you. You are meddling in something you know nothing about."

He saw someone up ahead, waved his arm, and said, "There is someone with whom I must speak, Sunniva. Good day," and strode off.

Left alone in front of the longhouse, she quietly spoke to his retreating back, "You are a coward." To have a friend who once was held in bondage or to marry the daughter of a freedman did not shield him from profiting from the supposed differences between a freeman and those men and women whom he kept in bondage.

Though men and women were bustling all around her, she neither noticed nor responded. Now that she knew for certain that her father would leave with Gevehard, she was convinced that it would be her fault if he never made it home.

Gevehard had not believed her. And worse yet, she had spoken the words that would make the attack come true. There was no way to quench the unbearable knowledge that something dreadful was about to happen.

If she were stuck here forever, it would be a fitting punishment to suffer the dreadful consequences of her refusal to have taken on the task Lady Blessed had requested. If only she had not been so reckless. She had acted too hastily.

Her gut twisted in knots. She could have wept for what she had done in a fit of rash, ill-temper. How could she live with the knowledge that she could have saved her father's life but, because of her cowardice, had done nothing?

She had only one option left. The sight of the three boats on the shore and the one that went missing were now held inside the amber bead. She would wrap it in an invisible piece of embroidery upon which she would picture a make-believe story about their safe return. She would tuck it deep inside her heart and keep it safe from harm.

To convince herself that the terrible things that she had seen, were now in a place so sheltered, they would never come true, she repeatedly affirmed that the pirate attack would never happen; the men would be safe for another year; and no one would ever see Wave Crestar engulfed in flames. Not for as long as she kept her prophesied visions hidden.

Edwina and her two assistants walked into the yard, followed by several of the household boys who carried the women's satchels and bundles. The smaller boys scooted around the largest puddles, but the biggest boys jumped over with dashing style, then snuck sidelong glances at the girls, to see whether they had noticed them showing off so nimbly.

For the last two days, Edwina had privately seen villagers who had asked for special healings and divinations. Now in a hurry to leave, she stood off to the side as Tate oversaw the packing of the horses. Edwina glanced impatiently around the yard and, like a hunter who has spotted the rabbit she caught in a snare, the wisewoman stalked right up to Sunniva.

"I know you snuck out during the cord-spinning ceremony and ran off afterward to hide," she said. "Where did you go that night? It was my ceremony. If you think you can usurp my position by taking a place higher than my platform, you had better tell me what you saw from up there."

Despite Edwina's rapturous dance, she had not only been aware that Sunniva had left the longhouse but was also aware that she had climbed onto the roof. Sunniva could not imagine how Edwina knew. Unless, that is, she had caught sight of her standing on the longhouse roof when she was flying in the guise of a sea eagle. But no matter how she had become aware of it, Edwina knew the truth.

Might Edwina also suspect that her own devious service to Lord Spider had been discovered? Might she also know that Sunniva suspected that her tale of a successful voyage had been deceitfully spun out during the ceremony to convince Gevehard that he had nothing to fear? Did the wisewoman see in Sunniva an enemy who must be neutralized by disparaging belittlement that would strip her of her confidence?

Edwina's cold, fierce gaze bored into Sunniva. "Nothing? You have nothing to report?" Edwina's accusations were blunt and to the point. "I have heard rumors about the stone carver and his daughter's plans to settle in the village. Just now, I saw you stop to talk with the shipmaster. Do you plan to serve Lady Blessed and to become Gevehard's wisewoman? Do you think that you can perform the cord-spinning ceremony yourself? Do you and your father believe that you can contest my place here and force me out?

"I come from a long line of wisewomen who have served these villages faithfully for many years. I cannot be pushed aside so easily. If you plan to come up against me in the otherworlds, you cannot win. You are not strong enough to fight me. I know how to pick my side in a fight, and I know how to win. I am a sea eagle. No other birds are bigger. Only one sea eagle can hold this territory. If you try to challenge me, you will lose."

Left speechless, Sunniva shook her head and wrung her hands. Though she denied it, she knew it was true. This was the advent of a challenge: a war of words between the sea eagle and the goshawk.

In her attempt to intimidate Sunniva with enticing references to what a wisewoman can accomplish, Edwina said, "The most important lesson, which you must learn, is to untie a knot and, thereby, to loosen your soul from your body. That way you may send it wherever you wish it to go. A wisewoman can spin her breath as she spins her dance and free her soul for flight. The things that you will find in the otherworlds are what men and women most desire. Riches may be picked up and carried back to this world. Is that what you want?"

Suspicious that Edwina was trying to feel her out in an attempt to catch her in a lie, Sunniva answered, "No. I want my soul to go nowhere. I want it to stay right here with me." She would have liked to have called the wisewoman an imposter but held her tongue. If she did, she feared she would be forced to prove her statement. She would be called upon to back her assertion with a description of what she had seen, and the secret would be out. And since she had no intention of allowing her vision to be belittled and stolen away, she chose instead to remain silent.

"Oh, but you do want to fly," Edwina said with exaggerated disbelief. "On the night of the ceremony, you wanted to fly away. You sought out the Lady as you have done before. I saw you. You cannot deny it."

Well, at least Edwina had gotten that wrong. Sunniva had not flown to the Lady. Nor had she taken on the guise of a goshawk. The Lady had come to her. She was the one who had led Sunniva to the top of the longhouse roof. Sunniva would never have done anything so rash on her own. Edwina had tricked her before, and she would not let her do it again. To safeguard the frightful possibility of grievous loss was now Sunniva's responsibility. She refused to be mocked, yet knew that Edwina would coax the truth from her if she tried to defend herself. The more the wisewoman taunted her, the more Sunniva vowed to protect the vision of the three boats coming ashore.

"My father's stone will protect the men and bring them home, not the make-believe boats that you pretended to pull home like toys on a string."

Edwina jerked back in response to Sunniva's disrespectful insult, and mocked her in a wheedling voice, "Your father, your father, your father. You look up to him as though he is a hero. But you cannot hide behind your father's reputation. There is nothing cunning about what he does. He is nothing but a self-important, renegade outlaw, an imposter who pretends to have secret knowledge.

"I see right through you, Sunniva. If you want to do what I do, think again. It is a hard and lonely life. I see both the desire and the fear in you. You are no different from many simple girls. You were attracted to the fine jewelry and pretty baubles I wore the other night. I saw how you stared at me, you, silly girl. You cannot deny it. You are not ready to give up your family for a few strings of beads. Go back to where you belong. Get married, have children, be tied down to a husband and your babies. If you never go anywhere, you will have nothing to fear. Soul flight and walking between worlds is dangerous work. If you are a coward, it is not the life for you."

Edwina turned on her heel and walked off.

Sunniva yelled after her, "I am not a coward," but knew she was.

The wisewoman chose to ignore Sunniva's childish outburst and sauntered toward the activity around the horses. But before she got very far, an odd-looking stranger stopped her, and they began to talk. His appearance was so unforgettable, Sunniva was certain that she had never seen him before. He was taller than other men by at least half a head and his limbs were so thin, he seemed to have been made from sticks. The clothes he dressed in were threadbare and patched. His long, tangled beard was streaked an ashy grey and his face was marred by a long, white scar. One, half-closed eyelid hung limply across an opaque, non-seeing eye.

The man looked up, saw Sunniva staring at him and tipped his head in a polite greeting. The way he nodded seemed to convey a friendly exchange between two well-known acquaintances. Dismayed and embarrassed, Sunniva was furthermore shocked by the implication of such intimacy and turned away in a huff. Yet, though she kept her back to him, an uncanny, tingly feeling warned her of his unrelenting scrutiny.

Adelheide walked hurriedly into the yard and, after she greeted Edwina, the two women walked toward the longhouse and went inside. That left Tate with nothing to do but watch the boys saddle and load the horses. She sidled up to Sunniva and, affecting a friendly manner, said, "My mistress Edwina has shown an interest in you. I, also, heard the tall man ask about you. Who is he? How do you know him?"

Sunniva brushed off the suggestion with a shrug of her shoulder and a shake of her head.

"Do you want to learn how to perform the cord-spinning ceremony?" Tate asked. "A girl may be given into a wisewoman's service if she has no family, or if her father is an outlaw, like your father is, and no one will offer her family the bride price for her hand in marriage. Not all of those who are given to Edwina may learn the ceremony but they may travel and see to the wisewoman's needs, as Kendra and I do. Or she may become a servant in Edwina's household."

Shocked by what she heard, Sunniva defended her honor, saying, "My father and mother would never force me into bondage. Nor is it true that my father is an outlaw."

"Come now, everyone knows he is," Tate said, with a side-to-side wag of her head. "Why else would a former warrior live in a farming hamlet with a woman to whom he is not wed and become a stone carver? If no one wants to marry you because you are a half-breed bastard, the spawn of an outlaw, Edwina will take you in."

Sunniva stared at Tate in speechless disbelief. Tate noticed the boys were yanking on the straps and knew they had finished saddling and loading the horses. She took a step, looked over shoulder, and said, "Edwina is gruff but kind." Then, turning to face Sunniva, directly, she continued to spiel out her insults in an offhand manner without, apparently, knowing how offensively she spoke. "Some of the other women in the enclave were also unwanted girls. Their fathers and mothers did not want them either. You need not feel ashamed."

"I am promised to marry at the end of harvest," Sunniva declared loudly. "You are jealous. My father and I are going home. Tomorrow."

"Believe what you wish," Tate said with a shrug. And, seemingly undeterred by common courtesy, spoke so loudly that everyone in the yard could hear. "I just heard from the men who escorted your father that the two of you are not welcome among the farmers in your hamlet. They think that you want to leave there for good. Or, maybe your father wants to leave you here. Maybe that is how he plans to get rid of you."

Whatever had Sunniva done to bring such hateful talk upon herself? Her jaw dropped and her face flushed. No one had ever been so rude to her before. She had never felt so alone. She longed for home. She wanted to run inside her house, to climb into her loft, and to curl into a ball and hide beneath the bedcovers. But since she had no place to call her own, she staked out a corner where she could defend herself. She set her basket on the end of a bench next to the wall of Gevehard's longhouse and mentally marked off the patch she considered her own. She leaned her back against the wall, tucked her distaff under her arm and set the whorl spinning.

In this world of uncertainty nothing was more important than the single thread she twisted. Nothing else mattered but the strand that was coming together between her fingers. It alone made order from the mass of fleece she had bundled atop her distaff. It alone could be measured at the end of the day and would add up to something of value. Everything else fell away. The women's voices in the cookhouse faded to a low murmur. Three boys running past became a blur. Edmund, the one-armed man, who Mila said shared Adelheide's bed when Gevehard was gone from home and might be plotting to overthrow their masters, pulled a sledge full of dung and clay behind him. He had been Wave Crestar's commander but now he was reduced to filling holes. She watched him stop and manage, quite ably, to scoop out the clay and dung with his shovel. He filled a puddled hole, tamped it down with the back of the shovel and then moved on to the next one. The more she saw of what happened to men and women who lived in this village, the more she hated it.

If only she had not asked the ironmonger to cut the jesses that Lady Blessed had tied around her ankle. If only she had not thrown away her chance to let her soul take flight in the guise of a goshawk. If, by her flight and song, she could give Gevehard a sign, he would know he must turn away, and the men would be safe from harm. But no matter how much she tried to lift and to fly away, her feet were stuck firmly to the ground. She also knew that if she were to keep Gevehard and his men safe from harm this year, they would not be protected from Erol's curse the next year or the next. No, there was only one way to negate the curse. The cup must be passed between the living and the dead, and those men and women who were born in servitude must be freed.

Instead, she determined to do as the women in this village did. As she spun, she would think of her father's and the other men's safety. She would tell herself a story in which Mila's betrothed bought her freedom. She, her husband and their children would live together in a house of their own. In this story Mila's brother would make it home safely, and the cookhouse women's lives would change for the better.

Then, once she had spun enough thread, she would dye them in pretty colors. She would get out her tablet loom and weave a world of goodness. It would be something that she could touch and hold. And as she wove, she would embroider pictures on it. She would make a world where people were fair and showed kindness to one another. She would weave and embroider it into existence. She could do that much, at least. Even an ordinary girl can make a story cloth. She would change the unspeakable suffering to something better.

Her reverie was interrupted when she sensed someone's fixed gaze boring into her. The tall man with the straggly beard had moved in closer. He now stood so near, he was only several steps away. To let him know how rude she thought it was to stare at her in that way, Sunniva lifted her chin and turned her head haughtily to the side. But, apparently, it was not so easy to ignore the tall man. He blatantly refused to take her hint, loped right up to her, bent forward clumsily from the waist and caught the dangling whorl in his hand. Straightening up, he held the spindle in one hand and wound the thread around the axis with the other.

Then, somehow, the cord came apart in his hands. He showed her the dangling ends. "Well, look at that. How did that happen?" Peering into her face, he said,

"There is no need to worry. A thread is easily fixed. What else is bothering you?"

Without even thinking, she just blurted out what had been on her mind for the last three days, "It is not the thread that worries me. I am afraid the four longships will be attacked and many of the men will die. The women in the cookhouse, the servants, and the ironmongers should be freed. And do not tell me that it is merely idle make-believe to wish it were so."

To protect the thread, with which she planned to weave that perfect world into being, and to keep it safe from his disbelief in her peaceable world, she wanted to grab the spindle away. He might pollute it, and she wanted to keep it safe from his defilement but felt too shy of his commanding presence to stand up to him and to demand he hand it back.

"So, you are worried about your father, are you? We can fix that too. We would not want anything to happen to him, now would we? I would like him to be my man, you know. As for the cookhouse women, that may be beyond my reach. Perhaps my Lady can help you with that problem. But, before we can keep the boats safe, we will need to tie these two ends together. My Lady tells me that I am good at knot-tying tricks," he said with a laugh.

What outlandish effrontery this man had. But before Sunniva was given a chance to protest, the odd man said something about taking a load off his feet. He fell back onto the bench so heavily it shook and creaked with a loud, ear-splitting scream. Although she told him not to bother, that she could fix it herself, he hunched his shoulders, bowed his back, and fumbled with the whorl, where it lay in his lap. He pulled the slack from the thread, and since it was attached to the fleece, which was wrapped around her distaff, Sunniva tightened her hold on it. She pressed her elbow into her side, grabbed the stick with her left hand and dug in her heels. But, the more she resisted, the more he yanked on the thread. Finally, because she feared the thread would break a second time, she was forced to step in closer to the man. Though he had turned slightly to the side, as if he had wanted to hide his knot-tying tricks from her oversight, she was able to watch his long fingers twist the thread's two ends together.

"Do you see things differently than others do?" he said in an off-hand manner. "If you do, I am a lot like you. I, too, see hidden things."

To focus better with his one good eye, he tipped his head to the side and bent so close to the whorl, his hands were almost touching his nose. "My Lady spins threads as light as clouds," he said, and added nonsensically, "Do you want to learn how she does it?"

How could he make such a ridiculous claim? Although she desperately wanted to get away, Sunniva could see no way out of her predicament. Her whorl was in his hands. She was connected to him by the thread and could not walk away. There was nothing she could do but stand beside him until he gave her spindle back. What would people think?

Then, quite suddenly, the man jerked upright and held his arms out to show her the string. Draped delicately between the pointer finger and thumb of each hand, the thread made one continuous strand.

Appearing to be quite pleased with himself, first, he pulled on it to test its strength, and then, since it did not break, he said, "Good as done."

Sunniva bent down to look at it more closely. There was neither a knot in it, nor a bulge where he had twisted the two frayed ends together. That odd man then wound it around the spindle and handed it back.

"To pass the time while you spin," he said, "we could share a few stories."

She stared at him, hardly knowing what to make of this offensive beggar's suggestion. Furthermore, the man frightened her. Reminded of what her mother said whenever she was taken with a fit of shivers, Sunniva recited beneath her breath, "Someone just walked over my grave."

She shook her head, tossed the whorl into her basket, picked it up by the handle, and rushed off, leaving the man alone on the bench in front of Gevehard's longhouse.

Fury shrugged off her rude behavior and called after her, "Another time then. I will catch up with you later," and added quietly, "You and me are not done yet."

NINE

Pearl
If you will bring forth truth
and prove loyalty.

Take this stone called Pearl which has the nature of the Moon. It is found in many shades of white, pink or black. It has been said such stones are hardened drops which fall from the full Moon into open oyster shells. Like the Moon, these stones will shine at night. If kept about one's person, it is good to enlighten truth about oneself and to flush out the truth about others. It is said to have this power only on the first day when the Moon is rising and waxing and again on the twenty-ninth day when the Moon is waning. So does Aaron say in the book of virtues of herbs and stones.

The Truth of Rocks, by Alwiss the Wise

I.

Though earlier, Lord Fury was cast as a man of undisguised lust and simple tastes, for those whose powers are less than are his own, his intentions are as unknowable as his namesake. Like the whirlwind, he both humbles and outrages those to whom he appears. Whenever he descends menacingly from leaden clouds, as a funnel of unleashed chaos, he sweeps menacingly across the land. And after he sucks-up, through the eye of his swirling vortex, all who lay in his path, he leaves behind an altered landscape.

To explain how a man, as enigmatic as he later proved to be, and to describe how he hid behind so modest a demeanor, yet got the better of us without arousing our suspicions, I must depict the time when he first appeared in our underground rooms. Claiming to be a seeker of knowledge and a lover of truth and wisdom, who was temporarily down on his luck, he called himself Meander and passed himself off as an itinerant, meadhall storyteller.

In hindsight, I cannot begin to fathom how such a master of illusion could have spoken so boldly of his love of truth. But, before we caught on to his talent for disguises, we invited him to stay with us for a while.

Though he and I go back a long way, somehow, he appears to look a bit different each time I see him. How that is even possible, when he has such an unmistakable face, I do not know. But I have never known anyone who could change his bearing and facial expressions to match the man, who he is pretending to be, as well as he can. As with any accomplished storyteller, he convincingly becomes whichever character best suits the attainment of his ambitions at the time. When he commands others, he looks ruthlessly hard and mean. But at other times, he has a thoughtful, sincere demeanor. Like any skillful imposter he can easily change his bearing without a second thought.

Admittedly, I count myself among those who were taken in by his deceptions. He became a sincere, trustworthy friend with whom I shared my intimate confessions. But because of his uncanny ability to detect other's weaknesses and to use that knowledge to influence his victims whenever their guard is down, I realized, too late, the things I told him were confidences I should never have revealed. Increasingly, the time I spent with him forced me to reconsider whether I could ever be certain of anything.

Though I remember he gave me a handful of pearls to gain my trust, I have never been able to find them. Of course, I was delighted to receive such a rare and valuable gift. Though I remember seeing the pearls clustered in the hollow palm of his hand, that was the last time I saw them. It seemed strange that, after he had given me the pearls, I somehow, immediately misplaced them.

He frequently asked me whether I appreciated his gift and went to great lengths to describe the pearls. He extolled their luster, saying they were so bright, he could see his reflection mirrored on each of the pearls' lustrous surfaces. Several times he told me how greatly he valued the irregularly shaped, lumpy ones. He described how it was possible to see a rooster's body or a man's torso in their unusual shapes and occasionally asked to see them again. But because I was embarrassed to have mislaid them, I was forced to make excuses and claimed to have had no the time to dig them out of my collection. It was so unlike me to lose something so precious, yet I never questioned my assumptions.

Convinced I had lost them, I did not want to admit my carelessness. It shamed me to think that I could have misplaced such a rare gift, or worse, that I may have inadvertently thrown them into the trash. But, after I began to mistrust him, I suspected that he had been playing me for a fool, all along. Although, I can see him, in my mind's eye, very clearly holding out his hand and fingering the pearls he was offering me, I suspect it never happened. Over time, he mentioned the pearls so often, I had falsely built up a belief in a memory of something that had never happened.

You would not think that such vividly recalled details could have been made up, but memory is a peculiar faculty. We remember some things very clearly, but others things not so well. Evidently, we can even recall things that never happened and will avidly defend our recollection of the event whenever the truth is challenged.

Truly, memory is a slippery thing. At other times, a memory will seize hold of me like a band of pirates pouring over the sides of a ship. When sounds, places, and scents evoke fearful memories of things that really happened and can never be forgotten, because they are so clearly and permanently etched upon my soul, they repeat endlessly. Though I may try to forget the memories that come back to haunt me, nonetheless, they force my thoughts to arrive at different destinations than I had intended them to go. Memories, like these, overtake my best intentions to use my mind to achieve its own objectives.

In exchange for the illusory gift of his handful of pearls I taught Fury—or, Meander, as he preferred to be called at the time—to read and to write the secret signs, and the Etruscan, Italic, and Phoenician alphabets from which they were derived. After he learned to read fluently, I allowed him to wander about in the library and study the texts. I was impressed with his linguistic skills and enjoyed the time I spent with him discussing deep and learned subjects. Because of his quick wit and phenomenal memory, he was able to defend his opinions unequivocally.

Allfrigg, too, was taken in by Fury's impostures and his talent for flattery. Over time, Allfrigg taught him how to make medicinal potions from herbs, roots, minerals and various animal substances—all the things that a cunning man would need to know. Worse yet, Allfrigg shared with him the secret, alchemical skills that he had acquired from those men of our own kind, who live in the far east, that will allow a man to stand on equal footing with the ruling powers.

It is for that reason, I fear, that we share some of the blame for the most audacious of Fury's impostures. For it was after he left us that he claimed to be the Lord of the Whirlwind, himself.

II.

But lest I get ahead of myself, I should like to describe in greater detail how he induced our trust. He was a convivial entertainer, had a good sense of humor, and readily engaged in conversation. At the time, we ate our suppers in a small room, the walls of which Grerr had decorated with bright and colorful frescoes. On one wall he depicted rolling hills, crowned with flowering plants, and two deer racing across the ridgeline. Above the distant hills, there are several swallows in flight. The lower third of the fresco depicts calm, blue water upon which a boat can be seen floating. Behind it, at the edge of the shoreline, there is a cluster of brick buildings.

On another wall, two well-filled-out, naked men appear to be running toward one another. About to engage in a wrestling competition, each man has one leg upraised, and an arm lifted to the height of his head. Opposite that wall, several men and women form a procession. They carry lambs, basketsful of produce, and numerous fishes strung on cords. The woman wears a crown encircling her head, made up of wave-like spirals. Her dark hair is long and flows down her back. Her full dress, pulled in tightly at the waist, is richly decorated with patterned trims sewn from shoulder to elbow and around the ankle-length hemline.

Equally rich, repeating, wave-like swirls border the tops and bottoms of the walls. Grerr painted the ceiling with squared, geometric patterns. Above the doorway he painted a large, long-handled, double axe framed by a pair of curved cattle horns.

Staring at these pictures and imagining the fruitful island they depict, I am readily fooled into believing I am somewhere that I have never been and never will visit. In this case, I can say that, convincingly, because the scenes, which Grerr painted on the walls, depict an island that was devastated by the Sons of the Fiery Realm. It is no longer there—it disappeared. When the mountain in its center exploded in an earth-shaking rush of ash and stony debris, the entire island and all its inhabitants were catastrophically swallowed up by the sea.

One time, after we had finished eating our supper, Grerr asked Meander to entertain us with one of his tales. He reached into the satchel, which he always carried with him, pulled out a flask, and uncorked it.

"What have you got in there?" Allfrigg asked.

"I filled this bottle near the top of the mountain where Juki and Bil tend the well named Hider-of-Something," Meander said. After he had taken a sip, he put it back into his bag, sighed heartily, smacked his lips contentedly, and added, "It inspires my storytelling."

"What kind of a potion is it?"

"Only the brother and sister, who live in the mountains, know how to make it."

"Will they share their recipe with me?"

"Good luck with that," Meander said with a chuckle. "But first you must get there. And the only way to get there is to catch a ride on Lord Moon's white-planked longship. After you arrive in the mountains where Juki and Bil live, you will need to ask the brother and sister to make a batch of the Mead of Inspiration. They will tell you to bring them a pail filled with the water with which they brew the mead. I warn you, however, that it is more difficult to dip a pail into the well named Hider-of-Something than I make it sound by my simple explanation."

Naturally, we assumed that he was pulling our legs and smiled to ourselves, but Allfrigg tried to trip him up, and said teasingly, "I would like to hear a story of that adventure. Will you tell us?"

"Unfortunately, I must save that tale for another time and a place."

"Well, then, tell us what else you have in your bag of tricks," Grerr said.

"Oh, I have many stories in here," Meander said. He stuck his nose into the satchel and added, "I am looking for something with which to begin. Perhaps a crow feather will do." He pulled one out, stroked its pinions several times to preen it and set it upon the table. He then pulled out a single strand of horsetail. Holding the two ends between the thumb and forefinger of each hand, he yanked on it several times before he coiled it loosely and set it upon the table beside the feather. Then, after he had dug around at the bottom of his satchel, he pulled out a single boar bristle and a small, whitish pebble, both of which he also set upon the table.

"You may think these things have little or no value—are nothing but the lint that sticks to your clothing, or the refuse you sweep up from the floor and throw onto the waste heap. But, I tell you, there is a story waiting to be told here in these items.

"I do not intend to fill in all the details of the tale. If I did, it would take me a lifetime to recount each of the incidents that drive my character's actions. And though your underground chambers are pleasant enough, and I do not mind spending my time here with you, I have other places to go and things to do, so I will need to weed out the multiple explanations that would otherwise lengthen and confuse the tale. Men and women's lives rarely go straight forward, as if they were following a paved, Roman road, but more often take a twisty route, like the ones you and I walk on, here in the northern lands, where over-grown paths and washed out roads lead to detours and switch-backs.

"Another night, I might tell the story a different way. I might follow a character who appeared peripherally in the first tale, kill off one of the characters in an untimely fashion, emphasize other facts, and weave in more complicated reasons and consequences for each of the characters' actions. I might even make a woman dress like a man or a man pretend to be a woman. It is impossible for one tale to tell you the whole story, you see. Nor are the stories I tell entirely factual. Therefore, I will leave it up to you to sort out the truth from the more dubious fabrications I weave."

"You sound like you are a student of Pyrrho."

"Perhaps. I am something of a skeptic. If there is one motto by which I live, it is to suspend judgment and to engage in constant seeking. It is by these means alone that I flourish.

"But now, let us get on with the story that I intend to tell you tonight. For me, the unearthing of a memory is like studying the pictures depicted here on these walls, which represent a land that is no longer there. To dig through the ruins of time is not about the discovery of what truly happened in the past but is about the act of remembrance. Since memory is imperfect, sometimes I choose to remember something in a manner that I know is only partially correct, is biased, or even mildly inaccurate. Every time that I remember something, I must make it new again and, by this act, I conjure a fantasy from my recollection by speculating upon how it may have been. I might need to make up what my memory otherwise lacks. I remember stories I do not like. I include stories I am skeptical of. If I like the story but I do not really believe in it, or if I have forgotten some of the details, I may move something from one place to another and tell versions of the past that suit my purposes better than another version that may, in fact, be more likely. I may even offer outright invention when my memory fails me. After all, wisemen say that the poorest memory is most conducive to invention."

He winked at me slyly, as if to imply that he had, in this unguarded moment, just spilled out some of his secrets. And, like a conjurer who shows his audience an empty hat from which he intends to pull a rabbit, he said, "I will, therefore, need Lady Remembrance's help in digging through the buried ruins of my memory before I can begin to recount my tale. Listen carefully, for there is a foretelling hidden inside it."

He bowed his head in a deferential manner and began:

I thank you now, for listening to this simple tale about a most unlikely hero. In the beginning, he was a lowly servant who lived in a fort town where a particular chieftain lived. The chieftain, to whom the lowly servant was in service, had been superbly blessed with abundant wealth and many allies. His handsome son's inner graces were known to surpass all others' to whom he was compared.

One day, his son mounted his horse and went on a hunt for partridge. But before he had gone very far he was set upon by thieves and taken captive.

Two days later, a messenger appeared before the chieftain. Carrying a green branch to show the chieftain that he came in peace, he described how the thieves had accosted his son on the road. They now held him hostage, the messenger said and, in return for a ransom payment, the chieftain's son would be set free. The chieftain, deeply troubled by this unfortunate news, called his steward forward, gave him four sacks of gold coins, and told him to take with him six of his fiercest warriors to deliver the ransom payment.

As it happened, the steward set out, accompanied by the six fierce warriors and the servant, (who is soon to become the unlikely hero of my tale). But before they had gone very far the steward said, "Look here, each of us will be rich as chieftains, ourselves, if we split the gold coins inside these bags between us."

The six warriors and the steward agreed to divide the ransom equally between them. To silence the servant, they threatened to slit his throat. But because his bitter weeping so evoked their pity, they agreed to spare his life on condition that he never betray them. If he did disclose their secret, they said he would surely die.

The steward and the six warriors then set out and left the servant behind. Left alone in the abandoned encampment he was so forlorn that, if you had seen the poor, foolish servant pacing back and forth, you would have concluded, quite reasonably, that he did not know which way to turn or where to go next. After a while, he gave up his senseless pacing, sat on a log, and held his head in his hands. He was kicking the dirt with the toe of his shoe when he unearthed a single gold coin laying in the dirt. He picked it up, said, "Oh, lucky day," slipped it into the pouch that hung from the belt at his waist and set out upon the road.

When he came to a village he saw several men wagering in a game of lots. The poor, foolish man thought that he should try his luck. After all, he had a lucky coin, and if his luck held, he figured his winnings might ransom the chieftain's son. He placed his coin in the ante pile and took his turn tossing the cup, but in the end, he foolishly lost the coin and was worse off than when he had begun.

Meander pointed to the crow feather, tapped it with his finger, and said, "Now let me see if I can get this feather to talk to me." He bowed his head so close to the table that his ear nearly touched the feather. After he appeared to listen for several moments, he sat upright, nodded his head and continued:

The luckless fool then set out upon the road again. When he saw a crow fighting a snake in a tree, he stopped to see who would come out the victor. The snake was threatening to eat the eggs in the crow's nest. To protect its nest, the crow struck repeatedly at its enemy with its beak until the snake fell from the branch. The crow glided down to attack the snake on the ground, but the limbless creature remained undeterred and twined itself around the bird's neck. When it seemed as though the snake would surely get the better of the crow, the bird looked up and, upon seeing the fool, said, "Look at my sorry plight and help me. I am worse off than you." The fool felt sad for the crow who was so valiantly defending her nest. He picked up the snake by the tail and, with one fatal blow, smashed it onto a rock.

The crow took a breath, saw the snake was dead, pulled a feather from its wing, offered it to the foolish young man, and said, "For your kindness, I offer you this feather. Keep it securely, and whenever you are in trouble, make a wish, blow on the feather, and it will turn into whatever you need."

The crow flew up to her nest to tend her eggs. The fool put the feather in his cap and began to walk along the road again.

Meander then pointed to the boar bristle where it lay on the table. He picked it up and held it to his ear before he continued:

When the fool saw a fat, gold-colored boar caught in a wicket fence, the boar said, "Look at my sorry plight and help me. I am worse off than you." The fool agreed. He pulled apart the woven saplings that formed the fence, put his foot to the pig's hind quarters, and shoved it, tumbling and squealing, from its entrapment. The boar got to his feet, shook himself out and, once he had restored his dignity, said, "For your kindness, pull a bristle from my back. Keep it securely, and whenever you are in trouble, make a wish, blow on the gold bristle, and it will turn into whatever you need."

The boar turned away to wallow in a mud puddle in the road, and the fool put the boar bristle into the pouch at this waist and continued on his way. When he saw a lame horse in a field, the horse said, "Look at my sorry plight and help me. It is worse than yours." The fool walked up to the horse, stroked its head and neck, and asked whether he could look at its foot. He lifted the hoof, saw a smooth, white pebble was stuck in it, and pried it loose with a stick.

The horse was so grateful, he said, "For your kindness, I will repay you. Pull a strand from my tail and pick up the pebble that you pulled from my hoof. Keep both securely, and whenever you are in trouble, make a wish, blow on either the horse hair or the pebble, and it will turn into whatever you need." The young man wrapped the long strand of horsetail around his wrist like an arm band, tied the two ends together in a knot, put the pebble in the pouch he wore at his waist, and took to the road again.

Meander then picked up the strand of horsetail and wrapped it around a finger on his left hand to make a ring. After he had scratched his ear with his finger, he continued:

When the road led into a deep, dark woods he wished he had a horse to ride. He blew on the horse hair, which he had wrapped around his wrist like a bracelet, and—.

"Now," Meander said, interrupting his tale, "if I told you that his wish was fulfilled when a horse suddenly appeared, you would, no doubt, refuse to believe me. And, furthermore, if I were to say that that was exactly what he did and what happened next, you would, no doubt, begin to mutter to yourself, stand up from where we sit so convivially at this table and walk away. But believe me, I beg you to stay with me a little while longer and you will see how it all works out for the better."

The single strand of horsetail turned into a horse, and the poor fool said, "Oh, happy day." He grabbed its mane, pulled himself onto the horse's back and set off into the forest. When he came to a glen he saw a pond. He led his horse to drink and the fool sat beside it to rest. When he looked into the pond he saw a small, gold ball lying on the bottom. He rolled up his pant legs and sleeves and waded into the pond until the water had come up to his waist.

He reached down to pull out the ball but, when he did, a despicable creature began to emerge from the water. It dripped and oozed with red-brown mud, its skin was lumpy, and its skinny fingers were tipped with long, pointy claws. In short, a hideous monster was coming after him.

When the fool saw it, he shook with terror but summoned his courage. Only a fool would try to fight a monster with a feather. But, nonetheless, he pulled the feather from his cap, waved it about in midair, wished it was a spear, blew on it, and turned it into a keen and shiny, black spear, shaped like a pointed feather. The fool fought the creature with the spear and while holding it off, he reached to the bottom of the water, pulled out the small, gold ball, put it into his pouch and said, "Oh, glorious day, oh happy day."

Spear in hand, he climbed ashore, leapt onto the horse's back and, to the sounds of the filthy, despicable creature's howls, the fool rode away from the glen in the forest.

The fool then continued on his way. When he and the horse came to the bank of a treacherous river, they stopped. Though the noise of the tumultuous river nearly drowned out a weeping woman's bitter cries for help, the fool looked to see where her voice was coming from. He guessed they arose from a house that was built of stone in the center of an island in the middle of the river. He leapt from the horse and told it to graze near the shoreline.

Because the water was too treacherous to cross without a boat, the fool broke a branch from a tree. He blew on the spear that had been the feather before, wished it was now a knife, and it turned into a small blade suitable for carving. He then sat on the riverbank, crossed his legs and began to carve a small boat. When it was finished, he blew on it, wished it was a boat large enough to seat two people, and the branch turned into a crudely shaped, full-size boat. He took another branch, whittled it into the shape of a paddle, and wished it, too, was full-sized.

He stuck the knife into his belt, got into the boat and paddled across the water. As he crossed the river, he heard the woman's plaintive cries grow louder.

"I can bear my pain no longer," she said. "Tears streak my cheeks. After the loss of my freedom, only longing and regret remain. Oh, for how long must I endure this cruel mistreatment? Save me, and you will remain forever within my heart."

The poor fool was saddened to hear her heartrending laments. Eager to release the woman from the stone house, in which she was so cruelly entrapped, he hastened to her rescue. When he got to the island, he pulled the boat ashore. But, upon circling the house, he was dismayed to find the house, inside of which the crying woman was entrapped, had no doors or windows.

The fool dug up a handful of red dirt and mixed it with water using a stick. He pulled the boar bristle from his pouch and blew on it while wishing it was a brush. He dipped the boar-bristle brush into the red mud and painted a door. He then wished the door would open. The woman emerged and, after she had walked through the door, the stone wall banged shut behind her.

She had a slender figure. Her face was as full as the moon and her skin was lustrous as a pearl. Her eyes were as big and innocent looking as were those of a deer. She had a lovely smile, wore a thin garment made of fabric that flowed like water and was embroidered with sparkling gold and silver threads. She wrapped her arms around the fool's neck and showed her gratitude for his kindness with a kiss on his cheek. The fool could hardly believe what was happening. Now that his luck was restored, he said, "Oh, lucky day, oh glorious day, oh happy day."

The woman told the fool how she had been imprisoned in the house without a door after she had been taken captive by a cunning man who was disguised as a red rooster. His feathers were like burning flames and, when he crowed, sparks had flown from his beaked mouth. The cunning man had overwhelmed her with his suffocating smoke, snatched her up, taken her captive and kept her in the middle of the raging river. The cunning man, in the guise of the red rooster, had tried to keep her from her destiny, she said. But nothing could prevent that which Necessity had decreed. And now, finally, she had been delivered from her imprisonment. She told the fool she brought with her a flask that she had filled at the top of the misty mountains where she was born and from which all the worldly rivers flowed.

The fool wished the brush was once again a boar bristle, slipped it into the pouch at his waist, led the woman onto the boat and rowed across the river. From where they stood on the river bank, he whistled for his horse. It came to him and nudged him in the shoulder. He first gave the woman a leg up, and then he pulled himself onto the horse's back. The woman wrapped her arms around the fool's waist. The fool almost lost his wits, but pulled himself together, and sharpened his resolve to see the task through to the end.

They followed the river until they reached the longhouse in which the chieftain's son was held captive. They stopped, dismounted, and cautiously snuck up to the closed doors. The woman and the fool peeked through a crack in the door. Inside the longhouse they could see a man seated at a table. At his side there was a large wolf seated on its haunches like a dog.

Before the fool could stop her, the woman opened the door and walked into the longhouse. The man and wolf were seated at a table near the hearth. The walls were hung with white draperies and tapestries. The longhouse was very large and extended so far into the shadows that the farthest end disappeared in darkness. The man seated at the table was very good-looking. He had dark, curly hair, a close-cropped beard that showed the strong, square shape of his jaw, and a fine mouth with a bow-shaped mouth. He wore a black coat over a black tunic. The woman asked him if he was hungry. When he said that he was ready for his supper, she said that she would bring it to him straightaway.

She walked out the door and closed it behind her. The fool, who was just daft enough to take on such dangerous adversaries as the thief and the wolf who were sitting in the longhouse awaiting their meal, reached into this pouch, pulled out the boar bristle, and wished it was a delicious looking, roasted pig laying on a platter.

The woman first opened the door, then she and the fool lifted the platter together and carried it inside. They laid it upon the table and stood off to the side. When the black-coated man took out his knife to carve the meat, the boar squealed, leapt up from the platter, ran across the table, jumped down, and took off out the door. The wolf and the man, upon seeing their supper run out the door, took off and chased after the roasted pig.

The young man and the woman then began to search the longhouse. The fool took the gold ball from his pouch. It miraculously began to glow as brightly as a small sun. By its light they advanced further and further into the depths of the longhouse. Following the chieftain's son's cries for help they turned into a long, narrow hallway. The white draperies that lined the walls began to flutter and wave about. It seemed as though the net-like curtains were alive and trying to trip-up the fool and the woman by wrapping themselves around their legs. As the fool and lucky woman fought their way through the curtains and moved toward the source of the voice, they could hear the chieftain's son's sad moans and cries for help getting louder and louder.

They came upon the final curtain. When they lifted it, they saw an open doorway that led into another room where the chieftain's son was held captive. At the far end of the room, he was caught in a web-like net that hung from a rope that was strung from a beam in the ceiling. Because it was too high to reach, the fool wished he had a ladder. The lucky woman made a ladder from her fingers. The fool climbed up but caught his toe on one of the rungs and almost tripped and fell. Once his balance was restored, he used the feather-shaped knife to cut the rope. He eased the net-wrapped bundle, which contained the chieftain's son, to the floor and climbed down the ladder. The woman's fingers once again became as delicate and slender as they had been before, but the nail on the finger on which the fool had tripped was broken.

The fool cut the boy loose from the net and slipped the knife back into his belt. The chieftain's son was pleased to see them and said that his father would reward them for their troubles with many favors.

The three of them took off, lighting their way through the longhouse with the sunlight cast by the golden ball. Once they were out the door, the fool stuck the gold ball into his pouch. When he whistled for his horse, his mount came out of the woods. The fool gave the woman and the chieftain's son a leg up onto the horse's back and then jumped up himself. He told the horse to take them back to the chieftain's hill fort, from which he had started his journey, as fast as it could carry them.

By that time, the black-coated man and the wolf knew that they had been tricked and out-maneuvered. The man got onto the wolf's back and they chased the horse and its three riders. Looking back, and seeing the thief and the snarling wolf on their tail, the fool reached into his pouch and took out the pebble. When he threw it behind them, it became a mountain range. Though its heights deterred the wolf and its rider for a while, soon the thief was back on their tail again. The lucky woman poured water from her flask and it became a flooded river. With banks that extended for as far and as wide as the sea, the river was impossible to cross.

When they saw the chieftain's hill fort up ahead, the young man stopped the horse. He jumped down and led the horse through the gates. Their procession through the village caused an uproar among the villagers. They all stood gazing at the chieftain's son who had gone missing but was now returning home. By the time the fool, the woman and the chieftain's son reached the inner stockade the whole village was cheering them on. The chieftain came out of his meadhall to greet them and embraced his son. Amazed by his servant's fidelity, the chieftain embraced the fool and said, "For your kindness, I will repay you with a feast tonight."

The fool and the woman were given the finest clothing to wear. The chieftain seated them both beside him at the high table. The fool told the chieftain what had happened from beginning to end. Amazed by their courage, skill and wisdom, the chieftain praised the fool. Exceedingly happy and in a generous mood, the chieftain bestowed upon the fool and the woman many honors, gifts, and other favors. He took the fool into his service and made him one of his counselors.

I should say, before we come to the end of this tale, I found out later that the poor fool and woman were soon wed. In time, they had a child who became a great leader. As for the chieftain and his son, they lived peacefully thereafter. And the fool, who had become an unlikely hero, said, "Oh auspicious day, oh lucky day, oh glorious day, oh happy day."

III.

Who is telling this story? Am I simply playing the role that Mother Necessity and her daughters, the Matrones, have assigned me? Or is it Lord Fury, himself, one of Necessity's prime movers who, by acting on her behalf, is calling the shots and driving this story forward by enacting Mother Necessity's rule? Are they getting even with me for some unknown infraction that I may have inadvertently committed in the past? And, now that they have insisted upon an appropriate pay-back, the means by which is to write this tale of the long-knife's birth in Berling's forge, have I unwittingly complied with their demand?

TEN

Agate
If thou wilt eschew illusions and fantasies.

Take this stone called Agate which is gray in color with white banding.
And it comes from the River Agates. If this be pierced and hung about the
neck, it is good against fiendish terrors and keeps the body safe against
adversaries. And this has been proved by men of late.
The Truth of Rocks, by Aluiss the Wise

I.

The layered, subtly shaded bands, pictured on this gray-toned agate,
remind me of the times I visited the shoreline after the tide went out
and walked barefoot on the soft, wave-sculpted sand. If I flip the small
stone upside down, back to front, and in reverse, I hear, as though
they were coming from out of nowhere, sounds like pebbles churning
inside a shaken, sand-filled jar.

At times like this, I question whether the world, which I bodily inhabit and
know with my senses, has any less validity than the spontaneous and instinctive world
I perceive whenever my awareness drifts in and out of the open doorway leading to
the dreamtime. When both inner and outer awareness merge to bring about something altogether new, I only know that if I respond to these mysterious notions, whenever they force their way to the forefront of my mind, things that have lain dormant
beneath the surface of immediate recognition may be revealed and, once they have
arisen, frequently prove important.

When even the least consequential fragment pops into my head I have learnt to
respond to the words, fleeting images, sounds, and random thoughts, and to further
convey them to this chronicle with a sketch or a note. And, in so doing, they take on a
trustworthy quality that lends believability to the information because of the mere act
of writing it down. In this way, the fragmentary thoughts become equally worthy of
my attention and arise more often. Over time, these ideas seem to bubble up more frequently from some underground spring in the dreamtime—arising, perhaps, from the
well named Hider-of-Something from which the mead of inspiration is brewed. And,
over time, the small trickle of astonishing, multiplicity of forms flows until it takes on
the strength of a mighty river.

If even a single word comes to mind and, acting like a recalcitrant child who, because it so desperately wants my attention, pursues me and forces me to take notice, I
neither ignore it nor shame it but write it down. Even if it demands to stand alone, in
its own sentence, insistently plants its feet, cocks its elbows out to the side, and dares
me, tenaciously, with a stubborn look upon its face, to eliminate it from the text by
drawing a line straight through it, I leave it there to stand alone and by itself.

I heed an idea, and since my mind just naturally follows whichever trajectory my memory has set in motion, my imagination comes to the fore. Reminded by this agate of the gloomy weather I encounter whenever I travel along the northern seacoast, a grayish-white, soft-edged circle in the upper left hand corner becomes a mist-obscured sun-disk hanging low on the eastern skyline.

II.

Although, the day before, the morning sky had been bright and clear, by late afternoon, the inhabitants of Gevehard's village were, once again, beset by the unceasing, sullen drizzle. And now, the following morning, the light rain, which had come so unrelentingly inland from the sea, had soaked the men's clothing, wet their faces, and strewn their hair and beards with what appeared to be tiny, glittering glass beads.

The dreary weather had dampened the crew members enthusiasm for training, yet he, along with the others, trudged down to the strand at dawn each morning. Though the sun gave off little more than a shadowless half-light, the men splashed in the puddles and went half-heartedly through the cuts and guards. But, unlike the others, he struggled daily to keep up with the men, who were considerably younger than he was.

Each night, after he drifted off to sleep, the bogman's gravelly voice lured him, unmercifully, toward that dark pond in the Ironwood. Shaken by the encounter, he then awakened in the night and lay abed, open-eyed, till dawn. Left weary and jumpy, on the third day following the feast, he had risen again to another dark day to carry the additional weight of the bogman who was clinging so insistently to his shoulders.

The commander saw him, dropped back from his partner and waved him over. Walking toward him, Jerold yelled, "Aiken, I want you to help me out today."

Meeting half way, Jerold drew Aiken off to the side and held his blade out horizontally. Pointing its tip in the direction of a young man, he made small, stabbing motions. "See that youth? Over there?"

"You mean Aart?"

"Yup. Well, Gevehard and me are locked in a dispute over his qualifications to join the crew. The shipmaster likes the boy. He says he is clever and observant and wants to train Aart to be a steersman, someday. But that day will never come. The youth is as fresh as a spring flower and should not be coming aboard.

"Aart's father pressured Gevehard to make his son a member of the crew. But the fact that his father is one of the biggest landholders in the region and has a lot of standing in the village is no reason to pick a youth who is poorly trained. Watch him now. What do you see?"

"The way that he holds his blade, shows me his lack of confidence. He reacts without thinking. Is scared but covers it up by acting cocky."

"Yup," Jerold said. "You got that right, Aiken. I say, we should leave the boy in the pasture where he belongs, along with the cows and sheep. I wager Aart will be hurt or killed before we make it home. You need to understand, Aiken, I cannot afford to lose a single man. Every man we lose weakens the entire crew and lessens our chances of making it home. Once we are out to sea, unless we take captives, there is no way to fill out the ranks when a man gets sick, is wounded, or dies.

"Men that need to be chained to the benches are untrustworthy and more trouble than they are worth. It is best to pick the most qualified men and to give them a place in the ranks. But Aart is a fool. He is boastful and acts as though he is too smart to learn from the men with whom he practices. Either they baby him or do not know enough to give him a good, hard licking. He needs to work out with someone who knows the guards and cuts and who trained with hardened fighters—the way you and me learned to fight. He needs to work out with someone who can show him up, someone who is not afraid to get on his father's bad side."

Jerold explained how the shipmaster's need to live up to his forebear's reputations often led him to offer men more than he could afford to give. If Gevehard had one weakness, it was his desire to please others with lavish promises. But his pretense of generosity and his easy-going nature were nothing of the sort. In truth, he was preoccupied with his leadership and was fixated upon keeping it.

According to Jerold, Gevehard had taken on leadership at too young an age. Because of his youth, he was forced to prove that he could lead the very same men who sought to undermine his authority. And now that his reputation was established, he often resorted to flattery as a means to maintain and build upon his standing and renown.

At first, Aiken thought that Jerold was referring to Aart and his father. But then he began to discern a different kind of meaning in Jerold's words. When the commander said, "Gevehard knows how to build a man's trust and confidence," Aiken knew Jerold had not meant Aart. Instead he was talking about the offer that Gevehard had made several days before.

Gevehard's plea to join the crew had, indeed, renewed Aiken's confidence. Now that a man of honor had shown faith in his observations, he was no longer ashamed to speak up. Instead, men listened to him when he spoke. And, though he doubted Gevehard's praise had been mere flattery, Jerold forced Aiken to question the shipmaster's motives.

"There is one thing you should know," Jerold said, looking Aiken straight in the eye and giving him a grim, hard look, "I am commander. I am the one who makes the final cut. I decide who comes aboard the boats. In the end, it is not Gevehard's decision. It is mine."

According to the commander, Gevehard's spontaneous show of affection had been nothing but a momentary burst of enthusiasm. After the shipmaster's initial interest in Aiken had subsided, he should expect Gevehard to rescind the invitation.

Though Aiken trusted the shipmaster, believed he liked him and had truly wanted him at his side when they boarded the ships, he reckoned Jerold had told Gevehard that he had no faith in a man who was beyond his prime and was blind in one eye. Aiken, along with Aart, was one of the men whose qualifications for membership on the crew were in dispute.

Aiken's heart began to race, and he cringed in that shameful side-ways twitch. To fight the inclination took an extreme act of will. In an attempt to maintain his composure and to tamp down the resentment that had begun to boil deep inside, he clenched his jaw, pulled his lips back from his teeth, hooked his thumbs in this belt, drummed his fingertips on his hip bones and stared coolly at Jerold.

Now that he was being paired off against a boy, who might not even make the crew, Aiken knew he had been sidelined. The commander had made his request sound like an honor but, clearly, Jerold thought that Aiken should not get in the way of the other men's training.

And, just to make sure his message was clear, Jerold drummed it home one last time before he returned to his practice partner. He slapped Aiken on the arm in an overly friendly manner and said, "Remember, I am the one who makes the final cut."

Aiken walked up to Aart and explained Jerold's plan to have them practice together that morning. Aart looked awestruck at the prospect of facing-off against a man with Aiken's reputation.

As Aiken prepared to face-off against Aart, he silently repeating what Jerold had told him: I am the one who makes the final cut. Jerold's humiliating rejection hurt. Yet Aiken hardly knew where to lay the blame. Had Gevehard misled him? Or had Jerold dismissed him without the shipmaster's approval? Who could he trust? Who should he believe? Maybe he had taken Gevehard's offer seriously when, in fact, he should have known it was mere flattery—that it was nothing but the false praise spoken by a smooth-talking man who only wanted to impress his listener.

Aiken slipped his left arm through the shield straps and crooked his arm at the elbow. His sore muscles rebelled against the weight. Mounted in the center of the heavy, iron-rimmed shield, the large, domed, bronze boss protected a man's hand-hold on the backside of the shield during combat. He lifted the rusty long-knife he had picked out of the pile of old plundered blades with his right hand and, to get a feel for its weight and balance, whipped it back and forth several times.

If what Jerold said was true, Gevehard was a liar. He was no better than a thief. If the man was untrustworthy, Aiken did not want to be on his crew. Convinced the shipmaster was no different from any other opportunistic warlord, a man who would use his best friend for a shield when fighting for his life, Aiken cursed the man.

Then, second guessing his angry assessment, he asked himself whether it was fair to be mad at Gevehard. Who should he believe, Jerold or Gevehard? Had the shipmaster's invitation to join the crew been based upon his fighting skills and his ability to draw inferences from his observations? Or had the shipmaster only wanted to flatter him? Did the shipmaster, truly, offer people more than he could afford to give?

He lifted the hilt to his right shoulder, held the blade vertical on the side of his left rear foot, and angled the knife slightly to the back. His confidence was unshakable, whereas the poorly trained youth held his knife straight out in front and awkwardly positioned his shield too high. It was easy to spot Aart's poor control of his weaponry. Any enemy would single him out immediately and Aart would be taken down in the first clash of the season.

Over the months when Aiken had been carving Hild, she had kept him shielded. She had kept the bogman at bay. But now that the creature was back with a vengeance worse than before, after Aiken had suffered through another night of restless sleep, the border that separated the waking, daily life in the here and now from the nightly dreamtime were broken-down.

With the dank Ironwood leaking so precipitously into his everyday world, Aiken was unable to hold the bogman back. The creature clung to Aiken's shoulders and squeezed its knees into his sides above the hips. Urged by the bogman to defend himself against the commander's slanderous insults, Aiken was told to show the commander what he could do. The creature stung Aiken on the legs with its whip and ordered his mount to move in toward the boy.

In response, Aiken took a passing step forward as he swung his blade to add momentum to the full power of the cut. But instead of finishing the full arc, he pulled the cut and ended with the pommel level with his own belly and the point aimed directly at Aart's throat.

In a vicious taunt that was sure to turn any untested youth's stomach, he raised the blade just enough to threaten Aart's face with the tip of his blade. Aiken growled deep in his throat to get the boy to look him in the eye and to draw attention to what a knife can do to a pretty-boy's face.

Aart cowered behind his shield and stepped back. Aiken kept his knife fully extended, then moved his hand toward his right, rear hip and dropped the point to angle it across his body. After he had effectively closed off any openings on that side with a guard that was hard to penetrate, he said, "Come and get me, Aart."

Aart foolishly lunged at him without understanding how hard it would be to break through Aiken's defensive position. Aiken moved forward to parry the thrust and threw Aart's blade off to the side. The silly boy was such an easy target, it was laughable. "Where did you learn that, you fool?" Aiken screamed, mockingly, "You fight like a little boy."

Aiken moved his weight onto his right rear foot and took the guard position he called ox because of the way it mimicked the animal's horn. To prepare for a powerful thrust, he pulled the blade back further. When he let go, he gave the cut all the strength and speed he had, without pulling it this time. The bogman screamed in delight.

Left in a state of uncertain bewilderment, Aiken asked himself whether he was awake or asleep? Was his opponent flesh and blood, or was he a figment of the dream-time half-light?

But there was no time to think it through. An opponent was in his face. On the back-swing, Aiken rapidly lifted the hilt to his shoulder and angled it down at Aart. The move forced the boy to lift his shield high enough to hide.

"Aart will never know what hit him," the bogman squealed in Aiken's ear.

Aiken moved forward with a quick, passing swipe of the knife, missing Aart by less than a finger's breadth. The slashing cut ended with the blade on the side opposite from where it began.

The boy leapt back, jerked his shield too high and, turning his back to Aiken, made a run for it. Aiken took off, all the time thinking that, for an old man who was racing against a boy, he was not doing too poorly. He caught up with Aart, pulled back the fist that held the knife hilt and took aim at the space between Aart's shoulder blades. The pommel struck the boy with the full momentum of the punch. Aart dropped his knife, and fell flat atop his shield. His right arm was splayed out above his head.

"Hah. You lose, Aart. You are dead," Aiken laughed pitilessly. "I could have killed you right now with a thrust to the back."

Aiken was sick and tired of men who did not want him around. The commander was just the most recent of the many men who had wanted to keep Aiken out of the group. He was unwanted when the warband took off on their final boar hunt. He had been unwanted in his cousin's meadhall, been unwanted at the Assembly, been unwanted in the hamlet, been unwanted in the quarry, and now he was unwanted on the crew.

Aiken taunted Aart further. "You are no good. No one wants you on the crew. You will be dead the first time you skirmish. You will be far from home. And no one will be there to mourn you."

Yet, seeing Aart splayed out that way, Aiken was moved to pity for the poor boy. "Aart, you are a pathetic creature." He tucked the knife hilt into his belt, bent down graciously, and extended his hand. Aart grabbed hold and Aiken pulled him up. "You will be black and blue there, you know."

Stumbling around, Aart sniveled while struggling to pull himself together while Aiken continued to abuse him. "In a fight, your opponent will not wait for you to rearrange your shield and weaponry. You drop your blade, it is gone. One mistake, you are dead. You got that? Look, I have seen men die. Every man I fought beside died. I know what I am talking about." He slapped Aart's thigh with the broad side of the blade. Then he knocked Aart on the helmet with the pommel. "Now you are dead three times. Are you angry yet?" When he got no response, Aiken screamed in his face, "What do I have to do to make you angry?"

"I am not mad at you," Aart said with a sour face. "I want to be your friend"

"Well, forget that. I do not want your friendship. If I hurt you, you will hate me and then I will become your enemy. Just like that."

"But you are friends with the men in Gevehard's household," Aart whined. "Will you put in a good word for me with the shipmaster?"

Aiken scoffed and shook his head. "Aart, why would I do that? You cannot even hold your weaponry like a man. You are a child. If you want to make friends with the men in Gevehard's household you must first become a man yourself. You must earn their respect."

This pampered boy was so ignorant in the ways of men, he should have gone home and played hide and seek with the girls. "Is that the reason your father wants you on the crew? To get in with Gevehard's household men?" It angered Aiken to think that a well-to-do farmer, who had never gone to war, was willing to throw his son to the wolves just to get in close with the kinleader's household men. Aiken had seen every man, whom he ever cared for, die. Out of an entire warband, he was the only one left. Did the fools not understand what awaited them out there?

"You are a hopeless baby. Did you know that?"

Still unable to get a rise out of Aart, Aiken yelled, "Do you think we are playing? If you do, you are mistaken. The fighting life is brutal sport. Do you hear me?

Now, get angry or you will be dead the very first time you see a man coming at you. If you turn and run the way you did just now, your opponent will stab you in the back. Now get ready, you pitiful creature. I will not wait for you this time. You have to plan how you will kill everyone you meet, including me. Got that? Are you ready?"

Aart opened his shield just wide enough to peer around its rim and extended his blade toward Aiken's throat when Aiken saw the face of the very first man whom he had ever killed. It was that trick of the light again. He saw with his blind eye what had, otherwise, gone missing. And there he was. The face of a man from Chieftain Kendric's warband was where Aart's face should have been.

The bogman screamed loudly, "Take him down. Take him down."

The same resentment and anger he had felt back then, when he was a small, bare-faced boy living amongst a band of large, bearded fighters enraged him. This was his chance to get back at those big, grown men who had come out of the woods and laughed at him after he had made such a mess of his first boar kill. Now was his chance to prove what he could do.

The man's helmet was dented, and his leather jerkin was poorly patched in places where it had been slashed and torn in previous combat. Mistaking Aiken for an easy take-down, the man was drawn to his youthfulness. Aiken's opponent came in close, drew his knife back and made the cut. But instead of parrying it, Aiken stepped off to the side, and the on-coming slash missed him, easily. Aiken dropped the tip of his knife and, because he knew what was coming next, he let the point hang low. When the man lifted his shield and moved it to the side just enough for Aiken's blade to slip in, he saw the opening. Now was his chance to show them what he could do. With the pommel held at his belly and the blade pointed slightly down, Aiken took a passing step forward, fully extended his arm, and angled the tip up with the thrust.

Undefended and thrown off by the surprise attack, the enemy's wide-eyed astonishment stared death in the face.

And, then the man became Aart again. Just like that. It had been too late for the boy to respond. He had not seen the on-coming thrust.

Aiken stepped back in shock. He whirled around, stood with his back to Aart, and dropped his blade-arm to his side. He was afraid to look at the youth but knew he had to check. He needed to see whether the boy was hurt. Turning slowly, he was relieved to see that Aart was standing there with a quizzical look on his face. Aiken took a deep breath.

Unlike the way he had finished the cut the previous time, when he had caught the man unawares in the groin and killed him, somehow, Aiken had known enough to pull the cut. He had managed it just in time, before he had completed the thrust and without even knowing that he was doing it.

His knife hung from his right arm. He squeezed the hilt so hard his knuckles went white. His fist rapped the shield. In a struggle to contain his rage, he paced back and forth. The stones rattled beneath his feet. And he heard Mildred's voice, coming from somewhere beneath the rumbling sounds of the sea, saying, "Settle down, Aiken."

"Settle down." That was what he would say to his mount, one that was neighing, pounding the earth with its front hooves and about to rear up onto its hind legs when they came around a bend in the road and saw a snake the length of over half the height of a man and as thick as his forearm sunning itself.

Aiken would say, "Whoa boy, settle down. It is going to be all right."

He staggered back and forth, swung the blade, heedlessly admonished himself to think it through, and said repeatedly, "It is going to be all right. Just settle down. Settle down."

He reminded himself of his single guiding principle, one which he held above all others: no more good men would die on his watch. All winter long, he had put everything he had into carving the big red stone. He had made it his duty to see no harm came to Gevehard's men. Hild was meant to be his redemption. He had engraved the stone's purpose upon his soul. After he had let his companions die, he had promised: no more men would die on his watch. And now that he had attached living men's names and faces to those anonymous men whom he had sworn to protect last winter, Aart's face was one among them. If he could teach this boy how to skillfully handle a knife, Aiken would take care of all the crewmembers. If he trained Aart well, he would help Gevehard's men survive.

No doubt, Jerold had noticed how hard it had been for Aiken to keep up with the daily practice. At the end of the day he was all worn out. For years, the hardest work he had done was chop wood, walk behind a plow, swing a scythe, and carve and turn bowls on the lathe with small chisels. He, along with Aart, should have been sent out to the pasture along with the cattle and sheep. He had lost the stamina and strength he needed to survive against ruthless fighters. If he had lost confidence in his ability to hold his own in a fight, it did no good to lash out at Aart because of his own frustration. The result of practice had proven one thing—he was old. He was soft. The door to his youth had slammed shut behind him and there was no way to get it back.

Good. He had talked himself down. He had gotten past the snake in the road. Aiken stopped pacing and stood facing Aart.

Though taut as a bowstring, and every sinew in his body was prepped and ready to send its well-aimed missile flying, he kept his voice low and controlled. He offered to show Aart a simple set of guards, cuts and thrusts that he could chain together. If he learned them well, he could move forward by pushing his opponent back. Aiken told the boy it was easy to overwhelm any combatant that way. "Aart, your youth, your height, your strength and speed give you an advantage over almost anyone you will come up against. But you must learn the cuts and defenses, or even those advantages cannot protect you against hardened fighters. Do you understand?"

Though he got nothing in reply but a blank stare, Aiken continued to make his point. "Now, listen to me. When I was a young man, no one wanted to come up against me. No one. I was nearly done-in because someone who had hidden in the weeds threw a cursed javelin at me. That was as close as any man wanted to get—he had to hide in the weeds. You got that? No one beat me when he was close enough to look me the eye. When you face off against me, boy, you are fighting a man who was an unbeaten champion. Understand?"

Aart nodded. Now he looked terrified. Good. Let the gutless boy be scared.

Aiken demonstrated the cuts. After he had done that, when he told Aart to prepare for a skirmish, the boy held his hilt confidently at his belly with the point facing forward. "That is good," Aiken said. "Now, if you drop the point you will be difficult to hit." And the boy did as Aiken instructed.

They walked together through all the guards and cuts. Aiken repeated the same positions in the opposite direction, all the time advising the boy on the methods he could use to fend off an attack and turn it in his favor. He told him how to bluff. He told him how to fool his adversary. He told him, "Make believe your blade will come at your opponent from one direction. But then, when he is about to defend himself against what he believes is coming at him, you get sneaky. You change the course of your attack. You have to be quick and think ahead. But if you do, before your enemy knows what is about to hit him, you come at him from the direction he least expects. His momentum will prevent him from correcting his course of action. His swing will be harmless, and he will be left wide open. That is when you make your cut. You got that? Outwit your enemy. That is the secret to staying alive."

Aiken knew that the skills he was teaching Aart were beyond the boy's grasp, but if he repeated them often enough, eventually the things he taught him would begin to make sense and Aart would put them into practice. Even in the midst of a battle, he would hear Aiken's voice reminding him of the way to tackle the most immediate problem he faced.

Aiken began to relish this opportunity to share what he knew with the boy. Aart seemed to be sharp enough to understand what he was told. Maybe Gevehard had pegged the youth correctly and Jerold was mistaken. Maybe he would make a good steersman and a good fighter once he matured. Maybe Aart was a farm boy who had simply needed the right teacher come along, a teacher who would make him into a skillful warrior.

When Aart looked at Aiken with an awed respect that verged on adulation, Aiken could not help but take a liking to the boy.

When Aiken had been a child, not much older than Bertolf or Gevehard's youngest boys, he had been mentored by hardened fighters who had trained him in the same manner. Blades had never been a toy. They were well-crafted tools meant for killing. Given names, they were handled with the respect that one gave an honored companion. Whenever Aiken was tested, he squared off against the best men in the warband. If those men had not stricken fear into a young man's heart, nothing would.

In contrast, Aart had only a few days to make up for years of lost time. When they faced off again, Aiken said, "This time when I come at you, I will not stab you in the back. When my blade guts you from the front, you will see it as it happens. Now, get ready."

After they had gone at it for a time, they both were tired and out of breath. Aiken called a break and pointed to the hull of an overturned fishing boat near the shoreline. They walked over and leaned against it.

"Have you ever killed a man?" Aart asked Aiken.

"You do not wear a knife on your belt just for show, now, do you?" Aiken scoffed. "A blade has only one purpose."

"To kill a man."

"Yes."

When Aart asked how many men he had killed, Aiken told him, "In the heat of battle, you do not stop to count. You have only one thing on your mind—staying alive. Men are not born to kill, you know. Wolves, bears, crows, stags, hawks, they do not kill others of their own kind. Sure, they challenge each other to fight, but they have an in-born reticence against killing one who looks and smells like them. They make themselves look big, make noise, and come at their challenger with teeth, claws, beaks, antlers, and talons, to scare them off, just as men do with their weaponry. The difference is that men are hunters who stalk the perimeters of their territory and purposefully go after other men with the intent to kill. It is not because men are born to kill. It takes practice to respond and not hold back. It takes anger, too. Then, when someone comes straight at you, threatening to kill you, you will know what to do. It takes only one time to become a killer. After that, you need to temper the impulse, to keep from taking the life of someone whom you will regret having killed."

"Do you regret killing anyone?"

"Yes, of course, but that is not the point I want to make right now. I was smaller than most of the men against whom I fought but I turned my disadvantage into a strength. I made up for my lack of height and shorter reach with a talent for spying out my opponent's weaknesses. I saw openings in their defenses no one else could see. Being light on my feet and having lean, taut arms and legs gave me an uncanny speed and a precise control of the blade."

Aiken looked down at his chest and thighs with a wry smile, and said, "I am not the sinewy light-weight I was back then, when I was young. I have a wife now who thinks it is her duty to fatten me up. You might not think that a man with a face as ugly as mine would have a wife but she says she loves me anyway. I hope that you can find a woman as good as mine."

"Your daughter is pretty."

"Well, forget about her. Sunniva is spoken for."

"I have no chance? None at all?"

"None whatsoever."

"Well, then, I am sorry that you and me will not be family. I admire you. Will you tell me, Aiken, what it is like to kill another man? What is it like to see someone go down who never gets up again?"

"You mean, unlike today? When you went down, I helped you up after I got you in the back."

"Do you ever think about the men you killed?"

"All the time. Not a single one of them lets me forget."

"What was it like to live in a warband? I want to join a warband and ride a horse like you did."

"Aart, stop indulging in foolish make-believe. Look at you. You already have fuzz on your cheeks. You are already too old."

"But I like horses."

"Well then, go muck out the stables. Listen to me, Aart. When I was half your age, I was practicing daily with spears and the heaviest knives I could handle. I may have had a thick neck, and a strong chest and big arms because I was handling heavy weaponry and shields, but I was still a boy. I was a bare-faced child, not even old enough to grow a beard, when I fought my first battle."

Aart proudly rubbed his hand over his cheeks and upper lip where a beard and mustache were beginning to fill in and pleaded, "Will you tell me about that battle?"

"Even when I was a little child," Aiken said, "I listened to my father, my uncle, and their fellow war companions tell stories. Since you are a farm boy, maybe you are deficient in that kind of learning so I will try to fill in some of the gaps in your training." He leaned the shield against the boat hull, stuck the blade's dull point into the sand and, folding his arms across his chest, he thought over the best way to begin the story.

"A feud arose between two chieftains, Kendric and Gareth. Kendric made the foolish mistake of killing the other man's nephew in a spat over a game of knuckle-bones. He accused the younger man of cheating, but since Kendric had a reputation for being a sore loser, no one believed him. The other chieftains said that he had crossed the line this time. They were tired of his breaking the peace among the clansmen.

"Gareth grieved the death of his sister's son and took to visiting his closest allies one-by-one. Each of the chieftains, with whom he spoke, understood that Kendric was no longer trustworthy. And they agreed to declare the good-for-nothing, double-dealing trouble-maker a rogue.

"If Gareth had taken the accusation to the Assembly, the worst reprimand Kendric would have faced was a fine equal to the worth of a young, fighting man's life. But for Gareth, the man-price was not a suitable punishment. Although he expected to win his case because there were witnesses to the crime, if Kendric had denied their testimony and claimed innocence, Gareth would have challenged Kendric to fight in single combat. But, even that possibility was not good enough for Gareth. He reckoned Kendric was too cowardly to defend himself. Instead, he would have pleaded illness and picked a champion to fight for him. In the end, Gareth chose the most reasonable solution: the only way to right the wrong was to see the man dead.

"My own chieftain, Torwald, was among Gareth's friends. The night we all feasted together, I was seated in the meadhall when Gareth stood up from his seat at the high table and proclaimed loudly, 'I want to see a large army come after Kendric. I want to see Kendric's band wiped out, his meadhall burned to the ground, his treasury plundered, and his lands split between those who agree to back me.'

"The following morning, Gareth left with Torwald's promise. Shortly afterward, Gareth sent the wooden knife to each of his sworn allies. Within a few days, over four hundred fighters assembled at the agreed upon rendezvous. From there we rode to a field just outside of Kendric's hill fort. Believe me, Aart, I was thrilled to be part of such a large army.

"As soon as we unsaddled our horses and set up our encampment, a group of the rogue chieftain's messengers rode up, holding a tree branch as a sign they came in peace. Gareth mounted his horse and, along with the other chieftains, confronted the messengers. Kendric's men presented Gareth with a charred wooden knife, along with their chieftain's order to clear off immediately. If Gareth's army did not leave at once, they told him, the trespassing warbands would be chased away the following morning.

"Obviously, it was an empty threat. Kendric's warnings were meaningless bluffs. Gareth gruffly told the messengers that Chieftain Kendric and his men were as good as dead. He called Kendric a puny, cowardly wretch and, to insult him further, offered his men safe passage. Gareth told the messengers that if they wanted to live another day, now was the time to foreswear their oaths and to come over to his side. He would accept their surrendered weaponry and allow them to go on their way after the battle was finished. But, because most men deemed masterless status equal to a fate worse than an honorable death, no one accepted Gareth's offer.

"After that, Gareth, Torwald, and the other chieftains rode back to the allies' encampment. The men in the warbands crowded around the men on horseback. We listening to them recount the incident and heaped scorn upon the rogue. I was still a boy, but I wanted to sound like the older men, so I deliberately deepened my voice and copied what they said. When they made fun of Kendric and the men in his warband I roared with laughter, along with the others.

"Kendric's men were outnumbered by four, or even five times as many as there were in the allies' army. None of the rogue's friends or kinsmen came to his defense. Certain of victory, the allies were eager to be done with him for good.

"In the past, whenever I accompanied the warband on small skirmishes and raids, I had brought the warriors food, ale, and water, cared for the horses, or helped the men with their gear. When the fighting began, I usually withdrew, along with the horses, to watch from a safe distance. But because Torwald thought the youngest men would not face much risk when fighting in an army of that size, he said it would be a good test of our battle readiness to take up arms along with the older men.

"That night we prepared for war the following morning. It was the first-time Alger and me had been treated by the other men as their equals. Since everyone was kin, the men sat around the small fires they had lit in the field and mixed it up. I stuck close to my uncle Otgar. As he wandered about, he caught up with those friends and relations whom he had not seen for a while. He introduced me as his young nephew and proudly told everyone that I was Eamon's son. Others passed the time singing, tossing the knucklebones, knife-dancing, sharpening their weapons, and checking their straps and belts.

"Some men never tire of looking over their war gear. They check their straps and buckles all night long. To make certain their hammers, axes and spears are well hafted and their hilts are securely connected to the blade, they do it over and over until it is time to go. It staves off the restlessness.

"Because I am getting to like you, Aart, I will be honest with you. You are a clever fellow, but you are too fresh. It is only fair to tell you what to expect. Most men do not want to talk about what happens on a battlefield, but I will tell you the truth. I will not lie and cover up the horror of fighting with fancy, meaningless words. As the night wore on, my building excitement mixed increasingly with dread.

"As jovial as the men had seemed to be that night, each one knew that he might die the following morning. A fighting man lives with fear day and night. He fears death, crippling wounds, humiliation, and dishonor. He fears everything that comes along with killing—pain, haunting dreams, regret, grief, and death. A warrior knows that when the Matrones spin his life-thread, they assign him death on the battlefield. Being slain with his weaponry in-hand is his certain end, and he struggles to contest it from one day to the next.

"After that first battle, I knew death was always there awaiting me. The Matrone who holds Endbringer is always prepared to take me down. She was the opponent who showed up every time I fought. I see her square off against me even now. I see her face in every man's face. Today, yesterday I see death looking at me. I see dead men's faces when I visit the dreamtime. I see them when I am awake. They are always there, staring at me, ready to come and get me."

"But the Matrone did not get you, did she?" Aart said, staring at the scars jaggedly crossing the right side of Aiken's face. "You were hurt and lived."

Aiken grunted. That was another story, one which he was not about to tell. To tell the story about Kendric and Gareth was entertainment for Aart but not for him. It ripped Aiken's heart out. These stories were not mere storytelling, nor were the heroic tales, the poets told, meant to be fun diversions. The poets could, through carefully composed stories, use orderly meter and rhyme to banish the battlefield chaos, the terror, and the shades of the dead. Their stories offered men the means to wash away with their tears, their pain, and their grief. There, within the holy walls of the ceremonial meadhall, a show of measured, deliberately restrained sentiment and suitable feelings could honorably be contained. If men did not glamorize war with the talk of heroic valor, but only recalled the brutality and gore, they would never go back to fighting.

Aart did not understand, but someday, if he lived long enough, he would. The horror and pain were hard to talk about. Instead, men talked in insulting terms about women they bedded. They spewed out hatred for anything that looked like weakness and looked down, contemptuously, upon anyone they could overpower with their own bodily strength. Men kept the forbidden feelings bottled up, or they related their tales with loud-mouthed, swaggering bravado just to keep the horror, shame, terror, and sorrow in check.

To both draw away from that place of loss and to remind himself why he was talking to this silly boy, Aiken said, "I am going to tell you the truth." He took a deep breath, sighed deeply, and picked up the story again. "Before dawn, we girded ourselves and took our places in the ranks."

"Were you scared?"

"Of course, I was scared. If I had not been scared there would have been something wrong with me. Or maybe I would have been too stupid to know any better. I was excited and scared at the same time. This is why you go over and over the same cuts and guards. Your training instills the confidence you need to survive because, when you come face to face with your enemy, you stop thinking clearly. Instead, the most ridiculous thoughts cross your mind. Because you can no longer comprehend the danger you face, that part of you goes numb. It wants to run away and hide. But since hiding is not an option, if you want to live, you must rely upon your arms and legs to act. Even when you are terrified, you will know what to do because of your practice. Otherwise you will be so scared you cannot move.

"You will wet and soil yourself. It will feel like your arms are bound to your sides with rope, and your ankles shackled. Some men freeze solid as ice. They just stand there. And after the fighting is over, if they survived, that is, other men have to pry their fingers off the hilt. After that happens, a man is no good for fighting any more. Or, a man will turn and run like you did. But you know what I said about running.

"So, I will tell you what to do when you are scared. Fear erects a wall against you, but there is a door in that wall. You know you practiced well and have faith that the doorway leading through your fear will open. After you go through it, you get to the other side. Then you are beyond fear.

"Aart, after you have listened to everything I told you, do you still want to be a fighting man?"

"Yes"

"That is only because you are young and untested. You think the Matrones will spare your life. But wishful thinking will not protect you. Only practice will."

To get back to the story of Kendric and Gareth, Aiken explained the strategy the allied chieftains had devised. "Right from the beginning, Gareth's scouts had chosen the battle site well. Although the field was flat and neither side had an advantage of higher ground, Gareth's army faced west. The morning sun would be low enough on the skyline to shine in the enemy's faces. Along with the size of Gareth's army, the sun at our backs gave our fighters an additional advantage.

"Our army formed a wedge-shaped shield wall. Gareth and the other chieftains were in the point. Torwald told us boys to stay in the back lines. But Alger and I pushed up front. We wanted to see some action. We took our places at the end of the far-left flank. If Kendric's men had not shown up, our army was prepared to march forward and to storm the stockade.

"But Kendric's men rode up, jumped from their saddles, and took their places in the opposing line. Those of us who were among the allies made fun of the opposing side's weaknesses. The enemy chieftain should have been out front, leading his men, but he was nowhere to be seen. Gareth was enraged because he wanted to be the point man facing off against his nephew's killer.

"We called Kendric a feeble coward. To undermine his men's courage and their willingness to fight on behalf of such a weakling, we screamed savage threats and insults. Then, we began to strike our shields with the flat sides of our blades." Aiken picked up the rusty long-knife and struck the bronze shield boss with its flat, steel side. Bang, bang, bang, bang, bang, bang. "It was hard and fast like that, but louder. Believe me, when you get over four hundred men beating their blades in time against the bronze bosses, the sound is deafening. You feel the drumming inside your chest.

"To challenge us, the enemy hurled the first spear. It fell short and dropped down in front of our line. Right there, we saw the sign of Kendric's inevitable defeat. Then it was time to go. To form the wall, each man lapped his shield over the one that was on his right. Ours was more than five ranks deep, bristling with spears, axes, and knives, whereas Kendric had only enough men to stack two ranks in the center and one paltry rank out on the flanks.

"Since the side that looks biggest and makes the most noise wins, we yelled at the tops of our lungs. The men furthest back banged on their shields. Then, in time with that bang, bang, bang, we stepped forward together, being careful not to break the lines. At first, we went slowly. No one wants to get there so they shuffle in little steps. Then, the inevitable happens. We met the opposing wall. Grunting hard, we pushed our shields against theirs'. The ranks behind me pushed their shields into Alger's and my back. He and I were in between, trying to break through. Men used axes to pull down the opposing shields. Others stabbed their spears over the tops of the enemy's wall. Alger and I used our shorter combat knives to lunge at the men whose shields were opposite ours. We aimed to get under their shields and to stab at their legs.

"The men in the center of our wall pushed forward with their wedge to break through the opposing line. Kendric's shield wall was so weak on the flanks, it fell apart immediately. We wrapped around to outflank them on both sides. After that happened, the whole wall broke apart. That was when the fighting opened-up. Men hurriedly sheathed their short knives and hefted their heavy, long-knives. Once the men were ready to fight in hand-to-hand combat we came at one another.

"I remembered my practice well," Aiken said, reminding Aart of the purpose behind this storytelling. "You want to know what it is like to kill someone, to see him go down and never get up again? I will tell you about the first man I ever killed.

"Coming at me, he called me a mommy's boy. Maybe it was meant to weaken my resolve but I thought it was laughable. He was a rugged-looking warrior who had picked me out of the horde because I was a youth. He thought a boy like me would be an easy match. Men will look at you the same way, Aart, so be ready for them. In my case, he was in for a surprise."

"You killed him?"

"Well not yet," Aiken said. "Even before Kendric's warband had ridden onto the field that morning, they all knew they were dead men. Not one of them accepted Gareth's offer. They looked as though they had spent the night in heavy drinking. The one who challenged me appeared to be no different. He could not hide the way he staggered. After we exchanged a few cuts, I saw what was about to become his final, fatal mistake. When he raised his shield up and to the side enough to give me an opening, I was ready and quick with the lunge. I caught him in the groin. My blade pierced his leather jerkin and dug into the flesh. The thrust only stopped because the knife point struck the back of his hipbone. I tell you, I was so happy I wanted to kiss my blade right then. I leaned into my back leg to pull the blade out just enough to thrust again. I made a forward, passing step to force my knife more deeply into the widening gap between his shield and belly. The second time I aimed higher and pushed in hard. The knife bypassed his hip and went all the way through his back. His knees buckled. As he went down, my blade arm twisted. I had to use my foot to push him off my knife.

"Well, Aart," Aiken said, "He never got up again. I did what I am training you to do. Just learn from my example."

Aiken told Aart how he had chained together his guards and cuts as he moved forward on the attack. He always stepped into the thrust and used the guards to recover. Never once did he step back or turn away. "Attack. Attack. Attack. Remember that, Aart. Attack, attack, attack.

"It was not easygoing. I was forced to walk over the bodies of wounded and dying men. Some screamed and grabbed my legs. Some were my enemies. Some I knew by name. Some were my friends. Some begged me to save them. Others begged to be finished off. But I just kept going. I never stopped. My knife hit the mark so many times it dripped with blood. The fabric on my trousers stuck to my thighs with sweat and blood spray.

"When I got to the back of the enemy line, I came upon the skirmish between several of Gareth's men and those who were in Kendric's honor guard. The killer who had begun the entire misadventure was cowering in the center of his men's encircling shield wall. Since Kendric was being attacked from all sides, he soon fell. The last of Kendric's honor guard called the retreat, turned and ran. The rest of the enemy's ranks were in shreds and trapped between Gareth's army's two opposing lines. That was when it became a rout.

"Aart, a battlefield is utter chaos. When men bearing weapons come at you from all sides, you will swear the wolf Treachery is loose. You will beg the Lords of Battle to favor you. Not to forget you. You will promise them anything, just to let you see it through to the end of the day, to join the celebration in the meadhall once it is finished. To see those meadhall doors open wide, and the flaming hearth fires burning inside, and the gleaming bronze, silver, and gold tableware. That is what you want to see, one more time. But before you can get there, you have to fight for your life.

"Remember, Aart, it is when your enemy turns and runs that a battle is won. It is easier to kill a man who is running like a rabbit than one who is coming at you like a wild boar that weighs twice as much as you do. Remember that Aart. Never, ever cower or turn and run the way you did today."

He patted Aart on the back and felt around between his shoulder blades. "How does it feel back there? Is it sore?"

Aart nodded, downcast.

"Good. I hope it is sore for several days. Every time you feel it, promise you will never turn your back on your enemy. Let me hear you say it."

"I promise. I will never turn and run."

"Good. If you do, you become a rabbit in another man's eyes, and he will cut you down from behind. You will be stabbed in the back next time, with the tip of a blade, not struck with its pommel. Got that?"

"Yes."

"Get at them from the flanks or rear. Make your enemy more scared of you than you are scared of him. You must yell and scream at the top of your lungs and build your rage. At a certain point, your rage opens that door and you run right through your fear to the other side. To stay alive, make your enemy turn his back. That way you will not be forced to look him in his eyes and see that he is one of your own kind, someone who has a mother and a father, a wife and babies back home. But once he becomes fair game, that is when the killing happens. That is when you become a wild cat in pursuit of a deer, and you stab him in the back.

"A feeling of battle madness comes over you. I cannot explain it, except to say that you feel as powerful as the Lords of Battle, themselves. You feel like you are on equal footing with the ruling powers. You know you came through the worst of it alive and there you are, at the top of your game. That is why men cannot stop fighting. They want to be at the top, again and again and again. You believe you are untouchable. Nothing can take you down. Nothing can get to you. That was the first time I ever felt the madness come over me, and I could not quit. I ran back into the midst of the fighting.

"Unfortunately, the combat was more bitter than anyone had expected. Despite the overwhelming odds of taking on an entire army, or maybe it was because each man had known that he was dead already, Kendric's men fought hard. Even after many were injured they continued to fight and gave it everything they had.

"Then, all at once, I stopped dead in my tracks and looked around. There was no one left to fight. The last remnants of Kendric's warband had thrown down their weaponry and fallen on their knees. They had given up and were begging for their lives. It was over, just like that.

"After you come down from the battle madness, you come down hard. Then you turn to seeking out your fallen war companions. It is a grisly ordeal, It leaves you numb because the anguish is just too great to bear."

Without warning, right there, on the strand, where Aiken was standing shoulder to shoulder with Aart, leaning back against the fishing boat, all the anguish, fear, grief, and battle madness combined to wash over him like a tidal wave coming inland from the sea. He felt the same as he had that day so long ago. He no longer knew where he was. The place where he stood took on a strange transparency. The sand and gravel overlapped that long ago, bloody field. Aiken was both on the shore of the Merchant Sea and on the battlefield outside of Kendric's fort town.

He was there because he had never left it. He was still looking over the broken bodies where they lay strewn in the dirt and trampled weeds. Try as he might to discriminate his friends from the enemy, when he looked into their faces they returned his gaze with blank, hollow stares.

"I had lost track of my best friend and was frightened I would find Alger amongst the fallen. Before the battle began, Alger and I had sworn to take turns covering each other's back." Aiken's throat was so tight, he began to choke and struggled to go on. "In the confusion, we had lost sight of each other and I feared I would find Alger lying on the field."

Aiken stopped the telling. He looked up at the sky. It seemed like iron bands were tightening around his ribcage and preventing him from catching his breath. His heart pounded so hard he felt light-headed. He feared he would fall over, gasping for air. And there he would be, laying on the sand, where everyone could see and judge him a deeply flawed man who was unfit to join the crew.

He pressed his back against the overturned boat hull and sank into a half-crouch. Taking note of his trembling hands and how they had tightened into claws, he clenched his fists, propped his elbows against his thighs, and dangled his hands between his knees. He bowed his head and willed himself to take long, slow breaths.

Whereas youthful, blameless Aart, unmarred by battle wounds, and the inevitable loss that comes with war, was oblivious to the signs of breakdown in a man. Unable to imagine what Aiken was going through, he only knew the story had stopped before it was over. "Did you find your friend alive?" he asked.

Aiken, naked and unprotected, struggled to retain mastery of himself. He straightened his back and looked up at Aart. "No, I did not find him. Not right away, anyhow. I heard someone call my name. It was my uncle Otgar, my father's brother. He was in Torwald's honor guard. After my father died, Otgar had treated me like a son. I lived in his house. He sponsored me when I became a member of the warband. And there he was, laying on the field."

Even then, years later, just the thought of that horrid day, made Aiken begin to cry. He stifled a sob and wiped his tears away with the back of his sleeve. "Otgar was so badly hurt, there was nothing I could do to help him. He lay there, dying. All I could do was kneel at his side. I held his hand and whispered my heartfelt gratitude for all that he had done for me."

To avoid Aart's gaze, Aiken looked away and stared into that emptiness. After that day, he had lost two fathers. He cleared his throat and described how he had hefted Otgar's body over his shoulder. "He was a big man, and I staggered beneath the weight. Another man came running to help me. Together, we carried his lifeless body to a wagon that had come onto the field to retrieve our dead and wounded."

"Did you think that it could have been you? Aart asked. "You might have been one of the dead men laying in amongst those bodies. If that had happened, it would have been your first and last battle."

Enraged that Aart did not, could not, understand how bad he felt, Aiken struggled to control his rising temper. He rubbed the back of his neck and clenched his jaw. That day he had lost the man whom he had loved like a father. Unable to talk to a boy who could not hear the story in a heartfelt manner, Aiken said, "No, I was angry that Otgar was dead."

Cursing the youth's simplemindedness with a threat that would, inevitably, come about in the future, Aiken spat out, "When you see your friends die, the same will happen to you. Take my word for it. You will see them die, unless you are the one who goes down first. And then you will be angry. The rage and fear and suffering does not go away. It becomes a part of who you are for the rest of your life. The screaming I hear at night when I sleep is the worst. Sometimes, the screams are mine and wake me.

"Now, listen to me," Aiken said, turning to look directly at Aart. "A man who knows he is meant to die—maybe tomorrow, maybe in the next raid, maybe in a surprise attack or an ambush, maybe in an attack inside the meadhall, or on the battlefield, or in his bed—is set apart from everyone else. Even after you get home, all that matters will be your warrior brotherhood. You are no longer one man alone. You are, instead, one arm or leg of the many-limbed warband. To maintain your warband is all you live for. Your desperate loyalty to one another is all that matters.

"Men yearn to jump into the fray. It makes no sense. Every day and night you live with danger. You are always alert, always on the watch against death. You eat and sleep and drink danger. There is nothing glamorous about it.

"Perhaps, the most wonderful thing about a warrior's life is the deep affection you feel for your brothers-in-arms. Every day you are alive, you are greedy to drink in the sweetness of life. You never know whether you will become nothing but greasy, bitter char and smoke tomorrow. And yet, you cannot give it up. A settled life is dreary, dull, tedious. You want to live on the sharp edge of the blade. That is all you desire. All you live for."

Dismayed, he shook his head and murmured to himself, "It makes no sense. It makes no sense. But the times when I was looking in death's face were the times I felt most alive," and added, in a subdued tone, "Why is that?"

But when all he saw in response to his question was Aart's puzzlement, Aiken said, "Go practice with the others. Story time is over."

Aart picked up his shield and blade and ran off. Whether or not the boy could hear his trailing voice, Aiken did not know, but yelled, nonetheless, "Do not forget what I taught you about chaining your guards and cuts together."

He pressed his back hard against the overturned boat hull. The sounds and sights of mock combat, the feel of the hilt in his hand and the shield at his side were as familiar as they had been that day when he had fought his first battle. His clothes were soaked through to the skin. His trousers and tunic clung to his legs and arms, same as they had done that day when he had fought on Kendric's field. The only difference between now and then was that his trousers had clung to him with the sticky blood that was shed by those whom he had hurt.

The practicing men's angry outbursts, their deep, booming voices and their calls of alarm, the clash of blades, the hammering on the shields and splitting wood all sounded the same as it had that day when he had fought outside Kendric's hill fort. Aiken confessed to thoughts that were buried so deeply he did not even know they were there. Hidden beneath his daily practice, they had been waiting in the darkest recesses of his soul for an opportune time to chase him down.

The day after his first battle, he had not taken pride in what he had done. Maybe his grief had something to do with his disappointment, but he had not felt the way he thought he should. Afterwards, when the poet praised him, he had not felt as heroic as he was made out to be. He had derived no glory or pride from his first kill. The old man was a staggering drunk. Aiken had done only what he had had to do to stay alive. If he had let up, even for a moment, he would have been dead, too.

He had stumbled around on the mired field looking for Alger among the dead and wounded. Hiding his face in his hands so no one could see him weep like the little boy he was, Aiken had crisscrossed the field screaming his best friend's name and saying over and over, "All this killing to avenge one death. It makes no sense. It makes no sense."

The day before, when they had laughed at Kendric and called him a puny coward, Aiken had misunderstood how many good men would need to die because one bad man had done something wrong. They had fought to get back at one guilty chieftain who had killed another's nephew. All the safeguards had failed. The means for taking a grievance to the Assembly, where the accuser stood before the judges and challenged a man to either speak the truth or admit his guilt, had failed to keep the peace.

It had happened because lust for violent retribution had built up an army. The threat of bloodshed and common hatred had tied them together. Feud was a treacherous hunger in the blood crying out to get even. The craving for vengeance led entire bloodlines to kill each other off. Families went after each other, time and again, sometimes for generations, until every man was dead. That was why Lord Glory had handed down the laws that were meant to rein in men's blood lust. But because there was no way to enforce the rule of law, it had been ineffective that day, and it still was.

Finally, when Aiken and Alger found each other alive, the two friends clutched at each other. Seated in the churned-up dirt, Alger did what he could to comfort Aiken while Aiken did the same for Alger. The fear, the loss, the grotesque horror, pity, blood-pounding excitement, anger, and hatred were all mixed up. Whether the bond, which Aiken had felt then, had been more than brotherly affection, he did not know for certain, because he had never been with a woman. But, right then, he thought he would never love a woman as much as he loved Alger.

Men were busily cleaning up the field, caring for the wounded, and stripping and plundering the dead. Others had gone into the village to pick off the stragglers, assert their control of Kendric's holdings, take captives, and plunder the treasury. When an older warrior saw Aiken and his friend seated in the mire, he did not tell them to get to work. Instead, he patted their shoulders and left them to cry it out. Because it was said that the battle needed to be relived again and again until the memory trailed off, young men, who were not yet hardened to combat, were allowed more time to let the memory grow faint. But it never went away, not entirely.

That day, the boy became a man. Aiken sat on the blood-soaked field crying alongside Alger. And now that the past was mixing up with the present, Aiken admitted to his friend how the memories still came after him, in unexpectedly devious ways, to remind him of all that he had done. Because the bogman rode him into the night battles, he feared sleep. The shades of those men whom he had killed never stayed dead all the way. They came after him night and day to force him to fight them all over again. Even in the daytime, the bogman played its tricks on him. Even inside his own house, he felt edgy, irritable, and fearful. He always sat in a place where he could face the door. Whenever he laid abed, he slept with his back pressed against the wall.

There were days when people crowding around him in the marketplace forced him to throw down whatever he was doing. He would walk off and leave Mildred to settle-up with those folks who were eager to buy his bowls, pitchers, cups or spoons. His heart raced so fast it skipped beats and thumped so loudly it sounded like a galloping three-legged horse.

The common men and women, who knew how much his craftsmanship was valued by the chieftains, wanted a piece of him, too. They wanted a bit of his luck, his worth, his standing, and his soul. The alarming dread cut his flesh all the way to the bone and never left him. Some days he was strung so tight, he felt harassed, ill-treated, picked on, and always on the defense. He begrudged every man and woman who challenged him. When he felt that way, anger was all he knew. He heard insults in unintended remarks. Tormented by doubt, he suspected men and women of playing upon his weaknesses and of getting back at him for unintended slights.

Back when he had been an untested youth, fresh as a spring flower like Aart, he had not been jumpy like that. "Remember, Alger," he said, "how we laughed? Remember, I was so light on my feet I could win any foot race? Back then, my restlessness came from joyful eagerness to move, not to recoil in fear."

It boggled his mind the way the terrible things he had seen so long ago still followed and tormented him. Holding that rusty old blade had brought it back, all right. But it was more than he had bargained for. The racket of clashing blades and shields, the din of men's screams and groans was more than he could tolerate. Aiken's head throbbed and felt too heavy for his neck to hold up.

Aiken stared hard at the fighting. The sounds of slaughter taunted him. He heard the ringing clamor of steel on steel, the wooden shields splintering, the madness of killing. He felt every harsh sound like a stabbing blade. The noise intensified the pains shooting through his dead eye, and he recoiled as though he was hurt.

Instead of passing through the opening in the wall that fear had erected against him, dead men were rushing through the wide-open doorway. Threatening him with hateful reprisals, the shades were on the attack and ready to take him down. Screaming mockery and insults and brandishing their dead, bent weapons, they were coming after him, ready to take him down.

And there, in the forefront was Alger, backing through the doorway. Long-knife in hand, and doing his best to protect Aiken from the onslaught, Alger yelled, "Get out of here. Let's go. Move out."

Aiken pushed himself up. He felt wobbly. He knew the haunts were coming after him from behind, but, otherwise, he hardly knew where he was. The damp mist hung thick as a curtain closing off his sight of the surrounding shoreline and the village buildings atop the mounds. A skirmishing throng was up ahead and the sea was at his back. That much he knew. There was no way to go but forward. If he did not get out of there in time, he would be trapped between both sides and be caught in the rout. He felt as though he had turned to a block of ice and strained to move. He ordered himself to take one step at a time—right foot, left foot, right foot, left foot. Passing the piles of gear, he tossed the helmet, rusty old blade, and shield onto their respective piles. Without a glance at Jerold, he took off. He was finished, done for. He mumbled a plea. Then it became an outright cry, begging the Lords of Battle to come to his aid.

The world he could see, touch, hear, and taste had become airy and dream-like. The world was not hard and fast. Instead he had come to an elusive, shadowy place where the world that he had known, years before, was more genuine than the actual one his body inhabited on the shore of the Merchant Sea.

An otherworldly wind came in from the land of the dead and threatened to blow him away and out to sea. Aiken lost hold. He became unmoored. Swamped by the all-pervasive fog, he floated amidst the flotsam. Bouncing on the waves, all that he had lost floated past: his name, his father, his mother, his home in the fort town, his war companions, his horses, his hounds, his hunting bird, and his honorable place among fighting man. Though they were gone forever, he had never stopped grieving their losses.

His wish to be seated at the high table alongside Gevehard floated past. All winter long he had anticipated being honored in the longhouse. He had wished to hear his name spoken again by a man of honor, to hear the praise for a craftsman like Wayland during the feasting celebration. All winter long the hope had kept him afloat. But now he was drowning, thrashing about. Belief that he would join the crew and would, again, become a member of a brotherhood of fighting men drifted past. He reached out to grab it, but it was beyond his grasp. All he had ever hoped to achieve sank beneath the surface.

III.

Aiken kept going. He made it past the skirmishing men and jogged up the sloping mound where the roofed, open-walled eating hall and the outdoors cookhouse stood. A quick glance behind him confirmed his fears. The haunts were still coming after him. If they had been embodied men, who responded to hard and fast steel, he could have stood his ground and taken them on. But these men inhabited a space beyond any kind of reckoning.

He slowed his pace to a fast walk. Several bonded men who worked in Gevehard's household sat on the benches arranged around the tables. Sheltering from the damp mist, they gnawed on bread, cold meats, and pickled roots before they would need to return to the ironmongery, fieldwork, carpentry, and other jobs that the shipmaster employed them in.

One of the men waved Aiken over and raised a cup. Aiken, in turn, inclined his head with a quick nod but, feeling too shaky to hold a cup steady, refused the offer.

He would have gone on his way, but one sidelong glance at what awaited him out beyond the edge of the open-walled eating hall convinced him to change his mind. The shades stood around in a horde with their bent long-knives and other weaponry in hand. Invisible to everyone but him, a warband made up of dead men, who came after living men in the night, were now coming after him in the daytime, too. They were threatening him with the blades that had been scavenged from the battlefield and folded cross-wise to prevent shades, like them, from avenging their deaths on the living men who had slaughtered them.

One of the shades heedlessly rested his weight on one leg. Another had tucked a blade hilt in his belt and stood with his arms folded across his chest. Another's feet were planted wide apart. His fists were stuck to his hips and his elbows pointed out to the sides. There was one who held a javelin haft. He held it straight upright and leaned his weight into the haft. The haunt who looked most threatening stood in a half crouch. Like a man ready to attack when the time was right, he flexed his arms with a two-handed grip on his long-handled double axe. They were waiting until Aiken was isolated and alone. Then they would come after him the way that Gareth's men had gone after Kendric and hack him into little, tiny pieces.

Aiken's heart skipped beats like that galloping three-legged horse. Though there was work to do in the holy grove, he was wary of going out there alone—not with that band of haunts in pursuit. For the time being, anyhow, Aiken preferred the company of living men, even if the group consisted of men for whom he had little respect—a bunch of bonded men and one itinerant freeloader.

The vagrant's garments hung so loosely from his bony frame, it looked as though his clothing were suspended from a hook. Judged on the state of his mud-caked, hooded cloak and heavy, worn-out tunic, along with his poorly made combat knife, and the way his gray, untrimmed beard trailed to the center of his chest in long, scraggly ropes, Aiken sneered at the man.

Aiken had first caught sight of the threadbare stranger the day before, when he had seen the fellow hanging around the outdoors eating hall. Some of the men, who were about to leave on the boat, had paid the old graybeard to forecast their futures with the staves—the long Hazelwood sticks upon which the twenty-four secret signs were marked.

Aiken was sitting on the bench, eating, when he had had the distinct impression that the man was eyeing him. Though he did not care to talk to the man, he privately questioned whether he might have come across him in the past. He might have seen him in a market town but was unable to place him. Aiken doubted that he had ever known him, back when he was a member of Torwald's warband.

Asked whether he knew the stranger, Edmund had shrugged off the question. Explaining that now, with so many men and women bringing trade goods from inland farms each day, there were folks filling up the village that even he, who had lived here all his life, did not know. Besides, it was not unusual to see wanderers stop by at any time of the year. Because traveling men offered gossip in exchange for a handout and a chance to sleep in one of the storage sheds or byres, Gevehard was reputed to pay wanderers for information about his neighbors, friends and enemies alike.

To explain the curious man's background Aiken and Edmund concluded that, first of all, because only highborn men read the staves, and secondly, because only warriors or former members of a warband carried a combat knife, the wanderer had been a fighting man at one time. But beyond that simple speculation, they could only guess that he had been deemed a masterless man who, after he had committed some unforgivable act of treachery, had lost his reputation. Or, maybe he had been on the losing side of a battle and, like the last of Kendric's men, had run off after he had escaped with his life. But whatever the circumstances that had led the unseemly man to his current, impoverished situation, Aiken and Edmund only knew for certain that he had been forced, by necessity, to read the staves in exchange for shelter and a meal.

Because Edmund feared that those bonded men, whom he oversaw in Gevehard's household, would spread hearsay that traveling men would pass on to other kinleaders and villagers, he discouraged them from gossiping with the vagrants who frequented the village. So, that day the men who were seated around the tables were careful to observe Edmund's orders to ignore the old beggar.

Treating the food laid out upon the table like his own private feast, the graybeard picked at the platters of bread, cheese, pickles, and meat and stuffed handfuls into his mouth. Since none of the fieldworkers or carpenters wanted a stave reading, the wanderer appealed for their attention with mindless chit-chat. But the bonded men's disregard for the annoying man's attempts at conversation had undermined any dignity he may have, otherwise, retained.

It was only when the old itinerant chose to entertain his captive audience with a riddle that Aiken perked up and listened:

> "A sunny beauty, my charm
> Is undimmed by age.
> Earth's child before I was pulled
> And carted from my homeland."

When the skeletally thin man lifted his arm out for emphasis, his tunic sleeve slipped down to his elbow to expose the knobby joints on his thin, narrow wrist.

> "Though shaped to thwart men's fears,
> I am deemed too weak for battle.
> Rather, I offer solace, fulfill desire,
> And reflect men's adoration.
> My power is greatest over those who love me most.
> What is my name?"

Finished with his recitation, the graybeard speared a hunk of meat and slipped it onto the slice of bread that he held in his other hand. He folded the bread, slid the meat off the blade, lifted it to his mouth and tore at it with his teeth.

Up until then, the hood on the man's cape had been pulled so low over his brow that his features were partially hidden in shadow. But, when he looked up to study his audience, he tipped his head back and the hood slipped down to his shoulders. One good look at his face revealed his high cheekbones, crooked nose, blind eye, and the scars crisscrossing the bridge of his nose.

Aiken stood off to the side, in a place from which he could watch everything that went on around him. Though he had chosen to keep his own counsel, when the riddler focused his sharpened gaze directly on him, Aiken inclined his head, took a step forward, and bellowed, "Gold."

The beggar's brows shot up. "You got it right," he said, and lifted his ale bowl in honor of Aiken's answer.

Aiken returned the man's approval with a quick nod, and asked, "Are you surprised?"

"Well, perhaps I am. Would you would like to test your luck by squaring off in a battle of wits?"

Since a verbal duel offered Aiken a chance to regain his footing and to sharpen his wits, if he were to come out the victor of a good contest, it might give him the edge he needed to take on the more daunting challenge of confronting the night terrors who awaited him on the sidelines. Thus persuaded to take advantage of the beggar's offer to contest with riddles, he said, "I accept your challenge."

The two contestants agreed to trade riddles until one of them failed to answer correctly. The primary rule all men agreed upon was that the contestant who asked the riddle must know the answer. If a dispute arose, the men on the benches would decide the winner.

As for the other men, an opportunity to watch a good riddle contest awakened them from their slouched lethargy. They sat a bit straighter, exchanged glances, and nodded enthusiastically. Clearly, because both contestants were knowledgeable in word-craft and the secret signs, it promised to be a good game. Looking back and forth between the stave reader and the stone carver, one fellow even wiggled in anticipation.

"What shall we wager?" the old man asked.

Aiken suggested, "Three copper coins."

The old man responded with a sour face.

"What is wrong? Aiken asked pointedly. "Do you prefer to wager silver?"

The beggar laughed, "You are joking, of course. I am a poor man."

"What do you suggest?"

The graybeard offered to read the staves for Aiken if he lost, but Aiken shook his head, "I have no interest in a stave reading." He dug into his purse and pulled out one coin. He walked over to where the man was seated, held the copper between his thumb and forefinger, tipped the far edge onto the table and, pressing the angled side down hard on the plank with his thumb, he laid it flat on the table with a sharp click. "One copper. Here is mine."

The man relented, pulled one coin from his purse and laid it beside Aiken's.

"Well then, let us get started," Aiken said, "You go first."

Right from the beginning, the way the graybeard stumbled over his words failed to elicit much confidence in his ability to win the ante pile:

"A fierce lot follows me all my life,
Though my courage means little.

In this savage world—"

He paused, for whatever reason, and after several moments of thoughtful deliberation completed the verse:

"I am no master of my fate.

In the storm of battle, I was broken—"

Again, he paused, stuck his tongue between his front teeth, and wet his lips before he continued:

"By the smith's iron handiwork."

He let out a deep sigh, and breathed in deeply. The way he halted now and then tended to increase both his opponent's and the other men's doubts as to whether he could pull the riddle together at all.

"I grope, blind of eye, without hands,
 Lose all hope that help will come to me."

Twisting his hands together, he looked despondently at the ante pile and let out a deep sigh. It seemed as though he had already taken leave of the two coppers, but shrugged his shoulders, and gave the riddle another stab:

"Without feet, I am dragged
And carried across the field of battle."

By then, everyone was embarrassed for the old graybeard. Finally, after a long pause, he managed to come up with two more verses:

"Weary of war, I fall.
I feel the flame ignite my bones.

My life is short,
My name is cursed and forgotten."

He paused one last time, before he managed to blurt out the final line:

"Tell me now, who I am."

Once he was finished, the old fool looked around at the seated spectators, gave them a weak grin, reached for a bite of cheese, and shoved it into his mouth.

Whereas the graybeard's poor recitation had, undeniably, elicited doubts about his ability to win the contest, Aiken responded with stunned recognition. The man had hit the mark spot-on. For the second time that day, Aiken felt time crumple.

Contrary to his earlier assessment of the man, he asked himself how the beggar could have devised a riddle for which the answer was his own, cursed namelessness. He, himself, was the answer to this riddle.

Aiken silently listed the things that had happened to the mysterious object who the graybeard had so acutely described: after he had fallen on the battlefield, he had crawled across the frozen soil and groped blindly in search of his weapon; the chieftains had stolen his identity, cursed him to lifetime of misery, and called him a nameless nobody; he was wracked by the pain the smith's iron handiwork had caused and, even now, was tortured by the invisible, iron point that was still lodged inside his skull; and the flames—the horrible flames which the old man had described in the riddle—corresponded to flames that he had ignited when he burnt his war companions' bones.

Aiken gasped for air. The bands tightened around his chest, the same way they had done earlier, when he was down on the strand. Though he tried to put a stop to the thoughts and struggled to shove them aside, they forced him to give in. Lost and unable find a way out of memory's entangled thicket, there was no way to go but through it—to charge into the ensuing anger, horror, and regret the flames stood for.

Events from his past had led to a complex, indebtedness to fire. Both the curse of fire, which he feared would plague his descendants for one hundred lifetimes, and the pyre flames he had lit the night when he had burnt his companions bones, remained persistently on the edge of continuous recall. His response was so immediate, even if he tried to keep from dwelling upon the pictures inside his head, he had no choice but to review that night and to think it through until it was spent.

How much of his memory of the event had truly happened? He never knew for certain. Sometimes dreamtime and waking memories got so mixed-up he was no longer certain of the truth. Whether or not his recall was a memory of something that he had seen in the dreamtime, or whether it was something that he had seen when he was awake, did not matter. Either way, this much he knew: he had burnt his companion's bones. Of that he was completely certain. He also knew that he had sworn an oath, that very night, to lay the fault for their murder at their killer's feet inside the hall of justice.

The memory and his oath had been carved into his soul the same way he had chiseled the pictures into the big, red stone. And like stone, the memories of that night were permanent and everlasting.

He had no choice but to let it play out until it quit. The memory rode him. It goaded him. It would not let him stop until it had worn him down to nothing. He kept going around and around, circling the memory until, like that day, so many years ago, he crawled out of the hole through which he had fallen several months before. In a reversal of the moment when he had fallen through the sink-hole beneath the tree roots and had landed upon the cave floor, he had pulled himself up and out of the same caved-in hole. Not as a shade of a dead man who was climbing out of an earthen grave to join the living, but as a living man who was climbing out of the earth to join the dead.

He had been told that Torwald and his war-companions were there and he had known what he must do. But he had not fully prepared himself for the awful sight that greeted him.

After he clambered out of the hole in the tunnel roof, the dew-coated, early springtime grasses felt wet and inviting beneath his hands. The earth was soft and buoyant beneath his knees. He glimpsed tiny, white flowers sprinkled here and there amidst the yellow-green grass blades. The sight of the blossoms facing the sunlight elicited a joy he had not known for a long time. But when he lifted his face and looked toward the river, the sight of his brother's decayed bodies knocked him flat.

The men were hanging by their necks from the branches of three, large cotton-woods growing near the riverbank. Their bodies had been gnawed on by foxes and wolverines, and pecked at by crows and magpies. Though their bones had withstood the scavengers and the ravages of snow, ice, and wind, not much was left of them. Clothed only in the sun-bleached fragments of the clothing they had worn the day they were killed, all that was left of them were their souls, still bound to their bones and haggard flesh, and his memories of them as vibrant, living men.

Helpless to do anything but weep, Aiken perched on one of the massive cotton-wood's roots. The last time he had sat beside the Warring River was the day when he had played knucklebones with Alger. And then his life had changed forever when the boy had ridden into the encampment screaming.

Aiken knew what he must do. He sighed deeply and stood. He was ready. Though he hesitated to look at their remains too closely, once he had stifled the dreadful disgust, he slowly approached the first tree and set to work. Because it was important to name each man, he identified each of the corpses by the ripped and shredded rags, and the hair that was stuck in matted clumps to their skulls.

Tears so blurred is one-eyed vision that he could barely see what he was doing. He climbed the first tree and pressed his belly flat against an overhanging branch. As he felt his way along, he eased out over their bodies and used Rushing Harm to slash through the ropes. One by one, their remains dropped and crumpled on the ground below.

After he had finished cutting down the bodies that hung from the first tree, he climbed the second and third ones and did the same. Once their bodies were all down, he picked up and carried the remains of each man to a place where he could lay them out in a row. He picked up the axe Berling had handed him on his way out the door and walked among the trees in the forest, searching for dry, fallen logs and kindling. He threw all that he collected onto two huge piles.

After Aiken had placed the men's bones atop the stacked wood, he kindled the fire with his flint and steel. He stood there, watching the flames consume all that was left of his friends, his chieftain, his name and the life he had lived before.

By then, the sky had darkened, and the first stars were appearing above the valley. When the first presence came to join Aiken, the uncanny realization made him feel so ill at ease he wanted to run. Along with the knowledge that he no was longer alone, a chill began at the base of his neck and spread outward and downward until he felt the uncanny cold course through his entire body. A shudder wracked him and he drew closer to the flames, but the chill remained unaffected by the heat. He felt so cold, he could have been staying the watch on the coldest night of the year. But if he had stepped any closer to the flames, he would have been scorched.

As each of the men came to stand around the blazing pyres, they celebrated their lives together, joked, and told stories, just as they had done when they had been alive. Aiken recited the praise songs he had composed in the their honor. He asked forgiveness for having outlived them, for not protecting them, nor for sharing in their common destiny.

That night had left him, everlastingly, with a foot on each side of the divide between the living and the dead. Even now, the sight of the shades of his dead war companions standing around the flaming pyre, seemed more apparent than the living men who were seated on the benches beneath the outdoors eating hall roof. Aiken was inhabiting both places at once, and the riddle contest between him and the old graybeard overlaid his memory of the riddle that Alger posed:

"Roads, fields and yards
Around men and women's
Dwellings are but borrowed places
Until the woods reclaim them.
All living things return to the soil,
Wash into the rivers
And flow into the sea.
Say now, what is my fierce power?"

Aiken thought through the clues to the riddle and answered, "All things are ruled by Father Time and Mother Necessity. In their dance around the egg, from which earth, fire, water and air derive, this world is given order by their eternal turning from birth to death to rebirth."

Alger took obvious pleasure in his friend's clever answer, tossed his head and joked, "Who gave you such a grand way with words?" His long, yellow hair tumbled down his back and glinted in the firelight.

At that moment, his friend looked so beautiful, Aiken felt weak-kneed with longing. But when Alger playfully punched him in the arm with his fist, the same way he had done countless times before, a sharp chill stabbed Aiken all the way to the bone. He shuddered and clenched his fists. There he stood, beside Alger's strangely transparent form, repulsed.

Aiken began to boast about his plan to champion justice on their behalf. He said that he, alone, would prove who had planned the ambush and, he alone would take the charge of murder to the Assembly and accuse the guilty of the men's unlawful deaths. Though there was no way to prove who had been behind the attack without testimony from witnesses, Aiken told them he suspected Leofar had planned it and Oswald had carried it out.

Of all the men, only their chieftain, Torwald, had refused to join them around the fire. He stood off to the side and kept his own counsel. When he was unable to hold back any longer, he stepped forward and loudly spoke up in defense of Leofar. "Aiken, I refuse to listen to another word of your slanderous accusations against my nephew."

Aiken looked around at his companion's faces, silently asking them to back him. But none agreed to accommodate his request. Instead, because the enemy's shields had all been blackened with char, each man agreed that the identity of the warband had been difficult to ascertain. But, because they had all seen Oswald astride a horse, they agreed, to the very last man, that those who had attacked them had to have been Oswald's men. No one had seen any of Leofar's men.

Aiken countered their claim with a description of the warband he had seen hiding in amongst the dried reeds and marsh grasses near the riverbank, directly beneath the bluff.

Torwald stepped up to Aiken and asked him, to his face, "How is it that you saw them and no one else did?"

"What did I tell you?" Sigmund countered. "He is a liar. He was in Oswald's pay all along. He was the one who gamed both sides and now he wants to lay the blame on an innocent man."

"No," Aiken said, "no one saw those men because the dried weeds were high enough to hide them. It was when Alger and I came over the top of the bluff that the additional height gave me a good view. That was when I saw the other warband. More men than I could count were hunkered down in amongst the reeds."

"Alger, did you see another warband?"

"No. The snow was falling so thick that it was hard to see anything ahead of me."

"Do you dispute Alger, Aiken? How can you prove it was Leofar's warband?"

Aiken had seen them so briefly when a wind gust cleared the snow, he had no answer.

And now, along with the passage of time, the memory of the men's ridicule, too, had changed. Along with his uncertain memories, when he looked back upon that night, he saw the hate in their eyes.

"You just showed up to see the job was done right. Admit it."

"That is how you managed to outlive us."

"You snake in the grass should be as dead as we are."

"Go ahead. Admit your complicity in our deaths."

Unable to counter their insults, Aiken defended himself by cruelly pointing out how ineffectual they all were as lifeless shades. "You may think of me as a reckless brawler who should have died long ago. Yet, here I stand, still fleshed out while the rest of you are nothing but rags and bones. I did not double cross you. As soon as I reached the bottom of the bluff I was hit with a javelin that came at me from out of the reeds. I tell you, I am not a coward nor a double-crosser. When I say I will go to the Assembly, you may not believe me, but I swear that if the guilty chieftain refuses to speak the truth, I will lay a cloak on the ground and establish his guilt through a meeting of the blades. Even if I lack a kinsman who will swear an oath to be my witness, I swear to discover the truth. Lord Glory and the Matrones will grant me victory through trial by combat.

"Listen to me," Aiken screamed, "blood cries out for blood."

But Torwald was unimpressed with Aiken's boasts. He shouted, angrily, "Oh, stop it, you noisy braggart. Aiken you are showing off like you always do. Tell us about your grief," he scoffed mockingly, "we are the ones who are dead, not you. You always look for reasons to challenge men. Now stop boasting about what you plan to do. Just do it."

"Do it. Do it. Do it," they all chanted mockingly.

Aiken stood there before their accusations, an innocent man. Though seething with rage, he remained silent in response to his chieftain's humiliating rebuke. He unbuckled his belt, slipped off Rushing Harm's scabbard, and said, "I will swear an oath to fight the accused fair and square." He held the sheathed knife out to Torwald. "Take it. I will swear an oath on my blade."

Torwald studied Aiken coldly. To him, the man who stood before him was nothing but a reckless brawler and a braggart. He had little faith in Aiken's boast to bring their murderer to justice. Aiken had always been easily distracted by whatever piqued his fancy at any given moment. He had a reputation for darting off to chase down an appealing woman. He became fascinated with warriors from other warbands who impressed him with their equally outrageous boasts, and often pressured them into squaring off against him in a friendly practice session. The other men in the warband said, behind Aiken's back, that his adulation of other men had shown his need for another father to replace the father and uncle whom he had lost. But Aiken claimed that, because his rivals were the ones whom he was most motivated to defeat, they became his greatest allies. If he befriended them, he could convince them to engage in friendly practice and teach him a few of their winning strategies. It had been a good way to improve his one-on-one combat skills.

Might Torwald have been jealous of Aiken's admiration of the other champions whenever he sought their attention? Perhaps. But, no matter the reason, just the sound of Aiken's name had become such an irritation that it set Torwald's teeth on edge. Of all the men who had served in his warband, Aiken was the last one his chieftain would have picked for this ordeal. Yet, the undisputable fact remained that Aiken was a clever strategist, had been unbeatable on the battlefield, was a champion when it came to one-on-one combat, and was the lone survivor. And now, Torwald needed to rely upon this annoying man to accuse the guilty, bring them to justice, and mete out the punishment.

Given no choice but to bend his left knee to the earth and extend his hand to accept Aiken's sheathed knife, Torwald placed the scabbard on top of his right thigh and rested the hilt upon his knee. He then laid his arm upon the sheath lengthwise and placed his right hand atop the hilt. Aiken knelt before his chieftain and slipped his right hand between the hilt and Torwald's knee. The way his chieftain's shade drew heat from the back of his hand felt as though he was resting it upon a block of ice.

"I call upon Lord Glory to be our witness," Torwald said. "You, Aiken, have removed my bodily remains from the gallows tree. When you lit the pyre, you freed my soul from the cursed fate of wandering this world as a shade. For this I am grateful.

"Aiken the Strength of Oak, you have withstood the lightning and the wind. You survived the storm. I command you to place your trust in Mother Necessity's laws. Keep faith in her decree. There are consequences for all men's actions. Fate shall provide you with the means to close in on the one who murdered us. Their guilty deeds shall be punished, and the murderer's debt paid. Whatever must come shall come to be. Aiken the Strength of Oak, I order you to become Mother Necessity's right hand of justice."

Aiken lifted his face to stare at the Lord's torch-lit wagon circling above his head. "Lord Glory, I ask you to hear me out. For as long as I, Aiken the Strength of Oak and the murderer both shall live, for as long as the sun shall shine and the worlds endure, I promise to track down the man who slaughtered Torwald and the members of our warband. I will accuse the murderer and will challenge him to speak the truth. If he refuses, I will challenge him to a judgment of arms.

"Just as Lord Glory drove the wolf Treachery into the Ironwood, so shall the man who breaks the peace be driven for as far and as wide as men drive wolves into the hinterland. Justice shall prevail over slaughter.

"For as long as I have two good legs and two good arms, and this blade named Rushing Harm, I promise, before Lord Glory, to force the man, who I hate, to kneel. I will look into his uplifted face, hold the blade above the place where his collarbones meet and will plunge Rushing Harm straight down through his heart. A fountain of blood will splash me, and the debt will be washed clean. Justice shall triumph over slaughter." Aiken then leant forward to seal his promise with a kiss to his liege lord's frigid hand.

"Aiken the Strength of Oak, stand now," Torwald said. He handed Rushing Harm back, and with the prescience of the dead, added, "There will come a time when the murderer, whoever he may be, will suffer the punishment he deserves. Do not lose heart, Aiken. Never give up the fight."

Aiken stood, slipped Rushing Harm's scabbard back onto his belt and took his place alongside Alger.

The pyre's fiery fingers continued to do their work. And as the flames unwove the last, thin strands that had bound the men's souls to their bones, each man's knotted ties to this world became undone. His snarled, dismembered sinews were untangled and his longing for this life became unfastened.

And, out beyond the light cast by the flames, at the edge of the woodland, hidden in the darkest shadows, the shapes of Lady Blessed and her husband, the Lord of the Whirlwind, were overseeing the attendants in their service.

Each of the Lady's attendants took a man by the arm to lead him to a place where he could join her for one, last, earthly night before he began his meanders through the otherworlds. And, after he was carried away on the eddying smoke, each man's soul dissolved in the nighttime sky.

When Lady Blessed realized that Aiken was still alive and not among the dead, she devised another plan for him. It was not till later that Aiken understood that his body and soul had been loaned out to Mildred that night, instead.

As the gray dawn began to appear in the east, only Alger and Torwald remained. Alger stepped forward to renounce the feast in Lady Blessed's Hall of Many Seats, and declared, "I choose, instead, to stay beside my friend until he has completed his promised retaliation. Not until he is finished, will I be finished too. Then we will leave together."

"Stay with him, Alger," Torwald said. "Do not leave until he has fulfilled his oath."

"Hey there," an unrecognizable voice seemed to come from out of nowhere. "Hey there."

Aiken was still watching the flames burn down. Soon he would begin to cover the bones and ashes with spadesful of dirt.

"Have you been struck dumb?"

Uncertain of what he had been asked and unable to answer, Aiken struggled to understand where he was. In an attempt to figure out whose voice he had heard, he looked around—all his war companions were gone. So, who was this graybeard?

Unable to place him, Aiken concluded that the man must be an interrogator who was about to decide his fate. He feared that he had been taken captive. His chest was so tight he could not breathe and thought he was bound with ropes. He lifted his arms and looked at his wrists. They remained unbound. For that he was grateful.

"Do you know the answer to the riddle I asked you?"

Aiken gulped air and tried to figure it out. He tipped his head confusedly to the side. He recalled a night when, after a small skirmish, he and the others, who had won the fight earlier in the day, had been feasting in Torwald's meadhall. A single, dazed captive was led in through the doors and forced to stand before them as they discussed his fate. In the end, they all agreed that a riddle contest would be a fitting way to reveal the three Matrones' judgment.

Although one could argue that the ordeal was fair because it offered the captive a chance to have a say in the outcome of his fate, it's true aim was nothing of the sort. Rather, it was an indulgence in cruel entertainment. Its purpose was to exact a taunting revenge on the last man who was left standing after his companions had all been slaughtered in the skirmish. With the full weight of either life or death dependent upon the captive's answer, they had posed a riddle and the man had made a wild guess.

As it happened, everyone agreed that he had gotten it right. They untied the ropes that bound his legs and arms and let him go. Once the man was freed from his bondage, he sprinted from the hall. The feasting men followed him out the door and laughed so hard they cried. Bent double by their hilarity, tears formed runnels down their cheeks. They slapped each other on their backs and held their sides, and said the captive ran with such speed he could have outpaced any rabbit.

Now, Aiken wanted to know, what was he in for? Depending upon his answer, would it be either death by hanging or a half-life of wandering?

"What was the question?" Aiken asked.

The graybeard repeated the last lines of the riddle.

"Carried across the field of battle,
Weary of war, I fall and feel the flame ignite my bones.

My life is short; my name cursed and forgotten.
Tell me, now, who I am."

He had been asked to give his name. His name was the answer to the riddle. But, he thought, I have no name. Those who stole my name took all that was mine and left me with nothing. I stand before these inquisitors, knowing that I am but a voice without speech. No one can hear me. I am nothing but ash, charred bone, and empty air.

"Speak up, man."

How had this graybeard become his interrogator? If it was possible to declare his name, he would. But he was unable to rouse himself enough to recall that part of himself that had a name. Lost in his waking dream, it was impossible to find his way out.

Armed men were walking up the sides of the sloped mound. They looked tired, out of breath and hungry. Long-knives and axes hung from their belts. They stood beneath the roofed shelter, filled cups and tore at the bread that the women had laid out on the table. The way they jostled and joked with one another, Aiken did not understand what they had to laugh about.

He was a nameless outsider amongst them. He had to get away. He needed to watch out. If only he could remember his name and solve the riddle, then, if he guessed the answer and got it right, they would let him go, and he would make a run for his freedom.

Trying to puzzle it out, he thought it through backwards. He remembered the graybeard had asked him a riddle. It had described that dreadful day when he had been hurt and his companions had all been murdered. Then, on top of it, there was the night that he had burnt their bones. In the end, all that was left of his chieftain and his companions had been the hot, glowing cinders. When dawn came, he had used the spade that he had been given to dig a hole. After that he had spread the ashes and their charred bones over the bottom and had mounded the soil over the top.

Never in his life, not until that day so long ago, had he felt so alone. Those men, whom he had always relied upon to stand beside him, were gone. Instead, they had trusted him to pursue justice in the defense of their honor and good names. That dreary morning was the first time he had known how unprotected and broken he was—and then he had it.

"I have the answer," Aiken said. "My name is Shield."

Though the graybeard's distasteful mockery of his friends' suffering disgusted him as no riddle ever had, when he saw the men nod heartily to show their approval of his answer, Aiken breathed more easily. Yet, he took note of the way his interrogator continued to stare at him.

The men on the benches turned their heads toward the graybeard to seek his final say on the matter. With all eyes on him, the man exaggerated the way he glanced at the ante pile. His mouth puckered in the same way it would, had eaten a sour pickle. He nodded regretfully, and said, "I accept my opponent's answer."

It was then that a young woman, whose age was about the same as Aiken's own daughter's, passed between the outdoors cook-house and Gevehard's longhouse. The fleeting comparison to Sunniva became another clue to the puzzle of his identity.

Absorbed, not so much in watching the girl walk past, as he was in watching the men who followed her with their eyes, Aiken recognized in those men, who sat on the benches, a threat to his own daughter's dignity and safety. The way they nudged each other and mumbled jokes about her shapely contours disgusted him. Others made obscene gestures with their thumbs and fists. When the men tried to catch her attention with whistles, she, in turn, ignored them, as any honorable woman should.

Aiken was coming back to himself. Though he was still dizzily needing to sort things out, his most immediate response brought his blood to a rapid boil and set his teeth on edge. Shocked equally by his urge to come to the defense of a girl, he neither knew, nor whose safety was his concern, he was taunted by his own past recriminations.

Although it might be said that a small measure of comfort could, possibly, be granted by the lack of recall of one's past, the more Aiken came back to himself, the more he remembered the times in his youth when he had lured young serving girls into his bed with hints of vacant promises. To possess enviable women was a privilege of wealthy men. The chieftains filled their mead halls with girls who were selected for their beauty and charm. Girls differed little from all the objects that the chieftains displayed to show-off their wealth and prowess. To use those women for their pleasure was one of the advantages the men in the chieftain's service enjoyed. The men saw in them fixtures of the luxurious meadhall feasting. Taught to serve a man according to his preferences and to give him whatever he wanted, the most sought-after ones were the youngest girls, had the smoothest, creamiest skin, and biggest eyes. Like a deer, they played the role of prey and the men played the role of the hunter.

To see his own past in this light disturbed and disgusted him. To acknowledge that he was as guilty as these common, lowborn men, he was forced to ask himself whether each of the girls, whom he had bedded, had had a father who would have chased him down and come after him if he could have. But because the young woman had been dragged from her home and forced into servitude like the gold in the graybeard's riddle, she had had no one to watch out for her or to protect her safety.

All eyes were now turned on Aiken.

"It is your turn," the graybeard said.

To maintain his precarious hold on all the random parts that made up this everyday world was like fixing a broken chair or treasure box. But now that he had been told what he must do, he called upon every last, left-over scrap of inner strength that he could muster, and put together a riddle on the spot:

"Now listen closely and be on your mettle.
Lay down your shield and sit astride my straight branch.
Together we shall slash the wind dispatched upon my arc.
My iron point shall pierce my target.
Identify your steed, and I shall be your fair friend."

Even after all the clues to the riddle had walked past, and the answer had been enacted with thumbs and fists, along with accompanying whistles and slurs against the young woman's pride and honor, the beggar struggled for a while before he admitted to being stumped. Looking down and shaking his head despondently, he mumbled into his beard as he thought it through aloud, "If an iron point and straight branch becomes a spear—whose weapon is it, anyhow?"

After he had given it more thought, he pulled himself upright. Seemingly, quite pleased with himself, he looked squarely at Aiken, and said, "Would it be a man's weapon?"

Aiken nodded approvingly, expecting the man to continue with this line of reasoning. But when the graybeard's voice dropped off at the end, Aiken was disappointed. The graybeard asked again, vaguely, "Would it not?" He rested his chin on his fist, looked down and off to the side, and stared vacantly at nothing. Finally, he said, "I do not know."

To see in the man's ignorance a chance to get back at his examiner, Aiken was increasingly self-satisfied with this opportune turn of events. He prodded the beggar, saying, "Either give it up, or answer: what is the target of a man's straight branch?"

The old man shook his head. Apparently unable to guess the correct answer, he threw his hands out to his sides and said with a shrug, "I do not know." He raised his brows, looked around at the other men, and pleaded for help. "Does anyone know? What sits astride the creature shaped for battle?"

One of the men seated on the benches cried out, "His woman, you, old fool. Or have you forgotten how to get it up?"

All the men laughed mockingly and shook their heads in wonderment. They turned to their neighbors and asked how any man could be so ignorant about something so obvious. When the stranger finally understood the meaning of their joke, he pulled a face to admit his chagrin. His foolish expression then led his audience to laugh even more loudly than it had before.

After the men had quieted down, the beggar adopted that same, confused look again. "But what does the man thrust?" he asked.

One of the men, after reaching unwittingly toward his groin, wiggled so gleefully at the obvious suggestion, the graybeard singled him out. "Well, tell me," he asked pointedly. "What does he thrust?"

Seemingly shy, at first, about naming aloud something, which he knew so well and with such intimacy, the man struggled to find a fitting figure of speech. He grinned broadly, looked around at the others, and said, "His fondest weapon is a man's greatest pleasure."

All the men lauded their friend's cleverness with whoops and cheers.

Ready to accept the answer, Aiken stepped forward to shake the hand of the man who had puzzled it out so skillfully, but before he was allowed to speak, he was interrupted by the graybeard.

Affecting ignorance once again, he asked meekly, "But, what is his target?"

Though Aiken was the contestant, who had originally devised the riddle, it was apparent that his opponent had plotted to usurp the meaning of his simple word game. And, though uncertain of what the graybeard was up to, Aiken chose to step aside and watch.

The man who had originally answered the riddle was stymied for a moment before he lit up and said, "It is the soft heart behind his woman's shield."

Without a pause, the beggar asked, "When does a woman lay down her shield?"

The unsuspecting men seemed none the wiser and remained ignorant of the danger this presumably simple-minded fool could pose. Rather, they trusted the graybeard's sincere stupidity. Only Aiken saw how the beggar had set them up to fill the roles that he had assigned them in this spontaneously devised game plan.

Each man, in an attempt to get in a word edgewise, used all manner of insinuating hints to out-do the others. Finally, one shouted more loudly than all of them combined and said, without subtlety, "When a man points his naked spear between a woman's legs."

Wildly amused by the answer, the old beggar clapped his hands, tossed his head back, and roared with laughter. He had taken control of his listeners, all right. "When does his target expect no danger?" he asked so blamelessly that there appeared to be no hint of risk.

One of the men, who sat on the benches, raised his eyebrow and wet his lips before he answered, "Neither he nor the woman expect danger to befall them when her husband is not at home."

Whereas those men, who had come from practice down on the strand, coldly narrowed their eyes and clenched their jaws, the answer raised a hearty guffaw from the bonded men.

It was almost too much to take in all at once. Dismayed, as he was at watching the answer to his riddle unfold in this way, Aiken felt his own possessive anger and resentment build along with the crewmembers'. If it came to a fight he had no doubt about to whose side he would be drawn. He would stand with those men who would soon be leaving their wives and daughters in the company of the lowborn laborers. The awareness of how they had been so cunningly manipulated made no difference. Only moments ago, all the men had shared a common purpose. All their lives had depended upon the success of the upcoming voyage and were working toward that end. But now, after the old man had drawn the line between them, they had separated into two, divisive camps.

The beggar could just as easily have been standing on the field between two opposing shield walls, only moments before the conflict began. With the enemies hurling insults and calling each other worthless cuckolds, all the graybeard would need to do was throw his spear. And when it landed, the battle would begin.

On one side were the freeborn men who were eyeing the men on the other side with distrust and thrusting their hips forward to make a show of the long-knives that hung sheathed from their belts. The men who sat on the benches were unarmed workers who did the heavy labor in Gevehard's household. More than willing to stick it to their superiors, just to get back at those men for whom they held festering grievances over the loss of their freedom, they were ready to use a man's wife or daughter to their advantage whenever an opportunity arose to humiliate her husband or her father.

Of all those men who were sheltering beneath the open-walled eating hall, the graybeard was the only one amongst them who appeared unperturbed by the rising tide of ill feelings.

To carry on with his line of questioning, he asked pointedly with mock sincerity, "What danger slashes the wind?"

This time it was one of the crew members who answered. He spoke the unspoken words that his fellow war companions all were thinking and, just to be certain that no one missed his threat, he drew out each menacing word, "It. Is. Her. Husband's. Blade." He followed his speech with an extravagant show of unsheathing his knife. By then it was so deathly quiet beneath the outdoors eating-hall roof that everyone could hear the blade ring as it came from its scabbard. He held the knife high overhead and brandished it. He then, held the sheath with his left hand and with one sweeping gesture slowly slipped the knife back into its scabbard with his right.

The two opposing sides stared at each other. And as the brittle silence stretched out in time, peace held between the men.

Meanwhile, Aiken, who in any gathering kept his back to the wall and his eye on the door, remained apart, and took the measure of each man. When a sudden stitch in his side reminded him of the bogman's presence, he asked himself whether it was inevitable that some inherent, ugly impulse, some untamed force lurking somewhere within each man and woman, laying hidden in the place where their souls visit the dreamtime perhaps, if given a little nudge is ready to call out to those who share common ends and unbending loyalty, to goad them on? And, after being supplied with the bogman's weaponry, are they so lacking in a will of their own that they will act out, unthinkingly, the roles and expectations that Mother Necessity assigns them? Hidden in the dark shadows, will this unspeakable power that awaits the perfect moment then enlist their participation in ruthless cruelty?

"I submit," the stranger said. "I do not know the answer." Affecting a simple child's guilelessness, he added, "Before we agree to disband, there is one last matter to take care of." He looked around, threw his arms out to his sides, and asked, "Do you all agree to declare Aiken the winner?"

By then, the riddle contest was forgotten. Other things of a more pressing nature had caught hold of the men's attention. The unarmed men eyed uneasily the hoard of armed men who were closing in around them. Reminded that, although a woman alone presented an alluring temptation, an offer to cure her of her loneliness held the risk of sudden death, each man nudged the one he sat beside and, altogether, they made their decision. They threw their legs over the benches and took off in all directions. The armed men banged their cups on the table, turned, and went back to their practice down on the strand. Within moments the shelter was empty, all but for the graybeard and Aiken.

Stunned by the graybeard's cunning, Aiken considered the many ways the stranger had set them up. Had he not created entire worlds within his riddles? By disguising one thing as another he had used rhyme and rhythm as if it were an incantation. He had invited people to enter the confused, upside-down worlds he described and, once they were all inside, he locked the gates. After that, they each became a marker in a game of tables. And the graybeard was the one who took command of the board. Right from the beginning of the contest, he had set each of the men on a square and, then, had pushed them around like ignorant fools who had no minds of their own.

First, he had described a young bride or serving girl's allure. Then, he had portrayed, in gory detail, a man's inglorious fall on the battlefield and the loss of his life, name and reputation. After that, he had taken over Aiken's own riddle and, drawn out the description of its full meaning to suggest the powerful threat that could befall any man who gamely satisfied his lusty appetites with a woman who, as he had described earlier, was tantalizing as gold. With nothing more than subtle implication, this silver-tongued trickster had suggested a risk greater than any warning a man might speak, even if he were he to stride into the central yard and to yell at the top of his lungs, "Keep your hands off my woman." Instead, the graybeard had directed the men to imagine themselves as the subject of revenge. And it had worked.

Both curious about this unseemly beggar's identity, and equally wary of a man who could whip-up a man's ire so readily, Aiken approached his opponent. As etiquette demanded, he respectfully congratulated the man on being a wordsmith of the highest order.

In turn, the stranger put forward a proposal. "You and me should team up some time. I think we did a good job protecting that girl. The men have been forewarned to leave her alone. Do you not agree?"

Clearly, Aiken was left speechless by the old man's devious suggestion and hardly knew how to answer. There had been no scheme between him and this itinerant beggar. He had never intended it that way, anyhow.

The stranger asked significantly, "You do not want those men to come after your daughter when you are away from home, now do you?"

"How do you know I have a daughter?"

"There are no secrets in this village."

"You are right in your assumption. I do have a daughter, but otherwise, you have it wrong. When I thought up that riddle my motive was to make the answer easy. I gave it away. I did not care if you won."

In contrast to Aiken's blunt insult, the stranger took the slight in stride and complimented both their skills. "For two men who are equally conversant in the secret signs, it was a good contest."

Aiken tipped his head to the side and asked, "How so?"

"I know who you are. Your name is written in stone for anyone to read. You are Aiken the Strength of Oak. I also know your daughter, Sunniva the Gifts of the Sun. She and I have passed a bit of time together."

The sound of her name being spoken aloud by the stranger so tainted his daughter's honor that Aiken's protective feelings were immediately aroused. But before he unsheathed his blade and held it to the man's throat, he caught a breath. He tamped down his risen anger, stuck his thumbs in his belt, clenched his fists and gave a curt nod to acknowledge that the man had gotten his name right. "You know mine, but I did not catch yours."

"Ach, I have been called so many things," the graybeard said, "some of which are not too complimentary, I would just as soon forget them." With a flap of his hand he listed a few of the unflattering names to which he referred, "Inciter, Blusterer, Meander, Riddler, take your pick. Any of those will do," he said, laughing with hearty self-mockery. "But, I think you know my game, Aiken. Why not call me Fury? It is good to meet a worthy opponent," he said and thrusted out his hand.

But Aiken's anger was not deflected by the man's praise. He did not like the way the man had overtaken his riddle and put it to his own uses. Furthermore, he was mad at being toyed with by a man who would not give his rightful name. Nor did he care whether a refusal to take the man's outstretched hand was perceived as an insult.

The result of Aiken's ill-mannered rebuff turned into an immediate contest of wills. The stubborn graybeard refused to back down, starkly fixed his opponent with a cool gaze, and let his right hand hang in the space between them. The gesture of trust, which two men agree to observe when they take each other's right hands in a show of willingness to withhold their weaponry, became another form of aggression. The two men continued to stare at the other until Aiken silently agreed to end the needless standoff.

When he grabbed the old man's hand, however, the graybeard turned the typical greeting into a death grip. Though Aiken tried to pull away, the man would not let him go. He clasped Aiken's hand so hard that both their knuckles turned white. The graybeard callously pumped his arm and pulled Aiken in towards himself. The tug-of-war ended when the graybeard dropped his hand and patted Aiken on the arm in fake congeniality.

The graybeard had gotten his message across. The hostile interchange had drawn attention to what Aiken knew already: his adversary was not a man to be taken lightly. He was one who, in playing a simpleton, sowed discord by prodding men wherever they were least defended. He could arouse their jealousy and fearful mistrust by playing both sides against the other. He could easily incite men to kill even those who posed no threat and shared their common destiny. For all Aiken knew, the contest and its aftermath, along with the threats of violence, had been but a pointless diversion that the man had contrived just to pass the time. By playing a potentially destructive game for his own, idle amusement, he had weakened the tenuous bonds that men in this village had forged between themselves but which, also, kept them perpetually on edge. It would not take much to tip the balance toward violence.

Aiken was unable to admire Fury's display of clever, underhanded ruthlessness. And though he had been drawn into the threatened confrontation unwittingly, he regretted his participation.

"Aiken, you won," Fury said.

"Neither of us were declared the winner. I will not take your coin. You keep both. You need them more than I do."

Fury picked up the two coins and held them out flat in the center of his open palm. "Here, take them. You won."

"I do not want the coins," Aiken said dismissively. The coins were now tainted by the unscrupulous man's touch. He turned on his heel and began to walk away. Then, after he had gone several paces, he glanced back over his shoulder and stopped mid-stride. Curious about what the slippery old man was up to next, Aiken turned a quarter way around and watched from behind his back.

Fury placed his worn leather satchel on the table and unbuckled it. He lifted its flap and gave it a suspicious look. Acting as though some kind of mischief may have occurred while he was not looking, he bent sideways to peer inside. Seemingly satisfied that nothing was amiss, he sat upright again. He stuck his hand in and pulled out a long, narrow package, wrapped like an infant swaddled in white linen. He moved the satchel aside and carefully placed the packet lengthwise on the table. The fabric's triangular corner lay neatly centered on the top. He grasped hold of it and with one long, sweeping motion, swiftly unrolled the fabric wrapped around the rattling, clustered staves. There lay a pile of long, flat, Hazelwood sticks, each scratched with a secret sign.

Aiken shrugged. He had seen enough. He took one sidelong glance at the haunts, turned and took off for the holy grove.

IV.

Like a drawn curtain, a long shadow stretched across Fury's inner vision. His resolve momentarily darkened. At most, this timely appearance served to confirm his suspicions. Outside forces were purposefully pitting themselves against his and Lady Blessed's intentions.

He held his hand above the pile and mumbled words to summon insight into the ways of Father Time, Mother Necessity, and their three daughters, the Matrones of the Becoming. The sisters names were What-was, What-is, and What-shall-come-to-be.

He tipped his head back to gaze overhead at the thatched roof. His breath quieted, and he mixed the staves lightly with his fingertips. To settle upon the first stave, he sightlessly touched several sticks, asking each one whether it would shed light upon those who had cut the cord that had bound Sunniva to his Lady.

When he was certain that he had fingered the correct stave, he picked it out of the pile and, without a glance, placed it to the side. Before he chose the second stave, he asked to gain insight into the identity of the forces that were currently at play. And then, he picked a third one to shed light upon the way things would come out in the end.

He glanced down to look at the sticks and immediately sucked in his breath. The staves lay side by side in their proper order—Need, Gift, and Yew. Need was the most troublesome of all.

Fury flipped one linen corner over the pile of remaining sticks, lifted them carefully and set them aside. Picking up the three he had chosen, he placed the staves before him, perpendicular to the table edge, and set his thoughts in order. Fury rested one elbow on the table and dropped his chin into his upraised fist. The eyelid that covered his sighted eye drew down to leave but a narrow slit.

The occasional sounds of crows calling to one another in the distance, the women's muffled voices coming from the nearby, outdoors cookhouse, and the sea rumbling in a constant, monotonous, rhythm set the tone for his reverie. And, there he sat, for a long while.

Eventually, Fury roused himself and picked up the stave upon which the sign for Need was written. As he studied it, he seemed to hear the Matrone who is named What-was, whisper a portion of the riddle that he had asked Aiken.

> In the storm of battle, I was broken
> By the smith's iron handiwork.
>
> I grope, without hands and blind of eye,
> Knowing no help will come to me.

Brief images flickered past. He saw a marshy bog on the edge of a dark wood; a dull light throwing glints; Aiken kneeling at the edge of a pond and groping for something beneath the surface of red-colored water; a dark chamber, its walls lit by small flaming lamps set in niches.

What meaning might he attribute to these visions? First of all, he knew that, unlike the shield that he had described in the riddle, Aiken had received help after he had been so grievously hurt. He was alive, was he not? Fury did not need to read the staves to learn that much.

Of the fleeting hints that had flashed across his inner vision, Fury found one especially meaningful. He recognized the room that was lit by flaming lamps set in niches. He had been there himself. Was that where Aiken had taken shelter after he was hurt?

Fury groaned at the thought that his wife had known, all along, the identity of the men he was up against. Fury leaned back, folded his arms across his chest, and snorted. So, now he got it. He was up against Grerr and his accomplices. His antagonists' skillful use of underhanded trickery should never be underestimated. As to whether or not he relished such a challenging battle of wits, he remained undecided.

Lady Blessed had purposefully hidden the knowledge. Why? It was just like her to do that. Whenever previous references to Grerr had come up, she had consistently remained tight-lipped. Furthermore, she refused to be drawn into any discussion about the gold neck ring her former lover had made her. Fury wondered, whether she thought that he would have refused her request had he known that Grerr was involved? She still pined for him. He knew that. His wife was not the kind of woman who was satisfied with only one bedmate.

He grabbed his forehead and gave it a squeeze. Perhaps he would have refused her request if he had known that Grerr was involved. Maybe, maybe not. He could tell her he did not want to get involved. But the truth was, his wife's method for handling him had proven more successful than he cared to admit. That embarrassing fact alone was as troublesome as the way he had succumbed so easily to the blatant flattery with which she had persuaded him to take on this thankless task.

Fury tapped the stave that lay between the ones representing the past and the future. He picked up the Hazelwood stick with a detached air, and said aloud, "Gift." He rubbed the shallow, scratched grooves with his fingertips and held the marks close to his one sighted eye. He then sat in silence for a while. Why was Gift the pivotal point between Need and Yew? Since all things must be paid for, if Aiken had bargained to keep his life, what might he have traded for it in return? Perhaps the debt that Gift represented was now coming due. And if that were so, no doubt, that was the reason the cord had been cut.

Frustrated by the signs that had, so far, revealed nothing but the obvious, he saw no clear answers, only murky questions disguised as oblique riddles. Again, he tapped the stave between Need and Yew but decided to pass it over and mumbled, "I will come back to this later." He took a deep breath, and sighed.

It was then that insight came to him in a flash. Perhaps he had been looking at it from the wrong direction. The clues had been there, right in front of him, all along. He had seen how Aiken stood on the edge of the open-walled eating hall. He had purposely taken a place from which he could watch all the men and anyone else who might come in from any, and all directions. It wore a man down to always be on the watch, especially a man who is blind on one side. Fury had an affinity for men who, like Aiken, had seen one too many battles, been hurt one too many times, and had lost one too many of his fellows. Forced to tread a sharp edge between self-control and utter panic, such battle-weary men constantly evaluate the underlying forces at work. Such a man is compelled to consider all that is happening around him, and to question how everything can possibly affect him. Such a man can never rest easy.

And, perhaps, Fury had seen some of those same behaviors in the man's daughter. When he met Sunniva, she had also stood ever-watchful with her back against the wall. She had shown the same edginess, there in the common yard, as her father had shown beneath the outdoors eating-hall roof. Yes, Fury was certain that both the father and the daughter shared certain likenesses. The Matrones had twisted their fates together, after all. What had affected the father had also affected the daughter, possibly since birth. And if it was war, then war had made both the father and his daughter.

Fury listed those qualities that a man with a battle-bruised soul might pass on to his daughter when he plants his seed in her mother's womb. Like the spears, arrows, and knife blades her father feared, his child will be fearful of things rushing at her headlong. And, like her father, she will need to seek out the truth, will need to root out whatever might threaten her, and will constantly ask questions, for which there may be no easy answers. Like the father, she will seek safe places, even beautiful places where she can find solace. She will want a protector who can save her from harm. These inclinations, Fury knew, became the necessary ingredients, like alchemical essences, from which one might brew an elixir that can give the imbiber the gift of far-seeing. A man or woman who is so disposed will be driven to get to the bottom of things by their insatiable curiosity. Bestowed upon one who is so affected, such a hunger can make for an outstanding talent. Were those not the same assets that Blessed had recognized in the young woman?

For one who is so gifted—or afflicted, depending upon how one looks at it—such talents will make a person's life hard. If there was any truth in this comparison, Aiken's dubious gift was a fearsome birthright to have passed on to his unborn child. Whereas most folks believe that hidden things are better left alone, such a woman will seek out those same hidden things that others cannot see. To exercise her in-born need to know, she will probe and dig until she can go no further. She will be dissatisfied until she hits rock bottom. She will never rest until all the pieces fit together to make a meaningful whole. This constant quest for knowledge may take her to the darkest regions of her soul. And in that darkness, she will find the greatest comfort.

Like having been given a key to unlock a door, those wisewomen, poets, storytellers, and inventive, visionary craftsmen with in-born, bruised souls, have the means to pass through the doorways that lead them to the storied, blood-drenched fields in the otherworldly dreamtime. There, they will find two jugs, which the Lord Creator, himself, molded from our earthen mother's clay body. One vessel contains terror, deprivation, and sorrow and the other contains hope, joy, and plenty. It is from these vessels that the visionary brings back both healing and grace for those who live in this world.

In this way, a wisewoman's easy access to otherworlds becomes a gift to ordinary folks who are, otherwise, deprived of such beneficence. But that is only true when she is properly cared for and given proper, well-deserved respect. Otherwise, this so-called gift becomes a curse. The constant barrage of otherworldly influences can leak out of that open doorway and assail the beholder so unceasingly that if she seeks to deaden her sensitive nature, she will fall prey to neglect and ill-treatment. At the point that a woman can no longer filter the real from the make-believe, her fears become exaggerated. This tendency toward excess must be held constantly in check. Likewise, this scent of peculiar otherness, which she carries with her after she has been meandering through the otherworlds, means that ordinary folks tend to keep their distance.

Indeed, one might say that if Gift were the pivot point in this stave reading, the narrows through which Fury must pass before he could fully comprehend the meaning of the staves marked with the signs Need and Yew, Gift becomes that point when one condition shifts to the other. It represents the moment between: when this Gift, this bruised soul, this burdensome weight becomes either the endowment of a talent or the ruination of its bearer.

Thus, to get a complete picture of What-was, What-is, and What-shall-come-to-be, the staves could be read both forward and backward—from either the past to the future, or its reverse, from Yew to Need, from death to life, from darkness to light. Like the story of the Endtime, when according to predictions, Lord Glory will fight Treachery one last time, the sun will go dark. After the final, world-shattering battles are over, Lady Blessed will plant a Yew from the single seed that she has kept safe from harm. The tree will sprout and grow from the fertile, blood-drenched soil. And from its trunk, a man and woman will emerge to become the heroes who will populate a cleansed world. And he, too, in his guise of the Old Man of the Forest, will wake from his long slumber and emerge from the inside of a dead tree.

This connection between that-which-went-before and that-which-is-yet-to-come is like Time and Necessity's dance of creation and destruction. From Creation comes destruction. From destruction comes creation. Nothing stays the same. Change is forever.

Fury drummed his fingertips on his knee and stared into the distance. Brief flashes of insight crossed his vision. With the speed of an eye-blink, he saw Aiken and Sunniva's futures unfold: a small, brightly colored bird, accompanied by a crow flies through a shadowy, book-lined room; the sun goes dark; a man rides the back of the Wind-bringer into the center of a battle; a woman walks through knee-deep snow; a long-knife is forged and spelled with secret signs; glassy, colorful leaves and flowers sprout from a marvelous tree's limbs, shatter, and collapse. Where it stood, a pile of shards is all that remains.

But something was missing. It had to do with the Yew tree and Aiken. Was it the shattered tree? He would need to sit with it for a while before the meaning became clear.

It was time to move on. With one scooping motion of his hand, Fury gathered the staves. He centered them neatly on the cloth, wrapped them with care, and placed them inside his satchel. He clicked his tongue and, as if he were speaking directly to those three sisters of the Becoming, mumbled, "Very interesting, Ladies—."

The Matrones' methods, though ambiguously cloaked in mystery, had made one thing clear. Before he could get to the daughter, he would need to get past her father.

What might he do to distract Aiken from so aggressively protecting Sunniva? To compare this situation with that of coming upon a viscous, three-headed dog who is standing guard before a treasure, if he were to merely throw the man a bone, it would, unfortunately, not be enough to serve his purpose. Before things could come out in his Lady's favor, Fury would need to find out what was riding that fervidly driven man. Yes, before he could deal with his adversaries and lay his plans accordingly, he would need to offer Aiken a distraction.

Whenever the doors to the dreamtime are not closed tightly, they become an opening through which dark terrors will steal into one's waking life. What otherworldly burdens, after they had leaked out of the dreamtime, now clung to Aiken's shoulders? If there ever was a time to create friction by rubbing two sticks together to spark the need-fire, Fury reckoned the time was now.

ELEVEN

Serpentine
If you will turn an enemy's words
Against himself and overcome all causes and matters.

Take the stone which is called Serpentine a kind of marble spotted like a snakeskin. If the stone be gripped straightly, it gives courage and victory, and it guards against all danger. It makes to overcome all causes, or matters in suit, and exposes truth.

The Truth of Rocks, by Aluiss the Wise

I.

The patterns on this small slice of yellow-green serpentine remind me of tiny, springtime willow leaves. Or, on second thought, perhaps the scalloped, overlapping shapes might be said to depict a small bird's feathered wings and body. Though either description might suit my purposes, this much I know for certain: in contrast to this stone's permanence, the mental images the picture evokes remind me of timely and elusive things like tree buds and the rapidly fluttering heartbeats I would feel if I were to cup a delicate, feathered creature in my hands.

And here is another. Similar in color, this stone appears to have been inked with random, chevron-shaped, black lines. This picture reminds me of a flock of birds in flight. But, I ask myself, earth bound as I am, would I not see a flock of birds in flight silhouetted against a blue, white, or gray-toned sky rather than a green one? To right this situation, I pretend to don a crow mask and a costume made of black feathers.

Now, if I were to look at a grassy field from a crow's eye-view of things, I would hover above it all like a sentry watching over a flock of garrulous birds feeding on seeds and bugs. They walk about, peck at the ground, shriek, and quarrel. And when a man approaches along the footpath, I squawk to warn my fellow flock members to lift and scatter. Most fly further inland but two remain, circle one time and settle down again, not far from Aiken's red stone.

II.

Entering the holy grove, he carefully wound his way between the white, lime-painted rocks. The two shades he had seen before, seated in their stone-outlined boat, were now accompanied by more shades, all of whom were, also, sitting in the small hulls making up the flotilla of white, outlined boats. Each of the men and women, who were crowded in amongst the others, were seated with their knees tucked up to their chin.

It seemed his ability to see the shades no longer depended upon the sight of his missing eye alone. Even when he looked directly at them with his good eye, he saw the dead. Something had changed, whether it was for better or for the worse he was uncertain. But it was mildly disturbing to think that the shades of the dead were always present, whether he saw them there or not. Like persistent memories of men and women, who once had lived here, they had been impressed upon this landscape forever.

A crow bobbed its head and, with its chest outthrusted, strutted toward him. Provoked by the bird to protect those men and women who were seated in the boats, he picked up a small rock and, with an intent to scare it off, threw the pebble. But instead of frightening the bird, the sound of the stone hitting the ground elicited its curiosity. To identify whatever the man had thrown, the bird tipped its head to the side and eyed it. When he saw the crow lower its head to peck at whatever lay on the ground, he ran toward it. Wanting to prevent the bird from defiling the dead men and women who were seated so placidly in their boats, he waved his arms, just as he had done years before, when he had chased away the crows who had alighted on the corpse-strewn battlefields of his youth.

The crow stretched its wings and flapped one time, provocatively. Once air-borne, it leisurely glided low to the ground and landed with a casual, elegant grace, only a short distance away from where he stood. Though clearly vexed by the bird's insolent behavior, he shrugged it off. He had more important things to do than chase after crows.

He took his accustomed place before the stone and stood there, just as he had done all winter long. But now that the carving was finished, his hands no longer held his tools. He placed one finger at the top of the graceful arc and, by this simple act of tracing the groove and following the long ribbon that formed the oval-shaped border, he came to know himself again. He was not the nameless character whom the graybeard had described in a riddle. He read aloud the secret signs which he, himself, remembered carving upon this everlasting picture of a ribbon. He was Aiken, the man who had carved this stone for Gevehard, son of Garr, son of Gerard, son of Glenn who had brought his people to this land. It said so, right here. And, now that it was engraved in stone, unlike the riddler's description of the man whose name had been cursed and forgotten, no one would ever forget his name.

The day before, Aiken had poured a sack of ground lime and salt into a bowl and had wet it with water. He had done the same with a sack containing powdered yellow ochre. He had mixed the yellow paint and whitewash until they were smooth as cream. Then he had covered the bowls with the empty sacks and set them aside beneath overturned crockery until today.

Now that the drizzle was letting up and things were drying out, Aiken wanted to add the final touches to the stone. He picked up his pig-bristled brushes, added a bit more water to the paints to ensure their consistency was right and stirred them thoroughly. He then began to fill in the outlines and to cover the flat planes with either the whitewash or yellow ochre. And as he painted, he spoke his words aloud so they, too, would bind to the stone and stay there, just as the whitewash and the ochre paint would remain stuck in the grooves and stay atop the flat planes after it was dry and hardened.

He told Hild that she would remain here for a long while. She would even outlast his death by many years. Though she was far from the place where the quarrymen had dug her from her mother stone, this holy grove was to become her new home. From now until the Endtime her presence would be a sign to all who saw her. The words and pictures he had carved would notify all the men and women, who read and deciphered their meaning, that Glenn's kin had established their rights to make their home here, on the shore of the Merchant Sea.

When he was finished, he was pleased by the way the white outlined grooves and solid yellow spaces shone so smartly against the dark red stone. Like a bride dressed in her wedding garment, she would soon be given away. All winter long, she had been Aiken's warrior stone, but now she would become a fighting man's wife.

Though it pained him to think that someday he would leave her, he had made her for Gevehard. She would become the shipmaster's weave-woman and battle-woman who, by weaving the seamen's protection into the warp and woof of the cloth that came together on her loom, she would ensure their victories.

Yet, Aiken did not want to leave her, not just yet anyhow. Though Hild was destined to belong to another, he wanted to admire her a while longer. He took a posture similar to the shades of the dead who were seated nearby, tucked his knees under his chin, wrapped his arms around his shins, and stared at Hild.

And, while he was lingering in that state of grace, his thoughts returned to the questions that weighed so heavily upon his mind. There were several matters he needed to consider. The first was whether to join Gevehard's crew. If he became one of the sea-going men, he, too, would be held within Hild's protective sphere, and that possibility pleased him very much. Though he had married Mildred and become a woodcarver, he still desired a more adventuresome life. To join the crew offered an opportunity to embark upon the alluring prospect of fulfilling that lifelong ambition.

But when he thought of Mildred, he did not want to worry her, nor did he want to leave her. Since their marriage, he had rarely been apart from her, and he missed her more than he had ever thought he would. He had told her when he expected to be home and she would worry if he had not returned by then. Admittedly, for an old, former warrior, he was more settled than he had ever thought would happen. Besides, there were things he had to do back home. He had promised to help with the fieldwork. And he had not yet arranged Sunniva's marriage—a matter that was becoming increasingly troublesome. He could not put off the deliberations with Werther over her bride price any longer.

Earlier, when he had been walking through the yard, Sunniva had stopped him to complain about not seeing him more often. The way she had asked him point blank, "Are you trying to get rid of me because you cannot find me a husband?" she had acted like a nagging wife.

He was so shocked he had hardly known how to answer. He stood there, so dumbfounded, all he could say was, "No, of course not."

"Do not lie to me."

"How did you come up with such a ridiculous notion?"

"Tate told me that no family will have me. She said that no one will pay my bride price because I am a half-breed bastard. She said that you plan to leave me here in service to Edwina because you want to get rid of me."

Aiken was so disturbed by her slanderous speech, he flat-out denied everything she said. He angrily turned his back and stomped away saying, "You are talking nonsense. I have no time for this."

But then, after he had given his initial reaction further consideration, he turned and glanced back. The sight of his daughter looking so downcast reminded him that he, too, often felt so lonely. Ashamed of his impatience, he turned and walked back. "There is no truth in what you say. Your mother and I are married, and you are a fine young woman."

"I do not believe you." Apparently, she had no interest in being placated by his assurances, but only wanted to spew out more accusations. "Everyone knows that you are highborn and my mother is a commoner. That makes your supposed vows unlawful and your marriage fraudulent."

Shooting one well-aimed grievance after another, she said, "What am I supposed to make of the cruel gossip that is being spread about me? Why am I not betrothed yet? Is it because no one will marry me? Tell me the truth."

"I am speaking the truth. You are an admirable young woman who has many suitors. I know that for a fact. I am the one who has been lax in settling upon the terms of your bride price. The fault lies with me. It is my fault alone and no one else's."

But no matter what he said, he had been unable to satisfy Sunniva. Instead, it seemed she only wanted to hurt him and to strip him of his authority and pride. "Is it because we are not going home? Are you joining the crew without telling me? Why did Adelheide say that she had a young man in mind for me to wed? She said he would make an excellent match when you and me settle in the village. She said Aart came from a wealthy landholding family and that I should be proud to marry him. She told me his father often sits at the high table with Gevehard just like you do. I cannot stand Aart. I do not want to live here. I hate it here. I want to go home."

What else could he say but, "Aart is not so bad."

There they were, standing in the common yard, his daughter glaring at her father, speaking slanderously of the shipmaster's wife and insulting Aart and his father, who was one of the most prestigious landholders in the region, and telling everyone how much she hated life in the village. Such opinions should be kept to oneself or shared with others only in strict confidence. Her slanderous speech would make them unwelcome here. One should never be rude but must speak well of one's hosts.

However, because he secretly agreed with her and plainly believed in truth-telling, he said, "The way you are contradicting yourself makes no sense at all. First you tell me that no man will have you. Then you tell me that Adelheide has arranged a marriage to the son of the most influential man in the village. Now, stop making such a fuss."

He resented being put on the spot this way and coolly lowered his voice, "Everyone is watching us. I assure you that I will speak with Werther as soon as we get home. Mildred and I will arrange your marriage. Just give it a bit more time."

"No."

"Sunniva, what do mean? The match between you and Wynn has been planned for a long time."

"Mother is the one who wants me to marry Wynn."

"Is there another young man whom you would rather wed?"

"I do not know whether I want to marry a farmer. Maybe I want to marry an ironmonger. We must get home immediately. We cannot stay here any longer. I want to go home."

Now that Aiken was alone in the holy grove and able to study their conversation from this greater distance, he realized that something drastic had happened to his daughter. Since the day of their arrival, Sunniva had changed so much, he hardly knew her. She had always been a willful child but, never before, had she spoken to her father so disrespectfully. She had treated him like a naughty child who had done something forbidden. He hardly knew what to make of her. She was no longer the simple child he had known before, but a strong-willed, adamant, angry young woman. How had that happened?

Unsettled by the exchange, he shook his head in despair. Could he never get away from other's scrutiny and speculation about his affairs? Who, besides the men who had escorted them to the village had known about his life in the hamlet and his unlawful marriage to Mildred? If this slanderous gossip had come from the very men whom he had entrusted with his and his daughter's lives, in hindsight, he was uncertain whether anyone in Gevehard's village was the man or woman he thought they were. Aiken had been led to believe that he was spending time among honorable fighting men, only to discover that the horsemen were no different from the nattering old women in the hamlet who relished every chance they were given to tittle-tattle and repeat their tales.

The fact that Adelheide had confided in Sunniva before first coming to him with a likely match worried him even more. Aiken was her father and he was the one who would decide to whom his daughter was wed. Gevehard was not his kinleader and had no right to use Aiken's girl as a prize when he was handing out favors to his men.

But on the other hand, the knowledge that Adelheide had sought a match for Sunniva may have indicated that Gevehard's offer to join his crew might still be in effect. Perhaps Jerold had not told the shipmaster that he had not made the cut. What was Aiken to make of that piece of information? Was he nothing but a little, wooden man, like the ones he carved for Bertolf? Was he just a toy sea-man, deprived of a will of his own, set into a child's boat, who was put afloat on a puddle in the yard, where he could be whimsically pushed about by others?

He had been masterless for so long, it was hard to let another man's intentions direct his actions. His service to Torwald had taught him to be wary of entrusting his fate to another man's weaknesses. He knew that any man to whom he swore his fealty might lead him into dangerous situations in which serious injury and death were probable outcomes. If he trusted no one but himself, how could he agree to follow a man when he felt so uncertain?

No. He could not—would not—allow another man to fit him and his daughter into their plans. If he did, he would be left, in the end, with no alternatives. As much as others might have wanted to push him in one direction or the other, it was his decision and he was the one who would choose.

Yet, the uncertainties plagued him. Even after he had studied all sides of the argument, Aiken remained equally torn between his desire to join the crew and his need to get back home to Mildred.

Overtaken by the weariness that had been dogging his heels since early morning, he gave in to the lulling sounds of the sea. He scooted around until he was sitting in a place where he could look out toward the bay. And, leaning back against one of Hild's unpainted sides, he rested in her protective shadow.

Here, on the island she formed, surrounded by small, stone-outlined boats, each of which were filled with shades floating on a sea of sand and grass, he was free of the troublesome bogman's pursuit. The band of haunts who had chased him, this far, stood on the edge of the holy grove, seemingly wary of entering another shade's territory. For now, with the red stone at his back, Aiken felt safe.

Soothing his reverie were the muffled noises coming from the direction of the village, the vestiges of last year's reeds, rhythmically knocking together like hollow bones, and the repetitious sounds of the surf. Like a mother dog who hides her teeth behind her lips when she kisses her young, the sea's full force was disguised as gentle waves lapping its deceptively passive, saline tongues at the sandy shoreline.

III.

Alerted to the sound of footsteps, Aiken shook off his drowsiness and immediately jumped to his feet. Here comes the old beggar, he thought, chewing on a hunk of bread. For a man who ate so constantly, there was little flesh on the graybeard's bones. Aiming straight at Aiken, he was stabbing aggressively at the ground with his walking staff. The satchel strap thrown across his shoulder was tied with a large bundle of branches and dried reeds. A sudden sea gust, combined with his stride, to whip at his dark, tattered cloak, and flap it like ominous, black wings.

Given a more discerning glance at this man, who called himself Fury, Aiken was forced to reconsider his earlier appraisal. What was different about the man's appearance? For one thing, he no longer carried himself with the bearing of a beaten-down, old beggar, who held all he owned in a large sack. Rather, the drained, gray pallor in his face was replaced by a robust appearance. The way he threw his long legs forward in a loping gait lent him the confident appearance of a man who carried himself with the full authority of a chieftain.

While Aiken was napping, he had been unaware of the two insolent crows who had taken advantage of his lack of attention to stake out their territory on the dune. When the birds called, kraa, kraa, kraak, the graybeard returned their greeting with the familiarity one generally reserves for well-known friends. He called them Thought and Memory—a storyteller's greatest asset—tore up what remained of the bread he held and threw the handful of crumbs beneath the low, spindly branches upon which one of the crows was perched. The bird spread its wings, floated down and landed. It thrusted its chest forward and looked about before it strutted toward the crumbs, bobbing its head with every confident step it took.

How is it that a crow carries itself with such elegant self-importance? Apparently, it knows that it can outwit all other birds, as well as a few humans. The crow picked up a crust, opened its wings and floated upward on the breeze. Its feather's glossy, metallic shimmer glinted in the pale sunlight as it gracefully perched upon the branch where it had previously rested. The bird's weight forced the gnarly shrub to whip up and down and back and forth several times before it adjusted.

"These are rightfully yours," the graybeard said. He held the two copper coins between his outstretched thumb and forefinger. "You should take them. You won the contest."

Aiken sighed with resignation. If he refused to take the ante pile, small as it was, he would prolong the unwelcome graybeard's visit with more ensuing arguments over whose riddle had been most clever. Aiken gave in to the inevitable, stepped up to the man, held out his hand, and accepted the coins. Though many men were bigger than he was, and Aiken was accustomed to that fact, he was, nonetheless, surprised to see the stranger stood over a head taller. Aiken had to crane his neck just to look up at the man's face.

Previously, when Aiken had seen the graybeard slumped down on the bench beneath the roof of the outdoors eating hall, with his legs tucked beneath him, he had looked frail and sickly. But now, Aiken could see that beneath those dirty rags, the man was made of lean, hard muscle. The man's height, combined with the taut strength and confidence he effused, lent him the appearance of one who routinely commands others.

Mildly bemused by his own willingness to have complied, Aiken asked himself: had the graybeard not demanded he take the coins? And had he not accepted them? Yes, he had obeyed the man as readily as one who knows that he is outranked and has been given an order by a superior.

The crow who was seated upon the bowed branch tucked its head beneath a raised wing and preened itself. The second bird, the first one's mate, no doubt, thrusted its head forward, spread its wings, and pushed off. It coasted away from the dune and headed toward a nearby, freshly planted field. When the remaining crow heard the other call, kraaa, kraaa, kraaak, it lifted its head and answered. Fury tilted his head, first to one side and then to the other, to listen attentively to the two crows as they called back and forth, kraaa, kraaa, kraaak.

After the birds' barking had ceased, Fury turned toward Aiken, and said, "It is an honor to speak with a man who has so worthy a talent. Will you tell me about the stone you carved?"

Flattered by the praise, Aiken dropped down in front of the stone. He sat on his heels, placed the fingers of both his hands in the grooves on either side and, as he traced the ribbon, read aloud, "Aiken carved this stone for Gevehard, son of Garr, son of Gerard, son of Glenn who brought us to this land. Help us now, Lord of Rich Waters."

"Yes," the graybeard said, "in comparison to the powers who control the sea, the wind, and the weather, a man can feel very small, indeed. Yet, when you offer to become a go-between, you give the men and women who live in this village hope."

"How so?"

"Through both the pictures and the written words you carved, you call forth forces that are mightier than Gevehard and all the men on his crew combined. You have created huge forces that can withstand even those that are as powerful as the Lords and Ladies, themselves. To know their names gives you great and convincing strength."

Though flattered, Aiken hardly knew what to make of that information. He went on to explain how the two ends of the ribbon met at the bottom. At the place where the two ends were tied together, they wrapped over and under and through three loops to form a complex knot. Aiken described how he had first scratched the design into a sand-filled box. He had smoothed the lines over and over and drawn them repeatedly until he was certain the knot was perfectly formed. If you followed the lines with your fingers you could tell it was right. The knot secured Glenn to Gevehard and all of his descendants. The forebear's goodwill was bound to all those who filled this village. Glenn's blessings were guaranteed to remain in effect for as long as this knot endured.

Aiken pointed to the top where he had carved Lady Sun's disk-shaped mirror. To represent a fast-moving, spinning wheel, and to lend it the appearance of forward movement, he had decorated the circle with four interlocking spirals. Beneath the sun and to each side, he had portrayed the Lady Sun's twin brothers, the great Lords of Battle who were known to protect men who go to sea. Carved in the likeness of a man's figure, each Lord held a long blade in one hand and, in the other, a shield decorated with a six-pointed star.

To stand-in for all the longboats in the fleet he had carved the picture of Wave Crestar beneath the two shield-bearing figures. The ship's serpent-head faced west, the direction the men would take when they left home. Her spiral tail pointed east, the direction from which they would return. Inside the ship, there were ten, little stick-figure men to stand in for all the crew members. Beneath the longship, the picture of a serpent's undulate curves mimicked the curled waves upon which the ship floated and were ruled by the Lord of Rich Waters.

It surprised Aiken to think that, here he was, speaking to this stranger, who, quite frankly, he did not like very much. Yet, he was honestly telling the man about the way he had thought through the designs. Over the years, Aiken had longed to talk about the objects he made, but was rarely given an opportunity to tell others about the meaning he put into his work. It was not because he wanted to keep it secret, but because, with the exception of the day he had met Gevehard, no one was interested enough to either ask nor to listen. Whenever he delivered the boxes and the high seats, he never saw anyone besides the chieftain's stewards. They accepted whatever he had spent months working on and, in return, offered him neither gratitude nor displeasure. After he had been handed the agreed upon payment, they expected him to clear out immediately so as to make way for the next people who were waiting in line to deliver their goods to the inner stockade.

And here he was, talking to a beggar who seemed to fully grasp all that he said. Grateful for this audience, Aiken continued to explain how, when he pictured the things he had borrowed from his surroundings, and the ideas and stories with which he was most familiar, he combined them with the knotted and interwoven cords and the words that he had spelled with secret signs, to make sense of a man's life in the best way he knew how.

The graybeard nodded distractedly and said, "You did well."

"I am grateful you should say so" And though Aiken was momentarily pleased by the praise, when he glanced up at the man looming over him, he felt a shocking chill. The old graybeard stared, not at the stone but at him. It seemed as though the man could see right through his skin and read the mysterious pictures and secret signs that the Matrones had engraved upon his bones. Instead of the knots, which Aiken had carved onto the stone, the graybeard was engrossed in study of the invisible, otherworldly picture of the knotted cords with which the Matrones had bound him to his fate.

And, here was Aiken, in the flesh, hunkered down before this perfectly balanced design on which his name was written in secret signs, when most of those for whom he carved treated him like an invisible, nameless, outcast. Whereas he had created a world of perfectly symmetrical harmony and goodness through the pictures and words he had carved on this stone, his own frayed life thread remained unattached from the Matrones' weave. Though he had acquired fame for the way in which he could tie everything together by unifying all the necessary elements with his carved braids and knots, through some quirk of fate, his own cord had become unraveled from the warp and been tied to the one man whom he loathed with a vengeance, the man who had destroyed the life that he had thought, at one time, he was destined to live. Though still bound to his enemy by a cursed oath, he seemed to have been forgotten by the three sisters. He had been cut loose and left to dangle free as they continued to weave the fate of the worlds with their all-consuming passion.

Although Aiken's sentiments had gone unspoken, it seemed like the graybeard understood. Fury nodded in agreement, arrested his gaze and turned back to his study of the stone. "What about these snakes?"

Aiken took a deep breath and explained how each of the two snakes looped once around the ribbon. The left snakehead pointed down, whereas the snake on the right pointed up.

The graybeard listened thoughtfully to all that Aiken described and nodded his head distractedly. He sank down to crouch beside Aiken and touched each of the two serpents. "Why did you reverse them?"

"I do not know. It seemed best for the balance of the design. There are times when the idea for a picture comes so naturally, I do not know where it comes from. To follow the impulse seems lucky, so I do not question it."

"The way I see it," the graybeard said, "the snakes represent the native strength that is inherent in the dreamtime." And to confirm the correctness of Aiken's hunch, he added, "That is where the ideas come from. As they rise from the depths, they carry with them the potency to make things happen. This stone becomes a doorway through which that teeming strength emerges. The snakes come from the place where the fundamental power lies lurking, breeding in the caves. When the door opens, the snakes carry with them tremendous power: one which is capable of bringing about change. The back and forth movement between the dreamtime world and the world of the waking expresses an elemental need. As the snake rises, it comes into this world to bring with it the vitality with which life creates life unto itself.

"And you, Aiken, are the picture maker, the word-smith. To infuse your carvings with luck, you bring that power with you. You have been given the means to open the way for this uncoiling serpent power to rise up from the depths. Unless carvings and stories evoke such other, dream-like worlds, they are nothing but idle embellishments and vacant entertainments. A carver, a storyteller must cultivate and nurture, must pray to, and bargain with, that dynamic, mighty force. The snakes represent your power. Your artistry becomes the gift you offer in return for its blessings."

"That may be so," Aiken said, though he did not feel very blest. He remained unconvinced of the snake's benevolence. The door to the dreamtime was open, night and day, and let in a chilling draught. He only wished he could close it, tightly. There seemed to be no way to hold off the haunts but by carving. Unless he carved these stories and words every day, the shades of dead men taunted him, and the bogman rode him into the night battles. With each of the high-seats, treasure boxes, spoons and trenchers he carved, he paid some form of tribute. Unlike the annual payments the chieftains collected from the hamlets, or even the objects they demanded from him in return for his freedom and safe passage on the roads, the very act of carving had become another form of tribute. It was a payment to another kind of power, a power he did not even know the name of, but which gave him a bit more time to hold off what would, in time, be the inevitable end of his story.

And now the graybeard had told him that because he did not know the name of that power, it too, controlled him. It wielded its power over him, the same way the chieftains and the bogman did. Unless he knew its name it would always hold him in its grip.

"Aiken, take my word for it: you are a talented sign maker. A man like you, who has a talent for directing his soul's flight between the worlds, may accomplish marvels. If I were a chieftain I would seat you at the high table along with my counselors. But, for the time being, anyhow, I am just a wanderer.

"After I saw the horrors of war, I went into the wild places to get right with the world again. To get by, I travel between the villages telling stories and casting the staves. My specialty is word-craft. When I compliment you on your skill, I know of that which I speak. I bow to your achievement. All I have ever done is scratch some signs onto sticks. What you do is more commendable, by far, and is of greater worth. It is an honor to meet up with a man who is as wise and as learned as you. Tell me, where did you learn to carve like this?"

Before Aiken was given time to resist, Fury grabbed his two hands. He looked them over closely. First he studied the backs and then turned them over to inspect the palms. He examined the mounded callouses that Aiken had built up, over the years, when grasping the chisels with his left hand and the hammer with his right. After Fury let him go, Aiken slid his hands down his thighs, uncomfortably, and rested them on his knees.

The graybeard asked, "Where did you acquire this skill with signs and words?" He leaned in closely and lowered his voice in the way that a confidante would do, "Of course, you may trust me. I do not gossip."

Aiken snorted. Recalling what Edmund had told him about the traveling men whom Gevehard paid to report on neighboring friends and enemies, Aiken doubted whether this man ever gossiped. No, he refused to reveal his secret to a man who made his way in the world by spreading rumors everywhere he ventured.

And furthermore, Aiken recalled the way, when earlier in the day, the graybeard had taken control of the other men. He had adeptly whipped up their passions the same way a chieftain would do before he led them into battle. Aiken refused to play into this man's hands or to become a marker in his game. Nor did he believe that all this man had done was scratch a few signs onto sticks. Tit for tat. Aiken would not let on about himself until the man had been more forthcoming about his own shames, failures, and achievements. Aiken was fed up with other men and women's curiosity about his life. He staunchly refused to give the names of his teachers to this man who had declined to reveal his own name. This was the one thing that the man could not order him to do. Aiken fixed his gaze past the man's shoulder and the tightly strung sinews in his jaw twitched.

Though he had gotten no reply from Aiken, the graybeard let it pass and continued to converse amicably. "Well, I would welcome you in my warband. But it seems that you have been spoken for by another. People do talk, you know, and of course I listen. It is said that the shipmaster offered you a place on the crew. Will you swear an oath to Gevehard? Will you pledge to be his man and to go out to sea with him? If you do, he is a lucky man."

Aiken merely shrugged in reply.

The man who called himself Fury pulled his cloak more tightly around himself, and said, "The sun is getting low and I feel a chill. Since we are both damp from this wretched drizzle, perhaps we should light a fire and dry ourselves out. I have a few reeds and sticks here."

And even before Aiken was given a chance to reply, Fury had laid his cloak on the ground and sat with his crossed legs near the edge. He untied the bundle of branches and reeds he had carried with him and placed them off to the side.

Since the graybeard seemed so determined, Aiken brought a small pile of kindling and dried dung that he had collected previously and kept covered beneath a basket near the stone.

Bending to the side, Fury looked through his collection of branches and picked out two sticks. One was short and squat, the other was long, thin, and straight. He pulled a short knife from his belt, carved a notch in the short stick and rubbed the blade against the long one to smooth the bark until it was free of rough spots.

Aiken handed him a handful of dried grass, the dried dung, and some twigs. Fury laid the kindling and blocks of dung on top of his cloak along with his own reeds and sticks, and formed the dried grass into a nest shape. He knelt with one knee on the ground, placed a foot on the notched stick, fit the lean, straight stick into the notch and, holding it upright between both hands, began to rub them back and forth.

It was an odd way to light a fire. The only times that Aiken had seen a fire lit in such a fashion was when the kinleader lit the Yuletide bonfire. "I have a flint and steel. That is a more efficient way to get a flame going."

But since Fury had chosen to ignore him, Aiken shrugged, knelt across from the beggar and watched. Wary, yet curious about this fast-talking fellow, Aiken found the man's oddities increasingly entertaining and his attention was soon absorbed by the man's repetitive movement.

Rubbing the stick, the graybeard's hands traveled patiently from the top of the stick to the bottom. Then, after he had stopped, time and again, he moved his hands from the bottom to the top and began to rub them together again.

"A man's ordeal is made up of the obligations and debts he carries," he said as he continued rubbing his hands together with the stick between them. "This burden can bog any man down. Or he can light the need-fire. He can use the friction and tension that builds from rubbing the weight, which his life demands he carry, against his desire to throw it from his shoulders. I have heard it said that at times of great necessity, when hardship is so overwhelming that there appears to be no way out of the troubles a man or woman faces, the need-fire is kindled to spark a flame that will shed light in the darkness. No iron, flint or steel is used to start the fire—only the heat generated by two sticks rubbed together. Offerings burnt on such a fire become gifts to the ruling powers. Carried upon its smoke, a man or woman's desperate pleas are sent to the Lords and Ladies of Earth, Sea, and Sky to bring about change for the better. If you like, Aiken, I will send a plea on this smoke. What do you need most right now? Is it to know what will happen to you and your daughter if you go to sea on Gevehard's boat?"

"No," Aiken said. He had no need to think it through. His need was right on the tip of his tongue. "Things are more complicated than that." Though surprised initially by his own spontaneous forthrightness, it felt so good to talk things over with some-one who seemed to understand, he continued to explain his dire situation. "My need goes back more than fifteen years. I want men to admit to the danger I saw coming. The lack of recognition of my accurate appraisal of the situation, which I and my war companions' faced at the time, and their refusal to heed my warnings has gnawed on my flesh from the inside like a worm. I want to take my grievances to the Assembly. There, in front of the chieftains, I want to charge the man who is responsible for my former chieftain, Torwald's, murder."

"And, what if the man you accuse denies the charge?"

"I will say he lies."

"What is stopping you?"

"I have no proof. There are no witnesses who will speak for me. It could be ar-gued that the guilty man is too powerful to care. He can easily dispose of anyone who challenges him or asks unseemly questions. But I cannot forget what he did to me and to my companions."

"Without proof or witnesses, you ask a lot," Fury said. He murmured a few in-distinct words, hummed tunelessly to himself, and continued to spin the stick between his hands.

As for the other problem that weighed Aiken down, he had never spoken with anyone but Mildred. And even then, the only reason he had disclosed the shameful secret was his inability to hide the way he awoke, in the night, with a pounding heart and breathing heavily. Perhaps if he knew the name of that other power, he might ask for help, but was unable to speak about the bogman, even to this unlikely stranger.

Yet, the way the graybeard looked at Aiken, it seemed as though he wholly understood the unspoken presence of the creature. Fury said, mysteriously, "It will not be easy to get rid of, but I will see what I can do. I will need some time to call in my allies."

More time passed before the friction between the two sticks had created enough heat to ignite the small bit of sawdust in the bottom of the notch. When a whiff of smoke lifted from the point where the two sticks met, Fury laid down the spindle and tipped the bottom stick toward Aiken. At the bottom of the notch, a tiny coal glowed bright red against the blackened wood. Fury set the handful of nest-shaped dried grass in front of his knee, picked up his knife, held the stick over the grass and tapped. The barely visible coal dropped in. He lifted the smoldering grass with both hands and, holding it close to his lips, blew gently. As if it were a rare and delicate creature, he breathed life into the ember until a smoke cloud began to billow around his face.

After he set it down, Aiken handed small sticks, shaved wood and chunks of dried dung to Fury, and let him build the fire into a small blaze.

Aiken spread out his cloak where he could sit nearest the stone and face Fury, who sat with his back to the shoreline. The two men warmed their hands on the small fire.

Sensing Alger's presence, Aiken looked around, and saw his blood brother standing in the thicket. The way Alger's mouth was set in a frown and his chest was heaving, Aiken sensed his friend's building jealousy over being excluded from amicably sharing the fire.

The old man watched Aiken intently but said nothing, only nodding now and then, as if in agreement with a silent conversation between them. Occasionally Aiken would turn his head to the right to check on the haunts who were still standing in a hoard on his blindside.

Perhaps, if he had ignored them, nothing more would have happened. But when he glanced in that direction, Fury also turned to look at the shades, and said, "Kipp, step over here."

The dead man who held a javelin approached and stood between the two seated men.

Fury looked up and invited the shade to join them. But, when he recognized his impolite indiscretion, he nodded at Aiken and asked, "If it is all right with you?"

Aiken allowed it was. He scooted over but was uncertain whether he could trust a shade who had been chasing him earlier in the day, especially one who held a javelin, and resolved to keep Kipp in his sight.

The dead man crossed his legs, laid the barbed spear at his side, and said, "Aiken, I have something that I believe is yours. I took it from you when I was one of Leofar's men and would like to return it."

"You were one of Leofar's men? Were you there the day he ambushed Torwald?"

"I was. That day, I took something from you. But it is yours and you should have it back."

"If you were one of Leofar's men you could be my witness. Would you agree to do that? Would you swear an oath to act as my kinsman when I present my accusations at the Assembly?"

"Aiken," Fury said, "a dead man cannot be a witness at an assembly of living men."

"Then, as the last resort, I will go to the Victory Hall to speak before the Lords who sit at the high table. Though Lord Glory neglected to favor me when I appeared before the men at the Assembly over fifteen years ago, I will demand he listen to me inside the walls of the Victory Hall. I will ask Lord Glory to send the peace-breaker, who killed my chieftain and my companions to the lowest land of the dead, and to insist he remain, between now and the Endtime, in Mother Torment's hall."

Fury shrugged a shoulder, "It sounds like a good plan. What do you think Kipp?"

"It turns out that Aiken and me are kinsman. And, yes, I will gladly act as a witness when you accuse Leofar."

"I am grateful, Kipp. I swear to speak the truth and to challenge the guilty man to do the same. I swear my cause is just. Now, what do you want to give me?"

"I have had it all this time," Kipp said, holding out his closed fist. "When Leofar spotted you he said, 'Get that man, he means trouble.' At first, Leofar thought that you were about to turn your horse and run for reinforcements."

"Perhaps I should have. It might have been a better plan," Aiken said with a tinge of regret. "But the thought never crossed my mind. I had never run from a fight."

"Leofar was afraid that you could identify him and would accuse him if you got away. But you dismounted and ran down the slope. When you hit level ground, I took this from you. It is yours, so you should have it back."

Aiken expected to be given something inconsequential, perhaps a small ornament or a buckle that had fallen off his war gear, something that Kipp might have scavenged from the battlefield when he was searching for his javelin in hopes of retrieving it. So when Kipp dropped a spherical object into Aiken's cupped palm, and he looked at what was given him, he was so astonished he nearly dropped it. There, in his palm, lay his dead eye, looking up at him. His good eye was staring at its twin. Aiken knew this eye. But it was useless, laying in his palm. He picked it up with the thumb and forefinger of his other hand and held it up to his empty eye socket. He tried to pry open the scarred skin, to pull it apart, somehow, but the lids were closed forever. "What good will it do me now? Take it back," Aiken said, angrily.

Kipp shrank back from Aiken's extended fist.

But Fury stuck out his hand, and said, "Here. Give it over."

Aiken dropped it into Fury's extended palm. He then watched the graybeard stand and walk the distance to the shoreline. Once he was there, Fury flung the eye into the sea.

When he was seated again, he said, "There, that settles it. One less thing to take care of, eh, Kipp? What next?"

For Aiken, this moment promised to put an end to years of waiting. Here was his chance to prove that Leofar had planned the ambush. He took hold of himself, looked hard at Kipp and asked, "You say you were in Leofar's band when he attacked us?"

It was comforting to see how the man nodded in agreement. Aiken just sat there for a moment, quietly relishing its significance before he asked, "Why did he attack Torwald?"

Before answering, Kipp shifted around a bit to make himself more comfortable. "Leofar keeps control over his men through fear and threats. He demands loyalty without giving it back. Men are afraid of him because of his harsh punishments. He is an ambitious man, hungry for power and prestige. At that time, he wanted to increase the size of his warband but, to do so he needed more land holdings to hand out to his men, and more gold to bind his alliances."

"Tell me how you remember that day."

"First, we need to talk about the Assembly. That was when they started to plan the ambush."

"You were there too?"

"Yes, I was."

"I do not remember you."

"You and me are distant kin. Our great grandfathers were cousins."

"I did not know you."

"You would not have known me. I was a low ranking spearman. But everyone knew who you were, Aiken. Because of your reputation for being good with a knife in close combat, I was proud to think that you and me were distant kin."

Kipp then went on to describe how Leofar and his men, along with the other freeman in the kindred, had attended the Assembly.

Aiken agreed with Kipp's description of the day. It had begun with petty disputes. But things heated up when some of the younger chieftains raised an objection to paying the tribute that their old enemies to the west collected annually. The payments had begun after their great grandfathers had lost a war between the tribes, shortly after the end of the Terrible Winter. Ever since their defeat, the kings in the west had demanded tribute to seal their allegiance. But because that disastrous war had been fought so many years ago, the younger men were no longer willing to pay it.

For Aiken, the act of talking over that day with Kipp brought the long-ago past into the present with such intensity, it seemed as though the events had happened only yesterday. It pained him to relive the treachery and betrayal that men, who had been Torwald's trusted allies, had perpetrated.

"I saw men being drawn into corners and speaking in hushed voices amongst themselves. I guessed the youngest, most gullible ones, were being poisoned by the chieftains who were arguing against making the tribute payment. I suspected they were secretly shaking hands, yet I did not know what they were agreeing to."

Kipp glanced at Fury to explain the dispute, "The older men were the uncles who had been chieftains for many years. Torwald threatened to force the younger men to pay their fair share of the tribute if they refused."

"I remember," Aiken said. "The older men tried to cut off further discussion of the arguments. They claimed that tribute was the price we paid to keep the borders between our lands open. For as long as we paid it, they said, the trade and coinage flowed both ways between their markets and ours. For as long as both sides gained from the agreement, there was no imminent threat of aggression.

"If we ceased paying the tribute, it would be the same as challenging our ene-my to war. Because the western kings and their underlings had standing armies, we would have to call an army together made up of the entire tribe, or even one made up of several tribes. To fight the western tribes, we would have to call a levy and to outfit farmers and merchants. The wartime preparation would have placed too great a burden on the chieftains' coffers. No one had the stomach for it.

"The wisest men claimed that the gathering of such a large army would dis-turb the growing season. Men's absence from the fields would result in famine. The merchants would complain of lost access to the ready coinage that the markets in the west provided. To bring an army together made up of many tribes would only work if everyone feared invasion. And that would only happen if all the chieftains agreed to withhold the tribute."

"It was when the younger men insisted upon a vote, that things got ugly."

"Yes, the following day, men from both sides stood guard at the doors to chal-lenge everyone who entered the Assembly. Each man was forced to prove his freeborn rights and kinship affiliations."

"I remember now. Both the younger and the older men set their own guards at the doors. They questioned each man relentlessly about his kin before he was allowed to enter the hall."

"I had to recite my entire lineage."

"In an attempt to intimidate the younger men, the older men leaned on them."

"Fights broke out. Brawling resulted."

"Some men were wounded in knife fights."

"Chieftains were wary of entering without the protection of their full honor guard."

"All this happened in front of the doors where men had sworn to find peaceful solutions to their disagreements. It was not right, I tell you, Aiken. I did not want to arm myself against my own kin but I had sworn loyalty to my chieftain, a man who did not feel the same as I did. What else could I do?"

"By the time the Assembly met for the last time, men came forward to argue both for and against the proposal. Those who found it unacceptable roared in dis-agreement, and those who approved shook and clashed their spears. The noise of men beating their hammers on their shields and stomping their feet and striking the floor with the butts of their spears made it impossible to take a vote."

"Nor was the responsibility for the final decision without risk of danger. In the end, the men seated at the high table withdrew privately to throw the staves."

"They figured the only way to come to a decision was to consult with the Ma-trones. When the chieftains returned, they called the proposal dead and refused to reconsider it."

"Though the men at the high table had consulted with the highest authority, Leofar and the younger chieftains stalked out, followed by their warbands."

"After that, more fights broke out in the yard. I was dismayed. My faith in the Assembly was damaged by the men who disrespected the law. They had no sense of right or wrong. Though I was certain that Leofar was behind the younger men's defection, I never spoke up. "

"If you thought that Leofar was behind it, then you were right."

"After Torwald's death, I learned from both a cousin and my mother that Leofar had planned the ambush. But even before anyone confirmed my suspicions, I suspected Leofar was slandering the old guard's leadership. But I had no proof. Because Torwald had a soft spot for Leofar, I hesitated to bring my suspicions to him. When I finally did speak up, he was so angry, he refused to listen. Torwald accused me of overreaching and, because I had sworn to follow him, he said that I could not question his decisions."

"Even after he had seen the conflicts at the Assembly?"

"In a situation like that, when you are at war or in the midst of a conflict, even if your leaders do something you disagree with, you are not allowed to question their judgement. That was what we were taught. Leofar's father and Torwald had been close friends growing up. Their own fathers were cousins and their families often traveled between each other's villages. Since Leofar had become a chieftain at too young an age, Torwald treated him like a nephew and defended him against other men's accusations."

"Well, Aiken, your forebodings were correct. Leofar went behind the older men's backs. He urged the younger men to take a stand, but never spoke before the entire Assembly on behalf of the proposal himself. By encouraging other men to put themselves forward, he stayed in the shadows and avoided calling attention to himself."

"Torwald was easily fooled by his fond feelings for Leofar's father. It clouded his vision. He refused to see how cruel, grasping, and heartless the man's son was. But I feared the warband's honor and safety were at stake. When I finally challenged Torwald, he threatened to charge me with disloyalty and treason if I spoke out against his nephew. I was called a traitor by the men in my own warband. I knew that if I kept it up I could lose my standing. Torwald would have seated me down at the far end of the bench with the lowest ranking men. Or worse, just to get rid of me, he could have purposely thrown me into a situation in which I would have been killed."

"Yup. That sometimes happened."

"I had hoped the grievances would blow over after the Assembly. But in hindsight, I see how the younger chieftains had agreed amongst themselves to get control, even if it meant picking off the older leaders one by one. There I was, a member of Torwald's honor-guard, armed with knives, spears, and axes, yet was unable to shield my chieftain from their slander. Now, in hindsight, I question how Torwald used his authority."

"There are chieftains who listen to their counselors," Kipp said and followed his statement with a gratuitous glance at Fury, who returned it with a wink and a sly grin. "And then, there are those who refuse to be second-guessed and, unfortunately, suffer from their errors."

"Yes, you are right," Aiken said, seeming to have missed the hidden meaning of the exchange between Kipp and Fury. "Instead of listening receptively, to his men, as Gevehard does, Torwald belittled the insights that his men brought forward for discussion. Instead he forced us to take orders. Those, like me, who questioned his leadership were accused of disloyalty. The men he listened to, like Sigmund, were only in it for their own selfish interests. To keep their rank, they consistently undermined the reputations of the men whom they feared might threaten their position in the warband."

"Chieftains can be like that you know," Kipp said, and cast a quick, embarrassed glance in Fury's direction. "But your chieftain made his fatal mistake when he treated Leofar like a mere child who needed his uncle's guidance and financial help. He humiliated Leofar when he offered to pay his portion of the tribute."

"I recall how Torwald laughed in Leofar's face and treated him like a child."

"To imply that his nephew was unable to pay the tribute himself because his treasury was empty was what tipped the scale. That was when Leofar decided to kill Torwald. For him, it was nothing to get rid of an uncle. Not after he had deflected suspicions following his older brother's death.

"Leofar spoke of his contempt for Torwald and the others and threatened to make his uncle an example. He said that the old men would see how dangerous he was. He claimed that no one would ever dare cross him again."

"Is that when Leofar planned the ambush?"

"He and Oswald planned the ambush together."

"Oswald hardly knows his tail end from his front end."

"True. But he was awed by Leofar's cunning. Of all the young chieftains, Oswald was the only one who had agreed to withhold his portion of the tribute regardless of the Assembly decision. As it turned out, the fact that Oswald's land shared a boundary with Torwald's holdings on the Warring River made it easy to set things in motion with a cattle raid."

"That explains it. Shortly after the Assembly was over and everyone had gone home, we heard about the cattle's disappearance. At first we thought it was a raid but then we suspected that either Oswald or some his people were behind it. That was when Torwald asked Oswald to meet with us. But when he was slow in coming, the younger men became impatient. We wanted to bring the matter to an end. The night we attempted to get the cattle back, the raid got out of hand. In one swift, impulsive act of angry retribution, the men in the raiding party torched the hamlet."

Aiken shook his head and stiffened his palm and fingers to make sharp, chopping movements in midair. "That night was the point after which there could be no turning back."

He looked into his lap, clutched at his mouth with one hand, and after a long pause, asked, "Did the farmers in Oswald's jurisdiction take the cattle?"

"No. Oswald's men were the thieves. They herded the cows and hid them in the low forest. Leofar and Oswald made a deal with the headman of the hamlet inside Torwald's holdings. Leofar offered the man gold and promised to take his son into his warband. He said he would make him a freedman and a warrior. Leofar laid his arm across the boy's shoulders and looked so fatherly when he said that he would treat him like his own son that the headman was immediately smitten with the plan. So at least one man in Torwald's hamlet knew what we were up to. The headman inserted some of the men who lived the hamlet into your encampment. They chopped wood, carried water, and generally helped out. That way, they kept the headman informed of the goings-on in Torwald's camp."

"Now I understand. That was how they knew the scouts had spotted the cattle. They were the ones who created the mistrust between us by starting the rumor that one of us was playing both sides. All that time, when we were trying to get their cattle back, they were spying on us and undermining our attempts."

"One afternoon, the headman came into Oswald's encampment and told us your scouts had spotted the cattle herd. By then, Leofar had inserted many of his own men into Oswald's warband. When they told us to paint our shields with black char we knew that whatever we were doing was secretive, and probably unlawful but still, we had not fully grasped the meaning of Leofar's intentions.

"It is hard work to move a herd and to pick up the cowpats. But that was what I and several men were told to do. The new-fallen snow helped us cover the tracks."

"The morning after we burned the hamlet, the cattle were in the pasture where they were supposed to have been all along. It made us look bad, like we were in the wrong. We were forced to forfeit our position in the negotiations. I will say this much though—my chieftain was loyal. Even after he learned about the younger men's foolish actions, he stood by us.

"I was the only one who got singled out for harsh treatment. I was the one who became the target of his discontent. Sigmund accused me of being the traitor who was playing both sides. And Torwald picked on me when I tried to warn him about Oswald and Leofar's deceit. But the old fool refused to believe me. He remained confident that he could work out his differences with Oswald. Because the cattle had been returned, Torwald was prepared to come to a settlement that included payment for both the damages we had caused when we torched the hamlet and the man-price for the farmers we had killed. To have gotten Oswald to admit that his men had stolen or hidden the cattle and then had snuck them back into the home pasture would have been impossible. Someone had to lose face.

"Because the two chieftains had agreed not to break the peace, Torwald assigned men, whose negotiating skills he trusted, to work out a fair agreement. We were confident we would come out ahead in the end. We had faith in the men because they had honed their expertise by working out deals in past. Everyone disparaged Oswald's foolishness. But I suspected something more sinister was going on."

"Yes, Oswald was too young to be a chieftain. He had done nothing to warrant the rank and prestige that goes along with leadership. He was attracted to the most powerful people in any dispute. Yet he resented the lack of respect that he thought he deserved from the older chieftains. In the end, because he was easily influenced by others, he became more dangerous than anyone ever guessed. Because Oswald wanted to prove his toughness and to show that he was a man to be reckoned with, he took foolish risks by aligning himself with untrustworthy allies.

"Even while Torwald's and Oswald's negotiators were meeting that morning to talk things over, Leofar set the trap."

"So Leofar was there?"

"He laid out the plot the night before."

"Did they also plan to burn down the hamlet? Was one of Torwald's men in on it?"

"No, that was not in the plan. The following morning Oswald was irate. He regretted his decision to side with Leofar and threatened to wage war on Leofar himself. He was about to throw us all out. But after Leofar filled his cup a few more times, Oswald settled down. That was how he got rid of his older brother. He just kept filling the cup. If Oswald had passed out, Leofar would have poured it down his gullet and drowned him in ale. But Leofar accommodated Oswald's grievances and promised to make up for the losses. Once he was promised the rights to collect tribute from the hamlets on both sides of the river, Oswald was proud of his skillful negotiation. By then, he was so tipsy that he started to celebrate his increased wealth. Apparently he had never heard the old farmer's saying that a man should not count his chickens before they hatch—Leofar later backed out of the agreement."

"He learned too late that Leofar was a liar and a cheat?"

"You got that right, Aiken. The following autumn when Oswald tried to collect tribute from the hamlet across the river, Leofar told him that he had misunderstood the deal. By that time, Leofar had given the holding to one of the men in our own warband, and Oswald was afraid to cross him. In fact, all the chiefdoms were afraid to cross Leofar. No one trusted him. They all started to pay men in his warband to spy for them. One chieftain's man even approached me, and I was not a high ranking man. That just goes to show you how desperate they were."

"Did you agree to spy?"

Kipp deflected Aiken's question with a shoulder shrug, and continued, "Leofar promised the headman from Torwald's hamlet that he could rebuild the burnt hamlet and absorb those lands and cattle and the surviving hamlet dwellers. In other words, he made two promises, neither of which he intended to keep.

"The headman was there the night they laid out the plans. To sit with chieftains who were plotting to take down another high-ranking man increased the headman's stature in his own eyes. But he was too proud for his own good. He should have known better. Because he had reasons to get back at the chieftain to whom he owed tribute, this situation offered him a chance to get even with Torwald. I will say this: a man should not rant about the reasons he begrudges another chieftain, even when he is siding with the man's rival. Leofar fed the headman's resentment, but after he had inherited Torwald's holdings, that headman came to a sudden and mysterious end in the forest.

"Anyway, that night Leofar acted like he was the headman's friend. He kept filling his cup as he explained what they wanted him to do the following morning. He was told to go to Torwald's encampment and to tell the men in your warband that the farmers had sighted a wild boar."

Aiken groaned and swallowed hard. "I remember. He came into the encampment that morning with news about the boar. He claimed his men had cornered the beast with the dogs. He told us that he and his men would be the beaters."

"But there was no boar. It was all a ruse. Anyway, he led your band into the trap. There was a marsh in the river bend. Our scouts had chosen it because the tall rushes made a good blind in which to hide. We rode the horses over the river and sent them back across to be tied up in a woodland on the other side."

"What about Oswald's men?"

"Oswald's men, along with some of Leofar's men, hid in the woods, on the other side of a low hill. Because we wanted to confuse Torwald and his men, and keep them from spotting our hiding places, the headman led them on a long, roundabout way through the woods. We knew exactly how many men there were in your warband and doubled the number of our own. The hunting party rode right into the trap. After Torwald and his men dismounted and tied their horses in the underbrush, Oswald's men came out of hiding and surrounded them. Once the conflict had broken out, Oswald rode across the river and told the headman's son to take a horse, ride it back to the encampment, and tell any remaining fighters to come at once."

From there, Aiken picked up the story. "The camp was not far from where the others had gone hunting. After Alger and I were alerted to the attack, we left as quickly as we could. The headman's son led us to a bluff where the river takes a turn. After I hauled back on the reins, I could see the men were fighting in hand-to-hand combat at the bottom of the ravine. The attackers had Torwald and the warband encircled. I still remember how my stomach clenched. I was angry at myself because I had not issued my suspicions with greater urgency. I was angry with Torwald because he had not seen it coming. And I was angry with Leofar, who was acting just as I had known he would. I had known that he was up to no good. I still ask myself why I did not speak up more boldly.

"The falling snow had hidden Leofar and your warband, but when a sudden gust cleared the snow, I stared into the marsh below the bluff and saw the men in your band who were hidden among the tall weeds, shrubs and spindly trees."

"Yes, you see, we did not want the men in Torwald's warband to approach from the side where the bluff was. That was why we told the headman to lead them through the woods and then circle back. It was marshy there, but the water was low at that time of year and the ground was partially frozen. We crouched down on the tussocks. From there, we could watch for any men who might either run toward the horses or come to the other men's aid."

"More men than I could count were armed with spears and javelins, bows and arrows. I even saw the horses tethered in that sparse woodland across the river. At first, I did not see Leofar, but then I recognized him. He was in the midst of his honor guard. He was not even wearing a helmet. I ask you, what kind of a liege lord is not prepared to enter the fray?"

"A cowardly one. We all knew that."

"When I saw how few men we were, up against three or four times as many, I knew that we were as good as dead already. But Alger and I dismounted and charged. When I reached the bottom of the bluff, I stopped for a moment to get my bearings."

Aiken took several breaths before he could look up and continue. "It only took a moment to see just how bad things were. Everything was happening at once. Cynefrid, Selwyn, Sievert and Willard were protecting Torwald with their overlapped shields. Six or seven of Oswald's men had them surrounded. Two brothers in our band stood back to back, fighting against four attackers. One brother took a blow to his shield from a man wielding an axe. He managed to slash his blade from upper right to lower left, and caught the man's upper arm. Blood spray soaked their jerkins. The injured man dropped his axe but when he bent down to pick it up with his left hand, the second brother slashed at him on the back-swing and got him across the face. Then he smashed him in the helmet with the pommel until the man lay flat on the ground. Just then, he had to fend off the second man's swinging blade and had no time to recover. Osric and Erwin were down and bloodied. One was kicking his legs and writhing in pain."

"By then, I was one of Leofar's best marksmen. When you and your friend rode up, Leofar recognized you. Fearful that you would turn your horse and ride off, he said to me, 'Get him before he gets away. No one remains alive. Understand?'

"Aiken, believe me, I had no reason to hate you. Throwing is not the same as fighting in close combat. I was not fighting to stay alive. At that distance I had no fear of getting hurt. The nearest threat I faced was from the man who stood beside me. If I had missed, if I had not hit you, Leofar would have slapped a fine or punishment on me or done something worse to humiliate me. Besides, it was my duty to protect the other men in my warband from your blade. I felt more loyalty to my own war companions than to my chieftain. But I was not angry at you. It disgusted me to attack a fellow kinsmen. I want you to understand that."

Aiken nodded. "I understand. Those were the rules, we all agreed upon."

"When I took aim I had to remain clearheaded, to plan the trajectory, and to account for the wind. I had to wait for the perfect moment. Although I did not want to strike you, I trained my sights. There was no honor in taking you down. But it was my duty to protect my own war companions from your on-coming assault. I hope you understand."

"I do."

"When you came to the bottom of the rise and stood there, I had a clear shot. Not a good shot. I aimed at your chest but ended up getting you in the head. Anyway, I figured I had the best shot when you were standing still, so I let her rip and down you went."

"At first, I thought I had been hit with wind-blown debris. What happened next? What happened to Alger?"

"The man who rode up with you? After I downed you, he kept running. One of Torwald's men was hopping on one leg. Blood was drenching his injured thigh while he parried blows with his partially shattered shield. The man attacking him just had to push his own shield into the wounded man to knock him over. He swung his axe high overhead, and brought it down across the man's neck. Your friend came up behind and felled him with one axe blow to the center of his back. After that, one of Oswald's men came at him from the side. Before your friend could fend off the attack, he was stabbed in the back. He tried to recover and to swing his axe but Oswald's man just hacked at him until your friend's knees buckled."

Aiken caught a breath. Though he knew that Alger had been killed that day, it was hard to hear about the series of blows that had taken him down. Aiken sat quietly for a time, looking at his hands. After a while he said, "I never found out what happened to the two negotiators who were sent to reach a settlement with Oswald's men that morning."

"Their throats were slit in the midst of negotiations."

"No." Aiken was so stunned he felt like he had been hit in the gut. He doubled over, grabbed his stomach and feared he might retch. The bogman leapt onto his back, folded its long arms across the front of his neck, and grasped Aiken so tightly he was unable to catch a breath. It then squeezed him in the sides and Aiken felt that familiar stitch. He struggled hard to straighten up but began to choke. He coughed and shook himself but could not loosen the creature's hold.

It was then that an abrupt sea gust caught the men unaware. Aiken pushed himself upright just as the other two men turned to look in the direction from which the wind was blowing. Fury and Kipp stood and, altogether, the three men saw two, thin waterspouts trailing from the shadowy underside of a cloud. They were whipping about like fingers feeling their way across the violently churning waves. The storm cloud was glaringly white on the top, so brilliant that it hurt the eyes. But it was shaded forebodingly dark on the underside. Several fishermen, paddling small boats, were attempting to flee the on-coming storm. Bobbing on the choppy waves, the men were rowing hard to make it ashore.

The crow squawked. Annoyed with the gusts tousling its feathers, it pointed its beak downwind, flapped its wings and took off. Tipping side to side, the bird flew off to shelter further inland.

The graybeard picked up his cloak, managed to pull it around himself, and lifted the hood to cover his head. Facing the water, he leaned into the wind as he stared at the clouds blowing in their direction. When a tangle of hair whipped across his face, he tossed his head to the side to dislodge it. Kipp picked up his javelin and stepped in close to Fury.

A broad, slanting, gray streak hung from the heavy clouds, as a sign of the downpour coming their way. Lightning zigzagged in a brilliant flash. The men aboard the small boats, fighting against the turbulent white-capped waves, were working their oars in their struggle to keep from tipping. Inland men splashed into the surf with arms extended to reach out and to help pull the boats ashore.

Aiken's memory of the fateful day was still so vivid that he felt as though he was standing outside himself. And even as his wrath exploded, everything Aiken did seemed to happen slowly. Time warped and he was aware of each thought as it crossed his mind. He told himself that although some men had fallen, now, along with Alger's and his reinforcement they were certain to turn the skirmish their way. Alger was beside him. And together, they stepped into the fray.

But even so, Aiken knew he was lying to himself. They were horribly outnumbered three to one, four to one. The odds were stacked against them. They could never win. In the end, they would all be dead. He tried to make his way toward the place where Torwald was surrounded. He drew Rushing Harm. Assured of his willfulness, once the hilt was in his hand, he hefted its weight and connected to his killing arm. Anger over the hurts his brothers were suffering flooded him. Rage filled Aiken's heart. He took one step, then another and another, thinking all the time: Leofar has done it. Leofar has broken the peace. He will pay for this.

Alger yelled, "Aiken, go up ahead. I have your back."

All the men were coming at him in a spinning vortex, threatening to swallow him up. He had to fend them off. A howl followed a crashing boom. Sucked into the eye of the storm, Aiken struggled to hold his ground against the squealing gale. The men were coming at him, thrusting their weapons. Closing in, more and more fighters were caught up in the turbulence. And along with the eddying sand particles, dried leaves, seaweed, and twigs tossing about and whirling chaotically, the men's feet were barely touching the ground.

Leofar's herd of gray-black horses were coming across the water on dark clouds, galloping swiftly above the earth. The men jumped on, kicked their mount's flanks, and lifted on the spray. And there, in the forefront was their chieftain. In the center of the swirling gale, he stood with his back turned. His arms were lifted overhead as he yelled gruffly above the roar, "Move out. Move out. Go. Go. Go."

Aiken now understood, or thought he did, and took off after their chieftain before he could get away. Aiken grabbed his arm and spun him around. Staring into Leofar's face, he looked directly into his enemy's eyes. He screamed in Leofar's face, "You sent your warband after me to chase me into a trap. You called me an unmanly, one-eyed outlaw, a useless cowardly wretch, a good for nothing braggart. Your insults are punishable by death. You murdered my chieftain and my friends. You cannot get away this time. Pull your blade right now. We will see who the coward is. We will see who tells the truth. Fight. Now. Without backup. Single combat. You against me."

Centered in the squall, in a flurry of sand and debris, his opponent appeared to be as comfortable as a man at home standing leisurely on the dais inside his longhouse. He flapped his free hand at the swirling wreckage as if nothing but flies were buzzing annoyingly around his head.

Aiken stared menacingly. His every move stretched out in time. He tightly squeezed his opponent's arm and held him in his grip. "You are going nowhere. You and me will fight right here. Without your warband to back you up. Unsheathe your weapon."

"Allow me to offer you one, final word of advice," Aiken's opponent said. He narrowed his gaze and eyed Aiken with cold indifference. "When you threaten a man with violence, I recommend that you know who you are faced off against. Shall we have one last riddle before we part? A combat of words? Perhaps that will satisfy your blood lust.

"Now, tell me this one last thing if you can,
If you are, at all, the wise man whom
You proclaim yourself to be,
What did the Lord of the Whirlwind
Whisper into his wife's bronze pot?"

Just then the man's face changed. It was no longer Leofar, but the graybeard who spoke with the grim authority of a chieftain, "Now take your hand off my arm."

Aiken dropped his handhold and stepped back. Uncertain whether the ground upon which he stood was solid as rock or thin as smoke, he asked: What just happened? Things were all mixed up. Was Leofar an imposter, disguised as an old graybeard or was the graybeard disguised as Leofar?

Either way, he had his doubts. But his blade had a will of its own. Supported by Aiken's arm, Rushing Harm knew its target. The blade arced. And, at the same exact moment that it was whistling through the air, the man's cape flapped and took on the shape of a black, fanned-out tail and two black wings. And, just like that, the crow was pulled into the slender, swirling eye of a waterspout.

The bird got away, all but for a single tail feather. The pinion lifted on a gust, tossed about briefly, spiraled in the vortex, and landed with its shaft poking upright on the dune.

The howling winds blew and the clouds streamed past. Then the storm was gone. The wind subsided as quickly as it had risen. The particles of sand, weeds and sticks dropped to the ground. The air was still as it had been before the squall came up. A mild breeze blew inland. And at that very moment, Aiken was certain of just this much and nothing more: only the Lord of the Whirlwind knows the answer to that riddle.

IV.

At first, Aiken was unsure where he was. It took some time to figure out. He lay curled up in the red stone's shadow. Groggy, but calm, he knew this much at least: somehow, he had gotten past the threat. He was on the right side of immanent death and would see the sun rise tomorrow. He looked around. The haunts who had chased him this far were gone, but the shades, who sat in the small boats outlined by white stones, were still there, peaceably staring at him. Somehow, Aiken felt at ease among them.

He walked toward the place where he had last seen the graybeard standing. A subtle breeze lifted the feather and twirled it about. It floated down again and, dropping slowly, came to rest on the sandy dune. Clearly, there was a feather lying there. It was something he could see and touch. It was solid proof.

To make sure that it was not made of dream-stuff, he stooped to pick it up. Sure enough, it was real. He held the bottom of the pinion shaft between his thumb and pointer finger. He touched it with the other hand and stroked it lengthwise several times.

Then a sudden gust grabbed the feather, lifted it out of his grip, and just blew his proof away. He tried to catch it, but lost sight of it. He dropped down on hands and knees. He crawled around on the wind-blown dune and brushed his hands across the tops of the grass blades. Searching relentlessly for that black feather, he clawed at the grass with his fingers. But it was gone. He was unable to find it. It was gone. Just like that, his proof had disappeared.

A sudden shudder wracked Aiken's entire body.

A voice, seemingly coming from out of nowhere, floated toward him from all sides like an echo. "When you come up against Mother Necessity's restraints, there is no way to free yourself but by untying the knots." And though he was unable to discern from which direction the words had come, he heard them clearly say, "Recon-sider my offer. You may need my help. If you do, just call me by my name."

Aiken walked past the thicket and out to the road. The heavy clouds were mov-ing off to the south. The air was fresh and clean. The dampness was gone and the sky was blue. He was certain that the man he saw up ahead was the graybeard. Carelessly on his way, seemingly without a trouble to his name, he kept time to what may have been a jaunty tune he was humming. Almost dancing, he was bouncing his head back and forth.

The man stopped to issue a sharp, piercing whistle, then resumed skipping down the road. The two crows, named Thought and Memory, took flight from a nearby field. Bobbing up and down, they circled above the man as he strode off down the road. Thoroughly unscathed by the storm and in no seeming hurry to get anywhere fast, the crows followed the man. Sketching broad scrolls against the sky, they rotated to the left and then to the right, one bird ahead, and one behind. Their wings tipped side to side. They broke into a slow-moving glide, interrupted it with a single choppy wing beat, and banked into an alternate curve.

For a man whose haughty pretensions could put even the proudest man to shame with his claim to be Lady Blessed's husband, the man who called himself Fury had dared to evoke the wrath of ruling powers. And though he tempted their retribution for such an arrogant act, instead of suffering the repercussions of their vengeful anger, the infuriating stranger was getting away free and clear.

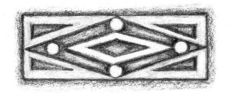

TWELVE

Lapis Lazuli
If you will cure melancholy in any man and make peace

Take this stone which is called Lapis Lazuli. It is like to the color of the nighttime sky, and there is within it little bodies of gold. And it is sure and proved, that it cures melancholy and makes the mind pure and devout. It strengthens the mind in good things.

The Truth of Rocks, by Aluiss the Wise

I.

It was dusk, the stars were appearing slowly, and this was all I knew: I was expected to arrive somewhere but was uncertain of where, exactly, I was meant to appear. Fearful of being late, I walked hurriedly between the high, anonymous-looking warehouse walls that lined both sides of the narrow street.

Pausing at the cross street to get my bearings, I saw, off to the left, a nearby river. To prevent erosion along this heavily trafficked stretch, the riverbank had been reinforced with travertine walls. A small crescent-shaped boat floated past carrying three seated people and one standing steersman in the back. On the grassy hillside across the river, amidst shrubberies and trees, there were several two and three-storied, cream-colored homes, roofed with red tiles. Two had porticos on three sides, but the portico on one roofed only the doorway. A woman and several men either stared vacantly at the flowing water or walked in a leisurely fashion along the riverbank. Otherwise, there were few people about.

Heading east through the nearly deserted streets, I was looking for a bridge across which I could walk. I had heard of a large, public library, which was located on the opposite side of the river. For quite some time, I have been on the look-out for a scroll that was rumored to have been written by a disciple of Pythagoras. And since I was visiting this city, I wanted to learn whether the library owned a copy I could either consult or would be permitted to make a facsimile of for my own collection.

The narrow corridors were poorly lit, but I could see my way well enough to keep from stumbling. Though my knowledge is second hand at best, and open to dispute, according to my understanding, when an ordinary man gazes at the clear, nighttime sky, most stars appear to shine with a sharp, white light. But due to this condition, with which the men of my own kind have been afflicted, our eyesight is said to be keen as an owl's. And because of this greater sensitivity to the light than an ordinary man's, when I look at the darkening sky, I see a multitude of colors. Above my head, I saw a red star light up and then a yellow one, followed by a blue star's appearance and, off to the left, a green one.

After I had left the warehouse district, I entered what looked like a commercial sector. To lend the area a festive mood, the merchant's stalls were decorated with frescoed pictures of garlands and complex, geometric patterns. Though most were closed and shuttered for the night, here and there, light spilled onto the street through the cracks between closed doors and doorposts and the slits in louvered windows.

Coming toward me, a man and woman, accompanied by a torch-bearing servant, exited an open doorway, which led into a dark, narrow alleyway. The man was dressed in a knee length, belted tunic, and leather sandals. A cloak thrown over his left shoulder was pinned on the right. The laughing, wide-mouthed woman who walked beside him arm-in-arm was dressed in a tunic, belted high above her waist, and an off-white, elaborately draped toga, which I assumed had been given her by a paramour. She had a very large bosom.

Upon seeing me, the garrulous woman acted as though she knew me and immediately began to recount an event that had happened the night before. Perplexed by her tale, and uncertain why she found it necessary to tell me, for I had never before set eyes upon her, I assumed that she was one of those people who cannot stop talking and will habitually accost anyone who appears to be willing to listen. Though I gave her my polite attention, I hoped she would pause to take a breath so I could ask directions to the library. But, unfortunately, she proved to be incredibly long-winded.

She touched my arm, drew uncomfortably close, and forced me to stare at that large bosom of hers as she described a house that she and another woman, named Melissa, had gone to visit the day before. Apparently, her friend had been hired to entertain several of the guests who had been invited to attend a dinner at Senator Cicero's home that night. The woman, to whom I was speaking, had agreed to accompany her friend. After the two women arrived through the back door, they had been shown into a dingy room in the servant's quarters and were instructed to remain seated until their services were required.

Though she bragged about her invitation to entertain in a home owned by a man of Cicero's stature, in the end, she had been disappointed. Her services had gone unneeded, and she had been forced to stay in the servant's quarters the entire night. Her companion, Melissa, however, had been led away. When her friend returned, Melissa had described the home in detail, including, in her account, a room filled entirely with shoes.

Melissa opened the long, narrow tube that she had walked in carrying, and shook out a scroll. Unreeling the parchment, she had then begun to read aloud a well-known Greek mathematician's commentary upon the cosmos.

As I listened to the woman's tale, I thought she may have meant scrolls or books with her description the room. Surely, someone like Cicero who, during his lifetime, was reputed to have been a learned man of scholarly pursuits, would have set aside a room for scrolls and books, but not for the storage of shoes.

At a loss for words, I leaned in close. But, tongue-tied as I was, all I could say was: "We may talk about shoes, if you like. I have several pairs of shoes and boots at home. But to fill an entire room with shoes is an extraordinary achievement. Senator Cicero must be an avid collector. Since I, too, am a collector, I would like to know where this house with the roomful of shoes is located. I should like to see it for myself."

She took ahold of my hand, raised it to her cheek, and caressed it gently. But before she had time to answer, I awoke.

Apparently, some clever prankster had intended to tease me by setting up a dreamtime drama with the express purpose of confusing shoes and scrolls. And, after I had come so close to the discovery of this long-lost manuscript's location, the adventure had only served to increase my frustration.

Several days later, it was nighttime, and the stars shone brightly enough to cast a shadow. Once again, I was walking through a cityscape similar to the one through which I had walked before. I still was headed east and was still close to the river, but apparently, had made some progress. The area through which I now made my way was a site where several buildings had been razed to make way for the construction of a large temple devoted to the veneration of Asclepius and the medical arts.

The earth was torn up so badly that it resembled a miniature mountain range. Lest I turn an ankle walking over the peaks, ridges, and valleys of dried, cracked mud, when I saw, on the right, a row of houses across from the building site, I thought the street, though unpaved, might offer me a safer place to walk and headed in that direction. Some of the houses were colored red, and others were pale yellow. The well-designed ornamentation on window frames, shutters, and doors made them pleasing to look at.

When I saw an open doorway I walked directly into the house. At the far end of the dark hallway a couple women were preparing food by the light of several small rush lamps and the softly glowing coals burning in a grated brazier. Small children crowded the kitchen. One, in particular, pulled repeatedly on a woman's skirt. The woman, who I presumed was the child's mother, took a fingerful of the porridge she was stirring and, to quiet the insistent child, stuck it into his mouth.

I told the two women that I was searching for Senator Cicero's home but had become hopelessly lost. One of the women kindly led me outside, offered me a seat on a bench beneath the portico, and sat beside me. She was barefoot and, because it was evening, I feared for her comfort but, apparently, she was unbothered by the cold. She assured me that I was headed in the right direction and explained where I should turn left up ahead.

I soon got past the torn-up construction site and came to a broad, paved roadway. After I had continued east for a while, I saw on the left, a wide staircase that led up a wooded hillside. This seemed to be the place where she had suggested I turn.

In time, the street led me directly to a double-doorway centered between two pillars topped with cornices. The wooden doors were elaborately trimmed in geometric patterns and painted agreeably with red and yellow ochre. Two men stood guard before the entrance of the magnificent home. When I told them that I had been invited to attend the gathering that night, they opened the double-doors, and I entered.

Once inside, I walked around the perimeter of a small, rectangular pool in the center of the vestibule. Above it, there was a similarly sized opening in the roof through which the nighttime sky could be observed. A servant greeted me, welcomed me to Senator Cicero's home, and showed me into the atrium. Here too, there was a pool, but larger, in the center of the unroofed courtyard. Arranged around the pool, several men and one woman reclined on couches. Without an introduction to the others, I was shown to a couch upon which I, too, could recline.

Here and there, flaming torches, set in iron stands, lent a soft glow to the atrium. In a corner, five musicians played lyres and pipes. The floor was tiled in an elegant, multi-hued lozenge pattern, made from small shapes cut from colored stones. Arranged beneath the peristyle-edged veranda, there were three life-size statues, each of which I believed was a representation of one of Cicero's forebears. They were all dressed in draped togas edged with the purple bands indicative of their status in the republic.

Several other sculptures were arranged around the courtyard. Carved of marble, the statues had been painted in colors so life-like that it was disarming to see them posed so breathlessly still. Some represented young men in athletic and heroic postures, and others were carved in the likenesses of young women garbed in semi-draped lengths of fabric. It was enticing to imagine one might drop what remained of her clothing and step naked into the pool.

Given the light of the flickering torches, the sculptures appeared to be so life-like that I was momentarily startled when a sculpture portraying a youth seemed to come alive. The boy walked directly toward me and offered me a footed, purple fluorite cup filled with wine. I accepted it with gratitude and admired the carved representations of grape clusters and leaves encircling the rim. Another boy brought me a platter of cheese, bread, and figs.

One of the reclining men said, "When I am asleep, that part of me, who visits the dreamtime, takes off without my willing it. Yet, once I am there, I never question the rationale behind this otherworldly landscape and am left to navigate it alone to the best of my ability.

"Though outdoor places, interior rooms and hallways are similar to those that I see when I am awake, somehow they seem different from the way I remember them. The other night, I was walking along a familiar street when I saw a cow—it might have been a brown one—aimlessly wandering about, oblivious of the traffic. I thought it had a pig-like face, but when a couple black and white spotted hogs came along behind it, I could see that the pigs' snouts were nothing like the cow's."

"Might they have been on the way to market?"

"No, there was no apparent reason for them to have been in a residential neighborhood. But what seemed even more peculiar was my reaction to their appearance. The single detail, which most aroused my interest, were the shapes of their snouts. I began to compare them without questioning the reason for my interest in animal snouts. Contrary to when I am awake, when I am the dreamer, I accept whatever occurs as readily as I would accept any ordinary, everyday event, no matter how absurd it is."

"I too, can be equally as befuddled as Virgil is and, upon awakening, will be unable to attribute meaning to the vision or to discover the context for its occurrence," another man said, and proceeded to narrate his vision from the previous night. "See what you can make of this. The sky was pitch black, and I was walking with a small group of men and women through a pleasant, pastoral garden. Apparently, I knew that one of the men in our group composed music, possibly for the lyre.

"As we were walking, I was winding a string around a ball of thread. Or I may have been unwinding it, laying the thread down on the path upon which we were walking. I am uncertain of which it was. Someone mentioned that the thread seemed to be rather loosely wound. I agreed and said that when I had made this ball of thread, several days before, even then, I had questioned how tightly I should wind it. I did not want to unduly stretch or break it and had hoped that someone could share their wisdom with me regarding this matter. After all, spinning and winding thread is an activity with which either my sister or mother are more familiar.

"Dreamtime incidents like these can seem so utterly absurd, that, although we engage in ordinary activities, things combine in such a bizarre fashion. People, objects, and activities get thrown together in unexpected ways. For me, a man, to be winding a ball of thread, while he is walking through a garden is certainly as absurd as Virgil's vision of cows with pig-like snouts. And yet, there must be some underlying logical organization to the dreamtime. Small tableaus are laid out in which I, the observer can participate. At times I seem to be both the character who is acting out the drama and the single audience member who is watching it play out. The director of my dream-time vision reshapes and recombines the things and events from my ordinary, daily life by giving those ordinary things new meanings that I may never have considered when I was awake. But without an understanding of the context, the drama seems so meaningless that I have no way to direct the action."

"That may be," another man said, "but I have heard that you can, in fact, direct your dreamtime actions. If Virgil had recognized how strange it was to see the cows, he may have become aware that he was both a visitor to the dreamtime and was awake at the same time. Aristotle refers to the common occurrence of this possibility in his treatise, *On Dreams*. I should think that, for someone who enjoys storytelling, Virgil might have invented a narrative out of the unlikely appearance of the cow and the pigs. A poet is always attentive to the details."

"Generally speaking," another man said, "Pliny dismisses the visions we have when we are asleep. He puts greater faith in the tangible world that he can observe with the organs of sensation."

"I agree. There does seem to be something inherently dangerous about dream-time activities," said the man who had been winding thread. "It is as though our nightly experience in that otherworldly place purposefully sets out to undermine our belief in the rational cosmos that we believe in and which we faithfully observe when we are awake."

"Possibly Pliny is right. But, it may also be said that the way we think in the dreamtime simply conforms to a different kind of logic than the way we think when we are awake. I ask you, how can we insist that the very things, which our forebears believed in, are incompatible with Natural Philosophy? When even the ancients believed in the existence of invisible beings like ghosts, gods, spirits, and the ability to prophesy, how can we, in all humility, label them delusional? Instead, might we say that such things do exist in some form but are shaped in a configuration with which we are unacquainted and are therefore ignorant? Homer gave shape and substance to Athena and all sorts of monstrosities. Can the whole history of humankind have been delusional? Apparently such beliefs have served men and women well in the past. Might Pliny have missed something when he insisted that all things must have a tangible, and earthly explanation?"

"According to Aristotle, visions correspond to the faculties of soul. On the first level we see with our eyes. The visions we see when awake or in a nightly vision, depends upon the imagination. And, thirdly, what we visualize with our intellect corresponds to pure reason."

"Likewise, although dream accounts are deemed untrustworthy and unacceptable as testimony in a court of law because they are impossible to corroborate," said the man who, I assumed was our host that evening, because he wore the draped toga, woven with the senatorial, purple bands, "and the highest regard is attributed to the intellect because it comes from a man's ability to reason, Pliny does admit that a man may, occasionally, have a significant experience when he visits the dreamtime. The way I see it, therein lies the greater problem. Answer me this, Horace, how will we know the difference between a meaningful nighttime vision and a random, nonsensical one?"

"I, too, agree that a well-ordered world should be our ideal," Horace answered. "The rational perspective, we are taught to observe, seeks to address our day to day existence with a sense of harmony and design. Like the sculptors who imagined the ideal human figure when they carved the statues, here in the atrium, these likenesses are well-balanced and lead the observer to meditate upon a peaceful world in which beauty, heroism, and athletic prowess are extolled."

"That may be the ideal, but when one has a body that does not act in an ideal fashion," Virgil said, "the more desperate nighttime visions affect me deeply. As you know my health is poorly."

"I too have had troublesome dreamtime experiences that seemed to foretell disaster," said Ovid, "but my fears proved to have been misplaced when nothing bad happened. Nonetheless, Virgil, you might wish to play it safe and treat the night vision in the same way as one that carries a significant message. To avert any danger-ous consequences, or to learn whether the dreamtime vision was a portent, you might want to describe it to the sun and the stars. Some men wash their hands in a stream or tell the vision to a river."

"I am grateful for your suggestions, but what works well for you, may not benefit me. Though we speak of the dreamtime as though it is a place known to each and every one of us, we all visit a different dreamworld. Everyone ventures there, but the worlds we see are all quite different."

"Virgil, you may also want to keep in mind," Horace said, "that many dream-time encounters are simply left-overs from the previous day's activities. I frequently go over the same thoughts and actions that had absorbed my attention before I went to sleep."

"If that is so, it is the same for me. But there have been times when I had a useful nighttime vision. Not long ago, I was absorbed in writing my *Histories,* when the part of me, who visits the dreamtime, snuck into Julius Caesar's tent. Playing the role of his scribe, I was hurriedly taking notes on a wax tablet while listening to the conversa-tion, in which he was engaged with his generals, after he had crossed the Rubicon."

"How did you manage that, Tacitus?" Cicero asked. "I should have liked to have spied on Caesar's dinner following the crossing of the Rubicon."

"I have read that Plutarch admitted to being so curious about his enemy's thoughts that he wished he could pry into their dreamtime activities."

"What a tantalizing temptation," Ovid laughed. "To think that I might open a small window through which I could peek at another's innermost secrets and observe an unseemly intrigue exposing my enemy's embarrassing weaknesses is a fascinating thought, indeed."

"Who would you spy on?"

"Augustus Caesar."

"That would certainly get you into trouble."

"But how would he know?"

"To hear another man's dream is like peering beneath the façade that he erects and from there, watch discrete, secretive scenes being staged," Horace said. "The observer is like the reader who spies on the writer's private thoughts when reading his texts. In many ways, what the poets write is not all that different from our dreamtime adventures. When I am taken with a fit of writing, I often feel as though I am reclining in the passionate arms of the Muse and am transported to a dream-like world. To read what the poet wrote can be similar to stealthily listening in on a conversation from behind a crack between the door and the doorpost, or to slip into a vacated room and to read correspondence, which was meant for someone else, or to peek at a man's secret journal."

"It is good to have so many poets gathered here tonight," Cicero said. "Do you not agree, Artemidorus? Perhaps a poet would be better at interpreting a scene in which a man is winding a ball of thread than those of us whose careers involve matters of state or writing historical narratives."

Now that all eyes were turned on him, Artemidorus, the author of the popular book, *The Interpretation of Dreams*, said, "Yes, the meaning of the dreamtime scenario can be revealed through proper interpretation. A poet cultivates the realm of imagination and his language is metaphorical. Because they spend their days in the realm that is overseen by Mother Remembrance and her daughters, the Muses, a poet will be well acquainted with the way that one thing can be made to stand-in for another. We shall ask the poets. Which of you would like to take a stab at giving meaning to Ovid's dreamtime vision?"

"I would," Virgil said. "If I, like Theseus, were meandering through the labyrinth, after I had killed-off the danger, I would follow the thread, winding and turning, hand over hand in fits and starts, to find my way out of the maze. The corridor is dark as the pitch-black sky, and I cannot see what is up ahead but must trust the thread to lead me. In the case of Theseus and the Minotaur, the greatest threat was to the children who were sacrificed to atone for the leader's transgression against the laws of Nature. In my case, perhaps the vision would refer to a loss of innocence and a feeling of displacement. To regain my sense of harmony I must trace the thread back to its beginning. It is the same as when I construct a poem. To mark out the path, to discover the plot, to find the way forward never takes me in a straight line, but, rather, the story is beset by numerous interruptions, looping diversions and switch-backs, which slow my movement to a snail's pace. I worry that I will die before I have completed the poem. Yet, according to this dream, if I am careful to keep the thread taut, I will manage to maintain its connection to the point where I started, and will be assured of reaching the exit. The danger lies in pulling too hard. If I break the thread, I will lose my way and, if I never get out of the maze, the poem will never be completed."

Ovid praised Virgil's poetic sentiments, saying, "The Matrones have given you a voice, Virgil, and by your voice you will be well-known."

Virgil tipped his head in acceptance of the praise. But Ovid continued, "However, your interpretation does not reflect my lived experience."

"There are many ways to interpret a dream," Artemidorus said. "According to my book, it is possible to categorize nighttime visions. Admittedly, the dream-visions that correspond to one's daily life require little interpretation, just as Horace said. But the other, more episodic visions are like little allegorical stories that illustrate a message about a real-world situation you face. To disregard the messages that are imparted by those who dwell in otherworlds can be perilous."

We all nodded our heads in agreement to express our satisfaction, and Artemidorus said. "Because the dream world is situated in a place between the worlds, there may be occasional nighttime visions in which a god will appear and impart a message. And at other times, a dreamer may meet up with those who dwell in the lands of the dead.

"It is there that Mother Remembrance presides over the pool of Forgetfulness," Artemidorus continued. "Because the dead exist outside of time, when they drink from this pool, they will forget the life they lived on earth."

"The poet may also venture into that world of souls," Virgil said. "As I have written, the Sibyl of Cumae is Aeneas's guide, but warns him that the way back is fraught with peril. There is much to be found there: wealth, pleasure, love, knowledge of the future, control over your enemies, and your beloved. To drink from Mother Remembrance's well of Memory is what the poet must do to find his stories. It is not unlike following the thread through the maze. He must plead with Mother Remembrance to be allowed access to that sacred well in the center."

"But, of the restless dead," Tacitus interjected, "those who were killed violently, or before their time was up, are especially bitter about their cruel, untimely deaths and may seek revenge. Polybius says that Philip of Macedon was haunted by night terrors."

"No doubt," Horace said, "they were the shades of the men whom he had killed and had left to rot on the battlefield. Lest they be forgotten, the dead want to tell their stories. They want those who are still alive to know how they suffered. They do not want to be pushed aside. At other times, they may appear and ask the living to fulfill a desire. They frequently seek blood and may ask the living to accept the risks that accompany the accomplishment of the task."

"Those restless dead who pursued Philip were, no doubt, requesting a proper burial and a well-spoken eulogy to lament their deaths," said Artemidorus.

"Will that be enough to forestall their anger?"

"The dead return because of a desire to collect some debt, and are said to come after those who victimized them until their suffering has been integrated into the memory we all share. You see, if their death finds its way into the storyteller's art, their memory lives on. Those living dead, who return, are the ones who feel forgotten. If the dreamer wishes to avert the danger that the dreamtime messages presage, or to avoid the dire consequences that the living dead pose, the nighttime vision's message should be acted upon. If Philip had wanted to rid himself of the shades who pestered him, it would have been wise to have done as they requested."

"For a man of his temperament, that hardly seems likely. It would have required him to respect each of those men's common dignity, something he would have been averse to doing. Nor would he have lamented their deaths."

"On the other hand, not all shades are restless," Artemidorus said. "Many wish to help the dreamer. They will speak to you in the human shape in which they appeared when they were alive. Though in the dreamtime, they seem to have a life of their own, it is your memory of them that you see and hear."

"If a poet has a mind to, he may give free rein to his imagination, Virgil said. "I, myself, wrote a story about the Trojan prince, Hector who, although he was dead, advised Aeneas to flee Troy with his family. He followed suit and, consequently, founded our great city."

"If that truly happened," Cicero said, "important historical events can hinge upon a dreamtime message. And, if that is so, what I cannot understand is why the gods or the shades of dead men would appear in a nighttime vision and not when a man is awake. In matters of such importance, it would clear up so much confusion if they appeared in the daytime."

"Of course, many men and women read the signs or visit Delphi."

"Though a dream narrative may seem mysterious at first," Artemidorus said, "there are clues to its understanding. When its significance eludes you, I recommend that you consult my book or ask a friend to help you interpret the message."

"But the dreamer's experience seems so personal, so impenetrable to anyone else."

"Oh, I disagree."

"Why is that Aristides?"

"Like Virgil, I too have struggled with illness. Because the dreamer's experience reflects the state of his body, a night vision can illustrate the dreamer's ill-health, or the best treatment for his disease. Nor do I agree with Horace when he said that he had been left to navigate the dream world alone. There are many otherworldly guides who appear in the nightly visions who may act as an advisor or a guide who will gladly show you the way.

"That is why men and women incubate dreams in Asclepius's temple and ask Mother Remembrance to help them with their recall the following morning. Frequently, these dreamtime consultations are directed toward one of the dreamer's deceased ancestors, a great hero, or an embodiment of the natural forces, such as those who are associated with the sky, water, and plants. If a man or a woman has a close relationship with one of the gods, they may even convince them to cure them of their affliction. My own successful career as an orator was inspired by Isis and Serapis. They each appeared to me in a nighttime vision, and Asclepius encouraged my literary ambitions.

"When a dream is incubated in the temple, upon waking, the dreamer sits in the Chair of Memory and recounts his night vision to the priests. The retelling then assists the healers in proscribing the best treatment for the malady from which the dreamer is suffering. Occasionally, a dreamer may also receive a token or a keep-sake while he is in the dreamtime."

"Do you mean to say that a dreamtime token can be an object that has weight and substance?" Horace asked incredulously.

"Sometimes," Aristedes said, "such objects have been known to appear, though it is unnecessary for the token to take on a solid presence in this world to work its power. I have heard of tokens that, somehow, came through the barrier that ordinarily separates the waking world from the dreamtime. These tangible artifacts have, indeed, been known to appear to the dreamer after he or she awakened. Of course, such a token will be regarded as unimpeachable evidence of the dreamtime landscape, and will serve as proof of the events that happened there.

"The token is like a gift that has been endowed upon the dreamer from the otherworlds. It represents something useful in the waking world, something that carries an otherworldly power. Such tokens, whether tangible, or intangible, may go on to inspire stories, pictures, sculptures, and other inventions.

"You might say that the dreamtime tokens have the power to create new and unforeseen realities in this world through storytellers, poets, and craftsmen's artistry. These objects, some of which are large and some quite small, along with written words, represent countless creators' lifetimes. The authors live on through their writings. In this way, their creations, also, become tokens of the dreamtime.

"When I think of the great libraries here in Rome and the one that was located in Alexandria before it was burned to the ground, I am awed by the many lifetimes that are represented on their shelves. For those, whose writings perished in the fire in Alexandria, it was like dying a second death. But the words written by the men who are present here tonight will outlast their own transient lives by eons."

There was a long pause in the conversation as each of these men pondered his own frailty and non-existent future. To break the silence, Horace said, "You speak as though you prophesy."

"That would not be unheard of. Aristotle said that not all prophetic dreams come from the gods or the shades of the dead. He attributes the potential for prophecy to the soul itself."

"Plutarch, too, claims that prophecy resides within the soul and, therefore, premonitions of the future can happen even when one is awake."

"But he also says that for as long as the soul inhabits the body, the power remains obscured. He says that the most reliable premonitions come from dreamtime visions."

"Yes, I have, also, found that to be true," said our host. He stood up from his reclining couch and began to address us in the same confident manner that I would have expected of an orator who frequently spoke to hundreds of men at a time. "I have in my collection a series of scrolls that were written by a follower of Pythagoras. After he escaped the fire, which had killed his teacher and so many of his fellow disciples, he took it upon himself to describe how the famed mathematician had interpreted the world in terms of numbers and arithmetical relationships."

Cicero then instructed the musicians to play in the old Greek modes. Entranced, as we were, by their interpretation of the music that Pythagoras may have played upon his lyre to quiet the passions of his disciples' souls, we all seemed to enter the dreamtime together as Cicero led us with his speech. "I ask you, now, to listen carefully. Because Nature and humanity are governed by the same principles as the musical overtones, to which you are listening, men and women will derive pleasure from combinations that share an affinity with the elemental, natural world. These harmonic laws of nature are said to both pervade and to predictably govern the cosmos. When you see and hear these impressions of proportional relationship, you experience these harmonic sensations as beauty.

"When I wrote my fictional account of Scipio's dream in *On the Commonwealth*, I was referring to Pythagoras's harmonics of the spheres. In it, I tell a story of Scipio's visit to the dreamtime during which his deceased grandfather showed him the mysteries of the cosmos. Led to a place above the earth where the stars shone with otherworldly splendor, Scipio's grandfather foretold his future, along with a description of a warrior's duty and his reward when, after death, he would be welcomed to everlasting life among the stars. From where they stood above it all, Scipio planted his feet on that great swath of light that crosses the sky and looked down upon the earth. In comparison to the greatness of the stars, Scipio could see how very small Rome was. It was then that he realized that the city was only a small speck when compared to the vastness of the cosmos.

"As Scipio stared in wonder at the starry sky, his grandfather explained how the nine celestial spheres, proceeding from the lowest to the highest, make music as they move from east to west, and sometimes in reverse. The moon, which is closest to our earth, vibrates with the lowest tone, and the others are set apart at fixed intervals. When played altogether, they make a beautiful harmony.

"The manuscript, to which I referred, explains, in mathematical formulae, the reasons that dreams prophecy. According to the great mathematician's concept, time multiplies upon itself forever in a perfectly logical manner. If one were schooled in dream interpretation, he believed that one could see through time. That is because the dreamtime is a place where a dreamer senses time differently.

"In the world of the dreamtime, time passes at speeds that differ from the one we are ordinarily accustomed to while awake. Time stretches and compresses, may skip a beat and back-track before moving forward once again.

"According to Pythagoras's teachings, the cosmos's inner workings can be explained by underlying, harmonious mathematical relationships. To acquaint oneself with these correlations will lead to a greater understanding of the structure of time. It is for this reason that a dreamer will sense time differently than when he or she is awake. In this way, a man or woman may participate simultaneously in both an event's effects and its causes by moving between the past and the future."

"You will lose me there," Virgil said. "I am not well-schooled in Greek mathematics. Are you saying that the dream creates the future by anticipation?"

"If you think of time in a musical sense, perhaps the idea will become clear. Whether it was Pythagoras, or one of his disciples, who proposed the theory, I do not know," said Cicero, "but either way, this manuscript describes the reasoning behind the mathematician's claim that dreams blend together both images of past experiences and future events. According to another of Pythagoras's mathematical principles, even a small fragment will contain the features of the whole. And for that reason, a single image from the dreamtime can carry great meaning. Because the cosmos is ruled by the universality of numbers, this truth may be found throughout Nature. These self-similar fragments are replicated in both decreasingly smaller or increasingly larger scales. If you look at the way crystals, blood vessels, tree roots, leaves, a snail's shell, and a fern frond builds upon the same pattern, you will come to see how the cosmos is intricately and infinitely patterned.

"Ordinarily, when the future is cut off from our waking sense of time, we are only aware of time moving steadily forward. We live in the present moment, and this experience gives us a curiously distorted notion. According to this view of time, the future is cut off from the growing past by a travelling present moment. He calls it an habitual fallacy owing to the mental error we all live with when we are awake. The mathematician claims to have worked out the arithmetic, and has said that he had formulae that could prove the way events are displaced in time from their proper positions.

"Since past and future events blend together in the dreamtime, that is the best place from which to observe time's backward and forward movement. The cosmos stretches out in time and can overcome the delusion that the future is unaccountably missing and cannot be observed."

"Is it possible to halt the forward motion and to prevent a predicted event?"

"Because the dreamer may cross back and forth between them when asleep, there seems to be no barrier between the past and the future. The greatest limitations are one's own acceptance of the conventional wisdom that blindly accepts that past and future are separate events. For those who are gifted in reading the signs, even when a man or woman is awake, an insight can slip over the dividing line and, occasionally, the future will become apparent in disconnected flashes that can result in small epiphanies that may be acted upon."

A soft, womanly voice spoke up to say, "Such epiphanies should not to be taken lightly. It would have gone better for Julius Caesar if he had heeded his wife's warnings not to attend the senate on the day that he was murdered. In her night vision, Calpurnia saw the pediment of their house collapse and grievously wept over her husband's dead body after he had been stabbed. Although she pleaded with Julius Caesar not to go to the Senate that day, a trusted friend warned him against making a decision that was based upon his wife's pleas for his safety. To be seen by others as a man who was ruled by his wife was hateful to someone as strong-willed and courageous as Caesar. But, unfortunately, he had been ill-advised. As it happened, his so-called friend was in on the plot to murder him."

This was a strange, and rather incendiary thing to say in Cicero's home, I thought. He nonetheless walked over to the couch upon which the woman was reclining. He took ahold of her hand and, bowing before her, said, "My dearest, Melissa, please join in our conversation. You have acquainted yourself with Pythagoras's secret teachings on this subject. Tell us what you think of them from a woman's perspective."

"Consider the similarities between one's future possibilities and the unshaped fleece on the distaff's spike," said Melissa. "As the spinner twists the thread she gives shape to the future in the same way that the past informs the present. And likewise the present flows backward to build upon the past.

"If time and space are, indeed, infinite then it is certain that everything that has ever gone before will, eventually, come to pass again. Like the alchemist's snake biting its own tail, the ouroboros signifies a periodical recurrence of patterns, events, and themes, which, by virtue of being revisited, time and again, gain complexity. The snake consumes time past to continually renew itself and thus become the future. And thus it goes on, into infinity.

"Another way to think of it is to imagine the weaver who passes her shuttle across the warp on her loom. The past shapes the present and, as it does so, the present continually changes and lengthens. Events laid atop one another add to the pattern. The same may be said of the future."

"How so? How can the future appear before it is woven?" Horace asked.

"There are many worlds, all of which exist side by side," Melissa answered. "At any given moment, alternate possibilities present you with several scenarios from which to choose. Because the repeating patterns are anticipated by your nighttime dramas, you may try out the different scenarios in the dreamtime. Just as Virgil described the labyrinth tonight, each intersection you come upon presents an alternate path, each of which will lead you to another set of possibilities. Though the future is unformed, previous patterns tend to prevail."

"Oh yes," I said, interrupting Melissa, "you are right. What you say is similar to the concept of the Matrones' woven tapestry. If you fold the fabric, that which was woven in the past will appear to lie side by side with an event that is happening in the present, as if there were no intervening time between them. The same holds true when one wishes to look into the future. Just pinch the fabric to see what the patterns reveal."

Now that I had become a participant in the conversation, I looked at each of the men who were seated before me in the atrium to see how he had reacted to my additional comments. But, apparently, my presence had gone unnoticed until that very moment. Scanning their faces, I saw how each man was staring back at me in shock. A lull in the conversation followed. And though I was but a stranger in their midst, I hastily changed the subject. "Senator Cicero," I blurted out. "I should like to see the scrolls to which you were referring."

"I warn you, they are rare and were written in the old Greek style. The words are connected and not separated into discrete elements of speech by a space between them, the way text is typically written today."

"Yes, I am familiar with the old linguistic forms and will have no trouble reading it."

His face lit up, seemingly pleased to meet a fellow scholar who was well-schooled in ancient, philosophical studies. He excused himself from the others and asked one of the servants to bring a lamp with which we could light our way.

With a wave of his hand he urged me to join him. I stood and, as we followed the servant's lamp light, he led me to the far end of the atrium. We climbed several steps and walked down a short hallway. From there, we turned into a small, square room. Bookcases made of citrus wood, inlaid with ivory, were as tall as the ceiling. Several busts of famous scholars and storytellers graced the shelves here and there. Among them, I recognized the head and shoulders of Plato, Homer, and Aristotle.

Cicero pointed to the box in which the scrolls were kept and asked the servant to bring a ladder. The servant placed the lamp on the table in the center of the room, set the ladder against the shelving, climbed it, and retrieved the box. After he climbed down, he set the box on the table. From among several metal tubes, Cicero found the one that we had been discussing earlier. He took it out and handed it to me. Knowing how old and fragile it was, I laid it carefully on the table. When he offered to let me copy it, I readily expressed my gratitude for his gracious generosity. He instructed the servant to leave the lamp and to bring me parchment, ink, and quills.

After Cicero had left, I picked the scrolls out of the box one by one. Each was kept inside its own metal tube. Reading the attached labels, I found the one with which I wanted to begin my copy. Inattentive to time's passage, I was wholly immersed in this incredible find, and did not notice the servant opening the louvered shutters that covered the window until it was too late. Unbeknownst to me, dawn was breaking outside the house. I leapt from my chair to stop him. A scroll was in my left hand, and I was reaching out with my right, when an early morning sunray pierced the window opening and struck me. I felt the pain as sharply as if I had I been struck by an arrow.

I knew only one thing: that I was certain of nothing. Unaware of the precise border where the dreamtime left off and world of the waking began, I feared that I was destined to become one of the stone sculptures in Cicero's home. And if that were to happen, I would remain trapped forever in this in-between place, disguised as a marble sculpture.

Slowly, I began to distinguish one thing from another. I lay abed with my eyes closed, uncertain whether I was truly awake or asleep. Fearful of moving, lest I discover the horrible truth, I nonetheless began to disengage from the dreamtime. When I managed to wiggle my toes and fingers, I opened my eyes and saw, above my head, the ceiling in my own room.

Satisfied that I had not been turned to stone, I reflected upon the men whose lifetimes had not, in fact, overlapped, but who, because the dream world compresses time, had been invited to sit together in Cicero's atrium. I felt honored to have been present when so many scholarly men had convened to converse, in such a polite manner, on so rarified a subject. To think that they had contrived to visit me while I was asleep, as if to clarify their thinking on this subject for my benefit, and to comment upon the very dreamtime activity in which they were appearing, was certainly an impressive feat—had I seen them wink at one another when they were talking about the messages that dead men may convey to the living?

I recalled what I had heard Ovid say: that if one wishes to avert a nighttime vision's dangerous consequences, it is good to recount the vision to the stars or the sun, along with a request for their protection. I returned to my reading room and saw, here, on my desk, a dark blue stone that looked like a small piece of the nighttime sky similar to the star-lit sky that I had seen in my dreamtime visions.

Here it lays, like a dreamtime token. After it had seemingly fallen to earth, it has now become an amulet, which will offer me protection from the dangers I had inadvertently encountered in the dreamtime. The small bits of gold-colored specks of pyrite that decorate its surface represent the stars, and a small, white, nearly round circle stands-in for the nearly full moon. A trailing, white, moon-lit cloud appears to be floating past.

II.

Several days before, the four longships had been rolled from their slips at high tide and anchored side by side in the shallows. Since then, a steady stream of men and women had hauled the men's food, gear, and trade goods from their homes and storage sheds. There were wooden trunks, baskets of dried breads, jars of salted cod, barrels of fresh water and ale, cakes of dried sea salt, bundles of weavings and furs, and baskets containing delicate amber nuggets, each of which had been carefully wrapped in straw. Other villagers walked down to the shoreline just to stare at the four serpent heads all lined up in a row and to feel the breathtaking, quickening in the blood, which the sight of the ships aroused.

That evening, Lady Sun had ended her daily ride across the sky and had met up with her longship, Nightly, where it awaited her in the west. And, in the east, a slightly flattened moon rose like a precious, thin-sided, shallow bowl made of rare, translucent porcelain. If such a marvel had travelled along the trade routes by wagon, horse, camel, and boat to its destination without having incurred any breakage, surely, that fact alone would have made it a wonder to behold.

The continuous drizzle had finally let up and, if the skies continued to look good, Gevehard said he and the men would leave in two days. Now that night was coming on, those sea-going men, who were planning to shove off soon, were heading for the hall where a feast of such grand proportions awaited them that it could be found nowhere but in either the sea-lord's hall named Haven, or in its earthly stand-in, the kinleader's longhouse. Greeting friends and fellow travelers as they went, the men, passing between the mounds, shared their excitement with the villagers who waved and cheered them on. When entering the longhouse like young boys, they slapped each other's shoulders, and shoved and punched each other playfully, but with a grown man's deep-throated laughter.

When a man entered this place of celebration where Lord Glory, the Lord of Rich-Waters, the Lords of Battle, and the holy forebears were honored, he was up-lifted to a good world. Here, within the longhouse's four walls, men found an orderly refuge, a perfect world where he was free from the unpredictability common to any man's ordinary, everyday life. The competition for food and water, the need for praise and satisfaction, and the conflicts one encountered with wives, children, servants, and neighbors, no longer mattered. When a man was inside the longhouse's four walls, he strengthened the bonds of fidelity and trust. The stories he heard assured him that his life had meaning, explained the reasons for the hardships he endured, recognized his bravery, and assigned blame to seemingly chance encounters, especially whenever he was at sea.

One man in particular caught my eye. Unlike the others, he walked sullenly up the steep slope and stood alone, off to the side where he could observe the other men without drawing attention to himself.

When the shipmaster spotted him, he yelled, "Aiken, come join us," and waved him over. Seeming to sense a need to protect some vague fragility in Aiken's bearing, one which was so out of keeping with what he, otherwise, would have expected from a tough, war-hardened man, Gevehard pulled Aiken aside.

"I am grateful for the attention you give Aart each day," Gevehard said as he accompanied Aiken to the place at the high table where he would sit.

"The boy is inexperienced, but, if given enough time, he will come around," Aiken said.

"I have no doubt that he will make a good steersman."

"Take my word for it, Gevehard, he will not live long enough to become a steersman unless he keeps training. I mean it. I like the boy and do not want to see him dead. Someone needs to pick up where I leave off."

"Aiken, you are the one who should be training Aart. My offer still stands. If you choose to jump aboard at the last moment, I will give you a hand up and pull you in."

Aiken shook his head and held a hand up at face level to ward off any more talk about his decision. He preferred to keep it that way. To leave it at that.

"I will miss not having you on the boat, you know that, Aiken. There should be no hard feelings between you and me."

"I am grateful you feel that way. Nor do I have any hard feelings."

Two days earlier, Aiken had told Gevehard that he needed to go home to discuss the offer to join the crew with Mildred. Assuming that Jerold would have cut him from the list of men who would be manning the oars, Aiken had presented Gevehard with a graceful way out. But when the shipmaster responded angrily, Aiken immediately back-tracked. To avoid being accused of an insolent refusal of a shipmaster's request, he had left an opening for another year, another time. It was as polite a rejection as he could muster. By the end of their, sometimes, heated conversation, Aiken had felt sad not to have accepted Gevehard's offer to take a place on the boats but had remained confident in the rightness of his decision.

He had told Gevehard that he would carve a set of doors, had measured the longhouse doorway with a piece of rope and had tied knots in it to indicate the height and width of the present opening. When he was finished, in another year or so, he would find his way north to deliver the new doors.

For years, Aiken had believed that if a chieftain offered to take him into his warband, he would have dropped everything and gone back to fighting. He had longed for that moment. But now that the opportunity had arisen, he had been too proud to tell Gevehard the real reason that he had declined the offer. Instead, he had covered the unspoken truth with a half-lie. His need to speak to Mildred was but a convenient excuse.

After he examined the leering fear that he had kept hidden and pondered only rarely—that he was incapable of fighting any more—he knew the truth. It was not because he was blind on one side and only half the world around him was visible at any given moment. No. He had held his own when he was practicing down on the strand. He still had it in him. His aim was still deadly.

But it was impossible to ignore the fact that he saw and heard dead men speaking, even in the daytime. Whenever the bogman chose to ride him, he became so enraged that the only way to keep from strangling another man was to walk away and hide. Sometimes he punched the walls in his work shed so hard he bruised his knuckles. How could he possibly live within a boat's small confines and travel with over a hundred and twenty men for months at a time? He need not ask. He knew the answer already. He could not do it. He was untrustworthy.

For years, he had longed for the companionship that he had had before, but now that he was living amongst these fighting men, practicing on the strand each day and sitting in a place of honor alongside the shipmaster at the supper table in the evenings, the life had lost its luster. Instead of joining in their banter, telling tall tales, and playing games, he preferred to sit by the hearth, carving small, wooden cows that not even Gevehard's sons had wanted.

For an old, former warrior, who had frequently been on the move between the chiefdoms when he was young, Mildred had turned him into more of a homebody than he cared to admit. Besides, how could he fight when the throbbing ache that replaced his missing eye was always there and never left him? There had been times when he was so incapacitated by the pain that all he could do was lay abed in the darkest corner of the house and cover his face with a cloth.

Nor did the shipmaster have him right. Aiken was not the cunning man Gevehard insisted he was. Aiken did not know how to tie or untie wind knots. Instead of being cunning, at any given moment he was ignorant of whether he was awake or asleep. As for being so perceptive, his constant scrutiny of others only made him increasingly suspicious of every man's intentions. Unable to discern one thing from another, he was more often mistaken than correct and frequently lost control of his passions. Yet, when he became crazed by his delusions, he was completely convinced of his accurate appraisal of the situation and of other men and women's motives.

For a man who, since early childhood, had set himself apart, who had watched the men who sat on the benches and kept his eye on the door, had constantly checked to see who was coming in and who was leaving, had always staked out a place where he had room enough to move in a dangerous situation, and someplace where he would have a quick way out, how could he expect to live within the tight confines of a boat? How could he trust himself to act responsibly when the experience several days before had shown him the plain truth. He was a danger both to himself and to other men. To put it simply: he was unfit to carry a weapon. To believe any differently only meant that he was fooling no one more than he was fooling himself.

He was not a flexible, well-crafted long-knife. Rather, he was nothing but a copy. He was like the worthless blade that a man straps onto his belt for show. Puffed up with meaningless swagger, he wears it in the marketplace like a costume to parade in. But because the knife is made of low-grade steel, it is inflexible and brittle. It will shatter in a fight. It invites danger. If someone were to call the bluff of the man who depended upon such a blade, he could not trust it. If he responded to the challenge, he may as well have a wooden knife of the sort made for a child. He was only a copy of a warrior and was as worthless as a toy blade. If he joined the crew, he would endanger the men who depended upon him. He would shatter once he came face to face with the enemy. Snapped off at the hilt, he would never make the cut.

The fighting life is brutal sport. Whatever a man does to another has importance. According to Necessity's decree, there can be no escape from the consequences of his actions. Over time, the effects add up.

Once Aiken had seen a man who had suffered from the natural, end result of all the conflicts that he had engaged in. To see what happens to a man like that, a man who becomes so filled with rage that he endangers even his own companions, one time is enough. Aiken never wanted to see something like that happen again. Never again. Nor did he want to be the cause of a deadly, rage-fueled fight like the one he had seen.

Aiken had been feasting among a group of men inside another chieftain's mead-hall. When, for no apparent reason, the man had erupted with red-faced fury. Before Aiken's very eyes, the man had turned into a beast who preyed on men. He had fought like a rabid wolf, and though the others had tried to temper his rage, before they could subdue him, he had killed six men, all of whom had been his close companions. The man had fought too many brutal fights. After he had seen so much suffering and death, he had become crazed by the fighting.

At the time, Aiken had been too young to make sense of it. But now, with age came understanding. The enraged man had been unable to discriminate the faces of his trusted companions from the faces of the dead men who had replaced them.

Haunted by those men, whom he had killed, when the madness came over him, the man had been impervious to injury. It seemed as though he was shielded by some otherworldly power. As hard as the other men had fought to constrain him, he had, nevertheless, come through the fighting unscathed. Though, clearly, his time had been up long ago, the Matrones had neglected to cut his life thread. And, in the end, his former companions had bound him with ropes and been forced to help the spinsters along.

After they had hung him that night, Aiken had seen men weep. No one wanted to see something like that happen again. But the chance of that uncontrollable rage erupting was always there. Like a smoldering ember lying hidden beneath the straw, rage lay in the shadows waiting for the right conditions to burst into flame and to burn the entire meadhall down.

And now Aiken knew, for a fact, that that same unpredictable, savage fire-beast lurked inside himself, as well. It was only awaiting a chance to pounce on some unwitting, blameless person who was guilty of nothing more than speaking the wrong word at the wrong time, or giving him a look he took the wrong way.

The truth was that he did not trust himself. Just to think of the fraught way he inhabited the holy borderland between the two worlds nearly brought him to tears. There was no one to whom he could turn for help, except perhaps his wife.

For Aiken, the barrier between the world of the standing and that of the fallen had broken down. Because he should have been dead, too, along with his war companions, he had been dislocated and left to wander the lands between. He no longer knew the difference between the worlds of the dreamtime and of the waking, the difference between the worlds of the living and of the dead.

In the same way that the holy grove, where the borders between the living and the dead were left ambiguously open and kept safely distant from the everyday, ordinary world where living men and women dwelt in the village, there was a need to keep Aiken apart from those whom he might taint by his presence or mistakenly kill. He was a man with a foot on each side of the divide. He did not trust himself to know when he might pull another man through the border between life and death and to make him dead, too.

There were so many conflicts inside him, he was constantly at war with himself. Struggling every step of the way with what it meant to be one of Mother Necessity's children was like wading waist deep through the effluvia of his life. All he could do was have faith that whatever must come, shall come to be. To make sense of it all and to put what he had learned into his carvings was what he lived for.

He longed to have his tools back in his hands again, and to study the patterns he saw in the wood grain. To feel the weight of the hammer, the sharpness of the chisels, and to see the fully dimensional forms emerge from the flat pieces of wood was all that mattered: to make something beautiful. Once he was back home and inside his work shed, he could stop worrying about what he might do when the door, the graybeard had spoken of, was open to the snakes' movement between this hard and fast world of everyday living and the other, less substantial worlds.

Aiken took his place on the left side of the table. He no longer held the coveted seat on Gevehard's right. Instead, he was seated near the end on the left, alongside Edmund.

In the light cast by the flickering hearth and torch flames Aiken could see his old war companions appearing and disappearing in among the last group of stragglers who were wandering in through the doors. Seen from amidst, behind, and in between those walking, living men, the glimmer on a belt buckle or a brooch convinced Aiken of Torwald, Alger and Sigmund's approach. Though Aiken attempted to explain the haunting shapes as mere tricks of the light and shadows, he knew the men were there.

Back when Aiken had been a member of Torwald's honor guard, he had been seated at the head table, just as he was seated at Gevehard's table that night, second from the end on the left, nearest the door. Back when the table that Aiken had sat at was Torwald's, his chieftain had greeted his guests at the door, just as Gevehard was doing now. And just as Torwald had done back then, his former chieftain was now making his entrance and taking his place at the center of the high table. Sigmund stood on Torwald's right and Alger was on his left.

Aiken whispered to their shadowy forms, "Tell me I was right about Leofar. Tell me I was right. I now have a kinsman who has agreed to be my witness. We can prove that Leofar that the who ambushed you."

Torwald looked at Aiken with contemptuous, frozen hatred. Hardened with bitter accusation, what he saw in Aiken was a coward. Aiken had been the last man standing on the field but had shirked his duty to avenge their deaths. "You threw down your long-knife and pleaded for your life," he said with a sneer. "What you did is unspeakable. Admit it. Even now, you continue to degrade yourself. You make wooden toys for the chieftains who slandered me. I curse your soul to remain forever in the lowest land of the dead where the oath-breakers dwell. May you drink the bitter ale of your shame in Mother Torment's hall."

Torwald's curse drained every bit of warmth from Aiken's bones. To defend himself, he said, "Listen to me. Go ahead and call an Assembly of dead men. I now have a kinsman who will prove my allegations. You were wrong when you told us that Leofar was trustworthy. He started picking off those who stood in his way with you. How can you dispute it? I am tired of being brushed aside. You should have listened to me then. If you had, maybe you would still be alive. Ask Sigmund who threw the first torch the night we burned Oswald's hamlet."

"Are you accusing me? It will cost you."

"Aiken, stop talking about it."

"Hear me out, Torwald. You threatened to sideline me and to take away my status. Instead, you lavished praise on Leofar. No one dared bring charges against him for fear of your reprisals. But now I have a witness who was there the day Leofar and his accomplices ambushed us."

"I refuse to accept your witness's testimony. You are accusing the wrong man, Aiken. Leofar is my nephew."

"Traitor, you are no brother of ours. The allegations you concocted against Leofar are worthless."

"Sigmund, You made up reasons for raids, ordered us to take needless risks, and attacked unarmed men and women. The night we burned the hamlet, we were there on your orders."

"We were getting back at Oswald. He started it when he stole the cattle."

"Even so, there was no need to boast about the number of men and women whom you killed. You never cared about anything but counting the number of men you took down."

"Aiken be quiet. Do not talk to Sigmund and Torwald that way. You know how it was. We had to stick with our own companions, no matter what they did."

"Torwald, even when men crossed the line that separated fairness from cruelty, you prized aggression and protected the wrongdoers."

"How dare you speak like that? Who do you think you are, to raise allegations against your chieftain? You know the rules. You do whatever it takes to win. You do what everyone else does. Those are the rules."

"Sigmund, I disagree. You killed unarmed men. When others were ashamed of what they did, you burnished your reputation with your boasts."

"It would be wise for you to hold your tongue, Aiken."

"Sigmund never shied away from a fight. He was a hero. He taught you how to be a hunter of men."

"He was no hero. What kind of a hero kills women and girls?"

"Do not insult Sigmund. Aiken, tonight, when the cup comes around, I expect you to show gratitude for Sigmund's service."

"Torwald, you remain stuck in the past. You refuse to see the truth. Sigmund threw down his honor long ago and trampled it in the dirt."

"Aiken you were taught to obey orders, now do what you are told."

"You never were one of us. You never did fit in."

"You are right. I am no longer a member of your warband, and I am now free to speak out."

"If you keep this up, I will bury my axe in your skull."

"How can you? Your threats are meaningless." Aiken sucked in his breath, "You are dead men. Go away."

The feast was about to get started. And, once again, Aiken was the odd man out. He did not belong there, among the sea-going men. Nor were the haunts he dragged behind him welcome.

Gevehard entered and took his place at the center of the high table. He extended the gold cup to his guests, and said, "Tonight we welcome those forebears who have come to feast and sup with us. It was they who brought their families here to settle on these headlands. We owe our prosperity to the hardships they endured. Let us honor their courage and praise their unyielding fortitude. Allow our memories of those men to speak, and listen to them when they do. They have important knowledge to impart. Our forebears want to share the stories of what they did on their travels, to tell you about their mistakes, failures, and successes. They want you to succeed, for they see themselves in you. You get strength from your ancestors. Your future is their future. So, tonight, though you will make a lot of noise, also listen to your forebear's voices and learn from them."

All the men raised their cups and erupted in cheers. Gevehard honored Glenn, Garr, and Gerard. And after he had supped, he handed the gold cup to the man on his right. That man then did the same. And as the cup went around the tables, it was refilled time and time again as each of the men affectionately honored their forebears by name and praised their memories.

To invite the ancestors to sit amongst them, additional benches had been set on the opposite sides of the tables and left empty. Some forebears had so many descendants they were forced to go repeatedly from one man to another. The living men who were feasting alongside their deceased fathers, grandfathers, and great grandfathers were, by sharing their food, sharing their fond memories of those men who had gone before. These were the men who had, once upon a time, sat on the same benches on which these living men were seated tonight. Those who had gone before had shown the way. They had rowed the oars and traded their goods in market towns, just as these living men would do. And now, all the men, both those who were alive and those who were dead, had come together to recall the sadness, the humor, and the grand adventures they had had. They remembered crossing the boundless sea and pulling ashore in markets where they had traded their goods with folks from far-away places.

Yes, to be a part of this generational brotherhood, which reached back into the shadows of time, meant that each man was making it possible for his children and their children to prosper and to go forward, just as the men who had gone before them had done. This, they told themselves, was why they endured the ordeals that set upon them, year after year, whenever they went to sea. And someday they, too, would be honored by their descendants after they had become one of the forebears.

Perhaps Aiken should have known it would happen, for when the gold cup came to him and he looked across the table, he was only mildly surprised to see his father's face appear. In the flickering half-light, he recognized Eamon's crinkly eyes and broad smile, the long auburn hair that was combed back from the peak in the center of his forehead and fell in waves past his shoulders and down his back. He saw, in his father's face, a man who was still the good looking young man he had been when Aiken was a child. Reluctant to have his father look at him and to see his own sun-scorched face, creased with age and disfigured by scars, Aiken would have hidden if he had had a place to go without looking foolish. But, unfortunately, he was too old to crawl beneath the table the way he had done when his mother and father were alive.

Now, Eamon's appearance made a ready target for Aiken's frustration. His deceased father was someone he could blame for all that had gone wrong in his life. All his suffering could be lain at Eamon's feet. His father's death became the source of Aiken's grief. And unlike the way that the other men were honoring their forebears that night, rather than recalling Eamon's honesty, fairness, and the respect that he had shown his men when he was alive, Aiken was angry. After all this time, now that he was finally face to face with his father, Aiken said accusingly, "Eamon, you broke your promise. You did not protect me and mother the way you said you would."

"I promise to make it up to you."

"You are an oath-breaker. Your promise is worthless."

"I will. I promise, I will," his father said. And then Aiken's sight of him was absorbed in the shadows, just as the others had been, and only his lingering voice remained: "I promise."

As for the men on the benches, those who were sitting, elbow to elbow in the crush around the tables, joked about getting familiar with being tight. Serving-girls edged through the openings between the tables and benches. Carrying trencher after trencher into the center, they skirted the fires and, being careful not to slop stew over the edges of the huge, wooden dishes, slid the steaming food onto the tables. Other women brought in mounds of bread, refilled the ale jugs, and carried large platters heaped with chunks of pork.

At one point, when Aiken noticed that Edmund was struggling to cut his meat single handedly, he reached over to cut it for him. Edmund looked at him with the same bottomless sorrow that Aiken knew all too well. No words were necessary. Silently, Edmund tapped Aiken on the chest three times with the backs of two knuckles. This they had in common: the daily hurt that comes from armed conflict and never goes away.

As the night wore on, the gold cup continued to circle the tables. Over and over, again and again, the men drank to their oaths and boasted with increasing abandonment. Aiken had been here before. He had heard the promises. He had seen what followed. When the unforeseen happens, nothing comes out the way it was meant to.

He asked himself, how many of these promises would, in time, be broken? Just give it time. Just give it time, he answered.

As for the shipmaster, nothing got past his notice. Nothing happened that he did not store away. He was a man of remarkable fortitude. He had weathered crises before and had held fast. There were few men like him: men who could hold up to the strain and still retain his sense of decency. And tonight, though Gevehard had carefully assessed each of the men whom he had chosen to crew the four boats, his oversight continued undiminished. Even as he laughed heartily, shouted, and extolled their upcoming trip, his eyes darted between them, observing each of the men's moods and weighing their words and actions.

The older men's self-assurance and stalwart grit was born from their skill at riding the waves, and from facing, head-on, the never-ending risks. They knew the uncertainty they would soon encounter. And, whereas Gevehard trusted those hardened sea-going men and respected their knowledge and endurance, he knew that the younger men had a lot to learn. But every year some of the men, whom he had relied upon the year before, quit or went missing and, every year, to fill in the ranks, he had to train in new ones.

Across the room, two young men came to blows over something that had begun in jest. When Gevehard saw them fighting, he raised his chin and tipped his head toward Jerold. The commander understood his shipmaster's unspoken orders, stepped away from the high table, and walked toward the sparring young men. With hands grown broad from rowing the oars and wielding the heavy long-knives, he pushed one man down onto the bench. The other man was pulled up by the neck of his tunic and dragged to another bench where he was seated between two mature, battle-hardened men. Jerold laid a hand on each of youth's shoulders and pushed him down hard.

After the two had been effectively separated, Jerold returned to the high table. He swung his leg over the high chair back, and said in a voice loud enough for everyone at the table to hear, "What do they know about danger? Nothing. They are a couple of young bucks eager to show off their antlers. But, hey! Their racks are still covered with soft velvet."

All the men glanced at the two red-faced young men and laughed hard. The older men knew that the only way to survive was to act together whenever they faced the inevitable hazards. But the young, hot-blooded men, who were proud to have been chosen by the shipmaster, were too full of their own, self-important swagger. Reacting too hastily at times, they displayed their excitement without giving a thought to the effect it had on the others.

Yet, the older men were tolerant and patient. They, too, had been young bucks who rubbed the velvet off their antlers the first time they went to sea. For the older men, their excitement was restrained by the fearful knowledge of the looming dangers. Each voyage was a game whose outcome had only one of two possible outcomes—a man either won or lost. Only the bottomless sea lay between success and failure.

Aiken recalled how he and his friend Alger had sparred, too, at times, but always made up the quarrel before the night was over. And, as if just the thought of his old friend was enough to make him reappear, a shadowy form crouched down on

Aiken's blindside. There, in the space between Aiken and Edmund, was Alger.

"I am glad to have you back," Aiken said. "It will be the same as it always was on feast nights when you and me sat side by side."

"Hey, Aiken. You still have the fighting skills you had back then. No one dared stand against you."

Heartened by the way Alger was, once again, the same man whom he had known back then, was a comfort. In their youth, they had worked together like a single man with four arms. Because of Aiken's ability to get through the tight spots up ahead on the field as they moved through the opposing ranks, to have Alger backing him up had changed his luck more than once. Alger had stopped the men who were coming at him from one side and Aiken had gotten the attackers who were coming from the other side.

But the praise was followed by the same, old recriminations. His friend's gaze narrowed to the familiar, cold, steely glare and, with an additional touch of mockery, he leveled the questions he had posed so many times before, "When do you plan to challenge Leofar? You claim to know that he was the one who murdered me. You know he is a fraud. He is afraid of single combat and is too cowardly to take his place in the front of the line. Call him on it. Show him up for what he is. When do you plan to do it Aiken? When?"

But Aiken had no answer.

"You stood there like a coward planning your escape."

"No Alger, do not say that. I was unable to protect you after I went down. I never saw the javelin coming at me."

"You stood there like a coward. I heard you say, 'We will all be killed.' I heard you say it."

"I will never stop blaming myself. Every day, I am haunted by what Leofar did to you. To know that there are men who remain free to do as they please, because the law cannot touch them, gnaws at me like a worm. The fairness that the Assembly once stood for has become nothing but a meaningless mockery of men's trust."

"You may be a man of fine words but are incapable of action. You offer excuses and stale platitudes. You tell me how much you suffer. But that is all you do. The opportunity to become one of Gevehard's men was your last chance to get back at the man who murdered me. Instead, you are running home to your woman."

"I never ran. Believe me. I never ran and I am not running now." Aiken put his elbows on the table, bowed his head and cradled it in his palms. "Stop it. Stop it. Stop it. You do not understand. You cannot understand." He raked his fingers through his hair, and mumbled, "Give it time, Alger, just give it time. I know Leofar was behind the ambush, but I have no proof. There is no living man who will stand up for me at the Assembly. Knowing it only makes the weight I bear worse than it was before. Unless one man comes forward to say that I am right—one man who will speak the truth and affirm Leofar's treachery—there can be no justice."

He dragged his face across his loosely curled fingers and open palms, slowly lifted his bowed head, and turned his gaze to the side. Though he sought mercy from his accuser, Alger was gone. Aiken jumped to his feet, slapped his hands hard on the table and leaned stiffly into his arms. In search of that one, familiar man-shaped shadow, he screamed, "I will never forget our friendship. I miss you every day," but Alger had mixed in with the other shades and disappeared.

Edmund touched him on the arm. "Aiken, can the girls get you something? I will call them over."

"No, nothing." Aiken fell back hard onto the seat and looked around. Burying his fists in the space between his knees, the nails on his tightly curled fingers bit into his fleshy palms. The encounter with Alger had so displaced him that he had forgotten he was surrounded by a hall full of men. He vaguely watched the living men, who were seemingly as transparent as the ghostly, surrounding shadows. They lunged and laughed and growled at one another. Separated as he was from the activity happening around him, Aiken asked himself whether he had ever acted like these men. If he had, he no longer remembered what it had felt like to rush so enthusiastically into the hard fight that awaited him on the morrow.

The men were gesturing with their knives as they ate, carelessly waving them about in each other's faces, and guzzling vast amounts of ale. They were so eager to set out on the boats and to fight their enemies, their urges could barely be contained. The ancestors celebrating another season on the boats were crowding in amongst their descendants. At times, their faces overlapped and blurred as they mingled. Some men looked so much like their grandfathers that it was impossible to tell them apart.

After the food had satisfied the men's hunger and dampened their immediate desire to be at sea, Edmund and another man took off their shirts, threw them into heaps on their seats, and strode into the center of the hall. When the men saw them standing there, they immediately quieted. Then, accompanied by loud whoops, two nearly grown boys rushed in through the open doors. Everyone turned to see them. Stripped of their shirts and with their trouser legs bound to their calves, they pounced onto the benches and leapt onto the tables. Like foals in the pasture, they pranced on the balls of their feet as they ran around the longhouse atop the tables. They jumped over trenchers and ale jugs and slapped the seated men's raised hands as they passed. At each opening between the tables, the acrobats leapt across the gaps, twisting and turning in midair.

Vaulting to the floor, they landed on their feet and raised their arms to accept the men's hearty cheers. Urged on to greater displays of acrobatic feats, the boys flipped somersaults in the space between the hearth and the tables and walked on their hands.

Edmund and the other man crouched to let the two boys leap onto their shoulders. When they yelled "Yup," the two standing men straightened their knees and the boys who were balanced on their shoulders flipped backward and landed. Again and again, Edmund and other man crouched so the boys could flip and turn in midair. One of the boys lit four torches and tossed two, one at a time, to the boy who stood on Edmund's shoulders. He then leapt onto the other man's shoulders. The two standing men straightened their knees and, standing tall, balanced the boys on their shoulders as they spun the four torches around in huge interlocking circles. Juggling the blazes, they tossed them back and forth, until each boy, once again held two. They leapt off, tossed one of their torches to each of standing men and jumped onto a nearby table. And, with the torch flames streaming out behind their backs, Edmund, the other man, and the two boys ran lengthwise across the tables and, to the accompaniment of the men's wild cheers, sprinted out the door.

The man on Aiken's left leaned in close and said, "We float the longships at the start of Yule. The men do the same feats then, but leap between the ships instead of the tables. The most hardy walk across the extended oars to prove their courage. Believe me, no one wants to fall into the water when it gets so cold. Then they run the torches ashore to light the bonfires."

Gevehard stood, lifted his cup and yelled, "We drink to Edmund who shows us the way to leap the gunwales and to walk bravely across the oars."

To honor of the man who had proven his courage, the year before, the hall erupted in cheers. Then, Edmund had leapt in front of Gevehard and taken the blow that was meant for his shipmaster and, in that way, had saved the lives of all the men and their families back home. Such was the shipmaster's legendary stature. Whether it was true or not did not matter.

For the men inside the longhouse, that night, Gevehard was the man who knew the trade routes to the markets and how to get them home again. They relied upon his leadership and his knowledge of the waves, the patterns of the swells, and the sound of the sea's pulse. He interpreted the seabirds' flights, measured the rise and fall of the sun and moon and the placement of the stars, and knew the shorelines as well as he knew the back of his own hand. Their trust in his leadership was so great, they believed that if he had been killed that day, they might have been lost at sea and never have made it home.

After the cheering died down, the two men slipped back inside the door. Edmund humbly put on his tunic, tucked it into his belt and sat. Aiken complimented him on the acrobatics. And as Edmund was tucking the empty sleeve into his belt, he gave Aiken a grin, wide enough to say: I still have it in me.

Several men entered the hall, stood by the hearth, and raised pipes cut and crafted from a swan's long wing bones. Covering the holes drilled along their lengths with their fingers and blowing into one end, they began to play a tune they all knew. The men joined in and sang along. Several men rose from the benches carrying steel long-knives. They walked into the center and formed two opposing lines. Pointing the knives toward the rafters, they all held the same opening position.

When the music began, they stomped loudly, sidestepping first to one side and then to the other in unison. This dance, with which they honored the Lords of Battle, set the two adversarial lines apart. But unlike the fights that the men would soon engage in, this one took on an orderly, ideal form. When each dancer crossed his long-knife with the one that was held by the man who was standing in the opposite line, their blades' flat sides slapped with loud, metallic clangs. The men on the benches clapped their hands and slapped the tables, keeping the rhythm and driving the dancers to speed up their footwork. Finally, the frenzied dancers turned in unison to one side and walked back to the benches. After that, table after table of sea-going men rose and danced with their weaponry.

After all the groups had taken their turn, one young man came forward alone, carrying two long blades. Rosy cheeked, fresh and sprightly, he looked as free of worry as a ship given a tail-wind by a gentle, summertime sea-breeze. He laid the two crossed blades on the floor. When the pipes began to play, he raised his arms high overhead and, following the rhythm of the pipes, began to step between the blades. Prancing lightly on his feet, he turned in mid-air, over and over, never once touching either knife. Because it was said that if he were to touch a blade with his foot, it could lead to a fatal blow the next time he faced a foe in battle, the men's attention was riveted to his daring display. Only a man who was confident of both his fighting skills and his footwork, would test his luck by tempting fate this way. The youth ended his dance, picked up the two long blades, kissed each one and held them aloft. The pipes trilled, and the meadhall echoed with the men's cheers.

Several more men had a go at the crossed blade dance. When one dancer kicked a knife with his toe and made it skidder across the floor, all the men gasped. Yet, the dancer remained undeterred. In an act of bravado, he grabbed both blades by their hilts and, mimicking a victor standing with one foot on his defeated antagonist's chest, held them, proudly, aloft. As he ran back to his table, the men on the benches cheered for the dancer but privately thought that his arrogant display had drawn the Matrones' undue attention.

The storyteller entered. Cradling a hand drum in the crook of one elbow, he took his place before the hearth. He raised the drum to the level of his shoulder and began to sway from front to back, first to one side and then to the other. Tapping an insistent rhythm, one long beat followed by three short, he began to tell the story that Glenn had come to hear, on this one night of year, when he joined his descendants in the longhouse to honor his memory.

There once was a man who was the son of Mannus, the Forebear of all the Tribes of Men. Named Glenn the Opening in the Clouds, he was said to be strong, and handsome. No one was his equal. Accustomed to hardship, brave and skillful in battle, he was wise in his counsel and generous to his friends but was, also, known to be equally ruthless when it came to his enemies.

And now I tell you this: Glenn had a hand in bringing about the end to the Terrible Winter. He won Lady Sun's heart and, with her blessings, led his kin to settle here, on the southern shore of the Merchant Sea where we make our home.

The time of hardship began when the Sons of the Fiery Realm burst from the place in the mountainous regions where they made their home. Unstoppable in their destruction, so great was their power that no one could stand against them. The Sons' breaths were so hot that men felt the heat burn their skin.

Spewing venom and fire as they went, the Sons' mounts threw-up dark smoke plumes in their wake that turned the sky pitch black. Their steeds shook the earth and made a deafening roar. Reaching the skybridge, in no time at all, the Sons of the Fiery Realm made a fierce assault. Wielding their blade named Burning Brightly, the span shattered with three mighty blows.

Once it was broken into countless pieces, the unity between the worlds was over. All exchange between the world of the ruling powers and the world of men and woman ceased. All that had gone before, all that people had relied upon came to a crashing end.

To take advantage of the dreadful devastation, Spider the Entangler released his longboat, Nail Ship, from its anchorage. He called upon his daughter, Mother Torment, to order the shades of dead who feasted in her hall to man the oars of his fleet, and she opened the doors. He called upon his other two children, the wolf named Treachery and the serpent of the deep named Tail-Devourer, to come forth and to wreak destruction.

Treachery the Grim Hardness of Iron broke his fetters, escaped the Iron-wood, and unleashed iron's deadly destruction. Freed from his captors, the wolf set out to devour the sun's goodness. Only complete chaos could satisfy his hunger. In no time at all, he took off running and chased after the flaming mirror that Lady Sun carried in her wagon.

Day after day Lady Sun fought valiantly. Though she spared no effort, her flaming long-knife failed to hold back Treachery's attack. The wolf broke so many chunks from her mirror that only a small, spent cinder remained. In the end, the defeated Lady Sun took to her deathbed.

The lack of daylight furthered the Frost Devourers' advance. Amongst their tribe were those who rode the backs of the mighty Wind-bringers and those who went afoot. Setting the icy winds in motion with each flap the Wind-bringers wings, those who rode the gigantic birds increased the size of their dominion. And the Devourers, who trudged down the ice-rimed mountain slopes, blanketed the earth with hail, snow, and frost.

The unceasing winds and the snow falling for three seasons out of four brought an end to good harvests. Along the seacoasts the monstrous Tail-Devourer came inland from the depths. The sea-snake was so thick and stretched so far that it was said to be everywhere at once. Its breath was so foul that all those who breathed its poisonous fumes suffered a miserable death. Entire villages and hamlets were left empty. Those few who survived the serpent's pestilence took to wandering but died of starvation along the roadsides.

The utter ruin deeply troubled those Lords and Ladies who sat at the high table in the Victory Hall. They feared the dreadful earthly devastation would bring an end to the world, not through fire, as the Sons of the Fiery Realm intended, but through unceasing, endless winter.

The Sky Lords sought counsel from the three Matrones of the Becoming. In answer to their entreaties, the three spinsters entered the Victory Hall. Seated solemnly atop the high platform, they twirled their whorls, read the threads they spun, and counseled the Lords and Ladies on the best ways to forestall their doom. First, the Matrones said, the Lords must rebuild the bridge that linked the worlds. Then, the serpent, who encircled the world and was everywhere at once, must be forced to return to the bottomless depths of the sea. And, finally, the wolf named Treachery must be taken captive and confined, once again, to the

Ironwood. In response to the Matrones' wise counsel, Lord Glory assigned the work that needed to be done.

They cast the lots to decide which of their enemies each Lord should engage in battle. On the first throw, it fell to Lord Thunderer to take on Tail-Devourer. On the second throw, it fell to Lady Blessed's son, White Fire the Bold, to take on Lord Spider. On the third throw it was Lord Glory's lot to take on the wolf named Treachery. On the fourth throw it fell to Lord Benevolent to take on the Frost Devourers.

Upon completion of the skybridge repair, the great linking road was restored and the continuity between the worlds was reestablished. The Army of Ten-Thousand Strong prepared for battle. The Lords and all their followers then dressed in their war gear and armed themselves. Lord Glory told Lord Guardsman to raise the call to battle. He blew his horn named Yelling, the doors to the Victory Hall opened wide, and the Sky Lords led the gathered star-warrior army across the skybridge in a great display of their might.

Those who were in the warbands led by Lord Thunderer swore to fight the sea monster who ravaged the coastlines. He and his men boarded ships and set out. Hauling back on the oars, they rowed hard and fast until the mighty fleet chased down the monstrous Tail-Devourer.

The weather grew foul. But valorous Lord Thunderer told his men to remain fearless in spite of the danger. He took his place in the prow. His helmet shone, his axe named Lightning glinted like silver, his shield shone like gold. A terrible gale began to blow and a violent storm broke out. The waves crashed loudly against their hulls. Yet, his men were unfazed by the howling din.

When the serpent named Tail-Devourer raised its head, Lord Thunderer hewed at it with his mighty axe. He fought long and hard to force the serpent into submission. In the end, Tail-Devourer withdrew and returned to the depths. The defeat of the monster brought an end to the pestilence, which had caused the deaths of so many, and Lord Thunderer was proclaimed the unassailable victor.

Lord White Fire, the Bold, stood in the prow of his ship with a Circle at the Stem. When a dark mist descended, Lord Spider's fleet came out of it, led by Nailship. A fierce battle ensued. Lord White Fire fought hard. Always at the front of his men, neither shield nor spear nor knife could match White Fire's bold display. Again and again he assaulted his enemy. Spears and arrows flew through the air, and the battle went on for a long time.

But Lord Spider the Entangler foresaw in this battle a way to get back at Lady Blessed for all that he begrudged her. He and his men boarded the Ship with a Circle in the Stem, encircled White Fire, bound him with ropes and took him captive. They returned to Nailship and took off for Mother Torment's hall where, even now, Spider holds White Fire the Bold for ransom. And, just as the Lord of Liars and Thieves had intended, even to this day, Lady Blessed continues to long for her son's release from captivity.

Now, I will tell you this: Lord Glory's ambition to protect Lady Sun's mirror from the hunger-crazed wolf was resolute. Lady Sun's youthful daughter took heart from Lord Glory's resolve. She approached her mother and knelt beside the bed where she lay dying. The daughter swore upon the flaming long-knife to replace her mother in the solar wagon, and vowed to overcome Treachery. Lord Glory's men armed themselves and mounted their horses. Lady Sun's daughter took her place in the wagon and held the reins. She cracked her whip and the horses took off from the Gates of Dawn. Escorted by Lord Glory and his men, Lady Sun's mirror-laden wagon once again crossed the sky.

Though Treachery saw who he was up against, he nonetheless vowed not to be outdone. Pressing forward, he slunk from the woods and took chase. Lord Glory spotted the wolf and led the pursuit. Whipping his horse to a full gallop, he came alongside the beast, leapt from his mount, and landed squarely atop it. He wrestled it to the ground, sat astride the wolf and straddled the beast with his knees. To constrain the wolf, his men threw a snare over Treachery's back and pulled the ropes taut. But the wolf bared his teeth and ripped a hole in the net.

It was at that crucial moment, when darkness was ascendant and light was fading fast, that Treachery sank his teeth into Lord Glory's right hand. He shook his head side to side, ripping the flesh from the bones in Lord Glory's hand. Lord Glory pulled his blade, lifted it high overhead, and with a single blow plunged the knife into the wolf's side. Shocked by the sudden assault, Treachery released his grip on the Lord's hand, reared up and threw Lord Glory onto his back.

Time stopped. And for that long, dreadful moment, when Treachery stood over Lord Glory, though he was prepared to make the fatal lunge, the wolf vowed, instead, to maintain their opposition. With blood dripping from his teeth, Treachery said, "We each opened a vein, and our blood is mixed. Now you and me are sworn brothers of light and dark. But, instead of ending the right fight now, regard this as an oath: I swear I will save you for another day."

Before the Lord's men could renew their attack, the wolf took off and, leaving behind a spattered blood trail to mark his passage, Treachery the Grim Hardness of Iron disappeared into the Ironwood's darkest depths.

The Lord knelt on the ground, bent his injured arm at the elbow, laid his forearm out flat, and ordered his second in command to cut off the damaged flesh. The man shook his head side to side and refused to do what the Lord commanded.

Again, Lord Glory ordered his man, "Do it."

His second in command grasped his axe with two hands, lifted it high over-head and, with a single, downward blow, lopped off all that remained of Lord Glory's mangled hand and wrist. His men cauterized the wound and took him home.

The wife of Lord Glory's second in command bound the stump with strips of linen and, to prevent him from remembering the pain, gave him the ale of for-getfulness to drink. But no matter how well she nursed him, the bleeding would not stop and the flesh would not mend. His blood had been mixed with Treachery's and, from then on, Lord Glory the Shining Firmament was akin to darkness and poisoned from within.

It was during those dreadful times, when Lord Glory lay dozing and was too weak to drive his torch-lit wagon, that men who depended upon their observation of the sky at night to keep their bearings, lost their way. The star-warrior army ceased lighting the star-torches and the sky went utterly dark.

At first, people pulled together to face the common enemy rather than to push apart. But, over time, men and women were so desperate, they forgot Lord Glory's laws. Because men and women believed that the Terrible Winter would never come to an end, they lost hope. Brothers fought brothers, and fathers slayed their children. Order broke down. People lost sight of goodness and had no respect for truth. Instead, they sought enemies to blame for their ordeal and followed liars who told them whatever they wanted to hear.

It was then that Mannus, whose lineage was mixed because he was born from a union between an earthly woman and Lord Glory, found his way across the darkened skybridge. Standing at his father's bedside, he saw how the poison boiled through his father's veins. It was Mannus, alone, who understood that the only means to restore his father's strength could be found in the roots of the mountains.

Mannus walked back across the skybridge and returned to his hill fort. He sent out messengers to each of his three sons' realms, ordering them to come at once. Glenn came from the lands along the northern sea coast; another son came from the deep inland forests in the south; and the third son came from the vast grasslands in the east.

Mannus told his three sons: "To restore my father's strength, you must enter the dark tunnels that thread through the mountain's roots. There you will discover the Water of Life that will heal my father."

Mannus's three sons agreed to do as their father commanded. They vowed to neither flee nor fear fire nor iron. They made preparation for the journey and set off.

At the mountain entrance, they came upon Lady Sun's daughter. She told them, "I come each night to ask the craftsmen inside the mountain to repair and relight the mirror in my wagon. But, so far, their efforts have been futile. Each day the wolf lays in wait for me and attacks. The solar mirror will not blaze up again until Lord Glory awakens and remembers his duty to bind the wolf."

She lit a lamp from the cinders in her wagon. Handing it to them, she said, "In return for freeing me from this place of darkness, I promise to become my hero's bedfellow."

"I was not born a coward," Glenn said. He dropped a knee, leant forward to kiss her hand, and said, "I promise you that the mirror in your wagon will blaze again. Do not fear. Never will I flee in the face of death."

The dim light from the lamp guided the three brothers through the dark passageways. In time, they came upon an immense underground room. They stopped and stared at the cavern. Lit with a hundred torches, its walls and ceiling were aglitter with jewels. At the far end of the vast room, the shadowy crafts-men's kinleader, the Old One, sat upon a high-seat carved from rock. At his side, twelve of his craftsmen stood.

The three brothers approached the Old One to ask for help. At first, he rebuffed their entreaty, saying, "I and those of my own kind were not consulted about where our sympathies lay. We know better than to be drawn to either side of a conflict between Treachery, the Devourers, and the Sky Lords."

In reply, the brothers told him, "You and your craftsmen have no choice in this matter. The Sky Lords hold the upper hand. You, the men who live in shad-ow, must do as they command. Their might is stronger than yours."

"When you put it that way," the Old One said, "I must agree to your de-mands. We will help restore Lord Glory's health."

The Old One then ordered those of his craftsmen, who were especially masterful in the restraint of the everlasting fires, to regain control over the flames that eat the air in the underground channels. And after the forges were relit, the Old One ordered the metalworkers to make fine, wire strands drawn from each of the seven metals. From these wires they twisted a cable strong enough to successfully bind the wolf.

In addition to the cable, they gave the brothers a gold pitcher with which to carry the Water of Life. To fight the wolf, they gave the brothers an iron blade that would never miss a stroke, would never rust, and would cut through stone and iron as easily as through straw. From the hilt, they made a deep socket which could be fitted to Lord Glory's arm. The Old One handed them an herb picked from the forest and told the brothers to place some of its leaves upon the wound and to steep the rest of the plant in the Waters of Life. If Lord Glory drank this broth, he said, their Lord would be healed within five days.

The three brothers then went in search of the healing waters. When they came to the heart of the mountain, they found the Water of Life, guarded by two swans. They dipped the pitcher into the pool and retraced their steps through the tunnels, left the mountain, and brought the water, the long-knife, the cable, and the healing leaves to their father.

Carrying these gifts from the Old One, Mannus retraced his steps across the skybridge and stood at his father's bedside. First, Mannus cleansed his father's wound with the Water of Life and made a compress with the healing plant's leaves to dress the wound. Then, he poured the healing water into a cup and held it to his father's lips. Lord Glory looked into the cup and saw a small, white, downy feather floating upon the water's surface.

Mannus shrank back, ashamed to have given his father defiled water to drink. But the Lord picked the feather out with his fingers and held it to the light. When he saw how it sparkled, a memory broke free from his forgetful-ness, and he remembered the sight of sunlight throwing rainbow colors upon breeze-rippled waters. And, along with this joyful memory, came a longing to recreate the embrace between earth and sky, from which all life flows. And thus, to help him remember light and life and goodness, he tucked the little feather, like a talisman, beneath his pillow.

That night, his body became a battleground. Again and again, he relived the fight with the wolf. The poison that flowed through his veins fought hard against the healing Water of Life. And as light and life struggled for ascendancy over darkness and death, Lord Glory became so cold that his body was wracked with trembling.

In the midst of his suffering, he envisioned how the water in the gold pitcher had grown wide as a lake. He held his arm in the water and let it wash over the wound. Looking up, he saw a swan floating across the surface. She came towards him, and once she reached the shore, she stepped from the lake and took off her feathered garment. She dipped a gold cup in the lake and invited him to drink. He reached toward the cup but took her hand instead. He drew her down beside him, put his arms around her and kissed her, and said, "There is no fairer woman than you." She was so beautiful Lord Glory wanted to keep her with him forever, so he took her feathered garment and hid it beneath his pillow.

When Lord Glory awoke, he saw that a woman lay beside him in his bed.

She told him, "Because you were shaken by the chills, I climbed into your bed and held you, tightly, in my arms to warm you."

Lord Glory sank into her embrace. He buried his face in the space between her breasts. He caressed her, smoothed her hair, and kissed her softly on the lips.

Thus, Swan-white awakened Lord Glory from his sleep of forgetfulness. She reminded him, "Most valiant hero, you are Lord of the Shining Firmament. It is your duty to fight the darkness. Others rely upon your leadership. Unless you rise to the challenge, darkness will prevail and rule forever."

Lord Glory accepted the truth of what she said and refused to drink the potions that made him sleep and forget. From then on, Swan-white stayed beside Lord Glory and became his ever-present consort, protector, and adviser. And it is said that Swan-white's face is clear and cloudless, and that their affection for one another sparkles like sunlight on breeze-rippled waters.

Swan-white dressed the wound with the leaves from the healing plant and soon Lord Glory's pain was gone. The next day the wound was healed. She cooked the flesh of a snake and a wolf and gave it to him to eat. She used serpent's venom to prepare a soup that would strengthen him and prepare him for victory. She told him to do as the Matrones had foreseen, for no one can withstand his destiny. She spoke charms to help him bind the wolf, and said, "It is with my help that your sunlit sky will once again free Mannus's children from their terror of darkness."

Swan-white poured a cup of the Water of Life from the gold pitcher. She offered him the cup to drink from, saying, "I honor you, Lord Glory the Shining Firmament. You are the greatest of the ruling powers."

He supped and accepted his duty. And though Lord Glory was limited to the use of a single hand, after he had regained his strength, he found that it was as easy to strike with the knife, which the Old One's craftsmen had forged, as it would have been if he had had the use of his whole arm.

Lord Glory vowed to renew his fight against Treachery. He called for his warband, ordered his horse saddled, mounted and led his men. That morning, when Lady Sun left the Gates of Dawn, she was accompanied by Lord Glory and his warband, along with his consort, Swan-white who was dressed in her feathered garment and flying overhead.

When Lord Glory saw Treachery come upon them, he rode valiantly and fought courageously. The wolf was overpowered and fettered with the cable twisted with wires drawn from the seven metals.

Once Treachery was shackled, he said, "For as long as the forces of darkness and light remain in balance, the truce between us holds. But, Lord Glory, I now have a taste for your flesh. Like blood brothers, our veins have been opened and our blood is mixed. May misfortune go with you. The legacy that will endure between now and the Endtime will be undying cruelty between men. Now, regard my spoken words as a sworn oath. A day will come when a shift will tip the balance toward the chaos, which I rule. Then, I will return. The fight will resume and I will complete what I began. From then on, darkness will reign supreme."

After the wolf was banished to captivity in the Ironwood, seasonal change was restored and the time of famine came to an end. The three brothers set out to find Lady Sun. Two brothers looked for a golden road by land. But Glenn followed the ever-brightening golden road by sea and he found his way west.

Within one year he was led to the harbor where Lady Sun ends her daily journey in the west. He came ashore and awaited her arrival. The Lady stepped down from her wagon. Glenn took her hand, led her to the bower in her longboat, and set her upon the couch that she reclines upon each night.

She offered him the cup to drink from and praised him and asked the Matrones to grant them a fair night.

He supped and asked to gain from all that she could teach him, for her wisdom was as boundless as the sky.

She answered, "If there is anything you desire, only ask and your wish shall be granted." She then invited Glenn to lay with her on her journey. And as her longboat, Nightly, crossed the sea on its way to the Gates of Dawn, Glenn sang to her and loved her.

It is said that when he returned to his home in the northeast, he told his people that Lady Sun had shown him a better place to live. He thus brought his people with him to settle, here, in the western lands.

They set off in well manned ships. When they arrived, Glenn ordered his men to prepare for battle. They went ashore fully armed. Not long after, Erol arrived with his motley warband. Glenn was at the front of his men, urging them to attack fiercely. Because Glenn's force was overwhelming, Erol's men soon gave way. And, in the end, Erol fell in the middle of his ranks, along with most of his men. Those few who were left, surrendered and fell to their knees. They were seized, bound, and taken away.

Glenn took over both the large farms and small ones and claimed the rulership that had belonged to Erol. Glenn thanked his men and offered them the abandoned land so that they could farm and pasture their sheep and cattle. From then on, he and his men, and their descendants have traveled the trade routes every season. Along with the wealth and the power that Glenn acquired, came his influence in the region. He was a fair, and fearless kinleader. He lived for a long time and his fame spread far and wide. All those who knew him sang his praises. It has been said that he outdid all other men as gold outshines iron.

When Glenn died, everyone grieved his loss. But no one grieved as sorrowfully as did Lady Sun. His body was placed in his ship's hull. After the boat was ignited, he took one last journey in flaming splendor. And the weeping Lady Sun picked up his soul and carried him in her arms to the Lord of Rich-Water's hall named Haven.

The story was finished. The hall was silent. The men had been carried away to that long-ago time when steadfast Glenn and their forefathers had manned the oars, and the salt spray had wetted their faces. And along with the storytelling, the men inside the longhouse, that night, had pictured themselves in service to their families and their community. And just as Glenn and his men had done, those who would leave in two days' time would bring home the wealth in the longboats' hulls.

First Gevehard stood. Then all the men awakened from the spell, the storyteller had cast, and they broke into cheers. The storyteller, turning and bowing in all directions, proudly accepted their praise. Gevehard waved him over to the high table and honored the man for his fine performance with lavish gifts.

Gevehard then said loudly, "In the autumn we will meet here again to celebrate our successful return. Then we will have new tales to tell."

The cheering went on for a long time before the doors opened wide and the men walked into the night.

And whereas those men, who had manned the oars on previous trips, knew what they were up against and set their jaws with conviction; the untried, younger men were ever more eager to test their valor and to prove what they could do.

For some men, this night would be the last time they ever set foot inside the longhouse. For others, there would be a celebration upon their return. Then the cup would go around, they would drink to their success, and recount their brave adventures with wildly embellished tales.

III.

Aiken stood beneath the brilliant, starlit sky. He looked up at the top of the domed sky and stared at the constellation men called Lord Glory's Wagon. To the south, he saw Lady Blessed's Distaff. And just above the skyline, he saw the brightest star, known to many as the Blue Star because of its blue and red flicker. It was there that the flaming red and blue torchlights marked the gate through which all must pass who wished to cross the skybridge. Along with the Lord's Wagon, this, too, was used for wayfinding, especially by those who wished to move between this world and the otherworldly meadhalls located at the far end of the bridge.

There, the bridge separates into two paths. The one that leads to the right will take the way-farer to the edge of the sea that encircles the worlds. There, on the shoreline, he will rest peacefully in the Lord of Rich-Water's hall named Haven. The road that leads to the left will take a man to the hill fort inside of which the Sky Lords and their Ladies live in their longhouses. It is there, in Lord Glory's Victory Hall that they assemble for both celebration and war-like entertainment.

The skyline glowed softly with the false dawn's golden light. The lingering blush would remain until Lady Sun's two chargers and her wagon broke through the Gates of Dawn to begin a fresh, new day. Aiken watched Day-farer breach the skyline and, carrying his white gleaming shield, lead the way.

Longing for Mildred's comforting lullabies and her hearty companionship, Aiken felt a sadness he could not shake. She was his best friend, and now, without her there beside him, he stood alone. He had hidden and lied about his true feelings. No one could understand except, perhaps, the graybeard.

He had had to deal with what had been a betrayal of all that he had ever known and believed in, alone. There was no such thing as honor or glory. There was no such thing as valor, heroism, or respect for truth and justice. His heart was no longer in it. Though he was ashamed to question those timeless values, he knew that powerful men used those words to convince children to throw down their lives like blood gifts on the killing fields to ensure their chieftain's victories. That was what he had been taught and had willingly accepted. But he could no longer defend the falsity of those claims.

Men blowing the war-horns were celebrating their last night in the longhouse before they left home. For Aiken, the mournful, eerie sounds and strange harmonic melodies conveyed his melancholic mood better than anything he had heard before.

Anguished by his belief that there was no one to whom he could turn for help, Aiken sought direction from the torch-outlined wagon. Lord Glory and his enemy, Treachery, had both been bound together by the mixing of their blood. Their un-relenting conflict was as constant and enduring as the bad blood between him and Leofar. For as long as Aiken remained pitted against the rogue chieftain, their conflict would continue, even if he had to meet up with his enemy in the land of the dead.

But, because Aiken believed his pleas had gone unheard, he turned his attention to the gate-keeper, Lord Guardsman, the one who opened the doors to the great sky-bridge, and to Day-farer, the one to whom fighting men asked for protection. Lord Guardsman was the one who guided those men, who had waged war on behalf of their chieftains, to the Victory Hall, and welcomed them to the star-warrior Army of Ten-thousand Strong.

It was those two Lords to whom Aiken chose to speak about his difficult situa-tion, not to the one who had turned his back on him. Because they would understand better than Lord Glory would, Aiken told them what he had learned the day that he had sat across from the graybeard with the need-fire between them. He told them about Leofar's betrayal and the execution of Torwald's murder. Aiken explained that, although he now understood how the guilty men had plotted against his chieftain, there were no living kinsman who would testify on his behalf. Along with his tears, his words expressed the stark and painful knowledge that, because he had been barred from the Assembly, he was unable to prove the rogue's treacherous actions. He would never be given an opportunity to seek justice on behalf of his dead war companions.

Alger's goading had hurt him badly. How much longer could he hold out before he set off to wander again? If he were to satisfy his oath, he knew, with stark finality, that this was how it would have to be: he would say goodbye to his wife and children; he would walk as far as Leofar's hill fort; he would force his way past the guards at the door and barge into the meadhall with Rushing Harm in hand; he would demand Leofar swear an oath to speak the truth; and if the rogue refused, Aiken would challenge him to a judgment of arms.

"Where are your kinsmen?" Leofar would ask. "Who will attest to the truth of your charge against me?" And, after Aiken had answered that no one had sworn to be his witness, Leofar would laugh. In the face of the rule of law, Aiken's foe would laugh and the hall would echo with the sounds of his gloating. Aiken would be mocked for his presumption, and the murderer would go free, unharmed.

Leofar would yell, "Seize him." And the result of Aiken's foolhardy action would end in being cut into pieces. They would start by gouging out his one good eye—a mixed blessing of sorts. To be blind in both eyes would prevent him from watching the rest of the torture. They would cut out his tongue to silence him. Then they would cut off each hand and foot. They would slip a noose around his neck, and Aiken would become another one of the men whom the rogue had strung from his meadhall rafters. Aiken would die without having been given a chance to hold Leofar accountable for breaking the peace. In the end, what good would he have accomplished?

Aiken's words became a gentle breeze, a whiff of breath, a faint, moist air. His plea floated above the reeds and grasses. It wound its way between the islands, passed the inlet to the sea, and drifted across the waves. His words took a turn for the south, found their way to the place where the most beautiful star in the sky, the flaming blue and red torches, marked the gated entrance through which all must pass before they are granted entry to the starry bridge. And Lord Guardsman waved the gravid words past.

Aiken's plea followed the broad, starlit path. Whereupon arrival at the opposite end of the bridge, his message was heard, repeated, and passed on several times before it was whispered in the ear of an expectant power. And the plea of a desperate man had found its way, at last, to the one who rides a horse named Slippery and who disguises himself, at times, like a common beggar.

IV.

Aiken stood outside the house where he had slept each night since his arrival in the village. He dropped his head and sighed deeply. Careful not to wake the sleeping householders when he opened the door, he quietly made his way inside. Stumbling around in the darkness, he found his bedroll, laid it out flat, unpinned his cloak, pulled off his tunic, and stepped out of his trousers. He folded his clothing and laid it atop his satchels. Exhausted, he crawled beneath the blankets.

On the verge of sleep, Aiken saw the graybeard come walking toward him. With his cloak flapping out behind his back, he rapidly stabbed the ground with the butt end of a spear. When face to face with Aiken, he said, "Come along with me."

And there he was, racing horseback. Thrilling to the chase, gripping the horse's flanks with his knees, he urged his mount to run at a full gallop. "Pour it on," Aiken cried to the sound of hooves ricocheting from the surface of the road. He looked back at Alger, yelled, "Race you to the edge of the woods up ahead," and pressed his legs into his horse's belly.

The horse's hooves ceased to touch the ground. Lifted above the road, Aiken and his horse were one beast soaring as if on wings. Smooth and weightless as the wind itself, the hard earth rushed away beneath them. Aiken's pleasure was so great, he wished to remain in flight forever.

Vying to take and to keep the lead, Aiken glanced to the left. His chieftain's horse ran neck and neck with his own. He felt the same gracious loyalty to Torwald that he had felt before everything went wrong, and they were driven apart. Torwald's lips pulled back in a snarl, to reveal his sharp, pointed dogteeth. He gestured with the point of his spear, and yelled, "Keep it coming. Keep it coming. Lord Thunderer rides with us. His lightning strikes promise a good kill."

Heedless of the lightning traces streaking parallel to the skyline, the men in the warband headed toward the clouds stirring like dark, muddy waves of froth. Eager to meet up with those frightful powers and to celebrate the boar-kill with a stewed pork feast, the men in the warband whooped it up, and their voices trailed like faint specters afloat on the wind.

Aiken looked to the left, expecting to see Torwald again, but everything had changed. Instead of Torwald, the man who now sat astride his chieftain's horse was the graybeard, the man who called himself Fury, and by implication, Lady Blessed's husband, the Lord of the Whirlwind. The cursed stranger's cloak fluttered above the back of his mount and his long wispy hair and beard were swept back from his shoulders. He turned directly toward Aiken and yelled, "You are my man now."

And in that single moment, Aiken knew he was stripped naked—less than naked—he was nothing but a bag of bleached bones: his ribs, leg bones and arm bones, breastbone and shoulder blades were staves marked with secret signs. Recoiling in disgust, Aiken knew that when the graybeard read the staves, he would foresee his response to each turn of the Matrones' whorls. All his thoughts, memories, and desires lay exposed to that dreadful man's uncanny vision. He would know precisely when the last sister would drop her spindle, lay down her distaff, pick up her knife named Endbringer and, holding Aiken's life thread taut between her fingers, slice it through with one final cut. And in that single moment, Aiken's breath would slip from his mouth one last time, and like a small bird, his soul would take flight and cross the Venom-cold River of life.

On the verge of the Ironwood, Fury lifted his spear above his head, gave the signal and reined to a stop. Up ahead, four villagers pointed to the forest where the beaters had encircled the beast. Their dogs, eager to go after the creature, paced and growled. The horses breathed in the beast's scent, whinnied and stomped in place.

In the distance, a horseman chased a rabbit. It broke to the side, feinted, and ran ahead but the huntsman's horse stayed with it. Coming alongside his prey, the hunter lifted his arm, pointed his spear and thrust. His aim was good. Without stopping, he lifted the speared rabbit, pulled it from the point, and dropped it into his hunting sack.

He nudged his horse with his heels and they went into the forest.

Fury hurled the spear named Attacker. The weapon flew from his hand, marked a straight path through the trees, and returned to his upraised hand.

Fury then handed Aiken a crow feather. "What good is this?" he asked. The strangeness of the feather reminded him of the one that he had had in hand before it had blown away several days before. This feather carried with it the knowledge that, just as before, when he had somehow chanced upon a place somewhere between the world, which he ordinarily inhabited when he was awake, and the dreamtime world, which he inhabited when he was asleep, he was, now, once again in that same in-between place. Fully aware that he was both awake and asleep, he could now control his actions in the dreamtime in a way that he had never done before.

Everything took on a sharpened clarity. Now that the feather, which had escaped him before, was in his hands again, it mysteriously changed its shape to become a heavy boar spear like none that he had ever seen. This gray-blue colored spear was marked on one side with signs naming it Charger and, on the other, with the secret sign that stood for Victory.

Assured that his fight against the beast would come to a successful conclusion, Aiken leapt from his mount. He looked around for his companions, but they had all gone ahead to meet up with him later. Now it was up to him. He alone would follow the spear-cut path through the, otherwise, impassible forest. And though he was uncertain of the beast's identity, he was confident that he would know it when he found it and would fight it into submission.

Wolves howled in the distance, and the wind blasted. To assure him of the ruling powers' presence, Lord Thunderer wrapped an iron-clad cloak around his shoulders. And though Aiken knew, somehow, that he was in service to those powerful forces, he neither understood the unfathomable depths of their natures nor the importance of his actions.

The dogs barked with sharp, excited yips and took off. Aiken stepped into the dark, smothering woods. The path, which Attacker had cleared for him, was straight and narrow. Oaks, maples, low shrubs, bowed fern fronds and blue flowers crowded the edge of his path. Escape was impossible. The only way to go was forward.

In time, the trees began to thin out. Sagebrush, buttercups, and sedges grew sparsely in the shade cast by slender birches and willows. Aiken came to a stagnant, slow-moving, red-colored stream. The stench of rot assailed his nostrils. He and the dogs gathered near the stream bank. The dogs bent to sniff and lap the water. Its oily, slick surface threw the familiar-looking, iron-dark, rainbow colors. And, as before, Aiken was drawn to watch the swirling red, orange, blue, and violet colors shift and pulse and mix together.

A long, scrawny arm reached out of the water and grabbed a dog that had ventured too close to the edge. It yipped and barked in terror as it was pulled beneath the water's surface. The other dogs ran off with their tails between their legs, leaving Aiken alone to wage war against the creature.

The bogman lashed out with its free arm. Threatening to pull Aiken under and, along with the dog, to suck the flesh from his bones and to drink his blood. Though it grabbed at him, unlike on prior occasions when Aiken had been hobbled by indecision and caught by the watery, iron-dark allure, this time Aiken was alert to the danger. This time he was armed with a steel spear marked with the sign for Victory. Aware that he could strategize with the sharp acuity that came with wakefulness, this time, he would be able to spot his challenger's weaknesses.

Charger's blue, green, and purple sheen matched the shimmering iridescent bog-water. And, just as the same old hurts and angers shifted and blended and swirled together inside Aiken, so, too, did the secret signs transform his doubt and anguish to self-assurance.

Aiken took a backward step. He held the shaft with both hands, a shoulder width apart, and anchored his right arm to his hip. Confident he could draw the bogman onto land, he lured it from the stream, calling, "Come to me. Mount me. Ride me into battle."

The bogman reached out with both arms, and answered, "My pretty boy. I know you clamor to be ridden. How you and me will pleasure in reliving the old battles."

The creature grabbed hold of the bank. To pull itself up, it lifted its right leg onto the soggy bank and then lifted the left one. It came toward Aiken on all fours, scrabbling and wheedling, "How I relish man's iron nature. Hand me the pretty spear. Give me the weapon. Let me lick the steel. Give me the spear. It is mine. I was the one who gave the smith the bog iron from which it was made."

To lure the creature away from the safety of the watery pit, Aiken took another backward step. And just as he intended, the bogman scrambled after him, singing:

"Like returns to like
      To feed my bog iron.
Steel cuts men's flesh
      To feed my bog iron.
Blood seeps into the soil
      To feed my bog iron.
Like returns to like
      To feed my bog iron."

To position himself for the lunge, Aiken was taking a backward step when a tree root laying underfoot on his blindside tripped him. He lost his balance and, twisting to the left, momentarily lost sight of the creature. The bogman leapt at Aiken from the right. To break his fall, Aiken pushed the spear's butt end into the soil and leaned to the side to avoid the creature's grasp. The bogman fell short, came down flat on its belly and, clutching at Aiken's ankles, caught hold. The creature yanked hard to bring Aiken down. His weight came out from under him, and he fell forward. The bogman reached out and took hold of the spear. Aiken and the bogman tugged back and forth. Aiken managed to twist to the side and to rise to his knees. He tried to stand. The bogman broke its grip and jumped at Aiken's back. Aiken wriggled free, got to his feet and straightened up.

To prepare for the thrust, he was grasping the spear with both hands and anchoring his right wrist against his hip when he saw, racing toward them, the huntsman whom he had seen previously in the distance. Now, Aiken knew the man. It was his father, Eamon. And right behind him, accompanied by two crows, flying overhead, was the man who called himself Fury.

The bogman, seeing how badly outnumbered it was, squealed and took off. Eamon gave chase. He held his spear high overhead and aimed. But the bogman leapt up and took on the shape of a creature of blazing fire. A red rooster, frenziedly flapping its wings, with neck extended, aimed its long spurs at Eamon's face. He threw off his arm to fend off the cock and, as it fell to the ground, wings aflutter, it flipped in midair to become a badger. The creature landed on all fours, scampered toward the bank, dove into the stream and paddled rapidly toward a burrow on the opposite bank.

Eamon's horse leapt across the stream to head it off. He jammed his spear into the mud to block the badger's entrance. The creature turned and headed upstream toward the pond. Aiken stomped through the water at an angle to cut it off before it could disappear underwater.

Fury leapt from his horse. Attacker in hand, he splashed through the knee-deep water. Aiken and Fury cornered the badger between them. It reared up, bared its teeth and flailed madly at their legs with claws sharp enough to rip a man's flesh from his bones. The men's spears fended it off. The creature contracted and changed, right before their very eyes, into a slimy clump of bog iron. As it began to sink, but before it reached the bottom, Eamon leapt from his horse. He reached beneath the water's surface to grab it. Once he had it in hand, he climbed onto the bank and was about to dump it into his sack when the nugget sprouted clawed feet, long skinny arms, and a lumpy head. Startled, Eamon dropped it.

The creature fell onto its back on the edge of the streambank. Aiken hurriedly pressed Charger's tip into its belly and said, "Move and I will gore you." Fury poked at it with Attacker. Pinned beneath their spear points, the bogman kicked out erratically in a fit of anger and frustration. Unable to get away, the bogman was reduced to yelling in foul language and calling the men filthy names.

Eamon brought the rope and handed it to Aiken. While Attacker kept the creature immobile, Eamon grabbed the bogman by the shoulders and roughly rolled the creature onto its belly. He pulled the creature's arms behind its back, so Aiken could wrap the rope around its wrists and bind it. He wrapped and knotted the ends of the rope to the creature's ankles. Grabbing it by its arms and shoulders, Eamon pulled it upright and set it upon its hobbled feet. Eamon pulled hard on the rope to force the creature to walk behind him. The bogman moaned and cried as it followed with small mincing steps.

The sounds of approaching horses caught the men's attention. Aiken glanced over his shoulder to see four lords and their attendants riding toward them in single file. Lord Thunderer was the first to appear. A proud, large man with a full, red beard, he was broad through the shoulders, his neck was thick as an oak tree, and his arms and legs were hard as stone pillars, ending in outsized hands and feet. He wore a black, iron chest plate, and a dark gray cloak. He was armed with a heavy, steel hammer polished to a silvery sheen that was inscribed with knots and secret signs. He eyed with evident disgust the three soiled men, dripping with red mud.

A great white swan soared overhead, followed by Lord Glory. He was an elegant, good looking man. His features were fine and well proportioned. A long straight nose, high cheek bones, a strong, pointed chin and ruddy cheeks, his mouth resembled a curved bow, curled up at the corners. His silky, burnished gold hair fell to his shoulders. Draped across his back, a blue cloak, trimmed with silver and woven bands was pinned with a silver brooch at his shoulder. The right edge hung free and the left edge was tossed over his shoulder. His silver-hilted, steel knives hung from a belt covered with gold plaques.

Next came the twin Lords of Battle and their attendants. They all crowded into the small clearing.

Aiken ran up to Lord Glory and asked him to hear his complaint. "Lord Glory, a terrible injustice was done. A chieftain named Leofar ambushed my chieftain and his warband. I brought my accusation to the Assembly but they refused to hear me out—."

"Let me go, let me go," the bogman whimpered pathetically, interrupting Aiken's pleas. , The creature had begun to creep toward Lord Glory before Eamon had finished tying the bogman to his saddle with another rope. "I promise to give you a treasured gold ball in return for my freedom. It is light and brilliant as the sun itself. Tell the men to let me go so I can retrieve it for you."

Lord Glory looked down on the sniveling creature and said, "I would like to see this gold ball, Eamon. Lead the bogman to its burrow and, keeping it bound, let it pull the ball out of the water."

Eamon released the bogman's arms and tied the rope around the creature's middle but left its legs hobbled. The bogman scrabbled on hands and feet to the edge of the pond, slipped down the bank and, dragging the rope behind it, disappeared beneath the water. Eamon firmly gripped the rope. The men stood around the edge of pond, watching the bubbles come from below. Each bubble floated momentarily on the surface before it broke.

Then the bubbles ceased rising. The rope became taut and, though Eamon tugged on it, it would not budge.

Aiken and Fury both jumped into the water. Grabbing ahold of the rope, they pulled hard against the creature. Forced to wade more deeply into the stagnant pool, the water came up to their hips, and then up to their waists. Aiken and Fury followed the rope, pulling hand over hand. Aiken took a deep breath, submerged and followed the rope until he had found and grasped the tree root around which the creature had wrapped it. Yanking on the rope beyond the root, he pulled the creature closer until he had the rope unwrapped from the root. He resurfaced and, altogether, the three men pulled hard to haul the creature up to the surface. But the bogman dug its feet in the streambed and refused to move any further.

Swan-white met the water with her webbed feet. She made a great splash and, in a storm of white feathers, beat her huge, outspread wings to attack the bogman. Like stinging sleet, she struck at the creature with her beak to force the bogman forward until she had forced it to the edge of the bank.

Several powerful down-strokes lifted Swan-white above the water. She came so close to Lord Thunderer that he felt the wind in his face and flinched from the big bird's approach. His horse whinnied and sidestepped.

Pleased to have made Lord Thunderer look so cowardly Swan-white called *hoop hoop* in a victorious cackle. Once she was above the trees, she circled graciously above them all.

Lord Thunderer had had enough of this disgusting farce, turned his horse, and he and his men rode away to the sounds of loud, overhead rumbling.

Aiken bent down and reached deep in the water. He lifted the bogman out of the pond and set it onto the bank. The creature was grasping the ball with both hands. It curled up, and lay on the ground whimpering. Fury and Aiken climbed out of the pond. Aiken grabbed for the gold ball and pulled it out of the creature's grip. Now that his hands had grown to twice or three times the size that they had been when he was a child, he was surprised to discover that the ball was smaller than he had remembered. It was now small enough to lie cradled in his cupped palm. Though the bogman continued to grasp for the ball, Aiken held it beyond its reach. He wiped the gold ball on the grass to clean off the dripping, red slime and showed it to Eamon, Fury, and Lord Glory.

"Let me go, let me go." The wheedling bogman screamed, "I gave you the ball, now let me go."

"Should we let this creature go?" Lord Glory asked.

"No, Lord Glory," Aiken said, shaking his head. "The ball is mine. My father gave it to me many years ago. This creature stole it."

Aiken bent a knee before the Lord, and said, "I beg you to hear me out and help me. I speak the truth. Leofar broke the peace. I was outlawed at the Assembly and accused of—"

Just then, Aiken realized that the bogman had, somehow, managed to slip free of the knot that Eamon had tied to his saddle. Aiken dropped the ball, leapt to his feet and ran after the scrabbling creature. Before the bogman could get back to the safety of its watery pit, Aiken grabbed hold of the detestable creature and tied more knots around it to bind it securely.

Yet, the bogman squealed:

"You need me,
     You want me,
          You want what I give you.
Without me
     You will have no iron.
Where will you be without me?
     You are weaponless without me.
You need me,
     You want me,
          You want what give you."

Eamon came toward the bogman, this time carrying a snare. He threw the net over the creature's head and tied the open end around its feet. He hoisted it up and threw it, upside down, over the leather blanket covering his horse's rump.

The bogman squealed and cried. It stuck its fingers through the openings in the tightly knotted snare, and cried, "You cheated. You promised. You promised."

For once, Aiken had the upper hand. And for the third time, he ran up to Lord Glory, "A terrible injustice was done—"

Eamon stepped up behind Aiken, proudly threw his arm around his son's shoulder, and said, "Lord Glory, let me present my son, Aiken the Strength of Oak."

Eamon looked Aiken in the face, and asked, "Are you a good man Aiken?"

"My wife Mildred says I am a good man."

"Well then, there you have it. On the recommendation of a woman, my son is a good man."

"Lord Glory, men have hidden the truth—"

"Aiken, we need more good men like you in our fight against injustice," Lord Glory said. "We need men who are not afraid to speak up in defense of truth. For now, the rule of law is broken and the fate of the worlds, as we know it, is at stake. An end through violence and terror is possible, perhaps inevitable. I fear the freedom that men honor at the Assembly is at risk. The Endtime has already begun. We must not give up the struggle for justice, even in the face of dire threats. We must do whatever we can to maintain the rule of law. Do not let the threats deter you."

Lord Glory pulled his reins to the side to turn his horse and led the Lords of Battle and their combined attendants in the direction from which they had come, accompanied by Swan-white who flew overhead.

Aiken watched him leave, despondently.

"What do we do with this creature?" Eamon asked Fury.

"Take it away." Fury said. He dug around in his satchel. And, as if it were some kind of enchanted piece of luggage from which everything came that a man would ever need, he pulled out a lock and key, handed them to Eamon, and said, "We will keep the bogman shackled with a locked chain in the common yard outside the Victory Hall."

Eamon took the lock and key and dropped them into the sack hanging from his saddle.

"No. Let me go, you cheaters," the bogman cried. "Let me go. Cheaters."

Fury looked disgustedly at the bogman, and said, "As for you, you sniveling creature, I will hold you hostage until your fellow bog creatures have paid the ransom I demand. In exchange for your freedom, they must supply me with a mountain of bog iron."

"Give me back my gold ball," the creature wheedled and cried. "Give it back."

Eamon waved farewell to his son, jumped into his saddle, and began to ride away.

Fury was mounting Slippery when Aiken asked, "Who are you?

"Who I am should be clear to you by now. But until you and me meet up again, let me offer you one, final piece of advice:

"Lest iron take control of a man,
A man must first take control of iron."

Aiken watched the two men ride off, accompanied by the two crows. Once they had disappeared in amongst the trees, he reached down to pick up the gold ball. He rubbed it against the inside of his tunic, the only place that was free of the red, sticky mud and shined it until it was gleaming.

To have been ridden by the bogman had been the reverse of an orderly human life. He had relived the chaos and carnage of war without end. It had made him act badly. But now he had something to hang on to, a shiny gold ball to show him the way forward.

He looked around. How long had he been standing there alone in the Ironwood? At first it seemed so quiet. But then, he heard the bogman's voice calling to him from somewhere in the distance, pleading to be released from the snare.

V.

It was before sunrise that morning when Aiken awoke. The man, in whose house he had been sleeping since his arrival in Gevehard's village, was preparing to patrol the roads around the village and the ones between the farms. Getting dressed, he hiked up his trousers, tightened his belt, put on his shoes, and wrapped his legs with cloth bands. The man's partner opened the door and stepped inside. The two men talked quietly, went outside, and closed the door behind them.

Aiken settled into his bedroll with a sigh and pulled the covers up to his chin. The familiar sounds brought to mind those that he had heard early in the morning when he was a small boy. Laying there, he recalled how his father had done the same things when he, too, had gotten ready to patrol the roads that day.

And while afloat on that deliciously trusting river of sound, Aiken heard his father's horse being led from the stable and, while it waited just outside the door, nicker and whinny. Aiken relished the squeak of leather his father's heavy belt made when he hiked it up and buckled it. The sheathed long-knife, side-arms, and steels clattered and rang along with the hammers and throwing axes that Eamon stuck into the belt rings.

Eamon bent over him, chucked his little son on the chin, kissed him on the head and said, "Bye now Little Acorn, go back to sleep. Your father is on guard duty today, and will keep you safe." He walked to the table and laid a key on the wooden top with a loud *click*. He then turned and went out the door.

Aiken heard his father swing into his saddle. He and the other men, with whom he was on patrol that day, flicked their reins, and were off. Then, he heard the familiar *clop-clop-clop*, the horses' clattering hooves made on the dirt outside their house.

Aiken lay there, still groggy from sleep. Though he knew he had awakened in a house, which was located in Gevehard's village, it seemed as though another part of him was still inside the house in which he had lived so long ago. It was so real to him, he knew the placement of all the furnishings. The door was off to the left. His mother and father's bed was in the back, right corner. His own trundle bed lay to the side of theirs and was slid beneath it during the daytime. The table upon which his father had placed the key was near the hearth, in the center of the house along with four, three-legged, elaborately carved chairs with high backs. Soon he would hear the servant woman come in to rake the coals. She would sing her greetings to the Hearth Mother, feed the fire, and once it was blazing he would smell the pleasant scent of fresh smoke.

Other sounds drifted in from outside as men and women roused and left their homes to start the fresh, new day.

THIRTEEN

Moonstone
If you will receive the gift of prophesy,
foresee one's destiny, reveal truth and unmask hidden enemies.

Take this stone which is called Moonstone. It is found in many colors
but the best has a bluish milk-like sheen. To bring an end to the old and to
start things anew, hold this stone in the light of the full moon. It will
change with light. When it is brightest it will aid one's inventiveness,
and give good fortune in love.

The Truth of Rocks, by Aluiss the Wise

I.

At times, a brilliant blue flash sparks at the center of this little round stone, and a transparent, moon-like circle, with a faintly blurred edge, appears to float inside it. A dream-like spell is cast and I find myself hovering upon a wave of gray-blue light.

II.

Tonight, before the men would leave at dawn, he had chosen to stand the watch beside the red stone. Crouched beside a pile of shaved wood, he struck his flint against the steel. The sparks landed in the kindling, and he fanned the faint embers, with his hand, until a flame caught hold. He fed the small fire with handfuls of dried grass, wood shavings, sticks, reeds, and crumbled blocks of dung. Occasionally his face or hand caught the flame's yellow shimmer.

Staring into the small fire, he was reminded of the night he had lit the pyres. Then, the blazes had stretched so high they had reached above his head. But tonight, there was no need for a large fire and mounds of fuel. Tonight, a small fire would do.

The numerous shades, whose names he had never learnt, sat in their small boats, outlined by moonlit stones. And, out beyond the reach of the flickering yellow flames, long, parallel black shadows striped the stark, blue-colored land.

Coming from somewhere in the distance, the shape of a man was walking towards him. The man's face was colored the same transparent, blue tinge as were the fields and pastures. But unlike the few, gnarly shrubs that were standing at the edge of the holy grove, the man's likeness threw no shadow. He tossed his blue-gray cloak back from his right shoulder, strode up to the fire, and tipped his head once in a silent greeting.

They stood there for a while, until, to break the long silence, the blue-tinged man said, "Aiken, let us not fight any more." His hand lifted in a gesture with which he had meant to convey his willingness to forget their quarrel. But, though he wanted to offer his friend a comforting touch upon the shoulder, after he reached out, he stopped and let his hand fall to his side.

Still that same, good-looking young man, he remained unchanged since that morning when the two men had sat together on the riverbank and thrown the bones. Back then, the cocky self-assurance, which their youth had lent them, had instilled the belief that together they could accomplish whatever they set out to do. But for Aiken, forces beyond his control had thwarted the endeavors he had sworn to accomplish so long ago. In the intervening years, life had changed him.

"I was the one who should have been out front, Alger. We swore to fight for one another and to watch each other's back. I let you down. You took the lead when it should have been me. I let you run to your death."

"You never could have stopped me. You know that. I take back what I said the other night. I do not hold my death against you. But you can still get beyond shame and regret. Atonement is still possible, Aiken."

"The night I lit the pyres, I was shaken by the sight of men with whom I had eaten, ridden, and slept beside hanging by their necks from tree branches. In contrition, I promised to seek justice for your murders. What else could I have done, otherwise? I had no choice that night. Loyalty to an oath offered me a purpose for which to live. But it has come to nothing. I have only succeeded in tying myself to a promise that can never be fulfilled. All I have accomplished was to bind myself to my enemy. The knots and braids I carve into combs, spoons, boxes, chairs, and bowls were meant to tie me to my former companions. But they have turned against me and now are my enemies."

Unmoved by his friend's confession, Alger raised his brow and looked at Aiken with a piercing gaze. "I refuse to accept your explanation. To claim your promise was nothing but an attempt to save face, after you were rendered so helpless, is nothing but an empty excuse." He looked at Aiken with cold, unwavering contempt, and said, "You swore to never back down. I still hold you to it. Do what you said you would. Avenge our deaths."

"I cannot. The night I swore to discover the name of the murderer and to bring him to justice for his crimes, I still had faith in the rule of law. But the chieftains have all turned against me."

A dreadful rift between success and failure was threatening to separate the two friends. On one side of the divide lay the fulfillment of what Aiken had sworn to accomplish, and on the other side lay the irredeemable losses each man had suffered. "The longer I dedicate myself to this pursuit, the more I suffer. My life has been a series of deprivations, breakdowns, and small deathblows. Humiliation has been never-ending.

"I blame Torwald for what happened. He was the one who led us, like a flock of sheep, into the paddock where the butchers awaited our slaughter. When I raised the alarm, no one heeded my warnings. I saw it coming but was unable to avert the tragedy. Even now, Torwald refuses to believe me. But you do. Say you believe me. I saw you standing in the thicket. You heard Kipp describe how Leofar planned the ambush. Tell me I was right. Stand up for me. Convince Torwald of Leofar's guilt and I will feel vindicated."

"No," Alger said, his cold and silent stare widening the gap between them. "I refuse."

"Your demands and misplaced accusations, Alger, make you no different from the others. Torwald was threatened by the younger men in the warband. He feared being pushed aside. He was unwilling to listen to those who were wiser."

"Oh? Are you presenting yourself as Torwald's most likely successor?"

"No. You do not understand. Torwald was unwilling to listen to the younger men's counsel. He feared it would weaken the appearance of being the infallible leader whom he had so carefully cultivated over the years. Either his trust in Leofar was simple-minded foolishness or, when he saw how the elders were losing their grip on the Assembly, he chose to end it all by leading us into a trap."

"Nonsense."

"Without a son to follow him, might he not have chosen to die recklessly instead of handing the leadership over to another man in the warband? Think about it, Alger. I cannot, and will not, forgive Torwald for his poor judgement. To keep his foremost place among us, he took all of you to his grave. If you cannot see it, you are still in his grip. Open your eyes and see how he wished for death."

Alger glared, stepped back, folded his arms, and shook his head. "No, I am proud to be Torwald's man, Aiken. You cannot know his thoughts."

Never before had Aiken questioned or disparaged their liege lord's authority in this way. But, even as he was expressing his bad faith in their chieftain's leadership, Aiken had known that he was losing Alger's friendship. His accusations had gone beyond all previous limitations. "I am not the man I was before. You are the same man you were the day you died. But the passage of time has changed me. I hardly know the man I was back then.

"To keep my hope alive, I built a private, invisible meadhall. I kept its doors open, night and day, expecting my former war companions to all walk in, and to celebrate our lives together again. I wanted things to be the same as they were before. But the belief that I can rebuild our meadhall from bones and ashes is delusional. I want to be rid of the idea that I can make it right again. The others will never come back to celebrate. They only come back to taunt me, and you only come back to shame me. Things will never be the same as they were before. I owe loyalty to no one but my wife and children. Sunniva will marry soon, but Mildred needs me. She needs her husband. Bertolf is still a child. He needs his father."

Breathing heavily, Aiken studied the small fire. He picked up a stick, stirred the embers, and crouched down to feed it more chunks of dried dung. He then gazed, thoughtfully, at the blue, moon-lit land, and said, decisively, "I thought this over long and hard and have made up my mind."

Aiken stood and said, resolutely, "Because there must be no dispute, and no mistake about my motives, you will be my witness. I will say it now, loud and clear: from this moment on, I have severed all ties to Torwald. He is no longer my chieftain."

Alger looked stunned. "No, Aiken, you cannot do that. An orderly life depends upon having a leader who draws men together. If it were not so, each man would live only for himself. When you swore your oath to Torwald, he became your chieftain.

When you joined our warband you promised to follow him. Even now, Aiken, you must obey Torwald without questioning his authority. You need to live by the rules."

"To live by rules, which blind a man to the truth and box him into a corner, only keeps him ignorant."

"Aiken, you took the vow. We all did. For as long as one member of the warband lives, it is his duty to avenge the death of their chieftain."

"And what was Torwald's responsibility to the men who had chosen to follow him? Alger, he did not observe the signs. Instead, he looked the other way. He based his actions on nostalgia for the past, poor decision-making in the present, and wishful thinking about the future. He should accept the blame. He led his men into a trap and, yet, he has shown no remorse for what he did. Instead, he laid the heavy weight of vengeance upon my shoulders."

"Aiken, your charges have become dangerously close to treasonous. Lest you be called a traitor and end up in the lowest land of the dead, you had better watch your tongue. I demand you carry out your promise."

"I am loyal to the cause of truth and justice, not to one man. I did what I said I would do. I took my accusation to the Assembly. There were witnesses there, that day, who could have given testimony and presented evidence, but no one spoke up. Instead I was mocked, lied to, kicked, and beaten.

"Without proof, Alger, it does no good to accuse the men who murdered you. It will accomplish nothing. I cannot restore yours and the other men's lives. Nor can I get my missing eye back. My eye is gone forever, and so are you and the others. I cannot make it right again. I cannot fix it. Before I can appear at the Assembly again, I will need to form a warband, made up of men who have promised to back me."

"And who might they be, Aiken?"

"Alger after all these years, I now understand that I have been going about my demand for justice the wrong way. I now have another plan. Though your killer has, so far, escaped judgement, my efforts to deliver justice will not end. My only witness is a dead man. Because the dead cannot testify against the living, I plan to pull together a kindred of dead men who will back me. My warband will be assembled from the dead men who have died in the wars the chieftains waged. The men who agree to be my witnesses and pledge their loyalty to the rule of law are the ones to whom I will pledge my loyalty. To see my duty discharged, I will take my accusations against Leofar to the Victory Hall.

"We will march together across the skybridge, drop a knee and vow to serve Lord Glory. There, I will call together an Assembly of dead men who will judge the guilty. I will accuse Leofar, Oswald and all the other chieftains who refused to hear me speak. I will prove that each and every one of them are guilty. Those dead men, who testify against the warlords, will be my witnesses to the slaughter. I will ask Lord Glory to divide the just from the unjust and to punish them. If you agree to join me, Alger, I will welcome you to my warband."

"No, I cannot do that," Alger said. Looking away, he crouched down, and stretched a hand out toward the fire. "There is something else I long for. I only know that it is something that I will never find here. But for as long as I remain tied to this world, I will never discover what it is that I desire."

Seemingly in search of that un-namable something that he had lost, Alger peered into the small flame and, as if he were speaking to the fire itself, he said, "I am uncertain what I am looking for. I only know that it is gone. I have not figured out, yet, what it is or how to get it back. Nor do I have any guarantee that, in the future, I will ever retrieve that un-namable something that I lost. But because I know that I will never find it here, among the living, I must leave."

Turning his face up to Aiken, he said, "You will find me in the Victory Hall when you and your kindred of dead men bring your charges to Lord Glory. I will hear your accusations and will decide, then, on Leofar's guilt. But, in the meantime, I will not leave Torwald's side. Now, it is time I left."

In response, Aiken laid one hand upon Alger's shoulder. "I will miss you."

Alger grasped hold of Aiken's wrist and, as he stood, crooked his head to the side to cradle Aiken's hand between his shoulder and his cheek. Aiken reached his free arm around Alger's back to clasp his friend and tightly embraced him.

Though overcome with a fit of shivering, Aiken was unable to let his best friend go. He rested his head on Alger's shoulder, and they held onto each other like that for a long time before Alger insisted Aiken let him go.

Aiken dropped his arms, stepped back, and wiped his face with his sleeve. "You know how much I will miss you."

No sooner had he said it than Alger's appearance split down the front. From the neckline to the hem, the tunic stood empty. There was nothing inside it. Just a hollow form stood there before him. All this time, Alger's presence had been nothing but smoke and air. Aiken began to gag at the sight but stifled the catch in his throat with a swallow.

Alger's weakened voice whispered, "Aiken, such are the bonds of our affection for one another that numerous strands are stretched between you and me like cobwebs. Even now, I struggle against the certainty of what must happen. But you cannot keep me here any longer. It is no good to try. You must let me go. I cannot stay. Help me."

The way the two pledge-brother's souls were enmeshed was no good. Aiken could not continue to carry another man's soul. Though it tore him apart to use a knife against the man, for whom he had cared so much, he had no choice. He unsheathed Rushing Harm and passed the iron blade between them to break the strands that had bound Alger's soul to his own. And, as the many strings snapped and frayed, the ends whipped about and Alger gave over to the necessity of his situation.

It was then that one of Lady Blessed's battlefield attendants stepped out of the shadowy thicket. She had come to lead Alger to the place where the dead go. She placed her hand upon his arm and asked him whether he was ready to leave.

Alger studied her appearance. He took note of her fine features. He reached out to touch the long, golden plait that was tied in a knot at the nape of her neck and fell down the center of her back. Her small waist was belted tightly to draw attention to her full hips. The way he looked at her, it seemed as though he was asking himself whether she might be that nameless something that had gone missing. There was no way to know for certain. The only way to find out was to follow her.

Might desire be the underlying, bottom strata upon which all living things rest? Is lust for union with another what drives the living to do whatever they must do? Or was it the very warmth that once had coursed through his veins that Alger had lost but still longed for? If that was what he wanted, he would not know it again until his soul had been reborn. Like the answer to the riddle that he had asked Aiken:

> All things are ruled by
> Father Time and Mother Necessity.
> In their dance around the egg,
> From whence earth, fire, water and air derive.

> This world is given order by their eternal turning
> From birth to death to rebirth.

A sudden gust blew at the smoke rising from Aiken's small fire. It mixed with the fog drifting across the stubbled field and separated into fine, curling tendrils as Alger and the Lady's attendant walked away hand in hand. To the south, the brightest star in the sky showed them the direction in which they should go to make it to their final destination. Aiken watched Alger and the woman walk toward the blue and red torch-lit stars until their distant shapes had disappeared amongst the slanted, moonlit shadows.

An owl cried, *whooo, whoo, whooo.*

Grief was easier to abide than anger—he preferred it this way. Whereas anger brought chaos in its wake and broke things apart, grief was honest and deliberate. Loss was similar to cutting away the wood to reveal the unformed shapes it held inside it. Suffering may have been in his heart but instead of weeping, he chose to carve meaning from his sorrow.

III.

The bogman's wheedling voice was like a constant ringing in his ears. Though it came from somewhere far away, it never completely silenced. At times the murmur called him terrible names: a lone wolf and a traitor who should be hanged. The bogman threatened to send the red rooster after him, to torment him with fire. At other times, its tone changed and it called Aiken it's pretty-boy. Pleading desperately to be released from its shackles, it promised to give him whatever he desired. Sometimes the noise was no louder than a hissing whisper and at other times it was so deafening Aiken found it difficult to hear men and women's speech above the roar.

The circumstances into which he had been born, and his attraction to the iron weaponry, which the bogman represented, had made him into a monster. Now, if he were to keep the bogman shackled, he would take the gold ball that he had retrieved from the Ironwood and let it shine as brightly as Lady Sun's blazing mirror. He would keep the gold ball safe from the bogman and the treachery that the wolf stood for. He would strip himself of all that had made him monstrous and would admit to his nakedness.

Wherever light and dark were poised in precarious balance, he would struggle to banish the darkness by shedding daylight. He understood, all too well, that the end had begun already. He knew that he could never stop the chiefdoms from waging a brutal war of attrition among themselves, and in so doing, weaken them all. Men honored those who waged war, not those who sought to keep the peace. Unfortunately, it would always be easier to attract followers by eliciting fear of others than by convincing men of the need to come together with their enemies and to settle disputes with the very same men, women, and children whom they had been taught to hate.

On one side of the divide that separated peace from war were those men who lusted for iron weaponry and wanted the bogman in their power. And on the other side were the men who had seen enough of war. He knew who benefited from war—the men who gathered and hoarded power and wealth—and he knew who suffered—both those men who blindly followed their leaders, and those men, women and children against whom the others waged their attacks. Harald had said it best: it is better to work the soil, to plant seeds, and to harvest the produce.

Was there goodness in this world? Aiken remained unconvinced. Fairness and justice would always prove inadequate. There would always be those who acted in their own self-interests and those who got away with it. The possibility that Leofar might go forever unchallenged for his perfidy left Aiken dizzy with anguish. Just the thought of the unfairness was so grievous that he was forced to a stifle wail.

Pressure on his arm led to a flash of understanding, and he knew that Fortuna, his lady luck, had come to join him. He patted the hand grasping his elbow, and he told her that his love for her was pure. How, he asked, could a nameless, dishonored woodcarver build an alliance of dead men? The only way he could pursue an undertaking of such vast proportions was to do the one thing that he was good at. He would do the one thing that he had done since he lost everything that once had mattered to him. He would use iron, not for killing and for breaking things, but for making things. To keep the bogman shackled was the only way to keep the creature from harming him. And to keep it shackled he would need to carve.

He did not want to take things apart, to hurt and to kill anymore. And it was she, his lady luck, who would give him the means to take on this riddle of a task. Fortuna would offer him the cup, which she had dipped into the waters of the world soul, and he would sip from it and luck would fill the emptiness he felt inside.

He had courted her and loved her. He had conversed with her and had learned from her how to shape the unknowable forces that lay beyond a man or woman's ordinary, earthly knowledge, and to make the unspoken into something knowable.

She was so attuned to those forces herself, she would act as his go-between. She was the one who had the power to help him turn one thing into another through his artistry. To make peace, he would need to be present with the tragedy. He would be a witness to war and would describe the suffering.

Now he understood, this was the oath he had been meant to take, all along. For years, he had carved the high seats and the treasure boxes, which the chieftains had forced him to make in exchange for their protection and guaranteed safe passage on the roads. But this carving would be different. He no longer wanted to make things that elevated the chieftain's rank. Nor did he have much to say about heroism and valor. Rather, he wanted to portray the horrors of combat. He would explain men and women's suffering on the door that opened to the meadhall he had built from bones and ashes. I was upon that door that he would tell others what had happened by carving a picture of each of those who entered.

He understood, now, that just as the living men had honored their dead forebears in Gevehard's meadhall several nights before, it became his duty to honor the men and women who had died in the wars between the chiefdoms. Instead of honoring the heroes, he would honor those whose lives had been thrown like scraps of meat to the dogs. It was the forgotten men and women who would tell their stories. And, in turn, he would lament each of their deaths. For as long as truth remained unspoken, for as long as there were no words with which to describe the way war-making corrupted and damaged men's souls, the knowledge would go unrecognized. And now he understood that the only way to bring about that change was to describe, through stories and pictures, the way the unspoken truth continues to hurt men and women's lives. It was through their stories that truth would be revealed.

Yes, he understood that much. He wanted to pass on their stories to others, to offer testimony. And the only means he had at hand was to tell their stories with pictures. He would carve loss and it would fill him. He would banish war and chaos by carving the emptiness and pain that all the dead men and women who had been hurt by treachery had suffered.

To do this, he would befriend all the men and women who had been hurt by war. He could honor the nameless men who had died fighting and the women who had suffered the consequences and been forgotten. Whether they had been his friends or his enemies did not matter. They all had death in common. He would include the faces of the victors and those whose faces had been erased. By repairing that erasure, he would write them into the story after he had heard each of them recount their hurts.

His meadhall would become their gathering place where, one-by-one, each dead man and woman could come to tell their story. These were the men and women who would become his kin. He would form a kinship made up of those who had suffered from war. Together he and his witnesses to war would fight the bogman and the fire and the wolf. All those who weighed in on the side of goodness, those who had been hurt, and those who had loved were connected to one another. And he, too, was connected to each and every one of them.

This much he could do. If justice for his fellows was impossible, he could, at least, listen to their memories, respectfully. In this meadhall there would be no competition for honor, approval, wealth, or esteem because, in this meadhall, they all were equal. They were all dead and all were entitled to respect.

There were so many dead, just to tell their stories would require a very wide, double door and a large doorframe upon which to carve.

Together, Aiken and Fortuna saw design for the doors take shape in the sky. As clearly as if it were being drawn upon the boundless surface of the steel-gray dome above their heads, an invisible brush, held by an invisible hand, painted faint, white lines. The brushstrokes seemed to connect the dots of starlight, and in this way, the lines made a network of shapes that bound them all together in a pattern. This was what he was meant to do. To tie make-believe knots and to mend the make-believe nets that bound those men and women, who entered his meadhall, together in community.

He had two good hands and he studied knots. Because his knots were make-believe knots, not real knots tied from string and rope, he would carve knots complex enough to hold the binding fast. The braided and knotted net that he would carve would need to be strong and flexible enough to maintain the uncertain balance between order and the everlasting chance that chaos could break out at any time.

Just as there were men who broke the peace and brought chaos in their wake, so too, there would always be those who formed the net that held men and women together. The men and women who joined his warband would be the ones who diligently retied the knots and repaired the holes after the net had failed.

The doors to his meadhall would open to any and all comers. He would stand in the open doorway to welcome all men and women who wished to enter. Inside the meadhall, each and every one of them would become a part of this net that bound the stars, the sun and the moon with those men and women who promised to uphold the truth. They would gather together, not to uphold the power of any chieftain or Lord or Lady, but to uphold truth, justice, and honesty.

Aiken and Fortuna watched the shapes shifting smoothly from one picture to another. The pictures he would carve were like puzzles. In this struggle for peace, the dark and light wrapped around each other in a circular design. Because every man and woman had within them this endless possibility, this eternal soul, as well as a possibility for participation in unimaginable cruelty, they each became that battleground where the well-being of others was pitted against survival at any cost. And this too, he would carve.

To make the monstrous beautiful he would blend the opposites to make riddle-like pictures of gorgeous grotesquery. Faces of men and birds and animals entangled one with the other. A bird changed into a man and a man changed into a wolf. Some came into view as others faded. Some popped-up quickly. Others took time to show themselves, as if they were too shy to come forward without his encouragement. And, somewhere in there, he would hide a picture of the bogman in the Ironwood and gold and treasure allure, where it lay at the bottom of the pond like a promise of all that a man wanted to obtain with iron's strong-armed might.

These pictures spoke in another kind of language, a wordless, riddle-like language that spoke to another form of truth in a way that affected a man or woman in a meaningful way when they saw how the mixed up things came together. The way that one thing was made to stand-in for another, the images had taken on meanings that words could never have described. When people saw these pictures, they would hear the stories being retold.

To make sense of the puzzles that he would carve on these doors, to give it time to enchant an observer, and to reveal the meaning behind what he wanted to say, a man or woman would have to look at them closely and to study them for a long time.

Aiken saw himself, too, in that design. Endurance was in his name—Aiken the Strength of Oak. Because truth was firm, solid, and steadfast as he was, he would make sure the truth he carved in pictures endured.

Shaped, formed and portrayed as one single man, one facet of the soul of the worlds, he was the sum total of a man who brought with him, when he carved, everything that he had ever known, lived and suffered. He had been driven into the depths and had resurfaced, bringing with him something of value from those dank regions below. The scent still clung to his clothing and to his skin, as if the air that surrounded him still reeked with the foulness of the boggy-pit where the bogman had drawn him in. People sensed his difference. Sometimes he frightened people because of where he had been. He had carried his doubts alone. He had been forced by circumstances to figure things out for himself. Now, after he had come to doubt everything that he had ever been taught by his elders, he was left with only the stories.

He was but one man standing alone beneath the majesty of the boundless sky. Glad to be free of the war inside his heart, he was filled with a sense of trust. Something at the bottommost level of his being had changed. To see it this way, settled Aiken. Composure filled him with quiet satisfaction, and he could say with certainty, "I did the best I could."

IV.

Upon seeing Day-farer breach the skyline, Aiken knew his sister was soon to follow. The early morning twilight dimmed the stars but subtly lit the design on the red stone. The way it looked, not red, but black, in contrast to the stark whitewash and pale yellow ochre, the signs and pictures seemed to hang freely in midair.

Aiken kicked out what remained of the fire and stirred the ashes until the embers were out. He took a wooden bowl and a small box from his sack. Each was carved with the same signs that he had inscribed on the stone. Aiken used a trowel to dig a small hole in front of the stone and placed the open box beside it on the raised pile of loose soil. This was a treasure box like none he had ever made before.

The men were coming. Led by Gevehard, over one hundred and twenty men, wearing oiled leather breeches, tunics and boots, gathered in a half circle around the stone, several rows deep. Those who carried torches, to light the way, took their places beside the stone.

The shipmaster carried a young rooster under one arm. He opened the cockerel's breast with a slash of his knife and, to awaken the dead forebears from their slumbers, sprinkled its blood on their graves. Whilst moving between the small outlined boats he asked their forebears to bear witness to his and the men's oaths. He pleaded with his father, grandfather and great grandfather for their blessings. When he was finished, he left the cockerel lying atop the heaped pile of stones.

Aiken poured ale into the shallow depression, he had carved into the top of the stone, to act as a cup so Hild, too, could drink to the voyage. Gevehard stood beside Aiken to lead the men. The shipmaster separated and lifted a thin, braided strand of hair from his head with one hand and they all followed his lead. He used the small knife, he held in his other hand, to cut the plait free from his scalp. He tied the two ends of the braid together to make an endless circle and, as he did so, all the men joined him in saying,

"I tie a knot in this rope,
braided from my own hair.
And with it,
I bind myself to my family,
To my kin,
To my homeland,
and to all these men
With whom I serve.

Their life threads
Now become
One with mine."

The shipmaster knelt before the stone. To give the land his vital, bodily fluid, he spit into the small hole that Aiken had dug into the soil. He then laid the braid in the open wooden box at the foot of the stone. He stood again, placed one hand on the stone's shoulder, took his knife, and slashed his forearm. Dipping his finger in his own blood, he used it to trace the secret signs as he mouthed a plea with which he asked the forces that ruled earth, water and sky to become their allies. And thus, his voice became a messenger that, by moving between the overlapping layers of both the visible and the invisible worlds, his words called upon the Lords and Ladies to help and to protect them on their journey.

After the shipmaster was finished, Aiken poured ale into the wooden cup. Gevehard lifted the cup in the eastern direction from whence the sun would soon rise, and said, "I call upon Lord Glory to witness this oath. I anchor this rope, which is cut from my own body, to this stone, which was carved in memory of my forebear, Glenn the Opening in the Clouds. I promise to return victorious. As an act of faith in my promise, I have given my own blood."

Gevehard drank from the bowl. He then walked to the line of men and handed it to Jerold, who swore his oath, and handed it to the man on his right. After the last man had supped, Gevehard took it from him, and handed it to Aiken, then stepped to the end of the front line.

Each man then followed Gevehard's example. He came forward, placed his cut hair braid in the box, spat into the soil at the foot of the stone, and rubbed his blood into the carvings.

After they were finished, Aiken buried the box. He mounded the soil to cover it. He then poured ale over it, patted it smooth and pressed his open hand into the mud to make a deep impression.

He sliced his forearm, dipped his finger into the blood and traced the signs just as the others had done, saying, "I, Aiken the Strength of Oak, made this stone named Hild the Battle-woman for Gevehard the Brave Heart."

He then addressed the stone itself, saying, "Hild the Battle-woman, I now command you to knot and bind Gevehard and his men to their oaths and to weave their successful voyage. Just as words once spoken may never be unspoken, the men's promises will never come undone. The men are now bound to one another by their words and actions. I command you now, Hild the Battle-woman, to weave the men's victorious return."

And Hild, after she had been created with Aiken's hands, words, and breath, and after she had been given the fluids from each of the men's bodies, became a manifestation of their thoughts and came alive.

Aiken poured ale into the bowl and carried it to Gevehard. They each drank from the cup and thus completed the circle. Gevehard raised the cup and greeted the risen sun to seal their oaths. Assured of Lady Sun and the Lords of Battles' protection, the men were certain of their return.

Led by Gevehard and Aiken, the seamen formed a procession through the village. All the villagers had turned out to see them off. Families pulled their men to themselves for one final leave-taking.

Gevehard turned to Aiken to shake his hand and then held out his left, closed fist. He said, "This is for you. Come with us after you have learned how to tie those wind-knots and tamed the Wind-bringer."

Aiken put out his hand and Gevehard dropped something into his palm. Warmed by Gevehard's body heat, it was hot, large, and heavy as was the man himself. Without looking, Aiken closed his fingers around it, tightly. They shook hands and the shipmaster turned and followed the men. They splashed through the shallow surf, walked up the steep plank, took their places on the benches, and slipped their oars through the holes bored into the strakes. Gevehard took his place in the prow and the steersmen placed their hands on the steering oars. The last men to board each ship pulled the anchor stones, ran up the planks, pulled them into the boats, and shoved the boats away from the shoreline with the butt ends of their oars.

Men lifted the curved, bronze war-horns to their lips and joined together in long, resonant harmonics. Their sonorous chords sounding like huge, long-necked water birds giving voice to the half-bird, half-snake longships.

The vaporous morning light brightened as the men drew their extended, winglike oars and the boats took flight, skimming the water so effortlessly that barely a splash was heard.

Though a small part of Aiken still longed to be among them, pulling on an oar, he was content to let his arms hang limply at his sides. The weight of his obligation to those men felt as heavy as the stone itself. The burden could have driven him so deeply into the sand, it would have buried him. After practicing with them daily, he felt like a brother to these men. He had shouldered the duty to guarantee their safety by means of the stone he had carved. He had done all he could. If he had been successful, no more good men would have died on his watch.

The longships disappeared behind a rocky island. The war-horn harmonics and the men's voices faded away until all he heard were the sounds of the wind, the waves stirring the sand, and the clattering beach pebbles rolling back and forth.

Aiken opened his closed fist. Laying in his palm, was a large bronze buckle. In the center of the design there was a complex knot framed within a square. On one side of the square there was a heavy, oval-shaped buckle, and on the opposite side there was an eagle's profile. Or maybe it was a Wind-bringer, and maybe the knot in the center was meant to represent a wind-knot. He smiled at the gift and the message it conveyed.

He turned away from the sea, and began to walk toward the village. He was going home today. And once he got there, he had a lot to do. There was the field work; he had to bargain for Sunniva's bride price; and there were bowls, cups and pitchers to turn on the lathe and trenchers to make. But first, he would have to cut new wood. He knew where there were a couple of ash and beech stands. And, more importantly, he needed to hew the trees from which to carve two, wide doors.

V.

Aiken finished packing the cart. Now that it was lighter, it would be easier for Smart-one and Plodder to pull. He gave Adelheide the wooden bowl from which the men had drunk when they had sworn their oaths. Adelheide, in turn, gave Aiken and Sunniva chunks of salt, two lengths of fabric, one for her and one for her mother, along with food and ale enough to get them home.

Aiken yoked the oxen and he and Sunniva took leave of Edmund and Adelheide. Sunniva hugged Frida and Mila, and told them each how much she would miss them.

The dead weight of the amber bead that hung above her heart continued to remind her of the questions that still plagued her. Once she had put more time and distance between herself and her refusal to take a stand, she hoped to come to an answer that she could live with. Should she have agreed to intervene and to forestall the hardship that a loss of the ships entailed? Or was it best to have increased, by the loss of the ship and trade goods, the chances of a successful insurrection? Or, were her beliefs, that whatever she did were important, nothing but foolish make-believe?

The horsemen who were to escort Aiken and Sunniva appeared, leading their horses. They checked the saddle straps and panniers, and asked, "Are you ready?" Seeing Aiken nod his head, they mounted, and said, "Well then, let's get a move on."

Aiken and Sunniva climbed in and sat on the cart bench. "I will drive the oxen," she said and reached out for the reins.

"All right then," Aiken said. He held out the reins and goad to his daughter and added, "Take us home Sunniva."

The last time her father had offered her a chance to drive the oxen was the day they had come home from the quarry. That day, he had implied that her disobedience could have gotten him killed. Now, she was taking her father home, just as her mother had instructed.

Though uncertain whether the animals would obey her, she sat forward, flicked the goad over the oxen's backs and, lowering her voice to convey the authority with which her father spoke, gave the verbal command.

When the animals began to pull the cart, she looked at her father, wide eyed and grinning broadly, said, "They did it."

"Of course they did. My boys are good boys. They know what to do. After all, I am the one who trained them. And, besides, they like you. They remember all those handfuls of flowering clover you gave them, and the times you scratched behind their ears. They, also, are as eager to get back to their home pasture, as you and me are."

Aiken sat comfortably on the bench and, interlacing his fingers, laid his folded hands in his lap. Though the worlds were continuing to overlap confusedly, he had faith that, in time, he would get used to the heightened acuity that accompanies the uncoiling serpent power that arose from the dreamtime depths. If it gave him the means to make the pictures on the doors, he would give himself over to whatever was required. Just as the graybeard had recommended, he would bargain with that serpent-like force. And in return for its blessings he would offer it his doors.

Rolling past the holy grove, Aiken took one, last look at the stone. He might never return to Gevehard's village. He might never finish those doors and might never deliver them. He might never learn whether Hild had brought the men home this autumn. He might never find out whether they had carried wealth home in the boat hulls. And, likewise, he might never know whether Hild was just a cold, dead piece of stone. He might never learn whether his endeavors had amounted to nothing more than a useless marker of men's folly, completely empty of worth. All he knew for certain was that he had given it everything he had.

And so they left the red stone in the company of crows and swallows, the hidden folk, and those shades of the dead whose names he had never learned.

Indian Agatestone
If thou will ward off misfortune

Take this stone which is called Agatestone. It is found in mountain streambeds which come from the East and flow into the region known as the Indian Lands. It is of many colors and is best collected on a full-moon day. And it is written in ancient hindu scriptures that whenever this stone is borne it has such power that it can make a beggar become a king.

The Truth of Rocks, by Alwiss the Wise

I.

Coinciding with each of Berling's hammer blows, something is resonating here inside my room. He is at his forge, striking a piece of iron on his anvil and I am here, in my reading room, searching for the origin of the corresponding vibrations. I walk about and bend my ear to various items, but none seem to be the cause. At times I lose track of the muffled sounds entirely, but then, when I retrace my steps, I once again pick up the faint, harmonic ringing.

At last, I come to the far side of my writing table, whip off the cloth beneath which I hide the long-knife, and discover the source. And now that the blade has been uncovered, its lingering tones increase in depth and volume.

I interpret these melodic, trailing tones to mean that the blade is content here, where it is close to both the place of its birth in Berling's smithy and to the hammers that were present at its conception. I also believe that the knife's musical, bell-like tones are indicative of the blade's satisfaction with my clumsy attempts at storytelling.

To keep its acquisition secret, I hide it beneath a cloth except for those times when I am seated here at my writing table. There are a couple of reasons to keep it covered. First, the cloth prevents its insistent demands from annoying me and, secondly, I fear that others may attempt to lay claim to it for themselves. I have no reason to show the knife to Berling, though both his hammers and his progeny were the ones who forged it. The fact that he may contest my ownership is, in itself, a good reason not to let him see it. Compared to my claim, which is justified by the fact that I am the one who found it and, also, am the one who promised, in all solemnity, to tell the story of its birth, I believe that any claim, which he might raise, would be less credible than mine.

Another good reason to protect the blade from other's possible ownership is my lack of trust in how other men or women might wish to use this long-knife if it ever came into their possession. Just as the shop-keeper had suspected, there were, indeed, spells worked into the steel. Most of the gold that was originally heat-set in the grooves forming each of its letters, is now gone and, perhaps, some of its power may be somewhat diminished for that reason. If so, it could easily be fixed. But in this case, I would not make such a radical departure from my ordinarily cautious approach to collecting.

Of those of us who collect wonders and curiosities, there are two camps. One type of collector seeks to restore the collectible to its original state whenever possible. They go to great lengths to glue broken pieces together, rebind old manuscripts, and paint over pictures whose colors have faded or been dulled by layers of varnish and smoke. Others, such as myself, respect the way that time has affected the collectible. The object is simply cleaned, mended, and polished without noticeably changing the condition in which it was found. For example, in the case of this long-knife, I would never replace the missing hilt, nor would I ask Grerr or Berling to fill the engraved grooves with gold wire.

To even ponder the possible consequences that such a restoration might set in motion is too frightful to consider. It is true that my kin have remarkable skill when crafting weaponry. The description of the blade, which the Old One gave Lord Glory, was not a storyteller's fabrication nor a fanciful delusion. There are, indeed, knives that come from these storied, underground chambers that never miss a stroke, never rust, and cut through stone and iron as easily as through straw. I add to that list of commendable traits, a knife that is marked with a sign that will assure the one, who carries it, of certain victory. Such blades should not be given out willy-nilly to all and sundry. To reinvigorate the spells would be foolhardy unless I was certain that whoever held it in his or her hands was capable of retaining a good moral compass.

What would happen if the long-knife fell into the wrong hands? What terrible powers might be unleashed? I do not know. Nor do I care to guess. So, for now it is sufficient to know that the blade is making pleasant enough music to make a man joyful. I shall thus give my unholy speculations a rest and leave it at that.

Sitting here, idly listening to the lovely, resonant vibrations, I share the knife's feeling of contentment. Gone is the annoyance with Berling's work that frequently sets my teeth on edge. Anyway, sticking my fingers or wads of fleece into my ears never did me much good. But, now that I can pretend that he is striking a bell, I feel at ease.

The long knife's request, or demand, depending upon how one wants to look at it, was what began this act of storytelling. I have not yet come to the story of its birth. Before I can finish what I originally had set out to do, there is more to tell. As I said at the beginning, it is a long tale. So far, I have only described two generations: a father and his daughter. But, inevitably, one thing will lead to another and before the long-knife's request is satisfied, I will need to expand upon a child's conception and to describe how it came about. The identities of the vessel and of the seed have been introduced. It is only a matter of time before l come to the part in the story that describes how they meet in this world, for real, and not simply in the dreamtime.

Listening to the lovely music, I gaze distractedly at stones laying here on my table. When two multi-colored agates catch my eye, I cannot help but recall the merchant from whom I purchased them. She was a restrained woman who, whenever I visited her shop, consistently refrained from disclosing much about herself. Though I never discovered her background, I guessed she may have inherited the shop and all its goods from either her father or a husband.

A collector, like me, is equally compelled by the very nature of the hunt for a long-sought-after item as by the acquisition of the object itself. To search diligently and to follow leads, the chase adds to the pleasure of the discovery and increases the satisfaction whenever I find something that fills a particular hole in my collection.

On the evening when I first made the woman's acquaintance, she was closing up for the night, but I managed to squeeze in between the door and doorpost before she could lock it. She begrudgingly let me in, seated herself upon her chair, folded her hands neatly in her lap, elevated her feet on a stool, and watched me with an eagle-like stare as I looked around. Although, that night, she kept her eye on me, her sly smile implied that she found something curious, perhaps even ridiculous about my demeanor. Nonetheless, she always let me in whenever I knocked. Nor did she question why I came to her door, exclusively, after nightfall. And after she let me in, she always pursed her lips, eyed me distrustfully, and grunted loudly before she took her seat.

Because this particular merchant rarely spoke more than was necessary to conduct our transactions, when she noticed my fascination with these agates, her vociferousness surprised me. She told me that the stones had come from a land far to east, north of the sea, and south of the snowy mountains. It was called Indian Land, by Herodotus, because the region lies beyond the Indian river. She also told me that those who live there claim descent from Lord Moon.

The traveler, from whom she had acquired the pebbles, had been to the Indian Land and had described how the moon-descended folk, who live there, pick the pebbles out of the river after they have washed down from the mountains.

These stone's colors convey a lovely sense of otherworldliness. One is evocative of an early morning sky, lit by a translucent lingering moon that is just about to set in the west. A second stone pictures a sandy shoreline in the forefront and distant, lavender hills, and a red sky in the background. If I turn it upside down, the red color becomes a sandy beach and the sky turns yellow.

II.

If I hold the rock crystal ball over one stone and then move it to the other, I seem to hear the sounds of waves lapping the shoreline. And then, who should appear but Lord Fury. Does it surprise me to see him? Hardly. Rather, it proves that no matter how much I try to leave him out of the story, there is no way to get rid of this notorious Lord.

He led his horse out of the tangle of shrubs and out to the side of the road. From where he stood, he could watch the four horsemen and their mounts trotting at a leisurely pace and the rumbling ox cart progressing along the road.

All right, so he had moved two of his markers forward in this game. Now, how would his opponents, the Matrones, move theirs?

Once the horses and the oxcart were out of sight, he tied Slippery's reins to a low, branching shrub and approached the red stone.

He stood before it, rapped three times with the tip of his staff, and said, "Good-day, Hild the Battle-woman."

Hild blinked her eyes and awoke from her long slumber. Dressed in a red gown, embroidered with brilliant white and ochre-colored threads, her neckline was trimmed with a ribbon naming her purpose in secret signs. Her shield was slung across her back and her knife hung from her belt. Seated on a chair-sized stone, she regarded her view of the sea as she sipped ale from the cup that Aiken had poured for her.

After some time had passed, she set her cup on the sandy soil, pulled hand-fuls of her long tresses to the front and combed-out her hair. From the pouch at her waist she pulled out a stack of square tablets, all of which had a hole cut in each of its four corners. She threaded strands of her hair through the holes and, by extending the long reach of her arms, looped the ends around Wave Crestar's spiral tail to make the loom's warp. Her tresses would thus form the warp and, over the summertime months, grow to the full length of the sea-going men's voy-age. She pulled the ends of her hair back to where she sat, wrapped them around her waist and knotted them.

She opened the small box that lay at her feet, took out each of the men's braids, untied the circle each one formed, unplaited it, and wound the hair around one of sev-eral bobbins. When she was finished she had a selection of russet red, yellow, white, brown, black, and gray threads with which to weave her design.

She picked out a set of threads then passed the shuttle and bobbin across the warp. Before each passage of her bobbin and shuttle, she twisted the tablets either to the left or to the right. This was how she defined the pattern that the longboats' voyage would take. Hild placed the shuttle in the shed, and beat the weft. And with each pass of the shuttle across the shed the men's hair unwound from the bobbins. Over and over, for as long as they traveled, she would turn the tablets, pass the shut-tle through the shed and place the beater between the separated strands and tamp the weft in the warp.

Following Aiken's instructions, she wove the men's safety: when storms arose the sea-going men would find shelter ashore; when the sun shone they would be hope-ful; when they pulled into harbors the trading would be good; and when they set out for home, the west wind would give them a hearty tailwind and blow them, safely, home. In this manner the seamen were now under her protection.

Each thread formed a series of small squares as it passed under and over the threads in the warp. When seen altogether, the squared patterns took on the appear-ance of four trapezoid shaped boats. Their diagonal lines represented the ships' curved stems and sterns. Several short, cross-hatched lines indicated the men's oars.

Fury watched Hild weave for a long while. From among the patterns, she wove, he distinguished a small image of a stick-figure man standing in one of the boats, just behind the stem. He guessed that the little stick-figure man represented the shipmas-ter. A series of squared, blocky-looking scrolls represented the water upon which the four boats floated.

Then, even without his willing it, sudden flashes of insight seemed to overlay the world in which he stood. Among the strange, otherworldly pictures there was one in which he saw himself standing alongside Sunniva. Though he heard her speak remorsefully, he could not discern her words. Another sight crossed his vision. A goshawk sat on Lady Blessed's gloved fist. She called the bird Storm-pale and, with a sudden flick of her wrist, the bird took flight. Then, the images faded to nothing and, once again, only the sight of the holy grove was apparent. He could neither identify nor interpret for certain what he had seen in those visions but because of their appearance simultaneously overlaying his vision of the woven pictures of the boats, the uncanniness seemed to hint at something ominous.

"That is all well and good, Hild. But, now, let your weaving move forward in time. Make the future become apparent. Fold and pinch the fabric you have woven to bring the present side by side with an event that will happen in the future, as if no intervening time were between them. Show me something I do not know yet, but should be aware of. Is there something worrisome up ahead for the boats?"

As instructed, Hild twisted her tablets, passed the shuttle and beat the warp. And as she continued to weave the pictures, several smaller boats appeared. Though they floated in the shallows near the shoreline, they were hidden from Gevehard and his men by a curtain-like, low-hanging fog bank, which Hild indicated with long, squared scrolls and cross-hatched, net-like patterns.

When an inverted chevron appeared in the weave, Fury interpreted the shape to mean that a large bird, possibly a sea eagle was working itself into the story. He watched the bird trace broad circles above the shipmaster's head, then suddenly swoop in to grab a fish from just beneath the water's surface. The large fish put up a good fight and forced the sea eagle to struggle hard. To see how the bird repeatedly slapped the water hard with its wings in its attempt to regain flight, any observer would conclude that the struggle could go either way. The fish could easily drag the eagle down beneath the surface and drown the bird. Or the eagle could stubbornly refuse to drop its catch and, in the end, win the fight. As it happened, the bird continued to flap frenziedly at the water until it was able to rise above the surface. Rapidly beating its wings, it passed low over the waves with the fish still clutched in its talons and began to regain loft.

Perhaps Shipmaster Gevehard would think that the struggle between eagle and the fish was a good sign. For just as the eagle was weighted down by the heavy fish, so too, were the longships heavily weighted. Riding low in the water, he and his men were struggling to make good progress against the waves. The trading season had been good. The men were strong and, no doubt, the shipmaster was confident that, just as the eagle had taken off with the large fish, he would make good time and successfully reach home within a few days.

But the story Hild told with her tablet weave was not yet finished. She then wove into her tale a similar but smaller, chevron-shaped bird. This bird, Fury guessed might be the goshawk that Lady Blessed had given flight with a flick of her wrist. Notoriously scrappy birds, who will fight to the death to protect their territory, goshawks have been known to take on birds even as big as an eagle. Fury dreaded what could happen.

Incautious and heedless of danger, the smaller bird came in fast. Flapping its wings hard, the goshawk soon caught up with the eagle and began to gain loft quickly by tracing small, tight circles. The large, solid bird was still recovering its strength after its exhausting fight with the fish. It cycled placidly, letting the updrafts lift and carry it higher.

If the smaller bird came at the eagle from a greater height it could surprise the bigger bird. The goshawk was sleek and fast. After it had reached a sufficient height, it tucked in its wings and began to fall out of the sky. As it fell head-first, it waited until it was positioned right above the larger bird. It then hastily twisted into attack position and pointed its talons straight at the eagle. The bigger bird, upon seeing the goshawk, dropped its fish and a mid-air battle of arms ensued. Grabbing each other by the talons, the two birds spun around and around like a wheel. As they dropped toward the water in their tug of war, each bird dared the other to be the first to break the bond. When they came to within a hand span of the water surface they broke apart. Each bird flapped its wings, regained loft, and went off in opposite directions. The goshawk and the eagle each circled higher and higher until they disappeared.

There was strong intent in this sign and no doubt its meaning was clear at once to Gevehard. He would know that the fight between a goshawk and a sea eagle had not been a chance occurrence. No, the eagle's fight with the fish had been a diversion, a false sign, a distraction. And now that the attack on the eagle had forced the big bird to drop its fish, the shipmaster knew immediately what he was in for. He was in trouble—big trouble.

Where was the danger lurking? He looked around. There in the low-hanging fog bank, near the shoreline, he caught sight of the smaller ships and knew. And, like the goshawk who is quicker than a sea eagle, especially one who is carrying a large fish, the smaller boats could easily out-pace his heavily laden boats.

"Turn. Turn. Turn," he yelled. "Blow the horns. Go. Go. Go. Head for open water. Go. Go. Go." Gevehard ran back to the stern and grabbed the steering oar from the steersman.

The men on the benches laid into the oars. The horns wailed and headed for the open sea to beat a hasty retreat. Those who were not seated at the oars picked up their shields and held their weaponry in hand, ready for an attack.

So, that was it. Fury tipped his head to the red stone, and said, "Interesting, Hild. Very interesting, indeed." Clearly, it had been imperative that Sunniva come along with her father on his journey north. And, in a matter of months, she would need to play the role of a goshawk in the enactment of the longships' protection. Little had Aiken suspected how integral his own daughter's fate had been to Hild's intentions and to the successful outcome of her weaving. But, for the stone's effectiveness to be as successful as Aiken had intended, somehow, Hild had, also, cleverly worked the man's daughter into the design.

Fury turned away, lifted his hood and pulled on the satchel strap that was slung across his shoulder. It all looked well and good, but for the singular hitch in Lady Blessed's plans. Something might still prevent it from happening as Hild had foretold.

One cannot go back in time and alter what previously happened. But the future offers unlimited possibilities. Like two facing mirrors that reflect into infinity, there are many worlds, each of which becomes a reflection of a reflection of a reflection of a reflection. Each passing moment splits the worlds into separate but consecutive occurrences, all of which are happening at the same time, and each of which will have a different consequence. This is the mystery of Time. Anything can happen in any alternative world. According to Time and Necessity's dance, multiple possibilities exist. There is no limit to what can happen.

As if there were a storyteller, somewhere outside time and space, who was describing the actions of each of the characters in the tale, as Fury had said, before, each time he tells a tale, he tells it differently. And, so too, each time a person makes a decision and follows through with an action, other versions, more than one can count, are each happening simultaneously, as each differ and continuously multiply. What happens in one world changes what happens in another world, across time and space. It is not just the person who changes, it is also the possible variations, all of which are happening in each of the storyteller's worlds. And when the storyteller's character stops to consider another option and chooses to follow another path, that too will change what happens in all the other worlds.

Fury had chosen to play a multi-dimensional game with the three sisters. And now it was up to him to make sure that things came out the way Hild intended. He tipped his head in the stone's direction, and said, "I am in your service."

And so too, was he in Lady Blessed's service. He had promised to bring Sunniva to his Lady. She always got what she wanted, and he, himself was the one who would make it happen. Though Sunniva's father had something to keep him occupied—collecting the men who would serve in his warband—Fury had yet to figure out how to get around the second obstacle before he could see things come out in his wife's favor.

He had not gotten a reputation for walking between the worlds by sitting on his hands and doing nothing all day. He would either complete the task she had assigned him, or no one would, ever again, call him Lord Fury the Whirlwind.

Stepping discreetly between the stone-outlined boats and saying, "Good day. Good day. Good day," he tipped his head toward each of the men and women who were interred in the holy grove. He untied Slippery's reins, mounted, looked out toward the road, clicked his tongue, touched his mount's belly with his heels, and he and Slippery took off at a leisurely pace.

III.

Two black birds soared past on tattered wings and landed near the surf to feast upon the mussels and small fish that had been stranded by the departing tide. Those who observe the crows tell me that they are most often seen in groups of three: a mother, a father and one offspring. So, where was the third? Perhaps these two were a nesting pair and the third was, as yet, unborn. Fury had called the two crows Thought and Memory. I shall name the third, Anticipation: a latter bird, who is about to take form in the shape of an egg.

After it is laid and the parent birds have kept it warm, its shell will crack. And like the egg around which Father Time and Mother Necessity dance, a new world will be born when the shell fractures. A chick made of blood, bone and sinew will peck itself free. And once it is out of the shelter, which it enjoyed inside its eggshell, the bird will become vulnerable to the final, puzzling enigma of life. On one hand are its expectations of flight and the allure of all that the living enjoy. And, on the other hand, are the limitations imposed by earthly, material structure and weight: a living body's need and desire to eat and to drink, to move about and to multiply, and to suffer its final fate and ultimate failure.

Acknowledgements

I wish to thank those who have, along the way, read the drafts and given me feedback and encouragement: Maureen McDevitt, Carol Slaughter, Greg Schaffner, Lynn Hazelton, Jay Hutchins, and members of Evergreen Mountain Writers. Thank you to Evergreen Artists Association for their award, the proceeds of which helped defray publishing expenses. Thank you to Karen Ober for assembling the family tree from which I gleaned the names of our family's more recent forebears. Thank you to Jeannette Stutzman for her expertise in designing and uploading this material onto the publisher's website. And thank you to all the librarians at Evergreen Library and the Jefferson County libraries, and all those librarians within the Prospector network who pulled and shelved many of the research books to which I have referred when writing this book.

The following works have proven invaluable: Language and History in the Early Germanic World by D. H. Green; Gods of the Ancient Northmen by Georges Dumezil;. The Lost Beliefs of Northern Europe, The Road to Hel: A Study of the Conception of the Dead in Old Norse Literature, The Sword in Anglo-Saxon England: Its Archaeology and Literature, The Journey to the Other World, Gods and Myths of Northern Europe, and Supernatural Enemies by Hilda Ellis Davidson; The Folklore of Ghosts, edited by Russell, W. M. S and Hilda Ellis Davidson; The Viking Way in the Late Iron Age Scandinavia by Neil Price; The Mead Hall, the Feasting Tradition in Anglo Saxon England by Steven Pollington; and The Lady with the Mead Cup: Ritual, Prophecy and Lordship in the European Warband from La Tene to the Viking Age, by Michael Enright; The Well and the Tree: World and Time in Early Germanic Culture, by Paul C. Bauschatz; Nine Worlds of Seid-Magic, by Blain, Jenny; The Craft of Thought: Meditation, Rhetoric, and the Making of Images, 400-1200, by Mary Carruthers; The Forge and the Crucible and Shamanism: Archaic Techniques of Ecstasy, by Eliade, Mircea; War Is A Force That Gives Us Meaning, by Chris Hedges; Myth in Indo-European Antiquity, edited by Gerald James Larson, C. Scott Littleton, and Puhvel, Jaan; Cabinets of Curiosities, by Patrick Mauries; The Well of Remembrance, by Ralph Metzner; Early Germanic Literature and Culture by Brian Murdoch and Malcolm Read; Taking up the Runes: A Complete Guide to Using Runes in Spells, Rituals, Divination, and Magic, by Paxson, Diana L.; (Magic) Staffs in the Viking Age, by Leszek Gardeta; A Feast of Creatures: Anglo-Saxon Riddle Songs, translated by Craig Williamson; Amber: The Golden Gem of the Ages, by Patty C. Rice; The Ancient Amber Routes and the Geographical Discovery of the Eastern Baltic, by Arnold Spekke; The Trueswordsman, by Adam Sharp; Everyday Life of the Barbarians: Goths, Franks and Vandals, by Malcolm Todd; Stoic Warriors: The Ancient Philosophy Behind the Military Mind, by Nancy Sherman; Why Homer Matters by Adam Nicolson; The Writing on Stones, translated by Barbara Bray, Dream Adventure, The Edge of Surrealism: A Roger Caillois Reader, edited by Claudine Frank, Man and the Sacred, and The Mask of Medusa, by Roger Caillois;

Teutonic Mythology, by Viktor Rydberg; The Love of Destiny and the website 'Norse Mythology for Smart People', http://norse-mythology.org/ by Dan McCoy; The Sagas of the Icelanders: A Selection, with a preface by Jane Smiley; The Saga of the Volsungs translated by Jesse Byock. The Poetic Edda, the Heroic Poems translated by Henry Bellows; The Prose Edda, Tales from Norse Mythology by Snorri Sturluson and translated by Arthur Gilchrist Brodeur; Seven Viking Romances, translated by Hermann Palsson and Paul Edwards; The Arabian Nights, translated by Husain Haddawy; Old Norse Religion in Long-Term Perspectives: Origins, Changes and Interactions. Edited by Anders Andrén, Kristina Jennbert, and Catharina Raudvere; The Chariot of the Sun: and other Rites and Symbols of the Northern Bronze Age, by Peter Gelling and Hilda Ellis Davidson; The Complete First Edition of the Original folk and Fairy Tales of the Brothers Grimm translated by Jack Zipes; Taking up the Runes, A Complete Guide to Using the Runes in Spells, Rituals, Divination, and Magic, and Futhark, A Handbook of Rune Magic and Runelore by Edred Thorsson; Insomniac Dreams, introduction by Gennady Barabtarlo; An Experiment with Time, by J. W. Dunne; Leonardo Da Vinci's Note-books, arranged and rendered into English by Edward Mccudy; The Writing of Stones, Cabinet, Spring 2008, by Marina Warner; Dreams and Dreaming in the Roman Empire: Cultural Memory and Imagination, by Juliette Harrisson; Warfare and Society in the Barbarian West, 450-900, by Guy Halsall; The Norse Concept of Luck, by Bettina Sejbjerg Sommer; Achilles in Vietnam: Combat Trauma and the Undoing of Character, and Odysseus in America: Combat Trauma and the Trials of Homecoming, by Jonathan Shay; Theophrastus On Stones by Earle R. Caley & John Richard; Crystal Enchantments: A Complete Guide to Stones and Their Magical Properties by D. J. Conway. translated by Barbara Bray, Crystal-Gazing by Theodore Besterman; Catastrophe: An Investigation into the Origins of Modern Civilization, by David Keys; Adventures in Memory, by Hilde Ostby and Ylva Ostby; The Catalogue of Shipwrecked Books: Christopher Columbus, His Son, and the Quest to Build the World's Greatest Library, by Edward Wilson-Lee; The Natural History, by Pliny the Elder, translated and edited by John Bostock, M.D., F.R.S., H.T. Riley, Esq., B.A., Ed.; Octavia Randolf on https://octavia.net/ and http://www.vikinganswerlady.com/ ; On the Ancient Inscribed Sumerian (Babylonian) Axe-Head from the Morgan Collection in the American Museum of Natural History, by George Frederick Kunz, as seen on http://www.palagems.com/babylonian-axe-head; The Keeper, by Massimiliano Gioni, Ydessa Hendeles, et al.; Honor and Shame, by Halvor Moxnes.

Thank you to all the journalists and editorialists at The Washington Post, The New York Times, the New Yorker, The Guardian, and the New Republic whose coverage of the news and opinion pieces are a constant source of inspiration.

And, lastly, thank you to the many anonymous writers on Wikipedia whose entries and research formed an indispensable source of information on countless topics.

To hear what a poet's song in the mead hall may have sounded like, listen to

'Edda Myths from Medieval Iceland' by Sequentia. To hear songs that may be similar to spinning songs and those which the distaff carriers used for achieving a trance state during their ceremonies there are the compositions by Veljo Tormis, based upon Estonian folk tunes and recorded in 'Forgotten People's' and 'Litany to Thunder' (specifically, "How Can I Recognize My Home"). To hear possible musical recreations of the bronze war horns, the lur, and music performed on instruments contemporary to the time of the meadhalls: 'Dragon Voices—The Giant Celtic Horns of Ancient Europe' by John Kenny, 'Ice & Longboat' by Ensemble Mare Balticum; and 'Spellweaving' by Campbell Colin.

Made in the USA
Coppell, TX
05 June 2020